Waltenberg

Hédi Kaddour

Waltenberg

Translated from the French
by David Coward

Harvill Secker
LONDON

Published by Harvill Secker 2008

2 4 6 8 10 9 7 5 3 1

First published with the title *Waltenberg* in 2008
by Éditions Gallimard, Paris

First published in Great Britain in 2008 by
HARVILL SECKER
Random House
20 Vauxhall Bridge Road
London SW1V 2SA

www.rbooks.co.uk

Addresses for companies within The Random House Group Limited can be found at:
www.randomhouse.co.uk/offices.htm

The Random House Group Limited Reg. No. 954009

A CIP catalogue record for this book is available from the British Library

ISBN 9781846550225

This book is supported by the French Ministry of Foreign Affairs as part of the Burgess
programme run by the Cultural Department of the French Embassy in London.
www.frenchbooknews.com

Liberté • Égalité • Fraternité
RÉPUBLIQUE FRANÇAISE

Ouvrage publié avec le soutien du Centre national du livre – ministère français chargé de la culture

This book is published with support from the French Ministry of Culture –
Centre National du Livre

Mixed Sources
Product group from well-managed
forests and other controlled sources
www.fsc.org Cert no. TT-COC-2139
© 1996 Forest Stewardship Council

Typeset by SX Composing DTP, Rayleigh, Essex
Printed and bound in Great Britain by
Mackays of Chatham plc, Chatham, Kent

For Lucienne and Habib Kaddour

Contents

Waltenberg

Chapter 1

1914

The Charge

In which the French cavalry is observed launching an assault on German dreams.

In which Hans Kappler remembers Lena Hotspur and the time when she took singing lessons with Madame Nietnagel.

In which Max Goffard defers his entrance and denounces toy machine guns.

In which a French commanding officer begins to speak of Africa and tells of a duel.

In which Alain-Fournier dies.

Monfaubert, 4 September 1914

Our dreams come to grief on the reef of dusk
When the dogs of day and the wolves of night
Do bloody battle for the light.

Robert Marteau

The jay has stopped its screeching. Hans has the tip of a sabre against his belly, a lightly curved sabre. The man who holds the sabre has a very pale, young face.

The blade trembles. There are other men behind him, on horseback, also young, red breeches, dark blue tunics, crested helmets: French dragoons.

Here in this wood?

But the front is fifty kilometres south.

The rabbits.

Hans does not cry out, he is ashamed of not crying out. Standing, arms raised, filled with such fear as he never felt before, he sees the rabbits he was watching only moments ago flee in the evening air, about fifteen grey rabbits which had rolled on the ground and climbed all over each other, with a hop and skip and a flash of white bobtail, coupling casually, all happening too far away to be able to tell male from female. 'Anyway, according to Saint Maxence,' Johann had just told him, 'they are incorrigible sodomites.'

Johann had slid to the ground, his neck half severed by a French dragoon.

Hans and Johann had stumbled into an enemy ambush at the edge of a wide clearing while they were out on evening patrol, or more

3

precisely out for a stroll, pipes filled with Virginia tobacco, swallows overhead, earnestly arguing in the still-warm air fragrant with the scent of mown grass.

Hans was watching the clouds, seeing shapes in them, and he began talking about a woman he had loved. Breasts as soft as turtle doves, he kept glancing down at them as she sat in front of him drinking her bowl of chocolate. She had disappeared, I was even told she was dead, it's not true, she can't be, the first time I saw her she'd just let the door slam behind her as she walked into the dining room of a large hotel, not out of carelessness or bad manners, it was the unaffected action of an American, utterly straightforward, a German girl wouldn't have dared, nor even a French girl, she'd just let it slam, she didn't need to do that to attract attention, no, it was done very simply, because if the door wasn't capable of closing itself quietly, hotel porters or no hotel porters, it was nothing to do with her, she had enough on her plate being a beautiful woman obliged to walk into a full dining room unescorted, and she had absolutely no wish to wait for some man to come along who would make the most of his opportunity to smile at her.

She was wearing a dark blue dress, shoulders held very straight, I never understood why she disappeared, one evening I came back from an outing, and she'd gone, left no address, I couldn't make it out but I should have known, something stupid had happened, I'll tell you about it if I have the energy.

White shoulders, long red hair, contralto voice, she was studying singing, she wanted to sing the *The Lovely Miller Girl* and *Winter Journey*, I told her they were both written for male voices, but that didn't bother her, musically it could be very interesting, a woman's voice singing a man's pain, the effect could be even more powerful, less expressive was how she put it, pure music and beyond the music, emotion, purified; it was all a bit complicated to follow but when she started singing *Das Wandern,* it was superb, it was anything but a march, you can't march to it, too many silences in the melody, if you take it at strict march tempo you drown out the silences, if you try it trippingly on the quavers you'll jounce, and if you do it with crotchets

4

it's too heavy, no, not really a march at all, more like a draft outline of a march. But I won't bore you with the details.

It's the song a young miller sings as he sets out to meet life, as he goes forward to meet the girl from the mill, he's marching along, it's delightful, a repeating round, a new element, the gurgle of the stream, even the stones are part of the round, the piano pushes on ahead, starting the round again each time, and each time there's a fresh energy, all right, I'll leave it there.

O Wandern, Wandern, meine Lust, a real pleasure, you should have heard Lena say *Lust*, that's why she wanted to sing a man's song, so she could say *Lust* in her woman's voice: pleasure. It was superb, *O Wandern, meine Lust*.

Hans sings, rather off key, flattening the notes and the intervals between them, she said that *lust* is much stronger in English, almost crude, at least it is when a woman says it, she loved it, singing a man's word in German which in her own language was almost crude, *lust*, she jumbled all this up and laughed and then untangled it all again when she sang. I'll stop now, I'm positive she isn't dead, she's gone to the other side of the ocean, gone home.

Johannn listened, paid the white shoulders, breasts soft as turtle doves and red hair the measured tribute that a man owes to his friend's girl. They were at war, this was men's talk and it grew stronger and more direct as the distance increased between them and the kind of life where a man needed to be discreet about what was called the inner self, that inner life which these days tended to be spread out for all to see, blood, guts and all, at the first salvo from the enemy's cannon.

Their talk deepened as the regiment moved from one staging post to the next, Namur, Charleroi, Saint-Quentin, Landrecies, Chauny, Fontenoy, Monfaubert, they talked about women with decreasing coyness but were never foul-mouthed, each making it clear that, however desirable his friend's girl was, he was not about to pat her on the behind.

The friend feels a growing urge to tell him she has an attractive behind, and on occasions his hand might even trace a curve in the pink and blue air of the clearing. Then, the friend being Johann, he acquiesces as he tracks the hand with his eyes, says a dreamy oof! even if the movements of his own hands over a woman's hindquarters are normally much more specific, more exploratory, more decisive than the graceful curves which Hans draws against the sky; he says oof! in passing acknowledgement of the girl's beauty, even if he's never seen her, as was the case with Johann who in peacetime would never have got friendly with this girl Hans kept telling him about for hours on end, until he was dreaming of her with his eyes open, tracing curves in the air with his hand.

And Johann would indicate that he had a very clear picture of the girl's shoulders, hips, buttocks, legs, that he understood exactly how exquisite it all was, and the swell of her breasts, soft as a dove's; he didn't agree about the turtle doves, he thought of them as being grey but he wasn't going to upset his friend, and anyway white doves do exist, a delicate white, he could see the girl clearly if he opened his eyes wide and then raised them to the sky, where the world regains something of its innocence.

Hans feels hot, Johann looks admiring, dreamy, he is one whom destiny has kept and will forever keep well away from the breasts and hindquarters of Madame Lena Hotspur, his friend's girl who has disappeared, and disappeared in the most mysterious circumstances.

But Hans might have suspected something, seen a warning in Lena's incomprehensible gesture; and, being his friend, Johann even found himself quizzing Hans. Were her shoulders really that straight? Yes, that's the first thing that struck me, usually women's shoulders are less prominent, more rounded, Lena's shoulders are like a boy's, her body is – how shall I put it? – very firm, she could wear any sort of dress, a dress on her hung as perfectly as in a fashion designer's illustrations, and yet you could see all her curves, everywhere, she must have gone back to live on the other side of the ocean.

Then the two men talked about rabbits and the place occupied by rabbits in mythology.

By way of defences, vehicles were simply parked in a circle, a large circle, more or less, with the vehicles well spaced out, a rough and ready arrangement, the clearing covered an area of more than fifty hectares, so it would have taken a lot of men.

They were still at war but the hardest battles were over and there was nothing to fear now.

Within a few weeks, following the plan laid down by the general staff, the Kaiser's army had penetrated deep into French territory, a brilliant strategic breakthrough in the form of a great scything movement through Belgium; four German armies, marshalled as though they were on manoeuvres, had come to a halt and regrouped on the banks of the Marne, which they would cross at any time now, their comrades had not died for nothing, it was the same situation as in 1870, the French forces routed and their President, Poincaré, already falling back on Bordeaux.

You could walk across the fields as if you were back home, wait for the moment when clouds and memories began to invent a woman, while observing the frolicking of frisky rabbits.

Johann talked endlessly about Easter bunnies, the descendants of the rabbits which according to our pagan ancestors escorted the goddess of spring, rabbits with giant testicles, creatures a metre high like pink granite, guarded by priestesses, with sterile women bringing them offerings though I've no idea of what, nowadays in my country women bring the healer a pound of butter, a bottle of schnapps and a pair of knickers, and the healer hangs the knickers on a hook in his barn and then proceeds to his fumigations, I've no idea if the wives of our pagan ancestors wore knickers or not, the Christian Church burned the priestesses at the stake, but it couldn't get rid of the rabbits, so it kept them but removed their bollocks and now we send children off to look for them under bushes, not the rabbits, stupid! chocolate rabbits.

The dragoons have bound and gagged Hans, they have knocked him to the ground, they are preparing for one of those charges of which the

French cavalry have been masters for centuries. Dragoons arrive from all sides, they line up in ranks of six in the space permitted by the forest track before they burst out in a serried column into the clearing occupied by the Germans.

Riders holding in their mounts, softly uttered commands, the rattle of bared steel, the horses clinking their bits as they try to nibble the young oak leaves at the edge of the copse: a late arrival, medium height, slim, brown hair and large projecting ears, tries to take his place in their ranks, he has a name well suited to the stereotypical Frenchman who tries to travel first class with a second-class ticket, just three syllables, one for his Christian name, two for his surname, the absolute minimum which enables a character to wander about in the wings but is perhaps insufficient to allow him to rise to the front row of what is about to be one of the French cavalry's most glorious charges.

The Captain of the dragoons eyes his troops who are now formed up, he has two fears: less than a year ago he was in Berlin, on manoeuvres, and saw the German infantry in action. Even through a telescope it had not been easy to pick out *feldgrau* uniforms against a background of greenery. He has just warned his men to keep their eyes wide open, but has said nothing of his other fear: the Germans are doubtless well-equipped with machine guns like the ones he saw being fired in Berlin.

'Industrialised death, my dear Jourde,' the British military attaché, an infantry man, had told him.

The Captain had replied: 'Oh, the big guns have been getting us used to that for a long time now.'

The attaché had responded with silence.

Later, over a cocktail, with nothing to lead up to it, he said to the Captain:

'The machine gun spells the end of chivalry.'

And Captain Jourde replied: 'Not if my dragoons charge with enough ferocity. Don't forget the new dogma: a shock strike will beat small-arms fire every time.'

Now the Captain groups his men closer together to give their action the semblance of a decisive blow, of a surprise, for surprise is the queen of tactical ploys. You can't fight the old battles again, Rivoli, Marengo, and the great charges which unseated the enemy at Austerlitz, Jena and especially Prenzlow:

'Finest charge I ever did see,' an expert, Prince Murat, would say afterwards.

Entire battles won with a charge, sabres at the ready, there's no way you can do that any more. There remains the element of surprise: locate the enemy, take him by storm, annihilate him and move on. The Captain has dismissed the sluggard with the second-class ticket and sticking-out ears, Max Goffard by name, it would be much too much of a *coincidence* to let him appear here, just for the satisfaction of providing Hans with a mirror-image.

Max protests, as a matter of fact Hans and he *have* coincided in many things of late, and they are not the only ones, and it all comes down to this: coincidence.

If there hadn't been millions upon millions of coincidences during that summer of 1914, the picturesque scene which is building up would have been replaced by a game of whist in a drawing room hung with tall dark-green curtains or alternatively by the monologue of a man who is about to go to sleep. Max would even agree to get on one of the horses whose backs have been rubbed raw by days and days of chafing and already give off a smell of death, it's too late now, said the Captain.

But even if it is too late, it matters for Max because of the friendship which is about to begin between him and Hans and will extend over a large slice of a century of which the year 1914 is the baptism of fire. And this coincidence must of necessity take place so that they may talk about it some day, it is this that will give godspeed and strength to their friendship which will end only in 1969, on the banks of the Rhine, when one of these two men will accompany the other to his last resting place, the funeral procession will perhaps pass by hillside, green with the embossed, fleshy-leaved Riesling vines that grow on the banks of the Rhine, a fine variety, in late spring the sheaths covered in a velvet cloak of innumerable fine hairs burst open and reach towards the light in tiny bouquets, the weather is dry and windy, a superb display of blossom, pollen flies up from the flower clusters, insects are busy, fertilisation in two weeks, a sweet smell, then the grapes start to look like fat, opaque marbles, hard and bluey-green, the heat shines on them, the nights turn cold, the days are grey, the sky clouds over with pale vapour, then one morning the wind from the sea spreads a damp mist which glazes the leaves, at noon the sun blazes down, and since last Monday there has been the honey-coloured translucence of grapes ready for picking.

For the funeral in 1969 there will even be a brass band with banners of red and gold, crowds of people, sunshine. And not only that, a beautiful young woman. People will ask who is the woman in the black hat, pearl-grey scarf and the boots, and a voice will say:

'Many things have passed away, but pretty women are always with us.'

There will be a large crowd, some men will even wear top hats in the sunshine, a vineyard with terraces of pink sandstone from Alsace or the Rhineland, a hill, the cortege winds along the flank of a hill in the autumn sun, climbs up to the forest, proceeds through the trees and past the low bushes, some eyes linger on the ferns, the leaves, here and there tints of gold and burnt ash, a spider's web is for a moment caught in a noose of sun. Other eyes look out for unlikely mushrooms, then the cortege descends once more to the Rhine, behind the band, the plumed horses and the antique-style hearse.

All this is precisely why Max wants to be seen *coincidentally* by Hans's side, now, in 1914, among the dragoons at Monfaubert who have just bound and gagged this enemy who shall be his friend. Max has grasped the bridle of a horse which has been rejected as being in no fit state to charge, the horse backs away; you can't say that it refuses to be mounted, it's an army horse, it tries to shy away without appearing to be looking for fresh grass, you never know; and at the same time it is already resigned to going into battle with a back that is a layer of pus and a rider he doesn't know.

Max strokes the horse's head.

Hans and him.

A coincidence.

One more, just like these millions of men coinciding in a war which they had opposed not all that long ago. And Max recalls that only a few months back he was fighting this war shoulder-to-shoulder with Jaurès and the socialists, a perfect coincidence with Hans who was doing exactly the same among the Germans. Coincidence was already there, and functioning, with each man trying to defend civilisation and culture by talking for hours on end in smoke-filled cafés, severally drinking schnapps or coffee laced with eau-de-vie, cheering the speakers, joining marches, convinced that the truth was emerging from the tramp of their feet, processing along boulevards gay with slogans and redolent of honest horse manure, buying newspapers which supported their ideas. Later they even left for the front for the same reasons, both wanting to defend civilisation once and for all against barbarism, we were the centre of the world.

The day war was declared, Hans and Max rushed out to march like everyone else, swept along like everyone else, one in Berlin, the other in Paris, by the same wave of coincidence and pride, each of them swept along by the wave and adding his own puny gravitational pull to the wave which sweeps them all along. Max even shouted:

'Long live Poincaré!'

Ten days previously, along with millions of men, he had called him a warmonger and a murderer, and in the café he joined in with his friends chanting a demand that all the manure in the barracks be gathered into a heap and that, 'in it, in the presence of all the troops and to the strains of a military band, the Colonel should plant the regimental flag!'

Gustave Hervé.

Then suddenly this great wave of men rushing to join the war to end war. Molecules feel the pull of the moon when tides are equinoctial. Few humans will remain standing on the sidelines like the man who was happy to note in his diary: '2 August 1914, Germany declares war on Russia. – Afternoon, went swimming.'

All the others are caught up in the swirl of molecules, swelling it and allowing themselves to be swept along behind the banners, waving their straw boaters, a hat for village dances, for pleasure, for summertime, what was it about the nonchalant swagger which a boater gives its wearer (in August, people would even stick them on cab-horses' heads, with holes cut out for their ears), what was it about the lightness and faintly rustic origin of its texture, about its colour, a light cream set off by the black of the hatband, what exactly was it that prompted the jerky movement of the hand which hurled it in the direction of Berlin, Paris or Vienna, up into the sky which contained the great ideas, the great beliefs and the icons which made a man want to run hatless across fields and with one mighty bound land on the streets of the enemy's capital? directly on to its streets, don't laugh.

So off they went to war. For a while, Hans almost forgot the woman he so longed to see again, whom he would certainly see again, one day, by working on himself, on his body, on his soul, he would be a vastly better person than he was on the day that stupid business happened, the day they parted.

Weeks on the march, camps lasting no more than a night or two, a pace which emptied the thoughts out of a man's head, then in this clearing the long halt, awaiting the crossing of the Marne and the final offensive, and then the woman came back.

Sometimes she surfaced in Hans's sleep. The sensation of a body lying on his. He would wake, nobody there, but someone was there in the hollow of his shoulder, on his belly; she was there, the weight of a body on him, afraid of waking too fully, of feeling nothing, close your eyes, go back to dream, the warmth steals back over his chest and belly, something moves.

But if he really goes back to sleep, it ends. Other times, it would happen in broad daylight, in the bushes a few metres dead ahead of him, in an autumn dress of ochre and dark green, woven of fine wool, he felt her presence less intensely than when he was half asleep but he could see her more clearly, she walked towards him as she used to once, carrying flowers in her arms.

Then again it could be more conscious, Hans would begin talking to the woman and she would be where he decided she should be. She would reply, she was there just next to him, they stood watching the countryside together, she was holding flowers in her arms. He didn't like flowers made up that way, people have such silly sentimental notions about bouquets of flowers. Now he could shed tears for them.

Then again she comes to me laughing, she is playful, she deliberately exaggerates the sway of her hips, when they went for walks it was always fine weather, but at times things turned stormy, the tone changed. Hans blames himself more and more, there'd been several incidents, but all the same those afternoons always turned out nice in the end. And here too, in the clearing, to smoke, to be himself, be alone by himself and sad.

At the same time, it could be very enjoyable to talk to her ghostly presence, to summon her, even if it turned out badly and she did not come. Then Johann would join him, together they would watch the rabbits' bacchanalian antics and the constantly changing clouds. And in the lull which preceded the storm, Lena would come back.

French dragoons, four troops of them, acting on orders from General Maisonneuve, commander of the 3rd Cavalry Division, orders which had been issued to the 2nd Squadron of the 12th Regiment of Dragoons for an operation to reconnoitre and harass.

A Sherman-style operation, so named after the Union general during the American Civil War who disrupted the Confederate rear with his cavalry. His trademark was rails ripped from the track, heated until white-hot and wrapped around telegraph poles so that they could not be used again, the so-called 'Sherman neckties'.

The dragoons headed north, beyond Soissons, a foray of more than 150 kilometres behind German lines. The motto of the 12th is 'Contending for Glory!'

On this late afternoon, the tally notched up by Squadron Jourde, so called after its leader, is meagre. Morale is low. Going home without glory, mocked by the song of thrushes, without having disrupted anything at all, riding back through fields littered with French corpses still in heaps or laid out in lines, flesh swollen, uniforms stretched to bursting over bloated, grotesque bodies, black faces, black buzzing entrails, mouths like rolls of purple flesh. They make what use they can of the forest's torpid shade, exhausted riders, three nights in a row without proper sleep, rocked by the motion of the horses, eyes fixed on the bobbing rumps ahead, sleep comes down on us like a fever, pinch yourself, talk to the man next to you, keep your voice as low as you can, sergeant-major I feel like a dumb animal, make the most of it, it helps you to put up with anything, sleep surges back, men slump forward, their chests touching their saddle-bags, they are ready to slide off their mounts, then they start, and the melancholy returns, as if it had been biding its time.

Second-Lieutenant Dutilleux tries to scribble entries in his notebook, ahead the sky rises like a wall, you see buildings that aren't there, trees, the shadows of trees, shadows which lengthen, the soporific amble of the spent horses, an officer rides back along the column rapping the men's helmets or making a point of asking them for their names, and then they go back to sleep. The horses are exhausted, badly shod, saddle galls, forty hours without let-up, the weight of rider plus kit, that means carrying more than 120 kilos, they stink to high heaven, the horses do not have the capacity for mind over matter to help them but they keep on going, with a look of gentle supplication, you could shove your thumb into the eye-sockets sunk deep in their heads, their gummy eyelids droop, on they go, sometimes they get in each other's way as, as when they see hanging in a tree, three metres above the ground, the corpse of one of their own kind which was blown there by a burst from a 320.

They halt. A peasant. He has pointed out a German position, three, maybe four kilometres off, in a clearing, a wide open space:

'They destroyed everything that was growing!'

Captain Jourde cried: 'Contending for Glory!'

Bound hand and foot in his ditch, Hans tells himself he should have been a hero and shouted a warning even if the sabre had left him only time enough to say the first syllable, even if his reaction had served no purpose whatsoever, given how far he was from the sentries. He should have. He is about to die anyway, and without heroism.

Hans is still shaking from having felt the tip of the sabre, from having heard Johann's bear-like growls change to a gurgle. The wound to Johann's neck. Hans curls up small. The minute you start looking at rabbits I know what you are going to say, Johann would remark, and then he'd add: it's a joke, we're not dumb animals, although if this war goes on a long time . . .

Johann growling, waddling, turning his growls into an impression of the call of a bear on heat. Johann is gamesome, playful, *lustig*.

Deep down, Hans knows exactly why Lena and he did not stay together, he told his friends then he didn't understand why she went away, but he knows full well. A stupid thing. He will see her again. What you want is first and foremost to become a better person. She will smile tenderly when she sees the change in him, better developed physically, better read, bolder, wiser: she will take his hand. No, I should take her hand, know what to do, wait until our hands brush against each other accidentally, exploit the accident, no that's a bit feeble, I'll just have to shake her hand.

That's it, shaking hands. They will both hold out their hands but Hans will take hers and kiss it, the most normal thing in the world. Not a handshake, we're not cattle merchants. Kiss her hand, lips on her skin and that kiss will contain all the kisses that have gone before.

Hans can picture the scene now, he doesn't describe it to Johann but he can see it very clearly. Lena is reserved, taken aback, she hasn't changed her perfume, L'Heure Bleue, either that or she knew I'd be there and wore the same Guerlain as she always did on our dates, as if time has stopped. But why so reserved? Because now that she's here again she is already regretting wearing that perfume. She wants to make it clear to Hans that he should have no illusions; politeness, she armours herself with politeness. He fluffs the kiss he plants on her hand, makes it the action of a possessive imbecile, and all Lena's prejudices are confirmed. The imbecile should be throttled, or maybe Lena just wants to leave me feeling unsure; she has chosen to appear reserved, she's flirting, no, not Lena, in which case it's politeness, no, perhaps she really is flirting. She is so cold.

She is not sure, that's it, Hans makes her feel unsure. He has changed so much, and for the better. Now none of that, stop giving yourself the best lines, you were always useless with women, you always strutted and swaggered for them and they were never impressed. The women who will truly love you appear when you're least expecting them, it's true, but Lena's here now.

Respond to Lena's politeness with even deeper reserve, ask her questions, get her to ask you questions, above all don't talk about yourself, don't wear that new suit, be at ease; and avoid trousers that are itchy or too tight.

What interests women? Actually, it's the fact that you aren't interested in them. That's a neat thought, you can try living with it and with those women who come when you're least expecting them. That said, you never know, the psychology of cheap novelettes may work, but my feelings for Lena aren't cheap fiction, we'll see.

So when Lena's there in the flesh, you do not ask her too many questions and you let on that you have another consuming passion, not another woman, certainly not, rather you speak passionately of what you will do once peace breaks out again, once the Marne has been crossed, it can only be a matter of days, then armistice, return home, the Baltic, wide beaches, the port, the third largest port in Germany, Rosmar.

The beautiful body of a seated woman, half-naked, memory hand in hand with death, Hans stands behind her, has a three-quarter view of her, he will find Lena again, he curls up more tightly, he is afraid, he is ashamed of being afraid. I have never forgiven them for putting me in this position, I knew what war was, hands tied behind my back, legs roped together, a gag over my mouth, you know your comrades are going to get killed and there's nothing you can do about it. It's partly my fault that my comrades are getting killed. I should have shouted a warning, but I couldn't. It turns out that I go on to have a good war, but I stopped believing in it from the very start.

The day he left home, Hans's mother gave him two pieces of advice. She said:

'I'm going to give you two pieces of un-German advice. Both are

16

far older than what nowadays go by the name of Germany or France, and I do not want to have to say one day: I'd give both France and Germany for him not to be dead. You know, as far back as you can go in my family, the women have always given their sons two pieces of advice when they were leaving home.'

His mother's voice is very calm, quiet, slow and distinct.

'Never volunteer and always keep thinking about the things you love most. I do not ask you to think about me but about whatever you think you love most at the time, I'd be happy if it was me, but I know men are more than just sons, so think about what you really love, that's what will see you through, and remember: never volunteer for anything.'

Hans crouching, feeling ashamed he hadn't shouted a warning, a French drummer-boy would have shouted a warning, like in those legends of the French Revolution which their nanny used to tell them back home at Rosmar. Hans and his younger brothers used to laugh at them, to upset Mademoiselle Françoise, the French don't do things like that, they never have time to be heroic, all they do is drink and sleep and when they wake up they run around like rabbits, they don't have time to sound the alarm.

Hans and his brothers would laugh, you know, Mademoiselle, at school nobody says *the French*, they say *the rabbits*, Mademoiselle Françoise didn't dare get angry and moved on to other stories, the children said sorry, they really liked that little drummer-boy and when they played games they made him a little Prussian drummer-boy, and they loved Mademoiselle Françoise and the stories she read them, about houses with three attics, mysterious lands with blue hills and wide tree-lined paths, Harlequins, Pierrots, dressing up, pony races and girls with fair hair and painfully sharp profiles.

Other families had English nannies. It didn't seem quite as good having Mademoiselle Françoise. She'd been with them for thirteen years. It was Hans who took her to the station, that was barely two months ago, at the start of July. No other member of the family wanted to come.

Françoise stood very straight and wept:

'Now I shan't have time to finish the book I was reading from, Master Hans. Please read them the end of *Le Grand Meaulnes*, they love it, one of the heroes is called Frantz, Frantz, and I saw in the paper that one of your greatest generals is called von François, there won't be a war, you can begin at the chapter entitled "A Day in the Country".'

There hadn't been time for Hans to continue reading the story.

The dragoons are now lined up many ranks deep the length of the forest track, three troops are required for the charge, article 1 of the *Provisional Rules issued 14 May 1912 for the conduct of mounted exercises and manoeuvres*, the cavalry shall attack by mounting a charge with bared sabres whenever a favourable opportunity presents itself.

Over a hundred riders, despite the losses of the preceding days, with one troop held in reserve, Captain Jourde has opted for an attack with sabre and lance, Jourde graduated from the military school at Saumur and our tactical answer to all situations was always a charge, otherwise your marks suffered, the lance is the latest model, number three, three metres of steel, it was solemnly delivered on the eve of the war to replace the old lance made from the male royal bamboo imported from Tonkin.

It was supposed to be used only by the leading rank in each squadron but it proved so popular that it was issued to every man. In normal circumstances, the lance is held vertically, its base secured in a holster fixed to the outside of the right stirrup.

As to the charge itself, the Colonel said it is 'the queen of any battle', especially when riders stay low on mounts measuring one metre sixty at the withers and weighing on average 500 pounds, with four years' military training behind them, not a contrary bone in their bodies, Anglo-Norman stock but fiery, great character, ready for anything, solid physique and blood pumping from stout hearts, eager for battle, never as strong as when they hear the rumble of the ground under their hooves, feel their rider press with his knees, give the lightest touch of spur, ease the reins, stand up in the stirrups, crouch over their necks to present a smaller target to enemy fire and see less of the danger, and cry as they ride, because the war has stopped meaning only the death of other men.

During the first days of the war, Hans's father wrote him a letter in which he spoke of his own shame at being no more than a shadow safe among shadows while ardent youth, which was how he put it, was entering the furnace, which was another of his expressions. And Hans entered this furnace where he and Max, on opposing sides, for some time behaved like men bent on saving culture and civilisation.

But neither Max nor Hans was mad or blind, neither had wanted this folly, and when by Christmas Eve 1915 the war will be well and truly dug in, Max, on sick leave, will be amazed by an article in *Le Figaro* and rush out to the corner of the rue Richepance and the rue Saint-Honoré and stride into the Blue Dwarf, the high-class toy shop in the most fashionable part of Paris, to see for himself if they really were displaying the machine gun for boys which had made *Le Figaro* write: 'Today French toys have acquired a soul.'

Max will tear a strip off the whole shop in the name of Voltaire.

He stands in the middle of the shop, next to Father Christmas, surrounded by model sailing boats, dolls from Alsace, miniature beds, tin railway engines, small figures of Jesus and toy machine guns and he shouts:

'Talapoins, that's what you are – a bunch of monkeys!'

Max still thinks he is in the land of Voltaire, the fight for right, for truth, we shall win and be worthy, he stands there watched by ladies who find this lieutenant with his arm in a sling rather good-looking, he has big ears but a nice face, a few of them would be only too happy to be admirers and perhaps more, if it were not for the objectionable comments he is making in a loud voice:

'Machine guns for monkeys!'

An elderly gent tells Max that he is undermining the morale of the nation, children must have something to defend themselves with, the Germans are cutting their hands off in Belgium and northern France, my son is at the front, sir, he has told me what it's like, and Monsieur Cocteau has published a splendid drawing in the magazine, *Le Mot*, showing eight large Huns with pointed helmets and knives drawn standing over a little girl who is kneeling with her hands over her eyes, and they are saying:

'Don't be afraid, little girl, we've just come to ask for your hand.'

Max answers the man saying that's all monkey propaganda, the Germans themselves believe that the French cut prisoners' noses off, ears too, this war is already crazy enough, and you really imagine that you can attract customers by dangling lies under their noses? They are perfectly capable of coming without any prompting, you know, it's never easy. It is due solely to his rank and shiny new medal that Max is not beaten up right there in the middle of the Blue Dwarf by the young mothers and the old gents now all hoarse with fury, Monsieur Poincaré himself, the President of the Republic, the President of us all, has just denounced German barbarism, it is a sacred task, get out, sir!

While this rumpus is going on, a boy strays from the machine gun counter and wanders over to the clockwork dolls, currently somewhat unpopular, he winds one up, black corselet, long skirt, blue flag, with a white apron, a chain with a large crucifix, clogs, a round face and pointed nose, she is carrying a pile of plates, suddenly the plates leap into the air then fall down again, and the doll raises her head, rolls her eyes like two marbles up to seek heaven as her witness. She is a Breton peasant and the model is 'Bécassine Drops The Plates'.

After the war, Hans will return to Rosmar, peace, the sea, writing, writing ten hours a day, no eight, and two hours of exercise, like an Englishman, or a long walk along the beach behind a coterie of curlews which fly off every time you get anywhere near and resettle thirty metres further on, keeping to the water's edge, the place where the waves finally disappear in the sand, you can walk without sinking in too much.

In January 1914, Hans has decided to resign permanently from the shipyard where he works as an engineer, his first book has been successful, he has the feeling that he has only used a small part of what can be done with a novel, after this war he will talk to Lena about the new one he intends to write, he will be passionate, this next book will be a family saga, an all-embracing novel, one in which reality returns to fiction. Where could she have disappeared to?

He will tell her that he'll come a cropper, that he doesn't care, it's worth it, a big story, at one and the same time it will be about what's going on inside the head of a character and what is happening in the world outside, he'll have to find the right rhythm to convey the flow of the man's thoughts, a new kind of monologue, a crazy idea, a little-known Frenchman already tried it, he called the result *The Laurels Have Been Cut Down*, it can be done a lot better using everyday language.

But that might never come to anything. It might turn out that in this opening scene of a war whose participants still believe they are the centre of the universe and from which Max is absent, despite his sticking-out ears, despite *coincidence*, despite the dumb resignation of the horse he was about to mount, it may turn out that Hans, contrary to what Max wished to believe, will also disappear without ever seeing Lena again and get himself idiotically killed by one of these dragoons who are the pride of the French army and who will write a page of history, perform a great martial exploit, that heroic cavalry charge which is the essential element of any strategic breakthrough, according to the last appendix of *General Army Regulations for 1913*.

Certainly, in the episode which concerns us, the dragoons have no other role than to act as a column whose function is to disrupt the enemy's rear, since up to this point it is the enemy who have performed all the strategic breakthroughs, but the dragoons spur their mounts with hopes of achieving glory with the benefit of surprise and the help of Saint George before they fall back to a position south of the Marne.

Max emerges from the Blue Dwarf, muttering denials as he goes, it's complicated, got to believe in the war not in fairy tales, remain cool, stay angry enough to shoot some fellow in the eye and cool enough to steer clear of all the bloody stupidity, the return of superstition, the salmagundi of religions, the talapoins, what's stopping me believing that the Hun chops children's hands off? I honestly never wanted to do anything like that, what man would, and if that stupid old sod is so keen to believe it that's because he'd like to do it himself, eye-for-an-eye, ear, hand, vendetta, he's got a son who might die, die trying to prevent the Hun chopping children's hands off, he dreams that his son will at least have died doing that, sometimes I almost believe it myself, that's not what I mean, why is that old man angry with me for not believing the same thing as he does? Max has resumed his soldier's quick march, he beats time to each group of words with his index finger, that old fool cannot believe what he believes he can make other people believe, if I tell him I don't believe it, then the game's up.

Max stares at his finger.

He marches on. Ahead of him he sees a woman pushing a pram without a baby; in it she has put a gramophone and she is singing 'O such a waste, to lose your life when you're a woman, alas and still young' to the tune of 'O sole mio', which emerges from the horn.

The woman with the pram isn't asking for money, she does not stop and ask for money. Max catches up with her. There's a saucer next to the gramophone. They both walk on under the chestnut trees of the rue Royale. The song is about a woman who was a victim of the Germans, 'such a waste' and 'lose your life', an English victim, Miss Cavell, Edith Cavell of Norfolk, who served as a nurse in Belgium; the Germans shot her, they shot a nurse whom they accused of helping English and French soldiers to escape; a firing squad for a nurse. Every newspaper reported it, Miss Cavell is proud and strong, hers will be an exemplary death, but, the newspaper says, she falters, her knees buckle, she faints.

The German officer commanding the firing squad empties his pistol into her head. *L'Excelsior*, a quality Paris paper, knows everything, sees everything, publishes a full-page artist's impression. On the page opposite there is another topical ditty, this one to be sung to the tune of 'The Girl from Paimpol', the ninth stanza runs:

> Punish the brutes who did this deed!
> Avenge a heroine pure in heart and creed.
> She was a saint, she is divine
> And dwells in heaven above, where heroes shine!

A thought is also spared for heroes in the first ditty, another stanza set to 'O sole mio', which has these manly words: 'but it's so fine to have the chance when you're a man to die for France', which are intended to avenge Miss Cavell. Max does not believe the stories printed in the papers but he drops a coin in the saucer. The young woman looks up at him:

'Now that he's dead, I've got to earn my living.'

Max walks faster to warm up, it strikes him as funny, the church of the Madeleine behind him, the song the woman sang, arrant nonsense, truth, talapoins, he walks past the red curtains hanging at the windows of Maxim's, hundreds of sandbags piled high, directly ahead of him are the Obelisk and the National Assembly, he's in the rue Royale then the Place de la Concorde, the sandbags, the cold wind blowing from the Seine, 'O sole mio'.

That's what a cavalry charge is, just a murmur of horses' hooves, a steady trot to begin with, then three hundred paces a minute, but not for long, to allow the riders in the rear to form up as and when they emerge into the clearing, with the enemy at six hundred metres.

The dragoons are much more than the sum of their history, according to *Regulations* they are a modern weapon, a group moulded into a weapon by force of discipline. They have the training, months and months of training, on ranges and in barracks, mounted drills daily, sessions of dressage, sessions of ground work, endless jumps, plus all the different exercises involving targets, rings, butts, dummies and, worst of all, the wooden quintain which spins vertically and has a weight which whips round and catches you in the back if you don't duck fast enough after hitting it, splendid sight.

And at least three times a year, they go through their paces in public, for a public thrilled to see its army, the riders are proud to be on show, keen to get the better of the spinning wooden effigy they call the Hun, the subalterns looking round, eyes hidden under the visors of their helmets, some for what might be on offer for that evening, others for a future wife, she would have to be pretty, of course, and come with a dowry of at least 1,200 francs in non-transferable government bonds, the Republic has made that the compulsory threshold: no wife for an officer if she comes with less than 1,200 francs. In 1885 permission was given for bonds to be replaced by an equivalent investment income from publicly quoted companies.

A young girl of good family glimpsed in the stands might be checked out the following day in church, or promenading on the mall, by a young officer in uniform, sheathed sabre held in the left hand, metal tip of the scabbard fore and sword-knot aft, all as discreet as you like, but the thrust of the scabbard and the swing of the sword-knot are unambiguous.

Add the special passes granted to those 'whose duty is to maintain the good name of the dragoons with the town's fair sex', *fair sex*, note, not those marriageable girls who keep their shifts on when they take their weekly all-over wash, because it's not done to undress completely, girls who shut their eyes when they change their underwear and cross themselves, never look at their navels, mammals with braided hair who wear corsets, contrivances designed to confine the bosom, clamp the buttocks, brace the stomach and keep the flesh safe from unmentionable pleasures and enervating joys, when you wear such scaffolding you might as well forget you've got a body at all.

As for the town's fair sex, Captain Jourde would say when addressing the regiment's new lieutenants, those middle-class ladies in their sleepy provincial backwaters have no equal, especially once they're married, Seyne, a brother officer, could put us right on that score but as it happens he's not here this afternoon, the lady wife of a notary, yes, a notary's wife, don't laugh, the message hasn't got through to you junior officers, if you set your sights on actresses, dancers, horsy girls, women who want you as trophies, on the flighty side, you're obviously doing it all wrong. Who can say how earthbound the flightiest girl can get when she decides she wants to be respected? I know what I'm talking about, one wrong move on your part and it's 'what you do take me for?', then again actresses will cost you a pretty penny, and if they pay their way then get out quick because they've fallen for you, they'll write to your parents. The notary's wife knows very well that what she's doing is wrong, but she's doing what she dreamed of doing the moment she saw you, which was long before you saw her.

The wife of the man of law makes a first-rate look-out, she can see everything coming a mile off, yes, I grant you, a fast woman will do anything, that's the truth, but she goes about it in a cool sort of way and more often than not – even after you've lived together for a couple of years – she isn't really very enterprising and will refuse to do what you think she is ready to do precisely because she knows you think she's ready to do it. But your notary's wife is all blushes, boldness, keenness, enterprise, and an inescapable mouth, Dutilleux! Don't you laugh when an old hand serves you up truth as naked as Eve, nobody ever told your lawyer's wife that where love is concerned nothing is off limits but she already knows, forbidden fruit is exactly what she wants, she's always known it, so make hay. One day these lawyers' wives will want to give lesbianism a try and when they do they'll drop you like hot bricks. So here's to notaries' wives, gentlemen, and to those who service them between the lotus hours of five and seven o'clock and have a damned good time doing it.

The weather was mild, water flowed unceasingly past the mill, water nymphs, a welcoming house, three half-red roses, the mill wheel, the water frothing, Lena looked at me as she sang 'if only I could make all the millstones go round, the girl in the mill would see how constant I am' and desire seized me, the girl from the mill is mine.

Once a week since the month of February 1913, Lena and Hans have been travelling from Waltenberg to Lucerne for her singing lesson with Madame Nietnagel. They would sit down in the drawing room, I want to see your canines, Madame Nietnagel would say, a voluminous lady, all sweetness but with crocodile eyes. Lena displayed her canines as she sang, Hans kept a straight face. Madame Nietnagel was simultaneously courteous and merciless. She liked Lena, considered she had talent. The dollars did not really come into it: Madame Nietnagel had money, she took pupils only to slow the onset of old age. She liked them. But when Lena objected to any of her comments, Madame Nietnagel would remark calmly:

'I will say one more thing: do not chop the air with your hands and please, less chin. You do not have a small chin, so avoid sticking it out, and have a thought for your abdomen.'

There would be a pause. Madame Nietnagel would smile, tell anecdotes, serve small biscuits with tea in pink cups. Then Lena would resume: 'my heart is too full . . .'

Tonight in the clearing, the time for manoeuvres is over, the sky acquires hues of cherry, riders in rows of six, the NCOs in serrefile, my sergeants are true warriors, re-enlisted men every man jack of them, the cavalry has been waiting forty years for this, swoop down on the Hun, the real thing, in the name of Alsace and Lorraine, in the name of all the cavalries in the world, to bury their reputation for serving no purpose, which every cavalry in the world has worn round its neck for fifty years, ever since one charge by a light brigade at Balaclava, when English hussars fell to the withering fire of Russian batteries, the Crimean War, there was a poem about it for children and young ladies but all cavalrymen everywhere have heard that the leader of the expeditionary force, Lord Raglan had only this to say of the English hussars: 'That's what comes of forgetting that the only thing the cavalry is good for is rounding up prisoners.'

It's the first time that the troopers of the 12th Dragoons are about to launch a real charge since the beginning of the war. Until this point, they have taken part in skirmishes, done more than their fair share of reconnaissance missions, taken pointless losses when they were shelled as they waited for an order to be issued, any order, but this is the first time that they have the honour of charging in full formation crying Saint George, and also to blot out the memory of those farmers who refused to sell them provisions the day before yesterday.

'We've got nothing left!'

'Come off it! Lieutenant, they want to keep the whole lot for theirselves, let's use the thumbscrews.'

'No! Remember the company motto: "Contending for Glory!" Now, to horse!'

Max many miles away, much later, new wounds later, in the trenches at the front on the Somme, watches clouds of brown smoke coming his way, the commanding officer standing next to Max is quicker on the uptake than most and orders a withdrawal at the double. A few men have begun to cough, a gust from a side wind blowing in from the sea saves Max, his CO and their men, but the attack takes a heavy toll a little further along the line.

It's another kind of war we're seeing the beginning of, the CO said, he thought he'd seen it all in Algeria twenty years before with those caves, after they'd set fire to bales of straw in the entry to the caves, old hands in the colonies called it wog-hunting, an old custom of the country, there was smoke, a lot of coughing and spluttering, the way it's done with moles, fifty years and it's still the only thing they understand, the settlers repeating 'old Pélissier was right, he shut their traps for them', and once, at the back of a cave, a narrow fault in the rock, a current of air, the natives had huddled there together, women, children.

There was only room for two or three to breathe in that space, and they'd have been crushed by the others while the chemistry of straw fires transformed the lungs of the natives into balls of red fire, a few men had tried to get out, there were rifles waiting for them.

'No prisoners!' the colonel had shouted. 'None, they don't take prisoners either, remember the comrades you found with their private parts stuffed in their mouths, also the Morins' farm, the entire family, got to make examples!'

The day when a lieutenant asked if the examples weren't becoming so numerous in their sector that there'd soon be no one left to follow them, he was given a month in the cells for insubordination, which in the event was commuted to a transfer to Paris because he bore a name which was six and a half centuries old and far too grand for cells, even republican cells.

'And that, my dear Goffard, is why, despite my seniority, I never made it beyond the rank of major.'

After the gas attack, a couple of weeks' rest then back to the front. In one of the deeper and increasingly sophisticated trenches cannily laid out by the men to make them disappear as completely from view as possible, in the lull that followed the umpteenth bombardment from enemy lines, the CO who was the product of six and a half centuries spoke at length with Max in the low, careful voice of a man who has seen it all:

'Before the war, Goffard, I killed a man, a duel, just after my wife died. A love letter in a drawer, it was all about their assignations, myself I'd never have told a woman a hundredth part of what it said. I tracked down the author of the letter and I killed him in a duel, stuck my blade exactly where I wanted it to go, in his throat. Day before yesterday, I received a note from my sister-in-law, she wants to defend my wife's memory, she can't hold back any longer, says that her sister was innocent, that I killed a man for nothing.

'Why am I telling you all this? See those two Boche gun emplacements directly ahead, they're called *pillboxes,* pillboxes, spanking new, very trim, see how our shelling has hardly scratched them? They say the Hun builds them with English concrete, just imagine, here we've been at war for more than a year and the Hun is using English concrete, you wonder how that can be. In twenty minutes I shall give out the order I've just got, our infantry is to make a "determinedly offensive" charge against those German pillboxes made of English concrete, using bayonets only. It is a bloody cretinous order, Goffard, "determinedly", such a moronic adverb, dying for nothing, as usual.

'And if my sister-in-law is right, then my role won't have changed one iota. You will follow me in the second wave, you can order a retreat if the going gets too rough. Will you go and see my sister-in-law? You'll find her address in my kit, don't wait, she'll explain what really happened. I won't be around any more to find out but if she does know the truth someone's got to be there to hear her tell it. You can tell her I always loved my wife. Can you feel the mildness in the air? It's time to tag on to the back of the queue of all the men who've died already. Go and tell the men to be ready.'

Somewhere in Europe or in her country on the other side of the ocean, the woman Hans wants to find will hold out her hand to him, he will have become a much better man than he was before, the war will be over, she looks at him as she sings: 'if only I could make all the millstones go round, the girl in the mill would see how constant I am', why had they ever separated?

A few incidents, no more. Such as the day Hans left, she hadn't said a word, but she'd seen him sneaking a look at his watch. Hans has never been able to look at his watch casually or discreetly, he always attempts to hide the gesture, one hand carelessly loitering near the fob while at the same time doing all he can to be seen, because it is not right to dissemble, he manages the thing in such a way that he can be observed in an attempt to dissemble though not quite obviously enough to be caught in the act, for then it would not be dissembling; the guilty hand slides over the cloth of his waistcoat, the thumb giving the impression of seeking support in the opening of the little watch pocket, the other fingers being already much lower so no one could suspect them of trying to slip round the watch nestling in that pocket, but as the hand creeps down, the reprimand will out.

Hans does not allow the opportunity for this to arise, he waits until the woman he is conversing with has her back to him before he looks at his watch.

And she who has observed him placing his hand over his waistcoat pocket is generally forced to keep what she knows but cannot see to herself, she is seized by doubt, she may have been mistaken, it shortens her temper, she must find something else to criticise, her back is turned to him, she looks out of the window, the woman who suffers faces the man who is bored and suddenly she blurts out:

'You don't look as if you are here.'

On this occasion, Lena had spotted the gesture and Hans's hand, caught in the act, instead of sliding had come to a sudden rest, Lena had said in French:

'Punctuality is the courtesy of kings.'

Had she really been as cross as that?

Still further along in both space and time, later, a year, three years later, in the middle of the war, at the end of the war, who can tell? Hans saw a comrade return from the firing line holding his entrails in his hands, and he thought of those first months of the war, of the day he had almost been skewered on the end of a French dragoon's sabre, then, seeing his wounded comrade, he remembered fabled King Renaud and thought or almost sang in French, the language which was always current in his family – and it mattered very little that they lived on the shores of the Baltic, at Rosmar, in a Reich which was increasingly adopting its true tongue, the French of Racine, Stendhal and, yes, even Tallement des Réaux was part of the air you breathed if you were civilised, even young people used bits and bobs of Parisian *argot* – seeing his comrade returning long after the others, Hans thought old King Renaud 'is come home from the wars', hummed it in French, breaking the word up to accommodate the rhythm, '*de gue-erre revient*', despite all they'd been saying lately about France.

And the comrade who was holding his guts like King Renaud wanted to go on walking with his knapsack on his back as he used to walk in the old days, in peacetime, the grape-harvest, with the pannier which stood out whitely against the green of the vines, at Grindisheim, in the sunshine, he had walked to fight off the fever he had caught one evening sitting by the fire with his back to the door, because walking cures every ailment, he had walked like Renaud carrying his entrails.

And two days later, the wounded man would write to his wife:

'I can't walk any more, it hurts like nobody knows when they fish bits of bone or shrapnel out of me, nobody knows how much, they gave me an enema which did no good, I'm in a bad way, I didn't want to say anything in my last letter, dearest, I didn't want to bother you.'

At Monfaubert, the dragoons are in action, the fire in their bellies stoked by thoughts of glory, country, the sergeant-major barking orders, revenge for the loss of Alsace-Lorraine, a single body, the anxious, tortured faces of those who have come under fire before, features twisted and apprehensive, the officers ride back up the ranks to enact part of the piece of theatre which is being staged, lithe, ramrod-backed in their boots, a light hand on the reins, a faint smile of excitement on their lips, giving out orders three centuries old, 'Lower lances!' or 'Draw swords!'; when they were three hundred paces from the Prussians, the Captain cried:

'Attack!'

Ride directly towards the enemy, without hesitation. A hundred dragoons, all ex-farmhands emboldened by terror but emboldened all the same, the column hurtles into the valley of death, it's hardly the pictorial grouping most likely to satisfy eye and soul, it consists of the two main lines of twenty riders, one line for each troop, the troops being staggered in echelons to widen the line of attack, here the Captain has formed them into columns six abreast to reduce the size of the target offered to enemy fire, it is less spectacular but makes little difference, they sally forth to the sound of the squadron buglers as if they're on parade, determined to restore the smile to their faces, to settle accounts, to avenge Sedan and Reichstoffen, to forget that once more the battle is taking place on French soil, that once more, as the major newspapers put it, the German army 'has been drawn into our national space'.

The German sentries facing the dragoons have not yet grasped what is happening. They see a coloured mass emerge against a background of foliage and tree trunks, they hear the bugles blow excitedly, the tune is not a German tune, the full gallop at three hundred metres, the dragoons behaving as if they are on manœuvres, gathering for the final charge in front of the stands when their speed draws from the lady spectators shrieks like those once heard at jousts in days of yore. Several dragoons fall during the headlong rush but there is no one now to rescue them despite the screams that burst out of their entrails. The rest bear down on Hans's comrades, the evening sentries who up to that point had detected nothing more sinister than the smell of peas and bacon and potatoes cooking on the embers. All Hans is aware of are gunshots and screams and he feels ashamed.

And Max, in another place at a later date, has watched his CO set off towards the pillboxes after being told one last time:

'Go and see my sister-in-law, tell her I was hit by a bullet in the forehead, and listen to her story, the one she wants to tell about my wife.'

An almost last, then one definitely last swig of brandy for all ranks and the CO climbs out of the trench at the head of his men, red trousers, blue greatcoats, everyone in full infantry kit, zigzagging in the deathly hush which settles when the men with guns opposite are adjusting their sights and before the bellicose cries which the attackers shout out to forget, Max saw the extinction brought on by the war, to which it clung as traveller's joy binds itself around the young elm, of everything that had gone before in the days when death still went under the name of accident or disaster, two trains colliding head-on on the outskirts of Melun, the passengers dodging between the flames before falling into the inferno which lit a chaos of shadowy figures, disembowelled carriages, twisted rails, heaped ballast and, looming over it all, the express's engine, immense, towering, spurting jets of steam.

At the CO's side marches Lazare, a ladies' dressmaker, he has written to tell his children that they mustn't do anything to upset their mother, he makes the company laugh with his jokes which are so much funnier than anything his comrades come up with:

'When I'm sure of a thing, I bet on it. When I'm not sure, I give my word of honour.'

He laughs with them, with the laughter he has provoked, and for Monsieur Henri Lavedan, a member of the French Academy, this laughter of the trenches is a special kind of laughter:

'It appeases hunger, satisfies appetite, and quenches thirst when the Hun is all a man has to fill his belly with. Actually, the French soldier could never dispense with laughter. When he fights as when he plays he must go at it heart and soul. He started laughing the day France was mobilised, so come on, my lusty lads, my chaffinches, my lascars! Laugh! Sing! Dance!'

Lazare was in the artillery, he asked to be transferred to us to be closer to the shooting, you have to, he'd say, when you've been French for only two generations.

Max knows Lazare is going to be killed, we have grown so old in so few months, death looms up in the midst of youth like youth itself, drunk with joy, while life grown sterile staggers along in dirty greatcoats to meet its end. Max stands on a threshold, he watches, feeling quite unreal, it's also possible to feel unreal when you know that thirty years from now Lazare's wife will not return from Ravensbrück.

On each day that preceded this determinedly offensive sortie against the pillboxes, Lazare wrote to his wife. In one letter, he even told her:

'The treats I like best are, first, biscuits and fruit cake, then chocolate, honey, oranges and acid drops, we do three compulsory exercise sessions a day, physical training, bayonet practice and community singing, they're teaching us "La Madelon".'

Max watches Lazare, the infantrymen, his comrades, the CO, all in red and blue as they move off, they've talked about these colours, especially the red, didn't they make it easier for the enemy to spot our soldiers? Contrary to certain allegations, the argument had not been ignored but one remark – in addition to worries about the continuing domestic production of madder from which the dye was made – had settled the matter from on high:

'In the matter of the dress of the French soldier, the disadvantage of the brightness of the colours is more than compensated for by the ardour which they inspire in him.'

The stuff of legend, by Saint George! On 4 September the troopers of the 12th Dragoons charge across the field of Monfaubert. Three troops of cavalry with fear in their bellies, thumping hearts, the sound of bugles and full battle kit of which all will end up being obliterated: army-red trousers with sky-blue piping, dark blue tunic with white trim to collar and facings, the clover-leaf shoulder tabs picked out in white cotton, blue collar-patch, silver buttons, red numbers, polished steel helmet with crest and black horse-hair plume (red for buglers), brass chin-strap, snuff-coloured horse-cloth, black gaiters, tan belts and straps, fatigue coat, saddle girth, blade-shaped cantle, greatcoat in a tight roll sixty-six centimetres wide, short under-saddle made of webbing, riveted girth-leathers, an explosive charge, lance-holder and Marbach key.

One hundred and twenty kilos per horse with rider, a hundred mounted ex-farmhands led by officers with aristocratic names, not all of them, but they set the tone, no need for them to keep their distance with the men to be obeyed, and no need for the ex-farmboys to touch their forelocks to keep their place, it's a genuine society in itself, with values, there's a positive side to everything, the officers don't give too much thought for the men, they know their horses better, though not all of them, the hardest ones are the NCOs.

They're every man jack of them heartily sick of these last two months of marches, counter-marches, retreats, nights when horses are not unsaddled and men sleep with their helmets on, bridle in hand. The fear comes little by little, not at the start, because at the start they're still living the legend, a new Reichshoffen charge and a victory, 'victory', they said, 'or death' because they hadn't seen death close up, brave words, no one would buckle, they didn't care a damn about the mounted gendarmes forming a screen behind the front lines ready to round up any soldiers who ran away, they repeated what the colonel of the gendarmerie had said in 1870:

'Gendarmes, remember that you have families and that your horses are your own property!'

All your gendarmes are good for is to make life complicated for the poor bastard who has got himself separated from his unit after a failed attack!

The fear came little by little, from sitting on a horse and doing nothing while being shelled, from being made to take a back seat by men on bicycles and foot soldiers, even by kitemen, from thinking about the kids, from an order to cross a road as last week, the order was issued well before the Germans brought their 77s to bear, but the road still had to be crossed, it was only after they'd crossed it that they received the order to retreat, which meant crossing it again while being shelled by the same 77s, you've got to carry out orders, a total shambles.

And so at Monfaubert the dragoons charge to demonstrate that they are good for more than rounding up prisoners or serving as target practice for German 77s, they are charging because more and more people keep telling them: 'You're in the wrong war.'

They intend to fight and win a battle such as was never fought and won, you'll see what we make of your modern warfare, they are charging for the legend, such is the view of the Captain, the subalterns and a few of the men.

The rest do it because they're there, might as well charge because this is a dream, trade fear for illusion for a moment, just as the young men of the Tsar's guard charged at Austerlitz so that Napoleon would say: 'Tonight many pretty ladies will weep.'

Bound and gagged, Hans lies curled up on the moss and dead leaves, they're going to kill him, like Johann, no, he's a prisoner, prisoners can't be killed, Hans is virtually certain of that, nor do they cut off prisoners' ears before killing them, they obey the laws of war, they've got to respect prisoners and the Red Cross, no officer would still dare shout at his men: 'No prisoners!'

Hans is not going to die, *das Wandern*, he walks towards a mill, towards a woman who sings a song about a mill, an immortal song, even the heavy millstones enter the refrain, 'Let me go in peace and walk', river where are we going? Later here is Madame Nietnagel, her voice that of a teacher accustomed to being instantly obeyed, she was speaking of jealousy and anger directed at the hunter, you are angry, you must be angry, Mademoiselle Hotspur, there is the sound of the hunting horn in your voice, the melody is overpowering the song, listen, listen, listen carefully to the piano, it plays what is written, staccato, the piano plays staccato, the voice stays with the piano's right hand, you must not stray from it, that's good, it's fast but you're not running away with it, you're going sharp, Madame Nietnagel's very fat fingers on the keys, small hands, very quick movements, she said that this *Lied* of the hunter is pretty much an exercise, the whole of the first section keeps the mood sombre, but it mustn't become too intense, and do not make it darker, and keep the second section in the middle range.

Madame Nietnagel's face lit up, she carried on in the same vein:

'This is the hardest passage, you think you're going to be able to rest the voice but this is the hardest part, and when you are well launched, you tend to go sharp, *scheut,* the highest – and loudest – note takes fright.'

Madame Nietnagel turned to Hans with an air of complicity which to her was the height of suggestive banter:

'A young she-goat frightened by the hunter's beard, do not contract!'

Madame Nietnagel laid her fingers on Lena's diaphragm:

'Keep your sides supple, and when you sing low you must save enough breath otherwise the stomach sags forward, which is not at all attractive, don't you agree?'

She was looking at Hans when she said this.

A war in which prisoners are not killed, the officers are far too busy dying gloriously, leading their men, a bullet in the head, a small clean hole, very little blood, just the red blotch which in the paintings of gifted artists serves to draw the eye of the beholder. The officers die for the legend, they will not sully their glory with an obscene order to have prisoners and wounded men shot, on the day war broke out President Poincaré spoke of 'the eternal moral power of right which neither peoples nor individuals can disregard with impunity', these lieutenants and captains die as Péguy died at Villeroi on 6 September, defending right, and from a shot in the middle of his forehead.

Péguy had demanded that Jaurès and his pacifism should be silenced 'by the drums of the guillotine'.

The officers pass living into legend even when no trace of their mortal remains is ever found, like Alain-Fournier, killed in action, like so many others, his death is summed up by the words of one soldier who survived:

'The lieutenant's bought it!'

Then come the phrase-makers, Alain-Fournier is dead, a mortal blow to literature, end of our childhood, the very trees of Sologne are in mourning, the village school is dead, the classroom that smells of hay and stables, everything, the red house, the virginia creeper, the lamp-lit evenings, Christmas, the great sacks of chestnuts, everything, good things to eat wrapped in cloths, and the pungency of singed wool when some boy stood too close to the stove to get warm, a body was never identified. Fournier's corpse was absent when they held roll-call.

'Henri Alban Fournier (the real name of Alain-Fournier) died from a shot in the head,' reports his brother-in-law, Jacques Rivière, who got it from a private soldier.

'He was killed by a bullet to the head,' says Paul Genuist.

'A bullet in the head, in a heroic action,' Patrick Antoniol states specifically.

It happened at Saint-Rémy, three weeks after Monfaubert, a bullet in the head, Fournier's batman said so, name of Jacquot, he saw it all:

'In the forehead, killed outright.'

Fournier had written:

'I've picked out as my batman a Zouave, a crapulous type who's good at fending for himself, seen service in Morocco, had two teeth knocked out by bullets, I'm afraid he's prone to exaggeration . . .'

Jacquot added:

'When I got back to him, the lieutenant was stone cold.'

Fournier's sister does not believe the story about the bullet in the head, Henri didn't die at all:

'The bullet in the centre of his forehead was something Jacquot made up, he'd told my parents: "I'll watch out for the lieutenant", but he wasn't at his side, he was in the rear.'

Yet Fournier's mistress, Pauline Benda – in January she was on stage playing Régine in *La Danse devant le miroir* displaying a surprising talent for the subtle nuance – Pauline Benda adds:

'At the exact moment Henri was shot, I felt a sudden pain in the middle of my forehead, as if I had been struck by something.'

In this war which never ends, a year, no, much longer than that, on another occasion altogether, Hans is very hungry, very thirsty, one day he is dying of thirst in a hole he cannot get out of, he tears out the last remaining handfuls of grass, he chews the grass, his teeth crunch on soil, he goes on chewing.

He vows that never again will he lose his temper when normal life returns, after the war, the trees, the paths, the woman he'll be reunited with, their walks together, he will not get cross when their horses pull on the reins and reach out with their lips to the grass which the dying day is now sprinkling with dew, Hans will turn to look at Lena, they will not waste the moment.

Henri Alban Fournier, killed in action while leading the 23rd Company of the 288th Infantry Regiment. A bullet in the head, his face otherwise unmarked. Rémi Debats, another soldier, saw Fournier hit by a bullet:

'But not in the head. *In the chest.* Killed outright.'

Yet another, Zacharie Baqué, a sergeant, sees Fournier leading the assault through the wood, under low branches, trampling the nettles underfoot, crushing the valerian just as Seurel and co. do in *Le Grand Meaulnes*, and Seurel himself stands at the forest's edge 'like a patrol which the corporal leading it has lost', along paths of green grass under the leafy branches they run, red breeches and blue frock-coats, to debouch, as if chasing game through the woods of Sologne, with the brambles snatching at your sleeve, 'suddenly,' said Seurel, 'I came out into a sort of clearing which turned out to be a meadow.'

Captain de Gramont and Lieutenant Fournier 'fire shots with their revolvers', Baqué sees Fournier 'on the ground, not moving', he hears a voice choking, it's Second-Lieutenant Imbert fatally wounded, he cries out 'Mother!', Baqué doesn't tell him what Robinson said to another officer who is dying:

'Your mummy doesn't give a damn!'

Instead he just goes on shooting at the Germans.

Now it's an Englishman, Stephen Gurney, who describes what happens to Fournier:

'Suddenly, stopped by *a bullet in the arm,* he dropped on one knee and was never seen again.'

Fournier, in that clearing at Saint-Rémy, like his hero at the end of *Le Grand Meaulnes.*

At Monfaubert the dragoons are about to find fame, at a gallop, skimming the ground, by Saint George! 'Contending for glory', and seven hundred paces a minute, a regulation cavalry pace being set at eighty centimetres, destiny is already flexing its muscles, at sixty paces from the Prussians Captain Jourde stands up in his stirrups and at the top of his voice cries:

'Chaaarge!'

The cry is taken up by all the officers. Some riders sit up straight to cut a more intimidating figure for the enemy's benefit, they drop their hands, dig with their spurs. One horse stumbles, a rabbit hole, it falls, rolls on its rider. Enemy fire starts up, still scattered as yet, ineffective. When dragoons charge in formation six abreast, only the leading line is fully exposed, it partly masks the rest of the column, horses and riders are hit but the devastating strike is rare, a wounded horse will continue to gallop long enough to smash into enemy lines, we have rediscovered our spirit, our drive, our bite, the column at full gallop, the rear presses the front to go faster, riders who fall cannot slow the overwhelming mass, we have stopped being only good for rounding up scum, it takes both arms to hold my mare, lying on her neck I aim with the point of my sabre, I have a pain in my belly, in my chest, I am hot and cold, a dragoon for the first time in all the years that he has been learning how to ride, falls, one foot caught in a stirrup, a lump of fear dragged over the grass by an animal determined to overtake the others.

Fournier isn't dead, Captain Juvin saw him, just wounded, he told the parents of Lieutenant Fournier:

'I can assure you that there was a German field dressing-station at the spot where he fell.'

'In that German dressing-station,' said Isabelle, 'lay all of our hopes.'

And everyone agrees: Captain Boubée de Gramont launched a pointless and dangerous attack. He said:

'It is essential that we go after the Hun.'

Testimony of Private Angla:

'The look-outs had warned us, Huns everywhere. The Captain was off his head, he said "I've got the black-rot all through me, say your prayers, lads, in my Company we're all dead men".'

Fournier was falling back with his infantry when the Captain made him turn and go after the enemy.

Suddenly there are shouts, all hell breaks loose.

'It's a German dressing-station that's been overrun,' said Baqué.

'I'm stuck with a captain who is a swine and so tiresome you could weep,' said Fournier.

A field dressing-station.

They attacked it, a 'desperate and heroic' action. Captain de Gramont, Lieutenants Fournier, Imbert and their men versus a field-station, the Red Cross and German stretcher-bearers.

Bugles, the gallop at Monfaubert, the earth shakes, Hans can see nothing, but he can hear. A French rider held back in reserve comes up to him, Hans stirs, the man puts one hand on his sabre, a voice says 'No!', it's a bad dream, wake up, dream something else, there's no sabre, none of it's real, Hans shakes, I know why I left Hans, because he was never there, physically he was there, he called me Lena, smiled when I looked at him, but he didn't like being there, or rather he didn't like the person he was when he was there, he called me Lena but it wasn't quite him, he always gave me the impression that I was dealing with a replacement, he'd sent me a replacement who was a great deal less interesting than he was, than the person he'd set his mind on becoming, and this replacement took only a blundering sort of interest in me. And in this story I became less desirable, I interested the Hans I had in front of me less than the Hans who would come later, there was this replacement who watched the both of us to see what we might turn into from the point of view of the Hans who would come later. He did not want me as I was, he tried to look at his watch, his innocent fingers crept towards his waistcoat pocket, all this is splitting hairs, I can sum it all up by saying that he was a pain in the neck, he didn't try to change me but he left me to confront someone who wasn't really there and with whom I couldn't really be myself, he was sweet, though still a pain in the neck, irritating and adorable.

The earth quakes, no one is going to kill Hans, it's not done, anyway it's a dream, dream another dream, think of the things you love.

Eighty thousand dead and two weeks later, on 22 September, came Saint-Rémy.

'Captain Gramont wouldn't listen, Lieutenant Fournier and Lieutenant Imbert wept because they could see the Captain was leading us to our deaths,' Private Angla told Jacques Rivière.

In Rivière's view, Alain-Fournier did not attack a dressing-station. The wood at Saint-Rémy is also known as Knights' Wood.

In his ditch at Monfaubert Hans is afraid and ashamed, he looks at Johann, his partially severed head, the blood has flowed copiously from Johann's neck.

The dressing-station attacked at a run, the orders of a captain who says:

'I've got the black-rot right through me.'

'A French war crime,' say the Germans, 'those responsible were shot.'

'Not a dressing-station but a cart carrying stretchers,' is the response on the French side.

'A fine, a great, a just war,' writes Henri Alban Fournier to Isabelle just before he was killed.

And to Pauline:

'We must not think anything that cuts the ground from under our feet.'

A dressing-station attacked by French forces: a report by

Commandant Uecker, officer commanding the German 2nd Medical Corps:

'At Saint-Rémy, a group of French infantry led by two officers killed eight stretcher-bearers and shot the three wounded men being treated in the dressing-station.'

On 24 November 1914, to a German military court, Private Meerländer:

'On 22 September, I saw French soldiers killing the wounded men on our stretchers, our men surrounded the Frenchmen and shot them all.'

'Untrue,' say the officials of the Association of the Friends of Jacques Rivière and Alain-Fournier, 'it is simply not true that Alain-Fournier was shot for attacking a field dressing-station, and anyway it wasn't a dressing-station ambulance but a cart carrying a few stretchers.'

Chapter 2

1914

The Lake

In which the intensity of the French cavalry charge reaches new heights.
*In which the achievement of President Poincaré is compared with that
of the* Pieds Nickelés.
In which we learn how Lena Hotspur fell in love with Hans Kappler.
In which questions are asked about the true death of Alain-Fournier.
*In which Hans and Lena suddenly hear cracking coming from the lake
on which they are skating.*

Monfaubert, 4 September 1914

It engulfs us, we organise: all falls down,
We reorganise: then we too all fall down,
Rainer Maria Rilke, *Duino Elegies*, VIII

Seven hundred paces a minute, Monfaubert, dragoons at full gallop, six hundred rounds in the same minute is the rhythm of the Spandau machine gun, two machine-gun posts at least have begun to open up but not until well after the start of the charge, where have these Frenchmen come from? The dragoons gallop on.

In close formation, the front line of riders six abreast per troop, three troops, less than thirty paces now from the objective, going at a tremendous lick, lashed by the devil himself. The machine-gun fire intensifies, shaking their tripods, cutting clear swathes through the horsemen who are closing fast. A few Germans, flat helmets with red flash, run hither and thither, rush forward, fall back, work the bolts of their rifles, hardly bother to take aim, fire at will, no time for concerted volleys.

Some dragoons ride into the crossfire from the machine guns and are shot in the back, the tide of dragoons is already on the enemy, a fusion of fear and furious voices lacerated by gunshots, lance thrusts, sabre blows, many riders have kept the curving sabre of 1882, despite the official ruling requiring the use of the straight sabre, the curved sabre is two-edged, cut and thrust, magnificent strokes, the point for the first shock, then slash with sharp blade to follow-up.

In the mêlée, the sabres rain down on a nest of machine-gunners, on heads not wearing helmets, on rifles held up to parry the blows, kill in order to live, screams from the Germans or perhaps the horsemen, no one can say, the advance continues, the breakthrough continues with bare steel, shock, speed, men leap forward or take avoiding action, we must achieve the breakthrough, strike at their very heart or else go down in the attempt.

Lena, Hans is no longer keen on the idea of horse rides at twilight, he is with her in autumn in a house with a garden, together they peruse catalogues of flowers and vegetables to plant in beds in the spring, they examine the packets of seeds, they open them, Hans laughs and jumbles up sweet peas and cress, broad beans, gladioli, pansies and spinach, she smacks his hand, they fool around trying to sort them all out again, they go outside, into the garden, it is morning, they walk a little way, the sun is still a pleasant red disc, a hazy round plate.

Lena is not dead, he is not going to die, why did they ever separate? That's not the way life should go. One night she simply stopped snuggling up with her back against his belly.

It was all so cosy, before. They'd hold each other's hand to turn the pages of a magazine, the advertisements, fashions even, was there a case for wearing divided skirts? Please, ladies, let us remain feminine, let us permit the elegance of the foot to intimate the slenderness of the leg which is discreetly encased in the bottom of a long skirt. Hans raised the hem of her skirt and kissed her leg in the Hotel Waldhaus in Waltenberg in 1913.

There is a vehicle in the middle of the German bivouac at Monfaubert now under attack by the dragoons. A voice rises above the battle, an *Offizier* who shouts orders, regroups his men. He stands on the running-board of a car. He directs his men to fire in groups, by bearings, in volleys: restore order, order is the better half of life.

The *Offizier* knows all about warfare, he is an old colonial hand, he was at Waterberg in Namibia, seven years ago already, Prussian troops against the Hereros, all the rebellious native tribes were driven back into the steppes of Omaheke, pursued from waterhole to waterhole.

And when there were no more wells, the savages dug holes fifteen metres deep looking for water. German patrols found large numbers

46

of skeletons around holes which were dry, the Herero people were estimated to number eighty thousand, and of them fifteen per cent survived, that was in 1907, the beginning of the century, all forgotten. The starkness of the final tally is to be explained, in diplomatic circles, by the relative inexperience of the Reich in colonial affairs. 'The cries of the dying,' wrote Oberleutnant Graf Schweinitz, 'and the ravings of the crazed rang out in the sublime silence of the infinite.' With mounting success, the *Offizier* on his running-board is heard and obeyed.

The subaltern leading the 2nd troop of French dragoons breaks off from the target and redirects his men against the car from which the orders are being issued, a horse is hit and its rider is pitched over its neck and put out of action, the rest thunder by. Some dragoons are now surrounded by Prussians, the Prussians fire at them, shoot each other, shoot dragoons, the dragoons surround the car, 'the mounted attack with drawn swords, which alone gives decisive results, is the principal modus operandi of the cavalry', later there are voices, wouldn't it have been better to attack on foot, with carbines? smaller losses, and the enemy well and truly put on the rack. Perhaps, but less panache that way. Before the attack, one of the French officers even shouted out 'You can't stop me dying in the saddle!'

The first priority now is to cut down the burly Prussian who is shouting the orders. In front of the car, a *Feldwebel* in a flat-topped steel helmet has picked up a lance, covers his officer, a dragoon runs his mount to the left of the lance, the *Feldwebel* turns the lance against the dragoon who lies flat on his horse's neck to pass under the point but receives a terrible thrust, at the same instant his sword connects with the Prussian's chest, another dragoon rides by, a thump in the ribs, falls on his back, brought down at point-blank range by a Prussian.

The rest of the dragoons have retreated to gather themselves for another charge, they close on the car and the *Offizier*, one dragoon goes down, another rides past, sabre held straight out stiff-armed, as if he is at drill and tilting at spinning quintains mounted on tripods, point of the blade angled up towards the chest, the point misses the chest, the strike is too high, the blade passes within centimetres of the man's neck, a trained reflex, the dragoon slashes as he draws back the sabre, the Prussian officer ducks, the blade saws off his ear, his cheek, the whole of his mouth.

Blood spurts, more shouting, the advantage of the curved sabre tells, more shots, the horse goes down, the dragoon is unscathed, three German soldiers leap on him, they scream, the dragoon on his feet, he has lost his sabre, get away, don't die in this abomination, war is an abomination, the dragoon hates war, he's a lawyer, and a good horseman.

A German soldier grabs him from behind, holds him in a headlock, this is no dress parade, parades were before, the rider does not want to die, bloody war, go back to what life was before, quick, start over again, the rider is a lawyer, spring of 1914, they were heading for the abomination of war, it was then that it should have all been stopped, Poincaré elected President of the Republic, the rider didn't want Poincaré, Fallières standing on the steps of the Élysée Palace sick at heart watching his successor climb the steps, says: 'Poincaré, so it's war.'

Another German soldier has picked up a bayonet and is trying to ram it into the dragoon pinioned by his comrade, Poincaré, man of the left, but a warmonger, still a republican all the same, the republicans had got together and nominated another candidate for the presidency, against the right, 'Stout Pams', these French bastards caught them napping, the Prussian is holding the bayonet awkwardly, he's a mechanic not really a killer, Pams would have made a perfectly good President, Poincaré only second in the ballot held by the republican camp, he should have withdrawn his name, that was the convention, but it seems Poincaré had been offended, on the grass of Monfaubert other cavalrymen fall, scream, no one to help them, when things have calmed down a handful of medical orderlies will come, the Red Cross, surgical saws, disinfectant, in Paris since 1912, a sensible precaution, nuns are allowed to work in hospitals, they learned to assist surgeons who were being trained to operate using disinfectant only, without anaesthetic, on the poor.

Her flesh is much lighter, Hans looks at Lena's bare back, the white fabric pulled down to her hips, her shock of red hair pulled up over the nape of her neck, the texture of her skin so smooth to his tongue. She is not dead. One night at Waltenberg her buttocks were all goose-pimples, how they had laughed, her laugh more raw, deeper than usual, Hans with his cheek against her hip had felt the strong flexing of her muscles as she laughed, her contralto voice. He can see the woman seated in the window with her back to the light, her back is three-quarters bare, her left breast just a little heavy in outline, it swells generously at a right angle from her ribs before curving roundly back to rejoin her body, he starts to get to his feet, makes it on to one knee alongside the armchair, is about to say don't move and cover the breast with little kisses, it is not the final image he had carried away of her, but it is the one which will protect him against the inferno.

The German soldier lunges at the Monfaubert dragoon, all he has is the bayonet in his hand, he tries to stick the blade into the chest of the dragoon who is being held from behind in a headlock by his comrade, the dragoon struggles, calls for help, kicks his legs out in front of him like a girl who's had too much to drink dancing the can-can or a tango, the bayonet catches him in the thigh, in the hands, he is bleeding, the German soldier aims for his heart, the bayonet just slides over his ribs, there is more and more blood, put a stop to the whole thing, Poincaré the warmonger, the 1913 election, the republicans had chosen another candidate for the presidency, yes, but there's the insult to Poincaré, what insult? the insult had left him free to canvass the votes of his opponents on the right, the warmongering hawks and those who still thought Dreyfus was a traitor, Poincaré, the war, and ready to do anything to become President of the Republic, not a traitor, freed of his obligations by the insults directed at his wife by the republican tittle-tattle emanating from his own camp.

In the guts! shrieks the Prussian who is holding the dragoon from behind, the blood trickles from a gash in his face, the Prussian is finding it increasingly difficult to keep the headlock on from behind, but the dragoon is a lawyer and isn't trained for hand-to-hand combat, doesn't know how to bend his knees suddenly, shift his weight forwards, and throw the soldier who has him in the headlock over his shoulder so that he lands on the bayonet of the soldier facing him, all the dragoon can do is lash out with his feet, 'In the guts!' screams the Prussian, the insult, Poincaré's wife wasn't really widowed in the United States and her civil marriage to Poincaré made her a bigamist, there was a bigamist in the Élysée Palace, but the Church stepped in, Cardinal Andrieu giving Poincaré his backing for the sake of morality, the cross, for Lorraine and a promise.

The bayonet slips, cuts deep into the hands of the German who is holding it, the dragoon yells for help, kicks his legs out in front of him, let us dance, said *Le Figaro*, since everyone else is dancing, the very dead will do a tango, the promise that the Poincarés would be married in church, the blessing to be given during the next parliamentary session, the session immediately following the presidential election, two unseated French cavalrymen come up scattering Prussians, whirling their sabres like windmills, the Cardinal goes to work on Catholic members of parliament and senators, Poincaré, vote for him, he's changed sides, his soul is in our camp.

The Prussian soldier finally gets a good grip on the bayonet, Jesus! don't leave me by myself, the dragoon's voice cracks, his two comrades wheel around the Prussians who will not let him go, and around them other Prussians come running, one of them gets his skull split from the top of his head to his teeth, a wounded horse rushes past at a triple gallop, its rider clinging on to his pommel, a church wedding is a small price to pay for entry to the Élysée, the people's mood is calm, he will go to war, you know, even the members of Bonnot's gang who were sentenced to death were executed without any fuss or unrest, it was enough to show them who was in charge, Poincaré the warmonger elected President, a republican to be sure, but one who had managed to get himself elected *by reactionaries*, it was treason!

No, there was no treason, the left, Poincaré said, had insulted his wife, a good argument, a U-turn and lurch to the right, the Prussian holding the dragoon from behind releases his grip, Poincaré became President, there were now two hopes for peace, the first was called

Caillaux, he was to become Prime Minister, he had already staved off one war with Germany.

The dragoon is almost free, another dragoon comes up on the Prussian who is holding the bayonet, at the last moment the bayonet pierces the stomach of the dragoon who thought he was safe, the full length of a bayonet slides into soft tissue, the dragoon screams, the Prussian receives a cut from a sabre, the other dragoons grab their comrade under the arms, must get away, sabre-thrusts right and left as they make a run for it, the Prussians give up, the two dragoons see their comrade's wound, don't leave me behind, with Caillaux as Prime Minister there would be peace despite Poincaré as President, and Henriette Caillaux, large dark hat with a feather and black muff, fires six shots with a gun.

'I smother you all over with tender kisses,' Caillaux had written to Henriette in letters dating from the time when she was merely his mistress.

Calmette, editor of Le Figaro, five or six shots, wanted to publish them, he is no longer a threat, three bullets, two fatal, in Calmette's carcass.

At Monfaubert, a bayonet in the belly, slower than a bullet in the head, really much slower, the two French dragoons lay their comrade on the ground, put a stop to it all in the spring, he does not yet know that it will take him four hours to die, Poincaré the warmonger has replaced Fallières, and Caillaux will not now be Prime Minister.

A woman sits half-dressed at dawn, a leather armchair, her back to the light, a cold crimson light, think about the things you love, his mother had said, Hans knows you don't have either the time or the right to remember the women you've loved when you've been thrown into a ditch and your comrades are being killed around you, it's so very vivid, images come in flashes, evening walks down the path outside the hotel, the names of a few stars above the snow, the gurgle of a stream, best give me your arm that way I shan't slip, holding his arm while they walk, that's all she'll ever do, they make their way back to the Waldhaus Hotel, a looming mass in the moonlight, a Belle Époque folly, a cross between a Bavarian *Schloss* and a fantastic overgrown chalet, two huge chalets eight storeys high standing on a common base itself three storeys tall, the third floor of this common base being occupied by guest lounges and the dining room, the north wing of the hotel terminating beyond the edge of a precipice, the architect having decided to make a bold gesture by extending the base of his building over empty space.

A twenty-metre overhang resting on girders anchored in the granite, propped up four-square, more solid than the Eiffel Tower or the piles of Brooklyn Bridge, the balconies of the rooms on the end of the north side hang over the void.

When he checked in, Hans had refused one of those rooms on the end of the north wing, I am a marine engineer, I built shapes that float on water not in air, the manager defends his hotel, there is no architecture without a gesture, Monsieur Kappler, and the overhang is the hotel's gesture, because if this were not so it would be just a very large kitsch gateau.

In the evening, the large bay windows lit the valley. They had returned arm in arm.

Later, a 'good night' in front of a door, the hand of Lena Hotspur reaches round the back of Hans's neck, Hans opens his lips.

There are two schools of thought in the matter of kissing, that promoted by the French postcard 'Ah, supreme embrace which melts all it touches, a kiss on the lips is the gift of the self', and that of modern medicine which recommends that when the kiss cannot be avoided it should be preceded by a thorough rinsing of the mouth with an antiseptic preparation.

Lena took Hans by the back of the neck and more or less bundled him into her room. The next morning, Hans opened the balcony window and realised that Lena had been given a room on the north side.

In all, twenty-one bodies lie in the common grave at Saint-Rémy, on their backs, heads to feet, two rows each of ten bodies, the twenty-first in the centre covering five other skeletons.

In it are also assorted religious medallions, a gold wedding ring, a rosary, several wallets, a cigarette lighter, a pipe, cartridge cases and cartridges, bullets, 1881 issue reservists' boots, sundry types of buttons, a pair of false teeth, a few ink pens, numerous gold coins wrapped in paper.

In most cases, the bullets were fired at these bodies from different angles and left wounds typical of traditional warfare: field combat, assault, retreat, what they call a princes' war. Some had been hit in ways that suggested they had been put out of their misery.

'Over here, quick!' Michel Algrain had been told one day in May 1991, 'it's beeping it's head off!'

A soldier's grave. In the places where soldiers die, enough iron and steel always remains for metal detectors to pick it up: eighteen privates and three officers, a captain, a lieutenant and a sub-lieutenant. The officers wear bespoke boots and are on average ten centimetres taller than their men. Dog tags, the number 228, which is the number of the regimental corps, clipped in brass to collar flaps, stripes sewn on the forearms and shoulders of the first three skeletons, there is absolutely no doubt: here lie Gramont, Fournier, Imbert and their men.

'The top joint of the right forefinger,' said an archaeologist, 'gives us the hand of a writer.'

Remnants of hand-knitted undergarments. A terrific find for an amateur archaeologist.

'But Michel Algrain,' commented the Association of the Friends of Jacques Rivière and Alain-Fournier in 1992, 'went too far. What do these German documents prove? What is the point of stories about some German field dressing-station which he went grubbing around for across the Rhine? Monsieur Algrain should remind himself that no one who goes looking in enemy territory for evidence with which to charge our own side with crimes they did not commit can ever claim to be innocent.'

On 10 November 1992, Algrain will be excluded from the ceremony when the remains are re-interred.

During the winter which preceded the war, Henri had written to Pauline:

'Somewhere there's a frozen pond where we would at this moment be skating, a white garden where I'd lead you by the hand, a road where we would go for a long, long walk before it got dark and a room where we would at this moment be sitting together by the fireside.'

A lovers' dream. The frozen pond, Henri and Pauline executing serene arabesques on the ice, in proper families they would be termed an unlawful couple. They dream of firesides.

Or then again they only speak in their letters of firesides and walks because it is not done in letters to speak of the predatory advances which are made in a bedroom in Paris as the evening gathers, the man talks like this to please the woman, or else he's the one who dreams he is in the white garden and offers her his dreams, and maybe both of them truly yearn for a happiness constituted by a white garden and a fireside, because nothing else is within their reach, no, what they really like is the dusk and the dark, persistent smells laden with oil fumes which fill the room whenever they have to heat it, but that is the one treat they can neither have nor write about, so they treat each other instead to a white garden, a log fire, chestnuts crackling, she seated in the armchair by the window, momentarily in repose, turned towards the landscape, the window blameless, the breast observed in profile, the snow has consumed everything, the only thing that stirs, faintly on the fence, is the black, white and blue stain of a magpie which had just landed.

At Monfaubert, the dragoons charge, that is, those who have not yet fallen to the rhythm of the noise which is for all the world like the sound of a very large sewing-machine, a Spandau no different from the thousands in service in the German army, manufactured under licence from the British and modified Prussian style.

'The target must not merely be pierced,' declared the Emperor, 'but riddled.'

The dragoons charge in a dream and what they take aim at with the point of their swords, of their lances, of their dreams, are other men's dreams.

If they'd been faced by ordinary troops, they would not have charged.

Facing them are dreams the colour of doves which have surfaced from the remote mists of time. And if it were not for these dove-grey dreams, there would have been no German victory against the Russians less than a month ago at Tannenberg, dreams which emerged from a labyrinth as old as the act of dreaming itself, but barely make it into the light of day.

At first, Max did not understand Calmette's death there in the offices of *Le Figaro*, the reasons for it, not Henriette Caillaux's reasons, a woman whose letters someone intends to publish is fully entitled to shoot the swine who would do such a thing, no, what Max did not understand at first were Calmette's reasons, such a serious-minded man, with no interest in scandal, he had just noted in his diary that *The Rite of Spring* was an offence against morality and that Nijinsky displayed 'gross indecency' in certain of his choreographed movements.

So why publish private letters? It was the sort of thing sensation-seeking newspapers did. And in *Le Figaro*! The same *Figaro* that went so far as to denounce the tango for obscenity, a so-called 'society' dance which, let it not be forgotten, requires the man to thrust one leg between those of his partner. Calmette had not dared write these details down in full, but he had spelled the message out to the men on the presses in the print-room: 'I will not allow such filth to corrupt the Family!'

And Max, ten years after the war, will be told that Calmette, normally so prudish and sober-sided, had a very good reason for turning his worthy *Figaro* into a rag filled with scandal and purloined letters, not a political reason, but rather a madness, because Calmette was mad and madly in love with another woman, *a woman of letters* whom Caillaux also loved to the point of wanting to divorce Henriette. Let's summarise.

Monsieur Caillaux, Madame Caillaux, Monsieur Calmette, and bringing up the rear, a *woman of letters*. Calmette, madly in love and jealous of this *woman of letters*, had unearthed Caillaux's old letters to his wife Henriette and was about to publish them. When she read the letters written to Henriette Caillaux, the *woman of letters* would lose interest in Caillaux. So Calmette decided to put an end to Caillaux, his policies and the designs he was said to have on a *woman of letters* who had the nerve to hesitate between a politician and the editor of *Le Figaro*.

A formidable lady, this *woman of letters*, all caustic and cream, a great name, a voice of her own, poison and poems, 'you have strength and I have guile; your strength is to be the one I love'. An ambassador, very much an admirer of the lusty male form, is about to sit down facing her. There is a hat on the chair, no point in sitting down, the hat's quite soft. A literary lady with genuine poems to her credit, 'even in my heart where your blood beats', then later the mistress of a married man, the man dies, the literary lady turns up at the funeral, very dignified, stays in the background, and when the mourners file past the open grave she throws her cloak into it.

The tango, the Holy Office decides, is an infernal dance, one final demonstration of this impious dance is given in the presence of Pius X by a couple of young Roman aristocrats, a brother and sister of irreproachable moral rectitude, who nevertheless wish to defend the tango, which tango did they dance? for the Pope commiserated with them on having to perform these 'very tiresome movements', nevertheless the tango is forbidden by the Vatican, and at least three of the shots fired in Calmette's office turn Calmette into a corpse, Henriette into a tragic heroine whom it is henceforth impossible for him to divorce even to marry a woman of letters, Calmette into political flotsam, and peace into a cause amputated of all leaders save Jaurès – whose voice Péguy would dearly love to drown out beneath the drums of the guillotine – who is a habitué of the Café du Croissant, with its carved wood façade and gold lettering.

He was young and good-looking, he said 'I love you, Lena', he put a lot of feeling into the way he looked at me, we were on a mountain, he didn't know where to begin, the back of his neck was soft, it made me want to drag him into my room, I did it, it felt good, I managed to say *Liebchen* and *Hansele* but it wasn't love, it was the mountain, I might have started to fall in love with him later on, when Marie-Thérèse . . .

He just went on staring at her, I was furious, I didn't want him to fall for another girl but that in itself is not enough to make a man love you. You can write books about it, but it's not enough. I thought he was very silly to stare at her like that, she started kicking up like a mare in season, she was insufferable, he just looked moony, a woman and a damp-eyed puppy, in a farmyard, I didn't bother to say anything, anyway I wasn't really in love with him.

He could have done whatever he liked with her, it wouldn't have bothered me. To start loving a man because you see him straightening his tie before going up to some Marie-Thérèse who jiggles all she's got for everyone to see, wears vulgar dresses, in that pink Liberty print, a pink muslin blouse, pink pearls and shows as much cleavage as it takes to attract looks from the morons, and very few from me.

I suddenly had this feeling that I had ceased to be anything, that I had no breasts, no backside, but I didn't feel that I had fallen in love. I didn't say anything and it didn't last. Anyway she's got peculiar breasts. I left the pair of them to it, he came after me, men are like that.

I know exactly when I started to love him, three months after we'd been together, Arosa, that farcical episode at Arosa, on the first floor of the chalet we'd rented for one night, with the raised bed.

I'd climbed into it, I was waiting for him, he was also already in his nightclothes, a little painted wooden chair, at the foot of the bed, the solemn look he gave me as he stood on the chair to join me, very amorous, as was only right and proper.

His foot went right through the chair, foot, calf, knee and halfway up his thigh, went clean through the flimsy wooden seat of a chair which was never intended for amorous use, a chair painted pale blue. He nearly fell over, he couldn't free his leg, it might have happened to me, he wasn't really hurt, only very annoyed.

He tried to extricate his leg but the splinters began sticking in his thigh, he swore, turned red in the face, a parfit knight with a chair circling his naked thigh, that's what set me off with the giggles, I shouldn't have, the most awful giggles, I bit my lip, I didn't want anyone on the floor below to hear me, my hot-blooded knight in a nightshirt, with one leg through a chair, we must get help, out of the question, he tried to break off the splintered wood but he was standing and couldn't do it, I was helpless with laughter, I bit the inside of my cheeks, we must have been making a terrible row, I could see he was in a bad way, I got down clinging to the bed posts.

He was beginning to be in real pain, I stopped laughing, I made him lie down on the floor, on his back, with his leg in the air, the chair clamped around his leg, I managed to slide the chair up his thigh to ease out the splinters which had started to dig into his flesh, he had good thighs, he didn't seem to be thinking about sex any more.

I kept my eyes on the job, I snapped off the splintered ends one by one to widen the hole in the chair and pull it off without doing him any damage, gently, and then I got the giggles again because I suddenly wanted to say: if only Marie-Thérèse could see you now!

Of course all that was already over and done with, but I still wanted to say it, naturally I didn't do anything of the sort, a fit of the giggles, my lover man, on his back, beautiful light of a candle, one leg in the air, his white nightshirt pulled up, with him doing his best not to make too indecent a spectacle of himself, come on try, with one leg in the air and a chair wrapped round it, I was laughing, I couldn't get the last of the splinters out and pull the chair down over his knee.

His skin was smooth, I wasn't laughing now, I kissed him, and suddenly I loved him more than I had ever loved anyone before, he didn't quite get it, for him love meant taking my breasts in both hands and gazing at me solemnly, I liked that too, though not as much as when he was on his back with that chair around his leg.

The staccato rat-tat-tat continues in bursts, riders are still falling in the clearing at Monfaubert, mown down by the chattering sewing-machine which has swung round towards them, but Captain Jourde can no longer react, regroup, respond, for the Captain is down, back propped against a tree, he has taken a burst in the chest.

He asks the lieutenant to sit him up, the lieutenant obeys, then walks into the throng of riderless horses and helmetless riders, some covered in blood and clinging for dear life to the pommel of their saddles, others screaming and thrusting and smiting, keep hold of this rage, keep the goal before you: destroy the Boches and their filthy dreams.

Captain Jourde is determined to die facing the enemy, but what he sees in front of him standing not two metres away is his own black mount, an Anglo-Norman thoroughbred, looks thin, has blood on its chest, it holds up one leg, which is also bleeding, the horse shudders, looks at the Captain who is saying to himself that the charge he led has failed, around him bullets whine, smack, slap, mew, ricochet, shatter a stone, a nose, the Captain's hand claws at the grass.

The regimental log simply states that the Captain died in battle, the press prefers 'on the field of honour' or 'for France', it makes a great deal of difference to a good many women who henceforth enter into what is called 'the heroic wakefulness of wives'.

Calmette, Caillaux, Henriette Caillaux and a *woman of letters,* after the war Max will be told that he's an obsessive, there is more to History than one floozy's flings, History is made by the mass of humanity, the prevailing laws, nations, passions, men of true greatness, great ideas or inter-imperialist contradictions, the hand of God, Max, or the wood that burns so that trees may turn green again, the act of righteous revenge which burns down the house which sets fire to the street, the act becomes a crime, then begets a new and more handsome street, war as a crime without punishment, undertaken to restore right: passions which at the last bring you back to the universal, or on the contrary the pure instinct of death, with nothing before it, especially not women, actually my dear Max, I challenge you to publish the name of that *woman of letters* who is supposed to have been loved at the same time by both Calmette and Caillaux, 'I hold the roses close so that my arms are pricked', the Swiss Ambassador talked about it in his correspondence, but he was Swiss.

Max gets under the skin of his friends on both the left and the right. He makes the Great War turn entirely on 'a pair of frilly lace knickers', it's too anecdotal my dear Max, wait a minute, at least let me tell the end of the Caillaux story, this woman reporter, a colleague, a friend, has just met Madame Caillaux, seven years after it happened, she asked her: 'When Calmette collapsed after you shot him, what was the first thing you felt?' What was Madame Caillaux's reply? I could give you three guesses but I'll tell you anyway: 'That I was not in love with my husband.'

Max is sometimes pretty odd, puts you in mind of Molière's cunning valet, Scapin, the sort of man who ends up thinking that everything's one big joke, that it was on Madame Poincaré's account that Poincaré the warmonger wanted to be President and that Madame Caillaux prevented her husband making peace, Max has a very odd way with him, all that talk of knickers, also quite incapable of hanging his mackintosh or overcoat on a coat-stand, he always leaves it draped over a chair, a desk, any old place.

He says he does it out of nostalgia for the coat pegs they had in the trenches, that's right, for more than a month one winter they used the feet of frozen corpses sticking out of the trench walls, bit of a bonus according to Max, German army boots, that didn't matter, they made decent coat pegs, then when the thaw came they turned out to be French corpses, their own comrades, in a perfect state of preservation: German boots and French corpses, imagine.

And so people will forgive the knickers and restore full conversation rights – this is long after the war is over, in the mid-1920s, in the Brasserie de la Paix on the Boulevard des Italiens – you'll have to tell another story, Max, so come on, let's have it:

'Out of the question!'

'Come on!'

So Max tells the story of the *Pieds Nickelés*, their last cartoon adventure in book form published before the war, in which it wasn't Poincaré who replaced Fallières, it was the famous gang comprising Ribouldingue, Filochard, and Croquignol, the Pieds Nickelés became ministers under Fallières, they had the same slogan as Poincaré, Republic, Duty, Country, a landslide for the Pieds Nickelés in the elections, men in frock-coats prevaricate, great junketings, big spending, gambling, living like kings only more so, Fallières gets worried and Ribouldingue comes up with: 'If Fallières tries to stick his nose in our affairs, we'll fettle Fallières, him and his bally heirs!'

Fallières went away, goatee, lips pursed and pop-eyed and opened a tobacconist's shop, leaving the Pieds Nickelés in the Élysée Palace to drink, thieve, and have lots of fun in frock-coats, this was late in 1912. Fallières and bally heirs. Ribouldingue, Croquignol and Filochard! If they'd stayed in power instead of Poincaré, there would have been peace.

'No Max, a true story, not this kid's stuff!'

'We would also have had peace if that serious incident involving France and England in April 1914 hadn't been speedily resolved.'

'Max, where did that come from? Your fifth beer? There was no such incident.'

'No, as true as I live and breathe, if a Franco-British stand-off had happened no one would have wanted war, a major incident of some sort, say a great dinner at the Élysée Palace, April 1914, King George having to lead off from the drawing room into the dining room with Madame Poincaré on his arm, and behind them would come the President and Queen Mary.'

Max lines up sugar lumps, one for each person, sets them out in a square.

'And a couple of hours before the dinner, Queen Mary is heard to say, "Me? Walk behind that woman? Never!" Panic, they toy with the idea of letting the Queen go first, with the President, but that would mean a king walking behind a president, Madame Poincaré threatens to boycott the dinner and the talk in the Queen's entourage is of bigamy, of getting back on the boat, you get the picture, a major incident, within an inch, France loses her alliance with Britain, therefore would tread much more carefully with Poincaré no longer

61

telling the Russians to just go ahead. At the time, he kept saying "I intend to force the Russians to be less feeble."'

'Max and his "ifs"! If, my aunt! Perhaps the French would have been more prudent, but the Austrians would have been more aggressive, I don't buy it, put those sugar lumps away.'

'However that may be, comrades, we did avoid a Franco-British incident, by a whisker.'

'How?'

'I didn't think you were interested, you really want to hear about my incident?'

Max reaches for the sugar lumps again and lines them up in a single row.

'Very well, it's very simple, in the Élysée, enormous double swing doors separate the drawing room and the dining room, all that they had to do was open both doors wide so both couples could go through abreast, though it's not as straightforward as that, both the ladies, the Queen and the President's wife, speed up, each trying to put a clear length between her and the other, so that the procession reaches the table at a canter.'

Max never liked Poincaré, he makes up all kinds of stories, yes, quite true, says Max, and I've changed my mind about Poincaré, I thought he wanted war and got it, I wanted a culprit, someone who'd betrayed his own side, Max, politics is primarily the art of betraying your own side, I know, says Max, and Poincaré is our collective sell-out, remember Pio Baroja, hugely talented novelist, late 1916: 'the French and the Germans are only fighting from cowardice; they are each under the thumb of a terrorist organisation and can do nothing about it.'

Max's points his index finger at his comrades:

'Robert, primary schoolteacher, Paul Robert, family holiday in the country, summer 1914, hot, only just arrived, 2 August, order for general mobilisation, had to leave his holiday cottage but the owner demanded payment of the full month's rent. And Poincaré remains a terrorist.'

Three troops at full tilt, charging at German dreams. At first they ride recklessly towards the machine gun. Later they're more careful. Charging dreams, their primary mission the Captain had said, the rumble of hooves, a rifle bullet in a horse's flank, the horse twists its neck and withers, rears up, is still rearing up when its heart bursts, the sound of a lance piercing a body, the whistle of sabre blades as they charge those German dreams, another rider is down, the bottom half of his face flops on his neck, a slice of soft flesh, blood, spittle, the lower jaw gone, blue eyes, intensely blue.

They haven't yet invented those marvellous operations for smashed jaws which will make the names of military surgeons famous, first remove a cutaneous flap two skin layers thick, from the top of the head, then bring it down and manoeuvre it over the lower part of the face, the quality of the skin taken from the scalp is far superior to that from the arm, which was previously used, the flap will be positioned over the damaged area, the patient can allow the hair of the flap to grow thus reconstituting an almost normal beard which will hide any scarring, though the effect is debatable from an aesthetic point of view. It's better than nothing, the patient will say. In the clearing, the dragoons charge the machine guns which destroy their momentum.

Basically when I was with Hans, I was jealous. In the end I admitted as much to myself. At first I thought of it as a branch of gymnastics. Before Marie-Thérèse, when I woke up I'd feel washed-out but now the moment I stirred I could see her and felt alive, there she was before my very eyes, she'd be smiling at Hans, I knew she wanted to take him away from me, I'd hold out a cup of tea to her, I wanted to tip it all over her frock, pink Liberty print again, why didn't she go, go away and wash and dry herself and change, and come back looking a fright, tipping the tea over her is so petty, if you really want rid of her throw it in her face, don't worry whether it's boiling hot or not, you're dreaming you're throwing tea in Marie-Thérèse's face because you know you'll never do it, whereas you could tip tea over the starchily creaking fabric at any time, and you tell yourself it's petty, result: you do nothing.

Marie-Thérèse puts her hand on Hans's forearm, like an old army friend. You could also take her to one side and threaten to kick her down the stairs if she touches him once more, you must smile at her, people are looking, they know everything and are enjoying it, dig your nails into her face, this new fashion is unspeakable, forehead uncovered on one side and on the other hair hanging down over the eyebrow, a sultry look for fast women, nails in the cheek, apparently if you use an ordinary lump of sugar to break the skin the scars never disappear.

What right did she have laughing like that? I knew she wanted to take him from me but I couldn't do anything until she'd actually done it, people would have said I was hysterical; and Hans playing the innocent, my darling girl, I don't understand why you don't get on with her, she'd smile, she'd blush, she wanted to take him away from me.

Tell us what happened next, Max, not what really happened next, except for the death of that teacher Robert, tell us another story, Max, it's true, instead make it the end of the story of the company officer who fought the duel, yes, the infantryman, I get confused with all these officers, cavalry Captain Jourde at Monfaubert, who was the infantry captain of Alain-Fournier who was himself a lieutenant at Saint-Rémy, those cavalry lieutenants at Monfaubert, the infantry CO with the name six and a half centuries old, the one Max later saw riding off to attack pillboxes with Lazare, the lad who liked sweets, yes Max's major's sister-in-law had told him the rest of the story of the duel when he saw her in Paris on a different leave, the lover who was no such thing, he had simply dreamed of being her lover, he used to send letters as if it had all really happened.

And very racy they were for a major's very Catholic wife, words expressing the thing, compared with them Caillaux's letters were elegant froth. But nothing had happened, nothing at all.

The major's wife had never answered any such letters and had never met the man. The sister showed Max the letters, well she did not show them exactly, she said they were in the black box on the table. She left the room, I'll be back in a moment, I want you to tell me if the letters are genuine, my sister always told me that nothing had happened, with me she just laughed about them, I never read the letters, she left them all with me for safe-keeping, except for the last one, but I never wanted to read them, Lieutenant, to read them was a sin.

Imagine that, my friends! the widow had never read them, that was her sister's mortal sin: to have read them. She told me I cannot entirely rule out the idea that my sister lied to me, I feel the presence of the Devil, I myself have lied to my confessor, I told him I hadn't found the letters, he wants me to hand them over so that he can destroy them, my sister is innocent, all she did was read them without telling her husband, she was afraid of being suspected of wrongdoing.

Maybe too the major's wife wasn't all that put out to find in the man's letters a reference to doings no one had ever taught her – 'darling, how I loved yesterday afternoon and the way you let me take that virginity of which even married women never speak, for they are only supposed to have one' – yes, the letters were the most awful rubbish, and he signed them 'Honoré, who loves you', which he had crossed out and corrected and given what he'd said, he felt justified in putting 'your darling Honoré, who loves you madly'.

Well, I'll spare you the boring details, oh no, Max, details are what makes the paper they're written on worth while, God is in the details, they're the reporter's first duty, I'm not sure the woman they were intended for understood them fully, they even mentioned such practices as a Cuban embrace and a crab's claw, the man had smothered everything with a sentimental Musset-type sauce, a lot of rubbish words.

In less than a week, the woman was dead of a nasty bout of bronchitis.

The major had found one of these racy missives in the deceased's writing desk and 'darling Honoré' had received a military sword full in the throat.

The major had saluted the witnesses, the man had died for something that really wasn't worth it, died for a joke, dear friends, Max would say, and many died for another joke, a joke on an altogether larger scale, on the evening of 29 July 1914, between Moscow and Berlin, it wasn't letters that were sent but telegrams, and these last official telegrams exchanged between the two empires bring war, one signed 'Your uncle Willy' and the other 'Your loving Nicky', war: a great big joke played by old men.

We even have photos dating from before the war in which Nicky and Willy, so fond of each other, are playing croquet, all very pally, with the façade of a château in the background, great game, croquet, very character-forming, they also go bicyle-riding, their majesties ride the first freewheel bicycles, freewheeling being designed to relieve the velocipedist's legs, such a devastatingly droll expression, so 'pre-war': 'to freewheel'.

The brasserie on the Boulevard des Italiens is enormous, noisy, hot, friendly, it is newly decorated, in the American style, large panels of dark wood, great stretches of light-coloured wall, it is the triumph of the panel and is echoed even in women's dresses, one panel fore, one panel aft, tall mirrors everywhere, very bright electric light, 1920s styling, no fancy curlicues, huge chandeliers but not of dangling crystals, made entirely of huge, clear prisms, and real live sparrows which nest above them and chirrup from one chandelier to another.

At a table just behind them, a woman stares at Max, Max sees her from the front and also from the side in one of the mirrors, he can see himself in another mirror, he can pretend he's not watching the woman, that he's looking at something else, and he can see her while she watches him talking. At the same time he can observe his own face, which he doesn't much care for, cauliflower ears, round head, flat profile, eyes slightly staring, a comic valet, the main thing is to keep talking, apparently when he becomes animated people don't notice how ugly he is, from time to time the woman seems interested, at least more than she is by her own table companions.

Fantastic face, thinks Max, high cheekbones, large eyes, not French, and not because of the cheekbones and the abundant brown hair, it's rather the way she is, it's the face of someone who does other things in life than try to please men, she's beautiful but she doesn't give a damn, her bearing is both restrained and free, is she powerful? A banker maybe? She gave a start when Max said the only ones left standing will be the arseholes, a foreigner who speaks French fluently then, get up? No, wait until she gets up, very *grande dame*, distinguished, make contact, whisk her off in a taxi, in taxis all women become tarts, and this one isn't likely to go at it in a half-hearted way, such a contemptuous way of looking at the people at her table, no not contemptuous, she wouldn't be so obvious, but her mind's not elsewhere either, she's there all right but no one's got her attention, in the back of the taxi, backside, lips, the lot, then get out and leave the taxi to her.

At Monfaubert, the dragoons thrust and slash and fall, and have gone much too wide on the left of the target of the charge, those dove-grey dreams of the Germans, riders carried by their momentum to the other end of the encampment, and the eight German dreams remain intact, it was easier on the Marne, two years before the war, Verzy, another war, a war fought with chamber pots, a charge through the streets of a small town, peasants panicking, the women especially, not afraid of animals, give the flat of the sword to a woman who's thwacking your horse's legs with a big stick, or the charge at Carmaux, it was miners that time, and ten or so dead.

In this clearing there are no chamber pots but there are rifles, bayonets and two, maybe three Spandau guns which have cut clear swathes in the first three troops, only just under half the riders have managed to traverse the enemy camp but without doing much real damage, too far to the left of those German dreams, the other half of the dragoons have been unseated, the relatively unscathed try to make it back to cover, a few Germans begin to gather their wits and shoot them down like rabbits.

There are also Germans lying on the ground, but their dreams are intact.

Then the lieutenant of the French dragoons who have been held in reserve in the woods orders his fourth troop to charge – to make the most of the enemy's disarray – a support troop which is in turn decimated by the tap and rattle of the sewing-machine while fifty dragoons who survived the first charge have wheeled round at the far end of the field, their dander up once more, a gallop, less than seven hundred paces a minute, two charges by wounded riders in a pincer movement that encircles the Germans, now to recreate the shock which spikes the guns, a mass moving forward at great speed in a century of speed, a steel pincer which is about to bite on the steel of German dreams.

The first time he heard the sparrows, saw them in the chandeliers of the brasserie, Max thought it was some sort of joke. When questioned, the waiter answered that many customers had asked that the sparrows be allowed to come and go and tweet in the assembly-rooms, ex-soldiers had asked.

'Well now,' Max had said, 'I know another tall tale, another extremely poetical story, extremely, provided you give the word poetical a meaning different from the one it had before our war: the story of the Martins and the Thomases.

'Max, they say you were with the dragoons the day they charged the Boches at Monfaubert, tell us about the charge.'

'I wasn't there!'

'Where were you, then?'

'Guess.'

'Headquarters?'

'Cheeky bastard!'

'Don't lose your rag, I give up.'

'Yes, more to the east!'

'I don't see . . .'

'Everyone's got it except you! Saint-Rémy! The place where Fournier was killed, I was there just before it happened, second lieutenant of dragoons, different regiment, I charged a flock of sheep.'

'Max, stopping messing about.'

'I'm not, the Germans were firing at us, I never say Boches, I never write it either, I've got a friend who's a Boche, we've been meeting up once a year since the Armistice, incidentally, do you write Boche with

68

a capital or not when it's a noun? The German artillery was firing at us, disgustingly accurate it was, we thought we were hidden by a small hill, a ridge, with something peculiar on the top, a man grazing his sheep, poor creatures have got to eat too, the shepherd must have been dead scared, we all were, but there he was, out with his sheep, brave man. We kept changing position, the Germans continued firing at us, the shepherd was in a blue funk, with your naked eye you could see him on the top of the ridge duck down each time a shell went screaming overhead, he tried to make his way back towards us, we shouted for him to stay up there, he couldn't hear, we made signs telling him to stay where he was, he wasn't in as much danger as us, but he changed position on his ridge when we did, staying in line with us, about three hundred metres away, a Frenchman who wanted to stay with the French, whatever the risk. We were taking a hammering from the German cannon, we kept moving to avoid their fire, and then the shells would find us again.

'In the end the penny dropped, the shepherd was a scout, all the German gunners had to do was aim over the top of the sheep every time the shepherd stopped, he was giving them the line of fire. So we charged the sheep with lances, we liked the lance, at that stage we were about to make a better world with our lances, we carried carbines slung round our necks, but it was the lance we liked best, a joust.

'The shepherd? We nabbed him, a spy who got two hundred francs a throw, he could have bought himself three overcoats at La Belle Jardinière for that, lined him up and shot him.

'We got hammered in that sector, then we were withdrawn and replaced by fresh troops, infantry, they were ready for a scrap, the 288th, that's right, Fournier's lot, and the Germans were eager for a scrap too, that's what Saint-Rémy was, a poxy wood and a war where you charged at sheep and writers died.'

The Frenchman at the next table with the big ears, most entertaining, he looks at me as if I were the only woman in his life, he talks in a loud voice, he comes out with some very French names, Martin, Thomas, he might be called something along those lines too, or maybe Duval. He's watching me in one of the mirrors with eyes that drink, eat, beckon, undress, would like to bite, disappear, garrulous eyes, very French, but not stupid. Now Hans didn't have garrulous eyes, his looked surprised, frequently surprised, if I'd made a scene about Marie-Thérèse he'd have come down to earth with a bump. He still hadn't noticed anything or felt anything or anticipated anything, and it was the scene I'd make that would open his eyes.

We were out walking, I was holding his arm, we met Marie-Thérèse coming towards us, she hardly knew me but called me 'dear Lena', she stopped and chatted, Hans was being witty, she laughed and touched his other arm as she laughed, do I dig my nails into her cheeks at this point? Or when she does it again, when she leans unambiguously on his arm, with both hands, so that through my arm I can feel Hans's body leaning away from me under the pressure of that woman's hands.

Marie-Thérèse blushed as she stood there, she wasn't ashamed of blushing, her neck was uncovered and her throat was suffused with red, Hans looked, he did not look openly the way you're supposed to when people push something under your nose unceremoniously, no, he glanced at it, pretended he wasn't looking at all, glanced at me tenderly, and then his eye sidled off again towards that bright redness.

Max raises one finger, like in school, not like a pupil but like the teacher when he wants to stress the salient point, what you need, friends, is the story of the Martins and the Thomases, names of large families.

'Max, how can you have a poetical tale about large families?'

'Easy,' Max replies, 'a dramatic story, group photos, white dresses, a swing in one corner of the photo, interchangeable names and oodles of conflict. Martin, Thomas! That's Pierre-Émile Martin versus Sidney Thomas, decades of confrontation spent chasing each other up and down statistical graphs, Martin, a decent old cove who hailed from Sireuil in the days of Napoleon III, Catholic, qualified engineer, concerned for the welfare of his workers, more than charitable, and

Sidney Thomas ten years later, an Englishman, long-standing quarrel, two names at loggerheads, each despising the other, and no sign of it all finishing, at stake world conquest, with little flags planted in the planisphere of their epic struggle.

'And at times quite staggering profits! shush, not a word, I'll carry on, at others catastrophic falls on the Stock Exchange, close-down, new start, cycles, crises, competing tooth and nail for markets, patent for patent, perhaps they even came near to pairing off two of their children, one of Martin's daughters and one of Thomas's sons, but in the end there is no marriage, production goes up and up, the women produce fewer offspring, but there are still plenty of faces in the photos, two names, competing, and so, starting from a story about iron ore, Victor Hugo . . .'

'Max!'

'Oh yes, Hugo, "O Nature, here are thy sublime beginnings".'

'Max, we all know you're mad about Hugo, you even went to his funeral.'

'You villain, I wasn't even born then.'

'In that case, spare us the rest.'

'One more quote and I'll stop: "At the sound of thy voice thy forces rise up from the glooms of the deep", to those forces we've added jaw-crushers, cone-crushers, cylinder-crushers, hammer-crushers, spiral separators, hydrocyclones, clean iron ore, it's crushed to produce molten pig-iron and clippety-clop, the carbon in the molten metal is oxidised, and then Bessemer . . .'

'Max, give me back my tankard.'

'It's empty.'

'Exactly, the waiter won't be able to see I need a refill.'

'Too bad, just drink out of my glass instead, I'll keep your tankard, you'll see, and Martin, no let's have Bessemer first, actually it all starts with Bessemer.'

'Or Cro-Magnon man.'

'If you're going to be like that, I'll shut up.'

'No, Max, you just carry on now but you can bring it to a speedy conclusion.'

'If you want a story, you've got to put in the time.'

Max holds the tankard at an angle, the Bessemer converter being slightly tilted, Max's forefinger under the tankard, cold air is blown into the bottom of the blast box at high pressure, the air passes up through the molten mass, a dry splashing, a burst of reddish yellow light, a shower of sparks, the blow eliminates the excess carbon, a bluish flame with a dark tip spurts out of the top, clouds of smoke, sprays of molten metal, the flame grows taller, turns white and clippety-clop, the tankard is horizontal, the Bessemer vessel is tipped up, the pig-iron is decarburised in a quarter of an hour, ingots are cast, Bessemer steel is fantastic, just one problem, the yield is inadequate, which is where my little chums Martin and Thomas come in, quantity, the future's in quantity, no more converters but vertical furnaces, here, take your tankard, don't cry.

Max stands two half-opened books upright in the middle of the table, large vertical smelters, menu for a roof, paper napkin for the floor, decarburise, dephosphorise, desulphurise, these tall furnaces are masters of the world, steel in huge quantities, Thomas's fining process involves blowing air through the molten ore, then lime and scrap-iron are added and pig-iron appears in the converter.

Max drops sugar lumps, matches, cigarettes, cigarette-ends between the two books, you wanted a story, well you've got one, unabridged, complete with forced air and incineration of all elements, the appearance of red smoke signals the end of the cycle, the cinders are cleaned out, it makes excellent fertiliser for crops, and then ferro-manganese is added.

Max adds coins and even his signet ring, glances up at his companions around the table, how's that for detail? long live Zola! now who's next? In Martin's process, it's even better, there's no blowing of air, instead a gas flame is used to raise the smelting temperature of the iron in the furnace, better quality of product.

The upshot is that there are two types of steel, Martin's and Thomas's, and then the fighting starts, Martin's steel is better, so he has all sorts of problems, one lawsuit after another for infringement of patents, no substance to the charges, but patents only protect the inventor for twenty years, the cases brought by his competitors slow down production, the ploy is to gain time until Martin's process has fallen into the public domain and can be used by anybody, meanwhile they fall back on Thomas's process until Martin's can be exploited without payment of royalties, of course Thomas steel is poorer in quality, but for rails and low-grade purposes it is adequate. And Pierre-Émile Martin? he doesn't go under but he doesn't see the financial returns he might have, he retires, an embittered man.

'Max, you promised us a poetical yarn, not a saga!'

'You'll get it all.'

Two simultaneous charges by battered dragoons, one from the east and one from the west of the clearing at Monfaubert, remnants of a captainless squadron, the dragoons mount a pincer movement, another dreamlike charge but there is fear and something else, the touch, the taste of horror, their blood is up: scream, do what you never did before, spit out and destroy those dove-grey German dreams, those dreams which face the cavalrymen as they charge from all parts of the field, German dreams which have emerged from a labyrinth, gay as a rower's straw boater, centuries of waking dreams, of red-chalk sketches, of regrets, architect's plans, pulleys, projects abandoned and resumed, like clockwork muffled by feathers, like floating drapes hanging by threads.

When did it all start? The day after Sarajevo, *L'Illustration* published a large sketch of the event which filled page three, the Archduke falling as he is shot, and opposite on page two the editorial written three days earlier is entitled: 'We are such spoiled brats'; one of the survivors of that war will be killed in 1944 in the Seine-et-Marne when his train is strafed by a US Lightning. Meanwhile Sarah Bernhardt has a wooden leg, in 1916 she makes a film, she wears a Greek-style tunic and carries a flag which flaps in the wind, she calls down the wrath of France's fighting men on the Boches, asking in alexandrines 'that one day by warriors shall their temples be destroyed, their children maimed and women raped', she also talks of monsters and the extermination of a whole race.

Hans was standing next to me but that did not stop him staring at the patches of red on Marie-Thérèse's throat, me, I never blush, I never blushed even when Marie-Thérèse called me 'dear Lena'.

I can't blush. All someone like Marie-Thérèse does is let it happen, she never tries to control herself, she lets herself blush and men interpret it as a promise. They must wonder if the rest of her blushes too, they call her type voluptuous. She was a lot less good-looking than me, she had short legs, it was no good her raising the waist on all her dresses, you could still see that she had short legs. One day, outside the Waldhaus, she had to lower the saddle of her bike, she wasn't at all happy about that, the Frenchman with the jug ears looks sad, or is it just a trick of the mirrors?

Max is now well launched, he talks in a loud voice to shut the others up, to forget, to find life again on the other side of despair, to have the time to watch that woman, and simultaneously he has the unbearable feeling of spreading himself too thin, of being less himself the more he talks, a mixture of everything, good for nothing except heaping cinders on the fire, pipe, beer, some day all you'll be fit for is talking to your slippers, you'll screw some girl from the Charente on your kitchen table and then tell her the story of your life, there'll be no one left.

Max sees the girl from the Charente now, on the table in the brasserie, while he talks to his comrades and watches the woman in the reflecting mirrors, the handsome face of a woman who has better things to do than listen to men talking, she doesn't smoke, you stand up, turn your back on all these boozy dimwits, and you go off with her, you become a different person, the man you wanted to be fifteen years ago when you walked into the Vieux Paris for a coffee before rushing home to read Aristotle, you look good, she has good breasts, Aristotle in the original and a good time with the woman, back seat of a cab, then throw her out head first, yes but she's not even looking at you, you haven't even managed to catch her eye once.

Listen, in 1914 or 1915, which is where our poetical story really begins, the Reich ministry in Berlin has a sense of its bounden duty, it rejects Thomas shells, Thomas steel is all right for shoeing mules but only Martin steel produces shells that pulverise everything they hit.

'And what shall we do with our stocks of Thomas shells?' ask the Reich's steelmakers.

'Sell it all to the Swiss, Swiss requirements in that department are huge, they buy twenty times as many from us as they produce themselves, where do all the shells go? That's beside the point, there's got to be profit, Swiss francs, and when the stocks have all gone make more Thomas shells for Switzerland, and ask top prices, respect the cartel, no need to bother your heads who buys them from Switzerland, in any case if Thomas shells fall on our German pillboxes they'll be landing on good English concrete which can only be bought for Swiss francs, it comes via Holland and Denmark, along with the copper and copra for our explosives, and if we run short of Martin shells at the front, too bad, we'll buy your Thomases too, says the Reich ministry to the Reich's steelmakers, jump to it, and you can drop your prices for us.'

Max glances up, the woman has gone, get up quickly, catch up with her, the cab, but finish the story first, protests from the steelmakers, and Hindenburg orders the Reich ministry to abide by the tariff set by the cartel and 'give them the price they ask, which is the export price'. I've also got a very good story about French army supplies in 1916, but that'll keep for later. Max starts getting to his feet, shall I retrieve my coat? my hat? They'll just laugh at me. Max sits down again, he's just noticed that there's no one at the beautiful brunette's table, they've all gone, you didn't see a thing.

'Another round!' says Max. 'On me.'

But let us not forget the real culprit, that straw boater, everything that preceded those few days during which it was waved this way and that under a burning sun, *union sacrée*, long live France, long live Poincaré, long live the Kaiser, war's a novelty, a joy, the sacrifice made for one's country, and last Tuesday morning in the Salle Gaveau Bishop Bolo gave some advice to a thousand young Frenchwomen on how to choose a husband, a long engagement is essential for you to get to know one another, for a fiancé is the most beguiling kind of liar, you will need time to get him trained, separation and the war are blessings in disguise, in the big stores, the girls who get paid three francs a day for a fifteen-hour day demand more chairs.

It will encourage laziness, say the directors, a sordid business having something like that brought up, the strike has been broken, and from Biskra, Monsieur Chiarelli, the distinguished entomologist, has sent us two splendid photographs of scorpions, one of a mother no doubt panic-stricken devouring her young, and one of an adult male devouring another, with the last three joints of the tail and the poisonous sting sticking out of the mouth of the victor.

For the dragoons at Monfaubert there are eight targets, eight dove-grey dreams as splendid as myths, each with its own great wings, a span of fourteen metres secured by wires finer than the guys of the finest sailing boats, forty square metres of aerofoil, a stream-lined fuselage made of canvas and light wooden struts, a stubby vertical mast between the engine and the pilot, a complex system of cables supporting wings (conceived and designed by observing the flight of a *zanonia* seed) with a span of fourteen centimetres, a perfectly rounded leading edge and a gracefully flowing trailing edge.

Igor Etrich, a first-rate engineer, multiplied the proportions of the outer shell by a hundred, added a pigeon-tail rear-end together with a six-cylinder in-line Mercedes engine, 120 horse-power, sweet dove-grey chargers, the century's new weapon of the skies, the *Taube*, one of them dropped two small bombs on Paris on 13 August.

The cavalrymen charge these new replacements on behalf of all the cavalries in the whole wide world, aircraft, airplanes, also known as aeroplanes, 'planes, the monoplanes Hans looks after, though in civilian life he is a naval engineer, novelist and dreamer, the army had turned him into a private in the infantry but quickly reassigned him as chief air mechanic in the first days of the war when the skies are still relatively free, pilots climb to almost 2,000 metres singing a snatch of song behind their propellers and return to base with bullet holes in their wings and a few snippets of information about the enemy, they smell of hot oil, their faces and hands are as oily as their engines but they wear fleece jackets costing a thousand marks a throw, are billeted in a château, drink champagne as they discreetly compare genealogical notes.

Up there, the war is almost clean, some opponents are still at the stage of saluting each other, they don't use parachutes, the dream of Icarus runs through their veins.

Marie-Thérèse almost fell off her bike twice, she had to lower the saddle, she wasn't at all pleased, Hans told her you mustn't have it too high, it's the wind that does it, the wind resistance, so funny, I didn't say anything and no one mentioned her little legs. After that Hans held her bike, one hand under the saddle and the other on the handle-bars, Marie-Thérèse laughed, she was wearing trousers, apparently where she comes from women aren't allowed to wear trousers except for riding a horse or a bike, but at home she never rode a bike, she laughed but she was trying it on, Hans had his hand under her saddle, and there was nothing I could say. She could blush at will, she knew how to make the most of her blushes, I've always been told I thought too much about love, Hans had shapely hands, smooth skin, every time I thought of it I'd tell myself that woman is going to find out what Hans's skin tastes like, that hand has no business being under her saddle. People say that being jealous can make you fall in love, it made me feel awkward, when she looked at him I thought he seemed so conceited. One evening, on the main staircase in the Waldhaus, he was telling me all about cycling, he'd read that bicycles spelled death for book sales, because people spent so much time riding them, cycling two or three hours every day, which was time taken away from reading, it was a real threat, he stopped one floor too soon, I couldn't keep it to myself, I said 'this is only Marie-Thérèse's floor'.

That sad-looking Frenchman with the big ears just now in the restaurant, Frenchmen stare at women a lot and just carry on talking to their companions, a woman like Marie-Thérèse would have got up.

Max knocks over the books on the table, returns the menu to the waiter, retrieves his coins and ring, empties his glass, the truth needs to be believed before it can be understood, the real culprit was the summer, the straw boaters we gaily tossed towards the enemy, the quick-tempered heat of that glorious summer when Jean Bouin ran the fearsome distance of nine kilometres seven hundred and twenty-one metres in thirty minutes, which was some going, we even hunted rats: identical hunting scenes on both sides of the front, rats hanging by their tails from wires strung between poles, the cook claimed he could make rat jam, we laughed, he's a real card, the style they called Charm, said the cook, I remember it well, I was head sales assistant, the skirt fitted very closely over the hips, swelled out in the shape of a bell and reached down to the ground with a train at the back, scooped-out necklines with satin-stitch, go on, cook, tell us more, some rats are as big as 75 mm shells, the .75 is the expression in metallic form of the marvellous qualities of our race, flooding brings the rats out, they swim among us at knee level, the general said we had to stay in the water, the CO said, 'Don't knock your brains out over it', and a voice piped up: 'The bullets will do that for us.' And on the role of the African infantry and the Moroccan cavalry one general would write one autumn day: 'Use before winter.'

And sometimes there's too much water, in one night at Neuville-Saint-Vaast, the trenches of both sides were flooded to the top, all the men climbed out and faced each other a hundred metres apart, and for hours and hours no one fired a gun, no one killed anybody, a wag said, 'If it goes on like this, they'll soon be building an Ark.'

At other times, much later on, there are men who don't want to kill or die any more, but they die pleading, wetting their trousers, their comrades dragging them to the stake, others stink even more, they struggle, they have to be tied to a chair while they scream, the colonel said, like women.

Bastards! screams one of the condemned men, you go on and on killing – that's why you'll always be slaves, the chair tips over, lash that chair to the stake says the colonel, the officers are forced to put more and more men out of their misery, some mutineers have been hit by only three bullets and none of them well placed, an officer yells at the firing squad he commands, every man who shoots wide is a coward, you ought to be ashamed, look at him, he's still moving.

Other mutineers die standing up, spitting defiance.

Two men different from the rest: they face the firing squad and sing the 'Marseillaise' and the 'Chant du départ'; first they embraced the officer commanding the squad, that's it, refused to obey the order to attack, found guilty at the double, a priest and a socialist MP had talked to them all through the night, an honourable death, you must do the decent thing, you say you're sorry and you face the firing squad and sing so that your comrades may still have enough strength to snatch victory from the shadows, the priest's cross and the MP's hands, you will set us all an example, we all want peace through victory.

Also a woman, who comes and speaks in the cell, what about our two daughters, daughters of a hero or a traitor, they said that if you say you're sorry, if you sing the 'Marseillaise', they'll just write 'killed in action' in the book, the officer said:

'What chance will a coward's daughter have of finding a husband?'

The daughter is two years old, not for eleven years will a friend tell her the truth, when Poincaré has become the man who laughs in cemeteries, yes, one of the two men sentenced to death was that schoolteacher, Robert, the one with the holiday cottage and the month's rent, the 'Marseillaise' and the 'Chant du départ', everyone could believe again, they embraced, they stood at the stake and wept.

Eight *Tauben* lined up, a plane of exactly this type and make has just set a new altitude record at 6,200 metres, the world spread out below is a marvel. The machine guns defend these dreams, they continue to cut down French dragoons, they decimate the fourth troop which charged in support, but one section of the dragoons succeeds in breaking through the line of fire, and others in position at the far end of the clearing also come riding up, one of the planes has had time to begin moving, it gains speed, waddles like an exasperated chicken on the churned-up grass. Two or three dragoons try to give chase, the horses take fright, still needs another three hundred, two hundred revs to reach the 65 kilometres an hour needed for take-off, in the bottom of his ditch Hans hears the signs, a hundred and fifty revs, he calculates the plane's chances, he knows each of the six in-line cylinders in each of his eight aircraft while the plane bumps along with increasing speed over the uneven surface.

Already its pilot has stopped thinking of anything except those trees dead ahead. The observer in the rear seat has a large repeating rifle and takes aim at the dragoons, keep thinking of what you love.

Hans hears the noise of the engine, a woman glides on to a frozen lake, why? The sound of the engine, death, he takes the woman's hand, puts his arm around her waist, a picture, a lake in the mountains, keep thinking of what you love, the sound of an aeroplane exasperated because it cannot take off, it battles with every tussock, never volunteer for anything, the engine is getting too much fuel, the pilot's going to flood the carburettor, pound to a penny it's Klaus, he never could do it right, and the second piece of advice, think, a village at one end of the mountain lake, a waterfall at the other, is this really the moment to think about what you love? Early winter keen-cold, sound of an engine, revs almost there, the sleeve now, robins panicking in the frost, early-morning skaters, light from a red disc, pale and austere, the same actions in unison, Hans and the young woman move out across the ice each leaning on the other, in turn.

Hans is not a very good skater, she smiles, you look like someone wading through mud, at first he put his right hand on Lena's waist but it was really she who wedged her hip against his, he dares not make too much of this, she has put her hand on Hans's right hand, the hand that holds her waist, and again she presses, presses herself against Hans as is required when two people skate together, around them are other couples, they brush past each other with a smile, the birches drop fine ash, Hans and the young woman are gliding, each leaning upon the other, the increasingly regular hiss of skates.

Sometimes to within kissing distance of Hans's lips come curls of red hair which escape from beneath her bonnet, Lena leans on Hans, then moves away from him, turns on the ice, faces him, he looks at her, her cheekbones are high, her mouth wide, he releases one of the young woman's hands, she begins to spin on the spot, the point of her skate, Hans's hand, her long-sleeved pelisse, black velvet, a short skirt which stops above the ankle, an unblemished quartz-blue sky, a peaceful morning, intermittent rook calls arrive on the breeze, a light, continuous icy breeze, a background of faint metallic sounds.

Suddenly at the edge of the lake a loud crack, Hans feels a stab of fear, he slows but Lena forces him to continue, the crack of frozen water, everyone has heard it, sees the dark water beneath the ice, a land of snow but there is no snow on the lake, only ice, everything just froze very fast and very hard, needles of cold prick cheeks, sting throats, lustrous dark blue water beneath the ice, Lena draws Hans away, a mist of breath from Lena's mouth, Hans tries to inhale the mist.

Another long cracking sound. Something angry stirs below, the birches white with frost, Lena has let go of Hans's hand, she skates off towards the far end of the lake, weaving about, Hans follows her, Lena's skirt and pelisse deliciously enhance her buttocks, Hans recalls a sentence from a fashion magazine aimed at skaters, we recommend that ladies should not take posterior flatness to extremes, Lena is far from taking posterior flatness to extremes, Hans is afraid, a cracking sound which lasts longer than the others, Hans moves closer to the shore, there is a reed-bank frozen solid and a boat with a blue prow trapped in the ice, the firs are encrusted with frost, a jay fights with a clod of frozen earth.

Hans calls out, Lena comes back towards him looking beautiful, a quick turn, her hip slides up against his, he rests his right hand on her waist, he does not dare apply pressure, Lena clamps one hand on his, the young woman does not wear corsets, we'd better go back, no, she forces Hans to make for the far end of the lake, the waterfall, every time she puts her weight on her leg Hans feels her muscles flex hard, and then a moment later the softness returns, another loud crack, the ice, the accident.

Hans deduces from the sound of the engine that the plane has managed to get airborne, one metre, two. The pilot begins a shallow turn to get round the trees, the lieutenant of the fourth troop of dragoons has dispatched two men in pursuit.

At full tilt, one rider finally succeeds in attacking the aeroplane's tail, slicing cables which control chord and rudder with his sabre, the *Taube* starts spinning on its axis, starts falling, the propeller slices open the side of the horse which rolls on the ground and likewise chases its own tail, legs flailing, entrails exposed and blood spurting, with his sabre the other cavalryman runs pilot and observer through, slashes the bracing wires, then backs away and stands his horse on its rear legs.

The rest of the squadron has begun cutting the *Tauben* to pieces with bare steel, canvas first and the bracing-stays, then the balsa struts, so fragile, the whole a miraculous balance of weights, volume, tension, resistance, female flesh, the other machine gun has stopped firing, the dragoons slash the wooden propellers, make the propellers pay for the deaths of their comrades, the aeroplane is the future of the world, you'll see what a cavalryman can make of the future of the world, a man with a leather flying helmet is skewered by a lance by the side of his plane, another lance pierces a fuel tank, a dragoon tosses a cotton-waste fuse on to it, other dragoons get the message, within moments all eight dreams are reduced to heaps of burning wreckage.

The meadow looks so beautiful, the reflections of red and gold from a sunset are prolonged by the flames, like a Midsummer's Day. A few shots are still heard, and shouts, bugles sound again, the surviving cavalrymen, barely a third of the company's strength but all the *Tauben* have been destroyed, they head as quickly as they can for the corner of the wood from which the jay fled, 'Lieutenant, what do we do with the prisoner?'

The crack of the ice, Lena lets go of Hans's hand, detaches herself, gains speed, leans forward, thrusts out her free leg, completes one loop, returns to Hans, skates off, noise of the engine still audible, bumps and jolts, the exasperated chicken bouncing over the tussocky field, the noise fades, the picture fades, then returns, on the ice the mark of the loop is perfect, think of what you love, don't be afraid, just a few cracks, we'll go like a train, get up steam, keep your skates in parallel lines.

Don't be afraid, Hans, you've got to know the lake, lift our skates together keeping in step, you understand, it's like a choo-choo, a train going full pelt, she laughs, detaches herself from Hans, speed, Lena legs apart, toes turned outwards, feet aligned along the same axis, a wide curve, legs and arms spread out, she leans back, the centre of the circle is at her back, she is at the very end of the lake, the ice cracks, she shouts out: it's called a spreadeagle.

She returns to Hans who's still moving as if he's wading through mud, we must get back, this girl takes crazy risks, no, we're staying, there's nothing to be afraid of, I know all about this cracking, it happens when the lake continues to freeze, it's not dangerous, it's not thawing, it's all very simple, the ice also goes crack when it continues to freeze hard, like this morning, north wind, we'll stay, come and see the waterfall, it's all frozen, it's wonderful. I was looking at Lena and I was happy. Something stupid, later.

As night fell, they beat Hans senseless with the butts of their rifles. Later his comrades came for him, he was trepanned under chloroform, sent to convalesce, then was returned to the front in early December 1914, they posted him to the infantry this time, without really punishing him for letting himself be taken off guard, but they deprived him of the things he loved, the open air, Mercedes engines and flying at 120 kilometres an hour.

The French dragoons fell back in disorder, pursued by a detachment of cyclists newly brought in as support. Between them and the French lines were von Klück's three hundred thousand men. Dragoons decimated, fleeing in knots along forest tracks, in the soft damp night, their wounded comrades left at farms, the rest made their way warily, strayed into in marshy bogs, turned back, got lost, starving, night marches, they halt on the edge of a level plain, their horses are lathered, heads drooping between their legs, lungs working like a blacksmith's bellows, German infantry attack on foot at dawn, they come creeping through the lucerne.

The dragoons rally, to die a more honourable death, one group succeeds in reaching the heart of the forest, half the men ride bare-backed, they strike their horses' flanks with the flat of their swords, they wander, they recross deserted fields, a horse never complains, it goes on until it drops.

Suddenly, there, just in front of me, hardly able to stand, a big mare, it's heartbreaking, she's lost her saddle, been abandoned, that speckled-grey coat, it can't be, it's Kolana, Kolana out of Esquirol, Thailhac's horse, he was killed two weeks ago, wonderful Kolana, a big-sized animal, holds herself well, plenty of muscle, good-natured, intelligent, so amenable in training, she won at Auteuil, twice, it was an honour to drill her, she trembles, she's finished, she was born to do so many things, war was not one of them.

The Monfaubert dragoons were mentioned in regimental dispatches, then were permanently dismounted: unsuited to trench warfare, the cavalry was forced to resign itself to watch while flying took over the role it had played for centuries. The airmen adopted the title of 'knights of the skies' and many cavalry officers applied to serve in this new arm, in which they could keep their boots.

Everywhere, from the Vosges to the Channel, battle was joined for points on maps, and Gilberte Swann wrote to Marcel to inform him that both the hillock at Méséglise, with the hawthorn hedge, and the cornfield through which the winds of adolescent love had blown, was now Hill 307 of which the newspapers talked so much.

May 2001, the *Frankfurter Allgemeine Zeitung*, Ludwig Harig reporting from Saint-Rémy. Monsieur Louis, one of the men who found the grave, showed him lot 357 and the spot where Alain-Fournier and the Frenchmen were shot.

'That's right,' said Monsieur Louis, 'shot for attacking a dressing-station. The clash of two companies of very young soldiers.'

A week later, a letter to the *Frankfurter Allgemeine Zeitung* from Gerd Krumeich, a historian with an expert knowledge of Joan of Arc:

'That Fournier was sent to face a firing-squad cannot be stated with absolute certainty.'

And Stéphane Audoin-Rouzeau, a specialist in the history of cruelty on the battlefield:

'In the matter of the incident at Saint-Rémy, both the excavation of the site and the archive evidence indicate clearly that something extremely violent happened, but not that it was accompanied by any particular cruelty.'

Further along, another cemetery, at Vaux-les-Palameix, other remains, those of eight German stretcher-bearers, killed the same day as the Frenchmen.

Max Goffard and Hans Kappler, one left with cauliflower ears, the other with the memory of a woman, had marched off to war full of hope. They had very quickly heard the din of a conflict which was to be the last before the great leap forward and it did not strike them as being in any way different from the thunderclaps at Christmas which frighten the children and promise them all presents on the big day.

Chapter 3

1956

A Remarkable Symmetry

In which Michael Lilstein remembers Hans Kappler and offers you a job as a Paris spy.

In which we learn what Lena owed to an easy-going American named Walker.

In which Lena disappears in the middle of Budapest.

In which Max tells several stories including the one which ends: 'We already know . . .'

In which Michael Lilstein unveils his theory of twin souls and introduces you to Linzer Torte.

Waltenberg/Paris, early December 1956

So it would seem you have a taste for espionage.
Faust to Mephisto
Johann Wolfgang Goethe, *Faust.* A tragedy

'Why so set on going back, Herr Kappler?'

It is with these words that Lilstein will make his approach to Kappler. Destabilise Kappler, force him to doubt, waste no time, make him change his mind.

Lilstein has just arrived at Waltenberg in the heart of the Swiss Alps. He strolls through the village until it is time for his first appointment, he walks across the powdery snow, slowly, each footfall a muffled sigh, walking slowly is such luxury, a layer of powdery snow, ten centimetres, a little less, which has fallen on lying, frozen snow, the air is dry, very sharp, Lilstein likes it.

This village in the Grisons is not his home ground, but he was born here, at Waltenberg, not born exactly but he spent his adolescence in this place: looking at women, having ideas, talking, onward and upward, drinking, smoking, always in a hurry, he loved speed, he completed the five-year plan in four, comrades! he smiles and slows down even more as he walks over the snow, looks at the forest which climbs up the side of the mountain and stops just before the sparkling cap of snow, quite a coup, two appointments today.

One man with a mind to change before lunch.

Another to convince this afternoon, two separate meetings but strikingly symmetrical.

Lilstein tells himself that it will be intellectually very gratifying if he can bring it off. It's a bit much to fit into one day but just now he can't afford to spend much time away from Berlin and the *Stalinallee*.

Mountains, sensations, ideas, this is where it all began a quarter of a century ago, in the spring of 1929.

He'd come from Rosmar, he was almost sixteen, he can still remember the first time he came up here, it wasn't anything like nowadays, a bus with the same hunting-horn depicted on the forward door but much less comfortable than today's, a very bumpy ride, very narrow road, ruts, ravines, all much harder going the higher you went, sometimes barely thirty centimetres between the tyres and a precipice, wonderful memories, would the trees just here break our fall? Will I have time to jump out of the window?

The bus skidded, lurched, Lilstein jumped out through the window, clutched at branches, the branches snapped, blood, screams. False alarm. He didn't jump because the bus went on climbing, small red flowers stared at him, saxifrage poked through the snow, the ravine was full of them, a series of bends, horns blaring, he shook, how stupid, felt sick, the nausea made worse because at the age he was then he did not want to admit to being afraid.

The nausea had not lasted, at Waltenberg, it never does. Quite extraordinary this sensation of having transparent lungs, pure air, it stings, beware nose bleeds.

These last few years, Lilstein has come back to Waltenberg quite often, yes, with dangerous frequency, but he knows the area well, has friends here, he'd be warned instantly, though actually he doesn't care, besides, the level of risk is the same every day, and his large East Berlin office is hardly the safest of places: the last time he felt at ease there, with a sense that he was making a success of his life, in 1951, two cars had come to get him.

A blindfold over his eyes, long hours in a plane, another car. At their destination, they removed the blindfold, sat him down on a stool a metre from the wall, allowed him to sit only on the edge of the stool, no way he could support himself against the wall, must sit up straight, he wasn't beaten, dunked in a bath, no electric wires.

They didn't want to leave any visible damage. Days and days spent on that stool, twenty hours a day: they took turns in teams of four, they call the approach the endless screw, the edge of the stool, a few punches, just to correct his posture, the feeling the stool reaches up to the back of your neck.

When Lilstein sags they drag him upright by the ears, they say they never saw anyone put up so little resistance, thump him in the kidneys, pinch his cheeks. But never in the presence of a superior.

A few days of this reduces a man to an aching pile of vertebrae, lots of questions, some of which he was unable to answer, but they didn't seem to want very detailed answers, not like the Gestapo when they'd demanded the names of the men in the network. In the Lubyanka, the questioning never stopped, an immense exhausting pain, for which Lilstein believed in the end that he alone was responsible. Then the blindfold again, the car, the plane, a new prison, a camp, in the cold.

When he was released, after the death of Stalin, he met the man who'd directed his interrogation, colonel's uniform, decorated like a hero.

'I had my orders,' the Colonel said.

'A good training if the fascists ever manage to get me again,' Lilstein said.

'You sound bitter, comrade, and you have every right to be.'

'Bitterness helps a man to grow old gracefully,' said Lilstein. 'It also makes a man efficient. You stop having illusions.'

Ever since Lilstein lost his illusions, he always does what he wants to do, whatever the risk, and he thrives on it. All the same, he remains cautious, he has come to Waltenberg circuitously, via Austria and Sweden, the Colonel was quite a decent man, he'd told Lilstein in an expressionless voice:

'Some of the men you denounced in 1947 did not have your luck, or protection.'

For a few hours here at Waltenberg, Lilstein can forget all about Warsaw, Budapest, such folly, and Suez, fortunately there's been Suez, that other folly, Lilstein hates events which just happen all by themselves then link up, gang up on you. He's had his fill of it these last few months.

Here at least he can breathe freely for a few hours, Switzerland, peace.

The little bridge at the edge of the village has not changed, in 1929 he used to spend every evening on it smoking his first pipefuls of dark tobacco cut with a Dutch honey mixture, numberless stars, the stars of deep mid-winter, the gurgle of the stream under the bridge is the same, things look smaller now than they did twenty-seven years ago but they're just the same, the bridge marks the entry to Waltenberg, Lilstein scrutinises the field of snow to his left, as far as the edge of the wood. Sometimes, if there's no noise from the village, you might spot a scampering stoat, but all is quiet just now.

Anyway, Lilstein hasn't time to stand there and keep watch, he makes for the houses, in the middle of the village are the church, the Hotel Prätschli, the grocery-cum-ironmonger's-cum-café with its large sign Konditorei, the garage, the red and gold petrol pump, and two large cowsheds. From the square, another hotel, the Waldhaus, can be seen on the distant side of a mountain, just where the ski slopes begin their descent to the north.

The Prätschli is a family hotel, the Waldhaus is much grander, a huge eight-storey double chalet, oversized, a bogus chalet trying to be a château, it disguises its inner structure of steel and concrete under wood cladding, beams, pantiles, rafters, joists, it dwarfs the valleys with its size, more than 400 rooms, a piece of Belle-Époque flummery, an hotel which draws its life from elsewhere, from people who travel hundreds, thousands of kilometres to live cocooned for a week or two in a land of chocolate, ski-lifts, simple joys and secret banking, it was built in the first years of the century, it started as a luxury sanatorium, with a bobsleigh run, it was accessible only by cable-car, in 1910 it was turned into a hotel and after 1918 a road was made, a heated garage was installed in the hotel basement together with an annexe which added a further hundred very modern rooms. The cable-car is still there, Lilstein read somewhere that in the days when it was a sanatorium coffins were sometimes brought down by bobsleigh, though that's probably a joke.

The Waldhaus quickly turned into a hotel catering for the winter sports and conference trade, Lilstein knows the owners quite well, has known them for ages, a couple who came from Alsace in the twenties, no money, a great deal of experience, became managers in 1939, were able to buy it in 1943, the darkest of the crisis years for tourism.

Lilstein strolls but he'll have to work fast, it's risky, two meetings in the same place, but the idea had caught his fancy and wouldn't let him be. The purpose of the first meeting is to make Kappler change his mind, Kappler, the great writer, the man who before the war had given him advice about life but that's all in the past.

The other meeting, with the man who needs to be convinced, a young Frenchman, from Paris, not yet thirty, if he accepts my proposal it could mean a very bright future for him.

That lands me with a very neat antithesis, it's dialectical, no, not dialectical, there's no synthesis, these two meetings form a symmetry, a thing and its obverse not its opposite, but what happens if it's the opposite that comes up?

I try to dissuade Kappler from returning to the GDR but instead he goes back and settles down at Rosmar; I try to persuade the young Frenchman to work with me, but he tells me to go to hell and denounces me to whoever will listen. You've still got your perfect symmetry but with both operations going wrong on the same day.

If Kappler does go back despite all I tell him it will be a failure only to me, in Berlin on the contrary I shall be congratulated for securing his return. But I won't be forgiven if the second operation goes wrong, long-term recruitment is the aim of all heads of external security whichever side they're on, a young man with a brilliant future, guide him over a period of years, tens of years, you're taking a big risk here, oh yes, but the problem is that you've not told anybody in Berlin about this plan to recruit the young Frenchman.

Or then again I fail with Kappler and succeed with the Frenchman, or else I succeed with Kappler and fail with the Frenchman, but I can also fail with both of them, which makes four possible outcomes in all.

To convince the young Frenchman I'll have to sound as if I'm convinced myself, with Kappler I'll have to sound bitter, writers like bitterness but if bitterness is all Kappler sees in me and if the Frenchman senses that I am too convinced, I'll be whistling in the wind, I'm the one who wants something, what have I got to offer?

Lilstein has known Kappler for ages, he first met him when he was already world-famous, it happened here, in 1929, Lilstein had come with his older brother, Thomas, a philosopher with a promising future, the 'Waldhaus Seminar', intellectuals, philosophers, economists, politicians, scientists, wealthy backers, beautiful women. People who wanted, as the expression already had it, to 'build Europe', all good bourgeois citizens and some of them even enlightened. Thomas is dead, he wanted to change philosophy, to find new relationships between being, reason and History.

What Lilstein wanted was to install telephone and radio in every corner of the globe and bring about the Revolution, sometimes people paid attention, affectionately, called him 'Young Lilstein', he was in love and he was rebuilding the world. These days he wonders exactly what it is he really wants to rebuild.

A few weeks ago in Berlin, he had been summoned by the Minister:

'Kappler wants to come back! Come back! Imagine, he's been gone ten years and now he wants to come back, at this point in time! It shows we were right all along!'

The Minister's huge paw strikes the top of his desk, hairs sprout on every joint of each finger, his voice rises:

'This proves it beyond the shadow of a doubt! Everything we've done this past year was harsh but it was fair, they call us "East Germany", even the "Soviet Zone", but Kappler said: "I'm going home", it proves we're a true homeland and not a part of somewhere else, you know him, don't you? known him personally for almost thirty years, you will go to him, you will give him anything he asks for, he must come back, it would be a stupendous coup. Kappler! he's abandoning them! I can already hear their hounds baying! He's coming back to the camp of progress, peace and socialism in spite of all the howls of their typewriter-pounding hyenas.'

The Minister pauses, looks Lilstein in the eye and adds:

'And in spite of our own mistakes! At last, some good news!'

And then the Minister did something very unpleasant. He stood up and scratched himself between the buttocks, a gesture which is appropriate only in private, as though Lilstein wasn't there. The Minister has short arms and this means he has to twist his spine backwards and to one side so that his hand can reach its objective, his head also has to bend back and to one side. To compensate, the Minister thrusts his chin forward and half-opens his mouth, a pose redolent of authority and deep thought, while his hand explores, locates and deals at length with the main item on the agenda.

Lilstein glanced out of the window, how can the Minister be told that the whole scheme is likely to come badly unstuck? Kappler back in Rosmar? He's done it once before, in 1946, he'd come from England, couldn't stand being at Rosmar for more than six months, and now he wants to come back again, Lilstein knows Kappler, and he knows the area he comes from, hammer and compass in a ring of rye, it won't work out, you won't feel right there, Herr Kappler, everything they say about us is true. Even in his head he still calls him Herr.

Lilstein has tried to reason with the Minister again, he has asked for a delay, he said maybe the subject's in poor physical shape, he's coming back because he's depressed, what'll we do if it turns out he'd come to us as a way of going to his death? The Minister said he'll be coming to the land of compass and rye, the scum flee, the best return, the compass, the rye and the hammer, not their filthy lucre, depression my arse, I thought you had a better analytical brain. The Minister's forefinger in Lilstein's direction:

'Think more politically!'

Lilstein ignored the short-armed Minister's arse: comrade Minister, we must tread carefully, this man won't be coming back because he thinks we're going to tear everything down, and the Minister said, but that's the point, we *are* going to tear everything down, urged on by the proletarian masses whose mouthpiece is the Party, and Kappler will be the positive living contradiction within this process which has been decided, directed and led by the Politburo under the authority of the general secretary, Comrade . . .

'Comrade Minister' – Lilstein has dared to interrupt the Minister – 'Hans Kappler does not give the same words the same meanings, let me remind you that in our country, when a writer publicly contradicts a minister, even the Minister of Culture, it's called antidemocratic propaganda, and he can be sent to prison for it. Now Kappler will not hesitate to contradict, he will exude negative contradiction, so at what point do we lock him up? The day after he gets here? Three weeks after? We will probably have to do it very quickly, otherwise we'll have to deport him or let all those who think as he does say their piece freely. Let's take our time, I say "our" time although this is not my area, I am not authorised for internal subversion, only exterior intelligence.'

As he speaks, Lilstein can see the Minister's tactic – success and it's marked down to the Minister, failure and it's Lilstein who fouled up – no, Minister, you fat pig, don't rely on me to carry the can, you think you're so strong, Minister, you have the support of a number of Soviet comrades, but they aren't necessarily the right ones any more, the funny thing is that you can't see it yet, one of these days I shall walk into your office and you'll be looking pretty sick because in the photo in *Pravda* the faces are different, not all of them, but you'll have this peculiar expression on yours, you'll scratch your arse because you think that you've got every right to scratch your arse in my presence, that I don't count, and you'll try to make sense of the new photo.

You might ask me what the photo in *Pravda,* all these changes, mean. What cannot be asked of a Department Head can be put to someone in whose presence you can scratch your arse, even if he's a Department Head, a brief passing conversation, one pig to another, you might assume I'll make it easy for you, and if my reply is that I have no idea, you can always bawl me out saying I never know anything, no, I know what I'll do, Minister, I'll pick up the photo and

I'll look even more scared than you, and that'll make you stop scratching yourself, you'll try to reassure me, the Soviet comrades have their own way of seeing things, they'll let us know when it suits them, sometimes they move very fast, you'll put on a brave smile when you say 'very fast', Minister, and there we'll be standing in front of the great slide, making polite noises.

You assure me that it'll be a straightforward descent, no more complicated than many other things in life, then all will return to normal at the bottom of the slope, say a quick hello to the new comrades, a kiss on the lips and then it all starts up again, so you'll want to go first, you'll try to push off gracefully, a straightforward descent, and there'll be only me who'll know, and I'll certainly not let on, that during the night the great slide iced up completely.

Lilstein looks the Minister straight in the eye:

'Comrade Minister, let us take steps to ensure we do not have an incident, at least let me sound out Kappler's intentions.'

And the Minister says:

'We must act quickly, you have your orders.'

He added nothing further. Correction: as he escorted Lilstein to the door he put one final question to him, keeping his tone formal:

'Are you for or against?'

'Against,' said Lilstein.

The Minister opened the door:

'All the same, those are your orders, and those orders express the will of the Politburo and Comrade Walter Ulbricht!'

The Minister had not needed to make him say 'Against', he did it for the benefit of his microphones and he took the opportunity to mention Ulbricht's name at least once.

Hans Kappler appeared to be in as much of a hurry as the Minister. To Lilstein's first message he replied that he didn't need time to think: in ten days he'd be in Berlin at the checkpoint on Friedrichstrasse.

At which Lilstein quickly arranged a meeting, in the greatest secrecy, at Waltenberg, to finalise the details.

'Do you like the Konditorei, Herr Kappler? Next Thursday, late morning? Shall we say eleven?'

Lilstein likes the Konditorei too, a kind of general emporium, groceries, hardware, ironmongery, confectionery, tobacco, bread and a few tables and chairs in the back to serve as a *Weinstube*. Low ceiling, narrow windows, gentle shadow, the smell of leather, specifically of harness and straps, the fragrance of bread and the tang of metal, nails are sold by the dozen, and all transactions are entered by hand in a great grey ledger, everyone who walks in says *Grüss Gott!*

What approach is he going to adopt with Kappler? The man's gone mad. Less than a year ago, he signed a piece in *Preuves*, for the people of the Congress for the Freedom of Culture who are anticommunists, which makes him a self-confessed anticommunist, and now he wants to go over to the socialist bloc, it's crazy. Or else, Kappler has turned into a lost soul floating on ideals as the current wafts him, frankly you'd be a lot more use to the cause of progress if you stayed in the West, Herr Kappler, representing us to the West, rather than coming back here spouting ideas which will be identified as Western.

It's all airy talk, and Kappler is very sensitive to how things are put, if it can't be said in ten words, then it's not true, not in fiction of course, the Kappler of old would point out, but true of life, of the way things are decided and action is initiated. You must learn, young Lilstein, speak last, use no more than ten words per sentence and utter only a few sentences.

Kappler, the master of the meandering sentence, my sentences are like centipedes he would say laughing; in 1929 Kappler gave Lilstein advice on the use of the incisive sentence in his undertakings, as if he were trying to relive his youth through Lilstein, but today he acts like anybody because he has begun to write like no one in particular.

Don't tell Kappler what he should do, destabilise him instead, why do you want to go back so badly? Lilstein also has another question to ask but he keeps it up his sleeve, because he doesn't know where it might lead them, he doesn't know how far this question he holds in reserve might take him, still it's what this is really all about, Rosmar is the idea of a man for whom everything's finished. Kappler is not a politician, his craziness is of a different order, so ask him the question:

'Did you ever see her again, Herr Kappler?'

No, not that question, if I ask him that more than likely I'll start shaking as I ask it, best water it down:

'Have you seen any of the people you knew in the good old days?'

Fool, it's the same question and it's not so upsetting to say.

'Have you seen her again?'

Make it just 'her', but my voice is bound to crack and he is quite capable of answering:

'How about you? Have you seen her? When was that?'

It would be a laugh to tell him, Lilstein thought, I'm sure that sooner or later, somehow over the next few years, Max will tell him, at least the parts he knows, a tale of cloak and dagger, I bumped into her, I almost bumped into her, our paths crossed but I never saw her again, it wasn't long ago, last August. Don't tell this to Kappler.

It might make him give up the idea of going back to Rosmar, but don't tell him, she comes out of the Budapest Academy of Music, the mood of the city is restless, end of August, they all reckon that 1956 will mark a new beginning, she has just done five hours' straight teaching, a master-class, I wonder what Max will make of her master-class, he'll not pick up on it and pass directly to what comes next, or else he'll use it as an excuse to try and talk about the music he loves.

It's after nine in the evening, she's happy, her Hungarian students are bright, a whole afternoon of Schubert, she has come up with new expressions to use on them, new ideas for exercises, a good singing teacher doesn't say:

'Put your whole soul into it!'

No, the good teacher finds graduated exercises which mobilise the multifarious moods of the soul, as a cover it was impeccable, very complete, it would have made the subject of a most interesting report, Lena's singing class in the Academy of Music, from an analysis of the *Lied* to her work on the perineum and 'when you sing keep thinking of your role, which is to inspire', the verb most frequently on her lips is *denken,* her classes in German, like in the good old days of the Hapsburgs, and in French, she speaks very good French, she is a genuine European, had a father who was mad about Henry James, in front of her class of young Hungarians she can try exercises, angles, snatches of interpretation.

She's just found one new phrase, she tells them not to try to express everything, your interpretation must leave the public wanting more, the audience must not receive passively, it must be drawn towards what you are singing, it's not hesitation, there's no mystery about it, it's a tension, you are offering an interpretation and the audience is thinking that something more is about to materialise, so don't obscure the message.

It is good to come up with new solutions and not simply be a rememberer of old inventions.

Night is falling slowly, there's a taxi free, she does not want it, she's walking to stretch her legs, one of her pupils has said, Madame, I'll walk with you, crossing from one bank to the next, towards Buda, the residential quarter, and her hotel in the middle of a park.

A lovely walk, a fit young pupil, sensitive too, they walk beside the Danube then cross Elisabeth Bridge. I love wandering through towns as it gets dark, crossing bridges, the mist, which blurs the outline of the monuments, when I was singing I had to take care, I was always pretty healthy but night mist is a little menace, you can easily wake up next day croaking. Lena puts her hand through the young man's arm, turns, forces him to do the same, look, that fantastic pile, it's the Parliament building, quite magnificent, they resume walking, her hand is still through her pupil's arm.

The suspension bridge vibrates with the steps of the pedestrians, at the end of the bridge her pupil stumbles, she clutches at his arm, a car is there, a door is open, the door slams shut, a pistol fitted with a silencer, one finger held against a mouth, the car speeds off, it swerves throwing Lena from one man against another, the one on her right says something, the car slows, other things are said, in fractured English, 'you', 'calm', they tie her hands, a hood is placed over her head, her head is forced down, fewer bends now, they are on an open road, much time goes by, her back aches.

Now the car is being driven fast, they let Lena sit up again, I must try to sleep, there's nothing else I can do, I should never have walked, it wouldn't have made any difference, they'd have laid on a bogus taxi, that pupil of mine was a good-looking boy, did they lean on him? Lithe, he walked lithely.

A long road, the car brakes, a sharp turn, ruts, then an unmade road, come to a stop, they bundle her out, a damp forest smell, they sit her down, back must be against the trunk of a tree, they remove the hood, a bad sign.

The air is dark and cool, night, moon, a soughing of leaves, a clearing, three men and one woman stand over her, two machine-pistols. The men smoke. Everything has a pallid sheen.

She looks up at the sky, hears the beat of wings, repeats to herself 'The stars and our lives are bound by hoops of steel', she is sixty-one years old, it's the end of the road, she is not unhappy, this afternoon's renditions of Schubert were very good. None of the three men look at Lena, the woman has the face of a mournful slave, rough movements and a revolver. She takes Lena by the arm and leads her to one side.

The Russians had kidnapped Lena, the KGB, it was Max who reconstructed the puzzle, it took him a good long time, he reconstructed it for Hans, to tell him the story of what happened, a very Max-ish story, with real facts, gaps, and cloak-and-dagger padding to fill the gaps, in 1956 Markov is Russia's deputy Minister of Security, in late August he arrives in Hungary, on its eastern border, a meeting of Warsaw Pact intelligence services, in a railway carriage:

'The Americans are making a nuisance of themselves, we need to give them a serious warning not to make a nuisance of themselves.'

'We could eliminate a few of their agents tonight, comrade Minister.'

'Like diplomats, you mean? And then what? If they've got

diplomatic passports, we'll have the United Nations down on us like a ton of bricks. If they don't, they're just the small fry.'

Lilstein is there, a better head on him than most of the other men present, he has a detached air, in fact he's had an idea but wishes he hadn't, it's a bad idea but it might produce good results, a doubtful gesture which might not turn out too badly, though badly for whom? He hesitates while all the rest put forward their proposals, round up one of the known networks and shoot the lot, hang them, do it in public, expel America's ambassador but not Britain's, it would produce the same rumpus and would have less fall-out, maybe there's something could be set moving in Berlin.

'What? Another world war?'

Markov is beginning to get angry, and the men who are there are afraid of Markov, it's late, it's dark and the later it gets the twitchier Markov becomes. It is dangerous to speak within earshot of a man with a record like Markov's, he saw off the Waffen SS with his foot soldiers, a forceful type, but tonight he's as jumpy as a cat, the other men speak when he gives them the nod and as they speak they can hear what is going into the report that contains a minute of what they've said together with an estimate of their abilities, at this juncture we need to come up with guilty names, if we're in this mess it's because there have been anomalies, if there have been anomalies it's because there have been failures.

Usually the way out of these messes is to recommend the strongest measure, pull coals out of the fire, only this time, pulling coals out of the fire when the result is a disaster amounts to sabotage, and Markov glares at the advocate of the strongest measures as if he were dealing with a mixture of Anglo-Saxon spy and Trotskyite snake, like in the good old days.

Then someone recommended to Markov the strongest measures, with safeguards, and Markov asked what exactly, and he doesn't know, and the report is filled out and he's marked down as a moron. Markov doesn't need to tell you in so many words, you might well be the head of Hungarian or Czech counter-espionage, and thousands, millions of people shake in their shoes at the mere mention of your name, but when you're facing Markov you're an undiluted moron.

And if you start talking of safeguards you immediately give the impression of being some sort of moderate and in the pay of the Anglo-Saxons to boot, and just at the very moment when the need is to come up with names, never mind, if we have to go in and clean up Budapest's mess we'll pick up anyone who doesn't have a diplomatic passport and we'll introduce martial law, without issuing any communiqués or talking about wasted bullets.

'Misha, you're not saying anything, are you bored? Is it complicated? What have you got to suggest?'

Markov smiles as he speaks and Michael Lilstein has a feeling that in that smile tragedy is choosing the object it will strike.

'We could snatch someone well known, comrade Minister, someone who is well-protected, who has never been bothered until now, and by snatching this person we would show that we know everything, we'd be returning the goods to the sender, at night, all the way to Austria, they'll get the message loud and clear.'

'A corpse?'

A trap, don't fall into it, you say:

'That's one option, comrade Minister.'

'It's still too complicated, Misha.'

Markov is not smiling now. Lilstein does not like seeing him in this mood. In January 1945, Markov was the first man Lilstein saw looming up in front of him, in woods close to Auschwitz, with his round, beaming face, Sancho Panza in a fur coat carrying a machine-pistol, part of the avant-garde of Konev's army, Lilstein fell into Markov's arms, he wept for a quarter of an hour in Markov's arms, saying nothing, and Markov smiled and said: 'It's all over, lad, all over' to a man who was two heads taller than him and weighed three times less. Markov was one of the political commissars of Konev's army. He was always in a good humour. He's done very well for himself. He's deputy Minister now. Tonight his mood is grim, he says:

'We're floundering, I must get some sleep, tomorrow morning, at five, we'll see what needs to be done.'

Twenty minutes after the meeting ended, Lilstein was called back to Markov's carriage.

'The Americans have an important agent in Budapest, an agent we've never bothered, and you never mentioned the fact to me?'

'There was a good chance the information would end up on a desk that wasn't yours, comrade Minister, I didn't have time to come to Moscow personally.'

And Markov adopts a very mechanical tone, why so many precautions among men who are fighting the same war, all the Ministries have their shoulders to the same wheel, Misha should have sent his message without delay. Markov ends with a wide, childlike smile, the look in his eye dictates Lilstein's response.

'I was aware, comrade Minister, that it wouldn't be long before you called us all together. I waited for the opportunity you've just created: it's a woman.'

Markov throws his hands in the air:

'We haven't been giving you all this protection so you could come up with hogwash like that!'

'She arrived here not long ago, comrade Minister, she was in Germany, she was already travelling in Germany and Hungary in the days of the Nazis and Horthy, and even before then, she has always known a great many things, she used to be a diva, by which I mean . . .'

'Misha, I too am a cultured man, I don't spend all my evenings questioning suspects with a blowtorch.'

'Everyone who matters goes to her public master-classes, comrade Minister, and they invite her to dinner, she's American.'

'The one from Berlin?'

Markov couldn't have asked for more, he doesn't want an answer, he smiles, a good smile, like in the old days, Sancho Panza, Lilstein wonders why Markov mentioned blowtorches, 'Comrade Minister, I'm certain that nowadays she's a full-time CIA operative, with no diplomatic status, if you wish we could pass the information to the Hungarians, let them shoot her, or alternatively wait and only shoot her when we've gone in to do Budapest's housekeeping, but if we send her back to them now, dead or alive whichever, they'll realise we know everything, everything that is less well guarded than the secret of this woman's role, they might settle for stirring people up with their Radio Free Europe broadcasts but if they really want to make a more specific response we must tell them that we know everything and are waiting for them to move.'

'Does she still sing?'

'Private recitals, just for friends, comrade Minister, apparently she's as good as ever.'

'Well, no more recitals! Lower the curtain! Put one of your men with mine, to keep an eye on things, this isn't a bad idea, you've got forty-eight hours, less if possible. You really didn't waste any time in sending me this information?'

Kappler doesn't need to know this part of Lena's story, not now, in the end Max will tell it to him, adding another episode, dating from in 1954, two years before Budapest, in the end Max will have to tell Kappler what he did in '56 and '54.

Max will turn it into a story in his usual style, with gaps, some invention, elements of the truth, and when the archives are opened fifty years hence it will be seen that Max was not very far wide of the mark, there'll be a few snippets of information for Max, about 1956 and going two years further back, to early 1954.

You really should talk about this to a couple of your poker chums, Max, one rumour about Lena is doing the rounds in Washington, McCarthy has a hankering, the McCarthy of the glory days, the communist witch-hunt, a minor scene in the office of Senator McCarthy, he is alone with his aide who is reading aloud from a file:

'This lady, this opera-singer who cosies up to the communists, she travels to the East whenever she wants, the FBI says nothing, the CIA lets her have a free hand, the State Department gives her trip its blessing, the KGB provides luxury hotel accommodation in Prague or Budapest, she's always had covert dealings, first with the Nazis, as early as 1931, she even cosied up to the Germans between 1914 and 1917, she left Germany in tears, twice, first in 1917 and again in 1941, each time just before we went to war, the Russians must have a helluva fat file on her, they've got her, we'll make her testify to the committee, under oath, diva or not, we'll fry her, she fraternised with the Nazis and she works for the Soviets and she's in cahoots with all the liberals in Washington, we've got her cold, a typical case, a Nazi, a Bolshevik and a Liberal.'

McCarthy makes up his mind:

'We'll subpoena her to appear before the committee.'

February 1954, McCarthy is about to put a large bomb under the communist and liberal networks, subpoena this woman, Max, you go too far, you talk as if you were sitting on McCarthy's knee, the bastard, if you knew anything about the man's morals, shush, not a word, down boy, this is guaranteed château-bottled stuff, aged in our own cellars.

McCarthy is out to get Lena, and two men ask for a meeting, two unofficial envoys from the White House, smart restaurant, private room, there'll be two of us, Mr Senator, you can bring your aide, there'll be no tricks, you can post one bodyguard at the door, not more, it will be a very significant meeting.

McCarthy has got the White House liberals, communist puppets, where he wants them, they've got their backs to the wall, they ask for a meeting and now they're sitting across from him, private room with a thick-pile carpet, dark red drapes, very quiet.

Two liberals for McCarthy: Walker, a member of Eisenhower's private office, the laid-back member of the team, tweed jacket, black-and-orange handkerchief in the breast pocket, Princeton colours, and the fairy, Garrick, grey suit, democratic Senator, two Washington fairies, both under thirty, each born with a silver spoon in his mouth, played football, law degrees from Princeton, muscles and crewcuts to give the lie, liberal fairies, they've had the nerve to send him these two, a single indictment will be enough, no cosying-up outside the door, no drinks even, McCarthy starts talking before he's finished sitting down, his hands are still on the arms of his chair:

'What have you two got that you want to say to me?'

'We've got nothing to ask, Senator.'

'What the hell are we doing here, then?'

'We come with a simple message,' says Walker, 'a message from the President, you are about to call a lady, please, let me finish, there's not much to say, the President says: "Don't".'

'Or else?'

'With all due respect, sir, the President told us to kick your ass.'

And Garrick adds:

'Until you stop liking it, Senator.'

No one has talked like that to McCarthy in a long, long while, and the two envoys are cool, provoking, the Chairman of the Committee on UnAmerican Activities lays one hand on his aide's forearm to calm him down, McCarthy is a good card-player, he started too fast, he's going to kill these two sons-of-bitches and do it without putting a foot wrong. They watch him, smiling, the blood has not risen to their faces which are not pale either, maybe they're not complete drag-asses, but they're pretty young, a Republican and a Democrat, here they are together, McCarthy should have made sure he was better informed, maybe they're not fairies, take care when you order them dead, he checks them out with a smile:

'You boys served in the war?'

'Yes, Senator.'

'Whereabouts?'

'Korea, Senator, in the marines both, volunteers' – this is Walker talking – 'a good outfit.'

'Yeah? What did you do?'

'Flame-thrower, Senator, for a year and a half, I wouldn't have changed places for the world, and Garrick here was a specialist sharp-shooter, his job was to look out for my butt, he did it for a year and a half too, I'm a Republican, he's a Democrat, we got on like good buddies, and we still do.'

'You did say: kick his ass?'

'Until he stops liking it, Senator, it's army talk, an image.'

'And what if I shoved my glass in your goddam face?'

'Senator, President Eisenhower said "or else it's total war". It'll only last forty-eight hours at most. Would you let me expand briefly, before you throw the glass? Actors, intellectuals, union bosses, writers, journalists, you can do pretty much what you want with them, foreigners too, have Thomas Mann dealt with as a communist, order *The Magic Mountain* removed from US cultural centres abroad, you can go further, tickle up Mr Dulles and the CIA, not too much, got to think of your credibility, all that stuff the President can understand, but when he sends us along to warn you to keep off the grass, keep off the grass is what he means. We don't like the smell of frying, Senator, but we can handle a fry-pan. This lady is gonna disappear from your plans and this meeting never took place.'

These events of 1954 will be related by Max, Michael Lilstein knows about a third of the story, but on the basis of the third that Lilstein will feed him, plus a few conversations with his friend Linus Mosberger, one of the top men at the *Washington Tribune*, Max will do something very plausible, he will add the events that took place in Budapest in 1956, and this will be crucial for the way people will remember Lena, the kidnapping, the car, a plausible story.

Which is why, soon, when he speaks to Kappler, Lilstein will not ask:

'Did you ever see her again?'

And no one's chin will start to tremble.

The other incident, the one which took place in Hungary last August shortly before Russian tanks rolled into Budapest, just a few weeks ago, Lilstein doesn't have to tell Kappler about it, he has reconstituted it but he won't tell the tale of the road, the halt, the forest, the woman with the revolver, she takes Lena to one side, Lena looks up at the sky, the stars and our death are bound by hoops of steel, no, the stars and the cold, what the poet said was the stars and the cold, not death, there's less pathos put like that, anyway death is there, belle of the ball, I've been belle of the ball several times, I've nothing to complain about, the forest surrounds Lena, she has always loved the forest, you have the feeling that this one isn't particularly beautiful, there's the noise water makes in the grass, the Waltenberg larches, we used to ski on the snow between the larches, with Hans, no not Hans, he didn't ski, at least not well enough for cross-country runs, and he never really wanted to come with me, it must have been Max who quoted the words of the poet to me, in Paris last year, the skiing was with Michael, young Lilstein, *nun hast du mir den ersten Schmerz getan*, the first pain I felt, you were the cause of the first pain I felt, and now, dear Michael, I am the one who's going to die.

It feels so good to enter the forest, the hiss of the skis on the snow, Kägli leads, the monitor, he tries out a new way of braking, a slide with skis aligned, in those days I wasn't very good at it, that was a quarter of a century ago, the braking action which slowed you from the convergent snowplough to the parallel christiania, hereabouts the forest is not a nice place, I don't like the dark, it wouldn't be much better if it were day, at least I don't have to think that I'm saved by a patch of blue sky, fortunately I don't have children, a woman with a revolver and a bullet for the heroine.

Not wild enough, all my life I have never been wild enough, the darkness deepens, the Hungarian forest, hurl curses at them like Tosca does, the way they'll look if I hurl . . . No, I've nothing to say to these people, why don't they get on with it, I'm only frightened that the woman will make a mess of it, my heart is beating fast, Max did warn me.

The woman with the revolver leaves Lena to be by herself for a moment, brings her back to the car, gives her hot tea to drink, looks into her eyes and says in a muffled voice:

'It's going to get very cold.'

A biscuit to go with the tea, again the voice says tonelessly:

'It's going to get very cold.'

The hood is placed over Lena's head again, the car, the long ride, in the end she falls asleep on the shoulder of one of the men. When she wakes, she is alone in the car. She hears voices all around her, American voices. A few minutes later she is in a large ambulance driving towards Vienna, men in white coats and a man in a tweed jacket, a black and orange handkerchief in the breast pocket, her friend Walker, he feels her brow, there are tears in his eyes. A doctor takes Lena's blood pressure, a syringe.

'What's in it?'

'A heart stimulant, Ma'am, that's it, no more field service for you.'

So in the end, later that morning, face to face with Kappler, Lilstein will not mention Lena's name. He'll just ask:

'Why are you so set on going back?'

Lilstein remembers Kappler from the days when he was so lucid, he used doubt like a drug. One day, Kappler had said to him:

'I am a doubter and you are a nay-sayer, that's the reason why we like arguing, at least for a spell, also because we're both from Rosmar.'

Lilstein knows Kappler but Kappler knows him even better, they have only run across each other two or three times since 1929, and then only briefly, but what happened all that time ago at Waltenberg has bound them together. Kappler is Lilstein's big older brother, he has a smile that makes him Lilstein's superior, it always will, he'll have no bother winkling out from beneath Lilstein's current demeanour old traces of the pre-war adolescent, the endless discussions they had in those evenings, in the Waldhaus, in one corner of the main residents' lounge.

They had their regular place by a window, near a very tall papyrus, a horticultural miracle in a pot at this altitude of 1,700 metres. Kappler always treated the young man as an equal, he would order two coffees and two Armagnacs, you look a lot older than your age, young Lilstein, and you don't smoke, which is a sign of self-control, but this will be your one and only Armagnac for this evening, are we agreed? Does Kappler remember everything that I can't even remember myself? I don't drink Armagnac any more, just coffee, did I take it with sugar in those days? nowadays it's one lump in the cup and the other in the spoon to dunk in the coffee, what the French call a *canard*, and if there's a third lump I leave it or treat myself to another *canard*, I never put two in the cup, or only rarely, and it's a bad idea, it makes me feel slightly nauseous, Kappler was already one of the world's great figures and – apart from the Armagnac – he treated an adolescent as an equal in furious arguments about ideas, he never took sugar with his coffee, he dipped his sugar lumps in the Armagnac, he had no children of his own.

Lilstein would contradict Kappler furiously, admiring him nonetheless, Kappler went out of his way to provoke his fury.

Even today Kappler knows more about Lilstein than Lilstein knows about himself, he knows that Lilstein is aching to ask him:

'Did you ever see her again?'

He knows all about that side of Lilstein that the years have covered over but that has not gone away, nothing ever goes away for good, everything that has continued to grow in Lilstein in a shadow which even Lilstein himself prefers to ignore, everything in him that is always ready to say no, the urge always to say no, the feeling that he has an inner strength that impels him not to align himself with a Minister who scratches his arse in front of his Department Heads.

On those evenings at Waltenberg, in the great drawing-cum-reading room of the Waldhaus, after that day's Seminar debates, Kappler would smile as he talked to Lilstein who, at fifteen or sixteen, was taller, looked older than his age and was building a new world with violence and adjectives, you are a rebel, young man, you are not sufficiently docile to be a true revolutionary and build new worlds, you must learn discipline, as it is you are merely a rebel, and even though you may not have broken discipline you have wanted to, the idea of making some seditious gesture is always at the back of your mind, you claim you want to make a new world but your true gift is for the rebellious gesture, even when you do not act you enjoy the pleasure of the rebellious gesture, a guilty pleasure, I'm pretty sure that the first time you were sent to school your mama slipped your hand into the headmaster's and left the room backwards, a headmaster so proud to have been entrusted with the progeny of two Doctor

Lilsteins, man and wife, you weren't the least upset when you saw your mother leave, rather you were curious about the new things that were happening, you didn't cry, though you did bite the headmaster's hand, I'm quite certain your brother told me about it, he laughed when he told me about that and the cuff the Headmaster gave you in return, freedom is useless if you can't bite the hand that holds you, the rebellious gesture, in the name of freedom, the urge to do anything, even burn the place down, anything, a look all around the room from Kappler, anything except the innocence of these people! yes, it's just bourgeois psychology, but remember: the taste for the rebellious gesture will always be part of you!

Kappler nodded towards the small groups of well-dressed people, like themselves, who were talking heatedly in the lounge of the Waldhaus, and Lilstein smiled with the satisfaction of having made a break-through, of seeing that Kappler was not far from sharing his own hostility to *these people*.

Not far from the corner where he and Kappler were talking, a man was sitting next to a woman in an easy chair, his name was Neuville and he was talking in a clear voice to a group of people who were standing, in his hand were several sheets of rolled-up paper, talking without being interrupted:

'The unit designed to measure human work called the Neuville or the N unit is a universal unit representing the quantity of available physiological energy which can be expended by a normally constituted human being in one minute.'

Neuville did not talk as if he were addressing a public meeting, he spoke in a steady voice, slowly, without giving the impression that he was delivering a lecture, but rather that he was sharing the pleasure of such a satisfying definition, he was wearing a double-breasted tweed suit, loose-fitting, grey with a faint green thread running through it, the same kind of suit favoured by Lilstein's father who, however, did not care for green thread on grey, but his mother said the green cheered it up and she had the last word, the man who was speaking in the steady voice had everything that life can offer, and to it he added a benevolence of word and look:

'In measuring the quantity of available human energy, allowance is made for the appropriate amount of rest required when the human in question, under normal conditions, carries out the actions and makes the physiological effort demanded by the industrial tasks for which he has been fitted and trained, at a rate which is equal to three-quarters of the normal rate of physiological exertion during the course of a normal day's work . . .'

A German woman stood drinking in Neuville's words, from time to time the woman in the easy chair gave her a very blank look, Neuville went on:

'. . . a level of exertion which must leave the worker still able to fulfil his familial and societal obligations, that is to expend each day the same amount of physiological energy without producing any deleterious effect on his health or individuality.'

Neuville, a man of clearly articulated speech, who used silences designed to enable the listener to ponder his words or examine his suit, like an actor who knows that no one will interrupt his monologue save to acquiesce. It was unbearable:

'Taylor failed to take account of fatigue and the need to renew the strength required for working – only the Neuville Unit measures the phenomenon in its entirety.'

To Lilstein, it was intolerable, a hotel lounge is intended for conversation, these people listen to him before he's even said anything, a servile bunch, shut this capitalist up, let him gather his lackeys around him somewhere else, Lilstein is sixteen, lashings of frustration to get out of his system, scandal, create a scandal, administer a public lesson to this mix of idealist visionary and evil bastard, he turns towards Neuville and hears him say:

'To earn my crust when I was a young man in the USA, I worked behind the counter of a whiskey store.'

Now for the story of my success! Lilstein waits for the pause, in it he intends to ruin the speaker's effect.

'We sold three different kinds of bottle at three different prices, quarter dollar, half dollar and one dollar, it was my introduction to capitalism: for all three prices they got the same quantity of the same whiskey.'

Suddenly Lilstein tells himself that he can learn something from such cynicism and he too begins to listen.

One day, much, much later, Lilstein would say with the categorical certainty that only a man who has passed through Auschwitz then the Gulag can aspire to:

'Capitalists are cynics.'

Smiles on the faces of the members of the Politburo's Special Economic Committee. Lilstein continues:

'They claim to lead crusades but basically they are cynics selling junk.'

More smiles. Lilstein goes on:

'But the trick is that they put a value on that junk, while we, who reject cynicism, are stuck with junk which has no value at all.'

No smiles now, the men newly appointed to run the economy just wonder why they were being attacked like this, in the name of what other group could Lilstein be speaking, for wasn't he a member of the group which had helped them up the ladder to their new responsibilities, Lilstein having even furnished them, thanks to his contacts, with invaluable information about capitalist products and techniques, why this observation about worthless junk? Was it an about-turn by Lilstein? A lurch in the direction of the reactionaries and fanatical advocates of heavy industry? Or was he in the process of reaching an understanding with some more advanced splinter group made up of irresponsible elements set on restoring capitalism on the specious argument that productivity is productivity? Or had he just been trying to be clever? He certainly had a reputation for never being able to resist a *Witz*, even of the sour variety. Difficult chap to keep a check on, just looks out for number one.

Long ago, in Waltenberg, the man talking about the Neuville system had added:

'Three separate prices but it was always genuine whiskey, my first lesson in capitalism, everything is relative, as our young friend Tellheim would say.'

Lilstein had decided not to create a scene. Tellheim was a young physicist who'd been invited to this same Seminar in the spring of 1929 to give lectures on relativity, he spoke of lifts, two lifts moving in parallel over the façade of an immensely tall skyscraper, like the ones they have in America, when both start to move the passengers in Lift One drop various objects out of the window, umbrellas, hats, handbags, the objects fall, dropping away beneath them at a speed of 981 centimetres per second, that is at a speed which increases by 981 centimetres every second, assuming the absence of any kind of resistance.

Tellheim did not try to grab people's attention, he just spoke of what he knew, that's all, you felt you were there in the lift with him, you couldn't stop yourself, and while Lift One starts going down in the normal way at the normal speed, Lift Two plunges into the void at a speed of 981 centimetres a second, impelled by the same force as the falling objects, which is to say the force of gravity, the passengers in Lift Two no longer feel their feet pressing down on the floor, their wallets cease to weigh anything in their pockets, and if they drop their hats, bags and brollies these objects remain suspended in mid-air before their very eyes, whether the hats be made of feathers or of lead.

And these passengers in Lift Two can see the objects dropped from Lift One floating just next to them, if you follow me, so that at exactly the same moment some passengers can see hats falling and others see them suspended in front of them, what does it take for a lift to be able to reach this speed? well, let's say provided there's no friction or resistance and that at the instant the lift started moving the cable snapped cleanly, a hypothesis that can easily be tested. Tomorrow evening, I'll tell you about trains and how, to an observer standing on the platform, a train passes through the station less quickly than for an observer sitting in the train, and the day after tomorrow it will be the curve which is the shortest distance in the universe between two points.

Tellheim and Lilstein had become instant friends.

In the drawing-cum-reading room of the Waldhaus in 1929, the women were very beautiful, and they looked the men straight in the eye.

'They've just discovered that ideas make eyes shine more brightly than kohl.'

This thought had been one of several to catch the fancy of the billiard players, but no one claimed to have said it first. Sometimes Lilstein watched the young French girls but his eyes lingered particularly on a tall red-haired woman who looked at him in the sweetest way, they'd gone cross-country skiing with some French girls, one of these had said to one of her friends:

'In three years, he'll be gorgeous.'

The other one had replied:

'What's wrong with him now?'

And whenever Kappler caught Lilstein looking at a woman he would repeat with a smile:

'Anything – except the innocence of these people!'

Sometimes a friend of Kappler's would join them, a French journalist with big ears, funny man, he was jealous of Lilstein and made scenes, shush! not a word, this is nothing to do with you, when he's with you he becomes young again, all I do is remind him of old horrors in the mud of long ago and the new horrors I go in search of in this vast world of ours, do you know in what receptacles the Head of the Medico-Legal Institute in Paris keeps the brains that interest him after he's completed an autopsy? chamber pots, and do you know why? He claims it's because nothing else fits the shape of the brain as well. Strange. Every time I say 'do you know?' it's to tell of some new horror. Do you know how French military posts in Morocco during the Riff wars were not so long ago supplied with water?

Kappler's French friend would take his time, twisting his glass round and round, giving the impression that he believed the answer would not be long in coming from his listeners, his ears gave him a comical, genial look, the ladies would press him, he would add, take twenty-five downtrodden privates with an officer who fancies himself as Roland and is looking for an Oliver to die with, and hundreds of Saracens all around them, Berbers, they're more chivalrous than Saracens except for one appalling habit, when they take prisoners they cut them open, stuff their innards full of rocks and camel dung, don't even wait for their captives to die before tearing their tongues out, experts who study these things call this rural rites of execration, obviously these men from the Riff are on home ground, their land has been defiled, oh yes, the water, it comes by plane along with a couple of military medals, no, the planes don't land, they drop supplies on the post. How do they manage to do that with water? The first time I heard it in a radio message I almost burst out laughing: 'Under siege, send blocks of ice.'

Maybe Kappler was mistaken about Lilstein when he spoke of his 'gift for the rebellious gesture', and 'guilty pleasure'. In those days, Lilstein gave short shrift to all that bourgeois psychology, those pronouncements about pleasure and innocence, but now he can see things he didn't see when he was an adolescent or even before he met Kappler, a gobbet of chewed-up blotting-paper splatting against a blackboard in school for instance, the teacher points to the gobbet and asks who did that, it didn't matter that the young Lilstein was innocent, he always turned bright red, he hadn't done anything but he could easily have had the idea of throwing the gobbet, his head was permanently full of mischief, he never actually did anything but when a gobbet of spittle-sodden blotting-paper went splat against the blackboard, he always thought it was a quality jape.

And he would blush bright red. Or maybe he was guilty of something else, the maid's armpits for example, he'd stare at them when she was dusting the chandeliers at home, and when the teacher pointed to the gobbet and asked who did that, Lilstein would turn red because he'd had the idea of the gobbet, because he was still thinking of the maid's armpits and behind the maid's armpits was another episode, the business of the grain of rice shot at the same maid's backside with an air-gun; blushing was his handicap, the minute anyone started talking about things that shouldn't be done he blushed crimson, it took him years to control it, sometimes he looked so guilty that he got sent out of the classroom and made to stand in the corridor.

There he would wait for the teacher on duty to come round, there was just a chance that the teacher might not appear and interrupt this really rather pleasant interlude in which crimes and punishments cancelled each other out in his imagination as he got his own back on the real culprit of a misdemeanour everyone got out of pretty easily, since being sent out of class was supposed to be the worst punishment going.

At breaktime, with his friends, Lilstein could silently enjoy being the character he'd just invented, which was that of someone who stood his ground and was consequently the moral superior of whoever it was who, by not owning up, had left him to face the full fury of the authorities.

And since the boy who had not owned up was generally class top dog, his kind was ultimately indebted to Lilstein for a portion of the cowed respect they extracted from their classmates with fist and foot.

However reassuring he found his status as an innocent but virile victim, Lilstein had finally come to see that a little emotion may also be taken as a sign that you are more innocent than those who remain stonily impassive, so that he who was forever blushing, you know, young and full-blooded, too tall for his age, is forever making up stories in his head, just you start talking about girls, you'll see, to the roots of his hair, it's unstoppable, or else make a few general remarks about spoiled brats.

Later, Lilstein's superiors, his colleagues, his instructors during his time in Moscow or the imprisoned comrades he knew in the camps, both the one run by the Nazis and the other one, all knew him as a quiet, meticulous man, he was always one step ahead of the game but a little fragile, always going slightly red in the face, he never looked as if he could lie, he was easily flustered, and his interrogators at the

Lubyanka who sat him on a stool and grilled him in relays twenty-four hours a day before sending him to a special camp all knew that he was a decent sort, that he'd got snarled up in the system, but that he was a decent type.

Now a man who blushes when a question is put to him is obviously guilty, but no more so than anyone else, if they'd put their minds to it they could have taken him apart, broken him, made him cry, made him say anything, but they couldn't go too far, especially not risk killing him, no one had given orders one way or the other, but everybody knew.

When Abakumov or his direct assistants failed to come in person and put their union seal on the work of the professionals, the professionals avoided doing too much, especially when the subject remained calm and blushed, though not too much. Lilstein had problems but went on being a decent sort, as if someone in the shadows had decided to anticipate the real enforcers and do Lilstein minor damage to save him from worse, some person or persons, or not anybody, perhaps nobody had taken charge of the matter, an empty box in the chart of the organisation's hierarchy, an oversight which had as many consequences as, if not more than, any specific action taken by a person or persons.

As if oozing out from its own inner void through this one place, the organisation began to act by itself, outlining solutions 'for a later date', no, hardly solutions more like contingency plans for later on, Lilstein's survival being one of these plans, without anyone in the organisation nor the organisation itself knowing exactly what 'a later date' meant, as if somehow a mechanism had been set in motion to save certain victims from the very worst.

As if the organisation knew, or felt, that some day it might well need to solicit the machinery of its own survival from the victims it had allowed to survive.

Now Kappler had known Lilstein before all that, the Lilstein who at Waltenberg in 1929 had been impelled by an inner force first to say no and then to work with the fall-out produced by his no, 'twas ever thus, he has always said no, even unto a mark of nought in science at the age of eleven so that his father would get the message, that medicine was out of the question, Kappler knew Lilstein as a revolutionary and the scion of celebrated doctors, a young man who said no to all-comers and wanted to scrap the world and start again, not because the world was suffering or made others suffer but because the world belonged to him.

'An anarcho-materialist, young Lilstein, an anarcho-materialist is just what you are, it makes you likeable but it will bring you a lot of trouble unless you learn to discipline yourself.'

It was Kappler who told him to read Lenin and, through Lenin, Marx. Kappler hated Lenin yet he told Lilstein to read him when Lilstein was just sixteen years old, because he knew it would help him to survive, you learned Russian so you could read Dostoyevsky, you can use it now to read Lenin. Lilstein became one of the German communists who knew Lenin's work best, in the original, and Kappler put him on his guard against his own personal sympathies, Rosa Luxemburg, no point reading her, Bukharin ditto, the sin of economism, Kappler admired Bukharin but he advised Lilstein against him:

'I'm not saying you shouldn't read him because I'm hoping you'll come to him against my advice, at your age you only read what you're told not to, but it'll get dangerous pretty quickly, Trotsky's dangerous too, utopia and militarism, his enemies say that he's a snake, it's not true but Trotskyism has lost its relevance, Lenin's your man, young Lilstein, the complete works, with Stalin, and Marx through Lenin and Stalin, and Stalin's going to be increasingly important, of course, not forgetting Engels and the rest of it, the permanent revolution, the worker's democracy, the end of alienation, all of it is an adolescent dream, there are no free gifts in this world and if you really want to change it then it's not pretty women you should be cuddling up to but the butcher.'

In 1929, Kappler telling Lilstein to do what he had never done himself, talking as he scrutinised the large potted papyrus near which they were sitting and Lilstein's face against the delicate green of the papyrus leaves, a young god, more than a young god, gods do not possess the same will to shape the future, nor wear their soul on their sleeve, Kappler felt behind his words the swell of a gladness he had given up on long ago, a young man's joy remembered from when the century was young, before the war, when Blériot flew across the Channel in 1909 we were all blissful Europeans, we harnessed forces and controlled explosions and converted them into machines worked by combustion, electric currents, even air-waves, decision-making was a grand affair, you aspired, you did the sums, you made the decision, you built, Hans wanted to build liners, calculate the fine lines of a hull, of airships some day, larger and larger airships, see the country-side from the skies, no more frontiers ever, and show it all to a woman who would have all the qualities of the new century.

And then one day, the end of joy, the autumn of 1914, the idea had begun to sink in, lights going out all over Europe and fifteen years later these discussions with a young man who dreamed as he once had, told his father he would not study medicine, was fervent about long-distance communications, about supplying the world with a vast invisible network of radiophony and telephony, millions of lines, of wireless beams, billions of words down these millions of lines, directly exchanged, uncontrolled and unexploited by money.

The young man also wanted the revolution, he'd get over that, perhaps he was right, at least he had the joy of it, he communicated its pulsation if not its contents to his elder. And for the first time since before the war, Hans felt his blood race once more, for the first time.

No, not the very first: at an earlier point there had been one occasion, shortly after the war, before Lilstein came on the scene. The last time to be honest that Hans had felt as fired up as when he sat talking to this young man in the lounge of the Waldhaus was in 1925, at the offices of the *Frankfurter Zeitung* in which he had just published a piece, October 1925, he'd received a postcard from the United States, it showed skyscrapers, with three words, in French:

'How are you?'

Just that, no name, Kappler knew it was from her, no address, she no doubt thought that if she had found a way of reaching him he should be able to do likewise, the postmark said New York, he'd set about writing agreeable, ingratiating letters to all the people he knew in the United States, adding a brief enquiry:

'Would you by any chance have any way of contacting a Madame Hotspur who wrote me a charming letter here at the paper without giving her address? I'd like to thank her, she may be living in New York.'

He had trotted off to consult Berlin's collections of America's leading newspapers to try to find some trace of Lena, he tripped from one paper to the next, maybe she was making a name for herself, research frenzy, go to America, cross the ocean and the States, he got answers to his letters, no information about Lena but replies containing good wishes for him and small requests which his amiable tone had prompted in his correspondents for information about Mr So-and-so whom the writer hadn't seen for some time, about some girl who would soon be completing her finishing year in old Europe and would it be too much to ask Hans to meet her for a little chat?

Replies to send, a waste of his time, he regretted having written those letters, a blind alley in his research, he went back to the newspaper collections, only went to the cinema in the hope that he might get to see America in the newsreels or a film, he could have booked a ticket to the United States straight away but his enquiries awoke feelings he feared he would not rediscover when he got there, he delayed his departure, he was afraid of failing, it was his dream. One card, three words.

That morning for the first time in many years he woke thinking of something other than the business of resuming ownership of his body which he liked less and less. He slept well, Berlin was sinister, Hamburg was sinister but he got up early and the moment he opened his eyes he could see the Manhattan skyline dead ahead, he was on the bridge of the boat that was about to dock.

There is no longer that roar from the horizon, but another sort of hubbub which stirs him, sirens, to these he sometimes added the water-jets from the fireboats, let's go, leaving was such a big thing, it wasn't his enquiries which detained him but the idea that he needed more time to become stronger.

He wanted a reception like the one they gave Dickens, crowds on the Long Island wharf, for him. Not too big a crowd, he didn't write popular serials for the newspapers, but lots of reporters, with microphones and questions which allowed him to show how smart he was.

To reconcile Germany and America, that's why he's come! Next he'll reconcile Germany and the Soviets. It's all so simple.

Germany is hungry, America needs markets, forget the fine sentiments, he had long talks with Rathenau before he was assassinated, reduce the debt claimed by the English and France, France especially, the French owe the Americans money, they reckon Germans owe them that money, it's all quite simple, straightforward, the Americans hold the key, still can't avoid the fine sentiments, but the solution's a commercial one.

All that remains is to devise suitable sentiments to facilitate debt reduction, it's just like literature, when you read me it's because you have faith in me, you allow me credit but at any moment you can shut the book and say 'What tripe!' or else you can take a chance on what comes next. Hans will say that I'm nothing more than a man of letters.

Talk to them about the things they like, the Americans aren't savages, they're as fond of the French language as Hans, 'The Pronunciophone Company', it was in *Time*, a full-page ad, 'Are you embarrassed by mistakes in pronunciation?', and to correct these mistakes in pronunciation a set of gramophone records which give the right way of saying *hors d'oeuvre, entente cordiale, déshabillé, Poincaré, objet d'art, faux pas, beau geste, en route* not forgetting *canapé*, show them that Germany is also part of Culture which is not just a French preserve, he will have won when 'The Pronunciophone Company' of New York will put out records declaiming *Gemütlichkeit, Sehnsucht, mein Liebchen, Schadenfreude*, no, not *Schadenfreude*, at least not straight away, make a start with *mein Liebchen*, so pretty, and philosophy, *Bewußtsein*, keep *Schadenfreude* for the Russkies, they know Marx, whenever I'm asked to translate this word I can't do it, all I can do is say, oh, it's so German, the pleasure we take from the misfortunes of others whether or not we've had anything to do with causing those misfortunes, absolutely essential to import the word to the United States, along with *mein Liebchen*.

Hans's words would cross the entire territory of the United States and finally reach Lena, one of his books in a shop window would catch her eye, she would come to meet him, she would show him New York, night-time, the cascades of lights, stars in the streets, stars in the sky, New York like Hamburg and Berlin only a hundred times more so, the billion stars of the dreaming city and sky, the façades of buildings throbbing with white light, architecture of glass, metal, stone writhing amid the whirling flashing lights, lights which flare aggressively from the shadows, rise dancing to the stars like Hans's dreams then fall back and project on to walls cascades of scintillating light and words written in fire, that's what Hans will say to them the day he arrives, at the foot of the gangplank, the microphones, I have come to you, I have come to the city of where the façades of buildings are made of white light, and glass, metal, stone writhe amid the whirling flashing lights which rise dancing to the stars then fall back and project on to walls cascades of scintillating light and words written in fire, New York's belligerent sleeplessness, machines competing with the sun, machines which murder the old moonlit night, the constant roar and high-speed kicks and pricks, quiet is for the war-wounded, music, rhythms from hell, everything that punches holes in the night, sometimes a light shows, atop a column of darkness, more than sixty floors up, like an eye, like a Cyclops.

By day they will walk between the metal towers, in the cold air, whenever he lets Lena go first he watches her buttocks, still firm and trim, sway in air as clear as ice which blows in off the sea, the arteries of poverty and luxury, the freshness of the pretty women scrubbed clean with soap and water, the huge litter bins full of the newspapers people have discarded, here you eat fast, you read fast, come on, just do it!

They hurry on past buildings made of light but built of steel, copper, stone and glass, standing stones in the city, and the bridges, their gateways built of Florentine blocks, passers-by transformed into gymnasts in the reflections, the shining chain mail that is the river, halt halfway across a bridge, feel the throb of power, and the tunnels under the water, and above them the huge transatlantic liners of iron and steel pass like toys.

The mountain range of the skyscrapers, the city on tip-toe, metal and glass, or else themes of Renaissance palaces multiplied by thirty, a snow-storm that is not to be credited, wind that takes the breath away, air like liquid ice, cars buried under the snow, and the magic of lifts, a single supple silky bound upwards, head for the sky, hardly time to draw breath twice and you're at the sixty-second floor, the approach of the boat as it arrives from Europe when the new skyscrapers of Manhattan rise suddenly out of the mists of the pulsating morning, all the centuries converge here, sometimes she didn't have the patience to wait.

She took him directly to a vast, greedy railway station, the sun pours down from high up on the walls through round windows at least ten metres in diameter and erects in the dust of the concourse giant tubes of light, a train of steel bound for Vermont, a sleeper, she wore pyjamas made from some ultra-soft material, behaved as if they'd been married for ten years, she laughed, it was a sweet time, sometimes he skipped the interlude on the train, saw himself back in a chalet in Vermont, where there are mountains and lots of snow, it was a surprise when he arrived.

She was by herself, was wearing the big Finnish pullover he'd just seen in a shop window in Rosmar, it reached halfway down her thighs, she is as beautiful standing up as lying down, and if it wasn't for the snow this could be a ranch, yes, in Texas, there are ranches in Vermont too, he got out a map of the United States and saw that Vermont was more or less on the East Coast, too European, not enough wide-open spaces, not enough appeal, go west, that's right, make for the Rockies, Colorado, he looked for a name that cast a spell,

Aurora, east of Denver, there's another Aurora west of Chicago, check the index of the atlas, at least thirteen Auroras for all the American States, Walsenburg, also in Colorado, it would be funny if she lived there, if she had a ranch just next to Walsenburg, or maybe she'd be staying in a hotel, not a big one of course, the clients would be regulars, in the evenings guests stay in and read in the lounge or play cards, or just talk, Lena stands, 'Goodnight everyone' in a warm voice, she takes the book from Hans's grasp and gently makes him get up, in front of everyone.

Alternatively he'd arrive at the ranch in autumn, just as Lena was being charged by a bull, he'd save her, don't go over the top, make it a horse in a bad temper, no not that either, make it a walking encounter, he would arrive incognito, he'd meet up with her as she was getting back from a walk, arms full of delicate branches and yellow flowers, in the light of the day's end, an ordinary meeting, you're just an ordinary man, apparently ordinary, the train, he would revert to the sleeping-car, they are both lying in the upper berth, side by side, they look out of the window, the back of Lena's neck is almost touching his lips, half a continent speeds by while they caress, Allentown, Harrisburg, Wheeling, Columbus, Champaign, Burlington, Des Moines, Omaha, her buttocks are bare, he is lying against her.

Lincoln, Sterling, then after Denver there's Alamosa, he's not sure if these are stops on a real railway line, so they stay in New York, they walk through the city, they've only just met up again, they walk side by side, the crowds, he has begun to like people once more, Lena, he counts the days they could have had together if he'd been able to keep hold of her, how many leaves during the war, she'd have come to Germany, at least before 1917, maybe they wouldn't have seen each other again during the war, but she'd have joined him in 1918, it's more than half a dozen years now since the Peace was signed, hundred and hundreds of nights, what a waste, they walk through New York, the ebb and flow of the crowds, now and then their shoulders touch, he takes Lena's arm to cross the street, no, he's been told that no true New York woman tolerates that any more, you don't grab a female New Yorker using the excuse that you're helping her to cross the street, anyway Lena knows the rules far better than you do.

They talk as they walk, she says talk to me, which makes him suddenly mute, two or three times during their walk their hands have touched, when she said talk to me it depressed him because in the old days those were the words which signalled that he was about to be scolded, when she felt his mind was somewhere else though he was with her, and here in the street in the middle of New York City, she says talk to me, so you must laugh, talk, whatever, he begins to resent her mentally for asking this so as to ensure that all of a sudden he can't say a thing, he refuses to look for the exact word for whatever it is when you ask someone to do something and by the very act of asking you prevent the person you've asked from doing what you've asked, talk to me, he closes up like an oyster, the reunion is already ruined.

The Lena who has come back is a Lena he had forgotten, the one who says talk to me, hawk-eyed, the one who says 'you don't love me, you don't know how', blink an eye and she's gone, he feels close to tears, they're standing in front of a shop window full of soft toys, huge cuddly clockwork toys, bears mainly, taller than grown men, and Hans starts laughing like a kid as he looks at these mechanical bears, childhood and innocence mixed up with a dirty story about a bear and a hunter, the hunter brings down a huge bear, two metres tall, dances round the corpse, kicks it in the ribs, returns rejoicing to his village, he feels a tap on the shoulder, he turns round, the bear's there in front of him, two metres tall, right paw raised, claws, the palm as big as the hunter's head, a smile on the face of the bear, can't tell the rest, around them kiddies are laughing, Hans laughs until the tears come, he doesn't want to leave the shop window, Lena laughs to see him like that, come on, she takes his hand to lead him away, won't let go of it, you're incorrigible, you deserve a good hiding, what's got into you?

He doesn't dare tell her the story about the bear, the hunter kills a bear two metres tall, he goes back to his village to fetch people to carry the animal back, on the way a tap on the shoulder, it's the bear, very much alive, on its back legs, two metres, right front paw raised, the bear's palm as big as the hunter's whole head, the bear lowers his left paw.

Hans and Lena walk hand in hand, as they did outside the Waldhaus, in the old days, before the war, their whole future is ahead of them, they're in the chalet in Vermont, no, in Colorado, she's cold, he says I'll warm you up, he is alone on the bridge of the ship, morning, Manhattan, the bliss of arriving, he knows the names of skyscrapers by heart, like he knows the peaks in a mountain range, he hears the boat's siren, he adds mist, tattered shreds of blue through the mist, it grows clearer and clearer, Hans has stopped wasting his life, that was all a long, long time ago, in 1925, one of his favourite dreams, four years before the Waltenberg Seminar.

Once again he is in the lounge of the Waldhaus for the 1929 European Seminar, he is talking to this obstreperous adolescent who wants to reach out and take the whole world in his arms, he feels invaded once more by the same fierce joy as a journey to New York produces in him, he could leave at the end of the Seminar, with this young man, not New York, this time, but Venice.

Sitting behind Kappler and Lilstein at the Waldhaus in his easy chair in the main lounge, the man holding forth on the Neuville index, he of the strictly measurable quantity of human energy, had concluded his little talk, he was speaking now of his château in Italy, grounds infested with vipers, only one way of dealing with them, offer a reward for every viper brought in dead, to begin with it worked very well but after a while we realised that it had given rise to a thriving trade in dead vipers which extended for over a hundred kilometres, and moreover the locals deliberately left enough reptiles roaming through the grounds to ensure that we went on being a weeny bit scared.

Kappler smiled, spoke of the usefulness of vipers in the world of politics, Kappler, the absolute democrat, told Lilstein to read Lenin and Stalin because he thought it would save him, Lilstein was a cultured young man who was hurtling towards communism while letting his mind stray from time to time to the maid's armpits and regretting the business with the air rifle, Kappler wanted him to be armed:

'And don't be one of those fools who shout out randy old snake every time some socialist gets up to speak.'

And very soon Lilstein was quite capable of making a connection between the instructions of Stalin and expressions used by Lenin, he even guessed several months in advance which of Lenin's phrases Stalin would actually use, he repeated snippets once or twice, without seeming to be quoting anyone, and one day that same quote surfaced in one of Stalin's pronouncements, it made certain comrades shake in their shoes, it's the sort of thing that enables a man to rise in an organisation, that and arriving at the right time, respecting deadlines, knowing how to handle the files, how to report back, in a few sentences of not more than ten words each, and doing nothing before receiving precise instructions, written or verbal but always in front of witnesses.

He had one other precious quality: he never seemed sure of himself; he appeared both remote and anxious, this is what saved Lilstein later on his stool in the Lubyanka, in the early 1950s, the impression he gave his captors of feeling slightly guilty, no indignant protests, nor stubborn resistance nor cooperation in making disclosures nor garrulity either, he looked at the lamp when they told him to look at the lamp and when they turned the lamp away he looked at the telephone, as if he were expecting a call which would bring this mistake to an end.

Occasionally he would look up at the man interrogating him, simply to avoid a possible 'Look at me when I'm talking to you', but not for very long either, so as to escape a 'stop looking at me with those cretinous eyes', and from time to time make a slip, say one word instead of another, or a 'I don't recall' to allow the interrogator to unload his aggression, never allow him to get to the hate stage, hands, look at their hands, don't provoke the moment when they form into fists or when they're placed flat on the desk, don't concern yourself with other people, the underlings, a slap in the face, or even the ear, that stuff doesn't matter, the one to watch is the man sitting facing you, or maybe on occasion it's someone who steps noiselessly into the room, you haven't turned round but you sensed he was there by the way the one who is sitting straightened, never let them fill up with anger or calmness, you've only one hope, the stool is vile but that's because it doesn't show any traces, they don't want to do you too much damage, if your morale remains good that gives you a way forward, they haven't yet handed you over to the butchers, there's no one yet who is anything like the ones he'd encountered before, *kein Warum*, here you can, you could ask, you still have a full set of finger-nails, make them want to keep you here.

Lilstein was a useful kind of a guilty party for the average accusers who are only too well aware that there isn't much in the file, he wasn't innocent, in those days they ended up liquidating the innocent, no one was going to admit to a mistake, with the guilty things were more violent, they howled like dogs as they died and then it was all over, whereas with someone like Lilstein with his little lies, his mild protests, his way of correcting previous statements, it all served to allow the mills of daily routine to keep turning, between two other much more significant cases, and he really did know Lenin's writings.

Lilstein would stare at the phone as if he were expecting a message, sometimes his eyes were completely focused on the effort of watching the phone, a toad made of black bakelite, circular dial pad, very ugly, one day the man in charge said to him:

'Obviously this is only a side issue, but do you really like my phone?'

The answer would have been very complicated. In normal life Lilstein feels increasing loathing for the telephone, especially at work, you think there's just the two of you talking, and an army of men in head-phones are recording your every word, it's a gruesome instrument, suitable only for people who won't find the time to deal with each other face to face, but when he was young he'd been mad about phones and radio, and telephone sets, the genuine article, the kind that had a personality, Berlin, 1925, an exhibition devoted to the history of the telephone – and one of the ways he had of holding firm at tricky times in his life, outside that is of reciting his favourite poems silently to himself, was to review in his mind his collection of old phones, the ones he had started buying when he was twelve, plus all those he had acquired later, the whole lot having disappeared during raids by the Gestapo and the KGB, his collection having disappeared twice, the memory of it having grown increasingly faint, he never tried to build it up again.

Henceforth he makes do with catalogues, all the catalogues he acquires whenever the opportunity arises, the ones his colleagues bring back for him from missions, as souvenirs, certain missions coincide sometimes splendidly with an exhibition or sale, no, that's just a piece of friendly libel, he no longer collects telephones, they take up too much room, the loss is too great when the cops come on heavy-handed and take them off you – catalogues you can find in a library – he also has sets of old instructions, and plans discovered in factory archives for installing and repairing equipment.

Besides, after all, it was with catalogues, designs, photos that he'd started, with pictures of women on the phone, one of them, from a very old magazine dating from around the turn of the century, a young woman standing, waist pinched tight, a low-cut dress, a V accentuated by the forward thrust of her bosom, she is holding the ear-piece of a phone to each ear, her arms are raised as required by the action, while below the belt which picks out her waist, her pose, which shows her turned slightly to one side, enables the viewer to devine the delicious swell of both her abdomen and rump, Lilstein recalls the words underneath which said that the girl was 'romantic', and there was also another woman, less beautiful, it was a photo of her, she had a definite edge over the bright young people of the time since she posed in a nightdress, with no corset, the result being a generous fullness which concealed her figure but let you sense nakedness underneath, the nightdress had a lower neckline than the other girl's dress, it had sleeves which allowed perfectly bare forearms to project, when you were thirteen the thing was to imagine the first girl with the tight corset wearing the other one's costume, and with the appropriate curves.

There was a third engraving, a greetings card, a source of further fertile elaborations of the image, an English drawing room, a young lady of fashion, her back three-quarters turned to the viewer, she was holding out with both hands and considerable grace a telephone receiver about fifteen centimetres long, her dress left the upper part of her back naked, the top of her shoulders, nape of her neck, ears, the pendant at her throat, arms bare from the shoulder-joint to the elbow where her gloves stopped, the eye returned to her back whose dynamically arched line launched sweet reveries, the arch ending at its most prominent point in a bow from which cascaded the folds of an ample satin skirt, Lilstein did not dare lock his bedroom door.

'Your son,' Herr Lilstein remarked to his wife, 'is for some incomprehensible reason obsessed by Belle Époque telephones.'

It was true, a magnificent model with magneto and cranking handle, in the style of a sewing-machine, with a plinth made of cast-iron, black cast-iron, lacquered, the combined receiver-and-speaker slung horizontally on a cradle which acted as a switch when the receiver was lifted, the cradle was nickel-plated and embellished with symmetrical bows and medallions, there were gold filaments running horizontally along each side of the plinth, or rather it was a framing strip, yes, an Ericsson 1907, and another model, a Sauerwein 1913, his favourite, a base of fine mahogany, darkened and French-polished, on which stood a chrome-plated lyre, I'm sure the upper part was decorated with laurel leaves, no, it was acanthus, and the fixed microphone was located in the top of the lyre.

Lilstein can no longer say how the receiver was held, he loved phones and the radio, the crystal set he and friends from school had made together, he was still dreaming about it in 1929, radio, telephones, you turn a knob or a handle and someone far away becomes your brother in a few words, another voice telling Lilstein not to mix things up, the telephone is not society, the society which advances by class conflict, but even so, if everyone is enabled to talk freely to everyone else, then there's hope.

'You know,' said the KGB officer who had searched his house in

Potsdam in 1951, 'all these handsets and catalogues and telephone literature, it's what they call a hobby, it's a very English thing, you have very English tastes, they could cost you dear.'

But no one ever raised the matter again. Lilstein tried to stop thinking about his phones and start concentrating on his poems.

The Gestapo, the camps, fealty, the KGB, the water torture, the stool, the telephone, his poems, May, the merry month of May in a boat on the Rhine, the excursion turned out badly, the telephones with their moulded materials, box, mahogany, each kind of wood carefully polished, walnut, pine, and also ivorine, he'd had to look up what ivorine was, plus the chrome, brass and nickel used for the cross pieces and uprights, shapes like stretching necks, patterns picked out on a small teak stand perched on four claw-and-ball feet, or on the contrary a thing of flight and fancy like the Siemens which looked like an ampersand or a treble clef, a simple metal chrome-plated stem braced itself at an initial loop before thrusting upwards, like a curved serpent, an arched and watchful serpent, and then steadied itself and ended in a scroll inside its own swirl, but allowing a budded branch to escape on which the receiver came to rest, this was his favourite, a treble clef, a snake, the colonel, the big office in Berlin, the minister who scratched himself, *Pravda*, the slide, frozen up or not: had Kappler foreseen all this when he'd advised him to read Lenin?

What is Lilstein to Kappler? Lilstein, an adolescent encountered once again after an interval of almost thirty years with all the allowances he'd made for the adolescent, thirty years, when exactly did bakelite replace ivorine? Someone who had survived everything, still 'wearing a halo of progressive light'? Or one of those types that officials in Bonn described to Kappler when they tried to dissuade him from returning to Rosmar, fair enough, OK, Herr Kappler, men of Lilstein's sort have been through a lot, Auschwitz or Stalin's camps or both, they've been put through the mangle but they're no angels, they're killers too, they have people killed to defend the purity of their Democratic Republic, they like having flowers on their desks but they kill, wound, break people for life, don't take our word for it, Herr

Kappler, we're policemen, you can despise us, you can tell us the only reason we're here is to keep an eye on the money in the bank vaults but over there it's worse, they keep an eye on everything, not money, there isn't any, but everything else, at least reread Koestler, or go and listen to what two or three exiles are saying, we know you're not afraid of anything but don't give your backing to those bastards, no, we're not alike, we don't go that far, we don't need to, we don't have an empire to hang on to, like those idiots the French, our hands are clean, have been for the last ten years, at least.

Max has also put Hans on his guard, he didn't want to see him go back to the GDR, those are gang bosses they have over there, they give an order, Hans, and people disappear, in the fog, those people keep an eye on everything, even in the fog, you might think I'm going over the top with this, with my big words, tyranny, terror, a journalist's words, you might not give a toss, but you can at least listen to a story, a very short story, you've always liked symptoms, six months ago I was in Dresden, with some English journalists, two English communist journalists, yes there are such things, and an official minder, a car, one of the Englishmen drove it, it was his own car, a privilege, drove very carefully, accompanied by the minder with hobnail boots, in the fog the Englishman strays on to tramlines, Hans, it wasn't anything, not even doing twenty, catches a low cement road-divider, no need even to straighten a bumper.

But the minder insists that the incident be reported to the police immediately, they start to laugh, eleven at night, suburbs of Dresden, fog, a minor bump, not even necessary to fix the bodywork, plus the fact that it's the Englishman's car, I say to the minder if you must you can put it in your report tomorrow, but now it's bedtime.

But the guy won't let it drop, 'Telefon, Telefon', he spots a light, a kind of *Weinstube*, very glaucous, when we go inside we realise our kraut is white as a sheet, he asks for the number of the police station, he's shaking, then the Englishman – a big noise in the British Party – takes the phone, he has seen the greasy smears on the mouthpiece, he takes it all the same, dials the number, talks to the cops, just a scratch, just the paintwork, not worth bothering with, you know what the reply was? At the other end, someone said, 'Yes, we already know.'

Max took Hans by the shoulders, Hans, it's the land where everything is already known, if you go either you'll blow your brains out inside two weeks or you'll become like them, you really think 'knowing everything already' is worth it?

When Lilstein and Kappler meet shortly in the Konditorei, Kappler will definitely see Lilstein coming, he knows everything, Lilstein won't be able to keep anything from him, they'll resume their conversation at the point where they'd left it in this selfsame place twenty-seven years ago, Kappler is the only man with whom Lilstein can speak in a different way, because Kappler remembers. From the very first minute they are together again Kappler will be confronted by two Lilsteins, not the adolescent and the adult but two adults, the adult that Lilstein has constructed and the adult Kappler will identify, the one who took over from the adolescent, the one the other Lilstein has suppressed, no, camouflaged, the one who goes on thinking filthy swine when faced by his Interior Minister, or moron when confronted by an article by Suslov. Actually, it's the best part of Lilstein, the part which still knows what a Minister is and what a Suslov is worth.

Or else this best part which is camouflaged not suppressed is dialectical, as they say, it allows the other part to exist and act, the part that lets Lilstein say 'close the file' as he holds out a list of three names to a subordinate, he can behave like a bastard because he knows that at any time, without much mental effort, he can reconnect with Lilstein the good, the clear-headed, the Lilstein who wants the good and the true, the one who rereads *What Is Englightenment?* and has the moral law inside him.

Perhaps those two Lilsteins are as nothing beside a third, older than both of them, who goes back a long way, further even than the adolescent, the one Kappler had sensed, he of the rebellious gesture, who from the start had always thought get lost the lot of you, as when he was small, he'd tried to repair his toy car, he'd taken the mechanism to pieces, then it didn't work at all, and he'd thrown the whole mess to the far end of the room shouting:

'Bugger and piss and shit!'

And he'd got a good hiding, because his father and mother and all their guests had heard him, despite the distance separating the drawing room from his nursery room.

'Bugger and piss and shit!'

It seems a pretty inventive verbal construct to him whenever he thinks about it, it was also a pretty good hiding, a father and a mother both eminent doctors with left-wing leanings, extreme left-wing, a damn good hiding, because such behaviour, such swearing, it's unacceptable, it's fascist, he'd taken a larruping from a belt, no not a belt but the dog's braided leash, to beat the fascism out of him, and he'd lost for good two small components of the clockwork car he'd taken apart, a sophisticated piece of clockwork it was, with two settings, the first made the car turn in a wide circle, the second made it do figures-of-eight, you wound the spring up with a hollow key which looked like a uniformed chauffeur, a real gem, fantastic outings, hotels like hotels are in dreams, in one of his dreams it was a limousine chrome-plated all over and he parked it outside the Adlon Hotel, but the car had had it.

Lilstein has no idea what became of that car, he drew a small lesson from the episode, became very meticulous when mending things, he soon learned how to put any clockwork car back together again, he can open the backs of watches and take apart lighters, musical-boxes, pens, locks, taps, Bunsen burners, telephones too, though that's not very interesting, but he can put them together again and often manages to mend them, there's a screw missing from the gramophone belonging to the camp guards, the one that immobilises the drive unit which prevents it moving when the spring is being wound up, he uses a nail instead held by a match splinter inserted into the hole, he remembers seeing a nail that very morning, just the right size, a nail not serving any purpose, in another barrack block, he asked permission, a real gift for make do and mend, he can work out the way things are designed, he doesn't need to use force to open the back of things, not watchmaker's hands exactly, but very clever even down to the nail of his right thumb which he uses as a small screwdriver, a handyman, in Buchenwald they spared Lilstein the most gruelling jobs, and there was always an extra piece of bread for him.

Which Lilstein is it who wants to say to Kappler whatever you do don't go back, and will tell him, despite the orders of the Minister and the directives of the General Secretary of the German United Socialist Party, comrade Walter Ulbricht:

'Don't go back, Herr Kappler.'

What's got into you, wanting to say something like that to a bourgeois writer who presents one of the finest opportunities our propaganda machine can hope to come by? Don't be a fool, just settle for doing what you're supposed to. If a tenth, a hundredth of what you want to say to Kappler should ever reach any one else's ears, you'll find yourself facing a real charge of high treason, and you won't be sitting on any stool this time, it'll be over very quickly. Or maybe that's exactly what makes you want to do it? The fact that where you live you can't say 'don't go back' to an old friend without *ipso facto* putting your life in deadly danger?

Ipso facto was the expression Kappler used to employ in those far-off days when he wanted to show Lilstein that the real never rises to seek the best under its own impetus and that it frequently finds itself biting its own tail.

Which Lilstein should he show Kappler? Lilstein doesn't know, it's only by talking to Kappler that Lilstein will be able to discover what he himself really thinks, you can tell him all sorts of things but you will have to make up your mind what exactly you're going to tell Kappler.

In any case, Kappler will go his own sweet way, so how do I manage to get him to trust me? no good talking reasons, Herr Kappler, there are three reasons why you should abandon this plan, Kappler won't even try to argue, he'll just say I don't give a damn, young Lilstein.

Why try to get him to change his mind? it's risky, virtually impossible, you'd be better off concentrating on the meeting with the other party, the appointment after lunch at the Waldhaus with the young Frenchman: the future.

Soon it will be eleven o'clock, Lilstein is outside the Konditorei, you're going to have to give Kappler something, a secret, that's it, people trust you if you confide in them, give Kappler something in confidence, but what? that you don't care for your Minister? Or get round to asking him the question he's expecting to be asked: have you seen her again?

*

It is three in the afternoon in the main lounge of the Waldhaus, you've come from Paris, you're not yet thirty but you're tired, you're sitting opposite a man named Michael Lilstein, his movements are unhurried and he says to you straight off:

'I'm particularly anxious that you don't become a spy, young gentleman of France. Spy is the word for the ones who get caught.'

A glance out of the window, the mountains of the Grisons, the high Swiss Alps, the peaks of the Rikshorn, Lilstein's face is smooth-skinned, hair blond, complexion fine, eyes foxy, eyebrows unruly at the ends, has the look of a student who's spent years dawdling here in the great lounge of the Waldhaus, which is deserted and dark once you move away from the windows, a few cabinets made of some heavy wood, which have already retreated into the shadows for the night, and a vast rack stacked with crockery standing just behind Lilstein, everywhere the smell of childhood, floor polish and beeswax, you winced when he said 'young gentleman of France'. Lilstein adds:

'Spies are voyeurs, thieves, miscreants, but you're different, I invite you to be my equal.'

Lilstein says 'I' very freely, not at all the sort of thing you'd expect from an East German, and he tells you a great deal about himself:

'My dear fellow, I'm forty-two but I'm already very old, I was over thirty when the Soviets liberated me from Auschwitz, it's not the sort of thing you ever forget, they also saved my mother and installed her in Moscow in a nice two-roomed flat, and me they sent to one of their Eastern steppes, to patch me up, goat's milk, mutton grilled over a wood fire with cumin, long walks, the plain stretching away as far as the eye could see, made the head spin, I marched through oceans of marguerites, growing close to the ground to keep death away, here it's more aggressive. So it wasn't you, young Frenchman, and comrade, who asked for this meeting?

'It wasn't me either, let's say it was good old Roland Hatzfeld who fixed it up, you don't know? The name means nothing to you? Forgotten it already? Oh, that's very good but, just between ourselves, quite unnecessary, you can trust me. Why? Because you want to and because I've a splendid story to tell you while we sit here looking out on this magnificent view which is so friendly to untruth.'

Lilstein gestures to the Rikshorn:

'Tremendous, isn't it? Crystalline rock fractured by layers of ice over millions of years so that today a man can whizz blithely down it in five or six seconds, it's not all over yet you know, it should yield a new peneplain in due course, the time-spans of physical geography are a comfort, so soothing, after all, man did not lose his tail overnight, but forgive me, that's the language of the guard-room and the Rikshorn ought to bring out the poetry in us, so, to say sorry, I shall now tell you my splendid story.'

A waitress with strong hands has set down two *Tee mit Rum*, Lilstein drinks his in tiny sips, lifts his head, looks towards the far end of the room, lowers his voice like a conspirator:

'Do you smell that scent of warm apple, slightly acid, rather pert, that comes from afar? The wife of the hotel owner has taken the tart out of the oven, a Linzer, Linzer Torte is her speciality, to me it's a drug, I can hold out for six, eight months without coming for a fix, and then I invent a mission for myself, a meeting, anything, just so that I can come here. Are there other places in Europe? Of course there are, but there's nothing to compare with what the owner's wife makes here. Before the war, I wasn't very interested in food, nowadays I love going to tea-rooms, pastries, I never let tea-times go by, but I only eat Linzer here. Smell it? Beneath the fragrance of the apple, an accompaniment of raspberry, sharp, sweet? Not too much raspberry, the raspberry should know its place, as an accompaniment, *Gut*, whether it was Hatzfeld or no, we can talk, and if you've come this far you're not going to turn down the chance of a good argument, even so at your age you should be ready to move things on, I'm not asking for your soul, young gentleman of France, we'll just work together to move things on.'

Lilstein has said 'work', he has placed the elbow of his right arm on the table, his hand is level with his eyes, fingers up, he gently rubs the end of his thumb against the tips of the other fingers, like a baker assaying the quality of flour, as if what he is about to propose is the product of some subtle craft:

'Work together, each on his own side, like equals, I won't ask for your soul, actually thanks to me you'll have two, two souls, the one you shaped for yourself, the one that's fine and great and revolutionary, the one that wants the good of all mankind because human nature is basically good and because all that's required is a better way of organising needs, means and talents, some day all that could be sweeter than springtime, you'd not forgive yourself for giving up your great soul, so idealistic, at last, the classless society.'

A pause. Lilstein really seems to believe in the classless society, and at the same time you sense that he doesn't believe in it wholeheartedly, though you'd be hard put to say what it is that makes you feel he doesn't believe in it and, on reflection, if you consider closely the impression he gives of believing in it, you'd find it just as impossible to put what he does mean into words, is he doing it on purpose? he looks straight at you and goes on:

'All the things you dreamed of in that great revolutionary soul of yours, my dear fellow, and then crash! the wretched let-down of

Budapest. Whereupon you feel like dumping your great soul, if you do, you'll have to adjust to a life of emotional inertia, you'll give up selling *Humanité* on Sundays in the market, reject the friendly greeting of the comrades, the roast chestnuts, I'll spare you the rest, it's so kitsch, you have problems justifying tanks that roll over civilians, and lurking behind soul number one is the other one, the soul that's realistic, lucid, disenchanted, bourgeois, cynical, the one that enables you to get an important job, to fulminate against the Russians and strikes, to remind yourself that solid obstacles must be placed in the way of human desires because human nature and so on and so forth.'

There's no one else in the room, Lilstein speaks slowly, in measured terms, it's dangerous, the place might be bugged, the waitress at the far end of the lounge who comes and goes at intervals might overhear snatches of their conversation, a professional like Lilstein must know, but it doesn't stop him:

'When soul number two, the soul of a young, concerned Frenchman, is thwarted, it might go as far as to declare that life is a struggle, just as the old one used to be actually, but now it's a different struggle, the triumph of the strong, the struggle for survival – you don't much like this second soul, it was bequeathed to you, it's the family soul, the soul of the nice part of town where you live, at first you hated it, but it's not always wrong, it is very effective, you might say it has the effectiveness of capitalism, it's in Marx:

'So you see, two souls, one full of dreams, the other believing it sees things as they are, but you don't really care for either one or the other, and as you leave the Party of your youth you find that you fall between two souls, ideas with no way of implementing them, ideas with no point, a pointless life before you've even lived, but I can show you how to keep both souls, how to make the most of both of them and act: a soul that dreams and a soul that does not dream.'

Lilstein has raised his right hand, it is closed except for the index and middle fingers which make a V to accentuate 'two', it also recalls Churchill's V:

'Two souls. Dreams? We'll dream them together, a just, classless society but you won't need to get your hands dirty defending that dream, I'll spare you the embarrassment of having to defend *Pravda* editorials, there's no point now, in future you'll bury your fine soul deep inside yourself and meantime, in public, you'll be the other one, the bourgeois, realistic soul, the one you dislike, the soul that would – dreadful fate – see eye to eye with Antoine Pinay, Joseph Laniel or Guy Mollet, a soul so lucid it does not believe in forgiving, leave it to do the dirty work, though it's not as dirty as all that, you'll denounce tyranny, show trials, anything from Bukharin to Stalin's doctors by way of all your Slanskys and Rajks.'

Two swallows of tea, a glance at the view over the Grisons, to allow the shadows of Slansky and Rajk to depart. Lilstein resumes:

'And I'm not entirely sure there won't be more trials, you know the old joke, a Marxist is a man who doesn't believe in life after death but does believe in rehabilitation after death, you will denounce the whole set-up, it will stand you in good stead, you'll condemn the economic chaos, the bogus statistics, the whole Potemkin village of Sovietism, the camps no one talks about, like the one I was released from in 1953, there are still party officials who want to keep them on, reopen them for Nagy or even Gomulka, Gomulka has already spent four years in a camp, he's used to it, like me. Not all the Soviet comrades are ruthless Kapos, but there are some who are best left well alone.

'You must denounce the whole shooting match, and make your denunciation pack a punch even if it makes people turn on you, because turn on you they will, they'll accuse you of turning on the Party, no one leaves the Party without some payback but your Good Soul will say your conscience is clear whereas if it was your good soul people had turned against, your lucid soul would never rush to your defence, all of which in short brings me to my proposition:

'You won't have to disown your ideals in degrading battles, nor defend everything Suslov or Thorez says, even if they say it in defence of the working class and the human race, on the contrary you will at last be able to say what you really think of the presence of the Russians in Budapest, in public, rather than publicly justify their presence and privately think it's madness, see how coy I am myself, the presence of the Russians, a splendid euphemism, you will embody lucidity, you'll tell the world Drop the masks! and the world will beg you to remove its masks. And it will make no attempt to touch yours.

'We shall go on dreaming, young Frenchman, but I won't promise you the moon and stars because I don't believe in them any more, I leave all that to the angels, the sparrows, the Party activists and the men with twisted minds.

'That said, there's still work to be done among men, beyond men, riding your luck, dreaming of a socialism cleansed of the scum, I'll go further: I don't know who will win. I'm speaking of a distant future, I don't know which of the two sides will win, our dreams or their capitalism, but you've nothing to lose: if it's your bourgeois soul that triumphs you can simply forget the other one, and if it's your revolutionary soul that emerges victorious you'll never have left the fold, I'll be there to vouch for it, two souls, and I'll always be frank with you, no not frank, frank is for hypocrites, I shall be unambiguous, we shall be equals, after all I too might have two souls.'

Lilstein has noticed that you have raised your eyebrows, he might also devise a mime to go with his two souls, eyes open wide, hands expressive, but he doesn't, his face is a blank and his words are cool:

'I propose we start with a straightforward exchange of information, not straight away, in a year or two, in the mid-term, anything that will help me rein in my more excitable comrades, the warmongers, the ones who believe you need tanks to help people think and camps to teach them to be punctual, do I surprise you? Already? None of this sounds anything like what you get from official spokesmen? But if I were just an official mouthpiece, I'd have disappeared long ago, in the camp they sent me to, not Auschwitz, a different one, six years after Auschwitz, one of the camps no one talks about.

'One day I'll tell you about it, I've a great fund of stories, meantime when you're in a position to, you can help me fight the warmongers, your Great Soul will tell me everything soul number two has garnered, I will pass on to you the secrets of the world I belong to, you will bring me yours, I shall today give you something that will make you very precious to your imperialist masters, you will become – you may smile – a keen supporter of the Cold War.

'A very sophisticated but rock-solid supporter, you will write splendid articles attacking communism, and very well-informed they'll be, it will be great fun, anyone who leaves the Party eventually turns into a supporter of the Cold War, but I suggest you become one straight away, you'll find it amusing and will leave the ranks of the Party without feeling that you're betraying anything, you have two souls, the disenchanted soul will remain the handmaid of your dreaming soul and will help it not to betray those dreams.

'A pact? No, we won't have a pact, the idea doesn't fill me with confidence, obviously one day you might be tempted to reverse the roles and betray me, betray what we'll have become, but I don't want pledges, I've got faith in you, young comrade, absolute faith, why? because I know all about you, if once upon a time you betrayed your family by joining the Party it was because you saw that your family was the betrayer, you know, we two are alike, if later on you betray the working class, such a pompous expression but there it is, if, I was saying, you betray the working class after betraying the bourgeoisie, you'll have nowhere else to go, and you're not old enough to return to the crucifix of your boyhood, your need not to be a traitor is too strong, just like mine.

'What did I betray? The world's youth, young gentleman of France. We've both lost our stake, we need each other, let's stay together, let's try to be civilised, and maybe thanks to us all these people will some day step back from the edge, it's what is called peaceful co-existence, we'll help to make the phrase fashionable.'

The Waldhaus is at an altitude of 1,700 metres, it's where forest gives way to rock, it's also where the Waldgang starts, a ski slope, not the highest but the most attractive, with its passage through woods, the stretch along the lake, the long diagonal over the west face, a balcony from which on a fine day you can see for a hundred kilometres.

Already there are a few early skiers here before the crowd of holidaymakers arrive, the descent starts with a 'wall' sixty metres long that runs parallel to the bobsleigh track but slopes more steeply, on the launching platform stand medics' sledges ready for service, each one numbered separately, black on a yellow background. From time to time, the wind blows the powdery snow into the air where it glows red in the last rays of the sun.

'Have I got you wrong, my dear fellow? I don't care much for "my dear fellow", I much prefer young man, my young friend, my young French friend, we'd be friends, I once was a young friend to a man I greatly admire, he still calls me young Lilstein, no, I feel that if I call you my young friend you won't care for it, you say you have no information to give me, that you are not important? I know that but I'm talking about the future, we have plenty of time, I'll start, I'll give you some hard information.

'And in a year or two Paris will be at your feet, doesn't the prospect tempt you? It's because you're young, let me be ambitious for you, at this juncture you don't like yourself very much, it's not healthy, a high percentage of the troubles I've had were caused by people who didn't like themselves, who liked other people because they did not like themselves, who were forever ready to sacrifice themselves, and to sacrifice others to save them, through self-loathing, through fear of themselves, but we shall know only constructive fear, welcome to the realm of constructive fears and feverish times, young gentleman of France.

'We shall combat the religion of war. Take us separately and we are sorry specimens, you, the man who is sick of action, and I, the apparatchik with no dreams, we're pathetic, but together we could make one very interesting person, a conciliator, a reconciler, a regulator, and there will even be moments when we can laugh, yes, laugh.

'In our line of business people laugh a lot, six months ago one of my colleagues in Africa, in a brand-new country, one Sunday morning, the whole day is devoted to voluntary farm service, he was a Special Envoy for Cultural Relations. The Africans put him in a field, with an

American, also a very important person, a Special Envoy for Economic Affairs, crewcut, with a cap of some sort on the back of his head, their job is to get rid of all the weeds in their field, so he and the American set to work, the two *specialists*, you know the song, it was a hit for a popular singer, left-wing, one of yours, "You only gotter bend a bit but that's the 'ardest part of it".

'By the end of the day, they're exhausted but happy, and friends almost, reconciled by manual work, the Minister for Internal and External Security of the host country comes and stands between the American and my friend for the photo, smiles all round, "A fine example of collaboration," he tells journalists, "and that, for our country together with our brothers in the East and the West, is our third way!" And then, in a whisper but still sporting his smile, he says to both of them out of the corner of his mouth: "You pulled up all the manioc."

'The story I promised you? No, that's not it, be patient, I really want to tell it to you.'

A woman walks quietly into the lounge, tall, red hair, ample movements, a midnight-blue linen dress, step springy and rhythmic, like a dancer's, very calm expression, she rootles for something in one of the cabinets then leaves.

'It's a story I've never told anyone, so I need a warm-up. So you're from Paris, sent by Roland Hatzfeld? That's right, he told me himself, is he still living in that little place near the Porte des Lilas? Not interested? You don't know? Good old Roland, still a man of sound habits, did you know that Malraux almost got him to join the Party? You didn't? You don't believe me? You do? See, you are interested after all, there was this public meeting in 1934, '35, yes indeed, those were very intense times.

'Hatzfeld turns up to hear Malraux, Salle Playel it was or maybe some other venue, the writer is just back from the USSR, a fast-flowing impassioned speech, it really was, that lock of hair falling across his forehead, the struggle against fascism, voice breaking dramatically and much gesturing with his hands, Malraux is being effective, "in the USSR," he declaims, "democracy is guaranteed by the fact the workers march with rifles on their shoulders", Roland Hatzfeld stands up, applauds wildly, the whole audience applauds wildly, and he decides that the very next day he will apply for a Communist Party card, he'd just finished his law degree, he'd pleaded well, people were already predicting he'd make a great advocate one day. At Party HQ, some sensible people told him he didn't need to have a card, that he'd be more useful remaining on the outside, but if he really wanted a card they would give him one as discreetly as he could wish, they probably didn't say "discreetly", most likely they said "privately", on a personal basis, it all went off very well.

'Why am I telling you this? To get you used to trusting me, though maybe that's not true, that said, Hatzfeld phoned me, it's not something he does often, it seems you're not going down well, Budapest, that report on Stalin's crimes, the rest of it, Hatzfeld advised me to offer you something you would embrace with passion.'

Chapter 4

1956

The Childhood of a Mole

In which you are invited by a friend of Michael Lilstein to eat lobster in a Paris brasserie.

In which you descend a considerable way into the bowels of the Gare de l'Est.

In which you meet a beautiful woman dressed in red in a first-class railway compartment.

In which Lilstein tells you why you should work with him.

Paris/Waltenberg, early December 1956

Every soul is a secret society unto itself.
Marcel Jouhandeau, *Algèbre des valeurs morales*

In Paris, a few days before your departure for Waltenberg, the Waldhaus and this conversation with Lilstein, Roland Hatzfeld had told you:

'You've been in the Party for more than ten years now, young man, it's time you thought of tackling more complex matters.'

He'd talked to you about Lilstein in a very odd sort of way, 'a victim of the Nazis and Stalin, but he never gave them anything, not Stalin, not the Nazis, and he's stayed up to his elbows in the slime of *praxis*, it would be useful for you to meet him.'

Up to his elbows, slime, a weighty image, and Hatzfeld had made it weightier by attaching 'praxis', but he'd opened his eyes wide as he said it, lifting his forefinger to a point halfway up his plump pink cheeks, articulating each word separately, smiling faintly, as if making a point of marking his distance from the obligatory language of the Party.

But he had taken care not to make this distance too obvious, the smile which was not a jibe, more a sign that no one was taken in by the minutiae of a ritual to which a man could remain attached even so, because it was a ritual which allowed people to acknowledge each other, people whom society refused to acknowledge. This conversation had taken place over a platter of sea-food in a brasserie near the Madeleine, wood panels, red leather, large lampshades, a great deal of brass, the men who came in had fat bellies, the women wore fox tippets or similar around their necks, both waiters and head waiters were got up like penguins, the maître d'hôtel was in evening dress: the slime of *praxis*.

'Don't sulk,' Hatzfeld had said. 'Makes you look like a puritan, puritans never do good work. Eat up, you're not thirty yet, you have your whole life in front of you, so don't behave like someone who doesn't know what to do with the claw of a lobster.'

At the end of the meal, Roland Hatzfeld had given you a return train ticket for Waltenberg, first class.

'It's partly to teach you to combat puritanism, but also because customs aren't as much of a nuisance with first-class passengers, but no sleeper, you travel by day, that means you won't meet the Madonna of the Sleeping-Cars, but it'll save us money. If the trip turns out to be a waste of time, you'll have had a short holiday, and you can pay me back if you like, but you're not obliged to.'

After leaving the restaurant, you went on talking as you walked with Hatzfeld towards the Place de la Bourse, a friendly stroll, you were flattered, you know he was part of a resistance network during the war, he was one of its leaders, they told you the day the network was blown Hatzfeld deliberately allowed himself to be captured, passing himself off as a simple messenger to point the Gestapo in the wrong direction, he was sent to Buchenwald. As you strolled along the Boulevard des Capucines, an almost tender note crept into Hatzfeld's voice.

He talked about struggle, never give up the struggle, stay on the side of life, currently he is defending a Frenchman facing charges of aiding the NLF who may very well be guillotined.

'I've been to see Coty, about a pardon, he said nothing but he told me a story, in 1917 he was present at the execution of a soldier who had refused to go up the line. To comfort the man, a general told him affectionately, "You're dying for France, my boy." '

Roland Hatzfeld also spoke about what he called the Great Mess, he gestured to a front page of *Paris-Presse* in the window of a newspaper kiosk, 'In the Hell that is Budapest'. You went pish! . . . to show that you wouldn't go that far, Hatzfeld told you that people shouldn't tell each other tales.

'Overall, you know, the bourgeois press is right, that's really what has happened, there are also barbed crosses, Horthyites, the return of the Whites, but it was the people that rebelled, sometimes I get so sick of it all . . . Go and see Lilstein and even if he fails to convince you, come back and tell me what he said, because I need to know. In 1930 I travelled from Berlin to Moscow by rail, it was interminable, a coach full of young people, Prussia, the Polish steppe, at one moment we passed under a triumphal arch made of wood, plain and simple.

'In the corridor of the train, a young German actress started singing the Internationale as she looked out at the landscape, I was happy, you should never be happy, today I no longer know what I should be doing. In 1949, in Paris, in court, I faced another woman, a German revolutionary, Katrin Bernheim, she'd fled to Moscow after Hitler came to power, she said that in 1936 she had been held in a camp in the USSR, at Karaganda; she called it a concentration camp, and she also said that in 1940 Stalin had handed her back to the Nazis who had sent her to Ravensbrück, you know what I did? I made a case showing that she herself had demanded to be returned to Germany, I was quite sure of what I was saying, she was a turncoat.

'Then one day, in 1954, Lilstein told me about the camp where he'd been held, we were just walking in Berlin, anywhere, an avenue, not the Stalinallee, that would have been too rich, but it was thereabouts, it was a sobering story, what they did to him, what he had seen being done to others, for two years he was in camp in Siberia, the two years that preceded Stalin's death, and the last months in particular, when he realised that things were getting tougher and tougher, until then he'd felt that the powers which had arrested him nevertheless wanted to go easy on him, but there came a moment when he realised that he was going to die, he told me that Siberia wasn't like Auschwitz, there was no *Selektionslager* for the kids, women, the sick, but from that moment on as far as he was concerned there was the same feel about things as at Auschwitz, he knew he would die during the coming month, he no longer tried to keep his head down, he took all the beatings, at Auschwitz he was saved by Stalin's troops, in Siberia it was Stalin's death, when Beria ordered the camps to be opened. Lilstein told me that, kept it very low key.

'All that was part of the information I needed, the turncoat Bernheim had been right, I made a mental note, but it was only a month later that I thought about her and what she'd said about the camps, I could tell you about breaking out in a cold sweat as I slept, recurring nightmares featuring female apparitions, about how memory takes its revenge at night, but it didn't happen that way, one day she simply came into my mind and ever since she has been part of my thinking, a great lady, she said Ravensbrück was cleaner and warmer than Karaganda, the Russians worked the prisoners to death by feeding them next to nothing, when they didn't fulfil the fixed work-quota their rations were halved, at Ravensbrück the food was better but prisoners died of the beatings they got, the guards were sadists, they were there to exterminate, the Russians were decent, scrupulous, they simply applied their system.

'She thought Karaganda was worse than Ravensbrück, Lilstein didn't grade them, I was only at Buchenwald, no one was gassed there, it was inside the Reich's own territory, gas was for the camps situated more to the east but all the same Buchenwald was hell, Nazi power with a hell all of its own, not the kind of hell to be used as a threat for the after-life, no, a hell in the here-and-now, a few hours away in a train from Berlin, and she said that Karaganda was worse, and the worst is that perhaps she was right, sometimes I get sick of it all . . . but can you really see us standing shoulder to shoulder with those bastards, while children are dying in Algeria?'

Hatzfeld motioned towards another newspaper with the headline: 'Our Flags Still Fly Over Port Said'.

By now you'd got as far as the Bourse, Hatzfeld stopped and looked at you:

'Never let virtue strangle virtue, make the trip, you can decide once you know the facts, leave the Party, don't leave the Party, whatever.

Go on, it's a birthday present, your twenty-seventh, and your tenth as a Party member.'

Before taking your leave of Hatzfeld you asked him where he'd met Lilstein, he stared up at the front of the Bourse as he gave you his answer:

'In a very smart place, a real debating club.'

'More specifically?'

Hatzfeld went into an English accent:

'In Buchenwald, in the latrines, a short while before they sent Lilstein to Auschwitz.'

Two days later, you went to the Gare de l'Est and caught the train, you got there with bags of time to spare, and just before you walked into the main concourse you gave yourself a moment to contemplate the huge picture by Herter which shows the departure of the soldiers for the war in 1914, contemplate is hardly the word, a daub, metre after metre, of grim-faced women, resolute men, it was painted in 1926, flowers, not so much enthusiasm as duty, there is something unintentional about the picture which for all its faults wins you over, in the centre of the composition, standing on the steps of a carriage, facing you, is a man holding his arms out wide and angled heavenwards, a bouquet in his left hand, a rifle in his right, with flowers in the spout of the gun, light shirt, eyes turned upward, towards Country and Values, and at the same time this man in the shirt, with his arms stretched out wide makes you think inevitably of Goya's condemned man, the man in the *Tres de mayo*, the civilian shot by a firing-squad of Napoleon's soldiers.

The war has not yet begun in the painting in the Gare de l'Est but that soldier in 1914 already has the look of a man condemned to death by firing-squad. With one difference: here, there is no firing-squad, the killers are out of the frame, they might be Prussians or whoever gave the order to go up against the Prussians, or again the killer could come from the heaven the man is looking at, it's not what Herter intended, but don't linger here, you know what you've got to do, you came early for a purpose, opposite the end of platform I is a small door, nothing remarkable about it, between two union posters, no sign on the door, it's closed, entry is restricted as you know, you wait discreetly until another man comes along and opens it with his key and then you slip in behind him as if you'd arrived at the same moment he did.

You find yourself in a corridor, you slow down to let the man get ahead of you, stairs lead up towards the administrative offices, you go up them, the steps are protected by a new floor covering called 'linoleum', this isn't the place, from the landing extends a line of offices, the corridor looks new, this isn't it, the last time you were here everything looked much shabbier, you've come to the wrong floor, you're about to be asked what damn business you have being here, you go back down the stairs, door on the left, corridor, you turn right, narrow staircase, you've never been down these steps, you are getting lost, but it's not that difficult in this bloody place, you are lost.

You're wasting time, you take the stairs which descend into the bowels of the station, now the steps are bare boards, a smell of old dust, you pass a man carrying a small case, another anonymous door at the foot of the stairs, a corridor, you're lost again, at this rate you'll miss your train, you must go back upstairs, you can't even find the stairs that will take you back up, this is stupid, and no chance of asking the way because you'd be challenged to say what you're doing here, you're going to be late, you don't trust your watch, you pass another man, he's got a small case too, it's cold, a door that creaks, the man had come out of it.

You're on the wrong track, you're lost, no, the smell, machine oil and hot dust, the smell particular to the contact of electricity with dust, you go through the door, on the left is a kind of lodge or records office, a woman sits inside, she doesn't give you a second glance, she is fully occupied with her index cards, the next room looks like a library, many tomes, glass-fronted bookcases, archives, the room is empty, it is very early, and then at the far end a door, above the door is an electric clock, at last you've arrived, you're not late, you may go in, people greet you though they don't know you, it's the way they do things here, you acknowledge the nodding heads with gestures which are more expansive, very deferential, you're the youngest person in the room.

It is a very large room, with a magnificent model railway layout on a raised dais a metre and a half from the ground, it occupies almost the whole floor space, despite the early hour men are going briskly about their business, each one has come with his own train in a small case, not many trains are running round the circuit, one of them has problems – I've got sixteen volts and the ammeter's showing zero – see what he wants, he'll get irritated, he acts like a kid, one man picks up a steam engine, it's not working, pound to a penny it's the brushes, no, it worked perfectly for me at home, it's the track that's the problem, it's not the track, look, Henri's Blue train has been running for an hour, if it isn't the brushes I don't see what it could be, a long goods train rattles along the rails and heads for a tunnel under a papier-mâché mountain.

As it re-emerges the train passes a half-built village, stops at the points, sets off again, many locomotives are lying on their sides, with their engine covers off, undergoing repairs or being tuned, a man in a Breton sailor's cap is re-winding an electric motor, another is feeding a bundle of thin wires into the coaches of his *Paris–Hendaye* to install night lights, you hear the rata-ta-taat the carriages make on the rails, you widen your gaze to take in the whole network, the Breton or Basque villages, the engine shed with its turntable, the sidings with a water-tower and coal bunker, and the trains go round, the Blue train, then a Michelin railcar, and those new electric engines, the ones christened crocodiles on account of their very long noses.

In front of a station are parked cars, a black Citroën DS 19, a Juva 4, not quite to the same scale as the rest, one of the men fiddles with a whistle which mimics the sound of a real steam whistle, you bend down to get a trackside view of a train coming towards you, you close your eyes, the sound of the rails, it's time.

You return to the surface, back in the station you walk to the end of your platform to stare up at the flanged smoke-shield mounted on top of the enormous metal cylinder which in turn reigns over a world of wheels, push-rods, fly-cranks, oscillating cams and injectors, the *Mountain 241* which will haul your train at 120 kilometres an hour, a *241 P*, double funnels, two new mechanical 18/24-stroke lubricators, you can't see the lubricators, they're on the left foot-plate, on the other side of the locomotive, what you're seeing is the right side and, bolted to the foot-plate, the large turbo-dynamo which looks small against the body of the boiler and the four drive-wheels each of which has a diameter of two metres, a superb dark green has been used for the combined engine and tender, darker than olive green, with red stripes running along the entire length.

So, a journey by day, with the pleasure of observing the landscape change as you travel across eastern France, the steeples which will grow more bulbous as the train rolls nearer to the mountains that are the heart of Europe, the pleasure of seeing yourself pass through towns without stopping, alone in one of those empty compartments where you can be yourself, such a delight, alone with yourself, with the current number of the review *La Nouvelle Pensée* and a popular magazine which has the latest news about the love life of some film actress and a light opera star, you took the liberty of buying this rag in the station, you swore you'd leave it behind on the train when you arrived, wanting to leave the Party doesn't mean that you have suddenly to acquire capitalist tastes, you'll throw the magazine away just as you'll throw your review away before going through customs, no need to draw attention to your political affiliations even if they are in the process of changing, yes, but where can you throw it away? in the toilets? A communist review abandoned just before the customs check would look even more suspicious, the toilet of another coach then? In second class?

Pretend to be going to the restaurant car and leave the review in a toilet in second class, or an empty compartment, you can leave the rag in your own compartment, keep one page, the one all about the camera of your dreams, the Paillard 8 mm with two Berthiot lenses, a focal length of 12/5 and one of 35, expensive, 73,000, francs, light, elegant, black-and-steel finish, very expensive.

A classical music record costs 2,600 francs, Schubert's *Winter Journey* sung by Fischer-Dieskau, for example, so ten times the price of the Schubert makes 26,000, so 73,000 is practically thirty classical records, three sixes are eighteen, three twos are six plus one makes seven, 78,000, take away two records, that makes twenty-eight records, in other words I can't buy records for two years if I want the Paillard with two lenses, that's not counting the cost of film, there are cheaper labels than Pathé-Marconi, that's further on, on the Phillips page, their 'Classics for Everyone', less than 2,000 francs a throw, true, but you've got to add local taxes, what's the local tax rate on records? And Phillips doesn't do the *Winter Journey,* nor the Brahms with Heifetz. How many packets of cigarettes make one Paillard?

Anyway, just go ahead and buy the Pathé-Marconi Schubert, the *Winter Journey,* I'm told the man singing it is fantastic, try with cigarettes, a hundred and thirty francs for a packet of Rallye, a hundred and sixty if you smoke Camels, they don't like Camels in the Party, but if I leave the Party I could smoke nothing but Camels, so if I gave up cigarettes, a hundred packets of Camel come to sixteen thousand francs, 'Camels, no other cigarette is so easy on the throat, regular smokers prefer Camels', a whole year of smoking Camels is sixteen times three hundred and sixty-five, hold on, it's more than a packet a day, what's a regular smoker? 'I'm a regular smoker, I prefer Camels, one packet, two, three packets, makes no difference, Camels do not irritate the throat', so let's say a packet and a half a day, just to keep the advertisers happy, it comes to more than five hundred packets.

Give or take it's eighteen months' smoking for a camera, but meanwhile I go on buying gramophone records, I'm wrong, it's less than a year of smoking, just four hundred packets, that would make four times six twenty-four, four and carry two, four times one, plus two, six, sixty-four plus the three zeros, that's already sixty-four thousand with four hundred packets, got to be accurate, in my head seventy-three thousand multiplied by a hundred and sixty, no, in seventy-three thousand how many hundred and sixties are there? No, sixty-four thousand buys four hundred packets, for five hundred packets it would cost another sixteen thousand, total eighty thousand, that makes the Paillard the equivalent of about four hundred and sixty packets, a year's smoking, if I'm careful.

I must brush up on my mental arithmetic, hello, we're off, something like a thousand kilometres to go, I've never been further than Mulhouse, no, another five minutes, it's that other train that's going, I always make that mistake, it's because I want to be off, the cigarettes, the camera, the reflection in the window, I'm twenty-seven, the face of the ballerina on a page of the magazine, she's the same age as me, she's made up as an old woman in a wig and a shawl, she scrambles through the barbed wire, Budapest is finished, she's leaving, I don't give a damn about the cardinal hidden in the Yankee Embassy, but the ballerina, and the University Hospital in Budapest, bottom right of the photo, a head, on the floor, a room in the hospital attacked by cannon, *fired by Soviet tanks,* the corpses of four patients, in a meeting of my cell I'd have said it was a fake photo got up for propaganda purposes, but Hatzfeld said have no illusions, almost everything they say is true, you just have to turn the pages.

In another photo it was Stalin's head that was on the ground, next to an advert for Vick's VapoRub, to be applied as a poultice on the chest at night the minute the infant sneezes, in *Humanité* it was a photo of a militia man at the headquarters of the Hungarian Communist Party, he was lying full length on the ground, a picture of Lenin placed on his stomach and a bayonet stuck clean through his throat, was the poultice mummy used to put on my chest Vick's VapoRub? It smelled of camphor and mint, that plus a soupspoonful of Rami linctus and I was ready for the night, I used to shut my eyes feeling slightly sick, it was better to be sleepy, read *White Fang* on the QT by my bedside lamp with a poultice on my chest and the after-taste of Rami in my mouth, which spoiled everything.

The Poles present Gomulka with a teddy bear to thank him for standing up to the Russians, the bear is enormous, it's in the station at Warsaw, a two-page spread, you try to look at the hands in the photos of Gomulka, Hatzfeld told you that, in prison in Stalin's day he had his fingernails torn out, can't really see for sure, this time the Poles come off better than the Hungarians, and then this pretty woman enters the compartment, a porter stows away her luggage, the pretty woman has no change, she searches through her bag marked H, comes up with nothing, she is wearing two delicate gold bracelets, the porter scowls, waits, he'll miss his next job.

You watch the little drama, the pretty woman's eyes are on you but she isn't looking at you, she is tall, under her coat a red dress, cut at the neck in an austere V, she doesn't want anything from you, you exist so minimally, but you are there, this she knows, had enough of this, you give the porter the coin, he goes without a word, he thought he might get more than the standard charge, your face feels hot, the woman thanks you with an irritated nod, pointed chin, broad forehead, she's taller than you, brunette, frankly she is not really happy about the way you interfered.

You sit down again, without speaking, don't exploit the situation, in any case you don't know how to, the train sets off, you are sitting in a corner seat next to the window facing the engine, it has not crossed your mind to offer your seat to the pretty woman, she has settled down on the same side as you but at the other end, next to the door, she can't see you now, a hundred thousand refugees have fled into Austria, you see people walking through the streets carrying loaves of bread, the woman has not yet taken her gloves off, she stands to retrieve one of her cases from the rack, you leap up to help, a 'thank you' in a discouraging voice, you've sat down again, she removes her purse from her case, closes the case, takes it by the handle, you leap up again, you put the case back on the luggage rack.

Again you are sitting, you stare out of the window, you are leaning forward, head turned towards the window and the landscape, tracking the houses the train has just passed. And in the window, the reflection of your head is also leaning forward, now you can see the reflection of the woman's face, her profile, it is rare for a woman to have such a beautiful profile, the prettier the girl the more like a grouper-fish she looks, it was a Breton friend who told you that about girls who don't respond, the woman has a large brow, a straight nose, as much chin as is necessary, you tell yourself it's like a profile on a medal, 'Monsieur,' the woman is speaking to you, she's not looking at you, she's searching through her purse, she takes out a coin, 'Monsieur,' now she's looking at you, she holds out the coin, you refuse it, 'Please', her voice is crisp, 'I insist,' you take the coin, she thanks you once more, her tone is not sharp now, it is cold, you say, 'Neither a borrower nor a lender . . .'

She says nothing, your smile is frozen on your lips, you feel foolish, you slip the coin into your jacket pocket, the left one, you hold the coin briefly between your fingers in your pocket, you stroke it, you look out of the window, you take your left hand out of your pocket, elbow on arm-rest, hand held up to your mouth, index-finger on your upper lip, a lingering smell of perfume on your finger, sweet, heavy, the woman must perfume her gloves, at moments it seems as if the perfume is coming from her whole person, it fights with the smell of the compartment, a mixture of smoke, polish and SNCF disinfectant, you look at her, she is reading, her legs are long.

Your hand returns to your pocket seeking the coin, you warm it between the ends of your fingers as you look at the woman's legs, you decide you are going to say something to her, being suave is not that difficult, you're a Parisian male and she's a middle-class lady up from the country who is going home, she'll be the one to say something first, you'll get to know her better, she'll invite you to her château, you'll go for long walks together, you won't be allowed to touch her, you'll chance your luck some evening, she'll grab a horse-whip, a stony look in her eye, she wants you naked but you mustn't move, big four-poster, chintz bed-curtains patterned with red flowers, outside the country speeds by, you fidget in your seat and hardly see anything of the landscape which you'd been looking forward to seeing.

You take the coin out, smuggled in your hand, it's warm now, you hold it against your left cheek, bring it nearer to your nose, you try to rediscover the perfume on the coin, a trace, what was the name of your mother's perfume? it was by Guerlain but what was it called? you shouldn't have held the coin against your cheek, now it's been tainted

by the smell of this morning's shaving soap, the perfume might well
be by Guerlain, but mixed up with the smell of your shaving soap the
result is not very pleasant, you try to discover a trace of it on the end
of your finger and in the air of the compartment.

You watch the reflection of the woman's profile in the window where
fields, woods and villages flash by, you have crossed your legs, your
magazine is open on your knees, that's not quite accurate, actually it's
your thighs, but the word thigh is indecent, does the woman spray
perfume on her thighs after she gets out of the bath? you're strolling
with her in the country, it's early evening, you are returning from your
walk, there's a whole group of you now moving across hill and dale,
sometimes a wisp of mist fifty centimetres above the ground, you walk
through it, the woman has caught you up and is walking next to you,
she has taken you by the hand, Gilberte, Catherine and Micheline are
there, they show off their petticoats, the elegant, sober 'Emo' model,
Gilberte's is made of run-proof Bemberg rayon, which is gathered
nylon over lace, Micheline's, priced three and a half thousand francs,
is virtually a nightdress, Empire neckline and the skirt flounced with
a lace insertion, two pages further on is the 'Boccaccio', a short
nightie, with a round neck and short sleeves puffed with coloured
smocking, and the 'Esmeralda', a very youthful style and impeccably
cut, youthful, impeccable, the words don't mean a thing, pointless as
adjectives, you can get a better idea of the 'Boccaccio' but I don't
know what smocking is.

Why not just ask the woman in the red dress what it is, in a moment,
as a conversation starter? meanwhile you turn to the next page and
you're bare-chested having just completed a month of the 'Dynam'
method, a course of psychophysical culture which turns you into a real
athlete, 'think about muscles and *Dynam* will see you get them,
work out in front of your mirror for just fifteen minutes a day – no
cheating! – for the length of the course and the end results are
amazing, thighs gain five centimetres on average!' You look out
again at the landscape, no, the grounds of the château, you're strolling

down a walkway shaded by heavy grape vines and reach a garden that
has run wild.

A profusion of parasitic weeds, a few pale rose trees well spaced out,
the silhouettes of women, bushes laden with fruit around a stagnant
pond, you see specific things, peaches fat and dark, a wall covered with
mauve flowers, the warm evening and Clara d'Ellébeuse, a flight of
rooks, the splash of an otter by the water's edge in the blue light, a few
patches of golden yellow among the leaves, the woman is alone now,
she is walking just ahead of you, she turns, her arms are very soft, a
forest slides past in the window, you have the feeling that you've been
asleep, you have been asleep, the woman in red is still there,
indifferent.

You lay aside your copy of *Paris-Match,* if you have indeed been asleep
you should be able to cope with *La Nouvelle Pensée,* it's your review,
you're still a member of the editorial board, three weeks ago you were
busy deciding the contents of the issue you now have in your hand,
with your comrades, under the chairmanship, exceptionally, of a
deputy member of the Politburo. It was bizarre, having a member of
the Politburo there, a deputy member but from the Politburo, though
not that bizarre in the circumstances, Warsaw, Budapest, these were
bumpy times.

But the fascist attacks on the Party's offices in Paris had closed up
the ranks, and then there was Suez – and in the presence of a member
of the Politburo no one had dared question the Party line, all the more
so since, at the start of the meeting, the deputy member of the
politburo had come out with two or three sentences astoundingly
critical of Rakosi and the former Hungarian leadership, very trenchant
sentences which went much further than anything the most outspoken comrade would have uttered on the subject.

Then they'd come to the business of settling the contents of the
next issue, a discussion about a piece roughly ten pages or so long, a
short story submitted by a bourgeois writer, it's entitled 'The
Rehearsal', the author is a foreigner, a German social-democrat, a Big
Name in European literature as they say, Hans Kappler, a harmless

enough tale, Kappler tries above all to achieve transparency, he explains everything, the love of a singer and a pianist, people with no worries beyond the accuracy of a note or the state of their feelings for each other, it was the opposite of what was required by the class struggle and socialist realism, a story of zero originality which nevertheless you'd liked and take great pleasure in rejecting.

It seemed bizarre to you that the Politburo should be so interested in the review, so interested that it had sent one of its members, a deputy member maybe but even so, to the last meeting of its editorial board, after all it's only a highbrow review read in intellectual circles, the comrade member of the Politburo had wanted to attend 'a no-holds barred meeting' of 'real' intellectuals who were 'aware of their historical task'.

As to Kappler's piece, some views had been very critical, others less so, you are the youngest member of the board, you were the most forthright, no doubt you were the one who liked the story best, you found it insubstantial but well-written and you were its toughest critic, as literature it was demotivating, its prose was fake-prole, the transparency was entirely bourgeois, Kappler almost made you forgive Proust, a comrade took up cudgels for Proust snobbish he might be but he understands feelings, besides he's very critical of upper-bourgeois values, much more so than Kappler, do reread *Time Regained*, the same comrade also defended the story, a weak defence, he was all at sea, he always backed the Party's political position one hundred and ten per cent, but he gave himself space on questions of culture.

But that day, with the comrade from the Politburo taking his time before saying anything on the subject, he wasn't sure which way to jump, the discussion covered socialist humanism, reality, and false consciousness, you took delight in destroying something you liked in the presence of a deputy member of the Politburo, but it wasn't important now since in all likelihood you'll soon be leaving the Party, yes, you could have defended 'The Rehearsal' but it reminded you too strongly of the sort of thing your family liked both before and during the war, books that were well-written, genteel literature, you criticised without believing in what you were saying because you have also stopped believing in the things you love.

At the same time you revelled in your ability to lie joyfully and effectively as you set about destroying a piece of writing which took you back to the age of eighteen, and your comrades as they listened refused to be outdone, when a few of you got together you found you had the same ideas, the same eclectic tastes for bourgeois authors, but with this editorial board you felt as if you were part of some ceremony in which each member of the tribe brings his richest possession and proudly casts it into the flames in front of everyone else, the member of the Politburo nodded his head with great understanding and kindliness, when he spoke he did so hesitantly, especially during the general discussion which opened the proceedings.

He stumbled over quotations from Thorez, especially when he wanted to say something complex, he struggled for words, he quoted Thorez 'there was no Stalinism', he'd started out as a boiler-maker, 'the word is part of our opponents' vocabulary', no one knew when he'd joined, he spoke slowly, hesitated, 'there has come about . . . although the policy was right and just . . . rooted in the principles of Marxism-Leninism', a comrade who was still young, about forty, a proletarian.

And the members of the editorial board took pleasure in prompting him with the quotes he found it hard to regurgitate whole, 'there has come about a retreat from these Marxist-Leninist principles in given historical conditions', they competed with each other, they vied to be the first to come up with the words the member of the Politburo was groping for, 'these conditions now exist', even statements they didn't much care for, 'there was no Stalinism', a real joy, putting words into the mouth of an important Party official, even if he's a deputy, being able to disappear behind words that could have no come-back, lending a helping hand to a comrade who was experienced but still young, a genuine member of the proletariat who was not in the habit of memorising essential quotes, no, he did remember one, it wasn't Thorez, it was Casanova, 'when we are fair and square with the revolutionary proletariat, then, and only then, will our conscience be clear.'

One comrade thought it funny to give only the first part of a Thorez quote, whereas all the comrades have always known that with Maurice it's invariably the second part that matters, 'The number of different roads to socialism has nothing to do with the content of the dictator-ship of the proletariat', this left the comrade deputy baffled by the violence of Maurice's contention, it was clear that he was thinking of the possible implications of such an assertion, a few words more and it would be pure Titoism, that is, the idea that there could be purely national roads to socialism, even if Tito had never stopped being a traitor and a monster, the comrade deputy was a man who missed nothing.

But another comrade, the biggest 'doubter' on the editorial board, gleefully supplied him with him the rest, 'that content being of neces-sity common to all countries which are marching towards socialism', everyone breathed again, they didn't agree with the comrade deputy, not really, but that was no reason for allowing a proletarian to flounder in a morass of hesitation, so you give him a helping hand, compete to be the most accurate, Thorez's idea is developed, it circu-lates, unifies.

To get back to the story, someone said he'd found it well-written, no, well-written means primarily that it engages with the real lives of the proletariat, go reread André Stil's latest novel and the letter which the factory girls in Nîmes wrote him, that's what's meant by well-written, no one had said nay to this, though whenever two or three of you linger over a meal there's always one who makes the other laugh by parodying André Stil's prose style, good-naturedly though, for he's one of the prime movers of *Humanité*, showed tremendous courage over Indochina, but in the end there was general agreement: no one was prepared to back the short story written by the great writer.

A German writer to boot, one of the comrades finally reminded them of the fact, until then no one had wanted to bring this up, and a German who lived among revanchists, who sometimes had dealings with the deepest-dyed right, the right of *Preuves*, that 'turncoats' rag' as another comrade dubbed it.

Then they'd moved on to other articles, philosophy, sociology, psychology, agreement reached pretty quickly on the line-up of the next issue, there was only the story to reject, they'd added an editorial condemning the fascist riots in Paris, when gangsters in the pay of the collaborator Tixier-Vignancourt had attacked Party headquarters, you were both happy and unhappy, unhappy with yourself and the others, and reasonably happy because you didn't have to fear the consequences of feeling unhappy, a splendid example of chiasmus, some of your comrades tore their hair, but you are turning into a permanent chiasmus, all in all a good meeting of the editorial board, the deputy member of the Politburo had a few more fairly harsh words for the former Hungarian leadership and the corrections that were needed, and when the question arose of who would reply to the great writer to inform him that his story had been rejected, the comrade member of the Politburo said the story would be published, it is politically necessary that the story should be published, Hans Kappler, a bourgeois writer of great eminence who is coming over to us, a German social-democrat, at the very time when we want to show a united front with the socialists.

In consequence of the wide-ranging exchange of views which has just taken place, the story will occupy a prime position, heading the line-up of the next issue, the publication date of said issue must accordingly be brought forward by two weeks, we can count absolutely on the cooperation of the printworkers' union, after these closing remarks from the representative of the Politburo the proposal was agreed *nem con*, the deputy member of the Politburo was a sound man, he'd succeeded in stimulating the critical faculties of everyone present and strengthened their discipline.

If you'd known this, you would have defended the story, on second thoughts, that would not have gone down well, what the members of a Politburo like is purity and discipline.

And the best test of discipline comes when you've expressed an opinion which is the very opposite of the decision that is finally reached, you liked the story, you damned it, they were publishing it anyway, all was for the best, you lied and the Party did not agree with your lie, both of you in roles which fitted like a glove.

In the train bowling along towards Switzerland you reread the story to the publication of which the comrade deputy attached such importance, and you still don't have the smallest inkling of the reasons why it was chosen.

At Chaumont, a man gets into the compartment, carrying a case, he glances at the woman, sits down opposite her, tweeds, brogues, a swaggering manner, she smiles at him, the man smiles back then looks across at you, it is not a stare but he continues looking, he looks you in the eye, thick neck, large ears, hands like dinner plates, hairy too, you feel uncomfortable, no wedding ring, your eye again catches his as though he's not stopped staring the whole time you've been observing his hands, his eyes are very pale, his eyes are on you, the woman reads her magazine, he is looking at you.

It's oppressive, you look up, you catch his eye, his probing eye, he does not smile, he seems to be thinking about you, thinking about something, he never takes his eyes off you though he has no justification for doing so, he doesn't bother with the woman, you are caught in his gaze, you bury your face in your magazine, there are women who give shirts as presents and in return get an electric coffee-grinder or a Hoover vacuum cleaner, there are no workers anywhere in the magazine, they only show workers when they are being fired on by Russian soldiers, the man makes you feel uncomfortable, you are nothing, but the woman had smiled at him, he does not look at her.

You try but fail to think of something other than the way the man's looking at you, you've tried reading but that didn't work, the man's hand grips the back of your neck, you're with him on a bridge, he slams your face against a wall, hurts you, the other hand reaches for your trousers, his hands are hard, he does not look at the woman, he sits facing her but does not look at her, the basilica of Chaumont recedes into the distance, a man selling refreshments pushes the compartment door open, in your pocket your grip tightens on the coin the woman gave you, suddenly the man speaks to her, very direct, anything but polite, the woman chooses a fruit juice, she has accepted the man's offer, the man has a beer.

You tell the vendor you don't want anything, the man holds up a note of large denomination to the vendor, the vendor can't change it, why don't you come back later, the woman laughs, takes out her purse, no, no, we're living in a modern world now, the man gets cross, he looks very annoyed, the woman calms him with a smile, I'm enjoying this moment, allow me, all right, but only on condition that I pay you back later, the woman smiles at the man as she pays.

The vendor says thank you and is about to move on, you say just a moment, please, you hadn't wanted anything but now you ask for a bottle of Vichy, and you pay with the warm, perfumed coin the woman gave you, you say keep the change, the vendor takes the metal cap off the bottle, gives the top a wipe, passes it to you, the man and the woman get out together at Mulhouse.

It was late at night when you reached Klosters, the hotel owner couldn't find your name on the register, he hurried off and woke his wife, she never told me we were expecting a young French gentleman, must have slipped her mind, but it's all sorted out now, one night in the hotel, already at altitude, you can't get off to sleep, the sheets are scratchy, you didn't abandon the magazine after all, you know it by heart, in Budapest a Russian officer reaches for his holster as he strides towards the photographer's lens, as if he was about to draw his pistol, 'Camels, no other cigarette is so easy on the throat', you've no more cigarettes, the soldiers in blue helmets have entered Alexandria, Eisenhower is a man with a Quaker background, he has allowed himself to be manipulated by the under-developed countries, the magazine dislikes Americans, not all of them, but it sure doesn't like Eisenhower.

He's an ally who forces the French and the English to get out of Egypt, the magazine doesn't care much for Cabot Lodge either, 'On colonial matters, Monsieur Cabot Lodge has ideas, ideas which he didn't get from the history of his native Massachusetts, where the price of Indian scalps ranged from a hundred dollars for the scalp of a warrior to five for the scalps of girls under ten, Monsieur Cabot Lodge believes that the new nationalist pressures are legitimate,' there are also pictures of Guy Mollet and Anthony Eden, Eisenhower has refused to meet the French and English ministers who'd come for the UNO session, the President's diary is too full to receive all the ministers of every delegation, 'the Americans are treating us as if we were the Sudan,' says the magazine.

An American official is talking about the French and the English, these people want to rebuild their empires, they still think it's 1910, they've got to learn, the Soviets had issued an ultimatum, they too could pounce on Alexandria and deal 'strategically' with the Franco-British fleet, for the military 'strategically' includes nuclear weapons, Puskas has not returned to Hungary, his wife has managed to flee to Austria, she phones him, at night, the Russian Vladimir Kuts has won the 5,000 and 10,000 metres in the Melbourne Olympics, in the 10,000, he makes twenty-three attempts to shake off Pirie, his great rival, twenty-three spurts in a 10,000 metres, the magazine shows him crossing the line but says nothing of the applause, as you turn the pages you find a high percentage of everything that's been happening these last few weeks but from a rather stomach-turning angle, a point of view that you do not share but which you soon might, you look for details of the deaths of the three militants killed during the fascist demonstrations against the Party in Paris.

You carry the names of the three men in your head, Ferrand, Le Guennec and Beaucourt, less has been said about Beaucourt because he was a member of Force Ouvrière, Le Guennec was wounded in the fascist attack on Party headquarters, on the Wednesday evening, he was a veteran of the Spanish Civil War, it was more complicated with Ferrand, he died of his injuries on the Wednesday evening, the same evening as Le Guennec, but with him it was a gun butt, at Montmartre Metro station, a gun butt, that meant the flying squad, at the time *Humanité* did not distinguish between the three, it just spoke of 'victims of the fascist riot' but didn't say anything else about the flying squad.

Next morning, you are cold, a long walk by yourself around Klosters, bus for Waltenberg in the early afternoon, an hour's climb up a road which must have been built by the Devil himself, you've still got your magazine, you reread it knowing full well that doing so will make you feel sick but you don't want to see the drop, another walk at the top, you feel tired, you shouldn't have agreed to this meeting.

*

And at tea-time you are back at the Waldhaus sitting opposite Lilstein, without knowing how or why, and it is now a bit late to ask yourself that, and Lilstein has left you no time to think about your own position, he promised to tell you a tale, and he goes off on endless tangents, like some Oriental story-teller or an alcoholic:

'With me, young gentleman of France, you won't be a spectator but a one-hundred-per-cent participant. What you ask your common or garden spy to do is to occupy a place in the sun while remaining a shadow, which is in itself very difficult, but you, you shall do much, much more, you are about to realise an ideal, you will not be simply the eyes or ears which perceive the drama, you will be the actor, you will play the lead in the great scenes.'

The woman with red hair has reappeared in the deserted lounge of the Waldhaus carrying a Linzer Torte on a large plate, she cuts two generous slices and warns that it is still hot, Lilstein thanks her in a quiet voice then carries on, removing his spectacles, an action which makes the look in his eyes childlike, avid.

'An actor is exactly what I mean! And it gets even better: on occasions you will actually be the author of the drama, you'll devise the whole thing, I pride myself that I never ever spy on events, I create them, and you'll reach the stage where you don't know if you are talking about some incident in which you participated or if you yourself created what you want to talk about, like some very keen scholar, like a creator, the artist of one's own life, we are going to fight against the warmongers, and in order to do that you are going to become one of them, "a hardliner", as the Americans say.'

Lilstein stares at his portion of tart but does not touch it.

'Are you getting the smell of vanilla and cinnamon? It's so faint as to be almost undetectable, it's absolutely essential not to be heavy-handed with these things, I promised you a story? No, I haven't forgotten, it's a story which means a great deal to me, it's the story of my mother, I need time. I've already told you that in 1945 the Soviets had put her in a very nice two-roomed flat in Moscow. A fierce militant, starting in 1916, she'd taken up the cause in the days of Zimmerwald and Kienthal, during the pacifist congresses which were staged while the Great War raged around them, women could circulate more easily than men, does that ring any bells? An ardent militant and a brilliant doctor, she knew a lot of people, she was widely respected, two rooms all to herself in Moscow in 1945 was quite something, when I was recalled to Moscow after my little trip to Kazakhstan, I was so pleased to see her again, she showed me round Moscow, then I started to get very busy.

'Moscow! I'd dreamed of it all through my youth, the future was already there, and I was made welcome, a few months of specialised training, then I was sent back to my own country, to my home town on the shores of the Baltic, I said goodbye to my mother and left for Rosmar, fog, dockside cranes, a handsome sea front and a quite superb brandy, finished your tea? Shall we order a small brandy apiece? No? The French don't really much care for brandy. Never been to Rosmar? One day I'll take you there and you can taste our brandy, *ein Kummel*, two salmon on the label, double distillation, forty-five degrees of pleasure and guile, flecks of gold in a flaxen robe, but no vulgar overtones.

Lilstein can wait no longer, he cuts a small piece of tart with his dessert fork, blows on it gently and consumes it slowly.

'It's still too hot, it doesn't burn the mouth but it's still too hot for you to get the full benefit of the aromas, when I was a boy, at Rosmar,

I was always too impatient to wait for the tart to cool sufficiently, I really must take you to Rosmar, we've rebuilt everything, excellent, sometimes I wonder how we did it because at the end of the war the only people still there were the halt, the hand-wringers and the thieves.

'Look, isn't that superb? the lattice on the tart, it gives the design added strength, it holds the jam, and it's not absolutely regular, that's important, you should never forget to have enough scraps of short pastry left over to make the lattice for the tart. The day I got back to Rosmar, a Russian general sent for me, in his office there were shelves, thousands of index cards, not all of them recent, he loved flicking through them himself, out of the window you looked down on the world, 1947, let battle commence, Rosmar!

'But let's not get carried away, I was pissing my pants as I stood before the general, those were days when it was more useful to have been an officer in the *Wehrmacht* than a communist in one of Hitler's camps, some memories are hard to live with, his office stank of orthodox pigsty, my Russian said "that lot need a boot up the arse!" His referring to the people of my home town as "that lot" presented me with a problem, if I also called them "that lot", what did that make me? Different? They were the ones who wanted to make me different, they would have even gassed me or similar if that's what it would have taken, the bastards. I wanted nothing to do with their difference nor with the Russian's difference, I was working with the breath of the dead blowing down my neck, "a boot up the arse", I was prepared to do that to the adults, I did it, you soon get sick of doing it, but the children? I wanted something new, "risen from the ruins and with face turned to the future", to rebuild with the children, and I even put one over on the general.'

Lilstein interrupts himself for a moment to look out of the window, a jackdaw, almost motionless, it is so near that you can make out the yellow of its eyes, it is flying into the wind, it pitches, rolls, adjusts its feathers to counteract the power of the rushing air.

'Childhood, young gentleman of France, does not interest you, not yet. Have you read Trakl, Georg Trakl? No? "Grodek", a war poem, written in 1914, captures the whole of the gangrene in a few lines, and at the end the poem becomes still and passes the baton to children against a background of golden leaves on a field of midnight black, the children who will be born and grow big, and Trakl dies and it's the war that grows big, our entire world was born in 1914, I was born in 1914.

'What did I put across the general? Don't you want me to tell you any more about my mother? Afraid you'll lose the thread? I'm very fond of digressions, still, too bad, I'm in Rosmar in 1947 with the general, I've reconstructed the adults and the kids I've turned into "Pioneers", quite delightful, the Internationale sung by corncrake voices along country lanes just before harvest-home, children returning with their little baskets full of poppies, a few wheat stalks, berries red and blue, and in town there were no more beggars on the streets.

'What? There weren't under Hitler either? That's not funny, I had no idea you'd sunk so low, you're being provocative, I'm not against it, and you wouldn't be wrong, factually, no more beggars, but I persist in believing that it wasn't the same, and so do you, of course. You know what the law was called that gave Hitler full powers to act, I know all about it, when the wonderful German elite went over wholesale to him, it was "the law for the elimination of poverty", how had this poverty come about? I'm getting back to the point, digression is my besetting sin, with my general in 1947 I digressed, I digressed for nights on end, I digressed with the aid of vodka and Kummel and one day I wrote a report, in it I said that the general was too fond of the army.'

Again Lilstein cuts a morsel of tart, raises it to his mouth, slowly, turning his dessert fork around to examine it, he tastes it, then sets about his portion in earnest. You do the same. The tart crumbles easily when bit, the shortcrust is firm in your mouth but also yielding, it breaks up and scatters amid the taste of apple and raspberry. Lilstein looks at you:

'You've tasted it before? Wasn't as good? You know, the secret of good shortcrust pastry is to take your time, don't go at it with too much vim, it must be left to prove for at least three hours, and you too, you must allow as long as it takes, I don't want you to get all tensed up, people who live in a state of anxiety make bad workmen, you must be the absolute master of your own rhythm, no emergency stations, that's what ruins the whole damn shoot, you really like this Linzer Torte? It's very delicate, hand movements precise but never vehement, the proprietor's wife does it without thinking, that's why she always succeeds.

'If you're heavy-handed your shortcrust goes rubbery, don't let the egg yolk be absorbed by the flour, it must first be beaten into the icing sugar, mix the flour and butter together lightly, ensuring that the flour is thoroughly coated in the butter to prevent it sticking, make a well in the middle for the egg yolks and add a mixture of sugar and vanilla, then you mix them together in the well with the tips of your fingers, lightly, like a cat's paw playing . . . Do you like Waltenberg, the French people I ask usually answer "The Swiss Alps! Ah, Thomas Mann, those were the days!" But do you know what else happened here, in 1929, the year you were born?

'The Waltenberg European Seminar? Great thinkers, philosophers, writers, politicians, industrialists, economists, beautiful women, a week on a tall mountain, great debates, seminars within the Seminar, economists at each other's throats over the question of value, fiercest were the ones who talked about hot cakes, they sickened me, value was not work but what they called marginal value, the price of bread when you're not hungry, and then there were the philosophers, a great philosophical tug-of-war between what bourgeois Europe had taken centuries to develop, the ideal of forms, the operation of rules, and, in the red corner opposite, a philosophy of Being, the notion of Being-in-the-World, which called for forms, rules and irony to be consigned to oblivion, while the participants stuffed themselves with chocolate creams, delicacies of the nouveaux riches, and tasteless, I personally have always been on the side of the Enlightenment.'

You can agree with Lilstein about the lure of the chocolate cream yet find it amusing that a communist should take up cudgels on behalf of the bourgeoisie of the Enlightenment, you might even smile a sceptical smile, but that doesn't stop Lilstein droning on about the Waltenberg European Seminar, Regel, Merken, Maynes, 1929, the fur that flew.

'Really? You never heard about it? But the French were there, there was a Madame de Valréas who financed the whole thing, gnarled hands, lips often dark red, violet eyes, very efficient, people said "the Waltenberg Seminar" or "the Valréas Conference", present also were Europe's lunatics, Wolkenhove, Van Ryssel of the steelworks, and Moncel, the great Christian metaphysician who is mad about theatre.

'He was young at the time, not as young as me, but a tyro, clenched, very reactionary, much more so than he is today, the philosophers asked one question, what was to be done about Kant's legacy ten years after the butchery in the trenches? "Dare to think", a small self-sufficient world of thinkers and writers, Hans Kappler, Édouard Palude, and politicians, Briand was there, it was the time of his "away with the cannon, away with the machine guns" and the United States of Europe, and scientists, wonderful lectures on the theory of relativity, the whole of Europe, the economists drew blood as they argued about the theory of value and their talk of hot cakes, in the end everything clashed, mingled, a whole world, along with the wives, the children, the mistresses, the catamites, they also knew how to have a good time, some went at it enthusiastically, and on occasions there were the imprints of knees in the snow.

'The coats of the women were fawn, grey, black, the hems, collars and cuffs trimmed with magnificent soft white fur, I found them very arousing, they wore small hats, and the men carried tomes bristling with bookmarks, between them in the space of a few days they redrew the intellectual map and reconfigured their wonderful Europe while they strolled, really major confrontations!

'And as usual behind the war of ideas lay questions of jobs, the presidencies of learned societies, arguments about finance and reputation, the sort of thing that drives the frailer brethren mad, and that's not reckoning with what was going on behind the scenes, in the streets of Germany, there was even one of the leading participants who had a manic outburst, a man who rushed into the hotel lounge shouting, "Infamy, infamy!" like something out of *King Lear*, there were also snowball fights, I was there with my brother, I was just sixteen, my brother had brought me, it was supposed to be good for my lungs, any excuse was enough for a snowball fight, I slipped, a woman was chasing me, she fell on top of me, I've been about a bit since then but I can still recall her breath on my neck, my brother was keen on the new philosophy, like many good people who "dared to think", not knowing that they were baring their throats for the dogs.'

Outside the window, the jackdaw was still visible and holding his own against the wind, suddenly he wheels on his right wing, rocks ands dives, Lilstein closes his eyes as he chews a mouthful of tart:

'She's put something else in it, she's changed the recipe today, what can you smell, over the raspberry, apple, butter, vanilla and cinnamon? Something else, try hard, trust yourself, say what's this on my tongue, ah yes, rum, a very good rum, you know what that back taste of rum means? No? What happened to the Russian general after I submitted my report? Are you really that fond of the army? Wouldn't you prefer to know the secret of the presence of rum in the Linzer, or a brief philosophical interlude or the story of my mother? The general first? Very well!

'The general disappeared, perhaps just as he walked round a bend in a corridor, they'll explain all that to you one day, the Russians sent another general, a hero of the Soviet Union, twice a hero of the Soviet Union, but this time he was the one nearly wetting his pants in my presence, he'd been at Stalingrad, panzers with hand grenades, he told me he would have attacked them with his bare hands if he'd had to, in the end the guy saw off the Reich's divisions, temperatures of twenty below, he faced me, a low-grade informer, and nearly wet himself, we became firm friends.'

Why is Lilstein saying all this? these are secrets and you shouldn't tell secrets unless you are about to trade them for other secrets, but

Lilstein has got into his stride, he says that after the business with the first general he hadn't felt any the better for it, to be perfectly honest, at the time he even considered taking French leave, as they say in England, some of his friends had managed to get away from Rosmar in '46.

'Once across the border, they stuck skull-caps on their heads and killed the language of the people who had killed them, they left, young gentleman of France, so that they might become strong once more, by moving rocks around for Ben Gurion, a new Sparta, they succeeded, nobody will ever make them disappear again, why didn't I leave? Because I can't stand the heat nor the Middle East, nor messianic missions, not messianic missions of any kind, you'll see, I've become very pragmatic, the Red Dawn, Promised Lands, that sort of thing is so mortiferous, personally I prefer fog, quiet brasseries, boring news-papers, waitresses with long legs, a world without God, and inter-nationalism, but above all I love my mother tongue, I am an internationalist infatuated with his mother tongue.'

Lilstein can't stand the Middle East but it's just like being in the Middle East, the talk will go on for hours touching on every subject but carpets, and it will categorically not be about money, in the window no more jackdaws are visible, lower down the mountain isolated chalets can be seen, you imagine another life: the stone sill at the door, at dusk a last cloud over the tree-line, and the hearth, all the resources of the mountain coming benignly together, the gurgle of a brook beneath the snow, a woman in a large woolly jumper, you need silence, Lilstein has caught your eye as it wanders towards the woman with red hair who is now unhurriedly busying herself in the room, he asks you if you think she's beautiful, yes, at first Lilstein also wanted to kill the language of the people who had killed him, he stayed in Germany but he never spoke German except to give orders:

'I used to joke in Russian, you have to!'

And as a precaution, Lilstein pretended to have forgotten his French and English, whereas he knows kilometres of poems in several languages, that means he can drive a thousand kilometres reciting poems non-stop or as good as, Shakespeare, Valéry, Baudelaire, Donne, Mandelstam, in particular he knows reams of Goethe, Heine, Rilke and Apollinaire, he'd almost killed all that off too, and then one day a book came his way which he had to read for professional reasons.

'Some bastard bourgeois scribbler! Listen, this too I know by heart, "German will remain the language of my mind, because I am a Jew, I intend to hold on to all that's left within me of a devastated country" that's good . . . "the fate of its sons is also my fate but I bring an additional legacy", that is generous, it's humanist! "I bring!" Now mark well the end: "I want to help the world to feel grateful to them for something", a double distillation, the catch in the back of the throat, if I were a great, strong Aryan, nothing would make me feel more humiliated than that sort of irony.'

So Lilstein decided he would stay, that he would help, he stayed with them, that is, he stayed at home.

At the time he read that forbidden author in bed at night, he would lie on one side with, against his back, a beautiful woman.

'It's wonderful, young comrade, no, too irritating, I can't go on saying comrade, you're about to leave the Party, it's wonderful to read a good book and feel against your back the breasts and legs of a woman who holds you close, her face was sweet and there were the rings of pleasure under her eyes, I did all I could to protect her, she loved me, she whispered in my ear that I took her to unbelievable depths.

'We liked walking along the beach, she denounced me in 1951, just then it wasn't a very good idea to be called Lilstein or Meyer, I could stroke her breasts for hours on end, I brought her bunches of irises, and she denounced me, or rather she signed a paper in which she said that I had said this and that and so on.

'In the Nazi camps I'd seen comrades die who could have obtained a stay of execution by denouncing me, and lo! my very first real woman managed to betray me! Unbelievable depths indeed!

'They hadn't even threatened her, they'd asked her questions, they'd dictated her replies, courtroom, men in uniforms, she was a good German citizen, she signed, I discovered everything together, love, *Realpolitik*, and vaginal follies, to me there are only follies, she denounced me, funny isn't it? I shed hot tears, but I had done some denouncing too, a general in the Red Army, but I wasn't sleeping with him at unbelievable depths, and the man who later asked me over and over to denounce myself while he kept turning the endless screw could easily have been one of the group who liberated me from Auschwitz where I hadn't been denounced, I really thought my number was up, do you know how people died in those times?

'Pneumonia, obviously, but you also got killed, young gentleman of France, from behind, as you walked along a corridor, never attempt to turn round, otherwise the bullet will shatter the bones in your face and then you can't be made presentable for the coffin, everyone wants to be present at their own death and they mess it up, you understand, the time I felt most scared was when I was in the corridor, I only breathed again when I got to the interrogation room, you have to do it, what saved me was the death of the Big Man with the moustache which also happened just in time to save the lives of his Jewish doctors from a walk down the corridor, I was much less frightened than they were, I soon realised that for reasons I couldn't understand they weren't going to kill me, they sent me to a camp, then the death of the Big Man with the moustache meant that I was released from one of those camps no one talks about.'

Sure, Lilstein saw the girl again, not very long ago, she came to see him in his big office in Berlin.

'I didn't feel I had anything to forgive her for, I said it wasn't anything to do with her, the investigation had been fixed from the start, and it's always better to be denounced by someone who knows you, there are fewer inconsistencies in the record, and therefore fewer beatings. It is a sweet feeling, having an ex-lover there in front of you torn between fear and remorse, it's a moment you've dreamed of a thousand times and when it happens you sit there and look, ten years on, the woman has not changed much, she is beautiful, deep breaths make her breasts rise, your hands remember her breasts, it's a very delicious position to be in, but you tell yourself you could have done without the circumstances which have brought it about, and that makes you change your mind as you watch the woman with such feeling.

'Are you absolutely sure you wouldn't care for a spot of philosophy, young man? I mean to say: Waltenberg! The famous Seminar, the intelligentsia of Europe reading the last rites over *Aufklärung*, such a rich word, and in its place proclaiming that we must inhabit the world poetically, go back to the earth, to the *Urwald*, to the great forest of Authentic Being, while the brownshirts were beginning to occupy the hearts of cities! The earth which does not lie, the forest tall with trees! Still, it was bound to get out, that in the end the tall trees always march in step with the warriors, across the earth that never lies. I was young, the people I loved called me young Lilstein, I liked that, I was sixteen in 1929, I had an older brother who was a philosopher and wanted me to understand it all, very taken he was with the new thought, that is the philosophy of Being, away with your concepts and your Enlightenment! In 1934, the Nazis grabbed him by the hair and beat his head against a kerbstone.

'Ten times or so, that was enough, "*erst wenn sie steht, die Uhr . . . it's only when the clock stops, im Pendelschlag des hin und her . . . between the swings of its pendulum, hörst Du, that you hear*", the clock's a lovely touch! "*sie geht, und ging und geht nicht mehr . . . that it's going, was going, has stopped going*", never heard that before? It was said by Merken, the great philosopher of Being, the *victor* of Waltenberg, a poem he dedicated after the war to his friend René Char, one of the very few genuine writers in the Resistance, Malraux of course was another, weapons at the ready, yes, Malraux was a bit later but he knew what strong links were, knew the best moment to forge strong links, you know, I always had a liking for Malraux, from time to time I discuss him with Hatzfeld, with old friends. Anyway, Merken dedicated these lines to his *friend* Char, a swing of the pendulum.

'Merken and Char, there's a magnificent photo, the two men walking along a forest path, taken from the back, they're walking side by side, Merken is short, Char is big and beefy, it's very moving, you really don't want to hear the rest? No philosophy? No poetry? My surprise when I saw the photo of these two men together, knowing what had happened to Merken after the Nazis took over? Later perhaps?

'Well shall we talk about the woman who brought all that splendid company together here at the Waldhaus? Madame de Valréas, French, an aristocrat, early forties, with a quite splendid derrière, you know, "the royal rear-guard when amorous battle is joined", no? You're so good at saying no, fair enough, I'm not here to put any sort of temptation in your way, not even Madame de Valréas's derrière which has changed significantly since those days, with or without the help of Verlaine, stick to serious matters, won't you try a glass of white wine with it? sure? Not even the story of my mother? Later?

'And you really wish to part company with your idealism? You don't care for my two-soul scheme? Turns your stomach? I can understand that, all those dead workers, that's right, workers, we're not going to start telling each other in full view of the Rikshorn that the Americans parachuted a hundred thousand imperialists into Budapest in one night, let's leave all that to the virgins, the eunuchs and our popular democratic press.'

A provocateur, Lilstein is just a provocateur, but where does he come from? an East German who can pass for Swiss when he wants to, but talks like this, does he believe what he says? He pretends to when he's talking but surely he can't believe it, and yet it sounds so right when he says it, is a German capable of telling a lie without believing it? But what else does he believe if he believes what he's been saying since we've been sitting here? In the omelette, in the broken eggs it is made of? Is Lilstein just a plain cop? But why should anyone be sending you to see a cop? Because in Paris you told two or three close friends that some Hungarian demonstrators were true socialists? And that not everything was false in Khrushchev's report? Or alternatively, is Lilstein a traitor? In which case Roland Hatzfeld has sent you to see a traitor, a traitor who is using his cover as a cop to say what he really thinks of the regime?

Or a cop who has stayed a cop but who is at least for once getting whatever is bothering him off his chest by playing the role of traitor they've told him to play? You can't get your head around any of this, you don't know if you should nod agreement at what Lilstein is saying, you rest your chin on your thumb with index and middle fingers aslant your mouth, you mutter sounds which might pass for assent or be taken as indications that you are paying attention, but from time to time you take your hand away from your cheek.

When you do this you uncover your mouth which is half open, a sign of denial, then you revert to your pose as Lilstein's docile audience, you're on your best behaviour, nor do you allow yourself to bite off bits of skin around your fingernails, sometimes you press your index finger into your cheek and hold it from the inside between your teeth, picking gently at the skin, taking care not to draw blood, Lilstein could also be a real traitor to the Party, a traitor in the pay of the English, so were you sent to see him by mistake or was it to cook a Frenchman's goose? A British Intelligence Service ploy? And why does the idea of being with an enemy of the Party you are intent on quitting make you feel sick to the stomach? No, Lilstein is a politician, a peevish communist but a real communist for all that, so why did you agree to come here to meet him if you are so keen to leave the Party?

'And so, young gentleman of France, the Red Army has just killed workers, including women workers, who were members of the Hungarian Communist Party, fact, it also killed fascists who were killing communists, not many fascists, they got out fast to Austria and Germany before the tanks came back into the city, it was the working-class suburbs which held out longest, all of which raises some very awkward questions for you, and because you have also read extracts from a "report attributed to comrade Khrushchev" in the bourgeois press, you are now thinking of resigning from the Party, of turning your card in, as they say.

'Why? to restore your innocence? to make yourself believe again?

Your father would be overjoyed, don't get angry, don't get up, spare me the dramatic gestures, I never found it very helpful being the son of a heroine of the resistance and I suspect it can't be easy to have a father who was a Pétainist and a collaborator, that may put me ahead morally but at least your father is still alive, stripped of his French nationality but alive, he plays boules in Barcelona, he's good at it, he lives in the Barrio Chino, am I correct? odd sort of exile for an ex-Vichy stalwart, in Franco's Spain yes, but in a red-light area of town, Work, Family, *Pimmel.*

'*Pimmel?* In German it means willy, all right, I didn't want to be coarse, I apologise, but don't be so combustible, sit down, my mother fought against Trotsky, she fought against him but she'd known him, the Party gave her a splendid funeral, in the photos there was not a single person of her generation left, I thanked the Party, our fragile organisations need grateful, gullible followers, who live longer, does it make you wince to be told all this? Learn to take life easier, I've been around, been around too much, seen too much History, you want some of mine? Leave the Party? The Party doesn't give a shit! There are hundreds, thousands of people ready to worship at the feet of the idol believing that they are thinking dialectically, but if you still have any ideas and ideals left, and if you want to fight for them, you're going to have to learn to stop being the kid who answers back.'

Lilstein looks at you, you hold his gaze and tell yourself that the Waldhaus is a trap, they can denounce you now whenever they want to, in Paris Hatzfeld said this trip would be like the journey to Zimmerwald, in 1917, in the middle of the war, when French pacifists travelled to meet their German and Russian comrades, but Lilstein is no pacifist, he's a stirrer, you look towards the dining room, empty, you look out at the Rikshorn, at Waltenberg down the mountainside, a small drowsy village, the boules, they know everything, what is your role in the drama, what audience are you performing to? the son of a French collaborator who is plotting in Switzerland with someone big in the Stasi? or the member of the editorial board of *La Nouvelle Pensée* who is having talks with a double agent of the Intelligence Service, less than a month after having discussions with a deputy member of the Politburo of the French Communist Party? Which newspaper, and on which side, will run the story first?

All you can do now is hand back your card, Lilstein has just one more thing to ask you, a small thing, and then he will let you depart in peace:

'Why did you join the Party which you now seem so anxious to leave? Didn't you know that the Party had done some terrible things long before this latest business in Budapest? In Berlin, not that long ago? In 1936, the show trials? And the "kulaks taken as a class", were they just a handful of parasites in evening dress as portrayed in some Eisenstein film? Or Cronstadt, a workers' council, like the one in Budapest, but you must know what the Soviets have always made of workers' councils, and the *Lumpen*, there are various books about it, are you an intellectual or a grand Lady Bountiful from some charitable organisation? Do you know by what means, as recently as three years ago, convicted persons were still leaving Moscow for camps – yes, camps – which don't exist, so it's hardly surprising that people find it so difficult to come back from them? In bogus refrigerated trucks, there were so many of them roaring through the streets that French journalists wrote glowingly of the abundant supply of butcher's meat! Fairy stories, the lot of it, one day we'll come back to them.'

Lilstein's eyes look larger now than they did a little while ago, his face less pink, the cheekbones more pronounced, you see more clearly the two inwardly curving lines running down from each nostril to the sides of his mouth, they are the lines that come to people who laugh, who consistently use their faces and expressions as pawns in the conversation, the better to impose on the person they're talking to.

A metre behind Lilstein, in the tall dresser, is a collection of decorated plates, mountains, lakes, goose-girls, old châteaux, group scenes, the late evening light floods through the window and warms the porcelain and the colours which decades of washing have turned pinkish, greenish, pastel-ish.

In the middle of the collection, two rectangular dishes, much bigger than the plates. The one on the left shows women emerging from a house and walking into the foreground in a swirl of snowflakes, severally carrying a lantern, distaff and gun, while in the background a group of men linger by the door holding straps and halters, it is the end of one of those country gatherings at which people would congregate around a ceramic stove and tell stories about the Devil, the lady of the lake or grapes, when the buds swell on the nodes of vine-shoots ravaged by the secateurs, everyone listened, the girls spun and wove their wedding trousseaus, the boys greased the horses' harness with goose-fat, Lilstein is calmer now, he resumes in a steady voice:

'At least your father is alive, and you're not obliged to smile nicely for his murderers.'

Lilstein is going to speak to you at some length, he will mix confidences, philosophy, crude words, the edge of tears, the thoughts of Bukharin, best of the Bolsheviks, the only one capable of coming up with ideas other than the knout and watchtowers, Schubert's *Lieder*, ah, you like them too, Fischer-Diskau, yes, but there's also Hans Hotter, it's an English company that distributes the recordings, the state of workers' pay, more Bukharin, the songs of Yves Montand, I particularly like the early Montand despite his legato, Schubert, I must get you to listen to the *Winter Journey* sung by a woman, rather unusual and quite magnificent, the death of Beria or rather the seven deaths of Beria, at least seven, in the Bolshoi they're performing *The Decembrists* by Yuri Shaporin, it's 27 June 1953, all the Party chiefs are there, *Pravda* prints all the names except Beria's, the approach road to the Bolshoi is closed off by tanks for the limousine bringing the comrade first deputy Prime Minister of the USSR and the Minister for State Security, he is shot in the prison of Lefortovo the same evening, the first of his seven deaths.

The second is Khrushchev saying 'One day Beria came to a meeting without a bodyguard and I killed him', Beria is the most interesting character of that generation, you shall hear all about him, young gentleman of France, Beria as a skirt-chaser, the guy has a reputation for having women brought forcibly in from the street and raping them in his office, over his desk, Bluebeard. When I was in prison I heard some hair-raising stories about him, a very complicated death.

Then there's the version by Sergo Beria, his son, 'my father was killed in his house' on 26 June.

Lilstein continues to jumble everything up, he drops the deaths of Beria, before he's done he'll tell you about the others, they're even more lurid, he switches to the atomic threat, comes back to his mother, Berlin, January 1919, she stumbled across the corpse of Rosa Luxemburg, he reverts to the atomic threat, back to Clara Zetkin, then something new, the colonial wars, Schubert's *Lieder* and his *Winter Journey*, I know a woman who used to sing it, marvellous, the story of the hunter and the bear, Beria's frolickings, his wife saying he had mistresses but not all that many, wouldn't have had the time, I must make time to tell you the story of the bear and the hunter, young gentleman of France, Picasso's paintings, I'm a noted expert on *Guernica*, the horse which turns round is fascinating, a whole story complete in itself, have you read the articles Blunt wrote about it, Anthony Blunt?

Lilstein raises his glass and begins to talk about a wide beach on the Baltic, you must be able to trust people with secrets, his life had begun again on a beach, everything had begun on a beach, it was 1948, he'd only just met the young woman, and when I think she denounced me!

He couldn't say now which of them had suggested the stroll along the shore, the sand and the sea, the desert that was the sea, the spume, the salt, the smell of seaweed, the cry of albatross and petrel, a small, low-roofed house loaned for their picnic, they'd walked for hours, defying the cold wind blowing in off the sea, walked without speaking, the wind stripped them of words, of any desire to speak, losing all sensation except that of a body walking into the wind, a body reduced to the sum of its movements and tears brought on by the cold and the brutal light, confronting spume and wind, walking over sand littered with mussels, sea-shells, seaweed, trident shapes left by the feet of curlews and gulls, seeking out the solid sand at the sea's edge to walk on as fast as they could to keep warm, they walked to where the sand is already sufficiently loaded with water to be firmer but not yet so saturated that shoes sink into it, just before the line where the wave dies, when its foam is simply froth and seems to be no longer liquid, when it is no more than a fringe of expiring bubbles at the extreme edge of all that water which continues to endure in its seething and rasping surges.

An immense beach, Lilstein tried to position himself so that he sheltered his companion but he was puny, made hardly any difference, even by walking backwards in front of her, he was buffeted by squalls and it was the young woman who, with a laugh, was first to set herself against the wind from the sea, at an angle, she swapped places, to protect him, saying, shouting into the wind, that she could stand up to the wind better than he could and as they changed places they grabbed each other by the shoulders, from time to time they passed little old men who were gathering firewood to warm themselves by, watching this floating plank or that end of a beam which in its own good time the sea would fling on to the beach, but it was that or nothing, sometimes there was more than one old man following the same piece of wreckage, they eyed each other warily and seemed relieved that Lilstein and the young woman did not represent youthful competition, and looked at them the way you'd expect them to look at people who did not need to rescue driftwood from the waves of the sea.

Lilstein and the young woman waved greetings, but did not stop to talk, bowled along by the expenditure of their combined energies, keeping in step, walking fast to keep warm, fighting sand and wind and the fierce flurries of stinging air which are on permanent duty for kilometre after kilometre under a storm-racked sky, lashed by gusts of wind which threatened to whip the hoods off their oilskins at any moment, forcing them to clap a frozen hand on the crown of their heads to prevent it, if they wanted to see around them they had to turn their shoulders or else partly swivel their heads inside their hoods, the wind was relentless, it blew at an angle, it swirled, always adversarial, finding a way in everywhere, laying its metal grip on everything, blasting, chilling, rending.

Yet for all that, their sweetness continued to seek the object of its desire, the cold wind denied it each time they exchanged a glance, forcing their heads down, making them bury their chins in their shoulders at an angle, the sweetness forced to retreat into eyes that looked out from lowered heads, sweetness suspended by the pummelling which left nothing in their thoughts except the wind, left them with no feeling but weariness, lungs raw, a kind of frozen-fingered intoxication, tears cold and salty, with nothing else for it but to go on walking, and when they returned in the middle of the afternoon to the white and blue room of the low-roofed house, once they were sheltered behind the closed door, they went on staggering for several moments from the fading effects of the wind.

What's to be done with Lilstein in this mood who insists on telling you about Picasso, *Guernica*, *Winter Journey*, and regales you with the promises he once made on a beach? You don't have a woman in Paris, at least not one sufficiently interesting for you to do the same and turn her into a story, you're going to have to find something else to tell, but for the moment Lilstein goes on talking, like a man who has decided to tell all, with no thought for prudence, and you are turning into the one who listens to his secret outpourings, who'll have to denounce Lilstein and Hatzfeld, to officials of the Party you are bent on leaving? Or to the Ministry of Internal Security?

'The girl I walked with on the beach, young gentleman of France, denounced me, it's funny, I can't stand the thought that I was denounced and you cannot stand the thought of having denounced, yes, the charges you made were solid, I mean the ones you brought four years ago against the comrades in your cell, you remember, communists who met unofficially, there were seven or eight of them, and held endless discussions of books by Rousset and Kravchenko, and the "alleged Soviet camps", and the Slansky trial and Tito and how to make the Party democratic? You got them thrown out of the Party by quoting Stalin and Thorez and lumping together Tito, Trotsky, Kravchenko, Slansky, the English, the police, Zionism, sorry, make that cosmopolitanism! Actually, a little too good to be true, if you will permit me a professional comment, which is why today you feel that what you did was squalid but that all you really did was cover up other things that were even more squalid, it must feel odd now to think of those you got excluded from the Party when at long last you know as much as they, Poletti, Warschawski, did.

'What about the Monclars? did you ever see Monclar's widow again? Nowadays you think like her, but the result of the charges you brought is that she's a widow, did you really need to be so thorough? Did you have to say that there was no proof that her husband did not have any contact with the Germans during the war? No proof *that he did not have*! That's good, very good, you could have kept a low profile, settled for saying that, objectively speaking, they were playing the same game as the Bonn revanchists, but you decided to add a clinching argument, to add that one basic issue was worth considering, the possibility that there'd been some contact between Monclar and the Germans in 1943 when a part of the network was blown, and by raising that question you made Monclar terminally suspect, tarred him with a suspicion "which unfortunately his current attempts to sabotage Party policy could only corroborate", this was tantamount to telling him you disapproved of the Party line in 1952, ergo you "very probably" did a deal with the Gestapo in 1943, and since we are now fighting a war we cannot afford the luxury of doubt.

'Obviously you didn't work all that out by yourself, you'd had evening classes which taught you that it's good to corroborate, did you know they used the same line with me too in Moscow when I was being interrogated? Monclar tells you you're a little shit, the comrade from the federation who just happens to be there that night says losing your temper does not constitute proof of innocence, good old Monclar, a perfectionist, he's excluded, no, you're right, he excludes himself, slams the door behind him, it makes him thoroughly miserable, and to make sure he doesn't miss he gets hold of two revolvers, one for each temple, he fumbles, manages to burst both eyeballs, not a pretty sight, hang on, I must finish.

'A week later he throws himself out of a window in the hospital, three floors, took four days to die, died like Brossolette but with

Brossolette it was the Nazis and different kinds of torture, have you written to Monclar's widow, I mean recently?

'One of my closest friends was in Monclar's network, a German antifascist with the FTP, today he's one of our leading poets, lives in Potsdam not far from my house, a real poet, he was the one who told me the story of the bear and the hunter, though maybe it wasn't him, no matter, sometimes we pass on secrets to each other, for the hell of it, not knowing if one of us will rat on the other, but we tell each other everything, that way the one who listens is just as guilty as the one who speaks, and if he does spill the beans he won't last very long either – "comrade, if your contact wanted to say such stupid things, how come he trusted you so much?" – he's for the drop too, which might even be a comfort for the friend he's denounced, absolute transparency! Are you beginning to understand what sort of struggle I've got to engage in these days?

'When I told my friend I might be meeting the Frenchman who had got Monclar thrown out of the Party, he said: "Ask him what he's got against people who were in the Resistance." There, I've done it. You think you're a real swine, you want to leave the Party which landed you in the mire and now you're going back to the nasty, sordid squalor you were trying to escape when you joined the Party, it would be so simple to have one squalid action to hate yourself for, such as what a young prosecuting counsel in a hurry once did, but we both know that there's something else, and that's why I've taken such a shine to you.'

Lilstein follows the direction of your eyes, turns round, stares at the dresser with you, a complete service of painted porcelain plates.

'Yes, very fine, especially the large dishes, the spinners, the country dance, I had it brought here, it isn't Swiss, don't you recognise it? It comes from your part of the world, it's French, Obernai-ware, from Alsace, the couple who run the factory are of Alsatian stock, they were already here in 1929, he was on the desk and she was housekeeper, a stroke of fortune for the pair of them, they both loved France but he didn't like being taught French by having his knuckles rapped.

'In 1927, '28, they applied for a seasonal job, they liked it, they went down well, they were kept on, when they saw Hitler beginning to stir things up in Germany, they concluded that sooner or later he'd try to move back into Alsace, so they decided to stay in Switzerland, they escaped the return of the Germans in 1940, moved up the ladder, bought the hotel in '43, bad times for tourism. She loves presiding over the kitchen range, she can make anything, especially Linzer, these decorated plates with country scenes, they're very peaceful, I like them a lot.'

Lilstein turns round in his chair to show you the plates:

'Can you see, there are eight different scenes for the plates, two per season, it's rustic stuff, not very valuable, but I'm very fond of it, some of the details, let me show you, that cat in a clump of honeysuckle, it didn't go there to take a nap, the cat creeps into the honeysuckle in the late afternoon, it lies down on its back on top of the clump just under the surface of the leaves, empty-headed blue tits beware!

'Throughout the whole of your time in school, in 1943 you were fourteen, when half of the Monclar network were rounded up, there was no chance that you'd meet him or admire him, you lived the life of a cosseted schoolboy in a gorgeous apartment in Paris, large rooms, very high ceilings, cornices, gold paint, ornate chimneypieces, an apartment your papa had bought for a song after the armistice in 1940, from a man named Blumental, Blumental was a man in a hurry! In the apartment sounds were deadened by carpets and bulging cupboards, a china service with a silver thread motif off which you ate your dinner, bed linen with Blumental's monogram, and even his children's books, did you ever try to find out what happened to the Blumentals? Shall I take you through it and help you recapture lost time?

'You suspected as much? Towards the end? There must be some details you don't know, a valley in Savoie, white walls, lauze roof, a well, a few motorised vans one morning and your father feeling obliged to exclaim "just smell that air!", it's not easy to become aware of life at such moments, there too you must have hated yourself and held your tongue, because you were brought up according to solid family values, respect for your father, reserve, the authority of your elders, it's not for you to judge them, and if the worst comes to the worst you take troubles to the priest who tells you to lift up your head to heaven, no, quite right, you're a Protestant, but you must have loved those values before you learned to hate them, and you once believed you could put it all behind you by basking in the crimson promise of our dawn, by throwing yourself enthusiastically at the age of eighteen into the ranks of the seventy-five thousand who had been shot dead, let's just say thousands, many thousands, and one day you discover that the Party you loved has put your best hopes to the worst possible use.

'Be content, you can now feel truly sorry for yourself, it will make a change from just despising yourself, but all those others, the gentle-folk of the old caste with the best addresses who foregathered around the family table, their words still reverberate in your head, the din-ners with Blumental finger-bowls, conversations about Judaeo-Bolshevism, saboteurs, the Greater Europe and the deafening silence of all these loud-mouthed people when your father had to flee the country after the Liberation, the silence of those who thought and said the same things as he did but never wrote it down or signed anything, the crimes of extreme civilisation are not crimes, these days all those people strut their stuff as good soldiers of the free world.

'The Great Family awaits your return, young gentleman of France, a place has been prepared, in your name, you now have extensive experience of the world of the proletariat, so you can explain to them how it operates, how to sack a worker without repercussions, I could even saddle the said worker with five kids, that's another so-called cliché, only society at large can manufacture clichés, but you know all this, you know what ends you will be made to serve.

'And when you look in the mirror, you now have two unpleasant faces to contemplate: Narcissus and his papa, Monclar's prosecutor and Pétain's minister. Please remain seated, you want me to reassure you? You're not the only one, and there's worse to come.'

And finally Lilstein gets round to speaking of the death of comrade Sarah Lilstein, Doctor Lilstein, 'a great figure in the international workers' movement', died of pneumonia, Moscow, 1946, pneumonia, a side-effect of Auschwitz, is Lilstein really speaking of his mother or of one of his own victims? Not long ago in Moscow, some well-intentioned soul passed Lilstein a manuscript, the notes the doctor took at his mother's bedside just before her death, it was an odd gift.

At first, Lilstein had had his doubts, just around the time that he'd also had doubts after learning of the report on Stalin's crimes attributed to comrade Khrushchev, there certainly were errors, with him as victim, not Stalin, the same blunders as you get in a war, a class war, but it wasn't Stalin who fouled up, it was his underlings, Michael Lilstein was summoned to Moscow, he was received at the highest level, so you're finding it hard to believe Khrushchev's report, Misha? You've been through the mill yet you see yourself as an unfortunate exception, an intelligence worker caught up in a regrettable shambles, the stool, the endless screw and the camp, all because of the fall-out from some stupid botch-up, and Iosif Vissarionovich wasn't in the know, nothing from which to draw sound conclusions, or better still, you sacrificed yourself after convincing yourself that it all served some useful purpose.

And while everything was collapsing around your ears, the others, taking their lead from the role of villain which you agreed to play, became more aware, harder-working, more disciplined, and were freer to be so, and you refuse to believe it when a report says you passed on the names of innocent people, because you did actually pass on names at the time, and you'd have talked so that the terror could go on in its mindless way, it was like giving a razor to a chimpanzee, you were willing to endure the worst in order to save the best, comrade Lilstein, and I don't want anybody telling you that all you did was to help a chimpanzee play with a razor.

My dear Michael, you don't believe wholeheartedly in Nikita Khrushchev's report, so you won't believe in the other report either, unless that report makes you want to reread the Khrushchev report.

And Lilstein was given an unedited copy of the report attributed to Khrushchev and then the notes written by his mother's doctor, we've always trusted you, we've taken a lot of risks on your behalf, Michael, a great many risks, when we decided to send you off in short order to the steppes in the east so that you wouldn't have to face the sorting of the sheep from the goats after Auschwitz was liberated, don't you remember the looks on the faces of some of your comrades when the Red Army pulled you out of the camps in Poland? The way they said see you soon? No, you thought you had nothing to fear, at the time it was a bit obvious keeping you well away from the screening process, true you'd acquitted yourself magnificently in the camps, there was no better organiser than you, and at the same time you had one thing going for you, you weren't popular, that is a valuable quality the way things are these days, a few months in Kazakhstan, the sorting of wheat and chaff became less urgent, a short spell in Moscow so we could have a closer look at you, and we quickly sent you home to Rosmar, that was just ten short years ago.

You did well at Rosmar, Misha, that general was a fool, but he gave you an opportunity to prove yourself, and then we redirected you towards the external intelligence service, that's what saved you, we needed you, we needed your pre-war contacts, it was urgent, an invaluable source, but you were also dynamite, you'd committed a mortal sin, at a meeting at the start of the 1930s you'd seen your comrade Ulbricht sitting on a platform with Goebbels, it was in the great hall of the Friedrichshain, now that should have got you sorted for good but you were lucky, you were closely acquainted with certain people whom we needed, you had a great big American secret within arm's reach.

You showed you had what it takes, the men at the top were very pleased, you could have blown up in our faces but you really did us proud, it lasted five very good years, we showed the Americans and the English a thing or two, in 1951 it was your other mortal sin which unleashed the dogs, couldn't you have phoned Adenauer or Bahr? or Bezukhov? no your name is Lilstein, that's bad, you had that bastard Abakumov snapping at your heels, even Beria was scared, he might have come to your defence, he could have gone to see the Big Man with the moustache and said this comrade is not a cosmopolitan snake in the grass and I still need him.

Beria didn't dare, all we could do was take some of the heat out of the situation, have you interrogated on the stool, keep your record out of it, even so at Magadan things got out of hand, and even when Stalin died and you were released and returned to your responsibilities, you had to pledge your enthusiastic support for Beria, it wasn't the right time, a neutral reunified Germany, a fine idea, but the timing was all wrong, but once again we saved our deposit, we told Malenkov and Ulbricht that you were our source of information about the trouble-makers, you spent your time making moves you shouldn't have made, a real gift for the inappropriate move, we took many risks for you: crawl out of the sandpit, Misha, you've got to play with the big boys now.

Lilstein thanked his Soviet comrades who said they'd taken risks so that he would be spared the worst, maybe it wasn't true, maybe nobody had been taking risks, maybe it was just a by-product of the bureaucracy, and at the time Lilstein had definitely had the feeling that he was being kept out of the limelight, that someone, perhaps the same someone who had pushed him into a car one morning with a blindfold over his eyes, was trying to spare him the worst by toning the treatment down, but after eighteen months in the camp he'd also felt that he was no longer being protected, he was sent out to do harder and harder labour, the sort you come back from feeling weaker and weaker, he saw those around him die more frequently, the comrades who said they'd always taken risks had been unable to take any more, if, that is, they'd ever taken any, but you could always pretend to believe the comrades when those who claimed to have taken risks seemed also to have taken over power, there had to be a side to be on, so some spring-cleaning is called for, open the windows, we've always trusted you, Michael, so here, read the notes your mother's doctor ran risks to take instead of letting the grave swallow the errors.

One morning, the doctor saw, drawing up outside the clinic reserved for high-ranking Party officials, the kind of car which normally brought only his most prestigious patients, just one army officer got out, silver-blue uniform, as worn by Kremlin guards, a colonel's uniform, a life or death rank, not the sort of man you'd want to meet so early in the day, but the doctor had felt relieved that it was that day and not another because he would be able to tell the colonel that he was going to save comrade Sarah Lilstein using drugs salvaged from the imperialists, he was very hopeful of saving her, a modicum of technical expertise borrowed from the West but also a sizeable input of Soviet know-how guided by the directives of the great Stalin.

The officer said that given the alarming nature of comrade Lilstein's state of health, comrade Stalin had instructed comrade Ivanov to prepare a speech to honour comrade Lilstein at her funeral and that he had come to make certain arrangements in connection with the ceremony, the doctor said that fortunately there would now be no need for any such arrangement and the colonel repeated that comrade Stalin had instructed comrade Ivanov to write the funeral oration.

The colonel had not understood what the doctor was saying, so the doctor repeated that he could, indeed was going to, save comrade Lilstein's life, he spoke with a cheerfulness intended to carry the colonel along on the tide of his enthusiasm.

And once more the colonel talked about Ivanov and the speech, and the doctor heard his guts rumble, he clenched his buttocks, and then contracted the muscles to prevent having an accident more befitting a toddler, and with the contraction and the cramps in his intestines came understanding, and with understanding his voice began to tremble at the moment when, for the third time, he was about to inform the colonel who seemed so hard of hearing that comrade Ivanov's oration would not be needed, his voice shook, his jaw trembled, the words made no sense, panic spread to his airways, lips, the rest of him, he said nothing.

He did not give her penicillin and he felt so bad about this that he kept as close an eye on her as if she'd been his own mother, he took notes of what she said when she grew feverish, a kind of shorthand record of her delirium, because he was meticulous, out of medical scrupulousness, a good reason, they were notes taken with a view to a 'Nosography of a Fever-Induced Delirium', and all the while he was taking his notes he experienced a terror even more intense than that which had made him feel like a private on latrine fatigue reporting to the colonel of the guard.

But a second visitation by terror did not stop him taking dangerous notes, this second terror had been forced to admit defeat for, unlike the first which had only morality to overcome, the second had found itself up against remorse which is, in regimes which require strict observance, the only means of achieving dignity.

And his notes had been found by *them*, some of *them* made it their business to ensure that the good doctor disappeared, but another group of *them* had arranged for the notes to be completed, in secret.

From the time she felt sure she was going to die, and this was in the month of March 1946, comrade Sarah Lilstein began to babble, it was, noted the doctor, as if she'd understood everything, the toing and froing in the corridor, the decision that penicillin was contra-indicated, the substitution of her nurses by others, it was as if she'd felt relieved by such signs of her imminent demise and had deliberately used her fevered state to let her thoughts run wild, so that she could say whatever she liked behind her ravings, think freely under the cover of the rambling state of mind they'd induced in her, think without being afraid of seeing death loom up before her, because death was there with her already, let her mind ramble without being afraid that friends and loved ones would be accused of plotting, since the proof of a rambling mind is in the excess of its rambling, in the things no healthy person would dream of saying.

Above all you had to avoid doing anything that might moderate the incoherence of your ramblings, in fact this would only prove that your mind was not wandering, so if your mind was really wandering you had no choice but to tell all and hold nothing back, so if you said you'd like to cut great Stalin's balls off with Lev Davidovich

Bronstein's rusty scissors you ran fewer risks than if you didn't dare go that far and made do, for example, with saying that the great leader had fucked up more than once on the agricultural policy front.

So Sarah Lilstein began to babble her way towards the worst things that could be said, she went on believing she could think under the cover of her ravings, keep control of her divagations, rave with the lucidity of the very drunk, and while she raved be both the Fool who raves and Shakespeare who makes him wise, Ariadne and the labyrinth, the egregious labyrinth, the eddy and the thing that thinks in the eddy, the eddy which scourges and dilutes everything in its wake, its history and its present, Sarah delving deep into her reserves, in the throbbing of her temples with a temperature of forty and eight tenths, and the fever entered into the very heart of her, took the place of the thought she believed she could control – and so, what she was trying to leave behind her to give a meaning to those fevered moments, now lost all meaning just when she was trying to find one, her ramblings were no longer a mask for her thoughts but the shape of the life she had led: her fevered outpourings were History itself.

Just a few images remained, the only ones that seemed still to have a meaning, a young woman in tears at the funeral of Rosa Luxemburg, then the young woman found herself in the clinic on the outskirts of Moscow and there unleashed a volley of curses even before she turned herself back into an old, dying woman Yezhov little shit Jdanov arsehole let Yezhov cut Stalin's head off and then into the blood pumping out, into the blood pumping out at the base of his throat, let him cast the whole decapitated world, a serpent-world, the poster that had so enraged her before the war showing homeland commissar Yezhov, massive in his red uniform, filling the whole right-hand side with his arm pointing out his hand inside a glove, wool or iron no way of telling which, throttling a viper under its chin its head is made of a number of heads belonging to homunculi, the men condemned to death in the thirties, Trotsky the viper's tail in the shape of a swastika the tiny heads Bukharin Rykov spitting blood squeezed out by Yezhov's massive gloved hand, tiny heads with big noses thick lips brown hair bloodshot popping eyes as seen also at the time in posters in Berlin or Nuremberg disgraceful at the time she'd only seen the poster, not the big noses.

Whenever Sarah, having nightmares within some episode full of nightmares, began to doubt, she remembers, the beginnings, when she had to tell herself this is a nightmare, it'll pass, it's passing, another nightmare, which passes, from nightmare to nightmare people pass, not the nightmares, a mortiferous process which swallows orders in Russian and spits them out again in a variety of foreign languages, those were the words of Clara Zetkin, 'the meaning and content of the Russian Revolution are being reduced to a set of rules like those of the Pickwick Club', Clara Zetkin attended the Party conference at Tours, she had spoken in support of the twenty-one conditions, and here she was, talking of a Pickwick-type club, of a mortiferous machine, she died saying 'through the midnight gloom I look to the future with optimism', that was in 1933.

Sarah whispering the whisper of her friend Clara Zetkin, and the hospital attendants did not dare go into her room, may Yezhov enter into Stalin and father a monstrous offspring, Beria saying when Yezhov was liquidated I realised that nothing was to be gained by always saying yes to Stalin, Yezhov plunging into the entrails of great Stalin and out of him siring the swastika-tailed heir who shall sit at the head of what the republic of soviets has been turned into, the optimists can go to hell, listen to the laughter of Bukharin, Kamenev and all those who scale the heavens.

Let them all laugh like hanged men who point to the sky with their third foot, let them watch while Stalin dies clubbed to death by Yezhov as they themselves died and may the diminutive Bronstein die a second death along with all those who believed in it all, the innocents who pledged their future to it and into the great receptacle along with the entrails and afterbirth shall go the Orthodox popes who manufactured terror and the rabbis who processed obedience and the men who worshipped organisation, the heroes of labour, the heroes of war, the commissars and the Vlassovs, the same vessel, Tukhachevsky and his fiddle.

May no one ever again sire believers, Nicolas the cretin, the imbecile Tsarina, the incompetent executioners, the innocents who confess, the martyrs who smile, Lenin who laughs, and all bide their time for the succession in the coming days, the child which Stalin held in the photo, the Bouriate girl, daughter of a regional secretary, she broke free from her parents at some reception or other and jumped into the arms of the Grandfather with the moustache, millions of copies of that photo were printed, the little girl with the slightly oriental eyes, behold, peoples of the world, the only union that is not racist!

The little girl wore a beatific smile and the grandfather smiled beneath his cap, the father is executed during the purges of the following year, the mother exiled in the north, and the mother dies of typhoid, though not according to a KGB note found later, the note asks Moscow what shall we do with this woman who most likely knew certain things? and the reply slip is rubber-stamped: 'For Elimination'.

The little girl was luckier than her father and mother and the great communist philosopher who gave philosophy lessons to the people's father, I would like, the people's father told him, to learn all about Hegel, and everything went smoothly, and when the professor reached the dialectic of reason he was dispatched to a camp, Sarah Lilstein hears the voice of her friend Aïno Kuusinen, wife of one of the leaders of the Komintern, said I was invited with my husband Otto, in 1928, Black Sea, a cruise, lovely boat, a small very ordinary cabin, a sailor brings champagne, biscuits, lovely song on the gramophone, 'Souliko'.

I myself shall serve my guests, says Stalin. We sip our drinks, Stalin replays the record, he drinks, stares at us, laughs, when the Georgian song ends he plays it again, serves another round of drinks, laughs louder and louder, starts to dance, plays the record once more, replays the same song all through the afternoon, it grows less and less lovely, Stalin jigs up and down, he shouts with laughter, he is drunk, from time to time he stands at the ship's stern, gazes at the water and the wake as it closes up behind the ship, then returns looking bored.

Again he starts jig-jigging to the music of the gramophone and all the while never stops observing us, the Komintern transmitted to the NKVD information given to it by the NKVD, you've got it, closed-circuit, Willi Münzenberg has links with Radek, Radek is shot, Münzenberg refuses to return to Moscow, a three-year reprieve, the NKVD finally catches up with him in a forest in France, that's the story, Stalin is happy, why did we ever allow that drunken Georgian to grow so big?

Why? Because you were bastards, cowards, fools, psychopaths, monsters, devils, that's the answer you'll get from the moralists, psychologists and believers, so lump them together with the Orthodox popes, the rabbis, the bastards, the cowards, the commissars, the psychopaths, it's no use, Stalin already did it, he had the brain of an Orthodox pope, a psychopath and a rabbi, and a commissar too; when they all landed up together at twenty below, each of them given a pick to hack at the permafrost, and among them some were innocent, Sarah tried to do something, no longer out of duty but from the remorse she felt at not having done what now clearly appeared to have been the duty she should have done when everything was already beyond the reach of remorse, or rather she acted not from remorse but because from that time on there could never be anything else, not remorse nor hope, even hope had become something dirty, Thälmann died at Buchenwald and his secretary Werner Hirsch died in the Lubyanka, Sarah spoke and talked and spoke out.

'So you see, young Frenchman, the worst of it was reading what my mother thought at the end of her life, my mother never betrayed anything or anyone, I don't think she ever committed a crime but when she stopped and looked back over the road that had been travelled all she saw was a petrified storm, even in *Doctor Zhivago*, at the end there is no paradise but there is still a desire for it, a hint of "in spite of everything" with the young people who will fall in love, a red scarf tied round their necks, it still reads like a progressive novel, whereas in the good doctor's notes was a half-century predicated on a paradise to come and it turned my stomach.'

*

That morning, in the Konditorei in the village, Lilstein's other interview had proved to be very difficult, much more so than his talk with the 'young gentleman of France'. Kappler had wasted no time and immediately barked at Lilstein:

'They put pressure on the Hungarians to fight and then left them in the lurch, CIA broadcasts told the Hungarians to take up arms, to set up a central military command, you know all this far better than I do, Lilstein, Radio Free Europe told the insurgents, go to it, reinforcements are on the way, the station was CIA-controlled and people believed what it said. That's why I'm going back to Rosmar.'

Kappler's voice booms in the dim light of the Konditorei, even the *patron* behind the bar does not succeed in ignoring a voice which threatens to explode at any moment. Kappler continues to speak and in his voice there is hatred for anyone who refuses to believe what it says. Lilstein has never seen his old friend like this:

'I'm going back to Rosmar because the Americans made the Russians believe that they would intervene to help the Hungarians, they said to the people of Győr and Budapest go ahead NATO is coming to the rescue, the Russians laid about them as only they know how, maybe they only went at it so hard because they thought NATO might turn up and NATO didn't budge, I know now that there'll be no cavalry riding in from outside, I hate Russian tanks but I hate even more the scum who are now shedding crocodile tears, they landed the Hungarians in the deepest shit and now they're staging a great international weeping-and-wailing-fest, there'll be no serious intervention from outside.'

And Lilstein knew then that he would lose, that Kappler had looped his loopiest loop, no hope of any intervention from outside, he has just one hope left, that something might turn up from inside the country itself, that's why he's going back to the GDR, Lilstein has twigged that Kappler still had that one hope left: he wanted to make a difference.

If he was to be prevented from returning, this last hope had to be destroyed, Lilstein had a choice, either kill off the object of that hope or cut the legs from under the man who hoped it, at first he opted to destroy Kappler's hopes, he did not draw pictures for him or offer an analysis, he just said:

'All my Minister's good at is scratching his arse, and he's the second highest-ranking minister of the State which you wish to join, he's the Interior Minister of the Socialist Workers' and Peasants' State and a member of the Politburo of the Unified Socialist Party of Germany, the second most important person in the country, and all this Minister is good at is arse-scratching, and that's the kind of country you want to go back to?'

That made Kappler laugh a long, optimistic laugh, he glanced up towards the *patron* of the Konditorei, pointed to the empty carafe, the man came over to serve them, Kappler joked with him, he was almost relaxed.

So then Lilstein decided to disable Kappler, he had a choice of allowing him into the GDR to be roasted on a slow spit or do him real damage so that he might live:

'I know exactly why you want to come over to us, Herr Kappler: eccentricity. You pretend to be eccentric because you've turned into a second-rate author, a writing machine, an old bruiser.'

And Lilstein put in the boot:

'You're trying to act like a somebody because nowadays you write like a nobody.'

Kappler flushed, Lilstein went on:

'You know what you're going to do once you're back in the German Democratic Republic? You will prevent our young writers developing in their own way, you'll cramp their style, the moment they try to come up with something new my Minister and his small-minded comrades will tell them to stop writing tripe, stop imitating the capitalist ways of doing things – at first that's what they'll say – if you imitate capitalist ways it will mean that we won't allow you to publish anything, if you continue making trouble they'll say you're imitating imperialist ways, and that's much more serious, capitalism is there, a fact of life, but imperialism is aggressive, which means that you're in cahoots with those who wish to attack us, that you imitate imperialist ways.

'From a literary point of view, that means nothing, Herr Kappler, but coming from them it means "we're going to put you in jail", thus far they've locked up young people who just wanted to be different, but soon they'll be jailing anyone who doesn't want to resemble what you've turned into, they'll say look at Kappler, the penny's dropped with him, he's come in from outside and he's setting you an example, he's seen through it all, and anyone can read his books, it's all perfectly transparent, so cut out all this symbolic or imperialistic petit-bourgeois posturing.

'So you do see what purpose you'll serve, Herr Kappler, don't you? You'll be used to prevent any other Kapplers coming through, I mean Kapplers like the Kappler of the twenties and thirties, now defunct. For a quarter of a century you've written nothing remarkable, nowadays you're just a biographer, that's why you want to go back, so that people will cheer the man you're ashamed to have become.'

That's how in the dimly lit Konditorei earlier that day Lilstein had advanced, destroying Kappler, feeling that he could weep, fabricating lies, lies which nevertheless were powerful, for they made Kappler turn bright red, made his chin tremble, Lilstein greatly admired Kappler's latest books, but he shot them down in flames while he looked on, all to prevent him returning to Rosmar.

'This notion that you would construct a narrative using the great days of the first half of the century was quite clever, Herr Kappler, a few dozen sequences, magnificent stuff, all the academies admired your last offering, but I know that the Kappler of 1929 would never have published it, he would have sat down in front of this succession of sequences and asked himself how it could all be brought together. He'd have buckled down to it, he'd have looked for a form.'

Lilstein lying to destabilise Kappler, using any means to ensure that Kappler does not go back:

'You're writing now like Turgenev or Anatole France, you write like they did before the war, I mean the 1914 war, it's so earnest and antiquated, how can you expect to have anything to say?'

And the deeper Lilstein goes in with his lie, the easier the words come, the more convinced he feels that he is right, the quicker Kappler's pages turn yellow, he knows what the ideologues of the GDR will do, threaten young writers, what's all this rubbish about disjointed narratives? and your petit-bourgeois monologues, stream of consciousness, conscious smut more like, pornography, you get these ideas from the Yanks, from a reactionary pro-slaver, that apple of their eye, Faulkner, or the traitor Dos Passos, now take Kappler, he's come back from there, from your precious West, he's tried it all and he's reverted to realism and a voice that tells things like they are, clearly, so everyone can understand, in the order they happen.

Lilstein talks to Kappler about what the Party ideologues will do, and the further he goes the more he feels he is right to say it, the more sympathetic he feels to those imperialist writers who are no more imperialist than Cholokhov who isn't imperialist at all, Kappler is old.

'Your books are closets for old clothes, Herr Kappler, as a form of writing the equivalent of antique furniture, too genteel, and to escape it you're opting for a freakish course of action.'

That's how Lilstein managed to get Kappler to snap:
'That's enough!'
Several times, and the last in a bare whisper:
'That's enough!'

And stop Lilstein did, he'd have liked to add that young people in the GDR had no need of the portable hell which Kappler has been dragging around with him since the beginning of time, he felt it wasn't necessary, they drank slowly, Kappler looked around the small bar area of the Konditorei, he didn't speak again, he seemed lost among the shelves of pots and pans and groceries, he allowed Lilstein to pay the bill, he then bought a few bars of chocolate, they left together, their footsteps were muffled by the snow as they walked towards the little bridge, they stopped, they looked up towards the edge of the forest, eyes peeled, Kappler asked:

'Tell me, young Lilstein, have you seen her again?'

Then they moved on and made for the village, the landscape was white but in shadow now, snow waiting for more snow, Kappler wanted Lilstein to escort him to the bus, at the last moment he said to Lilstein:

'I'm going back to Rosmar because you've done your damnedest to stop me, I'm going back because there must be people around you who think like you, I have no illusions about what the GDR is like today, I just believe that there is more to be done there than in the West, I'd still like to achieve something before it's too late for me, it's no good saying any more, I still want to write new things, and I also believe that you still have decent thoughts.'

'Thoughts aren't enough, Herr Kappler, a group of people who have fine thoughts can do a great deal of harm, and they are the worst kind.'

Hans said to him:

'Actually, young Lilstein, I like you best when you're trying to be stupid.'

*

Years later, one day when Lilstein has behaved very affectionately towards you, when he's called you 'young gentleman of France' three times on the trot, you will take your courage in both hands and raise the subject of Kappler, Lilstein will give you an unvarnished account of the talk he'd had that morning with his old friend before meeting you that same afternoon, when it was your turn. He'll say that it had taken a long time for him to forgive himself for failing to find a way of undermining Kappler's resolve.

Then you'll ask Lilstein what he would have done if you too had said no.

He'll reply that he'd have let you go, to live your life in the great wide world, but you have never been sure that this was true. Still, you never asked him outright if he would have arranged for you to disappear.

One day he'll say that even without him you would have taken the same path, you like influence, especially the influence which multiplies the power of the men who work in the shadows, ultimately it's an acceptable word, oh it's most unlikely that you would ever have acquired links, not with anybody, you would have been your own master. Lilstein knows two or three gossipy types in Paris who are paid with signs of consideration, not by him, by the Russians, loose tongues in high places, you would have played that game with much more finesse, but you would have had no real influence, not with any camp, whereas with Lilstein it was real politics, you went forward together, you gave each other presents, gifts, counter-gifts, you betrayed no one and you acted in tandem, really a most lordly occupation.

You were both standing at Klosters in front of the locomotive of a mountain railway, Lilstein told you that the first time he ever saw you in the Waldhaus in 1956 he was desperate because he'd failed with Kappler and he'd decided to speak to you as if you were his last chance.

There were ants in the grass between the rails in front of the engine, Lilstein spoke in a cynical voice:

'See? we're like them, ants standing in the path of a huge railway engine, some have given up wanting to know and just haul their grain of barley without asking questions, other ants say I'm going to make the engine back off, others again say it'll roll clean over me, there'll always be some people who get it right, but with us it's not the same. We've got the message: we play with model railways.'

Chapter 5

1978

Rumours and a Pair of Braces

In which a man named Berthier goes hunting for moles inside, no less, the French Embassy in Moscow, in a manner prejudicial to the interests of Henri de Vèze, whose love life is rocky, and also of Madame de Cramilly, who is bringing up a papyrus on her own.

In which de Vèze remembers a voice crying 'The Great Adventure is buggered!'

In which it becomes obvious that you've been Lilstein's mole in Paris for a very long time and that you have the ear of the President of the French Republic.

In which it becomes clear that Michael Lilstein is in melancholy mood and has almost stopped believing in socialism.

Paris, 4 June 1978

During the course of his life, a man is required to be
reborn several times, and all the help he gets comes
from chance and error.

Colette

Henri de Vèze entered the room without knocking, he is France's ambassador to Moscow, he was one of Free France's youngest subalterns and, in 1942, at Bir Hakeim, he cleared a minefield, his chances were one in ten.

He doesn't knock before entering a minister's office, even though it's now thirty-six years later, even though it's the Quai d'Orsay.

The Minister does not bridle: always agreeable, thinks de Vèze, spine of an oyster, a man of the centre, de Vèze is very angry, and the more so because he can't say why nor tell the Minister straight out that this meeting has forced him to abandon his mistress in the middle of a quarrel, twenty minutes it took twenty minutes for her to agree to give him back his braces, forced to negotiate with a harpy so he can be on time for a mollusc.

De Vèze and the Minister have known each other for ages, they joined the Foreign Office together in 1946 but not by the same academic route, the Minister sat the usual exams while de Vèze was entitled to attempt those set specially for ex-servicemen, for several years this did not matter.

And then de Vèze realised that he was not really part of the club, though not where promotion was concerned, no, they'd never screwed him around on that score, but when in certain meetings you're practically the only one in the room who never went to their prestigious École libre des sciences politiques, it gets to you in the end, especially the way they go about making sure you're not aware of it, sensitive people, uncivilised but sensitive, they take your coat while their chums look on because the secretary, bless her, has forgotten to do it yet again, and they oblige with that excess of attentiveness which proclaims that they're putting on a show especially for you, your scarf folded neatly instead of being stuffed into one sleeve, and everyone knows that you know.

The Minister is with a man to whom de Vèze takes an instant dislike, crewcut, thin lips, well-developed shoulders, the blue-eyed athlete of airport novels, though from the waist up only: below the belt, to speed things up, all parts have been shortened, more like a Mediterranean plumber, back bent and buttocks rounded, will never make second military attaché, talks like bursts of machine-gun fire with a strange rising intonation at the end of a phrase, to make him sound forceful, another one of those types who believe that being in charge means having to have a big mouth, a vulgar loudmouth, low-slung rear-end of a cockerel, how dare the Minister think he can lumber an ambassador with a jester like that?

And it was to be introduced to this moron that de Vèze walked out on his mistress this morning, bang in the middle of a big row, and they'd been back together again only a matter of days, they're both very good at rows, first a fit of feminine sulks, just a small one, the corners of her mouth turn down, her oval face becomes hard, her nose grows more pointed, a not-speaking phase which drags on, he was careful not to ask her what the matter was but to no avail, because she asked first, softly, gently:

'What's the matter?'

'Nothing.'

'You're in a bad temper, I can feel it.'

'Not at all, there's nothing the matter with me.'

'Yes there is, you seem to be in a hurry.'

That did it, the word 'hurry', it happened every time she says a

word she doesn't like, 'hurry', mentally you've as good as gone, de
Vèze knew what came next:

'Anyway you're never here . . .'

Within seconds, they'd got on to the actual length of his stay in
Paris, which was not certain.

'Muriel, you know I can't be away from Moscow for long.'

He was getting dressed, he added in one breath:

'You misheard, darling, I never said one thing while meaning
another, those two days in Dinard, it was just a thought, as you knew
all along.'

He paused a moment, to let the words sink in, it's true, Muriel does
always know but she invariably acts as if she doesn't, so that she can
keep the argument going, put him in the wrong, it's also true that he
pretends to believe that he'll have time to go to Dinard while all the
time he knows he won't, he makes much of it, he imagines going, but
she also behaves as if it were true, and he cannot see why he should
deny himself the prospect, and then when it all comes to nothing
Muriel makes a meal of it, although she too had been looking forward
to it. She seizes on his words:

'Knew all along? I never know anything with you, it's true, I never
know a thing!'

She has raised her voice to him, she breathes in through her mouth,
her voice drops:

'But I'm not going to get angry about it.'

Her mouth is a scornful curve, then her eyes relax, she smiles, he's
been caught without his braces, he smiles, he'll have to carry on the
argument *sans* braces, she's holding them in her hand, she has decided
not to get angry, she's just said so, he'd better believe her, she looks
down at the braces with a smile, all maternal:

'You know, I think this red is far too lurid for braces.'

She laughs, shaken by two little ripples of laughter, but there is no
real amusement in it, it's to get what's bothering her off her chest, she
repeats 'this red', exaggerating the movements of her lips, dropping
her chin, hollowing her cheeks, her voice scolds, mocks, 'this red', a
woman giving a young child or an old husband a good ticking off:

'And don't tell me it's maroon, maroon isn't as hot a colour, and it's more dignified, this is just red.'

She holds the braces up in the light streaming in at the window.

'Bright red, so unflattering. At your age!'

A silence. She looks him up and down.

'You wear braces when you don't need to, and when you do wear braces you choose red, it makes you look like an ageing dandy trying to look like a young man.'

Another silence, it's like an invitation, de Vèze says nothing, don't answer back, look sad, sad at being forced to leave her when she's looking so lovely, the crucial point is the meeting with the Minister, 'ageing dandy', 'young man', he doesn't answer, her malice should take the sting out of her mood, her voice is softer as she amends her words:

'Whereas you are neither one nor the other.'

She smiles, more relaxed now, her prettiness returns, de Vèze relaxes, armistice signed, she goes on:

'Tell me, when did you buy them?'

De Vèze knows that 'when' means 'who were you with when' because he wasn't with her, she is wondering 'with whom?' but will not put the question, it would be only too easy for de Vèze to say 'I was by myself, of course, I don't even remember where', obviously, there's no answer to that, she knows it, this way de Vèze could then take her by the hand and speak of jealousy in a gentle, understanding voice, 'I also buy my cigarettes by myself', maintain the tender note, and if she doesn't buy it you could ask 'do you really have to be jealous? Is it so hard to love someone straightforwardly?' Leave it at that, don't get schmaltzy, I don't do schmaltzy very well, but play up the jealousy angle because all she's got to go on is the purchase of a pair braces, that's the way to do it.

She knows all that, which is why she doesn't ask 'with whom?' but 'when?' it's not so provocative, de Vèze replies:

'I really don't know.'

The 'really' is good, say 'I don't know' by itself and you give the impression that you're clutching at straws, floundering, in the wrong, whereas 'really' is a clincher, it lends your answer an edge of exasperation, most effective, but not with her, she doesn't give a fig for 'really', she moves to what always comes next:

'You never know anything.'

She clears her throat, cigarette and venom, only moments ago she was saying 'I never know with you', and now it's 'you never know anything', it's not a particularly serious thing to say, 'you never know anything', it might just mean something along the lines of 'I'm feeling upset and want you to know'.

She holds your braces in her left hand, slides them between the thumb and forefinger of her right, the movement uncovers her breasts, a beauty spot high on the right breast, a chocolate chip, 'You never know anything', you feel her sadness, she's not wrong, a person could lie back and settle into sadness like that, life, circumstances, work, you promise you'll change, that you'll learn how to know, each of you contributes a quotient of inertia, and then you start all over again, you're back together for a couple of days, we've so little time, at least we shouldn't quarrel, but after saying 'you never know' she added:

'– ever.'

But there was nothing miserable at all about the way she said 'You never know anything – ever'. Always a bad sign with her.

De Vèze stands facing the double bed, Muriel shows no intention of getting out of it, well ensconced, shoulders leaning back on the cushions propped up against the wall, now she's playing with the braces like a catapult, like chest-expanders, she has always liked her hands, small, almost plump, but 'plump' is banned, much better say I love to nibble your fingertips, she's just lobbed ' – ever' at him and is waiting for him to ask for his braces back.

She looks him up and down, from head to toe, not possible to suck in his stomach or else his trousers will end up around his ankles, and if I hold my trousers up I'll just look stupid, now where's my other shoe got to, I must go.

A friend of de Vèze once lived for a week in Geneva with a lady chemist, a rich nymphomaniac who kept him under house arrest, she'd go out early in the morning while he was still asleep, she never locked the door, she just shut her pet lynx up in the hall, the lynx wasn't particularly aggressive but I never wanted to put it to the test, I didn't try to go out, every morning for a fortnight I read books, I also used the exercise bike, she'd be back at twelve-thirty, off duty until the next day, a whale of a time, absolutely, we'd go out for a breath of air in the afternoon, not for long, she was an expert, she could open your flies using only her toes.

Muriel has certainly chosen her moment, she looks at de Vèze, eyes dewy, eyelashes long, eyebrows arched, then a tetchy mannerism, her hand hooks her hair behind one ear, a little apple, at her best this woman is a little apple, vivacious, elegant, normally a couple of minutes at most would see him, braces, shoes, jacket, peck on the cheek, through the door.

He thought he'd left his braces attached to his trousers, but no, she had unfastened them last night while he was still wearing them, just playing, he's never sufficiently on his guard, and she has this way, as soon as she's swallowed the last mouthful of croissant, of kicking her legs out under the bedclothes, but he's run out of time.

'What are you thinking? You've as good as gone.'

And then a discharge of electricity, shoulders juddering fractiously against the cushions, I'm going to have to go looking for my shoes under the bed on all fours but I'm still in control of the situation, she's calming down, her face which had looked so hard is softening, she's forgotten the '– ever', she's not on the attack any more, soon I can bend down and reclaim my shoe from under the bed, she smiles, not a big smile, so as not to accentuate the quote-mark wrinkles around her mouth and nose, and she says:

'All right, see you this afternoon.'

Why ever you could not have just replied, 'Right, I'll ring you' when she said 'All right, see you this afternoon', why did you have to go into details:

'No, I can't this afternoon, some visits to make.'

It didn't go down well.

'People to see? Henri, you didn't say anything about that yesterday, you just talked about the Minister, no, don't lie, I'm not getting cross, but you didn't mention it.'

Talking about visits gives her an opportunity to say 'don't lie', it's not good when she starts saying 'don't lie', too late now to pick up on the jealousy theme, I should have kept the visits to myself and said 'Right, see you this afternoon, I'll give you a ring', and call her around two o'clock and tell her 'Something's come up, I'll phone you back', saying anything about visits was a mistake, though the visits were nothing special, the head of protocol and the bank, I could tell her that but it wouldn't help to go into details if what I get is:

'You prefer the bank to me, that's very nice, you're always saying you're not a money man, you've only got a few days in Paris and you prefer the bank to me!'

Best not mention the bank, the head of protocol perhaps, no, don't mention either bank or protocol, though actually she's making the running:

'These visits, which part of town will they take you to? Anywhere near Saint-Germain?'

I should never have mentioned those visits, Saint-Germain is a dangerous part of town.

If she's already got on to Saint-Germain it means that she is extremely cross, she has lit a cigarette though she's trying not to smoke before midday, she holds the braces in her left hand as if minded to lash out with them, she says not one word, she has opted for deadly silence now that she's mentioned Saint-Germain, Saint-Germain is deadly serious, whenever she says the words it's a point of no return, but if she maintains a deadly silence at least it's better than if she starts going on about the *quartier* Saint-Germain, in a deadly silence it's possible to make a getaway, it's hard but not disastrous, though it could get really serious if she started on about Saint-Germain, usually it's a reliable warning sign, when she says Saint-Germain she's saying 'Watch out, you're in for a rough ride!' and then she waits, and in moments like these de Vèze knows that she's asking that he be nice to her, that he point her away from Saint-Germain by unlimited attentiveness, promises, pleasant fancies, the prospect of Dinard, she has said Saint-Germain and now she waits for him to redeem himself with tenderness, reassurance and promises.

But this time she didn't wait, it's very unusual for her not to wait, for her to have got to Saint-Germain so quickly.

'Obviously you're going to visit *her!*'

It's what he was hoping to avoid, why did I ever bring up visits?

'You're going to visit your trollop.'

Didn't waste time getting to the crude abuse.

'You've been back there already.'

Chin starts to tremble, sob in the throat, she chokes it back, and to restore her voice she clears her throat and then snarls:

'Your whore!'

Straight into the tantrum.

'Does a good blow job, does she? The whore!'

She's angry, for God's sake don't say 'calm down'.

Say anything except that. Let the first squalls pass over.

'And your whore will do anything you want!'

This word 'whore' is new from her, maybe she's got mad just so she can test it. She threw the braces in his face left-handed, she missed and they land on the floor at the foot of the bed.

'She paid you, the whore, you've been back there, don't lie to me!'

A fine display of sobbing follows, jealous recriminations, body shaking, tremors, lulls, obscenities, she whips up her unhappiness with obscenities, catches her breath, the other woman isn't a whore, she's more the high society type, but it's her misfortune to be The Other Woman, not Another Woman, there are others and Muriel never says anything about them, the one in Moscow for instance, she knows about her, even that her name is Vassilissa, but she says nothing, acts as if she didn't exist, she doesn't want to give the impression that she knows, but this Other Woman, the one in Saint-Germain, dates from before her time, a friend of hers actually, she hates her, de Vèze hasn't been back to see her and it wasn't she who bought him the maroon braces, that was Vassilissa, but he doesn't want to make an issue of it.

The danger with tears is that she might go weepy on him, calm down, sigh, jiggle her legs about, pester him, she's quite capable of playing up in the most unsubtle way, to make him late, because she is more important than anything else, to ensure that de Vèze is unable to manage anything more than short visits, the very thought makes de Vèze angry, he breathes a sigh of regret and just says:

'Needs must . . .'

That's good, just the right amount of impatience in the truncated platitude to make him insufferable, it's my only chance, she has to think I'm insufferable, but she didn't calm down, anger and desire jostled together, as much was visible in the way she looked at him, her unhappiness was seductive as she knew very well, de Vèze remained firm, he picked up his braces, his shoe wasn't far under the bed, his visits, he should never have said anything about the visits he had to make that afternoon, a mistake, absolutely routine visits, but a mistake.

'You're just a coward, all this pretence for a whore, oh, just go!'

She will never forgive him for her descent into vulgarity, she, a distinguished university professor, wife, ex-wife, of a leading light at the Collège de France, normally so refined.

De Vèze managed to get away, he'll never understand why she is jealous, she never asks him anything about what he gets up to when he goes abroad, but the moment he's back in France he's not allowed to speak to another woman, he said nothing, he left without trying for a parting shot.

'A remarkable officer, Henri old man,' said the Minister as he introduced the plumber with the cockerel strut, 'and a great expert on matters of interest to us.'

An expert, in other words a tool, thinks de Vèze, not much good will come from this meeting, they didn't haul me back from Moscow so I could have a three-way chat with an expert like him, French interests or no French interests, God! wherever you go there's the same nauseating atmosphere, whether it's the Quai d'Orsay or the Élysée or any of the ministries; since getting back from Moscow de Vèze has not succeeded in having one serious conversation with any of his old colleagues, all he's met are edgy types, shiftier than usual, the smell of fear.

And the more scared they are the higher their rank, two of them, men he'd fought alongside during the war, accepted his invitation to dinner only to cancel at the last minute. De Vèze had never known anything like it, not even in the darkest days of Gaullism, during the generals' putsch, it's as if I've got the plague, and they'd been adventurers together!

The only one who came, not to greet him – in the Quai d'Orsay everyone says hello to everyone else – no, the only one who lingered longer than the thirty seconds demanded by etiquette and had, as they say, struck up a conversation, was Xavier Poirgade, he was coming down the great staircase as de Vèze was arriving, Poirgade, the grey diplomat, they'd known each other for over ten years, they'd met in Singapore, the least adventurous of diplomats, nowadays he's not even a diplomat, he left the Foreign Office to direct an institute for strategic studies at ten times the salary, Poirgade's got a good head on his shoulders, with his little beard, grey suit, manicured hands, has all the time in the world to chat pleasantly at the head of the great staircase with a man who's got the plague, does it because he likes to provoke, so pleased to see you again, Mr Ambassador, peculiar atmosphere, don't you think? A little tête-à-tête, people walk up, walk down, stare at them.

Poirgade stares at the starers, head tilted back, index finger under his chin, a defiant stance that says I refuse to allow the fact that de Vèze the bruiser is in a pickle to make me look like a poltroon in public, the Ambassador is wearing well, that little green ribbon in the lapel keeps a man young, he doesn't like me but he's happy to have me on hand so that he can be seen on the great staircase, I can't stand his sort, a skirt-chaser, a show-off, a big mouth, serve him right this business is catching up on him now, albatross around his neck, won't be long before he's all washed up, got to be nice to the flotsam so they last longer, I loved the interview you did for *Le Figaro*, Mr Ambassador, you won't have pleased everybody by reminding them of the Atlantic and the Urals, but really first-rate, enjoy it while you can, Excellency, you're nowhere near getting yourself out of the mire, you know, I'm younger than you, I never knew those days, not as an adult, but I agree completely with you, I support your ideas unequivocally, you have no idea how far I go to support you, Sexcellency, I support you as the rope supports the hanged man, and I am prepared to be so supportive as to untie the rope just as you're about to choke, but only so that I can pull it tight again.

De Vèze doesn't like Poirgade, he has 'I can talk to you because I'm above suspicion' written all over him, Poirgade tells him: look at these people, they say hello but when they walk past they stay close to the wall, they scuttle, de Vèze could have stayed silent, he's going to be late for the Minister, but he can't resist adding a word about his comrades from the days of that Great Adventure who are now making themselves scarce, do you remember, says Poirgade: 'The Great Adventure is buggered!' shows we're getting old, must have been a dozen years ago, I reckon? De Vèze remembers very well, the dinner in Singapore and over the meal the exclamation, the last word, at the time he didn't give a damn, 'The Great Adventure is buggered!' words spoken by a drunk, and today the fear is everywhere, old companions backing off, de Vèze can't stand Poirgade and yet here he is speaking to him in confidence, the weakness of his old companions who are ditching him, why are you telling him all this? you're a coward too, you're only talking to this grey diplomat because he dares to be seen with you in public, a beard which just circles his mouth, like a monkey's bum, you never did like the man.

Poirgade has made the most of his opportunity and now de Vèze understands why he wanted to speak to him, heard anything more about that couple? The historian and his wife? As if you didn't know, you hypocrite, it hardly seems possible that Poirgade is unaware that the historian and his wife have divorced, or that he doesn't know what the grounds for it were, he looks pleasantly at de Vèze who feels like replying: I don't know about the husband but the latest on the wife is that when I'm in Paris I still give her a good rogering, it works out very nicely, thanks, she's got a bit of a short fuse and doesn't care for red braces, but is very affectionate in her middle age.

Poirgade is a busybody who sprays gossip around, people think he sells information about strategy but in reality it's the gossip that interests his clients, his clientele is apparently drawn from the highest levels, international seminars, those dinners, he measures his words carefully over the coffee, heard the latest? Handsome de Vèze, still shacked up with Morel's ex! Wonderful example of fidelity, she leads him an awful dance but he always goes back, de Vèze is about to ditch Poirgade on the stairs, Poirgade senses it coming, I must leave you, Mr Ambassador, I gather the Minister is waiting, good day.

'The Great Adventure is buggered!' and it's not in this ministerial office that de Vèze is likely to retrieve it, with this other dimwit with the crewcut and cockerel strut they've foisted on him, and all on account of a rumour, hearsay, yes many tongues wagging and many ears flapping, it's hard to say exactly what's being said but it's common knowledge, it acquires credibility by sheer weight of numbers, no one's laughing now, and when the talking stops it's worse, there's a shabby silence every time you want to talk to the allies, you go to meetings, to begin with everything's fine, the flags flap, present arms, doors are opened for you, people greet you, there is warmth in the handshakes and because you're there they make the most of the opportunity to discuss the diameter of waste-paper baskets, even the Germans give you the treatment, though every six months one of them feels the need to jump out of the window of his office.

The Iron Curtain? The Wall? The Germans are all jolly good pals! Every summer they all get together in Hungary and after the fourth glass of schnapps there is only one Greater Germania, *über alles*, with Bayreuth as capital! And this stupid clod of a Minister allows the strutting plumber to say his piece, my God they're giving me instructions, a mole, at home in France, they take us for Englishmen, and today the English are laughing their socks off, saying we're just imitating them.

The worst of it is that everyone knows now, and the President can't come up with anything better than to put a woman on the case, of course he can bring women into whatever he likes, create all the State secretariats he wants for the distaff side, but he shouldn't bring them into serious matters.

And he did bring one in, intriguing name, Chagrin, Michèle Chagrin, a spinster's name, flat-chested, large chin, hair prematurely grey which she hasn't bothered to dye, the President made her responsible for the file, direct orders from the Élysée, Chagrin began her career in the Army Ministry in 1964 or '65, ex-student of the École nationale d'administration, did not graduate with flying colours, no way could she be called an intelligence expert, her field was administrative law, but for those military types even legal expertise was too much in a woman, they pushed her out, she left Paris.

What did she do then? she got herself noticed in the provinces for her serious approach to work, in the Auvergne, a prefect who says to the Minister of Finance I've got a remarkable woman in charge of my legal department, and the Minister poached her from the prefect, the minister becomes President with a capital P, Chagrin follows him, still on the legal side.

When the tale of the mole became a subject for a proper file, and a proper file is a file with a legal dimension, someone was needed to manage it properly, she was on hand, at least she was good at keeping on top of files, she ended up as overall coordinator, a woman of the shadows, never seen in receptions, never observed outside office hours, she was neither acolyte nor friend.

The men who came to report to the Élysée didn't like her, they'd found a nickname for her, and they'd made sure she knew what it was, she even used it herself on occasions: 'Lady Piddle', civilians had never accepted her any more than the military did, but there had to be someone – not to make them agree, that was impossible, and just as well – but to provide liaison, syntheses, avoid catastrophic short-circuits, yes, and years down the line it was still her nickname, a rather good one, don't you say it isn't, I like it, and it suits me better and better because I'm getting on now and I stay in my small corner, even if it is in the Élysée, and also because when they walk into my little old lady's office they get more and more nervous because they've got older too, because I know more and more about them and because I've acquired more and more responsibilities, not power, power is political.

I am Michèle Chagrin, civil service administrator, my responsibilities are defined by departmental order, I take no action which lies outside my official remit, I draft notes, and when a note seems to be satisfactory, then an officer, a colonel or higher, may be sent to Mourmelon or Lure, what a life, that's why it makes them nervous when they walk into my office, they're all incompetent, they see traitors everywhere, that prevents them from rooting out the real spies, especially the one who's been making life difficult for us these last ten years, yes, I've also been useless at winkling the swine out, but that's no reason for not managing the file properly.

Lady Piddle did not summon de Vèze, she bumped into him in town, as the saying goes, she was very nice to him, she looked like an unmade bed, we've got a lot of problems just now, she didn't ask anything of him, she talked about people with experience, ones you could still, thank God, count on, right?

At what point did people really start to be afraid of Lady Piddle? when she got the scalp of a minister, a blabbermouth, confidential documents – no, not top-secret defence documents, papers from Cabinet meetings, yes, one set per minister, and some of it very sensitive – documents which often made a public appearance on the front page of a certain large-circulation evening newspaper.

Little Miss Chagrin was endlessly patient, low-ranking and high-powered, it took almost a whole parliamentary session, she made small changes in the figures in selected files which were handed out to Cabinet members, doctoring the set of figures given to this or that minister, just one set, not all of them, a small alteration after the decimal point, she did it each time she switched her attention to a new suspect, until one day a figure she had lightly modified found its way into the columns of a well-known evening paper, even so that proved nothing in itself, a minister may have a score of close colleagues who have sight of the same documents as their chief, Chagrin didn't get excited, she multiplied the opportunities for temptation, one day she circulated three pages of a draft general budget to all ministers.

The minister under suspicion happened to be ill that day, the file was sent to him at home by motorcycle messenger, in it one of the figures that had been changed just for him, he got it a quarter of an hour before the leading daily was put to bed, and the figure in question was published on page one in the early afternoon edition, with the small alteration, the Lady went to see the President, very well, Chagrin, tell him I want to see him and you shall be present at the interview, you'll be there with the correct version of the file. No need to get unduly worked up, this sort of thing never goes to court, a month later the minister resigned, entered a clinic, he'd known the President for a quarter of a century, it was such a stupid thing to do, so why did he do it?

Illusions about the power of the press? or maybe the newspaper had something on him, or maybe for the fun of it, you'd never guess how many people do this sort of thing for the hell of it, I know a secret, I mustn't circulate it, if I circulate it I run the risk of being publicly disgraced, real Russian roulette, click, no one saw, didn't get caught, and I'm king of the castle, actually no one ever did find out what the minister's reasons were, it was even suggested that he was the Russian mole, a charge of culpable intelligence with the enemy could have been made to stick, but he didn't know enough, and besides the mole didn't stop digging.

And it was for this that de Vèze had been obliged to leave in his bed a woman who will never forgive him for the coarse words which had passed her lips, so there was a mole at the top, or in a major embassy, as seemed very likely.

A major embassy? could it be mine? Was all this designed to promote a few plumbers? The Americans had already tried the same thing under de Gaulle in '66, de Vèze remembers it well, it was a year after the famous evening in Singapore, the Americans and the 'porous' French! They claimed to have names.

At least at the time we didn't allow ourselves to be taken in by silly stories, no one believed that guff about having the names of dodgy individuals, they did it to pay us back for a speech de Gaulle had just made, in Asia, at Phnom Penh, a hundred thousand people, interminable ovations especially when he said that the Americans were facing 'a national resistance', that they should pledge to send their troops home, wild cheering, and then the best part, yes, it guaranteed everlasting hatred, that there was 'no way the people of Asia would ever submit to the rule of foreigners who came from the other side of the Pacific', Charles the Great, the Americans were purple with rage, a Moscow agent couldn't have done better, we'll teach you 'rule of foreigners', de Gaulle is just an agent for Moscow, Peking, any country that's coloured red, a radical act of betrayal, he never liked us, never forgave us for Yalta nor for our support for Algerian independence, no, that's not paying us back in our own coin, the domino effect, it's not the same, we'll explain it to you some day if you want to hear it, for the moment we'll destabilise you, there's a mole in de Gaulle's entourage, a hefty rumour, totally spurious, the Americans came clean about it much later, if you get the message, a load of codswallop, it was all part of the game.

But now, in '78, there's a full quarantine, it's already lasted more than a year, the counter-espionage people are very frustrated, they've been through all the biographies, pulled skeletons out of cupboards, set these people against those people, all hands on deck, plus a hunt for queers, like in England, suicides of a handful of men with wives and children, they also interviewed former members of the Normandie-Niémen squadron, why did you go to the USSR at that time?

'To have the pleasure of taking orders from a general who is a traitor!'

The same treatment meted out to old friends who had worked alongside communists during the Resistance, Guillaume, he'd told them straight:

'Go ahead, I'm used to it!'

And he pointed to his finger-tips. At the end of six months they'd had to tell the other African light cavalryman to call off his dogs, real moles aren't easy to catch, true, but we've still got this damned quarantine to deal with, rumours, echoes of echoes, and even the Italians seem to be keeping things from us.

It was so good, before, in the desert, 'de Vèze, you lead' and away they went, 'you'll link up with Amilakhvari and his Foreign Legion brigade, he's got six hours to make it, before sunrise', and away we went, over sand and shale Bir Hakeim or Qdret-el-Himeimat, 1942, an adventure on sand and shale against Rommel.

Then one day, much later, a formal dinner in Singapore, 'The Great Adventure is buggered!', some guffawing jester with big ears shouts these words at you, old but sprightly, had a way with him, shady type, like Scapin in the play who never lets anyone put anything across him, everyone around the table found it hilarious, and it takes de Vèze nearly fifteen years to realise that the jester was right, it took until the day the companions who'd shared the Great Adventure started refusing to have dinner with him because the morons in counter-espionage were busy setting up tradecraft here there everywhere.

Now if de Vèze has understood correctly, the Minister is asking him to take the strutting cockerel to Moscow, in his diplomatic bag, it's a provocation, stay calm, they're trying to force you into a wrong move.

De Vèze becomes engrossed in his scrutiny of the large brass inkstand which occupies the left-hand side of the Minister's desk, it must be a good thirty centimetres tall, two horses rearing up on hind legs over two hooded urns, two riders, one holding a drawn sabre, the other a lance, de Vèze wonders when this object might date from, it could be Second Empire, but are they cuirassiers? They don't have breastplates, hussars? no, these have helmets with a crest and slung over the flank of one of the horses there's a rifle, so they're dragoons, Third Republic then, but before 1914, when some people still pretended to believe in lance and sabre charges, grand-scale heroics, or the very first days of the Great War, charging at the Hun with sabres drawn before the statisticians at HQ had worked out that as a tactic it meant large losses for small gains.

De Vèze's father fought in the 1914–18 war, was in it until 1917, the year he lost a leg, never talked to him about the war, military medal, *croix de guerre*, Legion of Honour, mentioned in despatches many times, and never a word about the war, a silent hero, the house was all silence, his mother even more silent than his father.

All de Vèze knows about the First World War he has got out of books and from a handful of tales told by friends of his father, away from the house, there were also a few personal reminiscences of his junior schoolteachers or masters at his *lycée*, men who had gone to fight, the need took them sometimes, towards the end of the afternoon, instead of teaching the syllabus they'd look out of the window and start to talk, it was always the same thing, in the end we stopped paying much attention, we felt they had an urge to tell true stories, but at the same time they didn't want to put us off, and even when they'd started with a note of anger in their voice, anger against war, wounds, dying, the screams, the stupidity, that pointless war, it nevertheless always ended by sounding like what got printed in the newspapers on the eve of 11 November, no one was going to say we fought this war for nothing, we owed it to the dead not to admit anything of the sort, anger against war, anger against Germany which hadn't wanted to pay up, still hadn't paid up, nothing very specific about the war itself, de Vèze's friends knew his father, were proud of having a friend with a father like that, they also were proud of boys who were orphans, but that was less tangible than the wooden leg and walking stick of de Vèze senior when he crossed the school yard to go to his class.

One of his father's friends told him a tale or two of charges launched by the French cavalry at the very start of the war, follies perpetrated by dragoons, what a joke, an embryonic charge cast in brass on the desk of a minister who can't ever have been on a horse in his life, or picture the Minister sitting backwards on the horse, the sabre in one hand and the gee-gee's tail in the other, think Daumier, an urge to chuck it all in and shoot off for a week in Dinard with Little Miss Jealousy, he'll have to earn forgiveness for the disgraceful words she used, all his fault, a room with a view of the sea, a good way of getting it all back together again, breakfast in bed, croissants, she slices her croissant open, spreads red-current jelly, closes it and dunks.

And once she's finished, she stretches and waggles her legs.

She brings up their quarrel again, he replies:

'Bad language? You used bad language the other day? I don't remember, oh yes, what was it that woman did to me? What did you call her?'

And she would say:

'It was because I love you, you laugh when I get angry. That day, when you went off to see your Minister, I knew exactly what you were thinking.'

She would like to provoke him into saying something hurtful, she dreams of having a scene, I'm the only one she can have scenes with now.

'Henri, I'm sure you were thinking it was better when I was still married, I know you, I can read you like a book, you can come right out with it.'

No way! Dinard, you mustn't go there together, she'd have time to stock up on good intentions, besides in a railway compartment she can be unbearable, putting a hand on his thigh, fooling around, laying her head on his shoulder, getting all hot and bothered with her eyes shut, in full view of the other passengers, she doesn't see them, she knows they're looking at her, that they're looking at de Vèze, that it makes him feel uncomfortable, she loves it, she whispers:

'I don't care what other people think, I'm in love!'

Once she pulled a similar stunt in a cinema queue, she clung to him, said over and over I love your neck, I love your back, she was whispering but there were people not fifty centimetres away, she slips her hand round to de Vèze's back, under his jacket, her hand slides down, her fingers pull the tail of his shirt up, fingers on his skin, on his buttocks, she said I love stroking you there, they were going to see *Apocalypse Now*! There's nothing she likes better than putting him in that sort of situation.

This Dinard arrangement. Very nice is Dinard, families, dark blue sea, not too many pretty women about, they tend to go south, so not much danger of getting told off because you looked at one of them, like the other evening at Marty's when Muriel decided she wanted to swap places:

'What for?'

'Because I have no intention of allowing you to spend the whole evening ogling those two tarts sitting behind me.'

Or during an interval at the Comédie Française:

'Don't tell me you didn't see her!'

In the end he realised that a woman in a trouser-suit had stood next to him when he'd gone to fetch the drinks, she had smiled at him, he'd stepped aside, let her go first and replied to whatever it was she'd said. When he got back with his two bottles and two glasses, he'd had his ear well and truly chewed:

'Henri, if you want, I can go home and leave you here to carry on flirting, I see it's the mannish type now, she's flat-chested, go and check for yourself, but I won't be here when you get back.'

Dinard, swimming, there'll be breakers, watching the kites on the beach, there are more and more of them and they get bigger and bigger, a genuine sport now, with proper handgrips, great brutes with a span of three or four metres, forget all this talk of a mole, the kite nose-dives, finds lift just before hitting the sand, climbs whirring up into the sky, the boy standing next to his father, roaring with laughter, the wind, a rip in the canvas red yellow, some kites tear easily, others slip their lines, hurtle down and crash, the laughter too is extinguished, walking along old excisemen's paths, pass families on the way, see the craziest, the sweetest houses and think sweet thoughts.

The most attractive houses belong to the English, large picture windows with blue shutters, there's also a place that sells pancakes, that has photos of the twenties and thirties in dark brown beaded frames, the front page of a newspaper, also framed, with an article about the resistance in Madrid in 1936, the republicans with one gun for every two men, the article is signed Saint-Exupéry, also photos of a giant seaplane, something de Vèze had dreamed of when he was a boy, a Yankee Clipper, four engines, transatlantic flights in real sleeping berths, Dinard would be good, long walks, the waves crashing on the rocks.

Sometimes a squall there can be frightening, the air makes you dizzy, within moments you can't see the houses, the path is on a grassy slope, when a strong gust of wind comes along sometimes you have to sit down and hang on to a gorse bush, you don't have to but you never know, it can last a quarter of an hour, she nestles into my shoulder, her arms are around my waist, then we go on with our walk, I look at the gorse, I must take up botany again, then dinner for two, let Muriel choose for them both from the menu:

'Guess what I'd like.'

She'd answer:

'Oh, I know what you like.'

She would be terrifyingly tender, four days, don't suggest making it a week, say four days, maybe you could add a fifth at the last minute, days without braces or incident, until it's time to come back, which she doesn't like.

And instead of that, the strutting cockerel, Colonel Berthier, to be precise, but still in civvies.

That's why, two days ago at a reception, Maurice and Jacques told de Vèze:

'They promised you wouldn't make difficulties.'

Jacques added:

'Augustin, don't be daft!'

Augustin, his code name, a ridiculous name now but when he was young all the boys had wanted to be called Augustin, and all the girls dreamed of being Yvonne and smiling at some Augustin, that was when they were between thirteen and seventeen, in the Sologne, Jacques took him to one side leaving Maurice, who looked like a neurotic poodle, talking to the widow of a marshal.

Jacques with a mocking, snide smile:

'Get that Maurice, what a card, he's only trying to pick her up,' then Jacques added with a laugh, as if he were telling a very funny joke, 'and you can stop sleeping around, or do it with just the one, two at most, like me, but not in Moscow, you'll end up making enemies, some day you'll wake up with a great big bullet hole in the back.'

De Vèze did not care for that.

The Foreign Minister has almost stopped drivelling on, de Vèze has more or less understood, he has vaguely registered that he doesn't disagree, but that's as far as he'll go, stay calm, never react when you're riled, if you do react when you're riled remember that they'll have anticipated your reaction, smile disdainfully, show that you're treating this like a kid's game in a sandpit, as long as none of this gets in the way of your doing your job, say you'll complete your mission, the Minister replies, oh we've all got a mission, like hell we have, your mission as a minister is given to you by some Lady Piddle, you think you're Choiseul and Briand rolled into one, and you toddle off to some garret in the Élysée and report to a grey mouse who gives you orders, and you call that a mission, you've never known what a mission was, 'The Great Adventure is buggered!'

De Vèze, you lead, Koenig's orders had a certain panache. The meeting's over, the Minister stands up, he's getting a paunch, he tightens his belt a notch, he tries to lighten the atmosphere, he fiddles with his glasses, puts one hand on the plumber's shoulder and says laddishly:

'Henri, Colonel Berthier here is fully authorised to act, he could even make you turn out your trouser pockets if he wanted.'

Moron, a whisker away from a smack in the mouth. You didn't react, you've become like them, it's just like the devious oddball with the big, funny ears, like radar dishes, who'd been right in 1965, in Singapore:

'The Great Adventure is buggered!'

A large villa on a hill above the Strait of Singapore, a very attractive colonial villa like you get in the novels of Conrad, British Imperial Style, long-fronted, single-storey, façade a series of large dominos made of black and white panels, against a green background of tropical trees, they were in the garden, de Vèze, Poirgade, the joker with big ears, the French Consul at Singapore, his wife, a few guests, they were all waiting for the arrival of a man whom de Vèze had always admired.

You couldn't really say it had all begun at Singapore, though for de Vèze Singapore was beginning to have a portentous feel to it, but he also remembers something else that was said that evening, a comment aimed at Scapin, he of the big ears, by another guest, he couldn't say which now, it was intended to provoke, maybe it was Poirgade:

'No, not altogether buggered, just not a sure bet any more.'

*

Once again you've made the journey from Paris to the Waldhaus to meet up with Lilstein. A great many things have changed since you were a young Parisian making your first trip in 1956 and especially since the later one: in 1972 you became the general secretary of the annual Waltenberg Forum which welcomed you as a French intellectual, a Cartesian and Pyrrhonist who could be relied on to make the intellectual fur fly.

The Forum was a prestigious meeting of thinkers, politicians, top businessmen and economists. On the lines of what had already been done here in the inter-war years, the focus was on finding a principle of action, on being absolutely modern, you are accused of 'giving your allegiance to capitalism', you say it's quite true, and you proceed to defend capitalism.

In all this the crucial thing is to remember that in order to come here you no longer need to pretend to go to Lucerne or Zurich and then at the last moment take some meandering mountain railway so that you can meet up with Lilstein, you now have an excellent reason for making the trip: nowadays it's Lilstein who comes to meet you, he's the one who takes as many precautions as that fictional master-criminal Fantômas. Berlin, Warsaw, Stockholm, Brussels, Strasbourg, Basle.

He puts it about that he's a cousin of the hotelière, from Alsace, he always gives the impression of being up to something louche, as if he were her lover, he's fatter, he has a beard, looks older, eventually he admitted that his father was a theatre director, very well known in the twenties, it makes you laugh every trip, it's an age since you met in the great lounge, you each have your habits, the privileges of the old and valued customer, the hotelière was considerate enough to take a few of the painted plates you like from the dresser and hang them on the walls of the suite which she now keeps permanently for you, the two big ones in particular, on the phone Lilstein says:

'Ready or not I'm coming, young gentleman of France!'

You are twenty years older than when he first called you that, but he often still does. Now he bursts through a trap-door in the wall of your cupboard laughing, holding two helpings of Linzer on a plate.

'I come from the lower depths, from the bowels of the earth, like Punch but without the stick, like Harlequin, and I come bearing the best tart in the world.'

You laugh with him, he looks around your suite and adds:

'These are what we call "conspiring rooms".'

You laugh when Lilstein laughs but today you've started to feel scared, Paris is making big waves, you've even been told that de Vèze, the Ambassador, was being watched, you don't mind that, but you do wonder if this time there mightn't be someone taking an interest in you, you'd rather like to stay at Waltenberg, Switzerland does not extradite, still perhaps not, what would it amount to, spending your last years at the Waldhaus stuck between the spectacle of the Grisons and a view of a couple of painted plates? You watch the man with the slow movements who has just sat down facing you, it's Lilstein of course, but each time you see him again he strikes you first as the man with the slow movements, it takes you a moment before you get his name firmly placed again, you can't be afraid in this superb suite at the Waldhaus, it's not possible, you begin to calm down and Lilstein looks at you with a weary smile:

'Do you realise it's the twenty-second anniversary of our first meeting?'

You say what's an anniversary to me, add that you are more and more uncomfortable in Paris where you feel you're suffocating, you have this sense that a huge net has been cast and that you are about to be trapped in it, you can't feel anything yet but you are quite sure you're caught up in it, and all Lilstein has to say is:

'Jesters doing somersaults, it's the bells on their hats!'

Elsewhere whole networks are collapsing, large numbers of Soviets are going over to the West, as are some people from the GDR, not that many, but the ones who defect have a great deal to say, too much for your liking, and Germans are obsessed with index-cards and archives. If just one of Lilstein's archivists took a fancy to visit the Americans or merely his cousins in Bonn, your goose would be cooked.

'Quite,' says Lilstein, 'but we mustn't let that allow our Linzer to get cold, the only thing I'm certain of these days is that this is the twenty-second anniversary of our first meeting and that we're eating Linzer, not Sacher, praise the Lord! You don't know what the Sacher variety is?

'Sacher Torte is quite different, my boy, a Genoese pastry, a totally fraudulent reputation, chocolate and apricot jam, it's soft, gooey, whenever I've had to swallow a mouthful I've felt it had already been chewed by someone else, whereas this Linzer is as exceptional as ever, the jam is unctuous, the shortcrust pastry fights back exquisitely, as ever, and this time it again exudes a whiff of rum, do you remember? The hotelier's wife added rum once before, a long time ago, it doesn't make us any younger, did it never occur to you to wonder why, you might have guessed, do you want to know now? Think, it's simple, rum, a liquid, that means that the cook didn't use raw yolks but the yolks of hard-boiled eggs.

'Why? So that the pastry would be even more crumbly, but since a modicum of liquid is required and the yolks are hard, she added a spoonful of rum to the flour and butter before mixing, one spoonful, no more, just a splash, marvellous, at least the Linzer hasn't changed, not like everything else, are you really nervous? You know, speaking for myself, I'm more than nervous, I'm sad, melancholic, this may well be the last time we'll ever eat Linzer together, something I didn't fully realise when I got here, I went for a short stroll, as I always do, as far as the village before taking the cable car up here, for once I'd given myself enough time to construct a little hide, I wanted to see one of those lovely little rodents who suddenly panic when they realise how visible they are against all that snow.

'But I didn't see anything, or rather I saw the mechanical shovels and the bulldozers, Waltenberg is expanding, a heliport, it's an obscenity! For an annual *Forum*? The forums have always managed quite well without a heliport, as general secretary of the annual forum you could have lodged an objection, I'm joking, of course I know that was out of the question, and just as well they got their heliport, even more high-flying participants, more informal discussions, more data, a better return, an even more profitable undertaking, considerable productivity gains in information output, you see I'm up with modern economic thinking and the ethos of your Forum, but no matter, I'm still saddened, those bulldozers! That was when I realised how melancholy I'd got and that Waltenberg wouldn't lift my spirits, I look out at the Rikshorn through the window, and I feel absolutely nothing!

'There are too many jokers now, and as for us, we were the minders but we're turning into jokers, with one small difference between the two of us, which is that in my country they still shoot clowns, but it isn't the risk that depresses me, besides you run no risk whatsoever, from the start there never were any records, I told you, nothing written down, so there never was a records clerk filing everything we got up to, I never found any reason to write things down in black and white, that way no defector can turn you in, except for me, that's a joke, and if it proves necessary we'll stop meeting here, I won't come any more, you will say what you have to say directly to our hostess here, she'll pass it on, it's all very sad.'

And Lilstein adds something more depressing than sadness, more depressing than your fear, something which at a stroke cancels out all the reasons you still have for confronting depression and fear:

'I think, young gentleman of France, that we probably no longer serve any purpose. If I say "probably", it's merely out of consideration for you, in truth there is no "probably" about it.'

*

Berthier, Colonel Berthier, no first name, career launched by nabbing a traitor in the HQ of French Forces in Germany, following which he had swept France's Embassy in Rome clean of all the bugs which the Russians had accumulated there.

One morning, Lady Piddle had summoned him to her garret in the Élysée together with the Army Minister, she had told him in the presence of the Minister that from then on he would answer only to her.

A few days after the interview in the Minister's office in the Quai d'Orsay, Berthier stepped out of de Vèze's diplomatic bag and into the French Embassy in Moscow, he went wherever and whenever he wanted, sometimes he ordered the occupants out but most often he locked himself in with them, he was 'extremely sorry' but 'all the clocks had to be reset'.

He said 'extremely sorry' with a measurable emphasis on the last syllable, drawing out the 'ry', speaking through his nose for the fraction of a second it took to say it, an edgy drawl, an indication that the syllable could well blow up in their faces if the man who talked like that did not get answers to his questions right away.

And in the way he emphasised the end of the word 'sorry' there was a hint of latent, uncontrollable, vicious energy which was only biding its time before being unleashed from the restraints of common politeness and threatened the worst if Berthier were not helped as quickly as possible to stop him feeling so 'sor*reee*', such a polite word and ordinarily rendered anodyne because it figured so prominently in everyday speech, but in that edgy drawl it now regained the violence it once contained centuries ago when words meant what they said, when a man who told you he was 'sorry' was expressing the full extent of the 'sorrow' caused by the unhappy condition to which you had reduced him and at the same time gave him the power and the right to have you garrotted.

Berthier also used a thirty-page questionnaire and a ball-point pen in four colours, he spent his time clicking it, waited for the irritated reaction of people who can't stand hearing a ball-point pen being clicked, but no one dared tell him to stop. No, someone did, once: someone dared and had been told by Berthier that he seemed nervous.

And someone else had pulled a stunt, Mazet, in despatches, unimaginative sort, in a group meeting, fit of the giggles, every time Berthier clicked his four colours, Mazet did the same with his while looking at him innocently in the eye.

Berthier didn't stop, nor did Mazet, hence the fit of the giggles which convulsed the others, for a few days clicking ball-points was all the rage, Mazet became a star, eye more alert, voice stronger, and then Berthier told Mazet that there were irregularities in his records and took them away and kept them for three days. Mazet went back to being unimaginative.

Berthier went round repeating:

'The clocks are being reset, all the clocks.'

He was curt with the men, polite with the women. When he spoke to the women, he looked to one side, he became the major topic of conversation in the Ladies on the second floor, I'm telling you he isn't normal, got these cold eyes, everything about him is cold, he's asexual, I don't know about that, I haven't bothered to look that hard, and I shan't neither will you and that's a fact, you're just saying that, keep your hair on I was only joking, anyway it doesn't entitle him to walk into the Ladies without knocking, yes it does, he's already done it, twice at least, he did it yesterday, not here, on the third floor, oh excuse me he says but he barges in all the same! Into our toilets!

The nickname 'Bantam Bum' went round the Embassy like wildfire in competition with 'Lofty'.

One day Berthier claimed to have found traces of cocaine in the offices of the military attachés, these officers were minded 'to sock him on the jaw to teach him a lesson', they hadn't fought in the Algerian War to be treated like this, but not the naval attaché, he didn't mention Algeria, instead he stepped out into the corridor and yelled yes, I'm an addict, hooked on kerosene, drugs, treachery, I've got a secret to sell to fund my kerosene habit, two thousand seven hundred and twenty-two landings on French aircraft carriers, day, night, all weathers, it's a military secret, for sale to the Ivans, know this: French aircraft carriers are crap! the pilots on French aircraft carriers are crap! because they're all treated like crap! I'm going to tell the Ivans!'

Berthier asked for a dog, an Alsatian, to be sent from Paris.

'Just because you can't find anything doesn't mean you can do whatever you like,' protested de Vèze.

The way Bantam Bum went about his assignment even roused in de Vèze a certain fellow-feeling for the mole he was hunting, it must be priceless to be the mole and have daily dealings with the Bantam, a real hoot knowing you're running rings round him, you're facing this short-arsed nosy cop, he can send you to jail for ever and a day or even have you eliminated, and you're running rings round him, you're like a man sentenced to death who has managed to make off with the blade of the guillotine. Or rather you're like the invisible man, though you have an advantage over the invisible man, the invisible man is only invisible, he can see but runs no risk, that's all right for snotty-nosed boys, but a spy is visible and present, when people deal with him they think he's another person altogether, he makes that other person smile, a broad smile which dissembles his dissembling, he feels genuinely excited inside, you smile at people who are hunting you down to eliminate you, the tanks were hunting us too, we weren't smiling then, not a lot, but we were spying on them, we'd felt the same way when we were in our fox-holes, in the shale of the desert, waiting for the tank to drive over the top of us, so we could take him from the rear, a grenade lobbed from behind, a gap in the turret, the panzer was only vulnerable in two places, and when you managed to get one of them you could afford to smile, but sitting there in the hole while the great brute passed over without seeing you, that gave you a strange feeling, the effect was like some powerful drug.

The mole must feel like that, he – or she – lets Berthier walk past without seeing a thing, all the fun of an ambush, the mole cracks up when he sees Berthier at work. And de Vèze, pulling Berthier up short, 'just because you can't find anything doesn't mean you can do whatever you like', has the feeling that he's playing the mole's game, and the mole knows the game inside out.

De Vèze did not speak up too strongly for his military attachés, he'd never got on particularly well with them, they were drunks happy to be in Russia, the Alsatian finally arrives, he was called Baby, sleek black and tan coat, forty kilos of aggression, trained the hard way, he cocked his leg against the furniture, three drops each time as a marker, he sniffed around, marked, then sniffed some more. He was on the prowl.

One morning, he sniffed out a dachshund belonging to one of the officers, the dachshund stood its ground, as it did whenever it encountered a dog on a lead, it barked and stood its ground, Baby didn't bark, he wasn't on a lead, he upended the dachshund, he tried to rip its stomach open and the dachshund bit his bits from underneath, even an Alsatian trained the hard way gives his first thought to saving his bits, it was this that saved the dachshund, they were separated and then the Alsatian forgot all about cocaine and his three years of training, all he could think of was finding the dachshund and resuming their discussion, he went sniffing for him everywhere and drooled and peed every time he got a faint whiff of dachshund, at least this raised a laugh, and nobody found any cocaine.

All departments in the Moscow Embassy stood their ground, this isn't the place where you'll find traitors, moles winkle their way into your ranks, they're in counter-espionage like you, take the English, they have counter-spies to spy on spies, you recruit them any old how, Zorros and Pieds Nickelés, and when they're any good they use their skills to play a double game, even a triple hand, they're unstable types, here you'll only find people with traditional loyalties whom you can trust, straight-up people, some of them ram-rod stiff, but no dimwits, complete confidence, I can answer for all my colleagues.

Such solidarity! Wonderful! Berthier fiddled with his quadruple-clicking biro and revived his threatening sorrows, he put up with everything and got nothing, zilch, when he was weary of probing hearts and souls he turned his attention to walls and floors, then began a new round of interviews, but all he got were vague words and generalities.

They'd fob him off with generalities and he would canter off down the corridors on his hobby-horse, his questionnaire, only to be handed more generalities, there are far fewer spies about than people think, true sometimes there's loose talk, but don't make a big espionage thing out of the titbits anyone can read in the newspaper and repeat at cocktail parties, those are generalities, we can't avoid having conversations with the Russians if we want to know what's going on in Moscow or the country at large, what you've got to look at is the bottom line: we know a great deal about what goes on here, we've got to be trusted, we are people with traditional loyalties, with a sense of what's right, when I say 'we' I'm talking about people who have made this their career, the tenured staff.

These generalities were intended to make Berthier go to hell, and go away Berthier did, though he stayed within the Embassy, focusing on the non-tenured staff, saying where he'd come from and even which of their colleagues had sent him, or without saying so in so many words but letting the non-tenured staff work out who the bastard could be, because the harder you look the greater the need to believe in what you're looking for, and there are people who really believed that some bastard had dropped them in it.

Or if they didn't, they suspected that whoever was winding Berthier up by sending him away to get lost, i.e., in their direction, that someone was taking the piss, and they did the same, but a few of them started half-believing, A, what other people said about them, that they weren't as trustworthy as they thought, and B, what they themselves said about other people, though nothing ever went beyond the level of generalities, but no one much cared for any of these proceedings.

Berthier was told that his shabby little game would get him nowhere, and it didn't get him anywhere, a few titbits of gossip, people were above all that sort of thing, absolutely, an acerbic note in the voice, opinions changed about certain individuals of whom no one would ever have believed that they were so, oh, mum's the word, but we were above all that, we were happy just to pat the ball back, we saw clean through Berthier's little game and through everybody's little game, it was all so transparent, we retained our dignity, at least I'm not sleeping with just anybody, I never go out just anywhere, and Berthier starts peeking into the movements of those who do not sleep alone and those who go out, right, though at least you don't see those people hanging about the Embassy after office hours.

Berthier also questions the ones who stay late at the office, he tells them why he thought of questioning them a second or third time, still no names but a hot potato circulating at an ever increasing speed, keep alert, every man for himself, and not a closed door anywhere, no one dares shut himself up in his office any more, unless it's Berthier who closes the door, everybody remains on formal terms with everybody else, but no one really speaks to anybody and there are fewer contacts.

No one even dares go round with a hat collecting for a birthday or the rota for watering the indoor plants, so the plants shrivel, they are neglected, especially the papyrus on the second floor, the big one, the one on the landing by the window that needs so much watering, a papyrus in Moscow is not just any old plant, but with water it's possible, after all its name is 'feet-in-water', also a papyrus needs to be talked to, that's right, even plants need to be talked to, that was the view taken by Madame Cramilly, in the passport office, and by a few others too, including a man in security, but they were less forthright than Madame Cramilly in expressing their opinions in public on the real needs of certain house plants and notably the papyrus.

Besides, Madame Cramilly is not extreme in her views, it's true she talks to the papyrus, whispers to it while she's watering it or giving it a helping of the fertiliser which she arranges to have brought in the diplomatic bag, she speaks slowly but no one has ever made out what she says to it, when she's in a confidential mood she readily admits that she talks to the papyrus but mark this: she's never said that the papyrus talks back, it's not a dialogue, mischievous tongues allege that she has conversations with the papyrus, but that's outright slander, a bit of own-back because a few years ago she refused to contribute to the cost of a coffee machine to be installed in the office of Mademoiselle Legeais, whom she doesn't like, why her office? Because hers is the biggest, but Mademoiselle Legeais smokes like a man who has just hours to live, the image is admittedly brutal but that's how she smokes, she lights each cigarette with the previous one except when she intends to remove the filter from a cigarette, in which case she waits, she reckons that everything they say about tobacco is hooey, but that doesn't stop her waiting. When she has decided to remove the filter from her next cigarette, when she waits, everyone knows that she is going to remove the filter.

Madame Cramilly would never have set foot in her office where, to boot, people talk aimlessly, the coffee machine was a pretty low tactic aimed at Madame Cramilly who would have refused to go anywhere near it, so there is no coffee machine in Mademoiselle Legeais's office, no machine for making real espresso, a machine that works like the ones you see behind the counters in bars, they have several percolators, they cost a fortune.

At least thirty of you would need to club together, but even with the tax-free advantages of the diplomatic service, even a machine with only two percolators, and there is a really big difference in price between the two- and three-percolator types, the model offering best value-for-money according to Mademoiselle Legeais's consumer magazine was the one with two percolators, it would have worked with a bit of organisation, actually, that's wrong, actually it wasn't too expensive, though you could manage very nicely with two percolators, but faced by the cabal unleashed by La Cramilly it had not been possible to arrange a proper collection, Mademoiselle Legeais had only been able to purchase a machine which used paper filters, and there were already a lot of those in the Embassy, the big model, it's not exactly dishwater but it sure is no match for the percolator. And ever since then, the Legeais faction has never missed an opportunity to be nasty about Madame Cramilly.

No, Madame Cramilly doesn't have conversations with the papyrus, she just talks to it, while she waters it, yes, she has also arranged for a watering-can to be sent via the diplomatic bag, with a proper permit naturally, you know, in Moscow, watering-cans are poor quality, they weigh a ton and shoot water in heavy showers which leave holes in the soil and wash the best of it to the bottom, she talks to the papyrus so that it feels good, papyruses are social plants, all the encyclopaedias, all the specialist books on botany say so, and Madame Cramilly has read them all, at least all the chapters devoted to the papyrus, they are social plants, and when you force a papyrus to live in isolation, like the one on the second floor of the Embassy, you have to make it feel that it's not alone, that someone's looking out for it, which is why you've got to talk to it.

In her dealings with the papyrus, Madame Cramilly does the talking and has always been happy to do the talking, the rest of it, the stories about her having conversations with it, all the guff about Madame Cramilly actually imagining that a papyrus can answer her back, well, it's slander spread by Mademoiselle Legeais and her clan, they want to make Madame Cramilly look mad, but if they carry on like that it won't ever happen, everyone knows that papyruses can't talk, the papyrus has never once thanked Madame Cramilly for her kind words, no, Madame Cramilly is thanked by vibrations, the ones she hears of an evening at home, through the walls, they thank her for talking to the papyrus and taking care of it.

At first, Madame Cramilly hadn't believed in the vibrations, only in her own voice, and then one day she had made an astral contact when she was with some Muscovite friends, the Kipreievs, a lovely couple, both elderly, Madame Kipreiev was very fond of Madame Cramilly, they used to invite her round with a few of their friends, retired people, Madame Cramilly asked for authorisation to accept, séances are very entertaining, one evening, a series of rappings, a spirit came to the Kipreievs' table, it thanked Madame Cramilly several times but without saying for what.

It was not until six months later, in another round-table séance that the spirit had mentioned the papyrus, and the same spirit came back on another occasion, thanking her again, yes, quiet evenings, a small parlour, a mahogany table and a samovar placed not on the table but on a low chest behind the lady of the house, a most comforting samovar, deliciously pot-bellied, on the table was an embroidered cloth, little cakes still warm when Madame Kipreiev handed them round, aniseed cakes, very nice people who still remembered to hold their cakes over their cups before crumbling them.

Then Madame Kipreiev died, her husband became very depressed, no more evenings, no more rapping, no more spirits, Madame Cramilly continued to talk to the papyrus, she talked to it about the séances she had attended, about the spirit who had spoken to her on its behalf, and about her Moscow friends she now saw no more.

Then one day, not in her office but at home, Madame Cramilly thought she heard the echo of a voice, no rapping this time, not a spirit, a real voice, or an echo, then nothing, and two months later the voice returned, passing as a vibration through the walls of Madame Cramilly's flat, a clear voice this time, again it spoke of the papyrus and thanked Madame Cramilly, it was a vibration, and the vibration told her many other things. But now, with all this fuss in the Embassy, with all these questions, Madame Cramilly does not dare say anything, she doesn't even dare walk up to the second floor to speak to her papyrus as she used to, discreetly, but even so, remember, some people still poked gentle fun:

'And how's the papyrus today, Madame Cramilly? You know, we water it too, regularly.'

'Ah, how kind. But it's not enough, you know.'

'How do you mean?'

'Well, last week, I couldn't understand it, it was swimming in water, plenty of light, all it needed to thrive, the watering rota is fine, very well organised, but last week it started to droop, looked limp and drab, though it was swimming in water, but I spoke to it for longer than usual, the flowers perked up, it must have been depressed, papyruses must get depressed too, I'm like you, I find it hard to believe, but can you see any other explanation when everything is as it should be, water, the rota, and the papyrus starts to wither, then I talk to it and its lovely flowers brighten up again?'

Anyway until Berthier arrived, the papyrus had flourished, thanks to the watering rota in which all departments participated, plus Madame Cramilly's little chats, but now Madame Cramilly has lost heart, she no longer talks to the papyrus on the second floor, she doesn't dare walk up the stairs to water it, and no one does it in her stead, and certainly not Berthier, so with each passing day the papyrus is an increasingly sorry sight, and people have stopped speaking to each other, you know human beings, they have to talk, even Madame Cramilly, she even feels like talking to Berthier who is preventing people from talking to each other, if she talks to him, he'll go away and she can get back to normal and start talking to her papyrus again.

*

Lilstein has aged, we all get older, but for such a long time now you have thought of him as impervious to change, those clear eyes, the pale skin, he is tall, he used to hold himself very straight. Today, in your room at the Waldhaus, he slumps, there is less of him above the table, his shoulders have dropped, his eyes are dull, and he snaps:

'We no longer serve a useful purpose, young gentleman of France, our trade has become a melancholy one.'

Lilstein's hands dither, uncertain of what gestures to make, he syllogises, he rewrites history, he goes back ten years, he wants so much to be wrong, he struggles with a morsel of tart which refuses to be cut up with his small spoon, he gives up, points the spoon at you and says:

'Ten years ago, we fought against a stupid war in Vietnam, against the hawks who waved the star-spangled banner, it was a fine thing to do, and today in my camp there are fools waving the red flag who'd also love to have a war, one of their own, in the east, they're not proper soldiers or real politicians or even genuine fools.

'Shakespeare's fools have bells and a cap like a cock's crest, but there's great sense in their folly, they say "if you do not smile the way the wind blows you'll soon catch cold" or "let go when the great wheel rolls down the hill lest it break your neck".

'My fools are cretinous apparatchiks, high-hat Russians, Marxists who are still not done with the faith, holy writ, orthodoxy, they want to play at war, a real war, in some small country, far away, to close up the ranks and revive the faith, and in my part of the world, East Berlin as you call it, there are other cretins who give their backing to the dim comrades in Moscow, patriotic faith dressed up as a "proletarian intervention", imagine, one of them had the nerve to tell me that "proletarian intervention" is a "scientifically sacred" task, I'm still reeling with the shock of it, the same mistake as the Americans made, squared.'

Lilstein looks out towards the Rikshorn and gives a sigh:

'"Scientifically sacred"! That's going to cost us very dear. In Vietnam, we put an end to one war, now they're about to start another, in Afghanistan, perhaps it should be my turn now to give you information but I'm not sure if we could prevent this one, they've just appointed a new Minister for me to answer to, an oaf, dimmer than any I've had before, he's never seen a shot fired in anger, knows nothing about suffering or culture, he's one of Stalin's old informers, very interesting the career paths of those snitches, I wangled a seat for one of them in the Bonn government, and given what I can do with him, I'm not keen on having somebody else as Minister.

'But in Paris you too are scared of being the victim of an informer, I'm trying to put your mind at rest, but did you know that in Paris a list has been drawn up of seven hundred names and that yours is on it? Don't worry, it also contains dozens of ambassadors, prefects, ministers and former ministers, eat up, your tart's getting cold, you'll miss the aromas. Even the proprietor of *Paris-Match* is on the list as is the owner of *Détective* magazine, that says how serious it is! All the same, you are ready to jump ship and so am I, we're both in the process of having our Great Adventure shot from under us, they're going to win, they've set a woman on our trail, with a couple of eager blood-hounds, you can't get a decent dessert spoon anywhere, and here am I bewailing my lot, like a cat on hot cinders, that woman won't find anything but she's going to make the atmosphere unbreathable.'

Lilstein has resumed his tussle with his portion of tart, when he manages to cut it he ends up with pieces that are too small, he turns to you and complains:

'What's required is a spoon with a longer handle, for better leverage and more pressure, to help cut pieces from the slice, and one side of the spoon should be serrated, a kind of dessert spoon specifically designed for short-crust and puff pastry, otherwise we'll be like everybody else, have to eat with our fingers, one ritual fewer and one barbarism more, we do good work, but we do it for masters who don't deserve us, take mine: my first boss in the GDR, a weak and vindictive sort, and further down the line, yonder in the land of the bears, a second, master of all he surveyed, old, pot-bellied, you know he had himself appointed Marshal of the Soviet Union? And was awarded the Lenin Prize for Literature! Makes you feel sorry for Russian literature! Tolstoy, Gorky, Brezhnev, come one come all! Fortunately there are also Pasternak, and Solzhenitzyn, as you see I have tastes of my own. The old man, with his big belly, ensconced in the Kremlin, he spends his time arranging his medals in rows on his chest, he's got the medals already and would very much like to have his own war, in Afghanistan!

'But you also have two masters, one's in the Élysée Palace, a vain clucking peahen, doesn't bother much with medals, he worries about his baldness and his accordion, and such vanity, very touchy because he knows that in the long run he'll always have to kow-tow to a peanut farmer on the other side of the Atlantic.

'Even if we passed information to Mr Vanity in the Élysée, I haven't a clue what he would do with it, he could use it to put a spoke in the peanut farmer's wheel instead of giving him a helping hand, indeed he could, your chief has a lot of problems just now, because of us, we're working too well, the Americans are getting riled, we're really working well, but I don't know what we're doing any more, and here I am, no smarter than before.

'And no smarter than a fool, you remember, in 1956, I told you that we were going to work to let in the light, a rather portentous turn of phrase but there's always been a touch of that in the way I understood my role in spreading *Aufklärung*, and today I find it hard to see where the smallest glimmer of light would come from, I'd forgotten one thing though, wherever there is a lot of light, there is also deep shadow and that can be worse, a story about the death of Goethe: a play on words, on his deathbed the great man didn't say, as reported, *mehr Licht*, 'more light', but *mehr Nicht*, 'more nothing', I was a man of the Enlightenment and I produced more nothing.

'What information could I pass to your chief, dear boy? What would be the point? Our trade no longer serves a useful purpose, but listen, if your President were to forward a couple of choice details about Afghanistan to the Americans, it would calm them down and maybe call some of the dogs off us.'

*

No, in the Embassy people didn't start talking again overnight, and there's talking and talking, one word, two, a sigh, nothing definite, but as the days turn into weeks, Bantam Bum who had required people to talk to him has stopped asking, he no longer leans on people, is not so aggressive, sometimes he looks discouraged, stooped, human, not that long ago people would gladly have pushed him and his ball-point with four colours down the stairwell, but now, just because the days have turned into weeks which have ticked by, when Berthier sits down yet again to question someone he looks so weary, so shrunken, that you throw up your hands then let them fall on your desktop saying: what do you want me to say?

Nobody tells him anything, they just ask one question: what do you want me to say? They ask it so that he understands that the answer is 'nothing', so that he will go away, but at the same time the question you think you're asking him you are also putting to yourself.

It's just what people need to make them start talking, not a question that you asked to be put, you don't answer that one, you have your pride, especially when the person asking it walks like a bantam cock, no, the real question, which is the one you ask yourself when you put it to Berthier: what do you want me to say? You put it to him so that in the end he's forced to answer 'nothing'. But you've also put this question to yourself, and you've got to find an answer, and neither the word 'nothing' nor any amount of generalities will do, your self-respect requires you to come up with an answer that is true, and confronted by Berthier you start to answer your own question with generalities some of which are more specific than others.

Besides Berthier isn't that bad, for example, he didn't report the naval attaché, the aircraft carrier pilot who thought he was a piece of shit, or Mazet over the business of the biro and his records, no, Berthier understood certain things, and among the people who said that there were some things that he understood are some who said afterwards that if all this hoo-ha about a mole is true, then you need a lot of people to smoke him out, dirty work maybe but it has to be done, and to catch big fish you've got to get your arse wet, it's not about denouncing, Berthier actually loathed denunciation, he'd said so to two or three people, what he needed were pointers, generalities, some but not all needing to be more specific than others.

So that's where we stood, right, with 'generalities some of which are more specific than others', some generalities might give him a lead, he had packed up his questionnaire, now he seemed to be asking for help, he chatted, he still said he was 'extremely sorry' but did so without the earlier emphasis or menace, in the end he'd even put his four-spangled ball-point away, and when he was sitting, face drawn, eyes blank, he seemed to encapsulate the misery of a servant in a house facing ruin. He was becoming human.

People began to speak politely to Berthier, to chat, no one had cause to complain. The naval attaché had left on scheduled leave; on the second floor people had resumed watering the papyrus, the ends of its leaves had stopped turning brown, that truly stunning gold-brown that appears on the tips of the green leaves, but it's a deadly sign, the papyrus is a hardy plant but at the first hint of drought it dies.

And Madame Cramilly? No one had noticed if she'd started talking to the papyrus again, but it was likely that she was thinking about it, she seemed to be scared of Berthier but she always seemed to be bumping into him, she said hello, oh yes, people had started saying hello again, they were physically in Moscow, but they were among French people and living under French law! A guilty person was being hunted, but not ruthlessly, no one was being liquidated, so different from what the Ivans would do in the same circumstances. In the French Embassy the only thing liquidated was vanity, people spoke of this and that and reached an accommodation with their consciences. Until such time as consciences would become quite shameless.

And this included even Madame Cramilly, she had probably not started talking to the papyrus again but she now tried to talk to Berthier, scared though she was, she had already spoken to him, on two occasions, the second time at her behest, it lasted two hours, and subsequently it seemed that he was avoiding her and she was running after him, jokes were made about Berthier being harassed by an old lady who kept pestering him for another big session to go over important points.

What did Madame Cramilly look like? she looked like the old lady in *Babar the Elephant*, exactly like the old lady in *Babar*, small, a matchstick, thin lips, grey bun and pointy nose, no, she didn't wear a shawl over her shoulders, at least not at the office, a straight dark dress, cream collar, no jewellery, Berthier avoided her, but the old lady from *Babar* refused to let up, she had information of the greatest importance to give him, information that came from a very confidential source, she must have talked to Berthier about it once, he avoided her the way we seek to escape the agreeable and persistent caricature of ourselves that we all carry in our heads.

Sometimes Berthier looked happy, human. Had he discovered something?

Yes, a face in the carpet, or a pair of rabbit's ears in the shrubbery, things which vanish when you change the angle and stubbornly stay wool or leaves, he didn't discover anything at all but in the end he knew everything about everybody.

Only de Vèze had refused to talk to him.

'Her name is Vassilissa,' Berthier had informed him bluntly, 'and she's playing you for a fool.'

Berthier also went looking for hidden microphones, he tapped all the walls, he talked to himself in a whisper, affectionately you might say, he spoke vacantly to some person, to the furniture or his screwdriver, like Madame Cramilly and her papyrus, but the words weren't the same, do it for me, come on, be good, bitch, a whisper, a pointer, a lead, shit, he fenced with his screwdriver, do it for me, and his voice rose as he got to the last word, to 'me', grew almost strident, more so than when he'd been 'sor*reee*', then he started taking two-hundred-year-old items of furniture apart with a screwdriver, a hammer and the frenzy of the deranged, he started getting edgy with people again, he reverted to his previous vicious form as a persecutor of the innocent.

None of this discouraged Madame Cramilly, she was determined to have her long talk and seemed to know at any given moment on what floor Berthier happened to be, along which corridor he would pass, and she would lie in wait for him, she asked for that serious talk about important matters, or else when their paths crossed she said nothing but looked him straight in the eye to make sure he didn't forget that by refusing to talk to her he was committing a professional mistake.

At other times she would walk behind him without his being aware of it, and when he realised she was there he would scowl, though he never succeeded in putting her off.

True enough, people began to tease Berthier, they'd say 'good morning, Madame Cramilly' when they saw him coming down the corridor, to make him believe that she was behind him, it got so he no longer dared go up to the second floor and the papyrus, so the second floor became a haven for relaxed conversation, as someone remarked one day:

'I don't know if the papyrus really talks or if it's worth spending time trying to talk to it in private, but at least it allows us to chat among ourselves.'

So Berthier changed tactics, increasingly he would hole up in the wretched little room that de Vèze had allocated him, no window, only a sort of horizontal slit with a pane of frosted glass over it which didn't open, and when Berthier summoned a suspect to his rat hole, the suspect began by commiserating, it's grim in here, couldn't you get anywhere better than this? it's like being shut up in a cupboard.

He never responded, he would let the suspect score a point, sit down at a roll-top desk which must have dated from the 1930s, so that the suspect sitting across from him could see only the outside of the lid which Berthier opened after a few minutes, it was not possible for the suspect to see what there was inside.

With an ordinary desk, when you enter an office, you can see what's lying about on it, but not with a roll-top, Berthier would glance at intervals inside his desk and then look up at the suspect with his empty eyes, of course there wasn't anything in it, or maybe just an empty file, or the CV of an irreproachable civil servant, a few notes about the suspect from Intelligence, 'the concierge reports that . . .'

And Berthier would look into his desk like some small-time cop in a cheap detective novel, nothing to get nervous about, he could just as easily have left a file with the suspect's name on it lying around on his desk. All phoney.

Finally, he'd close his small-time cop's roll-top desk with a screech of slats made of old, dry wood, and too bad if all he had to go on were the few months that such or such a suspect had moved, at the age of nineteen, within the sphere of influence, as the expression has it, of the Communist Students Association, 'within the sphere of influence' because he'd never had a card, for someone had told the suspect that you should never sign up officially for any communist organisation, it leaves a permanent blot on your record.

The suspect had got a card under a false name, but he'd never trusted the secretary of the branch who had issued the card, a Stalinist, when the suspect had raised the matter of records the branch secretary had said 'no, in our records there are only aliases', and smiled, and in that smile the suspect thought he read contempt for his chicken-hearted petty bourgeois fears whereas what he saw was most probably the hypocrisy of the secretary who knew for certain that real names were also entered in the records, but in those days it was himself that the suspect did not trust and he'd been convinced that the branch secretary was sneering at him.

What had Berthier got in his roll-top desk? a note claiming that the suspect was once a sympathiser of the Union of Communist Students? Or a photocopy of the stub of his membership card, with both names on it, the alias and the real one? That was all a long time ago, the branch secretary who had enrolled the suspect as a member of the Communist Students was also a member of the Party, he was highly respected among the students, small voice, small build, small glasses, a tireless worker, destined one day to be a famous linguist, he'd been to a Congress of World Youth in the Ukraine and had come back with a small jar containing *tchernoziom*, that black earth so full of promise.

One day, the suspect learned that this sometime Stalinist branch secretary had left the Party to which he had been so attached, he had made his first trip to Peking and when he got back he had worked for six months in the front line of the class war, as a prole in a sardine cannery in Brittany; Prunère, the branch secretary who had become a Maoist was called Prunère, had been ordered to return to Paris, to join the Maoist organisation's central committee, his dialectical skills being needed in the ideological struggle against revisionism in the French Communist Party.

In Paris, the comrades could listen to Prunère for hours, fascinated by his dialectical skills, all the grassroots members who pasted and repasted thousands of posters on walls, those who handed out leaflets in the suburbs at six of a morning, those who stuffed newspapers up their lumber-jackets and anoraks as a protection against being beaten up by the lackeys of the bosses and/or revisionism, those who printed their leaflets at night on an old roneo machine which tore the stencils which then had to be retyped, those who helped the peasants get the hay in, or swept up on factory floors. You over there, go and dig in!

And You over there duly dropped out of his second year at law school to hump breeze blocks on a building site or can sardines, those who suddenly abandoned their studies when ordered to, so that they could meet the proletariat, they were all fascinated by the dialectical skills of Prunère, the Stalinist-turned-Maoist, and as the great work proceeded of sticking up posters, handing out leaflets, being smashed over the head, getting the hay in, and of wheelbarrows full of breeze blocks being trundled by the grassroot membership, Prunère the Maoist rose up through the ranks of the organisation.

The more the comrades put themselves about, the better Prunère was able to speak on their behalf at a senior level in the hierarchy, he had himself worked in a sardine factory, not for ten years like the others, just for six months, but it had been enough for him to acquire the kind of proletarian experience the organisation needed, he'd returned to Paris, on an even higher rung, he played a fundamental role in the 'revolutionary vigil' while carrying on with his university studies, he drew up documents containing charges designed to confound the forces of revisionism, both the objective revisionists and the bogus objectively bourgeois revisionists, he kept an eye on the proponents of autocriticism, and maintained the thought of Chairman Mao Tse Tung in all its purity.

One evening during a meeting devoted to maintaining the purity of the thought of Mao Tse Tung, Prunère singled out one comrade and demanded that she be sent away for a spell of manual labour at Nœux-les-Mines and then told another he should go and do likewise at Carmaux, now everyone knew that those two comrades were living together, he accepted but she kicked up a fuss, she was a sociologist specialising in the mechanism of the exploitation of the proletariat, a girl of solidly middle-class background, comrade Prunère accused her of continuing to exploit the proletariat she claimed to be defending, she then launched into a piece of very elaborate argumentation.

She said that by making a career in their revolutionary organisation Prunère was exploiting the work of grassroots militants, that if he was able to pursue a career therein as a permanent officer in it he did so on the back of the thousands of hours which the militants gave freely in the service of the organisation, all Prunère needed to do was say that her socialism was 'narrow and blinkered' to end the argument and, since the sociological comrade had quoted the work of a number of Yankee pseudo-scholars in her erroneous thesis, she was excluded without further discussion. The motion to exclude her was drafted by the comrade who was living with her.

The stub of the membership card carried only the alias, that was standard practice in those days, so Berthier has got zilch, but what about that little matter of the hashish when the suspect was working in Morocco, but his Moroccan friend, a colonel in the gendarmerie, had hushed it up, two hundred grams, not worth bothering about, but don't be so stupid in future, surely you know that the kids who sell the stuff by the side of the road are in cahoots with the gendarmes just a kilometre further on, if you must smoke, come along to the house, the family are away, everyone will be having a good time, there'll be dancing girls from the village, but bring some good cognac and some Havanas, I prefer them.

Berthier has got nothing on the suspect, the suspect isn't actually a suspect, but all the same the suspect searches through his suspect's memory, an over-payment of salary which he'd never reported, that business of the cheque that had almost landed him in it, so that in the end the roll-top can contain many, many things, and everybody appeared for a second time before Berthier and his desk, a stack of secrets, whether inside the roll-top or not, and a large number of suspects, a car which had been in an accident and had been sold on without full details being divulged to the buyer, a large sum which had been omitted from an income-tax return, a bank account at Klosters or Lucerne, because Geneva is for small-fry, two or three stupid letters written to friends who had sought asylum in Franco's Spain although you never shared their opinions about French Algeria, a gambling debt paid late, now that could cost you dear, a couple of days spent in Vienna with that Polish guy, true you'd never seen him again but you'd never reported it, a Pole or a Romanian girl, that could turn out expensive too.

Brother Berthier wasn't even in a proper office, he occupied a cupboard, without a proper window and without any form of heating.

'That'll teach him,' de Vèze had said.

Berthier couldn't care less, he's the one doing the teaching, he keeps his parka on, and he blows hot and cold on tenured colleagues and fixed-term staff, the civilians, the uniformed, the wise, the devious, the weak and the proud, his strength lies not in knowing people's secrets but in his success in convincing them that they have secrets from him, and they've always known that it's not right, Berthier waits, he lets the suspects sort through their secrets all by themselves.

*

In the Waldhaus you listen to Lilstein, he's not wrong, he repeats, 'we no longer serve a useful purpose, young gentleman of France', you'd better listen, call a halt to the whole thing, no records, no records clerk, if what he says is true you're in the clear, you've been playing this dangerous game for more than twenty years, you could get out now, without a scratch, you could go on living in Paris, meeting whoever you like and not have a worry in the world.

What does worry you is that Lilstein looks a broken man, his word was 'melancholy', but you've never seen him like this, if he doesn't stop, he'll end up clinically depressed, and then one day he'll say 'the hell with it' or something similar, and he'll throw his hand in for all the world to see, it would be to your advantage to anticipate events, to go over to the other side and be the one who turned first.

Are you going to betray Lilstein? He's never put you in any danger, you don't betray someone just on impulse, there's a small matter of honour, and beyond the matter of honour there's this: if you do go over to the other side, what baggage will you take with you?

If you have nothing of value to pack, it means at best fifteen years in a cell in the Santé prison, and everything you've done up to now will have been meaningless, it'll be your turn to be depressed, but here's the worst irony in this whole mess: you're about to shut up shop at the very time when at last Lilstein hands you a right royal scoop: Afghanistan. You remember your old pact: 'we'll be equals', Lilstein had said on that very first day.

Nor is Lilstein wrong in what he says about your respective masters, going on what you know of your President he'll give the Russians a free hand and carry on playing his accordion in the Élysée.

So all you need do is use Lilstein's information to force your President to take a tougher line with the Russians, he wouldn't be able to just let them get on with it any more, that would make him look as if he didn't appreciate the gravity of the situation, if he is given information or advice which will encourage him to be firm, he can't then say that it's all come as a surprise to him, and he'll relay it to the Americans, and the Americans will be pleased with France and her President, a win-win situation, you already stopped one war with the information you passed on.

No, that's not megalomania, Lilstein gave you the exact figure for American losses in Vietnam, no one knew it, you were given the real figure before even the American President got it, and you passed it on keeping everything low key, and now you're going to stop another war with the information you are about to receive. This time it'll be the French telling the Americans: 'the Russians are going to invade Afghanistan.' Ties of friendship renewed with Washington.

You don't need to stand on a platform or chant 'Stop the cannon! No to machine guns!', that sort of thing never served any useful purpose, you say nothing, you eat Linzer tart with Lilstein, and the war fades into the background. In the Élysée, your President is inclined to negotiate with the Russians, everyone knows that, you only have to read the newspapers, but the day he learns that the invasion really will happen he'll be forced to tell the Americans and he'll stand shoulder to shoulder with them and NATO will force the Russians to back off.

'The best thing,' Lilstein tells you, 'would no doubt be to call a halt now, that way they'd stop hunting for a mole, we'll have had a pretty good run, a Great Adventure, and you can stop worrying. Let's leave them to their war, after all, why shouldn't the Russians be entitled to a little colonial war, like everybody else? I'm not even sure many people will try to stop them.'

*

Everyone filed in and out of Berthier's cubby-hole except Madame Cramilly, who went and complained to de Vèze, and de Vèze sent her packing, and Madame Cramilly told him that she had seen Berthier coming out of his – the Ambassador's – office one day when he was out of town.

'That's his job,' said de Vèze.

He scribbled a telegram for Paris: 'It's him or me.'

Chapter 6

1978

Four or Five Lilsteins

In which de Vèze takes a ride on a merry-go-round near the Palais de Chaillot.

In which, despite your age, Lilstein continues to address you as 'young gentleman of France'.

In which we are present at the very first meeting of de Vèze and the niece of a Soviet marshal.

In which, in the presence of a lady, you have a reaction which might well compromise your activities as a mole.

Moscow, June 1978

. . . human beings who as they stood before me have
imperceptibly divested themselves of their first and
often their second and third simulated selves . . .
Marcel Proust, *Time Regained*

Berthier burst into de Vèze's office:

'You've got to hand it to them . . .'

He'd come straight from the telex room, a sleepless night, at last he'd found a number of bugs, not in the furniture, not in the walls, but inside certain machines, some of them dead simple, wires connected to a condenser with a shunt resistance, it modulates a high-frequency wave which can be tuned into remotely, better than tape-recorders any day said Berthier, he'd found his sharp tongue again, he gave orders:

'No one comes in, no one goes out until I've finished here.'

He asked Paris for reinforcements, they arrived within twenty-four hours.

'Why "Lofty"?' one of the new arrivals asked a secretary.

'Because he's so close to the ground.'

Virtual house arrest for all personnel, and a pretty good haul, electronic receivers in the telexes and especially the coding machines, high-quality work, built into the circuits, parts disguised as transistors and condensers, the equipment was pretty old, according to the technicians the appliances dated from the early sixties, and the instruments ditto.

Stout machines, sturdy, in the French mould, with a cast-iron base, the kind that don't often need replacing, riddled to the core with bugs by the craftsmen of the KGB, doubtless when they were being brought from Paris to Moscow, would you believe, by rail in sealed trucks, and they'd been checked on arrival, that's right, by unskilled workmen, early sixties, that meant the bugs had been installed in de Gaulle's time, that's almost fifteen years ago.

People in the Embassy breathed again, no one had seriously believed there was a mole, and when Berthier left everyone congratulated him on doing a good job, before the month was up, Madame Cramilly gave him a small papyrus in a pot as a present, he said very nice things about her, he told her that she reminded him of Céleste, the old lady in *Babar,* a lot of playful confidences were exchanged but no one told Berthier what they called him behind his back.

The naval attaché returned, this was Moscow, life there was not always easy, but the Embassy recovered and again became an efficient and happy community, with its dachshund, its papyrus, its military attachés, its four-colour ball-point pens and its old lady, a kind of scaled-down Célesteville, from which anger, discouragement, slackness, stupidity, fear, laziness and ignorance eventually faded under the benign influence of patience, knowledge, intelligence and hard work.

All minds now were focused on getting ready for the barbecue to be held in the Embassy gardens, the next big occasion.

In Paris, the President was not the least put out by this discovery, everyone calmed down, the aged Moscow equipment was repatriated and replaced by new machines which had the blessing of the Americans, who had even been allowed to give them a health check. Just in case, a team was set up to check out the staff who'd been involved with messages and codes during this whole period, some had retired and were living in the country, that too caused some problems for individuals without producing any positive results, there was an excellent report which summed up the affair, the point being to stop a few people sleeping easy in their beds.

According to this report, a great deal of information had been leaked via the interceptors, not things which were very secret in themselves: for the sensitive stuff the old tried-and-tested precautions were observed, no names, no plans, but a sharp eavesdropper could get a very clear idea of Western policy by putting together a few general principles contained in messages exchanged between the Embassy and Paris.

And that's how the Russians must have found what was more or less a green light for their invasion of Czechoslovakia in 1968, when a French ambassador asked to know what he should say to the Kremlin by way of caveats and was told he should say 'that it has been agreed with Washington, London and Bonn that we shall remain, within limits, flexible'.

Perhaps the investigators made too much of this in order to make their discovery sound important.

So the Minister had been right to send in Berthier, he summoned de Vèze to Paris, this time it is not known if de Vèze knocked before entering, what we do know is that the Minister allowed himself the luxury of apologising to de Vèze for Berthier's mission, it hadn't been easy, but it had been worth all the trouble.

'That's why, Ambassador, I assumed full responsibility myself, from the outset.'

Now if de Vèze were to feel like taking a spot of leave, it would be a way of demonstrating French disapproval to the Russians without going too far, yes, de Vèze could even go away somewhere, not for long, but he could breathe more easily again, the Minister could do no such thing, de Vèze was a lucky man.

On leaving the Minister's office, de Vèze ran into some very old friends, the corridors were buzzing again, his companions from the old days smiled, hands were firmly shaken, hands that had lobbed grenades at panzers and now suddenly rediscovered their warmth and vigour, de Vèze loitered, filled up on sympathy, and while he stood there, in the corridor, a lot of people seemed to walk past as if by chance, it went on a fair time. He even tried to cross Poirgade's path, did it casually, but he was told that he was away:

'He came up trumps, you know, always spoke up in your defence.'

In the late afternoon, de Vèze left the Quai d'Orsay, wanted a breath of air, felt like going at his own speed, he went out by the side door, thought he'd make a brief pilgrimage, walked by the plaque put up to the memory of the crew of the *Quimper*, a tank belonging to the 2nd Armoured Division, which the Germans had shot up on this spot during the Liberation, de Vèze had known the crew.

On the wall of the Ministry, old bullet holes had been left deliberately.

De Vèze walked on, turning right on to the left bank, along the tall iron railings of the Palace, the monument to Aristide Briand, very kitsch, the bronze bas-relief, Briand receives a procession of grateful women, the women vertical, very straight dresses, hair gathered into plaits and the plaits pinned up like crowns on the top of their heads, one frieze dominates the rest: a ploughman, a shepherd, cattle, ears of corn, the France of 1932, a blacksmith is included though, but tucked away in a corner, the age when Poincaré expressed satisfaction that France had achieved a balance, with half her people in towns, an ideal to be perpetuated, unlike the Americans who were descending into decadence and industrial chaos, well spotted, 1932, a France already behind the times by thirty years and happy to be so.

On the sides of the bas-relief, in columns, a hotchpotch of contradictory quotations about peace and country, disarmament and defending the nation, all jumbled up, but absent are Briand's most famous words, 'Away with the cannon, away with the machine guns', from his great speech in the League of Nations, it was the one their teacher had given them as a dictation, at Cluses, the great dream, and they'd had to learn the dream by heart. Didn't quite square with the plaque, thinks de Vèze with a smile, but at least it's got a certain something. He'd liked his teacher very much even if he'd only realised it much later. A fairly young man, a pacifist, who put on shorts to take them to the sports field, he taught them to walk in step in the street, football under one arm, because in the long run, it's discipline, it's team spirit!

De Vèze is fifty-five, but it's only now that he notices that he is a fifty-year-old man, your sixth decade a woman friend pointed out to him, even if you've given up wearing braces you are a man of mature years, he's not thinking straight, he looks down on the Seine, Paris, the water of the river, it has this green colour, it's weary too, the light scatters sparkles on it when a gust of wind blows against the current, Vassilissa hasn't written, de Vèze pauses uncertainly as he looks at the Seine, he invariably has a moment of uncertainty when he goes for a walk along the *quais*.

Shall it be the booksellers on the right? Or the quieter way to the left, towards Passy and the Île aux Cygnes?

He has nothing to read at the moment, he has many books in his flat but not one he feels like opening before going to sleep, such as *Capitaine Fracasse* or *The Count of Monte-Cristo*, a ripping yarn, nothing depressing, or how about a biography? it would have to be well written, with some thought in it.

He opts for the booksellers and turns right along the *quais* in the direction of the National Assembly, he's just received three invitations to dine with old wartime comrades but he's not taken in, all he has left are memories, he's like a stopped watch, which can make you do silly things.

He walks along the *quais*, another marble plaque on a parapet: it commemorates one of his best friends, Varin de La Brunnelière of the 1st Chad Foot, volunteered at eighteen, killed a hundred metres from the Place de la Concorde, gold letters on a white background, de Vèze reminds himself that he still has a few acquaintances hereabouts, on marble plaques, the same thought that occurred to his old friend Hatzfeld the day they walked up towards Belleville, Roland Hatzfeld, a communist, but not a card-carrier, or if he did have a card no one knew, a fellow-traveller as the expression went, a big lawyer with his feet under many tables, had chambers on the Île Saint-Louis though he still lives in the same part of Belleville where there's hardly a street where a Kherlakian or a Leibowitz wasn't murdered by the Nazis.

During their walk, Hatzfeld had stopped several times at plaques, the old pals circuit he'd said, then they'd sat down together in an

Algerian coffee shop, not big, with stools, and ordered baklavas, honey, ground almonds, real puff pastry, the proprietor had made a point of coming over to say hello to Hatzfeld.

'The most important element is the puff pastry,' said Hatzfeld, 'it should retain its bite beneath the honey, crunchy but not hard, baklava keeps for two days maximum, after that you've been had, I trust them here, and they don't use chickpeas or hazelnuts instead of almonds.'

With one hand Hatzfeld motioned to the streets outside along which they'd just walked:

'You see, the Resistance was like Marxism: lots of Jews and dagos.'

'Yes,' said de Vèze, licking his fingers, 'but there were aristocrats too, Boyer de La Tour, du Chastellar, and there was that man Robin de Margueritte who passed you your orders in 1944, they've got plaques too, down on the *quais* by the Seine.'

'Much grander, but on German posters our lot were scum, and we were proud of it, we wouldn't have changed places for a king's ransom, even if there are high-minded people nowadays who accuse the Party of sending us out to get killed.'

'I was sent out to be killed too, every day,' said de Vèze, 'they do say that's what war's all about.'

'You have to have been through it,' concluded Hatzfeld.

When they left the coffee shop, de Vèze laid his hand on his friend's shoulder, he squeezed it as he walked along by his side. Hatzfeld is the sole surviving member of a family of sixteen. After a moment, de Vèze asked:

'Your Algerian friend, is he in the Party?'

Hatzfeld, why not give Hatzfeld a ring, go back and eat more baklavas? De Vèze walks along the *quais* towards Notre-Dame, here are the first booksellers after the Place de la Concorde.

A short while ago, at the Quai d'Orsay, in the middle of all that handshaking, he'd been given a specific order, it came from the President, it had been passed on by the Minister: a month before going back to his posting, the President is only too happy about this, he thinks it will hang over the Soviets the threat of a recall of the French Ambassador, the fact is that Monsieur de Vèze is remaining in Paris, for talks, no, he hasn't been recalled, not officially, but we do not know whether or not he might also take a spell of leave, you know, life in Moscow isn't all that restful, yes, vital to maintain our great friendship but not, my dear fellow, at any price.

De Vèze walks along the *quais* and starts thinking about maybe a trip to Singapore, a short pilgrimage, a journey back to the sixties, to that evening in the villa, he wants to see it all again, why does he feel this so strongly? A colonial black-and-white villa bought from the English which was used as an annexe for the French consulate, the gleaming black of dominos on the façade basking in late afternoon sunshine bouncing the white back at the tropical green of the garden, the admirable pitch of the red-tiled roof and the huge living room displaying its collection of mahogany furniture to the plants in the garden, with a veranda where the table has already been set, white tablecloth, Sarreguemines plates, blue pattern; above the table there is a delicate chandelier, when lit it casts an indulgent glow over people's faces.

What de Vèze remembers particularly is the surprise he'd felt that evening, in 1965, he'd come specially from his posting at Rangoon, he'd travelled to Singapore specifically to say hello to a man he had always admired.

And instead, he'd met another man altogether, unexpected, genial, with big ears, who'd flung those words at him: 'The Great Adventure is buggered!'

On the *quais*, de Vèze has passed the Pont Royal, is approaching the Pont des Arts, suddenly he turns and retraces his steps, a moment ago he spotted a book in one of the booksellers' boxes, the title had caught his eye, he can't recall it now, a yarning sort of title, an author who wrote of faraway places, the sort of book that makes you want to pack a bag and go, or write something yourself, just the thing you want when you're on holiday, the volume was displayed face up, on the extreme left-hand side of one of the book boxes, who was it by? Not Pierre Loti, de Vèze passes along the boxes, who on earth is going to buy all those German newspapers published during the Occupation? no not a book by Morand either, Kessel maybe, there'd been only two booksellers with anything by Kessel, de Vèze retraces his steps, slaloming through the tourists, comes to a halt before the cover of a volume wrapped in cellophane, *Wagon-lit*, that was the title, and the name of the author guarantees that it won't be another *Madonna of the Sleeping-Cars*, Kessel, a name to reckon with.

Tonight, in his hotel room, de Vèze will have what he needs to go roaming, a big book, wide-open spaces, no big words, pace, but check first, the bookseller is rather unhelpful, he refuses to remove the cellophane, that's three times today I've been asked, it's a first edition, keep opening them and books get damaged, and the pages aren't cut, anything by Kessel you snap up, oh go on then, I'll open it for you, de Vèze doesn't care for the man, he leaves him to it and walks on, then he remembers that the book he'd seen hadn't been wrapped in cellophane.

He looks for the other bookseller, there it is, *Wagon-lit*, and it's half the price, and the pages have been cut.

A few metres from him, the bookseller is busy, he's talking about another author to a customer, a woman, yes, I've a copy of the first edition, de Vèze tries to overhear the conversation, blare of car horns, the swish of a bus passing along the *quais*, I paid five hundred old francs for it, the cover was badly damaged, roar of a passing motorcycle, did you know it was turned down by Gide no less? Which is why it was privately published, it has a dedication, I had it rebound for my own collection, I've kept it, sometimes I run my finger over the dedication.

De Vèze opens *Wagon-lit*, yes, an account of a long journey across Europe, going east, the Gare du Nord, one evening on a whim, Paris, Cologne, Berlin, Olsztyn, Siauliai, Riga, beyond, just took off, a woman, yonder, de Vèze reads: 'I felt the thrill of the fever, the frenzy, the wild call, gradually fill me, grip me, swamp me.'

No way! all those kilometres and what you get is shop girl effusions and words that come in threes, and that 'wild call', at this point the author has reached Riga but the phrase hasn't left Paris, de Vèze thinks he's not being fair, he looks for something more succulent, turns Kessel's pages with childish anticipation, he'd really like to go travelling with this book, 'as if she were regaining consciousness, a fierce fold formed in the space between her eyebrows', he holds the book in his hand, 'fierce fold formed', two thousand kilometres for a fierce fold to form, he puts the book down, his eyes fill with tears, you can't count on anybody, a Minister, a plumber, months of madness ahead.

He doesn't feel like reading any more, he's had a bellyful of book-sellers, he turns and walks back, still following the *quais*, finds himself back opposite the Place de la Concorde, thinks about crossing the bridge, he doesn't care for the Champs-Élysées, he stays on the left bank, quickens his step as he walks past his Ministry, carries on as far as the Pont de l'Alma, then, drawing level with the Eiffel Tower, the Pont d'Iéna, just at the start of the bridge is a small fair, with a merry-go-round framed by two rearing horses, each on a plinth, loudspeakers blaring the song 'Ah, le petit vin blanc', the horses in rows of three rise and fall along their axis as the merry-go-round turns, then 'Ah, le petit vin blanc' is followed by 'La Mer'.

Between the rows of horses are two elephants with seats for tiny tots, the horses are hideous, cream and gilt with manes that are variously brown, green, blue, purple, one of the tots is accompanied by his mother, he is crying, he wants to get off, the merry-go-round revolves; among the horses is a donkey, just the one, the ticket office advertises a free cuddly toy for anyone buying six tickets. There is also Snack-Go-Round which sells everything, popcorn, Belgian waffles, frites, ice-cream, two-scoop cornets, beef tea, candy-floss, crêpes, sausages: two cherubs float above the till. Next to it is a gift-and-souvenir stall which sells Eiffel Towers in various sizes, plus key-rings, scarves, spoons, ash-trays, paper-knives and pens, all with the Eiffel Tower on them. There is also a man selling roast chestnuts.

De Vèze does not linger, he looks over towards the other end of the Pont d'Iéna where the Palais de Chaillot rises, on the left, he crosses the Pont d'Iéna.

He reaches the other side: an even bigger roundabout, a two-tier merry-go-round, the horses are superior, the colours less gaudy, there's no donkey but there is a black horse, night is falling, there's no one on the upper tier, de Vèze strides up to the ticket office, buys a ticket, waits until the previous ride has finished, leaps boldly and decisively up the stairs to the top deck, loudspeakers are playing 'Ah, le petit vin blanc', de Vèze is up there all by himself, Paris spins around him, the decorated façade of the Palais de Chaillot, the ornamental pool, the roofs, the trees, the Seine, the pool again and the bas-reliefs, the bridge, the Tower, he feels good.

In Paris, the good times have returned, listening devices disguised as transistors, the whole business has left everyone feeling relieved, France had been caught out by machines, but there weren't any moles, moles were for the English and the Germans.

In the land of Joan of Arc, the native breed remained untainted.

After a six-week leave, de Vèze flew back to Moscow, a smile on his face, in the end he did not go on his pilgrimage to Singapore as planned, someone had told him that the black-and-white villa had been sold.

In Moscow he began seeing Vassilissa again, quite openly, de Vèze never hid any aspect of his private life, it means he doesn't have to answer questions put to him by underlings or short-arsed bantams, he notes everything in his desk diary, and makes no bones in doing so, entries that read 'visit from Mademoiselle Soloviev', or 'out with Mademoiselle Soloviev', often writing 'ma demoiselle' as two separate words, in the diary which after all is an official record, quite deliberately, hide nothing, you don't get bothered that way, Vassilissa is tall, blonde, a mathematician whose field is non-commutative algebras, niece of a marshal, no less, who has a seat on the Central Committee, that's the main reason why they are left alone, Vassilissa has brisk movements and a tight little bottom.

No one except Berthier has ever dared raise this subject with de Vèze. How would you do it? A man with a record like his is untouchable, the minute you ask him a question which he himself has not prompted, he looks straight at you, and you feel he is about to ask what the hell you did between 1940 and 1944, not in 1945 when there were already too many on the bandwagon, he has time only for survivors who were in it from the very start, like him, and when they send him a survivor who speaks to him candidly, the said survivor limits himself to making some trivial observation, because you don't treat a man like de Vèze as some minion.

Yes, things are beginning to look up, but you can't act yet, you'll have to wait until he does something stupid, he doesn't do that often, even this girl he has in Moscow, it's not very prudent, she does maths, knows all about non-commutative algebras, you never know, anyhow that sort of thing's just not done, and the Russians seem as wrong-footed as we are, but everything's clear and above board, that's their strength, they do something that's quite outrageous and never try to cover it up.

If the girl had picked up a low-level cultural attaché, she'd already be an inmate at Magadan, or at least at Yakutsk, alternatively Paris would have settled for recalling the cultural attaché, but as things stand she can look all and sundry right in the eye, it might be worth trying to make life hard for her because she'd slept with a hero of the Second World War, and the Russians know that if they ask for de Vèze to be recalled he won't be replaced by a Gaullist, Gaullists are an endangered species, so they prefer to hang on to him, de Gaulle might have called him in and said:

'Ha, de Vèze, go to it: to bed!'

But de Gaulle isn't around any more, anyway, who knows, he might just have muttered 'de Vèze? he's just doing what men do', and left it at that.

De Vèze and Vassilissa see each other Wednesdays and Saturdays, they prefer Saturdays.

Wednesdays are lively, they use de Vèze's flat in the Embassy,

275

Vassilissa knows she's there for only a couple of hours, she wastes no time getting into bed, she has given de Vèze a present, a small painting in the naive style which she personally nailed to his bedroom wall, it shows a couple of closely paired dolphins leaping the waves, she expends her energies directly, once she told de Vèze:

'If you want to know all about men, first you must wear them out.'

Saturdays are different, they can go off to the little house Vassilissa has in the country, it's not the same Vassilissa as on Wednesdays, one thing de Vèze really likes about the house is the wall bed, mattress a bit soft, a king-size duvet made of real feathers, but Vassilissa says: no, walkies first.

The wood is full of birch and sweet chestnut and is very old and overrun by bushes, but it blends the light into varied hues of gold and ash.

They walk along the course of a winding stream as far as the small spring where it starts, they pass anglers who start scowling and muttering as they walk by, they startle pigeons which splash through the pools in the middle of the path, and cats out stalking field-mice, they reach the spring, a barely audible gurgle of tiny bubblings which break through the turf close by an outcrop of velvety black roots.

They look around them, their eyes are soon reeling with the water, the sands, the reflections of branches and the sun, they stay there for some time, it all seems so uncomplicated, the grey of the iron-ore which changes to red, the surface of the water which sometimes gleams with rainbow colours.

'No, it's not oil, Mister Know-all, it's the composition of the ore, I'll explain, I love being able to explain things to you from time to time.'

The water laps low, a rustle of birdwing. A silence deep in the foliage holds everything together. On their way back, they pick sour but edible blackberries.

They have their slow times, de Vèze likes watching Vassilissa wash, he fetches water from the pump, he heats it, pours it into the cistern, a more than rudimentary shower, not much more than a trickle of water, Vassilissa laughs a lot and uses de Vèze to hang her towel on. Sometimes it happens that they spend a Saturday night in the house, they have a little time, de Vèze kisses the back of Vassilissa's heels then as he works upwards sometimes he hums two lines of a song they'd heard in some friends' house when the children were being put to bed, he only remembers these two lines, they don't rhyme, 'there is a jolly butterfly, it's like a flow'r that blows', Vassilissa lowers her hand, strokes his hair, it makes her tingle and she smiles because de Vèze sings slightly off key.

On Sunday mornings, de Vèze is woken by the squeak of the handle of a coffee mill being turned, he gets up, Vassilissa holds the coffee mill steady between her legs, he tells her that in another life . . .

'I know,' she says, 'you'd like to be a coffee mill in this house, but sometimes my aunt has first call on it.'

As soon as the weather turns warm, they hear the sound of birdsong through the blind. No one disturbs them, it's their gingerbread house, they are left alone, the days of Stalin are over, de Vèze is a big boy now, relations between France and Russia have always been special, de Vèze is a Gaullist, the uncle of the said Vassilissa Soloviev is a marshal, a hero of the Soviet Union, Stalingrad, storm troops; that must be it, that accounts for the affection the Marshal has for de Vèze: how did you throw grenades at a panzer? Toss them into the tracks or push them through a slit in the turret? Which is worse, sand or snow?

But perhaps they go out of their way to avoid wartime reminiscences, each of them knows exactly what the other one did, so they speak of the books and paintings they like or go for walks; and what they did in those old wartime days simply adds a background resonance to what they say, they also talk about nature, the fields of rape, oh yes, come the spring, all of a sudden, a great slap of bright yellow administered to thousands of miles of terrain, from the Atlantic to the Urals.

Marshal Soloviev raises his glass to the fields of rape, that's one plant at least, *tovarich* de Vèze, that continues to thrive, according to the directives issued by your Great Charles, from the Atlantic to the

Urals, your Great Charles now sadly no longer with us, I drink to the rape plant, to the Atlantic, to the Urals, and especially to Great Charles! you shall take me to see the Atlantic, shall we say from Brest, comrade Ambassador? in exercises for the general staff in Moscow, I was given the role of officer commanding the military region of Brittany, not the French commander, the Soviet officer who leads the occupying force, I always managed to get all the way to Brest with my men, very serious *Kriegspiel*, it went fine, you can show me Brittany, fields of rape that sweep right down to the sea, and on my side I'll take you to see the Urals after I retire.'

And the Marshall toasts friendship:

'*Za drouzhbou, tovarich!*'

*

There is no tall dresser behind Lilstein now, you are both ensconced in your enormous room at the Waldhaus, but the hotelière has, specially for you, hung a few painted plates and two of the large dishes from her complete Alsace service on the walls, so you can see, just as it was twenty-two years ago, as it ever was, the large dish showing the homely company leaving the party, the spinning-girls with lanterns in winter, and for the first time you look seriously at the other large dish hanging next to it, it shows country-dancing in the open air, you never paid much attention to it, you always preferred the spinning-girls, but now there's something that doesn't feel quite right about it and makes you stare at it. Lilstein picks up on your puzzlement:

'Yes, it's been changed, they never managed to find an identical replacement.'

And then you realise what it was that made you look at the dish.

'Someone broke it a few years back,' said Lilstein, 'and the hotelière never managed to find another with the original design, she found a different one with dancing, same size, but it's nothing like really.'

This new scene is more static than the other. Insofar as you remember the other one at all, having never looked at it very closely, it was richer, more boldly drawn; in the one hanging up now the people are as stiff as their high collars, the first row of dancers is observed from the back, they're easier to paint like that, the girls especially, only one of the girl dancers is seen from the front, in the background is a man with a trombone who does duty as the orchestra, and you're trying to remember something you never looked at properly.

The orchestra on the dish that was broken was a genuine orchestra, with trombone, trumpets, violins, and there were real girls dancing everywhere, even a couple on the right pretending to dance who were actually making off in the direction of the wood, a couple seizing their opportunity.

In the plate hanging in front of you, the people are stiff, unbending, there is a wood in the background here too but nobody heading towards it, there's just a curtain of trees, a rather amateurishly rendered curtain of trees, no one here ready to seize their opportunity, a rather sad scene of jollity.

You've remembered, in the other dish time passed in laughter, but that's because you can remember it, now that's water under the bridge, forget it. The first country dance scene has disappeared, someone must have looked at the broken pieces one last time before putting them in the bin, Lilstein turns round to look at the dish:

'This one, young gentleman of France, lacks the colourful rhythm of life.'

*

The way de Vèze and Vassilissa first met was like something out of a novel, a ball no less, in the presence of her uncle, Marshal Soloviev, a ball in Moscow, the Soviets love balls, in the mid-1970s, nostalgia for Tolstoy, full evening dress, not in the Kremlin, nor in the Ministries either, in the British Embassy, some Soviets begin to be fashion conscious, but style for the majority still means bulging paunches, pillowy bosoms and cheap perfume, and when a man is unmarried, like de Vèze, he is required to dance with the wives of Soviet officials or ambassadors' ladies, a thankless task if you like dancing, mangle a waltz with mature matrons, one or two exceptions but rarely more, it was the number two in the French Embassy, the resident minister, who drew up the pecking order, he doesn't like women, here's your dance card, Ambassador, he was really rather pleased to land de Vèze right in it like this.

De Vèze waltzed assiduously for a time then retired to a corner of the room to relax with his old comrade Soloviev, he tries to spot pretty women, meanwhile on the other side of the dance floor, near the refreshment buffet, in the middle of a group of starchy, sagely nodding diplomats, a young woman wonders if the French Ambassador is really that tall man over there wearing tails and a single decoration, which is barely visible, a small green ribbon with black edging, he looks quite young, why did my uncle give him an army salute when he's not wearing medals? There must be a rule, to be greeted with respect and affection by a marshal of the Soviet Union you must wear a single medal, one is enough; my uncle can't have made a mistake, maybe it was the light, he himself is wearing a kilo and a half of medals, that's what my aunt told me, nearly a kilo and a half by the kitchen scales, and even then he's not wearing them all, he doesn't want to offend certain comrades.

He's not talking to this Frenchman as he would to an ambassador, the way he talks to the English Ambassador for example, he puts one hand on the Frenchman's shoulder just as he would with an old wartime comrade, though I've heard that our officials should not have such close contact with foreigners, each time a hand is placed on a foreign shoulder there has to be a report, yet they're really doing the old pals act, but my uncle looks a great deal older, how old's the Frenchman?

It's complicated, my aunt explained it all, I'm only a girl, I'm not allowed to talk to high-ranking foreigners, I may answer if they speak to me, but I mustn't bother them, I can't walk over to this Frenchman and ask him why my uncle is putting one hand on his shoulder in that familiar way, I'm here with young people of my own age, artists, young diplomats with big careers ahead of them, to create a happy, carefree atmosphere, but without pestering the grown-ups, and since this Frenchman has better things to do than talk to me, we'll never talk at all, but he does have style, I've got to talk to him, I'm young, it's a court ball, I'm sixteen years old, my eyes are all a-flutter, I've pinned a rose in my hair, my heart is racing, I'm wearing satin slippers, I've walked across a red carpet, down a flower-lined staircase, at this moment only the Tsar is on the dance floor and no other couple dares join him, my arms are thin, my breasts are small.

I'm a good dancer, I know that at a ball you have to be asked quickly, I'm not going to be asked, you have to be among the first couples when everyone can still see you, someone is walking diagonally across the room, he's more than twenty metres away, I blink my eyes to check the tears that are starting, I won't be asked, he's a prince, he's coming this way, he's coming straight towards us, the room is very big, they say that he's one of the best dancers of the age, and he's a hero, he's going to ask my sister, or my cousin, he's so handsome, he almost got killed at Austerlitz, he was waving the flag, he's chosen me, what did he feel when he took me in his arms? we're dancing, everyone's looking at us.

No, I'm not sixteen, our present Tsar doesn't dance any more, he hasn't for at least thirty years, and I'm thirty, my arms aren't thin, my hair is fair, I'm a good swimmer, my breasts are large, I could wear a much lower neckline but my aunt looked unhappy when I tried on the other dress, she didn't say anything, she looked unhappy, that was enough for me, she knows, the only thing she ever dares say is that I could be married, I asked her to find me a hero. For her, it was easy, she saw a hero in 1943, she married him, he worships her, he's never laid a hand on her, when he gets drunk he sleeps at the Ministry, he's drinking less and less, I've tried to find a husband, nowadays all the men are wimps, they talk about cars, drink hard, get jealous and squash the life out of you on rough sheets, my aunt drove lorries during the battle of Stalingrad, my uncle told me she was a goddess, they had no children, they'd like grand-nephews and -nieces, the

Frenchman looked at me, I'm sure he did, are there any other good-looking women here tonight?

There are all these Western women, not all, but some are really beautiful, on the skinny side, and there are our women artists whom the Westerners always manage to invite, I'm not a dancer and I'm not a violinist, but I'm positive that I must look very pretty when I'm loved, I am a very good mathematician, more often than not I don't need to work out my calculations, I just see them, apparently this ability doesn't last beyond thirty-five, but for the moment it's working well, and I can play the cello, I should play more often, where did they get these pyramids of cherries? Nobody dares touch them.

That dancer from the Bolshoi has obviously spotted the Frenchman, she hasn't taken her eyes off him, dancers are shameless, they know that people make all sorts of allowances for them, this one is old, she's a star but she's old, that's why she often puts a hand up to one cheek, because of her white glove, not far off forty, and skinny, her back is very arched, and she's smiling at him, I always wanted to be able to walk like a ballerina, she turns her back to him, she's skinny but you can see how her body is already beginning to sag.

The Frenchman is looking at her, he must be thinking that she walks well, men only see what interests them, ballerinas can do anything with their pelvis, it's true that I don't walk well, I've been told I shuffle, but my shoulders go all stiff when I try not to shuffle, what I need is a firmer, more springy step, then my buttocks won't flop this way and that, the ballerina from the Bolshoi has vanished and now the Frenchman is chatting to my uncle.

'In my capacity as a marshal of the Soviet Union, I'm going to give you a confidential mission, *tovarich* de Vèze, and you will obey, so drink up and ask my niece to dance, she's the pretty blonde, the tall one, over there, who is smiling across the room, dance with her and tell her how wicked you Westerners are. She believes foreign men are more gentle than Russian men, she's attractive, she's unmarried, she's a great worry to me and my wife, she won't listen, she does maths, in this country we treat mathematicians like sacred cows.

'They do whatever they want until they get packed off to Yakutsk, I'm afraid she wants to marry a foreigner, it will only end in tears, she went out with an Englishman for a while, don't laugh, they're not all queer, or else they change, it will cause a lot of trouble, be nice, go and tell her that in the West men behave as badly to women as we do.

'Tell her that with an Englishman she'd still have two jobs, her maths plus the shopping, the kids, housework, cooking, just like here, but we won't be there to look after the children, and anyway she won't be allowed to go to England, she'll be sent to Yakutsk, she'll be forced to have an abortion, personally I don't give a damn about what happens to me, everyone knows I'm not ambitious, never was, Tukhachevsky taught me all I know, I admired him, they shot him, and it was on that account that I rose through the ranks so quickly, no ambition, because after the war I undertook certain little . . . undertakings for the good of the state.

'They can put me out to pasture whenever they want, I've always voted with the majority and I'm a hero of the Soviet Republic, I was made a hero of the Soviet Republic twice because when a lot of people get killed the survivors are decorated to honour those who did not, you know, seven and a half million soldiers died in four years, sixty per cent losses, that's a lot of dead heroes, so they turn the survivors into twice-, thrice-decorated heroes, I am a twice-decorated hero who votes prudently, that is, with the majority, here that sort of attitude is highly respected, I'm not afraid for me but I am afraid for my niece, especially when I won't be around any more.

'Go and say rude things about Westerners, *tovarich*, so she falls into line, as you people say, and blesses us with grand-nephews who are one hundred per cent Russian, I'll take them skating.

'You needn't even bother to go for her, look, she's coming over here, she knows she's not allowed to bother officials, but not being allowed to is a challenge for her, ask her to dance, tell her that your lot are just as heartless as our lot and that you don't know as many poems, no, she's stopping, it's the turn of those men to dance now, men in skirts, they'll dance with each other.

'See? she'd rather watch men in skirts dancing to that awful caterwauling.'

De Vèze and the Marshal stop talking, they are standing at the front of the spectators a few metres from the group of Scottish soldiers, you can't have a British ball without the crossed sabres laid on the ground, swords or straight sabres, points touching, and under the chandeliers, four men in pleated skirts and red jackets, hands on hips, they leap rhythmically over the swords, kilts flying to the skirl of bagpipes.

A few spectators exchange smiles, four other groups of four men in each corner are also dancing, but without swords, there must be some pecking order, twenty dancers in all, they are bare-headed, another dozen men are making the music, pipers and drummers, the men playing the drums are wearing black bearskins and golden yellow jackets, it's a small band with a tall drum-major, the sword dance is more than jumping up and down to music, it's light, heel, toe, half-turn in mid-air, or *entrechats*, not proper *entrechats*, that would be too feminine.

What they're doing is what soldiers can do when they're relieved of the burden of combat, their packs have been removed, they could almost be said to dance well; but with drums providing the rhythm, the spectacle keeps its military character, reaching out for the hands of their comrades, forming a harmonious group, even so it's not exactly *Swan Lake*, in the end they gather up their swords, amusing to see the face of one soldier who picks up his sword and salutes with it, lips together, jaw clamped shut, veins standing out on his hand and forearm, blade held vertical in front of his eyes, eyes fixed on some distant horizon, they don't see anyone, they call it 'a martial air', it means not looking happy, a woman looks up at the chandelier above the head of the drum-major, de Vèze likes the blaring pipes because in the desert these men had made up the main body of the infantry, and the reinforcements, the bagpipes had played 'Scotland the Brave'.

'I'm quite aware, Marshal, that you don't care for men in skirts, but at El-Alamein they were at the head of the infantry when we broke through Rommel's lines, the Germans had left an inviting underbelly exposed in the centre which was intended to suck in the Allied armour, but Montgomery steered well clear of it, the armour stayed at home, he dispatched infantry *en masse* to the German left flank, this plus the wailing of the pipes created an awesome effect. And that night in camp, those lads in kilts performed the same dance, with swords on the ground, I like it a lot, even if they also did the same to us at Waterloo.

'Anyway, look, they're going, here comes the waltz! You may well prefer the waltz, Marshal, which featured at the Congress of Vienna, you have reactionary tastes, your niece is coming this way, she walks a little stiffly, a military step, is she really your niece?'

*

And then out of the blue came the second alert, when the boffins in the lab in Paris disclosed the results of their analysis after the long summer holiday. True, all the devices discovered by Berthier in the Embassy in Moscow, all the recorders, dated from the sixties, but some of the soldered joints were much more recent, they'd been done more or less at about the time they were discovered, that is in about the spring of 1978.

They wasted no time.

Six vehicles outside Berthier's house.

'He's in hospital,' said his wife.

In the intensive care ward, Berthier had become a vegetable, with red, green blue pipes sticking out of him everywhere; a stroke, cause unknown, recovery ruled out.

Berthier's eyes were blank and staring, this did not prevent some investigators detecting in them the dejection of a man who, after he'd taken everyone else in, had himself been suckered. Others saw something quite different: the elation of a man who had made the ultimate sacrifice.

A traitor. But Berthier had a cast-iron CV, had only his salary coming in and not a penny more, never played politics, parents Catholic, not rich, graduated from military college, just one blot on his school record, he once got a nought in maths, it was when he was studying for the Saint-Cyr entrance exam, he handed in a blank script because he knew the whole class was cheating, wife a Catholic, no mistress, not even a mild flirtation, his sons were Boy Scouts.

They went back and looked some more. Nothing.

Served in a commando unit in Algeria, never had to take prisoners into the woods, never did any of those things that sicken a man and make him want to atone by doing something, anything.

A Gaullist, he'd opposed the putsch in Algeria but hadn't shopped anyone. After Algeria, he'd gone into counter-espionage, got interested in techniques of transmitting information, he had sailed through every stage of the very thorough vetting process each year, the man was a paragon.

Since his clean-up in Rome, he had been given full authority to sweep diplomatic premises abroad, the only thing they'd come up with was an uncle who admired Maurras and had been saved from the chimneys of Buchenwald by the camp's communist network, that's where analysts in the barracks at Mortier reckoned it all started, all his holidays as a boy and a teenager were spent with this uncle in Normandy, no doubt in hearing all about Stalingrad and the great struggle against barbarism in between fishing for trout, collecting mushrooms and setting a few snares, not everyone agreed that what followed started there.

Berthier will never speak again, and the uncle died in 1970, a poor man.

In the end, they'd had to face it: it was Berthier himself who had installed the bugs he claimed he'd discovered.

Why? Because the Russians had needed to make the French think that the leaks were coming from their own Embassy in Moscow, and to do that they'd risked blowing the cover of a specialist plumber it had taken them almost fifteen years to plant there.

The conclusion of the first security flatfoot on the scene: the aim was to protect someone they believed was even more important to them than Berthier, someone who'd been there for a long time. The most plausible hypothesis: a mole, operational since the mid-sixties, so the whole damn thing must have been set up nearly fifteen years ago.

When de Vèze was told, it struck him that this more or less coincided with the period he'd spent in Asia, when he'd been Ambassador in Rangoon, those were good times too, he pictures himself once more during a trip to Singapore playing croquet one evening on a lawn on some island which would still belong for a few months longer to the British Empire, he was waiting for someone he admired to arrive, killing time talking to an elderly man with big ears and a young woman in a yellow dress who wasn't wearing a slip.

In the world of counter-espionage, the Berthier affair at least produced one certainty: the mole was not a rumour.

Then began a new round of break-ins, they'd try anything, at the DST, the Ministry of Internal Security one of the senior managers decided to go to extreme lengths in the use of the ultimate capacities of the human mind: he imported a dowser, who waved his bent twig over lists of names of top civil servants, with a view to coming up with an astral link, the results were interesting.

They had another go at the veterans of the Second World War, especially the ones who had got on in life, next thing you knew ministers' offices were full of enraged people, throwing their Liberation medals on the floor, a torrent of foul-mouthed abuse, then the Gaullists kicking up a stink again, followed by a second visit by their leader and his colleagues to the Élysée, and one of them, with strong Corsican accent, told the President stories about patriots 'and not the puppets of international finance'.

The President remained firm, the investigations went on, everyone felt naked.

Then small newspapers, the kind which are delivered in sealed envelopes, began carrying stories dating from the time of rumour, fury, and reports from the far-right nationalist OAS of attempts on de Gaulle's life.

And of how young junior ministers had very probably handed the would-be killers the timetable of the movements of the man they called the Great Zohra, the specifics weren't easy to check but they were detailed and looked accurate, but what on the other hand was checkable were the photocopies of the founder of the OAS, General Salan as presented to the Special Court, it contained minutes of Cabinet meetings and had been discovered among General Salan's papers the day he was arrested, no comment was added, readers were allowed to work it out for themselves: who could have passed on to the head of the OAS details of what went on in Cabinet meetings? A hot potato, a dangerous dossier for everybody, it couldn't be checked out, the President cooled things down.

Actually, the whole thing eventually settled down, the President started saying and ordering officials to say *niet* to the Russians at every turn, a section of the Soviet Embassy was expelled, *Pravda* described France as 'jittery', then the Russians suddenly seemed less well-informed, the Americans seemed less aggressive, France's external intelligence agency the SDECE and military security went on turning up nothing, and the DST kept waving dowsers' twigs.

And de Vèze was made to pay for the Berthier business and the electronic listening devices, there are such things as counter-espionage procedures, you don't give a man like Berthier, even if he has full authority, a free run of the most sensitive areas of an embassy, with a soldering iron up his jumper.

De Vèze had taken Berthier to Moscow, de Vèze was responsible for him, reservations were expressed about the way he had handled the matter, but the Minister had defended him, with all the inflated eloquence of a junior counsel, the occasion was used as an excuse for recalling de Vèze to Paris, a spell in central administration before another ambassadorial posting, but de Vèze knows there'll be no other embassy for him, he won't be thrown on the scrap heap of course, he'll be offered unacceptable postings and get saddled with a reputation for being picky whereas we are all servants of France, he is no longer untouchable, at last they can forget all about Bir Hakeim, the minefield, the discreet green ribbon with black edging, draw a line under three decades of being upstaged.

One day in the Quai d'Orsay, de Vèze pens a note for the Minister, he tells him he feels that he has been the victim of a plot, his embassy could not have been selected at random, the investigators should have gone further back in time, they should have allowed him to remain in his post and prowled around him, waiting and watching. If he gets shunted into touch, whoever set him up will drop him and target somebody else, we need to start again from the beginning, he is ready to collaborate, to trawl through his past with the investigators, he's sure he must have crossed the path of the mole at some point in his career, everything would have to be cross-checked, meticulously, he is thinking of Singapore.

In his letter, he also tries to tell the Minister he has seen through his little game, he knows that in politics the biggest bastard is the man who speaks out warmly in defence of an opponent thus giving himself a clean bill of health so that he can shift the blame elsewhere when it suits him, you defended me like a lightning conductor, you directed the thunderbolts down on me as a way of covering the fact that it was you who saddled me with Berthier, you are a minister, you drop bricks so you can pick them up again later, it gives you a feeling of power, you ride on the backs of others.

De Vèze realises that his sentences are too complicated, two and a half pages, he feeds them into the shredder and settles for a three-line letter of resignation, it's the answer to everything, he drops his letter in the internal mail and leaves the building, giving the porter a doll as a present for his little girl who is sick.

He is alone, nothing seems to mean much, Jug Ears was right when he'd said 'The Great Adventure is buggered!' more than ten years ago. Today, there are only lies, and it's the laughter of Jug Ears in Singapore parodying the man de Vèze had come to meet, it is that old laughter which now has the colour of truth.

De Vèze decides to walk upriver along the *quais* of the Seine, as far as Notre-Dame, he passes the Pont de la Concorde, goes down the steps to the river bank to escape the traffic, he has plenty of time now, he can travel, follow his nose, or not, it's too late, he should have started earlier, he'll give it a go, buy a sailing boat or become an ethnologist, just take off somewhere, is he still fit enough for it? Or maybe write a book to escape the pack, to get away from the bastards, a bit late for that too, writing, de Vèze has missed out on so much, it's not easy to start telling stories when all your pen has under its belt is thirty years of diplomatic report-writing, and people like jovial Jug Ears from Singapore who could have stepped out of a stage farce and tell you with a laugh that it's all over, 'The Great Adventure is buggered!' people who mess up their lives and then give you the benefit of their failures.

'The Great Adventure is buggered!' De Vèze walks under the Palais Royal bridge, sharp smells, there's no one around, he shouts so he can hear the echo bounce back off the arch of stone and girders, 'The Great Adventure is buggered!' and in the echo he seems to hear once more the voice of Jug Ears, like the crack of a whip, just like that first time.

Resigning wasn't a very clever move, it's what they expected him to do, by handing in his resignation he has allowed a page to be turned, poor de Vèze, a casualty of the Berthier affair, and anyway it was his own fault, his wandering prick, in this profession you can't be too careful.

The trap had been laid a long time before, Moscow, it was no accident, he'd been fingered, and he must have met the man who'd fingered him. One day, a note had been made about him: a man who puts it about a lot, that's how it must have started, a ladies' man, plenty to say for himself, already in a senior post, a track record which will ensure that he'll go even higher, a juicy target, de Vèze would very much like to meet up again with the man who'd fingered him.

He's enjoying this walk along the Seine, a corridor, with a wind blowing along it chasing all that city smog away, de Vèze has now reached the Pont des Arts, he can see the Île de la Cité, the statue of Henri IV on his horse, it's de Vèze's favourite, he halts for a moment in front of it.

The French continued to look for the mole, without creating as much upheaval, but they didn't give up, the mole must have been part of an estimated circle of three hundred people, this was judged too small, so it was extended to six hundred.

One day, the Americans sent Paris a copy of a Russian document brought out of Moscow by a defector, an excellent survey of ten years of friction between France and her allies, very methodical, with high-grade information on NATO which should never have gone outside the family, one of the deputy directors of the CIA flew specially to Paris to discuss this document, a man named Walker, Richard F. T. Walker, a man who put his questions casually:

'Is what the Russians claim you're saying about us true? Is that really what you think of us? Or is it what the Russians would like you to think about us and you do genuinely think about us? Or is it what you say when you know the Russians are listening, so that we get the idea that you're doing it on purpose and we finally start trusting you? It's an amusing game, but you've got to come clean and tell us once and for all, because it's bizarre that the Russians think that you aren't a very easy ally to have, even though you've broken with Gaullist foreign policy, as your President has confirmed several times, personally, to ours.'

Walker, very Princeton, all tweed and corduroy:

'You know, what we can't figure out in this Russian document, yes, it's authentic, we checked it out, it cost two or three lives, notably the defector's father, anyway what's bugging us isn't the general political anecdotal material, no, but in it there is also intelligence about France's view of the weakness of NATO's southern flank, those shoot-outs between the Greeks and the Turks, the detail is too specific, the cliché of the nation of talkers, did you really say those things? You need to keep tabs on your military, otherwise we'll have to start looking up their asses, back home there's some of our people think we should take a closer look at your President, but they're neanderthals.'

Assurances were made to the Americans, they were given guarantees, more strenuous efforts were made to investigate the military, and the military began looking at the non-military, the whole business started up again, out of control, some slack had to be put into the loop.

To complicate matters, there were two suicides in the circle of the six hundred, they kept a lot of people busy for very little return, the first one had wearied of counting his multiplying malignant tumours and the other had almost certainly suffered some terrible blow, the sort that makes you shake and sob before making the most anodyne of phone calls, and you chew your fingernails down to the quick and you promise that starting tomorrow you'll leave your nails alone, you cry, you swallow a dose of Optalidon. Everything, except a lead.

They couldn't see a thing, like owls at noon, so the other hypothesis was revived, that there was no mole, that the mole was an invention of the paranoid minds who ran counter-espionage, people who dreamed of spies the way other paranoid persons imagine that their child has been killed so that they can unleash on the killers all the tortures they've been dreaming of ever since they stopped being children, a phantom mole which did ten times more damage than a real one, in any case he wasn't called a mole any more, they called him a traitor, someone lived behind his name just as he existed behind an unsilvered mirror.

He'd been a traitor since at least the start of the 1960s, they said 'mole' in English, their way of using a word to cover the slime of the thing, as if it were a cartoon, good-natured large bulldog, gleaming tan coat, who slips a stick of dynamite in a hole in the lawn and waits, and the little grey mole pops up out of another hole with the dynamite in its jaws and puts it down with a tee-hee just behind the bulldog, and the bulldog goes up with a 'Bang!', falls back down to earth, is flattened, then sets off in even hotter pursuit of the mole over five keys of a piano, it's one gag after another, the bulldog is so angry, turns red in the face, digs hundreds of holes in the lawn to chase the mole away then his master returns and lays about the bulldog who turns grey, and in the end the mole offers the bulldog, now a great big placid sleepyhead, a safe shelter at the bottom of the garden, 'that's all, folks!', a rather effective metaphor.

In Paris, no one used metaphors now, they said plain 'traitor', and twelve bullets were heard, whistling in the wind.

*

'Whatever happens,' Lilstein tells you, 'there's no risk, there is no record, no phone number, no address, no go-between, no dead-letter box, they know nothing, they're leaving no stone unturned but it's as if they were trying to make holes in marble with a spoon. And as for having agreed eight years ago to become the secretary of the Waltenberg Forum, why, my boy, it was a stroke of genius!

'You can come from Paris whenever you like, only the two of us know that we'll be together, excellent thing this forum, makes me feel younger despite the bulldozers and the heliport. Nobody knows a thing, when they look, they always look in the direction of the Russians, and in Moscow no one's ever asked me to name my sources, or, more accurately, when some of them wanted me to give names, I asked 'who to?', that created ructions between the various departments and after a while no one ever brought the subject up again, I always gave the impression that my information came from several sources simultaneously and that I was the only one able to cross-check them.

'The only thing a defector could ever say about me is that there's someone somewhere in Berlin who can see a long way, and they've not even got to that stage yet, so you've nothing to fear except your own reactions, a defector could finger some of my agents, but no one could blow your cover because you do not exist in any agency file, which means you do not exist at all, oh yes, I know the current state of play, the French are starting to put some very competent people on the job, but they won't find anything, no tracks, so we don't even need to scatter pepper to hide our trail.

'You have just one thing to fear, your own anxious French self,' Lilstein adds. 'If that's our only problem, everything will go swimmingly.'

His face goes slack, he asks if there's anything you still believe in.

'Because speaking for myself,' he says, 'I've had it up to here with them, our dogs of war have got the mange, I really feel like retiring, we'd leave the key under the door, you could stay on in your capacity as an organiser of this world forum, that would give you an influential role of your own if, that is, acting as doorman for a great banker ranks as an influential role, it's not really funny, only now am I beginning to understand what a German or Austrian aristocrat must have felt in 1918, or a revolutionary in 1935 around the time of the Moscow show trials, end of a world, a new world dawning in which there isn't a place for you, think I'm being morbid? So tell me instead how you're getting on these days with that female, Chagrin, aka Lady Piddle, it'll do us good to talk about something else.'

A few years back, there'd been a lively exchange of views about this woman between Lilstein and yourself when she began rising up through the ranks of the President's inner circle at the Élysée, you thought the safest thing was to handle her with kid gloves, talk things over with her, but Lilstein had disagreed.

'Make her curious, she has to suspect you, all the suspicions she had at the start will turn out in the end to be your salvation, I've always said it: don't try to be purer than the average man in the street.'

You disagreed with Lilstein, you told him he had no idea what the atmosphere inside the Élysée was like, and in the end you agreed to temporise, nor were you ever one of those who systematically called her Lady Piddle, furthermore you were never part of the President's inner circle, you don't work for him, you're an after-hours visitor, an unofficial adviser, wondrously rambling discussions about culture, politics, strategy, you never hesitate to ruffle his feathers, Chagrin was always trying to arrange to bump into you in the corridors completely as it were by chance, what she got was your cold shoulder.

'Always remember, young gentleman of France,' Lilstein had said, 'to be contemptuous, people like her can never be put in their place too often.'

One day the President himself told you that you should have a talk now and then with Chagrin, she'd like that, you could have said nothing but you said you found her irritating, that you didn't much care for ostentatiously virtuous people who are anything but virtuous. The President laughed.

And then Chagrin turned on you, it was in the President's ante-chamber, a room which preceded the Antechamber proper, Chagrin came in just as you were leaving, she'd arranged it deliberately, or maybe she hadn't, in any case she was sufficiently near the President's office for you to be unambiguously reminded of her importance but sufficiently distant for her to attack you, and savage you she did, the President must have had a word with her about your *irritation*, she attacked you although two security men were on duty in the room, Chagrin's words weren't meant for them, but they heard you being bawled out like some minion, Chagrin had a lot of pull, she was feared.

She marched further into the room holding a file, she stopped when she got to you and snarled:

'Why are you always so condescending when you talk to me?'

Chin thrust forward, and Chagrin had a lot of chin to thrust, you could have said 'Who, me?' and protested your finest feelings, instead of which you did something much more incisive, you looked at her with a smile on your face, she assumed she was being offered the hand of friendship, and more than friendship, but you said something to her you would not have dreamed yourself capable of saying, even now you have no idea where it came from, as though there was another person who had always lived alongside you without ever saying a word and all of a sudden, with this increasingly powerful woman standing in front of you, came out with a sequence of unexpected, unfore-seeable words which went straight to the heart of everything Chagrin held most dear and revealed to you a self you'd never suspected of containing such violence, you said to her:

'Because you're a spiteful slag.'

It wasn't too loud, nor said in anger, 'slag', but suddenly you remembered, that word had made life difficult for you once before, you'd forgotten, your wife had never forgiven you, she'd made you look a fool but you had made the biggest blunder by insulting her, your lawyer said that you'd spoken the word just once, your wife's lawyer pointed out to the judge, who was a woman, that his client had obviously lived for years with a man who had turned the word 'slag' round and round in his mouth without daring to say it out loud.

You'd so completely forgotten such violence that you'd stopped believing you could ever be capable of such a thing, it had cost you a divorce and now you'd flung the forbidden word in Chagrin's face with sufficient force that the two duty security men jumped and suddenly became part of the scene, so that Chagrin was both disconcerted that there should have been witnesses and immediately struck by the thought that now she had you, because you had just committed an irredeemable act.

You don't tell Lilstein about this episode because you have the feeling that you've just screwed everything up completely, twenty years down the tubes, and all for just one word, just as it was with your wife, all you say to Lilstein is that you get on very badly with Chagrin, which is actually what he'd asked, Lilstein changes the subject, bemoans the demise of the *Gemütlichkeit* which used to characterise Waltenberg and speaks once more of the old man of Moscow who is such a worry to him. He says that these days even success has a bitter taste.

'My greatest success was my greatest failure, it was the Haupt affair, everything the papers said was broadly speaking true, I'd succeeded in placing someone in the entourage of Chancellor Haupt, a direct line to the top, just like you, but even more focused, every confidential note passed through his hands, that's right, it was his secretary, Eisler.

'There was nothing for me to do, except see him when I needed to, or I would send someone instead of me, it was actually embarrassing to have so much reliable intelligence, we spent more time concealing what we knew than ferreting for things we would have needed to know if our man hadn't been in position. I tried to protect him, but he laid golden eggs, they made me work him as hard as I could, that's where it all went catastrophically wrong, Eisler was blown and when he went he also brought down Haupt who was the only German to have a clear vision of what Germany would turn into, we'd been protecting Haupt for a very long time, he was a genuine social democrat, an enemy, but of the highest calibre.

'When he was almost unseated by the right in the Bundestag, I bought two Christian-Democrat MPs, closed ballot, Haupt was expecting to lose, he was so surprised that he remained in his seat while the Bundestag rose, well at least his friends did, to give him a standing ovation, he was out for the count. That time I saved his skin.

'But only to bring him down later with a bump because we had a mole who was too good! That's why I always went carefully with you, young gentleman of France, I've kept you all to myself, I don't even tell the mirror in my bathroom about you, no other contact except me, and that only the strict minimum. From a technical point of view, the downfall of Willi Haupt didn't make life at all difficult, we had other sources, but something had been lost, which included our appetite for what we were doing.'

Haupt, Chagrin, the jokers, the feeling of disgust, it hardly made for the merriest evening you've spent with Lilstein. The next morning, he had disappeared.

You stayed on for a few days at Waltenberg, an informal session of the Forum, barely thirty participants, on the question of interest rates in Europe, dry-as-dust. You are the only French person there. You followed the debate but did not speak.

That evening, in the lounge, there was a freer and more political discussion, about rumours of the tramp of Soviet jackboots in the East, in Afghanistan, you thought about what you'd said to Lilstein,

you weren't taken in, you can see through his game, even his
melancholy, he is never stronger than when his morale is low, he loves
playing the part, he relaxes into it, he seems to be asking for help, but
you know he could give an order and have you liquidated, no, you
can't convince yourself that the thing is possible, you run through
your multiple Lilsteins, there's the first, the one you've only just left,
who eats his Linzer like a little boy, his spirits are low, he is against the
warmongers, he agreed to go to bed with the butchers to change the
world but the world hasn't changed, so he does all he can to make it
change, you are friends, and the world does change, only not the way
he wanted, he decides to retire and drops everything, he shows you the
trumps in his side's hand to prevent the worst from happening, just
like Cuba, because he hates the mangy dogs of war, as he calls them,
he passes you everything so that the Americans will react swiftly,
ruthlessly, and force the Soviets to back down, thus no invasion of
Afghanistan.

But you're not entirely sure of this first Lilstein, there is undeniably
a second, without scruples, we're not going to allow the said Asian
country to turn the clock back, revive the *droit du seigneur* and feudal
dues, progress has been made and must be preserved, there are the
frontiers of socialism to defend, an interventionist Lilstein who uses
both his own doubts and you to persuade the West that there are very
high-placed Soviets who are opposed to this intervention, intelligent
men in other words, and the West must help these intelligent communists by being flexible, and making the most of this flexibility the
Soviets, the warmongering crowd, will march into Afghanistan and
present the West with a *fait accompli*, yet maybe Lilstein is genuinely
opposed to this intervention, in which case he would use the flexibility
of the West to tell Moscow that American flexibility is in all likelihood
a trap set by the Americans.

The Americans demonstrate by their flexibility that they would like
the Soviets in turn to land themselves in a pit of shit in Afghanistan,
so going into Afghanistan would mean walking into an imperialist
trap, so they shouldn't go in.

But if Lilstein does favour intervening, he can also say that by making the Soviets believe that intervention is an imperialist trap, the Americans want the Soviets to back off the idea of intervening and thus demonstrate a weakness which would be prejudicial to the interest of socialism across the globe. That's Lilstein number four. You tell yourself that there must be others.

And then you'd got tired of pondering all this by yourself, you banished Lilstein from your thoughts that evening, in the lounge of the Waldhaus, so that you could address a few Forum colleagues and two or three good-looking women, and you gave your hypotheses another airing.

You delivered under several headings, in a thorough-going *Kriegspiel*, a sheaf of hypotheses, like an exquisite papyrus flower, from one end of a sofa, to ten or so people, sometimes a brief pause to savour the smoke of your Monte-Cristo, and the non-smokers smile and are happy to breathe in what is rare and costly, you are elated, you have never spoken as freely, you don't give a shit about Chagrin, Lilstein, his retirement, everything, you know that in Paris your slanging-match with Chagrin has thrown everything into the mixing-bowl, she will cut off your access to the President.

And when you got back, reception party at Orly, three tight-lipped men, a Citroën, the SM which you don't like, the suspension makes you feel car-sick, they drove you directly to the Élysée, taking you in through the garden.

The chief's floor, the chief's antechamber, he doesn't like being called 'chief', everyone is tense, you feel you are no longer the man everyone likes because he puts the chief in a good mood, you can't catch anybody's eye, one of the men who is escorting you knocks on a door, stands back to let you in, closes it behind you and then the President comes on to you like a jealous lover:

'My dear fellow, they tell me that at Waltenberg you gave a dazzling analysis of Soviet policy, you see I already know all about it, you mustn't be so modest, it wasn't you in journalistic mode, I was told that you made four points, the logic was incisive, but they weren't able to give me details, but really, when you hand out the brilliant analyses you could at least let me be the first to hear them, just the two of us, instead of shooting your mouth off in the lounge of a Swiss hotel, I'm jealous, I said just us two, you must know I never repeat any of our conversations. Way back, during the Cuba crisis, you gave first-rate advice, but let's not beat about the bush: if the Afghanistan situation were to develop, what would you advise?'

You tell your jealous chief you have no idea, he insists, eventually you say that now is the time to display those qualities of diplomacy which have been the rule since Choiseul and Talleyrand: neither prudence nor impulsiveness, allow time to look before you leap. If the Russians invade Afghanistan and win, it would still be just a dump, full of peasants, and if they lose, it will be a terrific result for the West.

'Couldn't agree more,' says the President, 'words of wisdom. Over Cuba you took a harder line, that was more like you.'

You get a smile from him, a smile of amused benevolence for your concern about the West as a whole and even the Atlantic Alliance, an acute analysis which in reality boils down to little more than a policy of 'wait and see'.

'But as head of state, I have to act, I have to think of the interests of France, not just of the Atlantic Alliance, this time the Russians must not be weakened too much, otherwise you can say goodbye to our national independence, there'll have to be a painful face-to-face with the hot-dog eaters, the Russians must not be humiliated and made to withdraw, Cuba was lesson enough for them, and that god-forsaken Asian hole can remain within their traditional sphere.'

You tell him maybe he's right, that you don't know, you imagined he would be a lot less like de Gaulle, he's very fond of acting up like an Englishman or a New Englander, and here he is talking about national independence, in the election he stood against a Gaullist who nowadays is reduced to attending parties given by the Marshal's widow, but once elected he pursued the very policies he had previously denounced and rejected, evidently with forked tongue, he runs a risk in doing so, he loves playing this role when you're with him, he probably doesn't do it often, but when you are his audience of one he doesn't pass up the chance, journalists reckon that this concern with national independence is the product of certain French constants, your man is constrained by history, geography, economics, *pommes-frites*, but you know that if he's acting this way now it's basically because for some time he's been increasingly drawn to doing things he doesn't like doing, he feels easier when he's doing them, it's a rule of politics: if you choose to do what you don't like doing it gives you better control, and you aren't so disappointed.

You reflect that there must be one last Lilstein, the one who antici-pated that you would suspect him of having at least four faces, that you would build four hypotheses, and that those hypotheses would eventually lead you to the office of the President, who will eventually tell you that he has opted for a policy of flexible response to the Soviets, that the Germans will follow suit, and then even the Americans have just confirmed that they won't push too hard on this one.

And you know that you will pass on this intelligence to Lilstein.

The President walks you to the door of his office, his tone is kindly:
 'There's someone here who would benefit greatly from talking to you, it would do her good, broaden her ideas, she has a difficult, a very wearing job, her horizons are narrow, true she loathes you, I know you never called her Lady Piddle, but I've heard about one very coarse word; she deliberately provoked you but it surprised me coming from you, I never realised you had such a short fuse, and now she hates you.
 'She says terrible things about you, though she doesn't really believe them, I'd like you to have a few sessions with her, I like the people around me to get on with each other, true you don't come here often anyway, now you mustn't start taking offence, you know how fond I

am of you, I try to keep it simple, you're the only one who refused to go with me to Africa, I know some who'd strangle their mother and father to go hunting with me, I'm not asking that, and I forbid you to tell Chagrin what you tell me, I want exclusive access to you, or don't talk to her, that's all right too, and when you're next in Switzerland you could try to be a tiny bit less brilliant, is that so hard? Will you come to dinner on Saturday? I command you!'

*

On the *quais* de Vèze continues his walk, he starts laughing to himself, a memory of that evening in Singapore in 1965, he remembers a gag, a practical joke that was played on him during dinner, he never found out who was responsible, he suspected Jug Ears of setting him up.

But he never succeeded in finding out who had played that damnable trick on him. It might even have been the man whom de Vèze admires, the guest of honour, no, it couldn't have been. Besides, the man de Vèze admires told the story of that dinner party in 1965 in one of his books, de Vèze was rather put out not to have been mentioned, the book said most about Jug Ears, spoke of him with affection, whereas in fact he had behaved very ungraciously with the man de Vèze admires, at one point they'd been on the verge of having a rather serious incident.

But basically, in the book, Jug Ears and the man de Vèze admires see more or less eye to eye, the man does not actually say 'The Great Adventure is buggered!' but in his introduction he does observe that comedy is as important in history as tragedy, that the presence of comedy is everywhere irrefutable and as elusive as a cat, that the Great Adventure is now just an empty apartment, that thought can never cancel time's lease, he is on the verge of pronouncing the end of History.

As he turned the pages, de Vèze thought it was all beginning to sound rather grim but here and there he caught echoes of what he had felt that evening in Singapore in 1965, words spoken from sheer enjoyment which buzz like bees in a hedge seen against the sun.

De Vèze continues walking along the *quais* of the Seine, he is beginning to feel tired, he remembers the Kessel book, just when everything seemed to have sorted itself out, try to find the bookseller again, buy *Wagon-lit*, he hadn't been fair, 'I felt the thrill of the fever', you can't get by without clichés and books of that kind have their uses, people say I could write as well as that, that helps, everyone knows what it is to have had the thrill of a fever.

Now *Lord Jim* or *Typhoon* are a different kettle of fish, but you feel so slow-witted, that is the paradox of Conrad's novels, when you're into them you feel both happy and stupid, and to be happy you forget you're stupid, it's only if you, personally, want to write that it comes back and hits you. De Vèze has a great many books, almost as many in Moscow as in Paris, often he has two copies of a book, he's always taking books to Moscow and when he feels like dipping into any of them in Paris he buys another copy.

And every evening always the same problem, which book to read before he goes off to sleep? Thousands of books within easy reach and not one to suit his mood, to help him make his peace with his own breathing even if it's only for a moment, something light to read before he drops off, every evening de Vèze runs his eye over the shelves of his library, a friend once told him if you've never bought a house in the country it's because you've got one here, on your bookshelves.

A partiality for fiction especially, these last few years, and all this so he can have something he can read or reread, he would hesitate, pick up a tome, read a page, put it back, hum-and-ha for maybe an hour while the moment for sleep passed, comes the evening and nothing takes his fancy, *La Route des Flandres* for instance, during the day he can get absorbed in it, saying he's not to be disturbed, but in the evening, he can't find a thing to read, to be fair he doesn't know what he wants exactly, one day he made a particular effort with an assistant in a Latin Quarter bookshop who was pressing him.

In the end he said I want a novel full of action with a happy ending, the young woman looked at him with a smile:

'You want him to get married? Or earn a lot of money? Or both together?'

She answered her own question:

'I'm afraid we don't have anything like that, or else if it's a classic you want, how about *War and Peace*?'

'Yes,' said de Vèze, 'that ends fairly happily, after twelve hundred pages the heroine has got fat, she has acquired homely tastes, takes up needlework and treats her hubby like her teddy bear, Natasha she's called, puts on twenty kilos, but all women end up fat, you're right, I'll have a copy of *War and Peace*.'

'You'll find it on the shelves,' the girl said frostily.

Then, more winningly:

'Unless you prefer it in the deluxe Pléiade edition?'

'No, I'll go on browsing,' said de Vèze.

He asked her where the crime novels were kept, crime fiction is simple, you just turn to the last page, not the back of the cover but the last page of the story, and you can see at a glance if it ends happily, then the first page, for how well the plot is set up, two basic conditions, and if he has time de Vèze skims two or three pages in the middle, to get the rhythm, the tone, as he did with the Kessel, ten years ago he was able to read an Ellroy last thing, even the murkiest of them. He can't do that any more, nowadays he can read them during the day, especially when he's travelling, but not the evening, in the morning an Ellroy works well, a whack with a baseball bat in the crotch or a headless woman, it inoculates you against pity and terror, you shut the book and you can go forth and confront the denizens of the new day with a soul that's been fortified.

But no way can he read *The Black Dahlia* late at night, so how did you manage it ten years ago? Ten years ago you could read James Hadley Chase, in one of those crime novels this guy has a model train layout, he rapes a woman on it, the woman could feel a part of the station dig into her shoulder, it must have been *Miss Callaghan Comes to Grief*, someone punished a girl by pouring turps over her pubis, it took her a few moments to grasp what was happening, the idea is to rid yourself of feelings of pity and terror with turpentine tales before you drift off into sleep.

You didn't like sleep, you fell into it still clutching a James Hadley

Chase or a James Ellroy, but nowadays you can no longer cope with violent crime thrillers before going to sleep, it means you no longer need to be inoculated against your dreams, you're not afraid of sleep any more, that's progress, so why do you spend an hour lingering in front of your books every night? you're not afraid of your dreams any more and you can't get off to sleep, and in the morning you find it harder and harder to get started, you stay up too late, you're losing your inner buoyancy, hundreds of bloody books within easy reach and you can't even find one in the whole mountain to keep your pillow company for half an hour, except, for the umpteenth time, *Les Secrets de la princesse de Carignan.*

De Vèze stops by the water's edge, life was good, it was inevitable that Bantam Bum would have turned up at the Embassy sooner or later, no, it had all started much earlier, much earlier, one day in Moscow or Berlin or Prague a bureaucrat had pulled out de Vèze's file and added a note recommending that he should be made the target of an operation, the note was circulated, it rose higher and higher until it reached the level at which the decision was taken.

Alternatively, someone high-ranking said find me a target, and the order went all the way down to the minor bureaucrat who sent de Vèze's file back up, and it was de Vèze who had beaten off the competition from other contending files, something to be proud of, he was made a target, he's certain of it, they used him for a propaganda operation, otherwise they'd never have allowed him so much freedom in Moscow, with Vassilissa, the French security services won't admit it but he is certain he has been the object of what is called a 'treatment'.

And now the French too are giving him the 'treatment', but as if he were a minor story, whereas he is certain he was at the centre of the plot, it ought to have been enough to leave him at his post in Moscow and see what happened, they might have learned a great many things, they might have made the people on the other side believe that France had known all along, that all they'd been given was duff intelligence, they could have turned the operation round, but no, the clique now in charge took the opportunity to eliminate a Gaullist, the new clique, the heirs of Pétain and the OAS, they'd wanted his hide for a long, long time.

Or again: it was the mole himself who'd fingered him, that's it, had the mole run into him one day in Singapore? In Moscow? Or here in Paris? It was he who had written the note, who had flagged up de Vèze's name for a possible propaganda operation, de Vèze had been under surveillance since the middle of the 1960s, and one day he'd been used to protect the mole, de Vèze spoke about all this in Paris, he had been listened to, highly ingenious, one of the committee members said it was the stuff of high art, thinking of how to protect the mole even as he was being planted, with de Vèze as circuit-breaker and Berthier as fallback, and anyway the whole thing was a shambles.

And now? go away? or write a book he'd want to read? not enough money to buy a boat, I don't even have enough money to live off, I've resigned, it'll be years before I start getting my pension, someone cannier would have negotiated some sort of paid part-time contract, have to look for a job in business, won't have time to write.

Thirty years, all of them defunct, de Vèze is now level with the Petit Pont, no, the Pont au Double, you're mixing them up, the Petit Pont is the one before, the one that leads to the Hôtel-Dieu, the wind sweeps the slates of the buildings clean, their roof-ridges too, everything is clear and bright, a man stands in profile, facing the river, grey overcoat, very worn, houndstooth cap, an old man, virtually a tramp, he leans on his stick looking distinguished, his eyes are fixed on the opposite bank, Notre-Dame.

De Vèze halts, thinks he is closer to this man than to his own youth, and if I've got time to look at him it's because I am now nothing, the currently powerful right has got rid of a Gaullist, even the Americans must have been consulted, for de Vèze it's the end of everything, he is certain that his Minister and the President wanted to keep the Americans happy, in particular the CIA man they talk about, Walker, the whatsit-thrower, they gave him the head of a Gaullist to keep him happy.

The end of everything, de Vèze wonders if he should try to get even, if I get even will my revenge have also been planned by whoever landed me in this mess?

At the far end of the Pont au Double, just before the square in front of Notre-Dame, a number of teenagers are roller-skating, they've set up rows of empty Coca-Cola cans, they slalom at crazy speeds through the cans, hardly ever knock one over, it's virtuoso stuff, they are virtuosos.

Still facing the Seine, the old man has not moved, grey coat, stick, cap, almost a tramp, suddenly he cries out:

'*On les aura*! We'll get them!'

Chapter 7

1965

The Uses of Croquet

In which Max Goffard meets up once more with his author in Singapore and recalls the Riff wars.

In which de Vèze speaks of Bir Hakeim and decides to seduce a young woman who reads novels.

In which you rejoin Lilstein at the Waldhaus Hotel so that you might share with him the scruples of a Paris-based spy.

In which Lilstein reassures you by relating the history of Tukhachevsky.

Singapore, July 1965

In traditional organisations, self-esteem
always begins as a provocation.
René Fraimond, *La Fin du monde rural*

The grounds of a large house, pre-dinner drinks are being served.

The guest of honour, the man de Vèze admires is not here yet. There are a good half-dozen of them waiting for him on the lawn, the French Consul at Singapore and his lady, two other diplomats both over thirty, one grey with a beard like a monkey's arse, the other pink in a salmon shirt with a double-barrelled Christian name. Also just arrived are a young historian very much in vogue, Philippe Morel, and his wife Muriel.

The most striking figure in the group is a man relatively advanced in years, quick movements, old-fashioned monocle, very sprightly, brings to mind a comic character in a play, the engaging con man, jug ears, he plays to the gallery while they wait, he has introduced himself to de Vèze: I am Baron de Clappique.

De Vèze would never have believed that there had actually been such a person as Clappique.

'It's not his real name,' whispers the Consul, 'actually he's a journalist, Max Goffard, he's promised me he will behave himself, but he's getting restless, he came expressly to meet our guest of honour, spring a surprise on him, I thought it would be a good idea to bring them together, they've known each other for ages, but our Monsieur Goffard has decided he wants to be called Clappique, I'm afraid there might be trouble.'

The journalist steps up his brusqueness.

'Ears, lie down! They are radar dishes not cauliflowers, for years I was called 'Cauliflower', I fought the first war with these cauliflowers, it was modern technology that saved me, I went through the second with my radar receivers, the war-correspondent's ultimate weapon! ah yes, I remember the soldiers in their red trousers, the summer of 1914, the Cossacks already close to Berlin, the Germans surrendering for bread and butter, and yesterday morning Johnson decided to unleash his B52s on Vietnam, it's a funny old business!'

Everyone on the lawn is outraged, the Americans haven't understood a thing, they've got to be stopped one way or another, or at least restrained.

The Consul has told de Vèze in confidence that the journalist fought all through the First World War and that in 1918 he was the only survivor of his whole Company.

'But the experience didn't turn him into a stay-at-home, did you know he was also one of the survivors of the *Hindenburg* disaster? Not easy, not easy at all. Between the two world wars he wandered round the colonies, Morocco especially, the Riff wars in the 1920s, they called him "African" Goffard. Ask him to tell you about it,' said the Consul, drawing on his meerschaum pipe, 'then maybe he'll stop calling himself Clappique.'

At seventy, Max Goffard is back in Asia again, working for a news agency.

'Yeah,' says he, 'I don't know if you're like me but I can't take Paris, the banks of the Seine, for a more than a week, that's my limit, so off I toddle to Vietnam, the last of the colonial wars, I'll have seen them all, all their struggles for independence since the Riff, the inter-war years, too right, that was a real war too, they were in a sense the fore-runners, with some habits left over from the old days, not in the best taste, Vietnam is the end of an era, I've come full circle, I also wanted to go to Peking, but no visa, and no one intervened to help me get one, I'm not liked everywhere, people complain that I cast a shadow.'

A smile, Max's eyes swivel towards the garden gate:
'But I'll get even!'

While they wait for the guest of honour to arrive, the Consul's wife suggests a game of croquet, there was no time for her husband to do more than glare at her, the others acquiesced, fancy, the best she can come up with is a game of croquet saying it was the latest thing in Singapore.

Max was enthusiastic:

'It's starting up again, 1914 all over, no, '25 or '26, I did play in 1914 but the last time was '26, in Rabat, in the gardens of the Residence, Lyautey's place, a great moment, I'll have to tell you about Lyautey, you know in those days I talked a lot with our beloved Lyautey, who'd overstayed his welcome, about the colonies, the Riff war. He was all Indochina, he'd interrupt me and say, Clappique, I'm an Asia man, absolutely! And I'd have to listen, and fascinating it was too, now and then I'd be permitted to say a word about the Riff, anyway, until he gets here, everyone look to their mallets!'

Max has explained the rules to the beginners, the Morels and the two diplomats, the grey one and the pink one: the nine hoops stuck in the lawn, the ball you hit with a mallet, but please not as in golf, you barbarian, watch me, face forward, legs apart, mallet swinging like a pendulum between the legs, eyes front, then a smart, sharp tap, clack, taking turns, in teams of two, through the nine arches, yes nine, I didn't make the rules, (to the pink diplomat) no sniggering! nine hoops, in order, and then turn for home, Rabat, though, was a different kettle of fish!

Max is starting to feel hot, he swings his arms about, shuffles his feet, blinks a lot, no, he says to de Vèze, I never liked being called 'The African', in those days, during the Riff wars, I wasn't very good at my trade, shush! not a word, at times Max goes off into a kind of trance and ignores all and sundry, he lets his eyes settle on the ocean, the lawn, the trees, not very good at my trade at all.

In one corner of the garden, on the side nearest the sea, there is a twisted knot, which looks beyond unravelling, of roots which turn into branches or trunks, branches that take root in the soil, a tangle of trees and leaves so intricately intertwined that you can't make out what's what, your eye returns to the lawn, the Consul said that his garden is a bottomless pit, you stop tending, draining, uprooting for just one week, and nature sneaks back, puts out shoots, you can't see it happening, and then one fine morning you find yourself with creepers swarming all over the veranda, and as for the lawn, don't ask! a very fragile thing is a real lawn, the soil, the climate, a true, even green, cut with shears once a week by gardeners on their knees.

Max surveys the garden, a large white patch stands out against the green, nine hoops, ages ago a chap in a white djellaba is playing croquet, only has one eye, in 1925 in the gardens of the Residence at Rabat, the man's right eye is fine, he's a quick learner, he plays well, he's one of the finest shots in the whole of the Atlas, old man, lost his eye in a shoot-out with our side, now he's one of us, one of the best formal surrender ceremonies we ever organised, you should have seen the way he handed over his rifle! Anyone would have thought he was giving it to us to clean, us the overlords! Pity that times change, a terrific do, yes that's really the scent of orange blossom, 1925, end of an era that no one sees coming, the moment when Lyautey is about to be pushed on to the sidelines by Pétain, but no one sees it coming.

Spit-roasted mutton, no, braised lamb, at the Residence the spit-roasts are generally left to the tourists, we have more sophisticated palates, a baked-mud oven, a very fierce flame, when the fire begins to make hot embers a bucket of water is thrown on to them, two or three sucking lambs are laid on the cinders, the oven is closed and made air-tight, it's left to cook for ten or twelve hours, the meat is incomparably tender, Lyautey is very partial to a game of croquet, see how considerate he is with the man with one eye, a government school, strategy, alliances, your shot, you'll understand.

In Morocco at that time things are not going at all well, so play a game of croquet, make an effort not to gloat too much over Spanish setbacks in the northern Riff, thirteen thousand hidalgos killed in two nights at the start of the revolt, they never recovered from that, lots of prisoners, the privates, had their throats cut; for the officers the Riffians demanded ransoms with fairly short deadlines, Lyautey likes watching his guests eat, Moroccan-style, with their fingers, looks down rather on those who use both hands and the ones who guzzle their food and leave nothing on their plates, it was better to be a prisoner of Abd el-Krim's regulars, with them you didn't get much to eat but at least they tried to abide by modern laws, whereas the others, the not-so-regulars who fought only when the enemy crossed their land, had no idea of how to treat prisoners.

The ones whose throats they did not cut were tied head down to a stake, then a fire was lit at the foot of the stake, to some they dangled the prospect of the fiery furnace and to the rest they talked of paradise, mind you, our soldiers didn't take many prisoners either, photos of heads lined up in a row on a low wall by grinning squaddies, they send stuff like that home, when they kept a prisoner, it was to make him talk, and their letters to their mates, yesterday we occupied a village, bints to bust your tackle. Lyautey's officers did not care for that sort of thing.

On the lawn of the Consulate, de Vèze has noticed the historian's wife, yellow dress, bare shoulders, wispy floating material, he tries to approach her, a reflex, for something to do until the guest of honour comes, because she's married, because he wants her to look at him, she's not a tease, not very tall, almost plump, light auburn hair, pointed nose, quick movements, not my type, it would be a change.

And the historian-husband has twigged what de Vèze is up to, like the dog which instinctively positions himself between its mistress and the passer-by, he spends his time coming between de Vèze and his wife, accidentally as it were, like Moine, Albert Moine, who also went to school at the Lycée Montaigne, Moine is in a restaurant with his wife, she is ten times better-looking than him, one day he was seen with this woman, no one ever knew how he'd managed it, dark hair, beautiful and, as in *Brave New World*, pneumatic, with eyes that shine. The moment he sees de Vèze coming towards their table Moine gets up, round face, small round glasses which make him look like Beria, he stands in front of the table, says hello, shakes hands, darling this is my friend Henri de Vèze, Éliane, my wife, it's twenty years ago since that happened but you can still hear Moine's intonation, very refined, 'my wife', intended to indicate that you're not such close friends as all that, he smiles, Moine knows you only too well, he stood in your path, with his left hand extended holding his napkin to remind you that he has better things to do than talk to you, no way will you be invited to join them, show's over, the women have been shared out and you sense that if you try to force the pace the distinguished husband will grab you and wrestle you to the ground, it comes to the same with the historian and his wife.

All de Vèze can do is glance at the young woman out of the corner of his eye, plumpish, vivacious, against a background of greenery, a weird display of vegetation obviously assembled by a collector who put tropical plants next to a few species imported from Cornwall, the ones that have survived, for broadly speaking European plants need winter, a proper winter.

Max has picked the croquet teams: the Consul and his wife, no, said the Consul, I have to keep an eye out for the arrival of our guest, must stick to protocol, very well, said Max, de Vèze I'll inflict you on our *Consuless.*

The Consul's wife is a tiny lady with a downcast mouth, a flat chest, 'Consuless' has not gone down at all well with her, Madame Morel, Max went on, you keep your husband who likes history, but let's have no domestic scenes, croquet is a less bloodthirsty game than conjugal tennis but can also have its moments, and the two inseparable great diplomatists of tomorrow, the pink and the grey, can stay together, I shall supervise, he surveys the scene and smiles, the first plays take place against a background of trees, the fan-palms, the Perrier bottle-shaped palm trees topped with thornless branches, and other successively taller palms which lift the whole space up towards the sky, why does Singapore look so small today? Nothing like what it was back then, maybe because I was younger? The same hoops, maybe not the bottle-shaped trees, but the same wooden balls, the same mallets, Rabat, lawn and gravel, same game, but it feels so cramped today.

Even the gravel in the paths doesn't seem of the same standard as in '25, you aren't up to the same standard either, the chippings are less uniform, not as well maintained, six small stones and a bigger one, a full-scale revolt, six small stones, we left the Residence at Rabat with its perfectly raked gravel, and the jacaranda trees, I've not seen any jacarandas here in Singapore, did four hundred kilometres of twisting roads, and then we were in the high jebel, confronted by more small stones, and you do not understand.

It's a game, explained the agent for Native Affairs who accompanies Max to the Riffian village, six small stones in one hand, with the other the little girl tosses the big one in the air, and before she catches it she has to put one of the small stones on the ground, and so on, I throw the big one up, I grab a small one, I put it down, I catch the big one before it hits the ground, I throw it up again, I grab a small one and put it next to the first one, when she gets to the end she starts again, she tosses the big stone in the air but this time she puts two little ones down, not together, one after the other, quickly, while the big stone stays aloft you look up, you keep your eye on it so it doesn't bang you on the nose, and the girls who manage twos can go on to throw the big stone up again and pick up and set down three little stones one after the other every time they throw the big stone up, the longer they go on the harder it gets, the likelier it is that they'll get hit in the face, no, I never saw it played myself, the agent for Native Affairs described it to me because on two occasions I'd seen little heaps of stones on the ground, at the entrance to a village that had been bombed, there were also traces of hopscotch and rain maidens.

An ideal husband, murmurs de Vèze as he observes Morel, worse than Moine, worse than a guard dog, a full back, a very close marker, never a moment to get anything going with the wife.

It's Morel's turn first, he hits his ball very quickly, rejoins his wife, Morel, you hit it too hard, cries Max, you've gone through the second hoop without going through the first, you'll have to come back through hoop two the other way, before you can go through hoop one, then you'll go through two again, the right way this time, otherwise it doesn't count, Morel protests, the rules mean he'll have to negotiate the second hoop three times, and de Vèze has stayed close to his wife; it's quite usual, says Max, you have to clear the backlog, you've racked up a number of errors, you're allowed to clear them, this is a very honest game, especially if you strike the ball properly instead of poking it cautiously with the mallet like our friend here! Max nods towards the grey diplomat, you're pushing not hitting, it's against the rules, foul stroke, you've got to make a noise, old man, a recognisable sound, wooden mallet against wooden ball, a distinctive 'clack', you went through the hoop in the right direction, but it wasn't a legal stroke, naughty naughty, you were seen, so you'll have to play the hoop again from the other side, so back you go!

De Vèze watches the young woman, her breasts move a little when she leans forward to play her shot but stay pretty firmly in place, that's the good thing about girls with fuller figures, young flesh, elastic, on a plate, a woman to spend a siesta with, the woman is lying naked on de Vèze, she straddles him, he takes her breasts in his hands, she smiles, arches her back, and Max, who has observed what de Vèze is up to and the husband who keeps getting in his way, finds the spectacle hugely entertaining; Monsieur Morel there's something I wanted to ask you, he gives the husband no option, don't you think there's a peculiar smell, comes in waves, acidic, it's not coming from the town, de Vèze tries to use the opportunity to make a masterly approach to the wife, and then Max, with one hand on Morel's shoulder, calls to de Vèze, can't you see it's your strike next, whatever are you thinking of?

De Vèze hits a ball, just goes through the motions, to be free of it, but Max detains him: tell Morel here how it works, contemporary history, events we have lived through, that'll get him out of his precious seventeenth century, but not now, good, now listen to me everybody, all you've had up to this point are the basic rules, they define a game suitable for morons, but there's more to croquet than that!

Croquet is a noun but also a verb, and 'croqueting' is precisely what makes the game human, aggressive, vicious, with its alliances, reprisals, betrayals, double-dealing, reconciliations, yes, patching things up, what does 'to croquet' mean, ladies and gentlemen? It means you are entitled to hit your opponent's ball into the sky-blue yonder, using his, as in pétanque, your opponent thinks he's nearly home then thwack, it's into the long grass with him, you're already past the turning post and making for home, you meet a player who's been held up, a dawdler, an innocent and thwack! the innocent knocks your ball all the way to Pétaouchnok, and you wonder if his innocence was really innocence, so, on with the game, it's all about strategy, shush! no talking, play's started, I'll be keeping an eye open.

Max smiles as he watches the first efforts of his pupils, in the end it's all about innocence, mustn't let anyone anticipate your next move, a clear look in the eye, a smooth lawn, Pétain's air of innocence, at Rabat.

Lyautey never saw it coming, the hero of Verdun disembarks, inspection visit to Morocco, because Abd el-Krim's Riffians have started to harass our lines of defence on the Ouergha, and the great leader of Verdun knocks his ball gently so that it rolls to a stop touching Lyautey's, which gives him the right to croquet, first touch then you can croquet, innocent smiles, may I, Marshal? Be my guest, Marshal! Pétain tight-croquets and Lyautey ends up in Pétaouchnok, semi-retirement, return to France, no one there to meet him off the boat, makes for Paris, the only thing waiting for me in the rue des Saints-Pères was a letter from the inland revenue, a demand for unpaid taxes.

Later a consolation prize, chair of the Colonial Exhibition committee, at the time I didn't see it coming, no one saw it, Lyautey didn't want a war in the Riff, you negotiate, you play for time, you divide and isolate and win back hearts and minds, I do note that the building of the Arabo-Berber School has fallen further behind schedule, so I'm asking you to take a personal interest in the work, you will report to me directly every two weeks.

A school for the sons of chiefs, the rebels want the Riff to be a republic, we won't give it to them, but we can negotiate a form of autonomy with allegiance to the Sultan of Rabat, ceremony, white

cloak, parasols, black slaves, Abd el-Krim will kiss his hand, it's nego-
tiable, he'd go to kiss the hand, and the Sultan would take back his
hand, no he must actually kiss his hand, and then the Sultan will
confer the accolade on him.

In receiving the accolade, Abd el-Krim must kiss his shoulder, no, no
kiss, which would you prefer? a man who pretends to kiss the hand and
will keep his word? Or another man who will lick the back of the hand,
the palm of the hand, the other hand and afterwards hatches some
underhand plot? Lyautey was seriously tempted to allow Abd el-Krim to
become firmly established, so as to boot the Spaniards out of Morocco,
teach them a lesson for staying neutral in 1914, the sky was bluer, more
intense than in Asia today, fewer clouds, a scent of orange trees and just
as much of a shambles, colonial troops getting a trouncing from
peasants who pour down from their mountains, not proper mountains
really, one morning the call goes out to the *harka,* twenty men from the
tents of each *douar,* a couple of *douars* per *leff,* no precise figures, a few
leffs per part of a tribe, plus a tribe, it soon adds up to hundreds and
thousands of men.

A mass mobilisation, an army of men who have no leaders but
know each other, here they come down from the hills, I hang on for
dear life, I am overrun, swept along by the rush down a slippery slope,
the meat at the Residence was succulent, Lyautey watching his guests
feeding off lambs served whole.

His own officers tore off pieces with a light, almost mechanical flick
of the wrist, three fingers of the right hand, without looking, choicest
morsels must go to the guests, to the chiefs who have come to be
honoured or to the Parisians who do not know what to do with the
titbits which are set politely down on the rim of the large dish in front
of them, red wine is served, to it ice is added, the ladies from Paris
laugh very loudly, gorgeous ceremonial tents, the largest for the
greatest personages and then lesser groups under progressively more
rustic tents, it's protocol, first the dishes go round to high-ranking
officials, next to low-ranking officials, then to their subordinates, and
when they have been poked at for the fifth or sixth time they reach the
attendants and, finally, the women in the compound at the back.

'Look at that, a show of breathtaking menace,' says Max, pointing to a galloping herd of leaden clouds over Singapore, 'there's going to be a deluge, dear people.'

'Not so,' says Morel, 'the wind off the sea prevents the clouds from massing, it won't come to anything much.'

'And the tree hasn't stirred,' adds the Consul.

From a tin of Capstan he has taken two small flakes of tobacco, which he proceeds to rub in his palm before filling the bowl of his pipe with it.

'Tree?' asks Morel.

'That one,' says the Consul, gesturing to a tree as supple as a large papyrus, 'when a real storm is brewing it closes up, but it hasn't stirred, so we're in the clear.'

'So come along ladies, play!' Max orders, 'since such is the will of the tree!'

Singapore, those were great times, some right, and the rest were wrong, those who had bombers were wrong to drop bombs, and those who kept to the forest, the paddy-fields, the night, were wrong not to negotiate. And those who'd spent forty years trying to understand, that is the English and the French, could play croquet in Singapore as in days of yore and tell each other that at last they'd been proved right.

*

This time it was you who reached the Waldhaus ahead of schedule, you arrived from Paris the day before, you stayed the night in the valley in the village hotel, the Prätschli, and next morning you took the cable car up to the Waldhaus. You are uneasy, you have a premonition, you are sitting by a window and you see Lilstein coming towards you through the lounge, stiff as a poker, moving as awkwardly as a student, he smiles, greets you, rubs his hands together and comes straight out with:

'They've screwed up, young gentleman of France, I know that

they've taken the decision, they're going to bomb Vietnam, carpet bombing, Johnson will make the announcement two weeks from now, you can tip the wink to your friend the Minister, it will give him a chance to make a prediction, it will do his reputation no harm!

'The Americans have fouled up, they can drop as many bombs as they like, it's a quagmire, they can fight a war from the air, but the more bombs they drop the less they'll be capable of establishing themselves on the ground, and they'll go home with their tails between their legs, as your side says, your de Gaulle is right about this, plus the two of us and a few of our friends, we're working to make reason prevail, reason will cut through this whole mess, but we've got to give it a helping hand, like at the time of Cuba, this isn't espionage, it's diplomacy, discreet, why so glum? This information is worth a pot of money, they're going to start bombing in two weeks, all's well! Let's just carry on.

'We'll need to be cautious, not go too fast, do nothing robust, just look at what we've achieved in ten years, you're no longer a nobody, Cuba, I gave you good information, "the Soviets will withdraw their missiles", you used it to submit a first-rate analysis of the situation, your friend the Minister liked it, today he is respected and he is grateful to you, not excessively so, he has a talent for forgetting services rendered, but he knows you can be useful to him, he regurgitated your analysis in a full Cabinet, with de Gaulle in the chair, hold firm whatever the cost, be strong, he's no Gaullist but in a tight corner he's sound, stand up to Khrushchev, give full backing to the Americans, Khrushchev will withdraw his missiles, you saw the result, we forced death on to the back foot, that's our only reward, so let's carry on, with all due humility.

'Our only reward is the outcome, your friend backed the Americans and he impressed de Gaulle, it must be done, and moreover comrade Nikita, a dangerous amateur, got the chop, nothing drastic, a five-roomed flat in Moscow, not to be sneezed at, and when people in the street ask him how things are, Nikita says, so-so, amateurs get the chop, I'm not sure that between Beria and him we gained much by the change, yes, I recall very clearly hearing you talking about the various deaths of Beria, you have a good memory, three deaths was it? no, at least six, and you are quite right, in the notes the doctor made about my mother's ravings the name of Beria did not appear.

'Not once. At first I thought it was the ultimate precaution, we'll have to come back to that, Beria, a sadist, a psychopath, a man sexually obsessed, the Russians love to frighten themselves by kicking their corpses in the ribs. If the Soviet Union is the kind of country that could be dominated by a man like him, then it isn't much of a country, or else Beria is much more than a man who ripped the panties off women, just think, Peter the Great died before he became Peter the Great and it was the great nobles took it on themselves to write the story of his life, or take the Emperor Augustus, he died before being Emperor Augustus, and it was Antony who wrote his portrait, Octavius the psychopath, which he most certainly was, like Beria, who was nothing like Augustus, or Iago, picture Iago, it'll cheer you up.'

Lilstein's digressions are of course intended to cheer you up and also to impose his ways on you. You've decided that you would go on looking grim to make him ask you what was wrong, you've thought hard about what you are going to say to him, that you've just reread *Faust*, that it's not working any more, and then he manages to make you listen again to his anecdotes or fantasies, by the time he's finished it'll be too late, he will have taken you by the hand once more, you will want to speak but won't be able to get the tone right, you'll sound hesitant or brusque, and appear to be missing the point.

'Picture Iago,' Lilstein goes on, 'an Iago who turns into an enlightened minister, an expert in maritime growth, he dies twenty years after that unfortunate business with the handkerchief, mourned by all, a statue facing out to sea for the centuries to come, I have a very bold hypothesis: what does Beria do when he succeeds Yezhov? What does Beria do after Stalin dies? He was always close to Bukharin's programme, a man of the right, work, profitability, a few market mechanisms, the Party worries about ideology and leaves the managers to manage things, let's have done with anti-Semitism and all that "Greater Russia" rhetoric, when he died some of the people implicated in the white-collar plot had to wait two years before they were freed, simply because the order for their release was signed by Beria.

'Each time he was fully in charge of security he ordered the doors to be opened, and in '53 he goes very far, he is ready to accept a form of German reunification on condition that it stays neutral, he has a clear idea of what growth means and what nationalities are, we'll speak of that later, yes, it's dangerous to talk about such matters, even today, that is why they went to so much trouble to kill Beria, one death but several versions, we can't make different models of the same motor car, but when it comes to death there's no one to touch us.

'So there is a fourth version, more fanciful, Beria attends a party at the Polish Embassy, shield decorated with a white eagle on a red background, we can add without fear of error that the Ambassador's wife has skin like a peach, and dimples and that she's wearing Chanel, Beria came in his own car, with Voroshilov and Bulganin, first-rate cuisine, meat that melts in the mouth, vast amounts of drink, Polish vodka obviously, end of the reception, they drive off into the night, the car, Beria, Bulganin, Voroshilov, everyone's pissed, they go to the Lubyanka, to Beria's flat, a drunken farce, with Malinovski and Konev in the car behind, Beria's driver has been changed, he's a colonel, three minutes later Beria is standing before a court presided over by Marshal Konev, judged, sentenced, executed in a cellar with which he was intimately acquainted.

'There are other versions, I'll tell you those another day, stories of bullets in the back put there by his friends, but we run no such risk, we trust each other.

'And then times started to change, between the two of us we made terror take a step back, we contributed in our modest way to push back the shadows of unnatural death, and your Minister friend cannot dispense with your conversation, we are moving forward, so you're rereading *Faust*? Now why did you tell me that?

'Because you have doubts? It's only to be expected, you're French and if you had fewer grandiose sentiments you'd have fewer doubts.'

*

The wives of the Consul and Morel are having cross words over a hoop, the young woman has quickly got the idea that you mustn't let people get away with anything:

'You went through four the wrong way, didn't you?'

Max, Morel and de Vèze watch them, the pink diplomat joins them, bald, ruddy complexion, an inane, unforgiving expression in his eye, a face descending in ledges towards his thick lips, he lisps:

'It's a very feminine game.'

'You look worried,' says Max.

The pink diplomat whines:

'It's so hard finding honest domestic help in Singapore, they don't know anything and they steal. There's this one I've got, this morning, in order to make him return a dinner jacket the police had to teach him a harsh lesson, like the English do, with a cane, it was painful to see, eighteen he was, skin very smooth, hardly smelled at all, for a minute he didn't understand what was happening, held face down on the table, he started struggling, they tied his feet to the legs of the table, white buttocks, he confessed at the fourth stroke but the sergeant said to go up to fifteen, I didn't care about the jacket, but you've got to have law and order, as the Anglo-Saxons say.'

The diplomat's chin rises and points to the horizon, tautening the fat on his neck which settles back into its regular folds when his chin comes down again.

Weird, de Vèze thinks, a sodomite singing the praises of law and order. They do it as a cover, a friend of his told him one day, but de Vèze thinks there might be more to it than that, there must be a visceral pleasure to be got from defending law and order in a society which puts you behind bars each time it catches you with a squaddie in a public toilet, de Vèze has known officers who were, as they say, limp-wristed but nevertheless laughed like drains, and quite genuinely, whenever they heard repeated what Clemenceau said about Lyautey, 'at last we've got a general with balls up his arse, though unfortunately they're not his', as though they gladly accepted the fact that they had two existences, one led in the dancing dark and the other in the light of day, in a society which dealt ruthlessly with the dancing shadows of which they were the – often heroic – guardians.

Morel, followed by the pink diplomat, walks away from Max and de Vèze towards his wife.

'They make a lovely couple,' says Max to de Vèze, 'I mean the husband and wife, but she must find him a bit of a bore at times, even if he does take her round all the embassies, did you know he used to be a member of the Communist Party? Actually, he's not the only one here this evening who came up via the Party, not you, you never had the time, anyway all these young people here this evening did, yes, I'm very well informed, it's my job, there isn't one of these youngsters who resisted the temptation, even the bearded chap in grey, likewise his pink chum, and maybe the young woman too, but Budapest, '56, went deep, they all jumped ship and then explained more or less why to the "bourgeois press", yes, I was there too, Budapest, I've seen a bit of everything.

'The hardest part? With those Russian tanks you're spoiled for choice. But if you want the biggest funk I was ever in: youngsters, a bridge over the Danube, just before the Russians arrived, a gang of kids, none more than thirteen, nobody knew where they came from, looked dirt poor, I was talking to passers-by who were carrying loaves of bread home, one of them shouted laughingly to the kids: aren't you a bit young to be playing with those? A quick burst of gunfire, the kids had sub-machine guns, the man I'd been talking to lying there in his own blood, breathing his last, the kids continue pointing their guns at us, they have the eyes of chicken-thieves.

'The people who had loaves put them down on the ground for the kids to see and then we all backed away, very slowly, you couldn't get to those kids, I've seen as much real war as you, but I never felt as scared as I did that day, so anyway, Budapest, for these young people who are here with us this evening, marked the break with their classless dreams, and today they're all Gaullists or congregate in the centre or belong to the "wait-and-see" brigade, that's why they think so much of this man who's keeping us waiting, he did exactly what they did, or rather they did what he did, though without the risks and the fanfares.

'Me? I never really felt tempted, never read Marx, I prefer Shakespeare, history always barks like a mad dog. By the way, Ambassador, were you aware that we've met before? Obviously you don't remember.'

Max leaves de Vèze, zigzags his way across the lawn, the sky has cleared, now and then the wind carries a few fading drops of rain or sea-spray, in the distance a few weak attempts at rainbows, a pale look to everything, the ocean and the moist air dilute and flatten, absence of anything to catch the eye, of high ground, *ars*, in Morocco there was more contrast, they called it *ars abu lhawa*, the clouds drift away, a still damp sun, the brown land shiningly wet, a rainbow against the sky, very bright, the agent for Native Affairs had translated for Max, *ars* is marriage, so 'the jackal's wedding', the jackal is truly their animal, their *Reynard the Fox*, and it also defines their politics, a jackal and a lion were sleeping on the edge of a ravine, the jackal says to the lion move over please, and the sleeping lion starts to fall over the edge, at the last moment he reaches out with his claws, pulls the jackal's tail clean off and as he falls cries I'll recognise you when we meet again! The jackal, minus tail, lopes off, gathers all the other jackals together, says let's go and eat apricots, they reach the apricot-tree, how do we get at the apricots? I'll tie all your tails to the apricot-tree, you shake it, then we'll eat the apricots, so he ties all their tails, then goes to keep watch while they shake the tree. He races back shouting, hunters! dogs! every man for himself!

And off he runs. All the jackals pull so hard that their tails come off, the lion catches our jackal, you made me fall, I pulled your tail off, our jackal says that all jackals are tail-less, send for them, they all come, now which one will you recognise?

The pulled-off tail is a political fable, Monsieur Goffard, here, as soon as a jackal loses his tail he does everything he can to ensure that he's not the only one it happens to, that's how you get them exactly where you want them.

Max rejoins the young woman, takes her by the elbow with the famil-
iarity that is allowed to men of his age, he brushes Morel to one side.

'We must talk rags.'

He whisks her off from under de Vèze's nose and just as de Vèze is
about to say something, Max steers her towards the Consul's wife,
leaves her there, I amuse her, I'm the person she feels most at ease with
this evening, I'm the oldest but I'm not that old, how old is Chaplin?
The girl's bored, we could see each other again in town, between four
walls, I wouldn't be a nuisance to have around, true, but I'm not
Chaplin, this convolvulus is lovely, that blue, the faded hues of burnt
sienna, you don't often come across convolvulus in those colours, it's
unreal, in the Chefchaouen region they had a song that went something like 'might as well try to separate me from you as to disentangle
the poppy from the bindweed', it was a war fought thicket to thicket,
rock to rock, pursuits over scree hanging on to branches of juniper, at
dawn along jackal trails, they know the terrain like the back of their
hands, God help those who abandoned their fields and went to live in
towns, magnificent clumps of oleander in the beds of wadis which
hadn't seen real rain for years, some roots would burrow down fifteen,
twenty, thirty metres looking for water, Abd el-Krim's lieutenants said
that after they'd won the war they'd rebuild Al Andalûs and its
fountains, but their men hated towns.

The pink diplomat walks over to de Vèze, asks him what he thinks of
Monsieur Goffard who is so keen to be called Clappique, rather
provocative, don't you think? don't you feel he's trying to create an
incident? the way he looked at the main gate saying I'll get even, yes,
he passes through here once or twice a year, the Consul cultivates him
for what he knows, we don't like him much, and tonight he seems
even more out of control than usual.

De Vèze gives the impression that he's listening to the pink
diplomat though he's really watching the historian's wife just a few
metres away who is standing in front of a bank of green leaves and
convolvulus.

'The garden is superb,' says the pink diplomat, 'you don't know anything about plants? I'll soon put that right, I won't say anything about orchids, they're all over the island, but have you seen the trees, the arboretum?'

De Vèze can't see it.

'I'll show you, not the coconut trees nor the palms or the bamboos, look there, clove-trees, and behind them, in the distance, on the left, that strange object that looks like a tangle, at the sea-edge, it gives off a rather acrid smell, like ammonia, decomposition, you must have heard of it? A speciality of the region, the man who used to own the property insisted on having one in his garden and it did so well that we've never managed to get rid of it, you need to keep an eye on virtually a daily basis, or just keep it dry, too much work, so we leave it to its own devices, it's not unpleasant to look at and it doesn't smell unless the weather gets too hot, it's a complete world of unlikely shapes, an underworld, larvae, transparent crabs, fish which breathe with lungs, tadpoles, globules of what looks like snot, all fermenting, sucking, roots reaching up and grabbing the air, water-spiders in the matted branches, I'm boring you, did you see? Something moved, you know sometimes you can see monkeys up in the leaves, real ones, on the lawn it's all so very different,' palm to the sky the hand of the pink diplomat gestures towards the croquet players only a few metres away, he gives the impression that he is sizing them up, he murmurs: 'This is what we fought two world wars to defend!'

De Vèze does not rise to this, the young woman's face is quite charming, dimples, pointed nose, lips not too big nor too small, teeth a tad rabbity, de Vèze watches for the moment when he'll get her profile, then abandons her face to catch the way the light behind her shows her legs through the material of her dress, they are almost sturdy, not exactly what he goes for, I prefer long legs, ah! the aristocracy of long legs! but hers have style, are muscular and cope very nicely without high heels, enough for an evening's entertainment but not worth ruining your whole life for.

And finally Malraux makes his appearance in the garden of the villa, charcoal-grey suit, white handkerchief in the breast pocket, dark tie, quick stepping, he no longer has that rebellious flop of hair over one eye, his baldness is spreading in all directions over his scalp from a central patch of stubbornly resistant hair, he emits a thin smile, he looks in better health than rumour has it:

'Please don't stop whatever you're doing! Croquet! I insist you finish your game, I didn't even know playing it was still allowed, fear not, Consul, I won't tell the General that his diplomats are in the habit of playing such a quintessentially English game, good to see you again, de Vèze, it's twenty years since the last time! Actually I think I'll join in the game, that way I shall be as guilty as you, oh just an ordinary pastis, Pernod if you have it, not too much water, one ice cube, thank you.'

Malraux with a magisterial flourish reaches for a mallet:

'You know, I played here in 1925, not at this villa, in the hotel, the Raffles, the English called croquet "the lord of lawn games".'

'"Lord, lord",' said Max in the wings, 'as well they might, croquet was invented by French peasants and it was passed on to the English via Ireland, the lord of lawn games has a whiff of the potato about it, anyway, this particular lord is on the point of extinction, killed off by baseball, ultimately the Yanks will kill off everything, except in out-of-the-way places like Singapore, the last gasp of empire, which will stagger on for just a wee while longer, though it's soon to be an independent republic.'

Max turns towards Malraux:

'My dear author, if you don't mind being my partner I shall be an active participant, as a matter of fact I was in the middle of explaining to these young people the rule of tight croqueting, to recap, a tight croquet is allowed when I have succeeded in hitting another player's ball with mine, this entitles me to a second shot, using considerably more force but still within the rules of the game, shush! don't say a word, I shall now fetch the ball which I hit with mine, watch carefully, I place it so that it touches mine but without moving it by so much as a hair's breadth, I put one foot on my ball, then thwack! I strike my own nice ball with my mallet and out shoots the other nasty ball, I can either hit it as far as I can or alternatively take careful aim and knock it through an illegal hoop, which is very much like diplomacy since it means pushing your opponent into making mistakes, which means the nasty ball has to be thwacked. You can peel as much as you like, but you'll not thwack everything into the long grass.'

They played on for some time while the daylight drained from the town and the ocean, from time to time Max would drift off into his thoughts, Rabat, his youth, barely thirty years old, in my head I've never got beyond thirty, I still feel that's how old I am, how I got around in those days! you could tell that young woman all about it, not sure if she'd listen, she speaks very well, very clipped, you're older than Chaplin was when he married his wife, she's not really paying any attention to you, she's watching the Ambassador from Rangoon, he's not aware of it, he's happy to strut and swagger for her benefit, he hasn't noticed that she's observing him back, there weren't any women like her in Rabat, this one can talk, has the voice of someone who isn't dependent on the way men look at her, she knows things, she can answer back, that 'didn't you?' to the Consul's wife just now was spunky stuff, in Rabat there were women who had a certain style but the minute they opened their mouths they ruined it, Lyautey just couldn't pick them, and Max was only interesting when he was talking, he got his best ideas from looking into the eyes of women, a friend once told him that a woman's look can sometimes be better than sex, he made conquests, today you're just an old story-teller who needs to be holding forth, I'll have to tell them about the rain maidens.

That doll on a manure heap in the Riff, at Chefchaouen, not the same smell as is now blowing in from the far end of the grounds, it was stronger, doll is hardly the word, a grain shovel, made of wood, a piece of wood nailed crosswise to the handle, the blade of the shovel is the hips, encapsulated a whole concept of Woman, then a small piece of cotton veil, red wool for a coat, a silk belt, a few Spanish coins around the head, the agent for Native Affairs said it's intended to invoke rain, they're dying of drought at present, and they're not allowed down on the plain unless they agree to surrender, woe to any who rise up in revolt only when their necks are already placed between block and sabre, so they make a doll, the children make a doll, they call it a rain maiden, they pour water over it and process with it from the mosque to the marabout, praying for rain, at the end of their march they prop it upright in a dungheap and go back home to wait for the rain to come, come on, de Vèze, wake up, dear boy, it's your turn.

De Vèze has almost begun to feel happy, playing croquet, drinking his whisky, watching the birds cross the sky, talking to the writer he so admires, and watching the young woman, Malraux and Max are paired, a team, they've been playing at a fantastic rate, with Malraux tending to invent new rules at every turn, they've even argued, Max has been behaving like a crotchety old man to ensure he remains in charge of operations, he has provoked Malraux, once he called him young man, he didn't do it again, he quite deliberately talked to himself or said As sure as my name is Clappique! and Malraux pretended not to hear so as not to have to follow it up, the Consul watched them anxiously, he had invited Clappique on his own initiative, he could feel an incident involving Malraux looming.

Something suddenly came over de Vèze at the thought that he would probably never see the young woman again, I must have her, she's got no business being with that man, the prissy bookworm, women belong to the men who love them most.

The young woman has seen a large bird in the clouds.

'An albatross,' said de Vèze, edging nearer her.

'No it's not,' said Max.

And the Consul's wife:

'It's a frigate-bird.'

'Four metres wingtip to wingtip,' adds Max, 'a bird that's all wing, it flies at ten thousand feet and sleeps on the bosom of the storm.'

He looks straight at de Vèze:

'There are frigate-birds and there are gannets, the gannet is the most ridiculous bird, the fat girl on the beach, you can kick her and she won't even try to run away, spends all the time stuffing herself, and she's drawn to frigate-birds, they've developed a technique for not overtiring themselves, they wait for a gannet to fly close to them, then they wallop it over the head until it coughs up the fish it's got in its craw, it's true, they keep swatting it, the fish falls from the gannet's beak and they catch it in mid-flight, frigate-birds don't have very nice manners.'

'It's not true,' says Malraux, 'in the wild frigate-birds and gannets get on very well.'

'It's just a story,' says Max, 'it's . . .'

'It's pure Goffard,' Malraux interrupts.

The young woman:

'As soon as you get these stories about male and female, people start making everything complicated.'

*

'Is it only because you have doubts that you're sulking?' Lilstein asks you in a patient voice. 'But doubts are vital in our line of work! And at your age it is a highly valuable commodity, can you imagine me working with a zealot? If you were a keen Frenchman brimming with the highest ideals, I wouldn't give myself six months, too dangerous! Look, if you want to stop for a while, get some perspective, do it, doubts about what? Still think you're a spy? Up to now I've been spying for you, Khrushchev and his missiles, a few years back, Khrushchev ready to give way, a hell of a tip-off, was I asked to feed it to you? Don't be sarcastic, it's politics, there are no free lunches, what matters is results, maybe my information did come from comrades who at the same time were urging Khrushchev to dig his heels in, knowing that he'd back down, so it would be easier to kick him out afterwards, yes, you're right, it wasn't a very nice game to play, you're a clever judge of these things, maybe too clever, not a nice game at all, maybe it did happen like that, maybe not.

'So not doubts exactly? Scruples, then? What you can't stand is being permanently surrounded by right-wing people? And you'd like to stay left of centre, protect your scruples, the gap between your two souls is too great? Oh please, no left-wing Gaullists, there's no future in it, let's be serious, in the end the General will go, so stay on the right with your friend the Minister, he'll go onwards and upwards and you'll go with him, he'll have to stop from time to time but he'll go very high; if you want to reduce the gap between your two souls, the dreaming one and the doing one, go easy on the dreams, though actually you're doing pretty well on the right wing, I know you've been invited to the Prime Minister's place, in the country, a ride on a mule, eh? wonderful, go ahead, you have doubts, you sulk, your left-wing soul aches, and yet you get an invitation from the Prime Minister! See? you only have to have doubts and things happen all by themselves.

'That said, would you mind if I give you a piece of advice? Go and ride your mule, but don't stay on it too long, pointless tagging along with the Prime Minister, you're not the same generation, you'd look like a callow arriviste, especially if you're riding a mule.

'You're not sure they're mules? More like big ponies? It's all the same, riding addles the brain, I'm not being fair, but a large percentage of the people who have taken much too close an interest in me wore riding boots, so it's time to dismount, we've plenty of time, see? I'm not treating you like one of my agents, I'm not telling you to do anything, I'm trying to put you on your guard, on the basis of my experience, if you really want to try something with the Prime Minister, go ahead, but believe me it's a closely watched circle; with your friend it's different, you're already a part of a group which is currently being formed, it looks natural, I can tell you this because I'm fifteen years older than you, I'm into my third life, we've got time, if I'd used you as an agent you'd already have been blown, the active life of a top-class agent is rarely longer than ten years, because you need a network, orders, go-betweens, archives.

'It's different for you, there's just me and you, and talk, like in Plato, and I try to shield you from accidents, it's like driving, it's not enough to observe the highway code, you must always give yourself a way of ending up in the ditch without breaking your neck, the right speed is the speed that allows you to get off the road if some road-hog comes at you head-on.

'I know you won't make any mistakes, young gentleman of France, but I try to protect you against the road-hogs, would you seriously prefer to have left-wing Gaullists? They won't get very far, it would be best to stay on the right, it suits you there, make the most of its surrogate pleasures, but if you really want some left-wing fun you only have to say that basically Lenin was right when he said that the State must wither away, say it with a laugh, if you still want to, and you'll be dancing to two tunes at the same time.

'Don't get close to the Prime Minister, when he's got a cigarette in his mouth the eye above it closes almost completely, but that's the eye he watches everything with, he knows people too well, he doesn't like your friend, he won't ever like you, it would be fun to get together with your friend and organise balls for him, he likes dancing, the moment there are women around the men start talking more loudly and say all sorts of things to drown out other men's voices, I'm not opposed in principle to the role women can play in our line of work.

'I'll say it again: this is not about spying! We are doing an important job, together we take the pulse of what goes on, we regulate the blood pressure, it's a noble calling, we do it with words in ears, the art of not unleashing catastrophes, that's odd, I can't smell our Linzer today.'

*

In Singapore, after the croquet, they went in to dinner, a round table, everyone can see everybody else without having to lean to the right or to the left, though it should be added that there is no right or left or centre any more.

'A table after de Gaulle's own heart,' said Max with a laugh.

'Over here, de Vèze,' said Malraux, seating him on his left.

The Consul's wife did not try to stop him. De Vèze thought his luck was in, especially when he saw that the young woman was sitting opposite him, Max, now well launched, continued:

'Left, right, port, starboard, tacking is tactics, isn't that a fact, you young people? Shush! don't interrupt, art of governing, art of sailing, to move the rudder there's a tiller that moves a half-turn, true of boats from the smallest craft to the largest caravel, so to tack right or left you reverse the directions of the tiller, you give the helmsman the command hard a-port!' Max's hand catches a wineglass which keels over, empty, and the boat veers to starboard. 'It works perfectly if you're a sailor.'

'And equally well if you're a Gaullist,' says the grey diplomat.

The Consul gives him a withering look, glances up at Malraux, Malraux smiles, the Ambassador relaxes his expression, the pink diplomat looks daggers at the grey diplomat, I don't know how often I've told Xavier not to overdo the right-wing cynic, it hasn't gone down at all well, Max continues:

'Very true, old man, the end of the Algerian War is a case in point, the General goes to Algiers, puts the tiller hard over to port, the crowd cheers, but every self-respecting sailor knew at the time that this meant tacking to the right, shush! not a word, I pick up where I left off, technical advances, pulleys, cables, reversing levers, tiller replaced by a wheel which eventually turns in the same direction as the course that has been set, all the navies of the world adopt it, steer to port now comes to mean that the wheel is turned to port to steer to port, or left if you prefer, shush! haven't finished, the English navy, so traditional, clings to the old system, obstinately: to steer a course to starboard, the captain of Her Majesty's ship gives the order hard a-port!, and on hearing 'port' the helmsman turns the wheel to starboard, God save Tradition, and the ship tacks to starboard; if you're English, it's plain sailing, all right, there has been the odd accident involving pilots in foreign ports, it didn't happen often, but the press got hold of it, hence the root-and-branch reform of the Royal Navy in 1933.'

As he sat down de Vèze's foot encountered another, he couldn't tell if it belonged to Malraux on his right, or to Max or even to the young woman sitting opposite him, he said sorry, very quickly, without looking at anyone in particular, no one reacted, they were served lobster mayonnaise, the pink diplomat looked startled, de Vèze has forgotten his name again, he remembers that the grey diplomat with the monkey-arse beard around his mouth is called Poirgade, Xavier Poirgade, Xavier suits him, suits his inflexible outlook, already one of our major strategy experts so the Consul told him, he is very well-connected in Paris, sometimes too close to certain American positions, an Atlanticist, but he has the ear of many people, the Consul raises his right hand to the right side of his face, palm slightly upturned, the pink diplomat's Christian name, it would be amusing, a less rigid sort of name, to complement 'Xavier' – Jean-Philippe, Jean-Jacques – de Vèze doesn't remember.

The pink diplomat stares at his mayonnaise, he should have known, here we are in the middle of Asia and the Consul decides to serve dinner *à la française*, and you give us lobster mayonnaise, why not give us *pan bagnia* while you're about it? afraid of Asian cuisine, there must be a halfway house between lobster mayonnaise and roast puppy with honey, but who around this table except me knows anything about good eating? Not the Consul, he's not eating anything, mostly he just puffs on his pipe and dyes his eyebrows and plays out time while waiting to be promoted to ambassador, nor his wife who is anorexic; Malraux? he'd be happy running on Pernod right through to the dessert; the young couple? not yet; the Ambassador at Rangoon, this de Vèze, probably scoffs tinned monkey when he's by himself to help him remember Bir Hakeim; and as for the esteemed Xavier he can't stand mayonnaise, yellow dribbles on grey silk, horrid thought, I wish he'd drop some down himself, this mayonnaise is tasteless, they must have made the olive oil go further by adding ground-nut oil, and no one here to notice, and the lobster has no flavour, overcooked, you don't get that aroma of iodine, it was a medical orderly who cooked it for sure, these people are only interested in words, instead of appreciating a meal they listen to a story and ask the limelight-hogging Max to explain that reform of the Royal Navy.

'Very simple, children!' says Max, 'in 1933 the Admiralty ruled as follows: henceforth, the command "starboard" will mean that the helmsman shall turn his wheel to starboard so that the ship steers directly to starboard, like everybody else.'

'Which put an end to the accidents,' says the pink diplomat, to shorten Max's peroration.

'Except those caused by old habits,' Max went on, '1942, the *Argus*,

English aircraft carrier, the Med, convoy heading for Malta, three Italian torpedoes, off the port bow, if the ship holds its present course it will be hit, the answer's simple, change course immediately in the direction of the torpedoes – to port – close the angle, the torpedoes will pass under the bows, the Captain has grasped the situation, not for nothing is he Captain of the *Argus*, pure instinct, he orders "hard to starboard", that's right, a slip-up, obtuse angle, the entire ship's side, 230 metres long, it will be exposed to the torpedoes, shush! don't speak, an English captain screaming orders, never been seen before, the helmsman panics, a pre-1933 reflex, puts the wheel over to port, and there you have it, the *Argus* veers to port, acute angle, torpedoes avoided, I love stories involving changes of direction.'

The conversation has reverted to the Americans, massive bombing of North Vietnam will never work, it works sometimes, says Max, it depends on the bombings but sometimes it does work, but only if you target civilians, they'll never agree to that intervenes Malraux, Johnson ruled it out precisely because he knows it won't work, he needs a failure, in his head de Vèze mulls over what he would like to say to Malraux, the day is ending, the sea-breeze, the yellow flowers, the young woman, behind her the trees slowly turn dark blue, no one dares ask Malraux why Johnson needs a failure, de Vèze hasn't been as close as this to Malraux since the Liberation.

What he finds surprising is that Malraux seems to be taking an interest in him, out of the blue he has asked de Vèze, in front of the assembled company, in front of the young woman:

'Tell me, de Vèze, Bir Hakeim . . .'

And the young woman has looked at de Vèze and smiled, how does she do it? only a modest neckline but so inviting, you feel you could slip your hand inside, any time, with every confidence, it would be the right move, neither aggressive nor shy, she's expecting it, she'd be a teeny bit miffed that you should behave like this, but she's expecting it, all you need is a manoeuvre to get you halfway there, hand suddenly very close, a few words away, but no pressure applied, just a stage, not like in the days of the first films you saw with a girl in the dark, when your hand settled on her shoulders in that relaxed, good pals sort of way, your hand was instantly shrugged off and that was it for that day, or else the girl let you do whatever and was ready for the rest without going through the good pals rigmarole, de Vèze had known one girl who had taken the hand he'd put on her shoulder and pressed it unambiguously to her breast saying now can we watch the film? Snatches of adolescence in the cinema, Morgan, Gabin, a few kisses, another time he and the girl canoodled and smooched their way through the entire picture.

He'd spent the rest of his youth in a Free French training camp and the films he saw then had been taken by movie cameras mounted on aeroplanes, he wanted to be a fighter pilot, but that took time, they sent him to Africa, but here, with this woman, she knows exactly what a hand on a breast feels like, the gradual approach is out, make a natural move, don't come at her from below, still maybe start by stroking the material, no, go straight for skin, the grain of the skin, start high from the shoulder, but where should he be positioned? Behind her? No, facing her, both standing, after dinner, behind the trees, look at her, extend right hand, crook wrist, fingers out, go in down the cleavage, palm over the nipple, change angle of wrist, fingers pointing down, the whole breast in your hand, its weight, one single move, de Vèze thinks of the inevitable pear, pretty pears, but pears are too hard, they don't say anything true about breasts, breasts shaped like pears, the whole breast in his hand, but you hardly squeeze at all and the breast swells in your hand, Moine's wife in the restaurant, she wore a low neckline, bigger breasts, with your finger-tips you feel something beating, you are aware of being clumsy, it's exactly what they expect, they expect you to be clumsy at such moments, for you are now entering a region in which all true knowledge is theirs, that of their pleasure, and they will run a mile from men who are too sure of themselves.

Or else do nothing with your hands, actually this business of dropping a right hand down inside a cleavage is pretty complicated, no, keep it simple, hands held behind her back, defenceless, drop head, kiss top of cleavage, the beauty spot, just a simple kiss, a stolen kiss.

*

'I'm sure you'll go on playing your part to perfection,' Lilstein tells you, 'because now you really want to be the character you're playing, you always half wanted it, to send me packing, become like them, a man of the right, of the Parisian right, very chic, it's like me, every time my secretary forgets something I act like a ruthless capitalist, but you, you would like to be a genuine reactionary with your feet under the table but at the same time you don't want to end up resembling your own family, not all the time, so sometimes, as they say in English, you chop and change, or as we say, you dance at two weddings at the same time.

'Did you know, young Frenchman, there was a lot of dancing here, before the war? I even cut my first dance-floor dash here, ballroom of the Waldhaus, sixteen, less than, I looked older than my age, there were balls, dancing parties, they opened all the doors wide, it made a very large room, during the day seminars and ideas, in the evening mixing with the ladies, I believed I was capable of doing all kinds of things, I was changing the world, but when I found myself in the arms of a woman it turned out to be no fun at all, tall she was, very straight shoulders, voice rather serious and husky, she asked me to dance, me!

'She wanted to avoid making some of the others jealous, but I didn't admit that to myself straight away, a waltz, fine, I had some vague idea about twirling round and round, but next up was a tango, I managed the first few steps rather grandly, going on how I'd seen it done and read about it in books, but as for what came next I hadn't the faintest, she led me, grip of steel, she did it as though she was being swept off her feet but in truth she was leading me, there was only one thing I could do, go limp like a rag-doll and follow her movements, one moment she was the woman who has been dominated, the next the woman who fights back, and it was she who directed the whole thing, it was great art, she was very lady-like but when she danced the tango she behaved like a bitch, she made it clear that it wasn't her but the dance which required her to grind her thigh against my hip and send her backside to hell.

'And later that evening, a friend of mine, a French journalist, came up to me, we watched her dancing with other men who were sleeker and more expert than I, my journalist chum said we've made a very famous friend there, but you get the feeling she'd give it all up and go some place where she could slit the throat of goat or fawn and tear it to pieces and chuck the pieces up in the air, look at her feet, Lilstein, she always keeps one in shadow.

'At one point during the ball, an Austrian girl told me I looked as if I'd been taught to dance the tango by Frederick II's soldiers, it wasn't true, I felt weak at the knees, the tall woman smiled, but she held me firmly with one hand, I came on strong, arch look in my eye, I was ludicrous, never come on strong, young man, just be someone who's indispensable, so indispensable that you won't need to have to impose your personality, it will simply be unthinkable that you're not there, the unthinkable empty chair, they won't be able to start without you, they call you to come, they wait for you and while they wait they sneer at the cheap shoes you wear, dark brown, to go with everything, this makes them warm to you, they'll poke affectionate fun at you, you won't need to scratch around for invitations, you'll have become indispensable, the man they're waiting for.

'Did I ever see that woman who danced the tango again? I don't know whether or not I'll tell you some day, what I do know is that I can see her now, here, all I have to do is shut my eyes, or even if I keep them open, just now as I was coming up, I walked past the swimming pool, which hasn't changed at all, it was very nice.'

Lilstein will go on telling you about the girl who danced the tango, a part of what he sees as he speaks will be for you, the rest stays with him, he is sixteen, an unlocked cubicle, no one screams, a silhouette in the shower, with the passage of the years he sees the face less and less clearly and what remains is what you sometimes find in museums, breasts, abdomen, thighs, perfection is the word for it, he closed the door, he did, he stayed outside, and for years he dreamed of what might have happened if he'd stepped inside and closed it after him, and even his dreams grew less torrid, he has a book at home which he never opens, wouldn't part with it, he'd lost it every time the police arrested him, the first time he'd bought it back, the next time one of his colleagues returned it to him together with a large part of his library, I took them home and kept them safe, I knew you'd talk your way out of trouble.

Lilstein said thanks but nothing else, he never opens the book, he's just happy to check that it's still there, in the binding of the copy which the Nazis burned he had hidden a letter, in the replacement he'd bought all he knows is that on a certain page he will find a picture of exactly what he'd seen that time in the shower, haunches, thighs, he is certain by comparing both memories, the shower and the page of the *Dictionary of Greek Sculpture*, that the two images are identical, haunches firm and long, breasts held high, thighs, how shall we put it, not fish, under me her thighs slipped away like trout, I had her on a river bank, not a river, not a poet, besides I never had her, sharp-buttocked, she cries out when you open the door, turns, three-quarter back view, sharp-buttocked, already you're not absolutely certain any more, what must have changed is your criterion of beauty, nowadays you'd find the Aphrodite pictured in the *Dictionary* too slim, her breasts not quite ripe, best not look in the book.

'In Paris, people in counter-espionage will have their suspicions,' Lilstein tells you, 'the same way you have doubts. They have to have suspicions, I mean to say we're in a risky business which operates on constructive fear and the charm of those frantic crises, no purpose is served by making yourself unsuspectable, one day someone will ask why you are so unsuspectable, so you're wasting your time staying whiter than white, because in the end somebody will say: "the man's too clean, if he isn't a Soviet agent he's burying his talents."

'There have to be blots on everybody's record, otherwise it's too good to be true, all the people I've ever known who were above suspicion came a cropper in the end, whereas everybody bears the mark of sin, they have to suspect people in sensitive jobs where suspicion is more dangerous than actual leaks, so they relax the pressure, they say that the cost-benefit ratio of hunting moles is too high.

'That's what the English thought, all those moles, even had a mole as head of their own espionage service, of course they suspected something, they spent years trying to nab them, not to protect old Cambridge chums or their little playmates in queerdom, there's real pleasure to be had in eliminating old friends, no, if the English hesitated for so long it was because the whole thing was so gross that it looked like a trap.

'The English have a memory for the wholesale traps, it all looked too much like the Tukhachevsky business, you'll never understand why moles operating in England were so successful if you forget Tukhachevsky.'

*

In front of everyone sitting round the table in the Consulate, out of the blue, Malraux suddenly asks de Vèze:

'Bir Hakeim, how did you manage to walk out of there in the middle of the night?'

'Our navigation point was five stars in the constellation Corbus.'

Malraux:

'What did you all reckon at the time?'

De Vèze:

'We reckoned it was perhaps a bit risky.'

Max:

'Is it true that at the time Berlin and Vichy both wanted you court-martialled and shot? you and your ragbag gang of French whites and blacks and the Judaeo-Bolsheviks of the Legion?'

'True,' said de Vèze, 'de Gaulle went on radio quick as a flash with his answer: he'd treat German prisoners the same way, and Radio-Berlin back-pedalled, they'd treat us as soldiers, but that didn't make us any more enthusiastic about the idea of being taken prisoner.'

'Were you really in jeeps?'

'No, there have been stories about jeeps but we didn't have any, I was on one of those vehicles with tracks called "Bren-gun carriers", one metre fifty high, you could get five men in it, didn't offer much protection but it would go anywhere.'

Three times de Vèze drove over the mines of Bir Hakeim, a way through had to be opened up, de Vèze, take one of the Brens and go for it, and when you'd gone for it and were still alive to tell the tale, you came back, got into another Bren and went for it again until there was a way through.

De Vèze has never talked about it in detail, not through modesty, but because he didn't like the Brens, what he would have liked was a plane and to be anywhere but Bir Hakeim, he'd have liked to start earlier in the war, whiff of knights of old, a fighter pilot over London, a Spitfire, like Mouchotte, when a few hundred men aged between eighteen and twenty succeeded in stopping Hitler, Battle of Britain, a dream, or with the Americans, the Naval Air Service, Battle of Midway, at the same time as Bir Hakeim, about ten in the morning, in just a few moments several dozen pilots sank the Japs' aircraft carriers and it was all over, Japan had lost, and he knew now that it was just a question of time. Each time, just a handful of men with everything depending on them.

In Africa it was different, a very small cog in an army of two hundred thousand men, it could be heroic, but not decisive, still Bir Hakeim wasn't a bad show even if it was a retreat, it was also an Adventure, it paved the way for El-Alamein, the real turning point, a lot of rocks, two armies.

'War in its purest form,' says Max, 'sand and gravel, soldiers, no civilians, a story that can be told, with radar, more and more radar.'

Without really wanting to, de Vèze stares at Max's ears. And Max smiles at de Vèze. He quite likes de Vèze, thinks he has a few too many illusions, heroism, an illness, not real war, we're having dinner, not the moment for Max to bring out his tales of racking coughs, purulent gobbets of tracheal mucous membrane expelled at a rate of knots by the coughing, large lumps nestling in armpits and groins which peel raw after two days, not to mention internal swellings, *ars abu lhawa*, the jackal and his wedding, didn't know how right they were, crafty Abd el-Krim, he succeed in re-grouping them, in a land where quarrels are so vicious that men are forbidden to go to the souk, only women, children and a few old men are allowed there.

Valleys of archaic violence, eye for an eye, where there could be a hundred dead in vendettas every year, a man has insulted my honour, I kill him at some family gathering, his brothers come looking for me, the old men discuss, they weigh the arguments, I pay the tribe a fine, nothing will happen to me, and the host of the party where the man was killed also receives compensation, the relatives of the murderer lay down their rifles in full sight of the tribal council, a value is put on them, the relatives of the dead man say 'more!'

The murderer's relatives add two or three rifles, then the elders cry 'enough, let us recite the *fatiha* over them', those who surrendered their guns may now buy them back, the remaining guns are auctioned off, when the sale is finished a deduction is made for the cost of the ox which was sacrificed for the meeting of the assembly, the cost of the oil for cooking it, the balance is shared out between each clan, and the assembly breaks up while the crier proclaims 'there is no God but God, we are all brothers, we hate no one except the Spaniard!'

Sometimes the relatives of the victim may continue to take their revenge on the relatives of the murderer, the dead man's brother has the right to kill my brother, and if the victims are women or children the blood debt cannot be redeemed, if the murderers have run away the injured party waits until their children are old enough to carry weapons and then kills them, cursèd be the nation in which each man behaves like a nation!

Actually Monsieur Goffard, it's even more complicated than that, the agent for Native Affairs told him, archaic violence, it's easy to say, but it's primarily about honour, it has to be defended when insulted, but the man who offends another man's honour is not only a delinquent, it's something he must do, he has to issue his challenge, if these people are archaic it is because they're forever challenging and defending, Abd el-Krim tried to turn all that into a republic, with phones and machine guns and honour and press releases, forbidding them to wage vendettas, we should add a few love songs for our female readers, 'O mother dear, it was written, for whom did I wash my dress? For a man with beautiful eyes, but he did not see me, tonight I'll throw myself into the sea's blue waves.'

Max, opposite de Vèze, ears like cauliflowers, now pink with drink and conversation:

'I'm very happy with my ears, a guarantee of a long life, like Picasso, he's got big ears too, when he was painting Helena Rubenstein, he said: "Helena, you've got ears like an elephant, they're as big as mine, how old are you?" and she said: "Pablo, you know very well I'm older than you," and he said: "Helena, elephants live for ever and so will we," and I'll be like Picasso and Helena Rubenstein, the Venerable Company of Jug Ears, I shall live for a long time yet, even if the world is getting less and less entertaining.'

Taking aim with his fork over his lobster mayonnaise, Max emits a laugh which he hopes sounds cavernous, as if it came from outside his body, from the very bowels of the earth, he looks straight at de Vèze and says:

'*The Great Adventure is buggered!*'

A cavernous voice, like a lesson from a place of darkness, with the waggish glee of some comic valet in a farce who has suddenly popped up out of the shadows, shot up from a world that is so dense, so elemental that de Vèze cannot recognise any of the things he has always believed in, a pool of magma in which great bubbles rise and burst one after the other and all the bubbles are of equal size, discord and betrayal all the way to the grave, chivalrous Adventure, Adventure is dead and gone for ever, the artful place their trust in the stars, Max punctuating his assertions with the rumblings of his stomach, oooh! aargh! groan, growl.

The sounds didn't come from the back of his throat or his nose, it was more a spasm of the abdomen, the muscles of the abdomen, but not a command transmitted to the muscles of the abdomen, muscles which instinctually respond to something which comes from the entrails, a place where time does not exist, snatches of an ancient voice in the depth of me, it's not my voice, I'll tell you everything, the truth is a bitch, a voice from before my time, a voice trying to get out, Max is not listening now, he is no longer looking, he is absorbed into the voice, that voice from before, and the dead people in my life, mud in mouths, the man is talking to you and next moment you're stuffing his right leg into a bag, a pal hands you something small, muddy, hairy, his moustache, stuck to what's left of a rifle butt.

He had no right to go away like that, taking with him whole chunks of what you are, of what you had shown him, without him you're nothing, what a mess, the kids, when they opened the doors of the cattle-trucks at Novosibirsk, gulag kids, *rigor mortis* well set in, you don't take notes because you know you have to make them forget you're a journalist, you say to the Red Army officer: war never *kharacho*, a show of fatalism you put on for him, actually you think it's as normal as he does, though maybe he doesn't find it at all normal but he hides it too, a fatalist, roll on peace, comrade journalist, we must be steel so that the bread of the future may finally be baked.

Mustn't tell him what you think of his half-baked metaphors, all your humanity has shrunk to an urge to puke and you hate yourself for not being able to puke, be steel, comrade dickhead, stay silent, the voices of silence, these are the real voices of silence, I have peeled my mind like an orange, both halves, and I've left nothing in the middle, that's what the Adventure is.

'They made out I was just a joker,' says Max, 'a silly, clowning Clappique, whereas my real name is Carnival, all the more reason for turning me into a jester.'

Indicating Max, de Vèze says to Malraux:

'He hasn't changed one bit, so why is he the only one you've allowed to come back?'

'Because he never asked me for anything,' replies Malraux.

De Vèze regrets having asked the question.

Max has heard and laughs:

'It was because our Great Author here wants to write *Twenty Years*

After, or even thirty, and also because I'm the most important character in *The Human Condition*, my friend.'

He counts off his fingers:

'Kyo, Katow, Tchen, and I'm d'Artagnan!'

And the young woman, to Malraux:

'He's not wrong, he's just as important as the others.'

'Ah, so you noticed,' said Malraux in a gentler voice.

'He's your anti-hero,' the young woman said to Malraux who is looking at her intensely.

Forgetting de Vèze, she goes on:

'It's Clappique who gives the story its true dimension, its reverse image.'

Malraux smiles at the young woman and de Vèze tries not to let his mouth hang open, many years ago someone told him it makes you look stupid, but if he clamps his jaws together he ends up looking like a martinet, just close your mouth without clenching your teeth, but he knows his face is on the full side, he stops thinking about the way the yellow material swoops down, what gives her the right to barge into the conversation like this? What gives her the right to get noticed by Malraux? This is de Vèze's moment, it doesn't belong to the wife of a historian, a blue-stocking, anti-hero my foot, do you know what you're talking about? When de Vèze and his friends took Amilakhvari back, no one felt like playing at being anti-heroes nor at being Clappique either, history and its obverse, give me a break, not with a cheeky comic valet like Jug Ears around.

To short-circuit the proceedings de Vèze murmurs under his breath to Malraux:

'I belong to the generation that learned Kyo's funeral oration by heart, I took orders from Amilak.'

Max has heard, he mimics Malraux's voice, his intonation descends from higher up in the pharynx, it is a voice that hangs an exclamation mark over the end of every statement, as if it was constantly at the pitch of Don Diègue's words 'that he should die!' Max exaggerating every characteristic, rubato, glissando, he recites the death of Kyo, as if it were pastiche, he almost bleats: '"He fought for what in his day would have carried the deepest of meanings and the greatest of hopes." Shush! don't interrupt, that's great prose, children!'

Max laughs the way you cough, between the words, expelling great bursts of laughter from his lungs and his very bones, he shakes with laughter, testing the limits of sarcasm:

'Chateaubriand, in that prison yard, in Shanghai!'

The Consul looks anxiously at Malraux whose face has turned pale.

The parody and the laughter have made de Vèze momentarily furious, he could kick Max, such a stupid thing to do, trying to pass himself off as Clappique, he could also have kicked the woman, he never imagined it would all turn out like this, this is his moment, de Vèze wanted to tell Malraux that he had recited the death of Kyo to himself at El-Alamein, after Bir Hakeim, a tricky business, there's a rocky outcrop bottling up the battlefield at El-Alamein, the Free French are sent in, Amilak, you've got two hours to take the position, go along the thalweg.

And Dimitri Zedguinidze, alias Amilakhvari, a Georgian prince forced to flee in 1917 by the revolutionaries, a lieutenant-colonel in the Foreign Legion, moves off to attack for France and for Montgomery, with a batch of French twenty-year-olds, Spanish anarchists and German Marxists, no artillery support, the attack fails, retreat.

Amilak brings up the rear, in his kepi, he was made a Companion of the Liberation, killed by a piece of shrapnel in the head, de Vèze stood before Amilakhvari's wooden cross and recited 'the deepest of meanings and the greatest of hopes' and the rest of it, he had to, 'the deepest of meanings', because the assault on the rocky outcrop was a shambles, a shambles that was followed three days later by victory, but a real shambles nonetheless and a hero who dies as the result of a cock-up needs 'the deepest of meanings', and here is Max parodying the whole thing, playing the fool.

Max is not looking at anyone now, he toys with his fork, for fifty years they've been saying I'm always clowning, last night I played poker again with two German officers, I first spotted them in 1914, they were running away just ahead of me, under shellfire, I mowed them down, two bullets in the back, range of two metres, 14 September, they didn't see a thing, sometimes they come back at night, we play poker, I can't make out their faces but I can see their cards, I let them win, I clown around, this man who was at Bir Hakeim has never managed to get away from it, he's a clown in his own way, the face he made when I said 'The Great Adventure is buggered!', you want wars fought by parfit knights, just like that agent for Native Affairs, a war of chivalrous warriors, like the first war with its photo-opportunity cavalry charges, there we were, facing courageous Arabo-Berber enemies, on the knoll, Colonel Corap, an old student of Pétain, five journalists around the Colonel who shouts: 'Bournazel, you may attack', he didn't actually say 'attack!' he didn't issue an order, he gave prancing heroes their heads, heroism doesn't stand around waiting, we all took it down in shorthand.

The Colonel's swagger stick points to the hill opposite, and Bournazel leads the charge with his three lieutenants and his seventy native mounted troops, pose for the photo; he's wearing a red cloak and a blue kepi, as Corap tells it, the insurgents believe that the bullets fired at the red coat bounce back and kill the man who fired them, got to show these types from Paris what we do in Morocco, here 'under a blazing sky, in this burning, pulsating wilderness of rock and scree', a war fought by noble lords against fierce warriors, courageous to the point of foolhardiness, one of Max's colleagues will write about 'what our officers are capable of: standing in their stirrups as they charge, red burnoose streaming on the wind, devil's gallop, heady excitement, hill captured, Bournazel lights a cigarette, trots back nonchalantly to his commanding officer, elegant figure carelessly wrapped in his cloak', the insurgents are beaten, one of them was found hiding in a cave, both thighs broken, his comrades hadn't been able to take him with them, or maybe he'd refused to go, he sat with his back to the rock wall, protected to the eyeballs by a low dry-stone wall, three rifles, water, olives, they didn't know he was alone, he delayed us for two days.

When they got to him he was dead, face serene, very dignified, maybe fifty years old, the agent for Native Affairs added: 'we've got two types of enemy, Monsieur Goffard, the savage who slits the throats of our wounded men, and the thoroughbred warrior who respects us as we respect him, we have both sorts, the problem is that they're often the same man.'

In the end, it was Corap who got his hands on Abd el-Krim, a full-scale raid, forced him to surrender, no fuss or bother, prisoner, parcelled up, packed off to La Réunion, Corap's claim to fame, his last, the rest was less brilliant, he made general, in May 1940 he has an army, the 9th, facing the panzers, this is a touch trickier than with comic-opera peasants, Corap screws up, army in disarray, sacked, or rather retired from active service, the rout of 1940, 'The Great Adventure is buggered!'

Preferable to behave like a buffoon, at least you weren't taken by surprise in 1940, the rout was the answer to the question put to me in 1918: Max, how did you manage to keep going? you said it was for love of country, because you believed in it, patriotic consent, you came back from the war with a military cross, a medal and several citations, rank of reserve Captain, twenty years later you find yourself up against the Germans with your medals, and you realise that in 1914 there'd been no consent given, you hadn't agreed to any such obscenity, you obeyed, it was obedience, if you went you died, if you didn't you died, gendarmes to bully us out of our fear, 'On your feet, you dead men!'

And in 1940 people remembered, no one waited, tell it how you like, the chiefs of staff screwed up, the holidays with pay which meant that aeroplanes weren't built, the ministers ran away, all the reasons you like, the truth is that if men kept their heads down, it was because finally they did what they'd been too scared to do twenty years before, what their fathers had been too scared to do, they had no wish to be guts hanging from a tree or have their heads blown off, 'so on your feet, you live men!'

And this time the living were too numerous for the gendarmes to arrest them all or for the colonel to have them shot, the firing-squads and the gendarmes kept their heads down just like everyone else, before everyone else did, meaning and hope? no thanks, we gave already.

De Vèze watches Max and the historian's wife, a birdbrain and a buffoon, and she dares to talk about anti-heroes, the obverse of history, what does she know about it? That's what you get when you let people speak who know nothing or laugh at everything, de Vèze feels like provoking an incident, another voice is heard, not Max's, 'he would die surrounded by men with whom he would have liked to live', the continuation of the death of Kyo, no, not that!

It's the young woman who is continuing to recite the words, why is she interfering? They're all the same, you look at them, they are aware of it, the hell with her, never touched a gun in her life and she talks about anti-heroes, she's wrecking everything, blue-stocking, the others have gone quiet, go on, recite away, it's tea-time at the Comédie Française, she goes on, 'he would die as each of these men had died, because he had given a meaning to his life', an odd look comes over the faces of the other guests as they listen.

As if it was some miracle that I should know the passage by heart, that a woman should be interested in anything other than bindweed in a hedge or the penises of the men around the table, the Ambassador might well be intelligent but he feels obliged to preen himself because I'm wearing a thin dress and am married, 'what value could be placed on a life for which he would not have been ready to die?' and Philippe who had no idea I'd read this novel, he thinks it's enough for him to love me, to marry me and now looks at me furiously because tonight I didn't wear a slip, a modern husband, I've seen him from all points of view, 'death surfeited with fraternal bleatings, a gathering of the vanquished where multitudes would recognise their martyrs', Monsieur Goffard's got a nerve, no respect for his author, he's usurped his role, actually Malraux is much more attentive to people than I'd have thought, has style, no tics, he acts out a lot of what he says, uninhibited, 'a bloody legend from which golden legends are made'.

*

'You probably know all about the Tukhachevsky affair? I won't press it,' Lilstein had said, 'at least that's one story I don't need to tell you.

'Anyway if any people in Paris ever pick up your scent, they have to be able to see a trail, don't be a perfectionist, don't cover all the tracks in your life, an adolescent's dream, some harsh treatment which might have given you cause for resentment, and don't behave as if you'd forgotten the story of your father's life, everyone knows it, you must give the guard dogs something to think about, they're only dogs, above all don't break off any relationships which might be held against you, they'll need to be able to hold things against you, lead whatever life you please, leave the same tracks as Mr Average, and everyone leaves the same tracks as you will, and your pursuers will go round and round in circles, they'll start admitting the possibility that there is a fake traitor (does more damage than a real one), the idea is that those who are looking for you will conclude that the hunt is costing them more than the game is worth, that's where the Russians showed real genius in running the Cambridge spies, the English only decided very late in the day to smoke out their moles because they'd been finding that trying to identify them was more costly than what the moles were costing them.

'You have only one thing to fear, sometimes you are too brilliant, much better be diffident, gauche, the sort of man who wipes his feet on the doormat when he's leaving your house, brilliant analyses, awkward gestures, you have to give people the feeling that they've got something to teach you, they like teaching people things, you're on a bike with stabilisers on the back wheel, a long avenue of chestnuts, autumn, sun on dead leaves, you're not sure of yourself, a great many people will want to teach you to ride your bike without those stabilisers, just for the pleasure of having shown young people how things are done.

'They will help a young gentleman of France such as yourself, they will back you, push you and watch you speed along the avenue of life, on two wheels, their hearts will swell with pure didactic joy and you too will laugh aloud to show them how so very pleased you are, you know who set up the Tukhachevsky operation?

'No, it wasn't German counter-espionage, not Canaris, I was right in thinking there are gaps in your encyclopaedic knowledge, a tremendous coup, the entire high command of the Red Army and the top echelon of Soviet espionage wiped out from 1937 onwards, in just over a year, no, it wasn't one of Stalin's mad moments nor was it just political, the tyrant who gets rid of senior army officers who might make a bid for power, Stalin of course would have liked to, and certain generals might also have been tempted, but that in itself wouldn't have been enough, it needed a small spark of genius, it was supplied by a piece of shit, which is why it's hardly ever talked about, Heydrich, the Nazis' top knife-man, the spark of genius did not come from a *civilised* German, a *professional* like Canaris or Gehlen, it came from a sadistic piece of shit, and the element of genius here was that it was not direct, the way Marshal Tukhachevsky made contact directly with the Nazi top brass was too obvious.

'Heydrich did much better, he began with a copy of a directive from Hitler ordering the Gestapo to keep tabs on the general staff of the *Reichswehr* because it looked as if German generals were plotting something with Tukhachevsky and his little Moscow comrades, the Hitler directive was quite genuine, Heydrich had asked Hitler to draft it for the good of the cause, and then proceeded to fatten up the file bit by bit, a few forged letters from German generals with signatures copied from cheques, plus various documents signed Tukhachevsky forged by an expert, references to meetings which might have taken place when Tukhachevsky was on missions abroad, banter, bogus banter made to sound bogus, in one of the letters a German general talks of their shared passion for violins.

'Yes, Tukhachevsky was the scion of an aristocratic family, studied music at the conservatoire, and he'd learned to make fiddles under Vitachek, the violins letter made Stalin absolutely furious, it was entirely about violins, reaction on the lines of 'I don't believe it, you couldn't make it up', vital not to pass him anything definite, leave him space to use his imagination, he is very good at imagining is comrade Iosif Vissarionovich, a terrible militaro-fascisto-trotsko-reactionary plot designed to help the Germans, Tukhachevsky is the link between

Bukharin and Trotsky, he has met German generals in London where he also saw the son of Trotsky, Sedov, no, that's not in the file manufactured by Heydrich, it would have been too obvious, Stalin himself said so, and better still Tukhachevsky admitted everything after one brief night in the Lubyanka.

'He even admitted the link with the chiefs of the NKVD, what was the link? A woman! A German Mata Hari, a rival of Fraülein Doktor, a certain Josephine Guenzi, Stalin himself told the story, she enlisted these men "on the basis of a certain part of her feminine person", a genuine piece of contemporary linguistic usage, and Stalin added something else in a very odd speech given before the military council of the Commissariat for Defence, June 1937.

'He added, "she is beautiful, she responds to propositions from men and then she destroys them", sounds like something out of the Old Testament, one day it will all come out, Josephine Guenzi doesn't like soldiers, she doesn't like Stalin, she doesn't like Hitler, she doesn't like men, she commutes between Moscow and Berlin, among Tukhachevsky's papers they found an X-ray picture, an obscene image, profile of a woman's face embracing a male member, no one knows what Josephine Guenzi is thinking, all you see is the outline of a female skull, and the man's penis, a *vanitas* in the form of an X-ray, normally the penis does not show up, no bone, so some medical students' prank, a montage, but the fake X-ray became one of the incriminating pieces of evidence, calling it into question would have been to call all the charges into question, and besides the erection was intended to make it absolutely obvious, things happened very quickly, no one dared say it was a physical impossibility, maybe Tukhachevsky kept the photo to have a laugh with his friends.

'Or else it was one of Yezhov's agents who put it among the general's papers, the cops descended on Tukhachevsky, you're for the drop soldier-boy, it seems they brought the Guenzi woman to see him, pleasing face, very sweet, like an Astrakhan doe, talk, we feel so very very sorry for you, the heart of a man is a box of secrets, we have all night to unlock that box, Guenzi was seen again at the time of the Ribbentrop-Molotov pact, such an innocent face, she disappeared somewhere into this immense world of ours, she knew a great many things, she knew how to hide the fact that she knew them, she was in love with everyone and everything, two or three of my colleagues ran into her before the war, she laughed like a child, all she thought of was loving and living, she must have watched Tukhachevsky die, you cannot share the death of another person, to relax she read romantic novelettes of an evening, the kind where the heroine gets into a hot bath to await the coming of her lover.

'The whole business is hard to swallow, on the one hand a plot at the very top, and on the other a plot that doesn't work and is uncovered before it's got going properly, the explanation given by Stalin – and you don't label yourself "a leading light of science" for nothing – was that the plot at the top could not have any roots at the bottom because "the USSR whose agriculture is now prospering is experiencing tremendous success on all fronts", the whole of the Soviet general staff decimated.

'No, decimated means that one in ten is eliminated, whereas then it was hardly one in ten who survived, and they weren't just any old victims, but technicians, modernisers, experts with advanced knowledge of field warfare, armoured vehicles and rockets, people from research institutes, and specialists from Germany working with the NKVD, they all disappeared in 1937, it took just one night for Tukhachevsky to confess, and it had all begun with a fake plot dreamed up by Heydrich in which Stalin developed an absolutely unshakeable belief on account of the violins, because appearances belong to those who look at them, that's what held the English back later, when they were told that parts of their espionage and counter-espionage services were in the pay of Moscow, they thought they were being set up for a Tukhachevsky-style hoax.'

Chapter 8

1965

The Locomotive and the Kangaroo

In which it is noticeable to what extent the Riff war is an obsession for Max Goffard.

In which Lilstein tells you the story of Selifane the coachman and asks you to continue thinking your own thoughts.

In which we are introduced to cyanide and soft-centred chocolates.

In which Lilstein attempts to translate for you what he understands by the word Menschheit.

In which the conversation between Max Goffard and his author takes a disagreeable turn.

In which de Vèze decides to play footsie under the table with the woman opposite him at the dinner table.

Singapore, July 1965

Novels are not serious; what is serious is mythomania.
André Malraux, *The Human Condition*

On the veranda the woman in the yellow dress has finished reciting, no one feels like talking, swallows swoop, sickles, down to grass-level, they shriek, wheel back up into the sky, waiters whisk away the empty plates, bring leg of mutton, flageolet beans, Beaujolais, the Consul indicates that the pink diplomat will taste the wine, he's our expert gourmet, he's very much in demand in the diplomatic colony, he even advises the Russians, it's his area of excellence, along with opera, old recordings.

The pink diplomat tastes the wine, reports to the Consul that his Beaujolais is excellent, he does not believe a word he says, a tightwad's god-awful rotgut, just what's needed to go with your leg of mutton, you pretentious careerist, these young Chinese waiters are rather alarming, any minute now one of them is going to drop food all over me, Xavier would blow his top, that said they seem nimble enough, how old do you suppose they are? Never seen them before, are they Consulate staff? Or were they brought in? Whom can I ask? That young woman is good value, just talks but she's upstaging old Goffard and the hero of Bir Hakeim, and given half a chance Malraux would make a play for her, look at the expression on the face of the hero of Bir Hakeim.

Before the War, de Vèze wouldn't have cared at all for her way of reciting, too neutral, anyway the death of Kyo isn't a number for women, but her voice is good, simple, she pronounces the syllables

359

clearly, she looks quite attractive when she recites, no histrionics, she just speaks it, very simply, lips neither too big nor too small, everyone's looking at her, even Malraux, she's no flirt, but does she know what comes next? Goffard could continue where she leaves off, I've had enough, why didn't they all shut up? The moment was mine, to think I came all the way from Rangoon for this!

Malraux looks at the young woman, his look is an encouragement, elbows on the table, his hands clasped on a level with his nose, just the eyes can be seen, the puckering of the crow's feet, silver cuff-links. The young woman resumes, voice very steady, 'how, with the glance of death upon him, was it possible not to hear the murmur of human sacrifice...' her husband looks surprised that she should know this by heart, '... which cried out to him that the virile heart of men ...' the hero of Bir Hakeim is just like the rest of them, he will like my voice, but it's too late, '... is a resting place for the dead as worthy as the mind of man ...' that beauty spot on her breast looks like a chocolate chip, this time the young woman falls silent, a chocolate chip on lightly baked, warm brioche.

The resting place for the dead 'as worthy as the mind of man', it sounds like a response to the Minister, says Morel, happy to have found this question to ask when his wife stopped talking, he is cross with himself for not knowing the work of Malraux as well as the rest of the company, but basically he doesn't think much of *The Human Condition*, he's a historian, he never got beyond what one of his teachers said of it, 'Chinese news items stewed in adjectives', exactly the kind of history that Morel loathes, fiction culled from newspapers, the instant seductive come-on, just like the Ambassador sitting opposite his wife, it's as plain as a pikestaff that he wants to lose no time in seducing her with that big mouth of his.

'That's right,' says Malraux, 'it was a response to Benda, he'd accused intellectuals of betraying the mind by opposing fascism, he was wrong, but anyway that passage is very oral, I wanted a voice to be heard, to release the novel from the silence of the page, I turned the thing almost into a canticle.'

Max:

'Good God! A song of praise, death of the knight, end of the hero, but in the novel I offered another canticle, struck a discordant note, the note that banjaxes emotion, canticles are complicated chaps, especially when they come with discordant notes!'

'What other canticle?' Morel asks Max.

'The *Pieds-Nickelés*-type canticle, the one he makes me tell before the death of Kyo,' says Max, 'when I manage to get on the boat leaving Shanghai, absolutely, while the others are imitating roast meat in the boilers of railway engines, I shake the dust of Shanghai from my feet with a dexterity worthy of the Pieds Nickelés, you must watch out for those Pieds Nickelés, the Master stuck a patch over my eye, said it was like Filochard's in the *Pieds Nickelés*, true, but not very nice, whereas I was hoping to be promoted to at least a Lear-type fool or maybe Scapin, a real out-and-out knave, but the Master has always been able to wind me round his little finger, he put one over on me first time we met in Indochina more than forty years ago, I helped to get him out of jail, and then he used my articles about Shanghai for his novel, and so that no one would notice he put me in it, he made me older, turned me into a dealer in antiquities and saddled me with the name Clappique, I had to kick up a stink to make him cut a scene he'd put me in, can you imagine it, a hotel, I'm in the dark, with a large naked woman, surrounded by men breathing heavily, a voyeurs' orgy.

'I act canny, he makes me run away, down corridors I go, trousers flapping, I would have none of it, I'm not sure if the incident of the voyeurs was something that happened to him, in the end he cut it, and the attack on the police station in the novel, a bravura passage, a triumph, it was actually I who first reported it in *Le Soir*, I was there with a colleague, Andrée Viollis, and Albert Londres, which, Monsieur Poirgade, explains my "Good God!" even though it pains you, I'll say it whenever I want, and especially when I feel low because my author made me a Pied Nickelé, not a fool like Lear's, not even permitted to read the future though I was born to be a prophet, oh I know, nowadays

I'd be allowed to say whatever I like, but there's nothing left to say.'

Suddenly Max has the feeling that no one round the table is listening to him, or that they are pretending to listen because no one wants to be rude and interrupt, they're just waiting for him to stop, he could say absolutely anything, don't tell the story of the canticle, he could be somewhere else, leave Singapore, don't go to Vietnam, still saying the same thing, I'll end up begging in the street, I should have been a beggar from the start, Max-the-beggar, beggar and madman, later the Japanese sacked Shanghai, rats in gutters don't distinguish between a baby and a dog, the baby doesn't move as much, the magnificent Samurai have stopped laughing, and these people sitting here smiling around the table while the moon comes up over the garden all take me for a beggar, the kids with their rain maidens, no more kids, all they'd found were Riffian dolls on dung-heaps, the little piles of pebbles, the rain maidens, the Riff and its tales of jackals, the songs sung by the harvesters in the fields, songs that promised 'for you I will screen the grain, I will riddle the grain, I will fetch wood, I will paint your cheeks, fold me in your arms, give me drink that the wicked may gnash their teeth', report submitted by Armengaud, chief of French airborne forces in Morocco, I have the honour to respectfully draw to your attention the results obtained by the systematic, intensive bombing of the souks, over a period of a few days five bombing raids left a minimum of five hundred victims, I have given instructions for the tallies to give only the number of victims, without specifying age or sex, the impression produced has been very great.

Terror reigns among the natives who actually have a tendency to exaggerate their losses, on 15 September 1925, several squadrons, one hundred and sixty-nine single-engine planes in the skies over the small settlement of Beni Zeroual, the heavy bombers, the Breguets and Farman *Goliath*s, have been reserved for Chefchaouen, an undefended town, they carry as markings the Shereef's star with a hand of *fatma* at its centre, the planes of the 1st Squadron had a swastika instead of the hand of *fatma,* the state to which the town was reduced by the bombing even impressed the Spaniards.

Bombing in waves over the town, it lasts three days, no fire returned, the warriors are about a hundred kilometres away, strafing of anything that moves in the streets, by lighter aircraft, on the left at the entrance to the town half a dead bull in the middle of the road, the gunners also used donkeys as targets to see them jerk their heads back like mad things when they were hit.

Fierce conflagrations, one woman finds herself with a breast full in the face, half a child between her feet, birds from hell, children and women throw stones at the Breguets, three days of bombing, the real number of civilian casualties at Chefchaouen is difficult to assess because the French pilots are reluctant to give exact estimates of the losses inflicted, Max and the agent for Native Affairs traversing what was once a small village, ochre dust, leaden sky, very grey, the greyness is everywhere.

Max saying you were telling me the other day about an enemy with two faces, one fierce one noble, very well, but how many faces do we have? Max putting the question a different way, your paladin upright in the stirrups, blue kepi, red cloak, how does he manage to defend widows and orphans if the widow and the orphan also start to disappear? When I say disappear it's because I don't want to talk about guts, stuffing your guts back inside you with your hands, smashed abdomens, skulls with strange stuff oozing out from inside, mouths gasping for air, air that doesn't come.

A loud Bang! and a man is no more than the sum of his nerves, flayed raw, especially when his skin has disappeared, let's be euphemistic and say disappeared, even if you still have in your nose a stench which only very slowly disappears from your surroundings, I experienced it at Douaumont, when you realise that an eye is only one organ among many, and the blast from a bomb can eviscerate a body in just one second, we used to say it was all about defending women and children back home, but here the only thing left untouched by some miracle is a dungheap, with one of those doll things sticking out of the top, among the smells of dung, dust, rotting flesh, cordite, it's all that's left, a doll and the smells that hang on the air which grows hotter, more oppressive, not a breath of air, smells layered in the air.

Dung and carrion give up the last of their moisture under the ochre sun, the people have been buried, there are now only parts of walls and the decomposing bodies of animals to testify to what has happened, in your statistics you count people on one side, livestock on the other, there must be some connection, a correlation, so many human corpses equals so many animal carcasses, I say this because by counting all the rotting carcasses here, and there really are a great many, it should be possible to infer a figure for people, just by counting the carcasses, the stench layered in the grey air, moisture which shivers in the heat, the stench shimmers suspended in the oppressive air, how does the paladin manage when there is no rain maiden to defend? Ask Pétain, Max, but pack your bags first, don't forget, we're here to put an end to the violence.

The agent told him about the four years he spent teaching in a boys' school, in the Middle Atlas, you know it can get pretty nippy up there between November and March, but each boy brought his own wood to burn, you should have seen how fast they learn French, and the black-winged storks on the roofs of the first purpose-built schools, you made the most of the opportunity to give them nature lessons, the preparations for their long journey, what do storks do in May? A boy puts up his hand, he has it off, sir, Max saying the natives have killed eight Frenchmen in Casablanca, we bombed the whole of the native quarter, we occupied Casablanca, they killed Doctor Mauchamp in Marrakech and we occupied Oujda, it's practically eight hundred kilometres from Oujda to Marrakech, but Oujda is a very attractive town, so we land there, they always manage to kill one of ours, result: planes, cannon, reprisals, occupation, the whole country, to civilise it of course, and teach it about storks and the present indicative.

In the Riff, the agent for Native Affairs had held his own against Max for as long as there was light to see by, but after dark around the fire he said I don't like all this, I'm in favour of a fruitful war, inevitable but fruitful, History advances because of the bad things History does, but I don't like it, and it's worse in the Spanish zone, I put Pétain in touch with Franco a couple of months back, it was unspeakable.

Max changes tone, turns to the wife of the Consul, just because the Master here turned me into a Pied Nickelé doesn't mean I shouldn't express the gratitude felt by my stomach:

'Madame, this lamb is remarkable.'

The pink diplomat has his nose in his wineglass. The mutton is hard and very rare, very rare and hard at the same time, how do they do it, yon bogus Clappique obviously knows, 'remarkable', the old hypocrite, an oikish compliment for uncooked sheepmeat that still reeks of farmyard, and Xavier has asked for more! He likes that sort of thing, all those uncivilised smells, should have seen him just now in the garden, standing in front of the mangrove, absolutely loves it, as soon as there are larvae, blobs that look like snot, embryonic life without arms or legs or eyes, jellyfish membrane, mudflat smells that catch you in the throat, all gurgles and effervescence, like the earth sucking itself off, all those bubbles and craters and spurting green sap, he'd like to splash about in it, and he claims he likes opera better than I do, that he'd comb Europe to get his hands on some recording by Tadeo, what he really likes is when things squirm, anything you get in places where things squirm.

Monsieur Xavier Poirgade likes crabs, he's come up with a crab to look out for, a horrible creature, first time he told me the name I laughed out loud, one claw is huge, the other one's normal, but the large one is as big as its whole body, they're called fiddler crabs, it starts at puberty, Xavier can spend hours watching out for one of these crabs, he's eating too fast, he'll spend all night complaining, and this red wine, a Beaujolais which has not travelled well, fit only for a spinster, doesn't even deserve to be pissed away, they're all eating without paying any attention to what's on their plates or in their glass, manners like savages.

*

'Yes, young gentleman of France,' Lilstein says to you yet again in the Waldhaus, 'in those days I really believed in the Tukhachevsky conspiracy, in '37 I was part of what was left of the secret Party apparatus in Berlin, Hitler was everywhere, and our first concern was to hunt down the Trotsko-Bukharinians, I do what everyone else is doing, I give names, I use Tukhachevsky to oil the wheels, a Bonapartist plot, they swallow it without any trouble, I am young, I am implacable, to say the least.

'But very quickly I get the feeling that I myself am starting to slip, the fashion then was for meetings around a table where every member had to denounce his neighbour, it was risky attending meetings like that and the point was for each of us to take pot-shots at everybody else, like they did in Moscow, I didn't care for that little game, it was crazy, you could come a cropper because you were right-wing, and if you steered clear of the right you got the chop for your left-wing tendencies, you kept a constant eye out for anyone with that bloodthirsty look about them and anybody who seemed in his right mind was your best friend, I once tried to get out of a fix by telling a story.

'Found it in Gogol, it's about the servant Pelagia who takes it into her head to show Tchichikov's coachman the way, now because she can't tell her right hand from her left she gets all mixed up, and Selifane the coachman bawls her out and yells "be off, you and your dirty feet, you can't tell the difference between right and left", we're all like Pelagia, right? Oh it was a stupid thing to do, and I knew I'd have to pay for it at the next meeting, one of us had already remarked that the things I said were amazingly irresponsible, I was about to have my very own plot, I'd last six months, if that is in the meantime the Gestapo didn't start poking its nose in.

'Three months after my little performance at the meeting, Stalin gives his speech on the draft constitution of the USSR, German translation, circulated clandestinely, and at the next meeting all the comrades gave me very strange looks, my story, the one about Selifane the coachman and Pelagia of the dirty feet had also been told by Stalin in his speech, I'd anticipated him by several months, I became an untouchable, a pure coincidence, we lived at a time when Gogol was probably the most topical read there was, but with Stalin there was no such thing as coincidence, I had also learned by heart numerous Lenin quotes, I managed to slip one in about the flexibility which all organisations must have, the atmosphere around me relaxed, a short while later a rumour went round to the effect that I was about to be summoned to Moscow, it was lucky for me the Nazis picked me up before I left, though maybe in Moscow they wouldn't have really had it in for me either, I've walked in a lot of rain without getting wet.

'The moral of the story is, in a nutshell: if you want to travel fast read Gogol, expect the unexpected, apply no rule too strictly, let the keepers of the laws have the pleasure of reminding you of them, always pay crude compliments to the lady of the house, use your knife to cut lettuce, even if you know the old story about oxidation by heart, it will let the people you have to deal with occupy the high ground, they love that, they'll want to teach you what they know, but you too will know interesting things, almost ten years ago you were one of the first to know that the alleged report attributed to comrade Khrushchev was genuine, soon the Americans will invade Vietnam, I will tip you many, many winks.

'To start with, the figures for their real losses, undoctored, you'll see, or rather it's your friend the Minister who'll see, so funny the expression on the face of an American Secretary of State when you toss the real figures at him, maybe he doesn't have them, perhaps he needs people like you to get the figures which his boss has given orders to be withheld from him, but you'll have them, it will be assumed that you've estimated them, I'll tell you how, a great commentator on international affairs, they need only give you your head, you will become an acute political analyst, your friend the Minister is already extremely taken with you.

'I want you to have the freedom to think,' Lilstein had told you, 'I want you to bring me contradiction, the freedom of a man who thinks differently, you'll be free, and you will convince, your friend the Minister will shine in Cabinet meetings in front of de Gaulle, and you will help me to be convincing in my meetings, I'm also on the side of the hawks, but I'm not shrill, I'm no warmonger, and the information I give is the kind that makes a majority of the Central Committee think that the enemy isn't as strong as all that, so that we don't need to tighten the screws too much.

*

'You still haven't told us what a *Pied-Nickelés*-type canticle is, Monsieur Goffard,' the young woman said.

'The discordant canticle,' replies Max, 'it occurs just before the death of Kyo, "he would have fought", but I don't fight, to get out of Shanghai I sling a matelot's broom over my shoulder, I stow away on board a fine ship, O memory! and my favourite author makes me tell a canticle story to a passenger who happens to be lurking nearby, it's set in South America, about how the bishop's flock learns a canticle of praise in readiness for his visit, six months of rehearsals in the open air, and the great day arrives, my flock line up in front of the mission, under the lofty trees, it's just like here, only less planned, not an English garden-style jungle planted with lots of different species, "one, two three" says the missionary who is leading the choir, and the flock are so tense, so nervous that no sound issues from their mouths, not a peep, but notwithstanding the hymn of praise still soars miraculously, old man, a miracle!'

And Malraux, imitating the voice of Clappique, something between Mr Punch and Scapin:

'A miracle!'

Malraux with a Clappique-like gesture, hands extended to the young woman, palms out, fingers spread very wide:

'A miracle!'

It suddenly dawns on de Vèze that Max's outrageous behaviour is a caricature of Malraux's, it always was, so much so that Clappique plays Malraux and Malraux plays a caricature of himself, as if he were a clown in a hilarious film where the images are even jerkier than the clown's gags, Malraux roars with laughter:

'A miracle! and all because over those six months the parrots in the trees had plenty of time to learn the words!'

'You're spoiling it for him,' the young woman said with a nod in de Vèze's direction.

She thinks him rather handsome, he was a hero once, he is very careful about what he eats, says no to bread though he helps himself to more mayonnaise, but eventually stretches out one hand for a crust, without looking at his hand, he's probably a bit fat in the wrong places and doesn't like being looked at when he's undressing; he'd be a good man to have in a tight corner, what would he do in the grass, in the clearing, when the gamekeeper turns up and tells us to hop it? And me, lying face down on a towel and I can't get up because I've taken my bra off to sunbathe, and the gamekeeper refuses to go away until we're both on our feet, this happens on the banks of the Rhine, it's warm and humid, the sap drips from the leaves.

De Vèze's mind is elsewhere, he watches the young woman, thinks about the way she recites, steady voice, precise, as the dusk settles, when the colours fade from things, removes their mask. He turns to Malraux:

'I really liked the death of Kyo, but now the canticle turns out to be a psittacism.'

'If you want drama, you still have the gift of the cyanide and the death of Katow,' the young woman said to de Vèze.

De Vèze does not answer, the young woman's backside, he is sorry now that he hadn't tried to get a good look at it before sitting down to dinner, he'd seen her legs, and all this time he's forgotten all about her backside, you're getting old, not legs from some hard-boiled crime novel, but neatly turned ankles, instep strongly arched, black shoes, heel just the right height, all that is now under the table, legs not too long but not coarse, given a little tenderness you could live with those legs. Immediately de Vèze regrets the turn of phrase, it undermines the kind of feelings he would like to have for her, rediscover the urge he'd had to kiss her breasts, your sex-drive does rather come and go, a woman had told him not so long ago, buttocks, they'd ideally be firm but yielding, he is surprised to hear himself say winsome.

Max, raising his voice:

'Cyanide, cyanide, there's more to life than cyanide!'

'But it's the high point of the whole novel,' says the grey diplomat, 'Katow who decides not to take his cyanide and offers it to two young men, both condemned to death, who are afraid of being fed to the boiler.'

The grey diplomat shuts up, swallows a mouthful of camembert, he is very fond of this scene where the young man who has been sentenced to death shakes Katow's hand, young men, well-built, disoriented, take your hand in theirs, and at last a spark of humanity passes between men, it's something very different from male squalidness, packs of males, and worst of all, those middle-class kids aping working-class violence, by the sea, when they'd hauled him out of the water, at Nice, after they'd pulled his swimming-trunks off, 'let the air get to it', with girls watching, one half of the boys chanted: 'Xav-i-er, new-boy, poof!' while the other half mimicked a choir of virgins, 'he don't use it, he can't use it!', they'd tied a little ribbon round it, and instead of handing out punishments the grown-ups in charge just laughed, and during his national service it was even worse, initiation rites, the only thing those swine deserved was a good thrashing, the grey diplomat adds:

'That handshake is very fine.'

Ah! He's waking up! de Vèze doesn't like friend Poirgade, charcoal grey, uses big words, podgy, weasel-faced, moustache and small beard fringing his mouth, like a monkey's arse, inquisitive, a pillow-biter, expert in strategy or not, well-connected or not, he can't stand him, a straight look to make sure he's got the message. Why does the Consul fuss over him so much?

'A compelling display of charity,' says the pink diplomat.

Well, you obviously find it more exciting than swishing your houseboys with a cane, thinks de Vèze, who can't remember the name of the hep cat in the pink shirt.

'Men, their death throes, charity which is all transcending, it's magnificent, pure Pascal,' says the grey diplomat holding de Vèze's gaze.

'It's exactly what they tell Boy Scouts round camp fires or in tents,' replies Max with his eyes fixed on the grey diplomat, 'away with you, death throes and charity my foot!'

Silence around the table, Max makes no effort to break it, gobbets of lung tissue, they have another game, Monsieur Goffard, with white beans and black beans, the agent for Native Affairs had said, it's played in the souk, while the women and the old men are selling or bartering, the kids play with beans or small stones, I'll explain later, but now we have to go, I don't like being here, I don't like it, it's orders, it's HQ that decides, they say the bombing is strategic, the Spaniards do a lot worse, they look at photos of dead or wounded comrades, then they get in their planes and give it all they've got, they forget everything, Pétain and Franco say it's strategic.

Max turns to Malraux:

'What we got up to was a lot more fun than the stories they tell the Cubs!'

Dessert has been served, a rather mushy *tarte tatin*, pastry rather rubbery, but with a good Sauternes, the pink diplomat likes Sauternes, it's the first decent wine of the evening, the Beaujolais was foul, when we get home, I'll have to tell Xavier he must do something about his habit of pulling on the lapels of his jacket, one hand on each side, to straighten his clothes, I can't bear it, he never stops, if he believes he's going to advance in his career behaving like that he's got another think coming! He's been getting more and more fidgety since the beginning of the year, and what's all this about cutting his lettuce with his knife? I don't really need to point it out to him, anyway there were at least four of them doing the same thing this evening, and actually I joined in so I wouldn't be out of step with the others.

'For Monsieur Clappique,' says the grey diplomat turning to Malraux, '*The Human Condition* is "entertaining", but that's only the opinion of a minor character.'

Malraux lets it go and turns to the young woman:

'There's another gift apart from the cyanide.'

He has his elbows on the table, his hands are crossed under his chin, his face forward, he is looking upwards and the whites of his eyes are visible below the pupils, his voice is sober but there is something about the pupils that seems to suggest that he is amused.

'I can't remember any other gift,' says the grey diplomat.

De Vèze can't either, although he thought he knew the novel by heart, he has forgotten, just as he has forgotten everything else he spent all those nights reading, glass of whisky at his elbow, during the war, after the war, read too quickly, reread skipping whole pages, all of Faulkner, all Dostoyevsky, Gogol, Flaubert, all Malraux, thirsting, like Malraux, as thirsty as the man whose education was cut short, could recite whole pages from memory, he can still remember odd sentences, read *The Human Condition* ten times, and he didn't remember the parrots or the offer of the cyanide, it's all he knows and he can't think of what Malraux calls 'the other gift'.

'The caramels! It's the gift of caramels!' cries Max. 'You don't read attentively, shush! no interruptions, you never see anything! On your toes! Caramels cremes, three pages after the cyanide in the novel, when he's about to write time regained, when Malraux himself behaves like Clappique, minor character my foot, an author who does that every three pages, children, no one gets it; right, dotty every five pages, it's the caramels, when the Finance Minister hands round little caramels in his office in Paris to Ferral and the bankers, chewy, stick to the teeth, it punctures the poignancy of the moment, all the selfless acts, the other twerp who offers his cyanide to the two youngsters to save them from being tossed into the boiler, a compelling moment of charity, well he's not the only one who puts something in the collection box, the twit, the caramels, history, recto, verso, 'The Great Adventure is buggered!' the revolution has gone down like a lead balloon, so it's cyanide and caramels all round!'

'That's a journalist's phrase,' Morel interjects.

'Get away with you,' says Max, coming back at him, 'a historian is only a journalist who looks back.'

Pow! take that! thinks de Vèze, as half-dreaming he sees Malraux's novel filling up with unexpected beings, a dream or something seen in a drunk's spinning head, an old man with a head like a cat who says I sell women, a Russian with a face like Croquignol leaning on a nickel-plated bar-rail, the corpse of a strangled man dancing the dance of the veils, a lunatic beaten to death, fat girls with huge breasts huddled on top of one another, and Clappique suddenly emerging from the heap as if out of some Pandora's box, skeletons in a trance, Hercules dressed as a woman, camera-eating rabbits, ah, if only alcohol didn't make you feel ill, trains full of whores sent hurtling towards Communist Party headquarters by connoisseurs of the human soul, a monster part-bear, part-man and part-spider coming towards you, a young woman standing at a top-floor balcony watching the sunset, de Vèze kneeling behind her, he removes her knickers, and in the street a coachman weeps for his horses surrounded by human victims and repeats over and over, all this for nothing, for nothing, the young woman says kiss me.

'I like these young people,' says Max, 'so modest, and they recite your work to you, they surely have great futures! Not like me, and that matelot's broom you hung over my shoulder, I can't forgive you that, you treat me as if I'm just some joker, you never believed I had a serious side, cyanide and caramels, recto and verso.'

Malraux doesn't react to this, smoothes the tablecloth by his plate, the Consul doesn't know what to say, he thinks Goffard is getting more and more out of hand, no one should speak like that to the Minister, he shouldn't even witness such scenes, mustn't say anything,

behave like it never happened or else intervene to stop it, but if that
fails you turn into the man who drew attention to something that
should never have happened in the first place.

Max has stopped talking, his head is spinning, he feels free but not
well, I burn, you eat, and then it is all repeated, everything smokes
and everything is repeated, everything smokes, the people throw
themselves on the ground, the red earth of the Riff, mouth full of a
metallic taste, something was falling, it was like sulphur, people were
going blind, their skin was turning black and peeling off, the
livestock swelled up and died, plants shrivelled within hours, the
people left with their animals and headed for the caves, you couldn't
drink from the streams any more, lungs flooding with white froth
which asphyxiates the victims who linger for two days, it's exactly like
drowning, at first you feel nothing, then it starts with sand under
your eyelids, Churchill saying 'we were the bees of hell', diphosgene,
chloropicrin and tabun, Berenguer, Spanish High Commissioner at
Tetuán, August 1922: 'I have always been opposed to the use of
combat gases against native populations, but after what they did to us
at Annual I shall use them with great pleasure,' and Alphonse XIII in
1925 to the French military attaché in Madrid: 'We must set aside
otiose humanitarian considerations, the urgent task is to exterminate
the Beni Ourriaguel, even Churchill did not rule out using gas on
villages in Iraq in 1919', if chemical gases are used before the great heat
of the day, they are very effective, directive of the Spanish military
command: 'I remind you once again that the regulation period before
entering zones on which special bombs have been dropped must be
strictly observed; in a regrettable incident yesterday, sixty of our own
troops were among the victims', and the whistle of the train in
Shanghai goes toot-toot every time a prisoner is fed into the boiler.

Around the table, no one says anything. So Max:
    'Shush! not a word!' Max resumes, '*The Human Condition* is the
locomotive and the parrot!'
    'Rather,' says the young woman, looking at de Vèze, 'it's the

locomotive and the kangaroo.'

Silence all round, she blushes, small red patches reaching down as far as her throat, Max has stopped moving, suddenly he seems smaller, but with him on the contrary the blood has drained from his cheeks.

'You're having us on,' he says.

'As you see, he doesn't know everything,' remarks Malraux.

Morel looks at his wife as if he had never seen her before.

'What kangaroo?' asks de Vèze.

And Max, his gaze faltering:

'Where's the kangaroo? you're taking the piss, darling, where do you get a kangaroo?'

Malraux, smile like a cat's:

'At the exact point where the ladies suddenly start paying close attention, tell them, Madame, while I enjoy both the pleasure of having truly serious women readers and that of tasting a truly excellent Sauternes, my compliments, Consul.'

De Vèze raises his glass until it is level with his eyes and tilts it forward.

'Now remind me, what's the word for wine when it slides slowly down the inside of the glass, legs or tears?'

My wife just has to look at him, thinks Morel, and he starts talking like some simpering oaf, and he's supposed to be a French ambassador!

'People say both,' said Max, 'legs and tears, you need both words, to keep everybody happy, the formula for success, make Wendy feel weepy and Andy feel randy, as an old boss of mine used to say before the war.'

'Joker or not,' says Malraux, 'I never made you say anything uncouth.'

'Monsieur Goffard, just let Madame tell us about the kangaroo,' said the pink diplomat.

*

'Is it more serious than I thought?' Lilstein asks you. 'Is it more than just doubts you're having? You want to stop? It's entirely up to you, I've always told you that you were perfectly free, let me set your mind at rest: your withdrawal, you will note that I do not talk of defection or betrayal, your withdrawal would not make life difficult for me at all. I could replace you in Paris immediately. You can withdraw, and if some day you ever wish to renew contact, if you need information, I shall always be there.

'How would I replace you? Perhaps I already have, maybe you have had a double from the beginning, not a double exactly, an understudy, someone who works with me in the same way, not with your friend the Minister but with somebody else who is also destined for high office, a man, a woman I'm having meetings with elsewhere, by the seaside, for a change, you have fears, doubts, you want to stop because you have still not got the point, you still think that I'm asking you to spy on a decision-making centre, you have no ambition, stand back, look at the wider picture: we are the centre where the decisions are made.

'The two of us, nobody else, when we're together and decide to do something nothing can stand in our way, and nobody can identify us, no gizmos to connect us, no phone, no radio, no codes, no cover, no letter-box, sleeping or otherwise, no go-betweens, no invisible ink, no cryptic grids, no microdots, no underhand stuff, if I ever stop coming here without letting you know beforehand, drop everything, at once, it will almost certainly mean that the ideas we support are going through a tough time, and me with them, never leave anything lying around that could look like evidence, everything in your head, traces yes, that's unavoidable, but never leave evidence, they have an obsession with evidence, and never admit anything, if I disappear don't try to find someone else to work with, "no longer mourn for me", no regular habits, no gizmos, you buy old recordings and sell them, from time to time you place an advertisement in the *Figaro*, and mind, you must buy and sell for real, five or six times a year, it's not a lot.

'All I need is the classified ad, three days before the meeting, you speak English, German and Spanish, you travel a lot, you'll have plenty of reasons, you like opera, it's expensive, isn't it? Opera is excellent, given the price of decent seats you can improve your general culture at the same time as cultivating your hatred of the rich, get yourself known as the sort of man who will go a thousand kilometres to hear a singer or a violinist, a few trips each year, West Germany, Austria, and you often go via Switzerland, in Zurich there are some famous record dealers, excellent second-hand bookshops, and a direct train for Waltenberg, if you decide you don't like all that travelling any more remember you can stop whenever you like, you have an understudy, though maybe you are his understudy, suspicion falls on you, among others, nothing can ever be proved against you, which allows me to shelter your understudy who is more vulnerable behind your more high-profile self, I'm only joking.'

*

'The kangaroo is sitting on Valérie Serge's bed in Shanghai's biggest hotel,' says the young woman.

'Madame Serge,' says Max, 'good name for a high-class couturière, most ingenious.'

'Baron,' says Malraux, 'let her speak.'

'This happens at the point,' the young woman resumes, 'where Ferral arranges for Valérie's room to be filled with uncaged birds, to pay her back for the business with the rabbit, on the bed a pair of soft pyjamas, all that's left of the woman he loved, red and gold silk, he picks them up, brushes them lightly against his cheek and starts to daydream.'

'About kangaroos,' says the pink diplomat who, as he looks towards the grey diplomat, turns a deeper shade of pink.

'No,' replies the young woman, 'about violence, as men do who like imagining what women secretly want to have done to them, anyway, he daydreams, while on the bed where they'd made love is a handsome, real, live kangaroo, a kangaroo with eyes like a terrified doe.'

'Shush! don't say a word!' cries Max, 'a hairy little kangaroo, superbly constructed, my dear fellow, that's exactly what your novel is, it's the locomotive and the kangaroo, a kangaroo with a moustache!'

'But no one,' the young woman says, 'apart that is from a few female readers who do not like empty beds, ever notices the kangaroo in the book, but it's there.'

'Maybe that's why it has fewer readers today,' Malraux observes, 'and why journalists find me lacking in humour, don't deny it, de Vèze.'

'Ah,' says Max, 'it's the absence of humour that explains why we have such large print-runs, revolutionary readers, moralists, the Classiques Larousse, right, left, Trotsky, Maurras's faithful, but those people don't need kangaroos, the rest of us do, I mean the fiction-reading public, in the end it all comes out, shush! don't interrupt! that's enough about kangaroos, today, Master, you're on your way to the land of the talapoins, and you're not taking me!'

'Who are these talapoins?' asks the grey diplomat.

'Asian monks,' answers Morel.

'Who are Voltaireans,' says Max.

'There's a word I'd forgotten,' says Malraux.

And Max:

'It was me who taught you it, you want to forget because a week from now you're scheduled to have a meeting with the great Mao, in the land of the talapoins, serious stuff in the offing, serious stuff is so depressing, I told you that Chiang Kai-Shek was going to dress the Chinese up in talapoin habits, but that was in '27, missed the boat, it was Mao twenty years later who dressed them like that, blue talapoins, I was twenty years ahead of my time, that's the joke, a machine for defragmenting time, just let it run, everything eventually turns into farce without any help from anybody.'

*

'I never asked you for any sort of bureaucratic involvement,' Lilstein tells you, 'you can put an end to it whenever you wish, it's a man-to-man relationship, *Menschheit*, young gentleman of France, do you know what my department is called? it's the *Aufklärung*, where you come from they say *Lumières,* enlightenment, what is my role in the *Aufklärung?* I never told you? I never hide anything from you, I have no official role in the set-up, don't really have an office, but all the big files pass through my hands, I answer only to the Minister who knows that I don't really answer to him at all but to a direct line, further to the East. Officially, my area of responsibility is international trade, I work hard at it, especially with our cousins in Bonn, they rather like me, I hint that I do more than just trade, that I am a man of shadows, that I have power, they think I'm either a boaster or a stirrer.

'Ever read the letter Kant wrote on the Englightenment? Wonderful stuff! "Dare to think!" You and I are Enlightenment Men, you too have an ideal, like all these people who are monkeys dangling on the stick of their particular ideal, but you are no monkey, you are an actor, you ask me how I'd translate *Menschheit?* As something between humanity and virility, not to worry, the sort of virility that has nothing to do with fascism.

'Though actually not virility, that's a bit strong, it's rather the simple fact of being a man, you could just say "humanity" but with an element of "integrity", think I'm exaggerating? There's also a notion of "fellowship" to it or again . . . not easy . . . it's daring to stand up and be counted as a man, to take that risk, it's somewhere between human and hero, between artifice and being true to your word . . . but not a halfway house, it's rather a third shore, everything we do is third shore.

'Was I in love with the woman who made me dance the waltz and the tango thirty years ago? For a Frenchman you ask very direct questions, I do hope that when you ask your friend the Minister questions you aren't so sharp with him, there was a swimming pool in the hotel even in those days, small blue tiles, burnished copper handrails, round windows, she was at full stretch in the water, on her back, moving over the surface, chin tucked in, head very mobile, finely arched neck, she was swimming lengths, leaving swirls of foam where she beat her feet, arm movements very expansive, not at all fast, it was a very new stroke at the time, I stayed out of the water, I didn't want to swim with her, all I've ever been able to manage was a sort of doggy paddle, sometimes she asked me to time her, or sometimes I'd leave, I'd go down into the maintenance gallery which ran all round the pool, that's where the round windows were.

'I'd watch her body, the way her abdomen swelled was captivating, she couldn't see me, she must have suspected I was there, she behaved as if she couldn't see me, her muscles were long and she was beginning to thicken around the middle, she'd do fifty lengths without stopping, she said she had to do the backstroke, a singer always works standing up, she had to take care of her spine, when I stood by the little round window at the end of the pool I could see her coming towards me head first, when she turned and set off again I was just on a level with her legs, when she finished I'd bring her bathrobe, I deliberately set it down some distance from her so that I could go to her and watch her as she came to me, at the time the other women said that her legs and her shoulders were deeply unattractive, too many muscles, you may well smile, mustn't let our Linzer get cold. Really? You don't understand what I meant by the third shore?'

Confronted by your dejection and your uncertainties, Lilstein eventually came out with this rather harsh thought:

'When people like us lose their nerve, they become as pathetic as everybody else, that's what lies in wait for us.'

*

'There was another tomfool story,' adds Max, 'the one about the man who wanted to send whole trainloads of prostitutes to Communist Party headquarters.'

'It was to soften them up,' said Malraux.

Max looks right into Malraux's eyes:

'According to what the Americans are saying just now about the great Helmsman and his whims, several coachloads must have got there, whole compartments crammed with little Lolitas for the comrade President who hasn't seen what he's got dangling south of his paunch for many a year, they've been trained to go looking for it.'

De Vèze observes the young woman, Goffard is out of order, doesn't know how to behave around a dinner table, too much alcohol, de Vèze wonders if the young woman will blush again, he imagines her with Mao, looking for it, she has her back against the twilight, hair almost black, the white of her shoulder, of her cleavage, the yellow dress, the clear look, the oh-so soft line of her chin, like a child's, if there were some of those cattleyas so beloved of tourists on the table I could stare at the pistil, that would be as vulgar as you could wish for, what the hell's she doing with a historian?

It's settled, at midnight de Vèze will reach out and take the young woman's hand in his, but he's not nineteen any more, he's not sitting next to her but opposite, surely I'm not going to have to play footsie under the table like some damned Russian? What else can I do? Wait for tomorrow? Pay formal court to her? By then she'll have gone away with her historian, goodbye brioche, her backside, assume softly swelling curves.

'Lolitas,' says Malraux, 'Baron, that's such a cliché!'

De Vèze taken aback, Malraux thrown off-balance, Goffard has gone overboard with Mao who is to receive Malraux in Peking.

'A cliché,' Malraux says again, 'Baron, you disappoint me, I wouldn't have thought you had this amazing appetite for CIA or Soviet tittle-tattle.'

Amazing appetite, de Vèze repeats to himself, coming from Malraux that means he is treating Goffard as an agent provocateur, a reputation he's been stuck with ever since the thirties, and the accusation is very Gaullist, the CIA and the KGB in the same bag, Lolitas was the word too far.

De Vèze, the Consul, the grey diplomat, all the guests try to find some way of changing the subject, but they can't think of anything, don't really want to, would prefer not to be there, can't be helped, something is definitely going on, no one can resist a tasty revelation, they don't say anything, they stand back and let it come, wrapped in its own shadow.

In the years between the wars, the albatross around Goffard's neck was the Russians and no one else, he was very critical of them but his information, which he got from Moscow, was first rate; and on Morocco he was every bit as well informed as the English journalists on *The Times,* everybody knows that *Times* correspondents also reported back to the Intelligence Service, Goffard touted information between Paris, London and Moscow, but no one in the final analysis knew on whose behalf.

Many would have liked to ask him face-to-face, but he played poker with Briand and Berthelot, and later with Daladier and Chamberlain, yes, in Munich, with half the ministers of Europe, so sitting here at the same table as Malraux is no big deal for him, he was taught by Bergson at Henri-IV, he was there in 1919 when Lloyd George remarked while looking at a map of Czechoslovakia 'it's not a country, it's a sausage', he undertook an unofficial tour through Europe for Briand, in 1928, the Pan-European Movement, very close also to Lyautey, he never succeeded in reconciling him with Briand.

Basically Briand agreed with Lyautey, but he hated him, had done so since 1916 when Lyautey had got the better of him in a Cabinet meeting. In Morocco, Goffard chummed up with the agents for Native Affairs who had been trained by Lyautey, he knew everything that was happening on the ground, the Spaniards were suspicious of him, he had managed to get his hands on a general order given by a *coronel*, collect all bomb debris, don't leave any lying around, if necessary the Spaniards would buy back any such debris from the same Riffians who had been under them when they fell, they used gloves to handle them, no, gas wasn't used at Chefchaouen, there they just dropped 100-kilo bombs, French sector, a town full of women, a strategic air raid, there's no evidence that the French used gas anywhere in their sector, Pétain was prepared to, to hurry things along, but Chambrun said no, those air raids broke the Riffians.

The women especially. They were fearsome, like the Gaulish women Caesar tells of, they got the men fired up with songs deriding cowards.

But after Chefchaouen they began to calm down, it was high time they did, the cataclysm was fast approaching, at headquarters there was talk of abandoning Fez, the trough of a wave, or rather a snowball, a Mediterranean country with lots of snowballs will . . . snowball, the parts merge, overnight thousands of men lining up behind Abd el-Krim, an impetus that carries all before it, an avalanche, a rolling snowball army, he even tried to create a state, a snowball state, he had begun as a good and faithful servant, an adviser to the Spanish governor, a journalist on the *Telegrama del Rif*, they were later dubbed the 'Beni-oui-oui', he could have taken a well-earned retirement, after thirty years of publishing jackal-bites-man stories in Spanish newspapers, he had no choice but to rebel, found himself between a country bent on destroying itself with vendettas and not overly civilised civilisers who let you see their motor cars and their aeroplanes and remind you at every turn that you, Abd el-Krim el-Khattabi, are still an ignorant savage; you end up thinking that this is the only reason they are there, to remind you.

And the French talk about the Spaniards the way the Spaniards talk about you, Abd el-Krim, trash, they also talk about you the way they talk about the Spaniards, but not Lyautey, and in France there are French people who actually sing your praises, you are a small liberty-loving people which would like to live in the twentieth century but without having settlers landed on you, the Riff Republic, Spanish officers sometimes talked about their own men, their Basques, their Catalans, their Andalusians from Jaén the way they talked about the natives, each level borrowing its contempt from the level above it.

Abd el-Krim probably didn't know exactly what he'd got into, he was a snowball too, *chérif, zaïm, fqih, raïs, amir, khalifat, mawlana, sidna, ghazi*, he'd picked up every title as he went along, even *sultan*.

Sometimes a strict old-style Muslim, no tobacco, no marabout, no dancing on hot coals, the right hand of thieves, the five prayers.

At other times he looks across at Turkey, Mustafa Kemal's fresh start, it's the religion of our fathers that has landed us in this mess, in four centuries we have not even been able to nail a long handle on to a brush and turn it into a broom, true, but at least Abd el-Krim didn't force that business with the cap on his Riffians, outside villages in certain parts of Turkey there was a gallows, with a real rope and a pile of caps; when they came to the village the peasants had to exchange their turbans for caps, there was a choice of caps.

Very complicated all these roles, but Abd el-Krim doesn't reject any of them, *khalifat* is virtually a successor to the Prophet, as *sultan* he replaces the Sultan of Morocco who is not best pleased, rid me of this rebel he is supposed to have said to Pétain, *ghazi* just means conqueror, a *fqih* is a holy man, *amir* is the director of the faithful but *raïs* is a secular chief, a sort of president.

Zaïm is what the English call a leader, *sidna* and *mawlana* are very traditional, somewhere between yer lordship and Our Lord, Abd el-Krim makes the most of them all, a mythical city, and he doesn't take anything for granted, swings of a pendulum, the Spaniards invade us, the tribes rise up, I use the insurrection to show the Spaniards that I'm indispensable, I demonstrate to the French that they need my support, I convince the Spaniards that they must negotiate, I mix holy war and Turkish-style revolution, the Europeans don't get the idea for five years, inconceivable that these people can fight to become something different from what we want them to become, Moscow's hand is behind it all, London's gold, and the voice of Berlin, a voice you could hear in beleaguered French outposts, came from the rebel lines, spoken in German by deserters from the Legion, 'come on you Riffians, by God, you got no balls!'

The Germans are prevented from crossing the Rhine, so they come to the Riff to stab the French in the back.

That said, they also helped the Spaniards: a purpose-built turnkey plant at Melilla for making Yperite and tabun, around ten thousand gas-bombs dropped in three years, Abd el-Krim believes France is incapable of undertaking a war, he gathers many men to him, those who come, those who don't come and are compelled to come, those he bribes – who sometimes prove more loyal than those who came in the flush of enthusiasm and will run away at the first setback – he also has hostages, as we do, a real snowball, but the snowball will come to a stop when it gets to the bottom of the hill, when it reaches the plain, where the great cities are which he does not dare to capture, woe to those who have forsaken their fields for the town, Goffard knew all that, they called him The African, and thirty years later he was also one of the first to get his hands on a copy of the Khrushchev report, it was his big scoop, it suited the interests of far too many people.

'The CIA and the KGB,' continues Malraux, 'are hand in hand, the Atlanticists and the Soviets, talking of Atlanticists, Baron, your friend Kappler, still as close to the Americans, is he?'

Max, face white, Malraux goes on:

'Kappler, difficult man, but instead of sticking to being difficult with women he had to poke his nose into politics, and now no one ever knows where he is, a friendly visit to the Russian zone in '47, neither here nor there, but he couldn't not return to the East in '56, did you discuss it? Which of you showed the other the Khrushchev report? Kappler going to live in the East after fighting the communists by the side of the CIA.'

'Along with you, Master,' said Max.

'True,' says Malraux, 'that business with *Preuves*, I wrote for *Preuves*, with Sperber, in about '52, '53, and with Kappler too, a great review, on the side of freedom.'

'Which had some very unusual financial backing.'

Malraux, without picking up on this remark:

'But Kappler certainly pulled the wool over our eyes, going off to live in the East in '56, after Budapest!'

'He only stayed three years,' says Max.

'He left for Switzerland in '59,' adds Malraux, 'and today his name crops up in CIA reviews, the reviews which publish him are subsidised by the Americans, a man for all seasons.'

'It's because he is a man of sincerity,' says Max.

'A man of every sincerity going,' says Malraux.

'He was incapable of telling the necessary lie.' Max has stopped clowning. 'But we're getting away from the subject, Master: Peking, the Great Helmsman and the little Lolitas.'

The two people around this table who have known each other longest are Goffard and Malraux, almost half a century of friendship, and they are now about to quarrel terminally, when Malraux said 'cliché' and 'tittle-tattle', he lowered his eyes, not wanting to see the man who had taken him in hand in the twenties, and Max too has had enough of his author, whole decades start falling under the hammer, an orgy of destruction, each man destroying what he had once meant to the other, I leave you my old clothes, enjoy, Lolitas, tittle-tattle, it's all meaningless, because it was him, tearing each other apart for the same absence of reason, because it was like this, because it was like that, or because they'd got too carried away, or because they'd never really been friends, or because one day the powers-that-be decide they don't like the edge one of you has over the other, or because what they had originally destroyed in order to become friends has reared its head again, what exactly is it that's been kept hidden for so long?

'Clichés, tittle-tattle,' repeats Malraux who has a reputation for his clinical approach to clean breaks, 'it's just snooping.'

Malraux doesn't mention the word 'Lolitas', but it's all those present around the table are thinking about, suddenly he relaxes, smiles, looks up at Max again and wags a forefinger at him:

'A story for you, your turn to listen, a poor man who had neither land nor a flock to watch, this happens in Bali, he finds a tortoise who can talk, he tells everyone about it, the king has him arrested and orders the tortoise to be brought to him, the tortoise refuses to say anything, the king has the poor man strangled, then the tortoise starts to speak, 'woe to him who, having nothing to watch over, can't even watch his tongue!'

Max smiles, says nothing more, the Consul makes the most of the opportunity:

'Basically, Minister, the tortoise is the tittle-tattle, the cliché which ultimately traps the gossip-monger.'

'Talking of clichés and Lolitas, Master,' asks Max, setting his wineglass down, 'do you know what Nabokov said about our novel?'

An old hand at debating, de Vèze says to himself, never reply to an accusation, bat the question back, but this time you're heading for a fall.

'Nabokov is often interesting,' says Malraux, 'but if you're going to tell me about him, then it's bound to be some nasty crack or an item of gossip.'

This time Malraux has spoken without looking at Max.

'Nabokov said,' Max ploughs on, 'that *The Human Condition*, with its Chinese rain, Chinese nights, Chinese streets, Chinese crowds is the Great International Cliché Company, he suggests readers try it in Belgian: "they went out into the Belgian night".'

De Vèze reckons Goffard won't go on being a character in a book for much longer, no one talks like that to Malraux.

A definite bust-up, everyone goes quiet, the Consul and his wife are not there, they are fiddling with spoons in their coffee cups, decidedly they are not among those present at a bust-up which has Malraux at its centre, that sort of thing can cost you dear, if Malraux asks the Consul to throw Goffard out, Goffard knows a great many people, he survived the *Hindenburg* disaster, and if Goffard refuses to go then Malraux will stand up and accuse the Consul of luring him into an ambush, and this was the Consul's last chance to have this Consulate made up to a full Embassy.

It's the fault of the Beaujolais, light, bland, they'd drunk it like water, a bust-up, and in front of Xavier, a junior attaché maybe, but he already has the ear of the Secretary-General and the Minister, he'll go far, with that inquisitorial look and his little monkey-arse beard, they're fast-tracking him, it's his private life, because they know they can get rid of him at any time, he's a threat to nobody, he'll go far, he's not the sort who'll speak up for me in Paris when what's happened around this table gets out in a couple of hours, you can trust them, they didn't drink too much of the Sauternes.

It's this middling Beaujolais that did it, the Consul should have opened the last of his Gevrey-Chambertin, there would have been just three bottles on the table but at least you don't glug Gevrey-Chambertin, if you do it hits you in the back of the throat, he should never have listened to his wife who wanted to keep those three bottles of Gevrey to celebrate his coming promotion, after all Malraux is only passing through, and he only drinks pastis, everyone knows that, and now there's been a major incident at the consular dinner table, still the Sauternes mixed with too much Beaujolais can't have helped much, a major incident at my table, and we'll drink the Gevrey-Chambertin when we have to do our flit, 'Belgian night', that's under the belt, and the others are in a funk too, they won't do anything, what went through my wife's head, nothing, nothing ever goes through her head.

She's like that, I only had to mention the Gevrey-Chambertin for her to say no, I should have said let's have the Beaujolais, and she'd have said no we'd better bring out the best bottles, and then Goffard would have behaved himself, she's been saying the opposite of what I say for more than thirty years, I should have left her while there was still time, when I discussed it with Jean-Claude, he said she makes you angry because she's always arguing, and she'll make you angrier and angrier, but if you do leave her it'll be worse, because you'll still be angry but you won't have any reasons to be, yes, but this time that's it, an incident, I know it doesn't sound much, old man, I wouldn't give your little incident a second thought, everyone knows what Malraux is like, this sort of thing is quickly forgotten, but as I was reminded by the Minister who is so sorry that he cannot see you, the essence of the diplomat's work is a capacity for avoiding incidents, recall to Paris.

No embassy, deputy in charge of a sub-department, and a three-roomed flat in the rue Vaneau, on the second floor, windows overlooking the courtyard, I prefer being on my own, she can go and mutter 'no' at people in the street or travellers on the *métro*, actually, she'll go back to her bloody country-living, with rubber boots, rubber gloves, rubber head, and mind you change your shoes as you come in, the Consul looks at his wife, smiles to encourage her to keep smiling in the midst of all the wreckage.

De Vèze says to Malraux:

'Nabokov is too clever by half.'

'Why do you say that?'

Malraux has pushed his chair back, he has folded his arms, polite expression on his face, an end-of-the-friendship politeness, these were most likely the last words he would speak that evening and he even looks as if he blames de Vèze, de Vèze isn't at all sure why he said Nabokov was too clever by half, he'd felt things were about to take a turn for the worse, so he came out with a smart remark, and now he's landed himself in a fix, he searches for a phrase incorporating 'destiny' and 'literature'.

'A cliché,' he says, 'is one form of destiny.'

De Vèze has the feeling he's not going to get anywhere.

'I don't follow,' says the pink diplomat.

Shut up, thinks the Consul, just shut up.

'I don't understand either,' cuts in Morel who is beginning to like de Vèze less and less.

That makes two of you, thinks de Vèze, three with the grey man who is pretending he understands, and four with me until I come up with something.

Those two make a funny pair, thinks Morel, glancing at the pink-and-grey couple, at least they're not ogling my wife, unlike this other character who's never succeeded in escaping from his legend, an embassy in Rangoon, a battle in 1942, he thinks it entitles him to undress other men's wives.

Morel would like to provoke an incident, yes that would be good, an incident would make people forget all about the tension between Malraux and Goffard, Mister Ambassador, my wife's neckline seems to interest you, once at a dinner Morel saw a woman with the courage to create an incident, are you going to sweep my husband off his feet now or can it wait? Who do these people think they are, they believe they can have anything because they are waited on at table, have a chauffeur-driven car, Morel cannot stand the breed, the title demeans, the function stultifies, he has known people who rang far truer, heroic but not self-important, who had gone back to their jobs as typesetters or pointsmen without hawking their medals around some ministry, Flaubert was right, Morel feels like hitting his wife.

'But this destiny thing is really quite simple, children,' says Max.

He lifts one finger and pauses.

Goffard to my rescue, thinks de Vèze, Goffard knows that these days without Malraux he is nothing more than an old man who is about to be forgotten by history, he has written thousands of newspaper articles, one occasionally worth a page of Malraux, but it's journalism, none of it will last.

'All our heroes die,' continues Max, 'victims of destiny, as they say in cheap novels.'

'Of destiny and repetition,' says de Vèze.

'They die, History repeats itself,' adds Max.

The young woman says nothing, all the guests have now raised their heads again, the Consul has finished his coffee, he plays with a pipe-cleaner, turning it between thumb and forefinger like an aeroplane propeller.

'A cliché,' says de Vèze carefully, though without knowing really what he's saying, 'is the portion of destiny in what we write.'

'That's clichés sorted out, then,' says Max, 'and that's why in Shanghai the tension is always terrible and the rain unfailingly Chinese and Nabokov is wrong, well spotted, Monsieur de Vèze, your phrasing is a touch awkward but if you'd like to do a book of interviews with the Master you've cracked it, and you've come to my rescue.'

'Come now, the idea that clichés are unavoidable is an old idea of Paulhan's,' says Malraux, who smiles again.

'Readers are morons,' cries Max, 'they're too busy sniffing out clichés to see the kangaroos!'

'You mustn't deny Monsieur de Vèze the pithiness of his axiom,' says the young woman.

Morel does not care at all for the way his wife defends the man, but he knows there's nothing he can do about it, nothing has gone right this evening, an insignificant moron, that's what you are to these people, your expertise, all you know about the peasantry in the eighteenth century, they couldn't care less, they have the power, they invite you, you give lectures, you have dinner in Singapore, beautiful plates, they separate you from your wife, tomorrow they'll tell you that you were rather grim.

'Monsieur de Vèze has a very elegant way of rescuing clichés,' says the young woman.

I'm going to go for the foot, de Vèze decides, but not with my shoe on. How can she possibly have hands like that? Bigger, heavier than you'd expect, lips that smile, hands that don't mess about.

'Well I at least wasn't a cliché,' says Max.

'Are you sure?' asks Malraux, 'cliché, pastiche, imitation, it goes to the very heart of the thing, writers don't express themselves, they imitate, what is the writer's raw material? The work of other writers, and the cliché is what remains of them at the level of language.'

Malraux, chin cupped in his left hand, right hand in the air, forefinger pointing, you have first to write down the adjective 'terrible' so that you can be free of it, you imitate, the finger lands on the table, there's no stopping him now, Malraux is launched, de Vèze presses the toe of his left shoe against the heel of his right shoe.

'It's better than not writing a novel at all, just because you're afraid of adjectives, isn't that so, Baron?' Malraux's voice is a hiss.

'But you had a very good story to tell in those days, Kappler had told me about it, in the offices of *Preuves*, the fear of adjectives, you need to stand back a little.'

Malraux draws a line on the table with his finger.

'You pastiche and you isolate the tenth which isn't imitated, and then you try to make sure the rest matches that tenth.'

Malraux has moved back, his hands above the plate begin to caress the thought like a conscientious potter.

'You go beyond pastiche, you play around with it, the opening of my novel, Baron . . .'

Little by little the fullness and the affection return to his voice:

'Obviously it's like a crime thriller, ordinary, night, car horns, suspense, you must ensure the reader's hair stands on end, nothing to feel ashamed of, take Hugo, *Les Misérables*, the tension that hits you in the stomach.'

Malraux's hands are together again, one index finger extended:

'It's a pastiche of a crime novel, or of Laclos.'

Slowly de Vèze eases off his right shoe.

'Valérie is a small-scale Merteuil,' says Max with a smile.

'That's right,' says Malraux, 'you pastiche Faulkner or twenties Russian novelists, your overripe pastiche becomes a filter which you use to look at the world through new eyes.'

Malraux puts his left hand up to his eyes with his fingers spread wide, like bars.

'You look at Shanghai through a haze of pulp crime fiction, or you strain the *Pensées* through the *Pieds Nickelés*' – the right hand up now, also with the fingers out wide, held against the left, like a trellis – 'a double filter, Filochard and the two infinites, put it all together and you get a decent book.'

He puts out both arms in front of him, forefinger extended on each hand, he beats time to his words with nods of his head, his face forward, chin in, pupils raised to compensate, eyes wide open:

'It takes a writer years before he can write with the sound of his own voice, get past other people's voices, at any rate his own is there, and if you don't pastiche as you imitate you're just a parrot, you rewrite Maupassant or Turgenev without realising it or pretending you've forgotten, like Nabokov or your friend Kappler, Baron.'

Malraux's left hand is on the table, arched like a spider, on the tips of the fingers.

'And it doesn't have kangaroos!'

'It also lacks cats,' says the young woman, displaying the large black cat which has jumped unnoticed on to her lap.

De Vèze decides that a woman who reduces him to this state in the middle of a dinner with Malraux is a pearl without price. At last he manages to slide his foot out of his right shoe.

A faint crackle in the sky, above the young woman's head, the first star, the star that favours the bold, a draught of air blows under the table, cools the sock, the floor of the veranda is warm.

'They say I don't do cats very well in my stories,' says Malraux.

He has backed his chair away, hands crossed on his knees, face down again, eyes looking up, he waits.

'That's not true,' asserts the young woman stroking the animal, 'actually, cats are your double.'

'What do you mean?' de Vèze asks belligerently.

He's not angry with her, not as he was a while back when he could have told her to go to hell, now he's scared, scared that he'll start thinking again what a blue-stocking she is, that she's read too many books, one of those women who pass their time picking you up on everything you say, a friend of his lived with a woman like that for twenty years, he's now in an asylum, scared to separate from her, scared to stop wanting her body, and now she comes out with this business of a double, and everyone is all agog because the minute you start talking about doubles at a dinner party people think you must be very smart.

'When Kyo watches Monsieur Clappique in the Black Cat, you describe the scene from a point of view that places you behind Kyo, who moves like a cat,' the young woman says to Malraux, 'and behind Clappique, in the background, there is the glow from the luminous outline of a cat which is watching us, which means that the scene is enacted between two cats.'

Malraux smiles, a rare expression on his face, never in photos, the delight of a cat who's been at the cream, perhaps a few woman are entitled to see this expression.

'Cat to the front!'

Max has shouted out.

'Cat to the rear! Cat everywhere. Raminagrobis be with us!'

A sudden hush, Max stares at his plate, everyone is looking at him, he remains silent, the Consul starts fiddling with his pipe-cleaner again, Max doesn't look at anyone, could these people guess how kids used to play with cats in the back streets of Rabat? Lyautey played croquet, the kids played shooting-star cats, in the towns, not in the Riff, there weren't any animals left in the Riff, nothing edible, like us in the trenches, a cat you caught was called a rabbit, the agent for Native Affairs said they don't even have standard scarcity fare, no wild artichokes, mallow stems, prickly pears, roots, nor tobacco or hashish to beguile hunger, hunger eats at your muscles, what with the bombs and hunger they eventually gave up, they came down hoping to get something to eat, they had nothing left to sell, they traded parts of their clothes, in certain *douars* in the Riff there wasn't a single man left alive, the women sold themselves, we behaved very decently, we staged surrender ceremonies, large gatherings, the colours of France and the flag of the Shereef, the whole shooting match.

An order, *atten-shun*! heels click, brains close, the conquered standing in a semi-circle, bugles, drums, let the ceremony begin, it's called the *targuiba*, the conquered chief brings a bull to the conquering chief, a single stroke with a knife, hamstring severed, the bull collapses, thrashes around, and thus the violence ends, allegiance sworn, pardon given, bull on its side, ten men to hold it, bull kicking out, a thrust of the knife to slit its throat, it's the only thing moving in front of the crowd which watches it die, the violence drains away through the aorta, the smell of warm blood in the noses of those in the front rows, if the tribe didn't have a bull then the military government provided the sacrificial beast, to be paid for in kind by forced labour, Bournazel was there, with his Arab scouts, no, he didn't die during the Riff wars, that was later, further south.

Foot of the Sargho hills, March 1933, very simple, he charges and takes a bullet in the stomach, legend has it that Giraud had ordered him to wear a grey djellaba over his red cloak, that took away his *baraka*, from the notebook of Dr Vial 'At the orifice made by the bullet I found a very large intestinal and peritoneal hernia, already strangulated and its pedicle twisted, extremely painful', Bournazel's nose looks pinched, bloodless lips, 'I'm cold, Doctor, I'm a long time dying, what a bloody way to go', that was it, had he kept his red cloak on? The shooting-star cats in the back streets of Rabat, the youngsters dipped their tails in oil, put a match to them, such brilliant flashes in the night, with added sound effects.

Max waves his right hand slowly in the air, watches it, comes out with one last phrase:

'The Cheshire cat from Alice's Wonderland!'

'Alice played croquet too,' said the young woman.

She looks at de Vèze, he says nothing, he's so gauche, he'd like to sleep with me, it's obvious what he means by sleeping: it means taking, then disappearing, and reappearing whenever he fancies, though there'd be a few walks together, at the beginning, and then you'd forget, Mr Good-Looking, you are so manly and I expect that when you can't do what you want a third time, you too will throw your pillow against the wall.

'The cat is the spirit of the place,' concludes the young woman.

'And of the writing,' says Malraux.

'Who does this thieving tom belong to?' asks the young woman as she prevents the cat getting its nose into her plate.

'To me,' says Max, 'it was a present from my author, I take him with me wherever I go, otherwise he yowls and upsets the guests at the hotel.'

'What did you call him?' the young woman asks Malraux.

'Orpheus,' says Malraux, 'I have one just like him in Paris, but I didn't have time to teach this one his manners.'

De Vèze tells himself that he will put his foot on the young woman's foot and do it as if it were the most natural thing in the world, she will throw the contents of her wineglass in his face, no, all she'll do is shoot him a withering look, why not wait for a better opportunity? Why not wait ten years while you're about it? You spend your life waiting, waiting to go away, waiting for a woman, you could wait for her to make all the moves, dream about it, where did I read that? A dinner, Louis XV, a man keeps staring at a woman sitting opposite him, he tries to be brilliant, witty remarks, best wines, the woman removes her shoe under the table and places her foot on the man's crotch, he has no idea what to do, can a woman really do that? You can dream about it and wait and then go away with nothing.

Max looks at de Vèze:

'A cat is less trouble than a kangaroo.'

Malraux:

'The kangaroo in the bedroom watching Ferral, it's because I needed something a touch grotesque, between the lines.'

'Only writing can still do that,' adds Max, 'in the cinema, a one-second shot of the kangaroo would be enough to get the whole audience laughing while Ferral is dreaming that he's tearing Valérie limb from limb and devouring the pieces.'

'Actually I didn't write it quite in that spirit,' Malraux corrects him.

'No matter,' says Max, 'there's a hint of Bluebeard in there, and also of kangaroo.'

'It wasn't done to lower the tension,' said Malraux, eyes down, right palm up towards Clappique, 'it was for comic relief, it doesn't go anywhere.'

'Ferral's mistake,' says the young woman, 'was to think we are little girls he could butcher and gobble up.'

She looks at de Vèze, thinks he looks like Ferral, only better, on the far side of folly, would he be capable of gobbling a person up? Can he do anything else? He'd like to eat me up, and it wouldn't be too unpleasant to be his supper for one evening, but could he also walk down the rue Lepic eating cherries out of a paper bag that we'd be sharing? It would be our first walk together, then on another day, when we're a bit more used to each other, we could buy shrimps, the little grey ones, wash them in the fountain ourselves and eat them just as they are, while we watch the world go by, he'd learn that there's more to life than erections, why not give it a try? Philippe is so distant, he sits there facing me, if it were someone else instead of him it wouldn't make the slightest difference to anything.

He doesn't love me, he wanted to get married, that's all, when I was little I wanted to marry a hero, what boldness is he capable of now, apart from the way he stares, what test could I set him? He says we're equals, we both work, we earn practically the same amount, he takes the rubbish out, but for him a loving wife is a woman who lives entirely through what her husband does.

He says he's all mine, but everything I like in life I'm supposed to feel through him, all the other couples we know, modern women, they all know their husbands' careers inside out, the wife who tells you straight out exactly what her hubby isn't after: the Cochin job, the Sorbonne professorship or the chairmanship, so-and-so is a bastard, especially when so-and-so is the hubby's rival, hubby smiles, darling you mustn't exaggerate so, he takes the bin out half the time, he's the one who chooses where we go when we travel, he never cried when I passed my exams, ah! so you are Morel's wife, and Morel always out in front.

And this is the man who went hopping and skipping through the trees in the Jardin du Luxembourg like a young puppy the day I said I love you, why do I like being in this situation? I live for him, he wasn't very good at philosophy, so I helped him without letting on, his thesis, I checked through the whole thing for him, and my own book isn't finished, he began to make his way and I loved watching him do it, he doesn't need me, I'm patient with him and it gets on my nerves, he won't let me smoke, because he loves me, he says I shouldn't have that second slice of cake, love is the sum of everything you prevent me doing, Malraux isn't like that, he calls me Madame, very entertaining the preface he wrote for *Les Liaisons*.

'The mistake men make,' the young woman goes on, 'is to think that women are still like they were in stories about ogres and Bluebeard.'

'Ah, ogres,' says Max, 'ogres are finished, whereas we at least took the century by the throat, terrifying ogres, tremendous romance, nowadays they call it an inner adventure, the time I spent screwing my way around the Quartier Latin seen through the keyhole of conscious-ness, no ogres, no story, no more stories, the blues as experienced by a moron who has lost his memory, bed and bored, no more playing a character in a book, personal pronouns, do I look like a personal pronoun type? Voyeurs, tight-arses or maybe the opposite, they guess the answers before they've read the book, game's up, there ain't no more ogres in the inkwell, nor in my lady's chamber, not nowhere, no more ogres, no more Adventure, shush! listen!'

Max casts an amused glance at de Vèze who has decided it is time to act, to place his right foot on the foot of the young woman, not a caress, just his foot resting on hers, as if it were an old habit, the arch of his foot itches, first he must scratch it on the back of the shoe he has taken off.

'Shush!' orders Max, 'don't say a word! The ogre: "Love shyly but slyly, Adore the fine lady and stay full of guile, But don't eat her child, Like the Russian ogre in my tale, Nor injure her dog or tread on its tail."'

De Vèze cannot locate the shoe he's just taken off, not on the right or the left, it's not anywhere, he moves his foot around on the wood of the floor while trying to keep his torso upright.

'I love those lines by Hugo,' says Malraux, 'that grotesque side he has to him.'

'Which poem is it from?' enquires Morel.

'It's the story of the Russian ogre who is in love with a fairy, he eats her brat because she's kept him waiting,' says Malraux, 'but also because he takes everything literally.'

'And also because brat rhymes with fat,' concludes Max.

De Vèze can't find it, starts feeling annoyed, somebody's moved my shoe, it's that big-eared bastard who's made my shoe vanish, or else it's her, that's why she's grinning like that.

Malraux again:

'In fact, no one knows if Hugo is mocking lovestruck ogres or if he's making a case for men to have the right to devour women.'

'He certainly,' says the Consul, 'had a big reputation as a man-eater.'

'His darling Juliette could have told you all about that,' says Max.

De Vèze feels the dinner drawing to a close, he'll have to stand up in full view of his fellow diners without his right shoe, there'll be jokes, worse: there won't be jokes.

The young woman smiles at Max.

'Is it true,' asks the grey diplomat, 'that towards the end of their life together Juliette refused to let him go upstairs and devour the maids in the attic?'

'Yes,' answers Malraux, 'she forbade him to devour anyone but he made her eat, she had cancer, swallowing was agony; at dinner, in front of everybody, he'd say "aren't you eating anything, Madame Drouet?" She'd force herself to take a few mouthfuls just to please her old ogre.'

'The end of loving,' says Max.

'The end of everything, my dear Baron,' says Malraux, right elbow on the table, hand open and palm up, carrying an invisible tray.

And in that 'my dear Baron' there is something surprising that suddenly holds the assembled company in its thrall, an unexpected tenderness, it's not irony, nor politeness, nor the affection a novelist might feel, all things considered, for the model for his character, but a tenderness which is exaggerated, yet also scrupulous and attentive, the sort of tenderness hands might show for a thousand-year-old death mask, as if Malraux – putting their present difference of opinion behind him – was remembering, and wanting now only to remember the time when, still very young, at the close of a war in which he had not fought, he had met a Goffard who used fits of the giggles and comments about James Ensor as a means of escaping the shadows of hell, look here, young man, Ensor's pictures are treee – menn – doussly— shush! don't interrupt!, its done, got our tickets for Brussels, and Antwerp, masked figures fighting over a hanged man, tremendously far in advance of real life!

Later, Malraux published his own account of that evening in Singapore, he did not mention de Vèze, who has always wondered why, nor did he mention the Morels, he spoke mainly about Clappique, with affection, but omitting any reference to the 'Lolita Incident'.

In Singapore, at dinner, there was one other moment of tension, when they'd talked about Churchill's funeral, in February, superb, what with Moulin and Churchill we've had some magnificent funerals recently, Max launched into one of his verbal flights, the beautiful spectacle of three hundred sailors pulling the gun carriage, the slow march, the foot which freezes in mid stride and then unfreezes, it's not a march, it's the celebration of a rite, no question of one-two, one-two, that's for the living who will go on, here – shush! not a word! – what lies in wait is a hole in the ground, so they go one, mark time, two, mark time, one, mark time, two, and it creates a kind of pitch or swell, three hundred sailors.

Three hundred white caps like the foam on slow waves bearing off the First Lord of the Admiralty.

'And not before time,' said Max, 'he was getting out of control, he started raging against what he called the "negrification" of the United Nations, when my friend Linus went to interview him ten years ago, Churchill showed him an English newspaper, in it was a photo of a black man and a white woman, both members of the Salvation Army, and he said to Linus "Is this what I'll find when I get to heaven? if so, I don't want to go anywhere near a place like that", Churchill's wife was much more dignified than him, he was really very old.'

In Malraux's account, he and Clappique get on swimmingly, mostly they talk about the script for a film which was never mentioned in de Vèze's hearing, Malraux also omitted any reference to the two diplomats, the pink and the grey.

Nor did he record the awkwardness which settled over the table when Max brought up the rumours about moles which were already doing the rounds at the time, Malraux had dismissed the issue with a wave of his hand, OAS officers trying to sell old floor-sweepings to the Americans, assassins sitting on their hands in exile while they waited for the next amnesty, Max had quoted his friend Linus Mosberger again:

'Shush! don't say anything! according to Linus there are a lot fewer moles in France than in England or Germany, because if you confront a Frenchman with a photo of his off-duty extra-marital activities he'll order half-a-dozen copies for his friends, whereas for Anglo-Saxons regular caning until the age of twenty tends to leave them vulnerable.'

Nor does Malraux seem to have had dealings with the same Consul, did he talk to Clappique next day at the Raffles and get this other conversation mixed up with the one of the previous evening? Did he make it up? After all, he was perfectly free to do so, certainly he makes Clappique quote the Hugo poem but he never said anything about the kangaroo on Valérie's bed, but he did talk about another kangaroo, the one belonging to Nina de Callias, a rich patroness of the arts, friend of Verlaine, who posed for Manet's *Lady with the Fans*, the magnificent Nina.

When he read Malraux, de Vèze realised that the young woman's neckline that evening had been the same as Nina de Callias's in the painting, but without the gauze, without the necklace at her throat, otherwise the beauty spot on her cleavage would have been less visible, nor feathers in her hair, nor fans on the wall behind her, there hadn't been a wall behind her, she'd been sitting with her back to the night, the white of her shoulders, the soft line of her chin, in his account Malraux recalled that the kangaroo had eaten all the green parts of Nina's large carpet during the siege of Paris in 1870.

Just as people were saying goodnight at the gates of the villa in Singapore, Max had shown de Vèze the sky:

'Look, see the moon that makes hearts ache, shush! we must see each other again soon, lots to tell you, we've met before, obviously you can't remember, you'd just turned five, we can meet in Rangoon or Paris, or in the Alps.'

Chapter 9

1928

Flaubert's Bust

In which Hans Kappler dreams of Lena Hotspur and has a conversation with his friend Max Goffard.

In which Max Goffard tries his hand at erotic writing and suggests that Hans Kappler might care to become a landscape painter.

In which Max Goffard finally gets on a train for Waltenberg and the European Seminar.

In which we learn how Max Goffard became a great reporter and is now a sports enthusiast.

Paris, September 1928

He was a member of a croquet club and
played assiduously on the paths of the
Jardin du Luxembourg
Georges Duhamel, *Salavin*

This happens in the Jardin du Luxembourg, Hans and Max are strolling, like old friends. One day they emerged from their fox-holes, came face to face, a ringing of bells, the Armistice, it's all over. Max sees a Hun officer who comes towards him and says, in French:

'Shall we exchange tobaccos? Tobacco is the recreation of a gentleman.'

They talk for hours; the Hun tells him he intends to go looking for a woman, while Max says he has no idea what he is going to do.

Since then, they have arranged to meet at least once a year. Today is a September morning, the first phase of autumn, before the cold sets in: autumn of fruits, a palette of brown, dark green, orange, rust, with hints of ash and lavender blue. Max and Hans saunter, make their way back to the gardens' north exit, passing sequestered nooks as they go, the bronze statue of Bacchus on his donkey with the nymphs writhing around him, the bust of Verlaine, there's rain at intervals, then a wind to chase the rain away, the trees drip and an emerald light bursts from the verges of the walkways.

They go as far as the edge of the orchard, head back to the centre of the gardens via the little Punch and Judy show. Through the foliage, the light forms patches of fluctuating brightness which warm the fragrance, to which the damp earth adds its quotient of sweet chestnut, plane and sometimes the tang and sweetness of spruce resin when the sun revives their scents and holds them suspended in the space where light turns to shadow for the delight also of the eye – trees, aromas and light join together to perform a fleeting role, for they are at the mercy of the cloud which will descend and wrap the gardens in unyielding grey.

By the ornamental pond, children with sticks launch their hired sailing boats which set off in pursuit of fierce pirates.

'Listen to this,' says Max, opening his newspaper, 'I'm quite fond of Monsieur Sarraut at present, you Germans can have no real idea of what a colonial empire is and the effect it has on the beauty of verbal expression: "Since the native population claim the right to express their wishes directly, Monsieur Albert Sarraut said he believes that this rightful claim must be examined before it has an opportunity to turn into a shrill demand." Shrill demand! Rightful claim! The colonials will flay Sarraut alive for saying such a thing.'

Max aims a kick at a pile of dead leaves.

'Hans, this is going to turn nasty, look!'

Another kick.

'The past is rotting before our very eyes.'

They continue strolling.

'What are you writing at the moment?'

Max it is who asked the question, anxious to know what the other man is up to, a concern which will make him speak about the thing which he finds hurtful.

It is both considerate and cruel, like all good questions; the two men get on famously together, Hans is the anxious type, Max feels increasingly that he is a failure, especially when he is with Hans, they are friends, Hans looks away into the shrubbery and answers, saying he's keeping a diary, that's all, he has already published four novels, three of them since the end of the war; he also translates a great deal of French literature for a Stuttgart publisher; he is what is called an established writer.

Max again:

'Have you really done with fiction?'

Hans doesn't know. All he wants for the moment is to keep a diary, like Jules Renard, write in short bursts, a vertical style, with no images, images put whiskers on a style, every day try to create an effect like the one of the shy friend who wipes his feet when he *leaves* a house, or the woman who remains silent at the top of her voice, do I really like Renard? Renard tries a fiction cure to get fiction out of his system, I need to do the same with his *Journal*, read it until I've had more than my fill, oh yes, Hans knows what Renard said, about a diary killing off the novel you might have written, Max's questions sting Hans who never knows if he can do better than what people have thus far admired in the tales he has spun. For Hans, Renard's *Journal* is a collection of hundreds of brief stories, life on the hoof, superb, I'd like to translate it, even if the style is a touch brittle for my taste.

'A very written life,' says Max, 'Renard always has a phrase in his head ready to lasso whatever is going on around him, 'he goes out hunting through the streets of Paris, all he lives for is his journal, and he calls that being free.'

'And what do you do?'

Hans has taken Max by the elbow, French style, he tries to put his question as delicately as possible, Max wanted to be a writer before the war, now he's trying to tell a story, a story which slips through his fingers.

'I'm a novelist who's started keeping a journal,' says Hans, 'and you are . . .'

'. . . a journalist who's begun writing a novel, you're extremely kind, but it's not exactly a *novel*; it's a true story, some people I met last year, in the Haute-Savoie.'

Hans didn't much care for that 'you're extremely kind', a hint of sourness, but he says with forced cheerfulness 'Haute-Savoie! Regionalism!' at any moment Max will start burbling on about a three-cheese Swiss *fondue*, the little chimney sweep and the kind-hearted maids, and unFrench Swissisms.

'It'll do me good, it'll be a change from journalism and spewing out words like a machine gun, a year ago I was still reporting from the Riff.'

'I read your stuff,' says Hans.

No, Hans didn't read anything, it was copy for press consumption only, what could be printed, not everything, Hans, you couldn't say everything if you wanted to stay in the field and not get sent home courtesy of the military, not easy being a reporter in the Riff with the military around, you stay on willy-nilly, rotten job, a month or two, you leave, you go back.

For four years, Max made the round-trip at least twice a year, each time I told myself I'd write about it later, I kept my eyes open, for my articles I kept mostly to the beauty of the branches of acacia in the beds of the wadis and the doctors who treated trachoma. When you write like that, you cut anything that oversteps the mark; the more you cut, the less your eye sees, what you preferred not to see resurfaces in the night, so don't let anyone tell us that the war should have acted on us like a vaccine, it was a soldier's world, now I hear screams in the night, no not in the night, in my dreams, and I wake up screaming, Hans I'm sick and tired of being a war correspondent, you get to see too much of what happens to the civilian population, or maybe I should take up sports reporting.

'And the best you could manage after the Riff was to swan off to Shanghai?'

Max had wanted a change of scene, Shanghai, the floating brothel, the first time he'd read about it was in his father's favourite paper, *Paris-Soir*, he was thirteen, he burst out laughing, it was in the drawing room, there were guests, he was sitting by himself in a corner, he giggled.

'What's so funny, Max?'

His father is very proud of having a son who reads newspapers.

'I'm reading an article about Shanghai, papa.'

The two words were hidden in a paragraph, 'floating brothel', Max reads them out to the whole drawing room, time for bed, in another family it would have been a clip round the ear and get up to bed, in our house no clip on the ear, just time for bed, an infinite iciness in my father's voice and no newspapers for two years.

Instead Max took up the piano, he played Bach, and Wagner

arranged for keyboard, it helped him when he became a journalist, a real asset in any drawing room, in the best families, throughout the whole of Europe.

China also means painting with a fine brush, people who spend three years learning how to draw a rock, the five shades of black ink, a waterfall as a living thing, the brush which makes the wind flow between the mountains, that's what Max was looking for, not floating brothels, but rather the scroll that is opened in the back of a shop, time which stops devouring the minutes, recapture time, before painting a bamboo first give it time to grow inside you.

Three weeks after Max arrived in China, Chiang Kai-Shek started liquidating his revolutionaries, Shanghai, stationary locomotives, boilers, screams, yes, the world's press reported it, the absolute height of horror said the papers, there were also more classical forms of giving quietus, the main square, men in single file, women too, the majority civilians, decapitation by sword, not easy, even when people have their hands tied, they lie down, they just won't kneel, some crawl around screaming, especially the innocent, they don't get far, scream hard enough to shatter their larynxes, not enough blocks to put heads on, the blade does not always strike clean, Chiang Kai-Shek's troopers roll up their sleeves, work in groups, yank them by the hair, use their bayonets, the work hardly progresses, the prisoners are lined up one behind the other by the hundred, occasionally one is calmer, steps forward without having to be pushed or pulled, shouts out a few words, no one will translate the words for Max, and Chiang's officers beat the more ineffectual troopers with English-style canes, they turn to Max, English-style jibes directed at those about to die:

'They'll never have toothache again!'

Not enough sand, not enough sawdust, men slip in the blood like in a Chaplin film, the officers put their side of the argument:

'No, no *coups de grâce*, we have to save money, my dear fellow, it's war, let's hope it's all over soon, no, you can't leave now, the streets around the square have not be made secure, yes, all afternoon, still, you're not too badly off here, I'd gladly change places with you,

neither victim nor executioner, and this evening you'll have hard
words for us in your despatch.'

*

In Max's story set in Savoie, there won't be any little chimney sweeps,
and not too much *fondue*, and nor of *tartiflette*, *tartiflette* is less well
known but if you use the best potatoes it's a dish fit for kings. Max
searches for a simple turn of phrase, as simple as the air up there,
simple as a Jules Renard anecdote, to forget Shanghai, to forget the
Riff, sunset of an evening over dun-coloured hills that ripple like a
horse's chest, in the Riff too prisoners had their throats cut, thousands
of Spanish soldiers in the hands of Abd el-Krim, no, not officers, and
the Spaniards gassed Riffian villages, three waves of bombers at dawn,
green-fingered dawn, the chemicals work more efficiently in the
morning dew, put all that behind you and tell a story set in the Alps,
a couple, they walk through fields on the edge of a village, they have a
dog on a lead.

'And in the background,' says Hans, 'we'll hear the soughing of the
wind, the rich earth, smells of the underwood, and a few clouds over
the mountain tops to catch the last flames of the sun, French-style
Alpenglühen?'

That's about the size of it, it would be good if Hans would agree to
write the descriptive bits, Max would include beneath the title 'Sets
and props by Hans Kappler', very smart, but don't give me any of
those meandering sentences with endless ramifications, subordinate
clauses, interpolated clauses, antepositions, breast-beating, details,
twenty lines of self-torment before we reach a full stop or the end of
the paragraph, exactly the sort of thing that goes down so well in
Germany, here readers are on the lazy side.

Hans smiles, Max does not realise that Hans is currently struggling
with a fit of melancholia, he shouldn't have mentioned meandering
sentences, he searches for a word that will correct his lapse, but Hans
goes on as if nothing had happened:

'You know, talking of descriptions, Colette went on writing
descriptions for Willy's books long after they went their separate ways,

one day he ordered a few pages of Mediterranean landscape for a novel, she started and then stalled, though she knew the Côte d'Azur well, she asked if she could change it for Franche-Comté, it didn't bother Willy, and when the book was going to press someone asked if it was true that if you looked out of a window in Franche-Comté you could really see the sea.'

Actually, Hans would do it much more seriously, look, we're being watched, Max and Hans are in a dark, unused corner of the Jardin du Luxembourg, a few badly parked wheelbarrows, a great heap of dead leaves and, in the middle, staring out at them, on a small plinth, a rather unprepossessing bust, an awkward-looking customer, a bronze done by some second-rater, modelled in haste, Flaubert.

Max and Hans immediately drop everything and start talking about Flaubert, there were moments when he loathed descriptions, the ridiculous accuracy, the lumbering effort, art lies in the imprecise, true but what about Madame Arnoux and her ribbons right at the beginning, pressing against her temples, and her grey hair at the end, and also in his correspondence, old Gustave, when he speaks of the detail which draws attention away from the larger picture but must be retained because ultimately everything falls into perspective, wonderful details, Hans has raised one finger, a scholarly gesture, then he blushes.

And for Max it is unheard of to see Hans do such a thing, Hans, eyes shining, cheeks red, finger raised in the direction of the front of the Senate building, a letter by Flaubert, he recites:

' "The woman . . ." '

Hans tries to capture the manner of a teacher dictating Thales's theorem in the middle of the Jardin du Luxembourg, but his face goes red the moment he starts, he cannot control his face, he recites in French:

' "The woman you fuck . . ." '

He hesitates, or pretends to hesitate, he specifies, it's a letter to Bouilhet. And for Max, it's unprecedented, if it had been in German Hans would never have dared. He recites in his virtually accentless French, one finger towards the Senate:

'"... who you fuck doggy-style, naked, in front of an old veneered mahogany pier-glass," Max, I think it was particularly the pier-glass and the mahogany that interested him, veneered mahogany.'

'You're right,' says Max, 'and in your novels you too have put some very fine furniture.'

'True, but not everything a man can do when he's enjoying the company of a lady.'

'Not even in a first draft?'

Hans does not reply, a short silence, Max restarts the conversation, how will Hans manage to make his descriptions stick? trade secret, says Hans, but why don't you tell me your story that has no chimney sweeps from Savoie in it but contains *tartiflette*, a true story, which I take to mean ninety-five per cent made up; no, Hans has got it wrong, it really is a true story, Max spent two weeks up there and was told it by the whole village and the valley; Hans continues to have his doubts, a couple, a stroll, a hunting-dog, that rings true enough, but it would be enough to hold the reader? it needs something which is out of the ordinary, and fast.

'What struck me,' says Max, 'is that the man had a wooden leg.'

'And these days is a wooden leg particularly striking? Did he come back with it from the war?'

'Douaumont. The woman had this strange look in her eye, intense and absent, a faint smile, she was physically stronger, but it seemed that he was supporting and guiding her. She looked as if she was miles away.'

'Yes ...'

Hans almost said *ja* or even *yo*, that ever-so-slightly below-the-salt *yo* used by his friend Johann, all those years ago, at the start of the war, just before the sabre-thrust, that's what's left of Johann in Hans's mind, a hesitation between *ja* and *yo*, has been happening several times a day for fifteen years, but Hans says *oui*, in Paris he takes more trouble, he forces himself to say every last word in French, to get *oui* to come as naturally as it does to any true-born Parisian is the most difficult thing of all, he says:

'Yes, the enigmatic female, that can give you up to twenty thousand readers; in Maupassant, she'd be the woman who has been spurned and has not forgiven, her burning jealousy will henceforth be unspoken, she has the smile of a woman who has every day the rest of her life to wreak her revenge, you could do worse, but watch out for clichés, and what about the dog?'

Max smiles, his face brightens, a splendid Irish setter, nothing delicate about him, Max's hands draw a rounded shape in space, a dog muscled from its runs in the open air, racing through the long grass, only two spurts of flame visible, its ears, at intervals. It's a story which is out of the ordinary, Hans, the man is a native of the place, the woman has come from Switzerland, before the war, they met in 1913, in Geneva, on the Pont du Mont Blanc, it was early one afternoon, she was leaving the Valais to go to France, he was going to the shops, he could never remember which one, maybe he was going to Payot's for some books.

Hans visualises the scene, you'd need to check if Payot's bookshop existed at the time, your hero sees the woman from a distance, that gives us time to sketch the background, he's reached the middle of the bridge, the water and the mountains sway gently, their looming bulk tinged with blue, a few well-fed birds watch the hands of the passers-by, on the roofs of the great hotels flags flap, bright sun, Hôtel des Bergues, we'll need to say a word about the Hôtel des Bergues at this point, you need occasionally to be able to do the postcard stuff, now for the woman!

'It's the fluid way she walks that first strikes Thomas,' says Max, 'the man's name is Thomas, Thomas de Vèze, old aristocracy badly mauled by history, I think I'll only use his Christian name, an attractive walk, somewhat unusual for a woman at that time, neither uneven nor constricted, as flowing as her skirt, steady rhythm, he told me that women often have one foot more forthright than the other, but not her, she comes towards him, brisk, resolute, dark hair, no hat, in Geneva, can you imagine? She's not wearing gloves, doesn't lower her eyes, her clear blue eyes.'

'It's as vivid as if I was there,' says Hans, 'when she passes Thomas he turns, like any self-respecting Frenchman he is inspecting her backside, that "royal rear-guard when amorous battle is joined", and he starts to follow her.'

'No, you're not even close, even today Thomas still has no idea what got into him: just as she is about to walk past him, he calls out, "You are so beautiful!"'

'This Thomas de Vèze is a novice, Max, even in Germany no one would do a thing like that.'

'She answered: "And who might you be?" They stayed together, they walked along the north side of the lake.'

'Max, I can see her, she's just eaten, she felt sated, drowsy, now she has forgotten how full she felt, for the setting I suggest initially a furtive note, a light breeze, from time to time it turns the leaves on the trees and shows their silver backs.'

Max has told Hans don't mock, Thomas wants to know everything, the woman says her name is Hélène, she has just left her whole life behind, for reasons which do not concern him, her voice is low.

'Right,' says Hans, 'a contralto, I've always liked contralto voices.'

And Hans's mouth stays open, his chin begins to tremble, like the chin of a person who is about to cry, Hans is completely lost for words, you think you're strong, you've managed to get everything in perspective, memories all in order, sorted, 1913, Arosa, Waltenberg, the giggles, the frozen lake, the large eagle, the bicycle rides, the raised bed, the hole in the chair, the recriminations when he looked at his watch, tea-time, the first time, her hand around the back of his neck, pink on the mountain tops, her breast outlined against the light in the window recess, and even that silly business one day at the Waldhaus, America too is tidied away, relegated to the distant future, transformed into the abstract idea of a destination, and Hans has met other women, some of them 'hurt' him as they say, an excellent feeling, to be able at last to say 'contralto voices' without shaking, without blushing, we used to go to see Madame Nietnagel, each week we'd go down to Lucerne, I loved it, we looked like an old married couple on an outing, when Lena looked at me as she sang, Nietnagel would say don't turn your head like that, it strains the vocal cords, puts a strain on everything, Nietnagel's crocodile eyes on me, she would say 'Kappler, too many consonants in this name', her crocodile gaze went over my head, became vague, I knew she was looking out of the window, she was watching for the sun, its rays on the pale yellow walls of the room, she really made Lena work, on the way back, in the train, Lena would lean her head on my shoulder, once she said 'Kappler, Kappler, *I* like your name.'

You think you've succeeded in settling everything down, you say 'contralto voices' and then your stupid chin starts to tremble, an itty-bitty muscle, a stupid spasm, you close your mouth, but then your lower lip starts doing it too, and the lower jaw joins in, actually during the war I'd stopped crying altogether, Lena could be there, in the middle of the track, she could walk down the middle of the track, a wool dress in autumn colours, or hold my arm instead of Max's, Max says nothing, he has taken Max by the elbow, he falls in step with him, he doesn't ask a question but Hans answers it all the same:

'I never saw her again. I've no idea where she is.'

A silence.

'If you want, I could try to find her for you.'

'No, Max, this is my business, if I'd wanted to I'd have already found her, I think about her every morning and that's enough, I'm waiting, I really wish I had changed.'

'So you'd find the same woman again? If you aren't the same man, she won't love you any more.'

'She didn't love me anyway, in Switzerland we parted company over something very painful, such stupidity, she behaved extremely well, I'm utterly useless, I'm going to change.'

Hans's chin has started behaving itself. Hans laughs softly, he will become irresistible, he will go to America, Max will come with him, but Hans will not go, all I'm good for is letting my mind wander, it's what I like best, I have a reputation for being a hard worker but in reality I spend hours and hours daydreaming, Hans's dreams are the dreams of a shop girl, of a megalomaniac, of revenge, this morning I dreamed that as I was on my way to the Jardin du Luxembourg, I was stopped by ticket-collectors on the underground, they called the police although I hadn't done anything wrong, I reminded them of my rights, the police were there, my German accent, I dreamed I got beaten up by the police, I was taken to the police station, an inspector who reads books sized up the situation, I'd been roughed up by the police, I got even, I demonstrated that what they'd done was totally and utterly wrong, the inspector talked to me about my books, in the end I got my own back, and quite right too, I dream daily, a vivid dream life, I see Lena again in my dreams and while I'm doing that I get older sitting at my desk, I am soluble in the air of my office, and also I dream because feeling guilty about dreaming gives me the strength to work. But for the moment, Max, I have to avoid saying 'contralto voices', so this girl of yours from the Valais will have to have a higher voice, but one just as good, which will easily rise above the noise of the traffic and the waves from the lake which sometimes beat against the embankment, wavelets.

In fact, according to Max, it was Thomas who did most of the talking. 'Max, I can hear him from here! This Thomas de Vèze talks like he's never talked before, either to other people or to himself, he has just had the encounter of his life, his own words sound strange to him, more indulgent about things in general, hesitant, he doesn't know anything any more, and at the same time he has the feeling that he is about to discover everything, he gets confused, keeps glancing at her breasts, she doesn't seem to mind, sometimes the gap in the material widens, he gets a glimpse of her collarbones, there is ten times less to see than there is of the women walking here in these gardens today, but for him it's a continent, such things could give a man a thrill back then in 1913, a glimpse of a collarbone. Look Max, since I am responsible for the props in your story, am I allowed to place a very fine chain around her neck, a brief mention, not one of those meandering sentences?'

'Very well, but no crosses or medallions, she doesn't believe in God and she's guessed that he's a Protestant from the way he sees things, by his clothes, a Protestant who does not hate himself and finds it difficult to pretend to be innocent, just like me. And towards the end of the afternoon . . .'

'One moment, Max! Leave them to me for five minutes, after all this is Lake Geneva! What is it about Thomas that caught the woman's eye?'

'Maybe my ears,' says Max, 'I think I'd like to lend him my ears.'

'Some people might think you're too sensitive about your ears, I know what they're like, I can see them!'

'You can see my ears?'

'Don't go on, I can see Thomas, and Hélène, they're walking along the side of Lake Geneva, they're pretending to identify the trees on the embankment or in the gardens of the houses, they're sauntering, the branches of some trees hang so low that the leaves kiss their own shadows on the ground, others still have just a soft dusting of buds, she knows that they are thuyas, she knows far more about all this than yon Thomas, some gardens are virtually well-tended parks, with whole expanses of violets or dahlias, or form large-scale arrangements in which the yellow of the hydrangea rubs shoulders with the pale blue of the asters, and the eye skips away only to alight for a moment on the musky orange, old-gold, ochre and burned-toast of a clump of helenium, the hardest ones to grow are the ochre, the trick is how to preserve that warmth without letting it turn shrill.'

With his hands, Hans traces a circle in the air, the warmth of the ochre, what Lena said about singing, smuggle ochre into the voice, a round voice, full, ochre is a colour which has retained a degree of chiaroscuro in its warmth. He resumes:

'Ochre is more difficult than the red you get in those poker-shaped flowers that stand on tall stems, Knophofia.'

Hans is getting heated, he always gets heated when he's speaking French, the names of flowers, the pleasure of manipulating rare words, lush flora, of course he has been cheating, Max points to beds full of flowers spread out before them, all labelled, the meticulous labours of the squad of gardeners responsible for the Luxembourg. Hans adds:

'I'm sure they have the same flowers in Geneva.'

Now and then Thomas and Hélène hear, in the bushes, a flutter of wings, or the raucous, caressing cry of the crows as they fly up into the oaks.

'No, Hans, in France the caressing cry of crows doesn't work, it sounds pretty but the word crow has been tainted by our anti-clerical battles and has never been the same since, so not easy to use it as a sound effect for a lover's tryst.'

'All right I'll make it blackbirds,' says Hans, 'males or maybe females, I need something to liven up the background.'

'Use rooks, I've no idea why but rooks seem to me to be more noble than blackbirds. Hans, we're not getting anywhere.'

'Did you or did you not put me in charge of sets and props? Right then. So what jobs do they do?'

'She's a nurse and midwife and he's a schoolteacher.'

'You're full of surprises.'

'He quickly realises that she is drifting.'

'Max! . . . And does he already know that she has just been left badly shaken by a first love affair?'

'He'll soon find out.'

'*Yo*! An affair with a married man . . .'

'I can't hide anything from you.'

There's only one way for Max to get out of this corner, and that is to ensure that the rest follows plausibly from this start which you might call novelettish, the only drawback being, if it's true, that people always guess everything, but maybe they'll like it even so. So how does the rest go?

'The rest? Thomas will take Hélène back home with him where they need someone just like her, this won't happen without the cat being set among the pigeons, a Swiss woman in the middle of Haute-Savoie.'

'She'll be terrified by your Savoyards, Max, she'll want to bring hygiene to the natives, to those one-room mountain hovels, cow on one side, humans on the other, a channel in the middle for the slurry, and the cow's tail attached with a line to ensure she doesn't spray too much, they'll have to wash, so there'll be confrontations in the offing, and the sheep sleeping under the bed, and the empty racks where they put the hay, and all those wonderful objects . . .'

'Talking of objects, Hans, did you know that in those parts the barber still charges you thirty centimes extra for the "spoon"?'

'What "spoon"?'

'He slides it into your mouth to make your cheek swell out for the razor.'

'And if you don't want the spoon?'

'He does it with his thumb.'

'*Scheisse!*'

'There must be the equivalent in your part of the world.'

'In the South, in Bavaria, but we must get on.'

'Thomas settles Hélène there,' says Max, 'but we've forgotten something, the boat trip, from Geneva to Évian, there's nothing quite like it.'

'You're right, the boat is called *The Simplon*, it was commissioned in 1911, it sails in a triangle serving Geneva, Ouchy and Évian, it's white, very wide, with one big paddle-wheel on each side, displacement two thousand eight hundred tons, can carry more than a thousand passengers; from the side, the sloped yellow-and-black funnel gives her a racing look, and in the prow, when there's fog, youngsters can imagine they're on an ocean-going liner ploughing through the spray on the high seas.'

'I was forgetting that in another life Monsieur Kappler was a marine engineer.'

'It's a thing of unalloyed beauty, Max, when you stand in the middle of the lower deck and get a good look at the Winterthur mechanism the builder left open to the elements: two steel rods each two metres long are propelled horizontally from the boiler and thrust into the cast-iron cradle which receives them, they are then pulled back by an invisible hand before being pushed forward once more, they alternate, a mixture of fury and concentration, turning the axle of the paddle-wheels by means of two enormous cranks, two great asymmetrical blocks of steel which once they start rotating first check then boost the thrust, and over each joint of the whole mechanism, over each friction point, is a glass jar with a brass cap full of oil which keeps all moving parts lubricated, a pretty amber-coloured oil.'

'That's more than enough about your Winterthur, we must get on, Hans, we must start climbing and install our couple up in the mountains, in a village a thousand metres high.'

'You want me to do it for you?'

Max takes his friend by the arm and makes as if to move him along:

'Must get on.'

'Did he marry her?'

'Not straight away.'

'We'll have to explain how they settle in, the formalities, how a foreign national can take her place in a French village, Max, but it'll be static, any ideas for livening it up?'

'A trollop.'

'A what?'

'A trollop, the one who was there before.'

'In the schoolteacher's life?'

'The daughter of a factory-owner in the valley, also a Protestant.'

'With big feet?'

'No, I was told she was beautiful, a bit on the thin side by rural standards, but beautiful, she made their lives impossible.'

'That's good, very good! In Germany, women wouldn't dare. What does it mean in those parts, made their lives impossible?'

'One morning, Hélène found thirty villagers on the doorstep of the house she'd been allocated, grim faces, the most awful scene. Hans, do you know who all those ladies were?'

Around them, statues of the queens of France, Hans looks up at Catherine de Medici, profile, shoulders, his mind wanders; twenty metres away, under the trees, girls wearing frocks are playing tennis, they've strung a red rope between two tree trunks, they shout, they don't have the proper footwear, one of them has just come from the fountain carrying a bucket, the bucket has a hole in it, it lets water escape in a thin jet, the girl carrying the bucket redraws the markings of their court with the jet of water, where have these tennis-playing young women come from?

'Probably working girls,' says Max.

'What sort of working girls?'

'Girls in the rag trade, it's their midday break, an apple instead of lunch, helps them keep their figures, a spot of exercise here before they go back to their Saint-Sulpice workshops, I wrote a piece about them a couple of months back, the girls working for Mavillon were on strike, furs, big patriotic firm, their employers say they are the elves of the fashion business, eighteen francs a day for ten hours' work and a canny technique for keeping them up to the mark: they give them all the same job to do at the same time, the last three to finish get the sack and the time taken by the first becomes the standard for the job.'

'Did you publish that?'

'Don't be silly, it's Bolshevik stuff, I just told one of the girls to write a few lines for *L'Humanité*. But let's get on, Hans, thirty villagers are gathered outside Hélène's house, the factory-owner's daughter has spread the word that this stranger is a witch who casts spells, people believe her, the same people who get work from her father.'

'They are factory workers?'

'Locals who work on the land, during the winter in Haute-Savoie they make moving parts for watches and turn out screws for the industries in the valley, it represents half their income.'

'Will you let me describe the machines, the way they work? the screw-making will have my special screw-tiny.'

'What has made the daughter so furious is that she's been told that Thomas doesn't actually sleep with the nurse, rumour has it that "he respects her".'

'Whereas he didn't waste any time having his wicked way with your young, Protestant factory-owner's daughter, as though she were a farm-girl.'

'She didn't put up much of a fight, and Thomas wasn't the first. She wouldn't have minded if he'd actually slept with another girl, she'd have got herself another boy, but it was the "respect" that stuck in her craw.'

'And elsewhere.'

'Max, you've got a dirty mind.'

'So did Thomas go to bed with Hélène in the end?'

'It was she who decided that's how things had to be. He was perfect, behaved like a beaten dog. He atoned for the faults of the other man, back in Switzerland, the married man, the one she walked out on so dramatically.'

'And probably an abortion, with uterine scrape. Have a care, Max! this is turning into melodrama.'

'You want to describe the uterine scrape?'

'Absolutely not! What's next?'

'Eventually she is melted by Thomas's impeccable manner.'

'Will you let me do the crucial scene, Max? I never dared write one.'

'I've already written it.'

'In that case you can let me have Thomas's chalet, I've always wanted to do a large chalet, such a play of stresses in the timber frame of a chalet.'

'Thomas's isn't all that big, people in those parts don't like big chalets, too hard to heat.'

'Mustn't worry about that,' says Hans, 'a large chalet built of dark wood, which creaks in the wind, just as you enter the village, a large family chalet, in fact two families of schoolteachers could live in it but your schoolteacher lives there by himself, you go in by a small door, under a rather fine lintel, with a date carved on it a full century ago, a corridor, a coat stand, door on the left, the main living room, it opens into two others, you return to the corridor, on the right are a kitchen and three other rooms, at the far end there are stairs, not a staircase actually, steps without a banister, you have to hang on to the risers, you reach a sort of mezzanine, then more steps, no a ladder, long and warped, when you get to the top a huge cross beam blocks your way across the whole width of the loft, thirty centimetres from the floor, you have to climb over it, there are two others exactly like it in the middle and at the far end of the loft, they're called tie-beams, in the middle of these beams is a vertical beam, like a thick mast, the whole attic looks like a three-masted ship without the sails, another beam is aligned along the top of the three masts, it marks the apex of the roof, the ridge, a huge loft, it's very solid, more than solid, it's intelligent, the weight of the roof ridge, the weight of the roof, all that weight flows down through the three masts,' Hans holds his clenched hands out in front of him, makes a movement which sweeps downwards along imaginary poles, 'a force which sweeps down the entire length of the masts, along the tie-beams, it pushes down, trying to bend them, to snap them in the middle, but simultaneously it is opposed by the collective resistance of the tie-beams which strain with every fibre, and there is yet another pressure which arcs diagonally from the ridge and follows the sloping sides of the roof, then along the rafters, forces which run slantwise down the sides of a triangle, placing huge strains on its base at both ends and pushing them outwards,' Hans's hands have flowed slantwise down the side of the triangle, 'the three cross-beams are as taut as hawsers, and the forces cancel each other, the forces which drop vertically along the masts are cancelled out by the resistance of each of the tie-beams and the forces which flow slantwise down the sloping roof and bear down on each end,' Hans holds his hands apart horizontally, 'the weight becomes weightless, interplay of forces, the three stout masts are technically speaking crown-posts, or king-posts, Max, let me tell it, the details will be forgotten, what will stay in the mind will be cement, tie-beams, rafters, crown-posts, a ship, a set of beams, of interlocking forces, when the wind blows it creaks like a glorious sailing ship, I'd love to live in a place like that, I'd turn it into a library, make it my study.'

'Mainly you'd be cold,' says Max.

Hans and Max are again walking past Bacchus and his nymphs, a large bronze, the god, pot-belly to the fore, riding his donkey, lithe Maenads writhing around Bacchus, one has fallen flat on her back, arms and legs pointing in all directions, Hans stops:

'It's not as vivid as Flaubert.'

'True, but they're highly sexed, he's rather a fright but they're trying to do all sorts to him.'

They move off, walk down the steps leading to the middle of the gardens, take a turn around the boating pond, a little boy is crying, his boat has got trapped in the middle of the pond, at the base of the fountain, where the wind does not reach, where the falling water creates a gentle vortex, where sails droop; the boat cannot escape, its fate is certain, it's doomed, the little boy's mother tells him, serves him right, what he deserves, else they'll come and pinch it off of him, so stop that row, you're a big boy now, the mother gives the boy a slap on the hand.

Two weeks ago all the boats on the lake were stolen, for a laugh, vandals broke into the shed in the central avenue, the whole flotilla was found a week later, nonetheless, a boat can vanish, especially a sailing boat, the boy who's crying knows a legend about a boat that vanished, it's what is about to happen to his boat now, it will disappear beneath the central fountain, answering the call of all the sailing boats which have already disappeared down all the years, it will go to join them on the great ocean, an armada of sailing boats on the mighty main, the boy will command his boat, next in line to the admiral's ship, huge waves, captains courageous, he looks up towards the façade of the Senate.

Waves as high as buildings, the ships do battle with the storm, the last battle, but the man who owns the sailing boats and his assistant come with a thin rope which they hold across the pond, they loop the rope over the mast of the foundering sailing boat, haul it into more navigable waters, the wind blowing over the surface of the small pond can now swell the sails, the sun laughs in the playing fountain, the child has to go, no, you can't have another turn, you do it on purpose, you do it every time I'm nice, never content, you always manage to blame me and cry, you were told one turn, a turn is a quarter of an hour, not longer, you agreed, and now you're crying, you're a naughty boy, every time I let you have your way you take advantage and ask for something else and start crying, if you don't stop you'll never get anything ever again!

Hans would have liked Max to let him tell at least part of the love scene between Thomas and Hélène, he's cross with Max for having beaten him to it:

'A scene on the steamy side, Max, you've taken the best bit! I long to write something like that.'

'It won't be published.'

'But you'll let me read the scene you've written?'

'No,' says Max, 'I had the nerve to put it down on paper but I wouldn't dare let anyone read it, I'm afraid of what they would say.'

'If you wrote it, it means that you did meet a woman.'

'You know how it works, the only assignation you have is with your reader.'

And Max explains to Hans that he finds it hard to face the public, to abandon the public he imagines while he's writing and face the real public, he has a very complicated notion of the public, obviously he has a number of imaginary allies who accompany his every sentence, but always looming before him, on his right, is someone who keeps an eye on him and never approves of anything he writes, and someone sitting in front of him, who cannot read the sentence Max is writing but seems to know it even as it is being written, it seems as if it is being written in the head of this person at the same time as it is being written on Max's page and the sentence brings a smile to the face of this faceless person, a smile which is unbearably knowing, it isn't a friendly reader who might say I can hear too many iambic pentameters in that clause, too much blank verse, too many things that are self-evident, do you really want to say that the milkman came at ten past five? No, the person who sits opposite Max and smiles is a person who is ready to deride everything Max thinks particularly fine in his writing.

Not a person as kindly disposed as the Hans who warned him he was perilously close to melodrama, not someone meticulous like his boss François Mérien, who told him this sentence lacks rhythm, take out a verb here, put a full stop there, no, someone who doesn't need Max's book but in Max's mind is nevertheless a person of some importance, a person who smiles when he says:

'Does this serve a useful purpose?'

Max hasn't called this faceless face names as he most assuredly would if he were dealing with some stupid critic, the blank face is that of both the public he needs to win over and the public which will never be won over, the public which Max masters for all its peevish ill-temper and its ideas about what a proper novel should be, the public which is there every time Max removes or amends a word and whispers in his ear:

'Surely you don't think you can get away with just doing that?'

The loathsome, indispensable public with its insane and insatiable demand for nebulous quality, everything that makes Max feel furious with himself for not responding to the madness that is his, and angry also with this public which asks so much of him, he has finally grown to resent everyone who constitutes the real public, people like him, his contemporaries, everyone, every phrase becomes a cage and he resents all the people he invites to watch him in his cage, he feels he'd like to stuff their heads down a lavatory pan.

He begins to hate people who never did anything to him, simply because he himself admits he's no good at anything, and sometimes Max turns pragmatic, holds forth, what comes closest to it in tone is the small, shrill voice of the modish journalist, a touch limp-wristed, a touch corrupt.

Max knows that limp-wristed and corrupt are idiotic words, but he needs them to give a name to the hate which seizes him, to give a name to what will be his failure, he has laid his book before that faceless face, saying here you are, know me, I who have done everything to ensure that you will recognise yourself in me, a struggle for recognition, he will lose, limp-wristed, corrupt, a name for the someone who would make fun of his love scene, of the fornucopia, as Flaubert might say, which Max wrote at a time when it could still cost an author dear, when at the very least it would get your book banned in public and limit you to the market for erotic books aimed at lawyers.

And Max is all the more wary because not long ago, in Paris, a writer was found guilty of uttering an obscenity, Victor Margueritte, fined, stripped of his Legion of Honour for having written in *La Garçonne*, 'she was picking the dark-hued lavender, seeing her crouching loins he had seized his chance, he had pulled up her skirt and she had felt the fiery god possess her.'

His Legion of Honour, they say he got it for gallantry in the field. Stripped of it for crouching loins. Plus two or three paragraphs of Sapphic delights. Max wrote his sex scene because he is jealous, not of

Margueritte, a novelist whom you can see pulling the strings rather too obviously, but jealous of an Englishman whose book he has read which in London circulates under the counter.

This book has infuriated Max because as he read it he realised that it was exactly what he would have liked to write himself, it would have established his reputation in a blaze of lightning as a novelist out of the ordinary run of novelists, and he begins to hate the novelist he would like to have been as much as he hates the reader he would like to have.

So it transpired that this middle-aged Englishman wrote the book Max should have written, it wasn't so much the story of a gamekeeper and a lady, but the man's direct way with words like hole, penis, fuck, balls, and at the same time a great tenderness, a taste of apple, delicate gestures, everything that made Max want to say that this happened with Thomas because Hélène could no longer put up with Thomas's hangdog manner, she took her decision, despite all the smiles of the reader whose sarcastic comments already ring in Max's ears, she will give him what he has been wanting since the day they first met, only Max will use fewer metaphors than the Englishman, and Hélène will take the lead, for she will no longer allow herself to be taken.

One evening she goes to Thomas's house, a nightdress under her cloak, goes up to his room, he is already asleep, she takes off her cloak, the rustle wakes him, don't move! she gets into the bed, pins Thomas on his back, prevents him making the movements which men always think necessary for the seduction of the female, she doesn't want him to try to seduce her, men always hurt her, so she will undress him.

Thomas's penis when she removes his short drawers, but she has no wish to touch it, she is not a whore, she comes to him out of tenderness, now Thomas is naked the skin softer than she expected she is melted by it she repeats don't move! and lowers herself on to Thomas laying her head next to his neck, the penis, an apprehension, Thomas makes a movement which hurts her, she says sh! she takes the penis, and Max thinks that the word penis is not entirely appropriate but what other word is there? penis is medical, phallus, too erudite, sex, that's it, his sex.

It's the word Max thought of first on the *métro*, when the

frightened look in the eyes of a woman passenger made him realise that he'd just said it out loud while searching for what he wanted to say, but actually the word came to mind too soon, Max amused himself trying out other words, cock, tail, prick, dick, he changes his mind, and Hélène guides the penis with her hand saying 'gently', she is the one who thrusts, the contact surprises her, it's more than a year since she felt it and the sensation is not the same as with the man then, Thomas does not dare look at Hélène, he has closed his eyes and breathes more loudly, she says 'don't hold back'.

She prevents Thomas from moving, she does not want him to go off as they say, she'd be afraid, and though she had not planned it in advance she's the one now who, I'll have to reread the English author thinks Max, he can prolong, describe, change the metaphors the one about melting her all molten, the one about the sword, the one about heaving waves breaking over the very quick of her, leave all that to the poets along with the one about the yielding scissors and the cloth, Hélène moves slowly, just think about what she's doing, faster keep an eye on Thomas his breathing thinks of herself she tenses suddenly, and when it's over don't have too many flowers not as many hyacinth bells as the English writer has, nor meadowsweet nor bluebells, Thomas has given a little cry, she is prone on top of him, from time to time faint stirring between her legs, how many years has she wasted? She kisses Thomas's face, licks the tears on his cheeks, he tries to caress her she restrains him she does not want to find just another male, with their jerking, their writhing, that stupid look they put on their faces when they dominate, the ridiculous thrusting of their buttocks, some really bite, others just leave unbearable lovebites on the neck, one of her friends told her, 'They learn about love in the army, at the same time as they learn to march in step.'

She licks Thomas's neck, lips, breasts, armpits, desires crowd in on her, she kisses his navel, moves down to the cloud of dark hair, thinks his man-hair is beautiful, his sex has shrunk in the calm shadows, no more threatening than a comma, as on a Michelangelo, she swings her hair over it, she begins to sing softly.

'So I'm not going to be allowed to read the scene which steams up this chalet in the mountains, Max, couldn't you at least let me add a fireplace, a blazing hearth?'

'Or a pier-glass in veneered mahogany? Now it's you who are writing novelettes, the story hasn't even begun yet.'

'You mean this fornucopia isn't the climax of the tale?'

'I shan't be publishing any scenes of fucking.'

'Sixty years from now, Max, on the manuscript, it would make an interesting variant, variants give life to books.'

'No variant.'

'So there won't be any culminating point to your story, nor even a climactic turn of phrase such as you get in the *Arabian Nights*, a moment of pure poetry, "the buttocks of the young man were so beautiful that the eighteen young girls began to sing"?'

'No scene with fucking, I shall be elliptical, I'll pick up the story just after.'

'And what did Thomas do just after?'

'He did what you or I did.'

'He went back to sleep?'

'He went off to the war, after marrying Hélène, she didn't agree with the war, but she was Swiss.'

'He was like us, bit of a socialist, hostile before . . .'

'His name on the B list of people to be arrested on the first day of the mobilisation.'

'And in your country as in Germany nobody was arrested because everybody agreed with everybody else, it was to be the war to end war.'

'He acted with heroism.'

'Your military medal?'

'To which you can add the Legion of Honour and the *croix de guerre.*'

'*Und ein* leg less.'

'Hélène didn't care for that at all, Thomas came home in 1917, a hero, even the Paris papers had reported his gallantry, an exemplary record, schoolteacher, a pacifist, a son of the people, a captain within three years, six times wounded, defended his position at Verdun to the last man and brought back his wounded CO – one of the Langle de Carys, a Catholic and a royalist – crawled, though he himself had very little feeling in his right leg, genuine front-page material, with coloured-up sketches, they had a field day, but Hélène didn't care for it at all.'

'1917, your best period, there was some wavering in the ranks.'

'In yours too,' says Max. 'Hélène was working in an armaments factory in the valley, she was discreet but well-informed, when Thomas came home she starting talking to people: Zimmerwald, Kienthal, the conferences supporting revolutionary peace, she took part in strikes.'

'Was she arrested?'

'Don't be silly! In France, my dear fellow, you don't touch the wives of heroes.'

'They gave her her head?'

'They took good care of her, but that too is a long story.'

Hans and Max are sitting on two metal chairs, a woman in a dark anthracite uniform appears behind them, they didn't see her coming, she has a small metal cylinder hanging from her waist, a cylinder with a handle, like the ones bus conductors have, we were just leaving, I can't help that, two turns of the handle, she holds out two tickets, ten *sous* please, she moves off in the direction of a small boy who has just sat down and leaps up the moment he spots her, hey you there, the boy runs off.

Max and Hans have stood up, they have walked on for another hour among the flâneurs, the children, the gardeners, they watch the women walking and try to spot feet that might stumble, with her it's the left one, you lost, it was the right, they never agree, they lingered to watch the chess players, Max took Hans by the arm when he sensed that his friend fancied a game, they went on their way until they came across the croquet players and there it was Hans's turn to make Max walk on, Max laughed saying that for once I have a temptation which is easy to resist! They passed quite near the cluster of hives just by the gate that opens into the rue d'Assas, bees were still busying around, flashes of brown and gold.

They spoke of the not-too-distant future, for once they would be spending a longer time together, a meeting in the mountains, intellectuals, politicians, artists, economists, scholars, philosophers, neutral ground, an obscure mountain fastness, in Switzerland, Max is to go there for his paper, Hans because he is a member of the 'Committee for the United States of Europe', it will take place in six months, right at the beginning of spring.

Max has asked Hans if he'd have time to accompany him to Brussels, I've promised a young writer I know that I'd take him, Brussels and Antwerp, we're doing a tour of the paintings of James Ensor, *Skeletons Fighting over a Herring, King Plague*, he's been mad about the artist for ages, he wants to see the originals again, the great Belgian orgy, delicate doesn't come into it, *The Exception Giving the Rule a Kick up the Backside.* Do you know Ensor's work?'

'Not really. Who's the young writer?'

'Shows real promise of becoming a great writer, we met half a dozen years ago, he ducked out of school to write, he's already knocked about the world a bit, he was in Indochina when I was in the Riff, we used to tell each other about the things we'd seen, he was braver than I was, war reporter, anticolonialist, slap-bang in the middle of Saigon, now he publishes art books, he has already written a novel, it's a very ambitious novel, East v. West no holds barred, and on the side he publishes short, funny tales, I'll introduce you and one of these days too I'll take you too to see Ensor's paintings, the truth of the century, *Christ entering Brussels*, terrific, Christ riding a donkey, banners saying 'Long Live the Social State', honest wives being groped in the procession, foaming glasses of beer and Jesus, three sheets to the wind, delivering a blessing on the whole shebang.

'He's a painter of great character, if you don't want to buy one of his paintings he takes it off its nail and puts it on the floor, like a mat, he's also got a gift for turning a brilliant insult, "demolition man with a sucking mouthpart" for instance is not at all bad to describe a critic.

My young writer friend loves it. Ensor also does small drawings from life, the beach at Ostend, men playing croquet on the sand, and girls too, Indian ink, three strokes of a brush, and it's all there, the nine hoops, the mallet swinging like a pendulum between the legs, and the wind blowing among the players, the air is the hardest to do, did I ever tell you I played croquet with Lyautey? It was in Rabat, at the Residence, two years ago, just before Pétain had Lyautey turfed out of Morocco, look, some people never see anything coming!'

Max shows Hans a young woman sitting on the knee of the young man she's with, the chair lady comes up, the man laughs.

'Hang on,' says Max, 'just watch.'

Hans and Max stand stock still.

The young woman has stayed sitting on the man's knee, both of them snigger at the chair lady who goes off and comes back almost immediately with a policeman, the man and woman get to their feet, move off, blast on a whistle, the forefinger of the gendarme points in their direction, the couple turn, freeze, everyone is staring at them, the policeman's finger bends into a hook, reels them in with an imaginary line, the couple walk back to the policeman who marches them off to one of the police boxes outside the Senate. Max takes Hans by the elbow once more.

'Amusing, don't you think? Yes, Ensor also does pastiches of Rembrandt, Doctors Pouffamatus and Transmouffe examining the stools of King Darius after the battle of Gaugamela, to determine if the defeat can be attributed to the disorders of the royal intestine, which is quite an undertaking! The Belgians reckon him to be a great painter, but they can't control him, the burghers lose sleep over him, he paints a strike and demonstration, he has this man with his skull split open by a rifle butt, people living on a second floor spew their dinner over police underneath, while on the top floor a man with a pig's head kisses a woman who makes a face, I'm going to take another look at all that with my boy genius, sure you won't come to Brussels with us?'

Hans has run out of time, at least that's what he tells Max, what he doesn't say is that he wants to call in at the Paris office of Cunard, information about transatlantic crossings, perhaps even cross on the *Queen Mary* from Le Havre to Southampton, just to see what it's like to stride around the decks thinking of Lena, Hans makes up a story about having to be in Berlin in two days, shall they meet up again at Waltenberg, at the Waldhaus, in March?

Sure, says Max. It's not that he's that terribly keen to make the trip to Waltenberg in March, but his boss wants him to go. Max would much rather cover some sporting event, yes, write a novel and report on a sports event, lend his support to the French rugby team which is going through a bad patch, that's what I need, creativity, play, it would make a change from the Riff and Shanghai, you know what I'll miss by going to Waltenberg? I'm going to miss the Six Days, I'll miss the France-Portugal football match, France-England at rugby at the Stade Colombes, and I shall also miss, here Max does a shuffle with his legs, jabs the air with his fists, a child stares at him, Battalina v. Genscher, the world light-heavyweight title fight, because I'm also going to have to report on a session of the council of the League of Nations before travelling up that mountain, I'm quite happy, long live Waltenberg and its yahoos! And meanwhile I shall continue to beaver away at my story set in Savoie, I'll leave blanks for you to add landscapes and objects.

Max stops, grabs Hans by the sleeve and brings him to a halt, an affectionate look:

'Hans, wouldn't you like the both of us to go to America and look for her? Mérien would find me an assignment. You could tell me why you're afraid to find her, why you're such a difficult man. What happened up there, all those years ago?'

*

Silence, the silence and the stillness must have woken him, Max listens, a moment later metallic clangs, voices, then silence again, Max does not like it, it's not long ago since silence like this was a direct threat to life and limb, his and those of any number of others, a silence which was a prelude to earthquake or apocalypse, depending on the ideas and beliefs of the individual, ideas and beliefs which in the coming minutes would no longer carry any weight whatsoever, the grotesque lull which turns you into a lump of meat smelling of fear, flattened to the ground, ready for the mincer.

Max listens, dispersing any remaining sleep in his state of high alert.

Creaking sounds. They come from outside, though not entirely, the creaking of metal and wood, very clear in the silence, small jolts, bustle and activity at one end of the coach. Max pulls back the curtain over his window, it's very dark, he must be in Switzerland, he scrapes away enough frost to make a hole to see through the glass: feeble light cast by two lamp posts, a clock, nobody about, a quarter to four, no sound of any machinery, and the world, or what is left of it at this hour, has ceased turning.

On a sign Max reads *Landquart*, it's the start of the Grisons, the high mountains. The coach has stopped rocking. More jolts. Max realises now that his coach is being hitched to a high-altitude train. Silence again, a voice says something in German, a lilting kind of German, and slowly the coach starts moving, accompanied by the puffing of a shorter-breathed engine than the 'Mountain' which Max had admired before boarding it in the Gare de l'Est. The platform slips past, then a few houses, they scowl under an uncertain moon.

He's on his way to Küblis, from there he can get a bus or car to Waltenberg, his left shoulder aches, and it will get worse and worse, he tells himself, as he thinks of his wounds for the first time that day, of the after-effects that will be his legacy into old age.

The spring of 1929 began officially a few days ago and it is even colder here than it was in Paris, all Max can make out through the fog of his own breath are the high walls the snowplough has left along each side of the track, they're so close to the sides of the coaches you could almost touch them with your hand. In places the sides of this corridor are lower, and permit glimpses of a landscape muffled by snow under the moon, dimpled with occasional swellings, like large bubbles: buried villages.

Even during the winters of the Great War he had never seen as much snow, under the stars the land is broken white, as far as the eye can see, a cold planet.

The train is not travelling fast, Max tries to get back to sleep, try to keep off that left shoulder, he lies on his other side, shuts his eyes, but he hears the blood thumping in his temples, a sure sign of insomnia, he is cross with himself for waking up, don't get all het up, breathe slowly, stop thinking about it, try inventing one of those conscious dreams you use for getting off to sleep, he closes his eyes, imagines he is a policeman, a superintendent, calm temperament, and he embarks on his favourite plot, a story about a beautiful suspect who says she committed a murder but whose innocence he sets out to prove and thus unmask the husband, but the woman is strange, the more she wins Max over to her side and makes him want to get her out of trouble, the more inextricably guilty she seems, and on the contrary the superintendent's well-meaning enquiries merely multiply the charges against the woman whose name he wants to clear.

Ordinarily, it's a pretty effective dream, his mind, unable to break out of the labyrinth and come up with some way of saving the woman, overheats, gives up and surrenders to the security of real dreams which he can feel gradually encroaching on his initial reverie, they provoke short-circuits which last longer and longer, commotions, things that happen for no reason: the suspect he is interrogating suddenly turns into the teacher he had when he was little or a dead friend with whom he sallies forth to buy a bunch of violets in an unknown town.

Max fights against these genuine dreams, he takes back the initiative, questions his suspect with glee, brings her to the edge of a confession, then the friend returns, turns nasty, the violets disappear, his old teacher takes off her overall, the motor races wildly and Max swings into a copper-bottomed sleep.

At least that's the theory, but in this train which will take more than another three hours to deposit him below Waltenberg, Max senses that his little subterfuge isn't working, he is much too wide awake now, all the problems of his waking hours will start up, he's thirsty, he knows that if he gets out of his couchette and puts the light on to pour himself a glass of water he will start something irreversible, he won't be able to go back to bed.

Sleep? what's the point? sleep, silence: death's antechambers. Not feeling too cheery this morning, he gets up, drinks the glass of water, he feels another need, he opens the small cupboard, shuts it again, without using the chamber pot, he doesn't like them, even the ones provided by the *Compagnie internationale des wagons-lits et des grands express européens,* with gold border and blue monogram, he smiles, Mérien's neat observation:

'I want a journalist to be as curious as a piss-pot.'

He pulls his coat over his pyjamas and puts on his slippers, as a young man he loathed the slippers his mother bought him, he preferred leather mules, even in winter.

One night, in the trenches, a comrade had said:

'When it's all over I'm going to buy myself some slippers, and I'll kill the first bastard who laughs.'

Max steps out of his compartment and walks all the way to the toilet at the far end of the coach.

When he gets back, he is no longer sleepy nor does he want to be sleepy, he just feels stiff and sluggish, with a migraine in the offing, he opens one of the windows in the corridor, holds his face into the icy air, reaches out with one hand to snatch snow from the walls that are so close and rub it over his eyes and cheeks, not such a good idea, the roughness under the crystals, no more hand or even no more arm, it only takes a moment, like that time at Véneux, at the start of 1918, a series of appalling howls and hissings, the trench is about to collapse, they'd looked at each other: a whizzing shell bursts, just metres away! they were all there, Stéphane with his mouth hanging open, eyes like chapel hatpegs, short of one hand, he wasn't screaming yet as he would in the seconds that followed, Max remembers that at that moment he'd thought:

'So that's what's meant by looking surprised.'

Then the screams, which gangrene had turned into moans a few days later in the battalion infirmary, Stéphane whom they comfort through the smell of disinfectant and rot:

'Thought we'd come and cheer you up, take you out of your shell.'

And the medic who sees no point in further amputations:

'The gangrene has spread everywhere.'

Max closes the window, he looks down the length of the corridor of his sleeping-car, the designs on the lampshades overhead, he runs his hand over the grained lemonwood veneer, the discreet brass handrail, and proceeds slowly, so that he feels the thickness of the pile of the carpet under his feet, everything is so very orderly, luxurious, calm, he enters his compartment, gives up all thought of his couchette, sits on the seat opposite, somewhat put out that he's not facing the engine, but if you're that pernickety then you're going to find growing old something of a strain.

Stéphane's father was Mérien, François Mérien, owner of *Le Soir*, more than a million copies sold daily. Six months ago, in September, he'd said to Max:

'I'm sending you to cover these shenanigans because I want the real behind-the-scenes story, what they're saying about Europe, their thinking, their politics, all their discussions, what's behind it all, cash? Power? Treason? A conspiracy? They'll talk about values, that's good, I like values, I want every man jack of them stripped bare! You'll be staying with them at the Waldhaus, all expenses paid, keep the bar bill down, off you go, and make the most of it.'

That was the boss for you, short-fuse, but he was very fond of Max, Max had written to him immediately with an account of Stéphane's death, without frills, death of a hero, Mérien had been grateful to Max, he'd never tried to check what was hidden behind what he had written and, as the years passed, he, who was obsessed with clarity, assuaged his fatherly grief with the myth of a bullet in the head on the field of honour that he would never have entertained for one moment if it had been someone else.

'So what are you going to do now?' Mérien had asked Max at the very start of their relationship, when he took Max to lunch so he could hear him talk about his son.

It was just after what had been called the Victory. Max had not answered, he was drifting; before the war, he'd wanted to be a writer, he'd given that idea up. One day, Mérien had pressed him and the only thing Max could think of to say was:

'I'd like to be a Nosy Parker.'

Mérien had given him a job and turned him into a reporter:

'From this day henceforth, subject, verb, object. For adjectives, see me first!'

He'd also ordered him not to write any sentence more than fifteen words long, then he'd loosened the reins. Max had become one of his best reporters.

As the years passed, Max had come to like François Mérien very much. His boss had a reputation for being a coarse man, but Max knew that he set aside one hour every day to translate Pindar or Tacitus, he had known Mallarmé, Jules Renard, Gabriel Fauré, and at least once a day he would go into the editorial room and shout:

'Make Wendy feel weepy and Andy feel randy! And let's do it with style!'

He had interests in a company that made a vitamin-enriched cordial, he handed out bottles of the stuff to politicians terrorised by his paper and its two and a half million readership, an ambiguous gift, some ministers tried to find out through Max whether the cordial was a friendly gesture or if it meant Mérien considered that they were finished.

Even Poincaré had been scared the day Max asked him for his opinion of the cordial:

'Tell your employer that I partake regularly. And that I never felt better in my life.'

Another minister had offered to make the cordial part of the weekly rations given to colonial troops, Mérien had refused and laughingly told Max:

'That would be like something out of Feydeau. It's best if all this stays between him and me.'

And Max never did discover if Mérien seriously believed in the effectiveness of his cordial.

In the train, too late now to go back to sleep, too early for breakfast, Max tries to think, morning is his best time for ideas, before midday you can still put one thought with another and shake them up with a stub of pencil and a notebook, a number 2 lead pencil, not too bold but soft enough to keep up with your thoughts, a 2B. After lunch, all Max is good for is living.

He shuts his eyes, opens them again, it's daylight, the frost has gone from the window, slopes now figure much more prominently in the landscape, Max muses, remembers, lets his mind wander, abandons his memories, stops tapping a pointless rhythm with his pencil, these European conferences, find a subject for a real think-piece, with more punch than usual, make it dramatic, deep down it's all theatre, difficult, when they're on stage the characters refuse to play down their personalities, or rather Max himself finds it difficult to keep his distance, you feel much too much at home with these people, money, power, you were a pawn in the game, not insignificant but a pawn nonetheless, surplus to requirements.

Max never completed his studies after the war was over, a writerly vocation, I'd have been better off becoming a respectable solicitor, with wife, in some market-town, then I wouldn't be hearing someone like Wendel saying you know, a job like mine, pure fluke, and if I stay it's because I don't really have a choice, no one else would do it.

All these people want to spend time with Max, they need him, he is the intermediary between them and the hoi polloi they all want to nobble, organise, direct, control, and above all be loved by.

'Single-minded about collective action': a phrase that goes into the notebook, Max is not entirely happy with it, come back to it later, big people convinced they are right to bully the little people they rule and

become even more authoritarian and inflexible, make this clearer, find
an image, a parable, newspaper readers like a parable, a story:

'Max! find me a story!' Mérien would say sometimes when one of
his pieces seemed too abstract.

A life spent as a famous reporter, you drink champagne with Van
Ryssel who owns a fifth of all the steelworks in Europe, you lunch as
the guest of Duissard whose bank holds a large percentage of Van
Ryssel's shares, and you even bought a hat with Merken, at Freiburg,
as if you could care less, Merken put one hand on your shoulder saying
good choice I'll get one too, Merkel copied you, a dark-grey bowler,
we have the same tastes, true, but it's not you who goes home, picks
up a pen and writes *What is Metaphysics?* No, you go back to the paper
to churn out copy and you never made anything of that meeting, you
were taught for two years by Bergson and you never made anything of
that either, at least Merken got a hat out of it, Max also likes Willi
Münzenberg, one of the men Moscow never fails to send to congresses
like this, and there's also Hans who doubts everything and is the only
really new writer to have emerged since the war, Max even recalls the
beauty spot on the thigh of Madame de Valréas, their common muse,
whose strength of will is the driving force behind these conferences,
everyone here likes Max and wants to be liked by him.

Throughout his entire youth, Max sought to win them over, I am
becoming the finest writer of my generation, all doors are open to me,
wonderful pages you put in the waste-paper basket without even rereading them, and it's only when you can no longer be bothered to
write any more pages wonderful or otherwise that people start swarming all over you asking for articles for newspapers, parties at the
Valréases, highly enjoyable, until the day Mérien yelled at you:

'No fancy literary stuff! An article is only something you've got time
to read in the bog!'

Max knows all that, he forgets, the dream of writing that will endure,
he pulls himself together, keep at the daily task, he learns to forget just
enough to allow him to cling to his dream, to make the most of it, like

a good cigar or a liqueur, reread Maupassant, Turgenev fast enough for you to come away with the impression that you could do as well.

Madame de Valréas! Universal muse to the fine assembled company, a Baroness, and there is no shortage of Baronesses in these circles, but she has a genuine ancestry, money, the talents which go with money, good legs, teeth extremely suitable for smiling with, has a certain *je ne sais quoi*, as they used to say before the war, Max has slept with her, just once, at the close of the Belle Époque, a fine house, the property of a banker, in Brittany, with a wheat field which sloped directly down to the beach, the gold of the sand, the green of the ears of corn dotted with bright red freckles, ribbons, parasols, and all of it whipped by squally showers and blustering winds combined with whatever the cloud-factory threw up at the sun, the gleam of molten metal, the flap of flags, the tumults of opium, sandstorms, blowing with a strength which lent an aura of bravery to the little dolls in their Sunday best who had come to the beach to kill their germs in the foaming brine and uttered coltish shrieks of terror each time a wave nibbled a crinoline hem or a shoe, in May 1914, the good times.

By about two in the morning, all the couples had formed up, Max and Madame de Valréas had found themselves alone in the lounge, Max is not very susceptible to the charms of La Valréas, a state of affairs which allows him to risk a remark:

'It looks, Baroness, as if we've been left to ourselves.'

Was she really tight? Just drunk enough for you to be allowed to do whatever you wanted? She'd followed Max, glass in hand, and had made him go first as they went up the stairs, saying:

'The best bit is always the stairs.'

The Baroness is a virtuoso conversation-maker, when she speaks she backs her words with movements of her hands:

'You know, I'm from the south of France.'

Not quite. The way she speaks is altogether more calculated than loquacious, she makes a point of flexing the joints of each finger and puts you in mind of a crazed orchestra maestro, or a spider's legs, her voice is metallic, her eyes violet, her body a touch on the skinny side, but buttocks which fear no man's scrutiny, she is an expert, she knows that what she does with her hands takes in only the simpletons, and that it captivates men who are receptive to well-oiled gestures, she has a dream: to reconcile France and Germany and help build a Europe free of Russians and Yanks, from Danzig to Bordeaux and Athens.

'Not forgetting Italy, where very interesting things are happening.'

A Europe with clout, with workers who turn up on time, who are paid fairly but not excessively, well-behaved adolescents, large families, full churches and respect for success.

Max tries to sum up all that in one phrase, for a cross-title for the paper, he notes: 'The Values of Wartime Togetherness Applied to Entire Continent'. He puts his pencil down, stares at his reflection in the window and murmurs to himself: 'with La Valréas having the right to open her legs whenever she feels like.'

In the corridor, a bell, a voice:

'Breakfast! First Sitting!'

Already. Max gets washed and dressed quickly.

He is sitting at a table in the restaurant-car, he has half an hour before he arrives at Küblis, he makes a few more notes, the main points of what will happen, four or five people are already in the process of drawing up the Seminar's end-of-conference resolution, this sort of conference only works if the organisers know in advance where they're going, it's only a talking-shop but it's precisely on these occasions that they fine-tune ideas on which political campaigns and votes in parliaments will later turn, an old-fashioned free-for-all, Max had seen what had happened in London the previous year.

Six days spent on a few odds and ends of phrases, 'how we must give shape to the natural momentum of the European economy', that was included at the behest of Van Ryssel and the steel cartel, 'maintaining the status quo of frontiers inside Europe', one for the Poles and the Czechs, 'safeguarding the sovereignty of nations', for the Germans this means withdrawing the French and Belgian occupying troops, and then other forms of words, rather more cryptic, 'to give full scope to initiatives taken by industry', trade unionists insisted on the addition of 'with proper regard to social justice', so it gets added, all under the beaming smiles of the bankers and the socialists, the carp, the rabbit and a sickly-sweet sauce.

And behind all that, other arguments about words among philosophers or economists, even artists get stuck in, apparently at Waltenberg a great deal will turn on the question of values, value, what actually defines value? In economics, in morality, in art? The value of a loaf of bread, of a painting, an idea, a machine, an alliance, Max feels exhausted at the mere thought of having to write it all up, he ought never to have accepted the *Globe* assignment, should have just stuck to reporting it for *Le Soir*, *Le Globe* is a stylish weekly, glossy paper, fine photos, in-depth articles across two pages, prestige.

For *Le Soir*, no problem, a piece of five hundred words maximum every day, the most common words in the language, make absolutely clear what's at stake, 'between the supporters of the United States of Europe and the defenders of old-style nationalism, who will run out winners?' or possibly 'tension at Waltenberg between theorists and pragmatists', no, that would never get through, Max can hear Mérien's voice, journalism, Wendy and Andy, imagine the look on Andy's face if you plonked him down in front of Merken's musings about 'the spatiality of available intrasocietal being', no point including anything about philosophy for *Le Soir*, or else find another angle, turn it into a fight, the boar, Merken is a definite boar, now what's Regel like? Battle Royal between the Heron and the Boar, in François Mérien's view this argument between philosophers would turn out badly:

'In private the Germans, at this juncture, aren't doing themselves any favours.'

With *Le Globe* it's altogether different, almost too much space, in it Max has just read a remarkable article it has published, three full pages on the theory of relativity, a major paper by a young physicist, name of Tellheim, you can follow it as easily as a detective story, you can understand every word but it's not over-simplified, Max has been told that Tellheim would be at the Waldhaus, the thought of sharing the hospitality of *Le Globe* with such a clever man paralyses Max, he should have stayed in Paris, covered sports events, the light-heavies, Battalina v. Genscher! And the Vel' d'hiv!

Chapter 10

1929

An Artichoke Heart

In which we observe many philosophers, economists, politicians, artists, and even young Lilstein, as they meet in the Swiss Grisons to help make Truth manifest.

In which Hans Kappler feels dizzy as he hears a Lied *being sung in the Waldhaus Hotel.*

In which the Swiss Army suddenly looms.

In which young Lilstein gets drunk on French cognac.

In which Max Goffard spends his one and only wedding night.

Waltenberg, March 1929

Philosophy must constantly exercise
within the heart of Europe's humanity its
function of straightening what is crooked.
Ernst Cassirer

The mountain, the Waldhaus, the peace to begin with, the clientele of skiers, and then on the Saturday morning within hours it all starts to buzz, Baroness Valréas in the vast lobby like Napoleon at Austerlitz, with her staff officers, secretaries, her executive director, her daughter Frédérique, and Erna, the debates secretary, she calls them her 'brigade', and Merken's wife and the wife of Regel, Merken's rival, the room booked for the philosophy seminar is too small, maybe, but it's out of the question for the philosophers to be put in the room booked for the economists, and the large lounge-cum-library has been earmarked for the political sessions which will be chaired by Monsieur Briand; the private secretaries start to play dirty tricks on each other, the chamber-maids and valets of the principal guests meet up again, yes, last time was London, then again there's the whole of the hotel's staff, less sophisticated, who keep an eye on the valets from the city, to see how they do things but refuse to be taken in by their fine airs, they're the same as us, they obey orders.

Some arrive by car, the bodywork of some cars is made of different kinds of precious wood, others prefer the cable-car, more amusing, each time a cable-car arrives it brings two or three guests and the next cars come up with their trunks and their servants, each time a car passes a pylon it dips, some pylons are very tall, if you're sitting in the

447

front it's quite terrifying, like being on the Figure of Eight, the passengers got very cold and Max found a moment to say:

'The last time it was just here the floor gave way.'

The seats of the cable-cars are covered with midnight-blue plush, the plush is changed annually, large trunks being wheeled round and round the lobby, the frantic bustle in and of itself is hardly worth a second glance, it's when one of the trunks cannot be located that it becomes entertaining, Maynes's wife, for instance, the ballerina, has lost her main trunk, not hysterical, never in public, merely on the verge of tears.

The husband in a panic. John Maynes, Sir John, is reshaping the economy of Europe and he's in a panic about a trunk, yes, it's his wife's, no, there are no gems in it but even so, important things, a cabin-trunk, one side for hanging clothes, the other with drawers, no, not monogrammed canvas, nothing common or garden, genuine English leather, dark, very handsome, must have been left on the Paris train, the train that has carried on to Coire and not just Coire, it goes to Vienna and Istanbul, Maynes, one metre ninety, stands out head and shoulders in the lobby, don't worry, I'll get a car and catch up with the train.

Madame Valréas says no you won't, but not to Maynes, to him she says:

'John, we'll try and find a solution.'

She cannot in any way contemplate the prospect of his tearing along the road to Vienna, a disaster, he'll be gone for at least two days, that's without reckoning avalanches, all this fuss over a bird-brained ballerina's knickers, oh yes, in the end Maynes told me that the most important item in the cabin-trunk was his wife's underwear, he's one of the major figures attending the Seminar, he's not to budge from here, we'll find another solution, we'll send a telegram.

In the garage, Mrs Maynes's trunk was in the garage, a silly mistake by a servant, not one of the hotel's employees, they know their business, it must have been a servant of one of the participants, good, that's all settled, Madame de Valréas has embraced Maynes's wife.

The merry-go-round could now start up again, in full swing now, ladies' maids in dark coats, cloche hats, they size up the hotel maids, they soon get the picture, don't be nice to them, you tell them what to do, but careful how you go with the head housekeeper, she gives no quarter, she treats you as if you were a guest but if you're not on the right floor or if you use the guests' stairs you get a ticking-off sharpish and you're reported to the Baroness's office, so know your place, it's the rule, and the lift is out of bounds.

In the lobby, Maynes is very pleased to meet up again with Édouard, Van Ryssel's French novelist friend, they haven't yet got the key to their rooms, the trunk has been found, they take time to talk, and Mrs Maynes knows she mustn't interrupt her husband when he's talking to a writer.

Whenever she loses a trunk, all she has to do is look glum and John can think of nothing but her, it's delightful, but one day I interrupted my husband when he was chatting to Mrs Woolf, I can't stand the woman but they say she writes wonderful novels, I told them if you'd care to come back down to earth we could go in to dinner, John didn't say anything, they got up pleasantly enough and all through dinner they made small talk, I would have liked them to continue their discussion with us, when I'd interrupted them Mrs Woolf was talking about the gulf which splits masculine intelligence in two, I thought she'd be keen to pursue this with other women but actually she went out of her way not to say anything interesting, and every time it seemed that she might John always managed to bring the conversation back to small talk, he's very English that way. I didn't say anything, not even afterwards, I truly think he doesn't realise what he's doing when he's like that, if I made a scene he would know and it wouldn't make a scrap of difference, I prefer to reserve any scenes I make for the women who run after him.

So Mrs Maynes leaves her husband to chat with his friend Édouard. It's an Édouard who's on top form, smooth face, black hat, long cape, long legs, he is very proud of his long legs, Maynes doesn't let him get a word in edgeways, he has read Édouard's latest novel in French, all this novel-within-a-novel business isn't the crux of your book, what I like about it so much is the way you deal with those hearts of gold, family men who want morality to be the gold standard of existence, the character who's a judge, his name is Moulinard, I think he's so funny! side-glance from Maynes at the fair young man who is with Édouard, Édouard hasn't introduced him, Maynes would like to ask him his name, but that might make Édouard cross.

If Édouard hasn't said anything to me it's because he doesn't trust this young man who can't be all that attached to him, don't say anything, the young man won't always be with dear Édouard, this Moulinard of yours, Édouard, the more he demands total truthfulness from his children, the more they lie to him, a heart of gold who asks for words of gold, the ultimate value, and all he gets in return are lies, false coin, it's exactly like economics, no good trying to base anything on the gold standard, it was all right before 1914, your novel is spot on, gold is a folly, Mr Churchill re-established the gold standard in Britain, it led to inflation and unemployment, I've explained all that in a short tract, I'll give you a copy, *The Economic Aftermath of Mr Churchill*, what's needed is what you make your young hero say at the start of the novel, 'let's give credit', obviously you aren't talking specifically about economics, but the young man eventually decides to 'give credit' to his mother's good taste, does he not? he discovers that his father is not really his father, trust is dead, he has just lost his gold standard, if I may so express it, belief is dead so he says 'let's give credit', and to his friends he offers an exchange, it's a brilliant idea, now don't say it isn't, I do realise that you aren't an economist but you've said something quite new that we could act on today.

Why doesn't the young man look at me when I'm talking? Is he bored? Am I boring him? No, when I'm bored I always look at the person I'm talking to, he won't look at me, he's good-looking, he knows it, a little too much, it would be delightful to make him feel unsure of himself, Édouard spoils him, he mollycoddles him, the generalised offer of credit, Édouard old man, essence of trade, that's what you've hit on, it's what we need, circulation, healthy circulation, without dogma or gold standard, a glance from Maynes at the young man.

Out of the corner of her eye, the Baroness watches Maynes and Édouard who have finally got to their feet, she'd like to talk to them but she has Hans Kappler on her hands, he is already anxious to get back to Germany, one of the key men of the Seminar, an important humanist, classed as left-wing, a great one for bringing people together, yet he wants to be off when he's hardly got here, it's not on account of a trunk but because of a woman, you couldn't make it up, he is in the lobby with Madame de Valréas, he can hear singing, a rehearsal, *die Welt ist leer*, the world is empty, it's coming from out-side, Schumann, not a soprano, a fine, rounded voice, Hans thinks fast, he blanches, Madame de Valréas is suddenly worried, Hans does his best to reassure:

'It's nothing, Baroness, it's the altitude, I should have listened to my doctor, I feel slightly dizzy.'

The Baroness puts it down to the heat, the central heating, she makes Hans step out on to the terrace, lean on me.

The voice that sings is coming from somewhere above their heads, one of the rooms at the front of the building, Hans cannot pin it down, the Baroness puts a hand on his shoulder.

'You like Schumann, Hans, I know for a fact, it's a surprise I organised with you specifically in mind, it's for the last day, you are so pale.'

'Touch of altitude sickness, Baroness, my heart, I don't know if I'll be able to stay.'

'Hans, what on earth are you talking about? Don't be silly, every-one gets it, the body needs to adapt, that's all, and you're not to tell me some story about this being the first time you've been here, that time before the war, I know everything.'

The Baroness's violet eyes bore into Hans's, she lifts an eyebrow, raises a half-smile to make her mouth more interesting, arches her neck, he was trembling as he stood next to me, I held him by the arm, it was no good blaming the altitude, I knew at once that there was a woman behind it, he was trying to identify the window as if it was a matter of both death and salvation, I didn't let go of him, I made a mistake about the recital, a genuine recital, Hans, and that's not all,

God he's shaking, the recital was a mistake, Hans leaving the Seminar the day he arrives, it's crazy, I was told he might know her, he's shaking, he's playing this up, turn the knife in the wound without further ado:

'Come along, Hans, let's go and say hello to the singer, or should I call her a prima donna or a diva? I never know what to say, she'll be delighted.'

'First I must rest a while, Baroness.'

No, he must see her, kiss her on both cheeks, then he'll stay and stop being a nuisance, find some reason, I'm sure she's read your books, Hans, a very personable young woman, come along, damn he's digging his heels in, her name's Stirnweiss, that's done the trick, I've said the name and he's stopped looking green at the gills, he's stopped shaking, he has a silly grin on his face, she's not the one he was thinking of, he's turned back into a man, shoulders back and eyes forward.

'An excellent programme, Hans: Schubert, Schumann, a closing recital, a little bird told me you like romantic *Lied,* you see I'm not just a wicked aristocrat in the pay of the steel cartel and ruthless capitalists, I have a heart and a soul, and my European soul chooses music of which my heart makes a gift to my friends, come along!'

Hans does not wish to take the lift, Madame de Valréas holds Hans's left hand and puts her right arm around his waist, they make their way up the great staircase which rises in a spiral from the middle of the lobby, Hans is not as thin as he looks, she leads him, third floor, corridor on the left, Hans is alert, nonchalant, you change very quickly, what play-acting!

'Stirnweiss, you say, Baroness? I never came across the name, except perhaps in an American newspaper a few years ago.'

'Impossible, Hans, I think she did live for some time in the United States. But I gather that Stirnweiss is her stage name.'

The sound of singing comes nearer, Hans can hear it quite distinctly now, the *Lied* of the widow, a pseudonym, the voice is not as low but rounder than before, with more feeling, she has come back to feeling, it's her, the song of the widow, she used to sing it, the end of love, *die Welt ist leer*, the world is empty, I'm the one who's empty, I shall stand before her clothed in my foolishness, as I did once before, is it fifteen years already? a stupid gesture, I am as empty as I was then, not one drop of blood left, a stage name, and it's her voice, with feeling, she's nearly overdoing it, she must always have been emotional underneath but she hid it, it was Nietnagel who couldn't stand sentiment, she used to say that if you want sentiment in music listen to a military band, I'd rather anything than come face to face with her now, Baroness Valréas's hand tightens on Hans's faintly faltering hip, she blames herself, I never know when to keep my mouth shut, I only had to say stage name and he blanches, this man was a hero in the war and he turns white the moment you say stage name, where's Max got to? never there when you need him, he could look after his friend, keep him here. On the third-floor landing, Hans and Madame de Valréas see Maynes coming towards them.

'There, Hans, you see one of our greatest economists.'

'Yes,' says Hans, 'we've already met, in London.'

One hand is kissed, another is shaken, a few friendly words, no need to hurry, mustn't give the impression that we are in a hurry, Hans latches on to Maynes, delighted to see you again, you know, I didn't altogether follow what you said in London about public works and the exponential effect; Maynes isn't going to pass up an opportunity for converting someone like Kappler, a European with influence, to the cause of public works, even on the landing of a hotel, it's simple, it can be summed up in a few words, if you permit, Baroness, such works always provide a greater return than the sums invested in them, one Deutschmark invested in public works gives a return of two or three for the overall economy, it's precisely what happened with the great pyramids, it's the same with the aftermath of earthquakes.

Maynes leans on the aged oak rail which runs the length of the landing and tries to make it vibrate, fails, smiles, ditto with war, wars have always increased the wealth of nations, you have to know how to spend, bankers don't like spending, but it's the same with their gold mines, a very fixed smile on the face of Madame de Valréas, Maynes talks too much, she hasn't let go of Hans, you spend money digging holes in the ground, adds Maynes, and you call them gold mines, in fact they're large-scale works, but when it's about gold, bankers call it sound finance.

Madame de Valréas does not want him to be cut off mid-flow, but Maynes is telling stories about bankers, next time she'll ask Van Ryssel:

'Do you believe all this business about public works as much as Maynes does? He spends his time telling me all about it, he's very nice but I find him just a trifle dogmatic.'

And Van Ryssel will understand that Madame de Valréas speaks on an equal footing with the great and the good, he will ask her when she'd had this talk with Maynes, Van Ryssel is suspicious, a man does not produce a quarter of all Europe's steel without acquiring a suspicious mind, he is convinced that here in the Waldhaus meetings are being held and will continue to be held without him, since he himself spends his time organising secret meetings he believes everyone else is doing the same, Madame de Valréas will not disabuse him, she will invite him to take coffee with Briand and Wolkenhove, and Van Ryssel will think he's being invited to a secret meeting, afterwards it will be easier, just between ourselves:

'My dear Van Ryssel, I'm going to have to ask you to do me a large favour.'

'You have no need to ask, Baroness, no sacrifice is too great for our cause, besides sacrifice is not the word, it's an investment.'

Smile on Van Ryssel's face, they're wrong to call him a toad, he can be very charming:

'My accountant has already taken care of it, Baroness.'

On the landing, Maynes is in full spate:

'If you decided to sink a deep hole, bury bottles full of old bank-notes in it and then pay private companies to dig the old banknotes up again, you could almost get rid of unemployment.'

Hans is grateful to Maynes for having detained him as he

approached his time of trial, Madame de Valréas sets the example of the mine and the bottles to one side, Maynes drives on, that said, it would be better to build houses and dams to bring electricity to the houses, but for many of my colleagues that would be tantamount to communism, Madame de Valréas will have no truck with the word communism, it's always the same with Maynes, give him his head and he says the most inappropriate things.

'John, we could listen to you for hours, you have such a wonderful flair for economics, but you must excuse us, there is someone Hans and I positively must see.'

'I haven't forgotten,' says Hans, 'why don't you come with us, we're going to see Madame Stirnweiss.'

The Baroness decides this is an excellent idea, they will bear Maynes off with them just as far as the end of the corridor, Stirnweiss will be delighted, but I know for certain that you'll never dare set foot in Stirnweiss's suite without your wife, you miserable economic worm, you'd like to but you're scared of your lady wife, you'd do anything rather than come with us, she repeats the invitation:

'Come along then, John.'

Again the voice in the corridor, *Nun hast du mir*, you first made my heart ache, *la re re re*, she repeats the first bars, the ache, more rubato than ever, but no tremolo, Hans has the impression that the voice at times comes perilously near to a tremolo, you're not being fair, if there's a tremolo it's in your own voice, whereas she is actually singing, she has changed, a stage name, but it's her, Maynes has disappeared, Hans and the Baroness are just a few steps from the door, Hans asks:

'How does the end of this corridor relate to the rest of the building? It's the end of one wing, is that right? The north wing? I seem to recall that the north wing extends outward over a precipice, twenty metres of building projecting over nothing, a crazy idea.'

'I've no idea, Hans, but twenty metres is an exaggeration, it's all supported on steel girders sunk into the granite, they're a great deal more solid than the Eiffel Tower, and the views are stunning, it's not the neatly tended kind of landscape but then we are in the heart of the high Alps after all, young mountains.'

'I am convinced. Baroness, that these rooms here look out over a void.'

From the start, in the hotel, everything has been going round and round at high speed, ideas, glances, forces, words, around the rooms and through the corridors, out on to the terraces, over the dance floor, down the gravel walks outside, in the rooms, even as far as the village to which you sometimes went down by the only permanent means of access when snow blocked the new road, the cable-railway, with its yellow-and-black cars, forces and rhythms, people don't talk over aperitifs the way they do in the formal sessions, over drinks or in the lounge it's speed that counts, words are tossed around to tickle up thoughts, no time is given for thoughts to develop, they're shot at like guinea-fowl, what we want is the abolition of private property, the communism you're so fond of means misery all round plus watch-towers, have you seen that photo of Venice on the front page? All the canals frozen solid, that's crazy, you get watchtowers because of war and wars are caused by you and your steel, in the world weather conference in Prague they're talking about global cooling, what happened about that colonel who was arrested in London charged with being a crook? A hero in the Great War, an Australian, the times we live in are a disgrace, Europe must get back to the ethnic superiority which made it great, the Neuville system is the key to the way the world will be organised, a system which will be neither capitalist nor socialist.

It will be simply scientific, it's a crisis of culture, nothing will be achieved without a return to God, if we are to end the current crisis we must invest in public works, the idea of God is the sign of a lazy mind, oppression comes from the state, if the state withers away so will oppression, and meanwhile what are you doing? As certain men talk they eye some young girl who they believe would be ready for anything because she's wearing long eyelashes, fascism is the absolute form of democracy, others look at the hands of young men, a clash of concepts, never pure concepts, concepts connected with power, money, jobs, red dawns, vested interests, profits, even dedication yields a dividend, it's when passions are roused that terror enters the fray, a great deal of blood needs to be shed before men return to their habitual indifference, that's an expression of Édouard's, a little further off you hear 'is Spinoza relevant in today's world?'

Sometimes a quieter group, after dinner, with Maynes again, one of the stars of the Waldhaus, always surrounded by people, a famous book on the economic consequences of the 1919 treaties, catastrophic consequences, he is rich, he defends capitalism, a wily defence, young Lilstein puts this to him 'communism means the Soviets plus electricity', to which he replies by quoting Edison's 'I'll make electricity so cheap that only the rich will be able to afford candles', he told Lilstein this is a game where you'll always lose.

None of which prevents Maynes from hating gold, the gold standard, received ideas, received values, he is in friendly disagreement with those he calls the neighbourhood bakers of laissez-faire economics, it's true, they don't like public expenditure, the creative deficit, they want a market of the pristine kind, the fox to be free in a free chicken-run.

'Why bakers?'

'Bakers,' says Maynes with an amused glance at Lilstein, 'because they make bread, liberals are always talking about bread, it's not labour that creates value, you're hungry you're willing to pay a hefty price for your first loaf, wonderful golden crust outside, soft inside, warm, but the fuller you get the less you are prepared to pay, so you reach the margin, the marginal usefulness of the loaf,' continues Maynes, 'is what defines its value, a relative value, the value which clashes with the usefulness of another commodity, your newspaper for example which until now you have refused to buy because you were thinking of your stomach, now that is what for the bakers constitutes the value of a commodity, it's a trifle strong but it allows them to express value in equations.'

It's at this point that Lilstein loses his temper, swindlers' equations, true value is the work of the producer, that is, of the worker, and one of Van Ryssel's aides calls him a Bolshevik, equality in slavery. Young

Lilstein is clumsy and rude but the ladies love him, a cherub standing one metre ninety in his socks. Do you really think so? Cherub? He's not so bad, darling, but he's an overgrown colt, a tall bony colt. Lilstein is very sharp-tongued, categorical, your relative value is a mask for exploitation.

Eventually Maynes takes Lilstein to one side and says:

'I share a good many of your ideas on the exploitation of workers, but if there is a real intra-social war as happened in Russia, that war will find me on the side of the cultured middle class.'

He pictures himself baring his chest to receive young Lilstein's bullets or alternatively imagines himself taking aim, this image makes him fall even more deeply in love with the adolescent and he becomes aware that another man is also watching Lilstein, it's Édouard, he was there, Cadio is watching Édouard.

Édouard is also watching young Tellheim, who is there at the personal invitation of Madame de Valréas, a discreet individual, quiet voice, unhurried gestures, middling height, fleshy, a disciple of Einstein.

Madame de Valréas welcomed him saying my dear Tellheim it's time my guests learned all about relativity, I loved your articles in *The Globe*, when you explain it, it all seems so simple, your armoured train, for example, with the guns mounted in the same turret, one facing forward and the other facing the rear, which fire simultaneously at targets the same distance away, have I got that right? And men with stop-watches under each target, Madame de Valréas slows her rate of speech, you see I've remembered it all, she puts one finger to the right, the shell fired forwards will take less time to hit the target, the other finger to the left, than the shell fired backwards, it's amazing, you must also tell us about the lifts, but not this evening, not just before bedtime, it scares me.

Young Tellheim is brilliant and pleasant, a rare mixture, Lilstein is fascinated by Tellheim who is only a few years older than he is yet people treat him as if he had already won a Nobel Prize, and Tellheim likes Lilstein a lot, his passion for willing the future lives of others.

He finds Lilstein's ideas simple but attractive, he promises himself he will read Marx more carefully, just now he doesn't have all that much time, I'm busy with the structure of the atom, I correspond with Monsieur Nils Bohr, but as soon as he has a moment Tellheim will read the book Lilstein has lent him on the State and the Revolution, he told Lilstein for me communist society is like a large laboratory full of free people.

Lilstein and Tellheim promise to meet up again this summer in Berlin, at the swimming baths, a young Christian philosopher, Moncel, hogs the conversation, science is like a clearing in the dark forest of mystery, man is continually widening the circle which borders the clearing, but at the same time, and by virtue of his efforts, he finds himself in contact with the shadow of the Unknown on a growing number of points.

'Max,' asks Madame de Valréas without a glance at Moncel, 'which do you prefer? The loaves of bread or the guns of the armoured train?'

She doesn't wait for an answer:

'Max, be good, why don't you too tell us a story about relativity?'

Max can no longer bear such drawing-room small talk, right now he'd much rather be at the Six Days, with his friends from the professional cycle track, Grassin, Boucheron, Wambat, the smell of embrocation, ether, dirty bunks, greasy food and ladies' perfume, last year Wambat had told him: 'the Six Days slims down me arse.'

Max will also miss the France *v.* England game, he remains polite, smiling and diffident.

'Tellheim tells it so much better than I, Baroness.'

'No! It's your turn, you annoying man, otherwise I shall wave my wand and turn you into a toad.'

'Once there was a flock of sheep which . . .'

'Max! I know all about this flock of sheep and the artillery fire during the war, you told me all about it last year and it has nothing to do with relativity.'

Madame de Valréas thrusts her palm out in Max's direction, long fingers spread like a spider's legs.

'But Baroness, there was indeed a flock of sheep, but not during the war, no guns, a flock, a hyena, and as much relativity as you could wish for, the hyena prowls round the flock, gruesome creature, the sheep poke fun at the hyena, it comes closer, coat stiff as a long-handled scrubbing brush, it growls, shows its teeth, stinking breath, the rams lower their horns, it backs away, the sheep sing in time "oh the lying beast he's in love", the hyena goes looking elsewhere, finds the corpse of an old wolf, enough there to eat for several days, and it gives the hyena an idea, it puts the wolf's skin on its back and runs back to settle the score with the sheep, panic in the flock, look out! a wolf!'

Hearing shouts people gather round, it's Max, the French news-paper man, he's so funny, he's telling a story about a hyena disguised as a wolf.

Max turns his back to the fireplace, not the one in the library but the one in the bar, an avant-garde fireplace, it is situated in the middle of the room, a concrete bowl three metres across under a circular hood made of brushed steel, a metal used for the manufacture of aeroplanes, with a fire-guard in the form of a fine steel-mesh curtain which hangs down from the hood and encircles the bowl, more a large brazier than a fireplace, it looks very fine but you cannot lean on it like Chateaubriand and hold forth, you are no longer in the centre of the picture, there are little centres everywhere at three hundred and sixty degrees around the brazier, adjacent circles, and people move from one to the next, the circles grow smaller or get bigger according to the relative interest generated.

Max always wants to have the biggest circle, he cries, watch out! a wolf! the sheep flee in a panic, a young ram cries chief it's not a wolf, chief, listen to me, that's no wolf, that's a hyena laughing, it's only a hyena disguised as a wolf, chief, no need to run away, it'll make the ewes' milk curdle, just a hyena, you deal with this with a quick flick of the horns, he starts to slow down, the chief bawls him out, Max also takes the part of the chief, he pumps his arms like a runner, run, imbecile, but chief, run I tell you, everyone knows it's a hyena but they don't mind in the least, because in the meantime the wolves will leave us alone, but chief the wolves also know it's only a hyena, exactly, lad, they hate hyenas, the hyena is pretending, we're pretending, everyone's happy, and at the same time we are practising running away for such time as we are confronted by a real wolf, but chief I could settle this hyena's hash for him, a solid thrust with my horns, I'll teach him what we sheep have got under our coats, all right go ahead, the hyena will also teach you something, Max turns towards the logs burning in the hearth:

'I've yet to find the right range, my nostalgic voice, do you think it's better with a traditional fireplace with fire-dogs, mantel, shelf and embossed back-plate? But it's amusing, being able to look through this steel curtain, I can see the ladies on the other side, through the flames.'

'You can also see the gentlemen, Max.'

'True, but I'm more interested in the ladies, with the old style of fireplace, you looked at the flames in the company of a lady.'

'Now, Max, finish the story!'

'To hear is to obey, Baroness: Go to it, says the chief ram to the young ram, the hyena will teach you that there are a lot worse things than hyenas disguised as wolves, idiot! And worst of all is the sheep who thinks he's only disguised as a sheep!'

An embarrassed silence falls upon the listeners, all eyes turn to Madame de Valréas, her ruffled feathers.

'Max, I fail to see how that story has anything whatsoever to do with relativity.'

A Pole moves to the front, shoulders sideways on:

'It is very clear to me, the story is a symptom.'

'Well if it's a symptom, that obviously changes everything,' says Madame de Valréas.

She scrutinises the Pole very closely, then moves away from the fireplace.

'No, wait a moment, Baroness.'

The Pole is afraid he has offended Madame de Valréas, his voice is a mixture of entreaty aimed at her and resentment intended for Max:

'It is truly a symptom, a symptom of moral relativism, the rationalist cowardice in which Europe has been mired since the eighteenth century, the generalised relativisation of values against which . . .'

Max does not flinch under the Pole's scrutiny and interrupts using his grandest manner:

'I am not at all surprised that you do not care for the boastful sheep, since your country is entirely governed by . . .'

'Please, gentlemen, this is a friendly gathering,' sighs Madame de Valréas.

She takes them both by the hand.

The Pole smiles, kisses the hand of the Baroness, this man Max is exactly what I was told he would be like, he's been ordered to under-mine the reputation of our newly regenerated Poland, he loses his temper the moment anyone denounces moral relativism, he is a Franco-Bolshevik agent, a godless spy, who scoffs at all values, Max smiles at Madame de Valréas, the Baroness places Max's hand in the hand of the Pole, she is happy, people tell her amusing stories, there is a clash of ideas but people shake hands, this is the greatest week of her life, she is surrounded by French, Germans, Italians, English, Luxembourgers, Poles, two Scots in kilts, socialists, almost every nationality in Europe, pacifists, a general, agrarians, free-marketeers, federalists and nationalists, a Buddhist, suffragettes, Christians, Marxists, colonialists and conservatives, adolescents and emanci-pators, dignified matrons, Luddites, a physicist, economists and steel-men, there are no communists in the strict sense but some intellectuals here agree with what is happening in Moscow, and Madame de Valréas herself invited them, must get them to speak, must know what's going on in Moscow, otherwise their revolution will come here and put the wind up our body politic.

There aren't any Nazis either, because as a party they are discredited, marginalised, with just twelve per cent of the vote they are less and less of a force in the political life of a Weimar Republic which now, early in 1929, is back on the road to recovery, Madame de Valréas goes out of her way to give star treatment to certain participants, Neuville, of course, but not forgetting Wolkenhove, Kurt Wolkenhove, born in Japan, brought up in Bohemia and Vienna, he heads a movement which he has simply called Europa, it's the biggest idea of the century, to build Europe, Aristide Briand chairs the French committee of Europa.

Wolkenhove is a friend of Madame de Valréas, for some months now she has been trying to bring him closer to her industrialist friends, my dear Kurt, ideas are all very well but you must be able to base them on tangible ground, if you succeed in convincing people from the iron and steel cartel and their bankers, then the future of our European movement is guaranteed, Madame de Valréas is also very fond of Hans, he has one passion, to reconcile France and Germany, one day he declared 'we were all born in France', he has thanked Madame de Valréas publicly, with your invaluable help European thought is about to give a tangible form to the teachings of Kant, you'll have to go careful with Hans, don't talk to him about the iron and steel cartel, Hans thinks in terms of the destiny of peoples, he might not go along with us, even so he must be made to agree to serve as chairman of the Committee for the United States of Europe which is to be set up at the end of the Seminar, he's so inconsistent, so difficult.

Hans found Elisabeth Stirnweiss very likeable, he'd never seen her before, young, chubby, fair-haired, turned-up nose, she was in the middle of a rehearsal but she gave Hans and the Baroness the warmest of welcomes.

'May I introduce Werner, my accompanist, he is also my husband, my producer, my manager and my teacher, we never agree about anything, we were about to have an argument, he always says I sing with too much feeling, he would like me to sing in public the way I do when we rehearse, but singing is life, it's supposed to express something, even tears, but if I do tears he says he can hear rain in my voice, I think that's hateful, yes, I'm more mezzo than soprano, it's quite a recent thing, you never know what's going on with a voice.'

Hans congratulated Elisabeth Stirnweiss, her husband found Hans very intimidating, he used the Baroness's departure as an excuse to stretch his legs, actually he's going out to smoke a cigar, says Elisabeth Stirnweiss, I don't let him smoke when we're working, he can't abide it, but I can't abide his tobacco even more, so whoever can't abide the most wins, I'm one of your admirers, says she, and I am fast becoming one of your admirers, says he, Hans isn't thinking too clearly about what he's saying, in his view not enough thought has been put into what Elisabeth Stirnweiss does, but nonetheless he tells the young woman that he is fast becoming one of her admirers, it's relaxing to pay an artist compliments, and too bad if you end up believing that you mean them.

'So everything is all right,' says Elisabeth Stirnweiss, there are red blotches on her neck and shoulders, 'let's talk about cheerful things.'

Thus Hans was able to listen in on a whole afternoon's rehearsal in Elisabeth Stirnweiss's suite, she sings without asking herself questions, Hans finds that relaxing, she has a body of full, soft curves, when she breathes, you might almost think she is offering herself.

That evening they met again around the table of Madame de Valréas, along with Briand in the place of honour, Max, the Mayneses, Madame de Valréas's daughter, her name is Frédérique, by means of some slick footwork she has managed to sit next to Hans, Madame de Valréas is on Briand's left, Briand looks across at another table, the second from the end, just next to the large papyrus plant, Madame de Valréas says to him:

'Keeping an eye on Professor Merken? I must invite you to tea with him, there's a gulf between you, I want to bridge that gulf.'

Hans is sitting on Madame de Valréas's left, Max and Maynes are directly opposite, Briand having glanced across at Merken now launches into a eulogy of Great Britain, he revels in provoking his hostess, he speaks nostalgically of what might have been, Max knows Briand like the back of his hand, he waits for the cheese and the salad, for the wines to be changed, a 1911 Burgundy, Briand looks at the label, relaxes, selects a goat and a little of a camembert that is not too ripe, Max delivers a eulogy of Madame de Valréas, I'm sure that you'll be able to bring the Chairman and the Professor together, women are invariably on the side of reconciliation and unity, Madame de Valréas summons a modest blush, Briand snaps:

'Not invariably, not invariably.'

Smiles, Briand helps himself to the lion's share of the salad, tastes it, raises his glass to his lips.

More smiles, putting salad in a mouth with a 1911 Burgundy, the man's a boor, no, Baroness, women are not invariably on the side of reconciliation, and I'm not thinking only in terms of dalliance, which always goes hand in hand with opulence, his right hand moves through space and designates the whole table, Hans thinks that Briand has rather short arms, my dear Baroness, in fact she is a republican Baroness, she couldn't care less about her title, especially when it's Briand who uses it on her, but all the same there's etiquette, silver knives and forks, they bear the Valréas crest, all brought here by the Baroness's staff so that everything shall be as it ought, Briand sinks back in his chair, the more he ages the more like a hunchback he sometimes looks, but he does not slump, he's a frump, his nails are clean but Max saw him in the lift ploughing them with a visiting card, Briand is happy to believe that the barony is now just a crest on a set of forks and that the Baroness doesn't care for the idea, the important thing is that the title should be retained in conversation.

'Not invariably,' Briand says again, 'Max here is a demagogue, Max is always trying to please the ladies and casts them as reconcilers, but he's wrong.'

Briand has a fine voice, full, he uses it the way singers do, he places the sound of his voice in front of his face, with chiaroscuro effects, and as you listen you forget everything else, women are not always on the side of reconciliation, it's not just a question of dalliance, I could, adds Briand, tell you stories about musical Maenads whose way with a suitor could hardly be described as dalliance, but we'll let that lie, I'm thinking particularly about politics, always about politics, where women can be the real cause of disasters, smile from Briand at the Baroness who is wondering where President Briand is going with this, she knows that he is her friend, she also knows that he'll do anything for a witty remark.

Max has set Briand off, he wouldn't like to be in the Baroness's shoes, she needs Briand, she smiles back at Briand to show him that everyone's listening, and in part of her smile there is also the idea that eating salad with Burgundy is something that's simply not done, at least in the manuals written for young wives, but it's all right if you're someone like Briand, always assuming that you do it in the presence of someone like the Baroness who has seen it all before, the idea of getting Merken and Briand together over a cup of tea isn't terribly attractive, Briand's Anglophilia.

'I'm quite serious,' says Briand, 'women and disaster, I'm speaking of the past, of History, Joan of Arc, for instance.'

Silence, even Max says nothing, Madame de Valréas ventures with a thin, rather forced smile:

'It's a good few years since I've been anything like Joan of Arc.'

But Briand, in his full-bottomed voice, launches forth, in tragic vein:

'Joan should have stayed in her field counting her sheep and spinning their wool, instead of behaving like an amazon! There would have been excellent Plantagenet marriages, a Franco-English kingdom which would have been invincible and would have maintained the peace in Europe for many centuries, ah! the monstrous regiment of virgins!'

Briand turns to Madame de Valréas pointing his fork at Max:

'As for the salad, you should know that I'm not a barbarian, the dressing was made in the kitchen by my favourite gourmet, it's a Goffard dressing, that's how it shall be known from this day forth, Max perfected it last winter, a salad dressing designed to go with red wine: olive oil, hazel-nut oil, a home-made vinegar derived from a very good wine, sea salt, mild pepper, Strasbourg mustard with herbs, a sliver of Emmenthal, and an artichoke heart.'

'A quarter of an artichoke heart,' says Max.

'All right, a quarter!'

Briand holds up a lettuce leaf and a small piece of camembert on the end of his fork, and let us not forget the yolk of an egg, a thick but creamy dressing, brings out the flavour of the lettuce, he turns his fork round and round before his eyes, it discreetly enhances the cheese, with his left hand he raises his wineglass, and with the wine it is unassertive, an accompaniment, Max, once more I take my hat off to you!

Behind Briand, at another table, a small one, in a corner, two men engrossed in their plates, they speak without even looking at each other, Maynes looks at them, says to Max: do you know them?

'The tall one, yes,' says Max, 'he's called Münzenberg, Willi to his friends, and they form a large constituency, he's everywhere, Paris, Berlin, London, I'm surprised you don't know him, he's the sort of man who in forty-eight hours could find you a couple of thousand bodies and by no means of the humblest class to fill a cinema or a music-hall provided that it was in the anti-fascist cause or to defend Bolshevik Russia.'

'A Moscow agent?'

'It's more elegant than that, he's a volunteer, enrols in great causes, an artist, he is capable of creating a first-rate newspaper in forty-eight hours, or of financing a film, he doesn't mince his words, says he doesn't understand what's going on right now among the Soviets, I don't know the man with him.'

Münzenberg glances up, looks across at Max and Maynes, Max gives him a little wave.

The man sitting opposite Münzenberg says this Seminar bores me, Willi, you're right comrade Vaïno, these capitalists and their guard dogs are boring, but there are two or three young people here who should be of interest to you, especially one of them, very committed, he wants a revolution, he's very cultured, he's older than he looks, in two, three years he'll be absolutely ready, he's more or less ready now, just a small Trotskyite tendency but I think that could easily be taken care of, I have every confidence in you, you'll find a way of getting him to denounce two or three saboteurs, there's also a girl, a philosopher, but I think she is less committed, she's the daughter of Baroness de

Valréas, our fascist Baroness, not a hundred per cent fascist nowadays, I've heard her say better the Reds than America, could be useful to us, the international movement is going to need people like that, the girl has a very logical mind, she lives under Merken's roof, he's the favourite philosopher of the ultra-conservatives, but she should be coming back to Paris one of these days, she doesn't like the old world, take it from me, these young people have great futures, the young man is called Lilstein, anyway, I leave you to judge, you'll be the one who decides, I mean the appropriate authorities.

The man who answers to the first name of Vaïno is less than keen on this mention of the appropriate authorities but he says nothing to Münzenberg, Münzenberg is very good at getting things moving, he does much good work in the struggle against fascism, and Vaïno Vaatinen fully acknowledges his worth, he finds him a little casual at times, Münzenberg has told him that this is necessary for his work, but if Münzenberg is allowed to remain for too long so far from Moscow, in Paris or London, he'll deteriorate, he should be called back more often, you realise we're being watched? Yes, says Münzenberg, it's the Frenchman, the journalist who's sitting next to Maynes, steer clear of him, I nearly forgot, adds Münzenberg, there's another very interest-ing young man, a physicist, a disciple of Nils Bohr, he was born in Prussia but lives in France, his mother is a dressmaker, his father is a mechanic, he's young, has no ideology, but he has the right class reflexes, his name's Tellheim, I saw him turn pale when Neuville explained the experiment with the two working-girls, when he was explaining his model of the scientific organisation of work, he has the gall to call it scientific, the young physicist could have strangled him.

Neuville on his couch, the circle of admirers around him, elegant exposition delivered in a slow voice, the omniscience of the rich, two working-girls, seated side by side, in front of them two heaps of pens and two display cabinets, the young man is sickened by Neuville who talks about them as though they were guinea-pigs, they put the pens vertically in the slots in the cabinet, one of them picks up a dozen pens in her left hand and inserts them one at a time with her right hand, when no pens remain in her left hand she takes another dozen and continues to insert them with her right hand and so forth, there are fifty slots in the cabinet, when she is two-thirds of the way through her task the other girl has already finished and is resting, hands on knees, she hasn't worked any faster, but though following the same rhythm she has not inserted the pens in the same way, she also picked up her pens from the pile one by one, but using both hands together, her two hands doing the same thing at the same time, moving directly from the pile to the cabinet without an interval between, rationalise, you see she has time to rest, she previously worked in textiles, she made dresses by machine, the kind you work with your legs, with your feet on a treadle which rocks and engages the pulleys, which make the needle move, apparently this movement of the lower limbs gave the girls ideas, so bromide was added to their food in the canteen, nobody asked them.

It was when Neuville smiled as he mentioned the bromide that the young physicist almost lost his temper, said Münzenberg, I whispered in his ear that anger makes you give the best speech you'll ever regret, he allowed Neuville to drone on and on uninterrupted, he spoke enthusiastically of pen-sorting, without bromide, yes, the rhythm could be speeded up, not too fast to begin with, set a standard, with the same salary since they don't get so tired, even more pens and fewer hands, or increased volume with the same staffing-level, or again greater volume at a higher rhythm, I propose, said Neuville, to call that an adjustment variable, as physicists do, Neuville smiles at Tellheim, we too are turning into scientists, the scientific organisation of work, there are around three million motor neurons for every thirty grams of human flesh, which makes two and a half billion motor neurons to enable the human machine to function, I have set myself the task of calculating the quantitative value of the work of these motor neurons if a workman does exactly what he's told, how he should lift an object using five movements, how to carry, how to walk, how long each step should be as a function of his height, how to put the object down in five other movements, the rhythm by which he should return and repeat the operation, in terms of output it's possible to move from twelve tons of steel a day to forty-seven, from twelve to forty-seven! that's a gain of three hundred per cent, you install cameras to record movements, you attach lights to wrists, all the joints, you under-expose the negative and you get a film which is a finished time-and-motion schema, the system can be set up in three weeks, express fatigue in equations, learn how to calculate, I landed in the United States in 1906 with less than a dollar in my pocket at the same time as a million others. Today, I am one of the best-paid men in the world.

Neuville also tells them about his expedition in the Canadian Great North, fifty-three cowboys paid four dollars a day, one hundred and thirty-three horses, of which one carried sixty-five kilos of ladies' shoes, everything required for a full expedition into an area which still has no reliable maps, aluminium tables, the latest thing, crystal glasses, French saucepans, a hundred and eighty kilos of books including *War and Peace*, a few kilos of foie gras and, the last word in up-to-date equipment, five ultra-modern half-tracks, two broke down, beyond repair, I organised a photo session for the cameras, a trail down the side of a cliff, two of the half-tracks were pushed over the edge into the ravine, we sold the pictures for more money than the two vehicles had cost, it's communication that matters nowadays, it's through communication that capital and labour will be brought together, and it will be done using the Neuville index.

*

On the Tuesday, the third day of the Seminar, coffee time on the terrace, sunshine, flags flapping, good fun is had with a telescope chained to the safety rail, five centimes for three minutes, people gather nearby, around the panoramic table, they throw bits of bread or crumbs of fruit cake for a few jackdaws, huge Swiss hotel jackdaws, far off to the north-east rises the Gehenna Pass.

'I can see a red dot,' says Max.

The eye that is drawn by the red dot also detects the movement of a white streamer, the trace of sinuous movement on the slope, something not quite as white as the snow.

'It's the army,' explains Merken who has taken out his own binoculars and is also looking towards the Gehenna, 'the Swiss army, white anoraks, mountain light infantry, white trousers, white skis, probably come from Davos.'

Through the telescope Max eventually picks out an orderly, regular line, broken white against the dazzling white of the snow, with a serrefile officer in bright red, they are still a long way away, a waving streamer and a red dot, Max says gaily:

'The young ladies will be delighted to learn that e'en now a pack of hearty young men is bearing down on us on skis, all in white, with a fine figure of an officer in red.'

An entire squad, the squad's careful winding progress, it's easier for the officer, his twists and turns are more expansive, the euphoria of a long descent, nothing to impede, pure Telemark turns, Merken speaks to Moncel, he has put his binoculars away, no one dares ask to borrow them, at intervals Moncel nods a yes, a good relationship, the exhilaration of the descent, moving bodies which enfold space in sinuous motion, the virgin snow, space which excites, that's why I like skiing, says Merken, clear a space for oneself, these words aren't very accurate, you can't clear a space for yourself, it's more hair-raising, euphoric and hair-raising, you discover that space persists whatever we do, the moment there are no more goals, it opens up.

Max remains glued to his telescope, the Swiss army which dresses its officers in red, you know, they'll have to have it explained to them, our first months of the Great War, three hundred thousand-odd dead, our rich experience was to serve some useful purpose, another one of these types who want to die with their boots on from proper wounds, I can already hear the order to fire, aim for the red dot, one good skier less, I'll never ski as well as that, he puts me in mind of my dragoon officers, Max goes on looking a while longer, also Bournazel, no one knows if he died dressed in red or grey, I'm certain he'd kept his red cloak on, to feed the myth; Max gives up his turn to Elisabeth Stirnweiss, Stirnweiss leaning forward with her eye to the telescope is also a sight to behold, one that doesn't last.

Stirnweiss offers to surrender her turn to Hans who declines politely, you're very kind but it hurts my eyes, he turns away and goes back to talk to young Frédérique, Madame de Valréas's daughter, he's not thinking now of Schumann or the rest, he's watching the dark-haired girl talk philosophy in the excitable voice of a sports reporter.

Two days ago, Hans had a long conversation with Max, told him about his attempted trip on the *Queen Mary* between Le Havre and Southampton, a disaster, Max, I was sea-sick, I couldn't think of anything else, especially not Lena, but it set me to rights again, I decided it was time I grew up, no more distractions, an end to fond imaginings, no more Renard-style diaries, yes, a great novel, on the decline of values, Max had reservations, it'll be seven hundred pages of pure ideas, too bad said Hans, and anyway you can always put me right, at this point a girl with dark hair approached and laughed as she planted two kisses on Max's cheeks, Max introduced Frédérique de Valréas to Hans, when I first saw her she was running up and down the stairs with no clothes on, Frédérique didn't take offence, I was three, and the day it happens to you, Max, I'll tell everyone about it too.

Ever since that meeting Hans and Frédérique have had a half-dozen private conversations, I'm thirty-eight, she's nineteen, Lena has disappeared, he will take the girl by the hand, they'll walk in the forest together, and then she will take his hand.

On the terrace, Frédérique says to Hans:

'Are you listening, Monsieur Kappler? I'm talking to you but your mind is elsewhere, my mother warned me, authors are unbearable, you think you're talking to someone and their mind is elsewhere, with which of your characters are you walking in this forest at this moment? A pretty woman?'

Frédérique behaves like a woman who is cross, but she is delighted to have caught him out, Hans looks like a clumsy teddy bear.

It's Max's turn again with the telescope, Hans and Frédérique move away from the group, Max searches for five centimes, then five more, the movements on the snow remind him of Bournazel, he was another one who slalomed down slopes, on a horse.

Max again offers to pass his turn to Hans who declines, to Stirnweiss, but she has suddenly disappeared, he puts his eye once more to the telescope, Hans! Come and see, it's a tall, handsome, blood-coloured officer, Hans is very busy at the other end of the terrace, Max calls Tellheim, Come here! resistance of the snow, angle of the slope, resistance of the air, elasticity coefficient of the human body, you can express all this wonderful zigzagging as a mathematical formula, you can tell us if time passes *relatively* faster for them than for us, Tellheim has the telescope, people are enjoying themselves, everything is relative, handsome officer, Tellheim wanders off.

And then the punch-up started, not exactly what you'd expect to find behind the word, a brawl in a gutter, not as vulgar, but more a tasteful brand of competing, a form of rivalry that was nonetheless unremitting, a struggle to occupy the high ground, score points, have the last word, capture attention.

It started below them, outside the entrance to the hotel, the arrival of the squad of mountain light infantry, when Mademoiselle Stirnweiss helped Lena Hellström take off her bright red anorak.

She said I don't know how you can, I'd never dare go on a long hike like that, half an hour in this cold and my throat's on fire, for me to go out skiing counts as a professional blunder, but you put on a red anorak, you take your planks, you're away up a mountain for ten hours with a squad of infantrymen and you emerge unscathed, skiing across country for ten hours or more, Hellström, you're a public menace!

Everyone was looking, Tellheim wondered if Max knew something when he said come and see to Hans, then he thought I want her, perhaps he didn't actually think that, maybe his body simply moved and found itself in the path of this tall woman with red hair, go down from the terrace, go to where the soldiers are removing their boots, being there, being gripped by an unexplained rage against Lilstein who somehow is there ahead of him, and Max is also ahead of him, even

Hans, because Frédérique de Valréas always behaves perfectly, you must never let a man feel any regret for being with you, not even one teeny-weeny regret, you take him by the arm, like an old friend, an uncle, come, fifteen athletes, you shall be my alibi, she whisks him off to meet the woman who has just arrived, there is no sharpness in her voice, come along, Hans.

'No,' said Lena Hellström to her friend Stirnweiss, 'not a ten-hour hike but thirty, thirty hours, we set out yesterday morning, a detour by way of the Hirschkuh Pass, we built an igloo outside the refuge, we spent the night in a large igloo, Swiss cold doesn't bite, it's all right for tourists, it's nothing compared to Montana, I slept with fifteen men.'

'The army agreed to take you along with them?'

'I had a job to do.'

'Now you're pulling my leg,' said Stirnweiss.

'No, a real job, I was studying the effect of Mozart's *berceuses* on the sleep of mountain infantrymen on patrol, I sang them some Mozart round the fire in the igloo, a single oil-lamp, all those men, they taught me mountain songs, rather coarse, it was most satisfactory, be an angel, Elisabeth, I couldn't walk another step, would you order me a hot bath, tell the housekeeper that I want a very large hot bath, hello Hans!'

Hans doesn't tremble, he is very calm, he is surprised by how calm he is, he says pleasantly:

'I'm so pleased to see you again! *Madame Hellström?*'

'Yes, Hans, it's my real name, my maiden name, the other one, Hotspur, was a made-up name.'

And Tellheim has already butted into the conversation, you ski admirably, and Lilstein says nothing but he's the one Lena is looking at, and Max says:

'I'm sure we've met before.'

'Me too,' says Lena, 'you have the sort of face people don't forget.'

'Say ears, you recognise my ears?'

'Your friends called you Max, 1926, Paris, that enormous brasserie, the Brasserie de la Paix, you were watching me in the reflection of the mirrors and I heard you telling some appalling story about steel-makers, don't look so surprised, it was my dark hair blue eyes period, you were fiddling with a wineglass and sugar lumps, you made your friends laugh but there were tears in your voice, I almost came over to your table but apparently that isn't done, it was for you to come over and speak to me!'

Lena turns to Hans:

'Men rarely dare make the first move.'

And Lilstein, Tellheim, the others there present form a small circle around Lena, she takes off her hat, shakes a fine shock of thick hair free, Lilstein thinks that she's the only woman for him, Hans intro-duces Frédérique to Lena, eyes peering in a semi-circle, furtively watching, eyes vying and prying, then the moment when Lena Hellström cried out John! and planted a loud kiss on Maynes's cheek, Paris, it can't be ten years already!

Tellheim notices that when Stirnweiss looks at men they feel handsome and suave but to talk to the beautiful red-haired skier they straighten their backs, Mrs Maynes smiles at Lena Hellström and strokes her husband's cheek.

Merken has remained up on the terrace with Moncel, they carry on talking about space, Merken in lyrical mode, free-wheeling, leaving the sparkle on what is free, the complicit slope, space: the dispenser of being, Merken glances down at the skiers, comes out with a remark which surprises Moncel, about animals.

*

The antithesis of Merken in the Seminar is the master of classical philosophy, Regel, the man who has the most self-control, Merken is a boar, Regel looks more like a heron, long, delicate, quick neck, one morning people remain in the lounge for a few moments before going to their various seminars, Regel comes in singing:

'Let's take a walk in the woods while the wolf's not about, let's take a walk in the woods . . .'

They thought Regel incapable of the smallest jest, and he begins talking to everyone and no one, raising his voice, shouting:

'Aaah, villainy! villainy and its cohort of ravening beasts who disguise themselves the better to tear out the throats of the unsuspecting.'

Regel arms aloft, head down:

'Villainy, and worse than villainy, the moment when villainy takes its hat off instead of allowing us a little longer to bask in our hopes after letting us build them up for so long, we all know what's going to happen, and yet we prefer to go on hoping!'

He sings another snatch:

'Are you there, Mister Wolf? Do you dare, Mister Wolf?'

Those present do not understand what is happening, young Frédérique is the first to react, Regel is oblivious to the furniture, watch out! he'll hurt himself! no one dares restrain Regel, dares put a hand on him, so everyone starts moving things to one side, the seats, low tables, easy chairs which might get in his way, Regel advances sightlessly, in a straight line, like a curling stone whose passage is brushed smooth to facilitate its progress. He repeats:

'Are you there, Mister Wolf? Do you dare, Mister Wolf? Don't give me that, Mister Wolf has been here among us for a long, long time.'

He points to the far wall of the library, a section without shelves, just wallpaper:

'The Wolf, long before the most stupidest kid in the class would have spotted his ears in those leaves which form the background to our playtimes, ah, dances without villainy! dancing round and round, flowers, ideas, when the friendly breeze fills the space with fine abstractions, villainy and the warm embrace of friends!'

Regel has begun to waltz:

'*Ich hatt' einen Kameraden, einen bess'ren find'st du nicht*, the swine even use death, *die Trommel schlug zum Streite . . .*'

He turns and comes back to the middle of the room, his arms less agitated, his voice likewise, he now has a dreamy look:

'Villainy, you are their god, why would they accept principles and allow the captious law of men to deprive them of what is offered them by the slimy copulation of power and cunning?'

Everyone is looking at Regel, tall, gaunt, thin blade of a nose, very elegant in his light-coloured suit, handkerchief in his breast pocket, pine-green tie, holds himself very straight, strict self-control, as always, except for his staring eyes, everyone hesitates, maybe this is his idea of a joke, but Hans senses that Regel has lost his mind, Max tells him:

'Wait, he's still saying things that make sense.'

Regel starts to make his case:

'But why brand them with the name of villain and wild beast? Why? After all, they derive more strength and glamour from the sensual pleasures of lying and raping than we find in the dismal bed of precept and convention from which we produce only spineless cretins whom the herd are already quietly driving to the very edge of the abyss, our way of extricating ourselves from the old herd was very fine, two consciousnesses face to face, living people who acknowledge each other, each demonstrating to the other that they are there, without one killing the other, and the other one has no need to run away, not like animals, each one needing the other, a struggle which leaves a place for the weak, the loser, attached to life he stays and becomes a servant, and he wins, he is told that he has won, but the master can see in his servant only an object, which means he has no one facing him to acknowledge his consciousness, whereas the servant sees in his master the perfect form of the self, an authentic being, this being deigns to look at him, it is enough for him, he sets to work, and he can contemplate his own self in the fruits of his labour, his labour and a master, a false master, it was a fine thing, except that no one foresaw that the masters would begin killing in earnest, return of the herd! Spineless cretins whom the herd are already quietly driving to the edge of the abyss while all the time telling them that some blessing or other mingles with the mountain dew.'

Regel has moved closer to the window.

'See how the dew makes the leaves of the tall poplars sparkle and cools our presence in the world! No more need to think, it is enough just to be, to celebrate being, to contemplate the forest, the poplars will march in step with the warrior populace, the tall poplars, let's take a walk in the woods, yes, and in our absence we are robbed of the space in which we might have struck a discordant note against the night-black diapason even now in rehearsal! *Ich hatt' einen Kameraden, einen bess'ren,* while, albeit making space for us, they enlarge the cemeteries.'

Regel looks at Hans:

'Be quiet, Hans! I don't need any help, I'm not raving, this is a moment of lucidity, Berlin, headship of the Department of Philosophy, forty years of toil, the votes of thirty professors, a life's work, twelve hours a day! A life played by the rules, a life of rebuffs suffered in silence and with the most respectful politeness even when I felt like ramming a dustbin over the head of the most arrogant of the two-faced hypocrites, the one who broke open the champagne when his little friends killed Rathenau, Rathenau whom I loved like a brother, one of the great men of the Empire and the Republic! The man who opened the champagne is with us now, which is no trifling matter, he had the nerve to say on the day those swine sent by the extreme right and the *Casque d'acier* killed Rathenau, he said the major ministries should be reserved for men of more "intrinsic" origins, that way there'd be less resentment and violence, bastards! I had right on my side! And the law! And the fact of a democratic majority! But I'd for-gotten one thing and some snivelling boot-licker, a member of a government of snivelling boot-lickers incapable of standing up to the scum in brown shirts, some gutless wimp at a desk decided I wouldn't get the Berlin job, that the job should go to someone more intrinsic! More intrinsic! To the friend and colleague who only moments ago greeted me with open arms, though that friend and colleague knew everything, long before the telegram, more intrinsic, more radiant! It's all so obvious, when the supporters of people like him turn a spotlight on the power which makes cowards keep silent! Do you enjoy seeing me behaving like some demented puppet on a string? And the philosophers? They say their farewells, they form a circle to applaud my old friend Professor Merken whose origins are much more intrinsic! Make a circle, not a circle, a ring, these days there are no reserved seats for philosophers, they have to put on gloves and fight, like everyone else!'

The only person who dared register a protest with Regel was Frédérique, she tried to treat him as if he wasn't raving, she thought that by arguing with him they could bring him back to reality.

'That's unfair, Professor, the man you refer to has never compromised himself either with the people you say point spotlights or the brown shirts.'

Regel:

'Him? Never! He is pure thought, never an obscene word, a direct gaze, so straight it never pauses to settle on the person he's speaking to, his look is lost in thought, in the purity of thought, the wonderful flow of ideas, such new ideas, so necessary, so strong, so true, leave it to others to tamper with votes, get their hands dirty grubbing around in the mud.'

Regel's body suddenly crumples, sags to one side, his elbows pressed against his stomach, hands clenched, knees bent, Erna, his secretary, has tried to talk sense to him.

'Erna, is that you? Erna, they've given your dear old mentor his marching orders and you haven't downed tools yet? Serves him right? Red Erna, watching while the old social democrat is used as an arsewipe by the riff-raff, Erna's little ultra-Red comrades warned her: old Regel is enemy number one, got nothing to say, Erna? You like wolves?'

Erna also talked back at Regel, it was the right way to keep him here with people, talk to him just as if he was fully compos mentis, she told him he was a bit late in the day finding out they were wolves, after believing they'd make very obedient dogs, she started talking as though addressing a public meeting, the place to strike is the fertile womb that spawns the wolves!

It hasn't calmed Regel down.

'Ah! the revolutionary exhilaration of knowing you were right all along! Erna is overjoyed when the centrists are flat on their backs!'

Erna going on:

'The matrix, that's where we must strike the beast!'

Hans realises that she's going too far:

'Professor, won't you sit down? we can think about this together!'

Regel:

'Think, sleep, hope, we shall all disappear, Hans, anyone who's *extrinsic* is going to have to disappear to make way for certifiable madmen!'

He backs into the lounge. The madness contorts him, doubles him up, propels him, swoops down on him again, releases him then puts out its claws almost playfully, he becomes calm, in a slow voice:

'Nothing to worry about, friends, a passing upset, you know, there are times when I admire what Merken says, it's very fine, it's poetry, except that no one should be allowed to poeticise philosophy, meanwhile the poplars, the warriors, I don't want him to shake my the hand, let's take a walk in the woods while the wolf's not about, are you there, Mister Wolf? can you hear?'

Then Regel disappears.

*

A week of ideas, of battles over ideas, of monocles, splendour, courtly manners, the men make the rules and the women set the tone, there are Pan-Europeans, nationalists, internationalists, conservatives, defenders of the giant dirigible, socialists, liberals, economic liberals who are conservative in politics and vice versa, progressives, advocates of the four-turret battleship who are there to plan the forthcoming naval conference, anticolonialists, economists, philosophers of rule and balance, jurists, imperialists and proud of it, criss-crossing battle lines, for example supporters of the League of Nations internally split between those who remain faithful to the cellulo-linen choker-collar and those who have gone over to the close-woven, lightly starched, semi-stiff collar, it doesn't catch the folds under the chin as much, but the soft collar is out, you can leave that to the moneymen.

Mustn't leave out the ones who only want the League to act as a gendarme to police frontiers, and the ones who dream of a universal republic much larger than just Europe, the ones who talk to other people and the ones who talk to themselves, like Madame Merken, she is extremely proud of carrying off her little intrigue so successfully, her husband will go to Berlin, in the end he accepted the job despite the scandal, he told her he was accepting it on one condition, he was going to need a new secretary, he would have to employ young Erna.

Madame Merken gave in, but pondered the matter, why is she always the one to give in? still, he'd agreed to leave Heidelberg, the thousand-year-old university where the professors swell with self-satisfaction when invited to dine at the home of some sausage manufacturer. Berlin, invited to the feast! But keep quiet about all that, keep even quieter about Germany, unite, close ranks, advance, I'm just a philosopher's wife, but I know two things that philosophers forget, you achieve nothing without politics and in politics prudence gets you nowhere, the future belongs to those who push at doors which open into the unknown, kick down doors, unleash fanaticism, make things happen, create the moment for things to happen, the only philosophy which will survive is the philosophy which keeps abreast of the times, bold men stand ready and waiting, they are rough, they laugh at philosophy but they hold the secret which sets History moving once more, I want to join them, in silence, my husband's job is to philosophise the silence, but he mustn't be too aware of what he's doing, just do his job, no more.

A week of battles over ideas, to begin with it meant genuine exchanges of views but that didn't last, Max laughing, saying I'm not sorry I came, I feel as if I'm taking part in a football match wearing crampons, no, that's too simple, let's say a game of *soule*, an old sport played back home, one third football, one third rugby, one third wrestling or boxing with a cycle race thrown in, all taking place in the same stadium-cum-velodrome, the Europa team of Pan-Europeans are first out of the north bend, Wolkenhove in the lead sets the pace supported by his team-mate Kappler, fifteen metres up now on the Nationals team, they pick up the pace, Kappler's magic pedals, the Pan-Europeans flash past along the yellow track in full view of a public of dark suits and white shirt-fronts, cheers, hooters and pretty women, now thirty metres up on the pursuing riders, but at the tail of this group there are signs of flagging, three men, the team's weakest links, one is Berthelot, Briand's deputy, they are finding it hard to keep up the pace set by Wolkenhove and Kappler, signs that they're tiring.

And behind this group, Bainville puts on a spurt, Bainville is leader of the team in pursuit, the Nationals, Bainville and the Prussian Kuhn, an alliance of opposites, the rebirth of Germany is a condition of the rebirth of the West, absolutely not so, Europe must gather under the intellectual aegis of France, meantime they swap the lead with each other until such time as they are able to catch and overtake the stateless Pan-Europeans, Bainville and Kuhn are now only a dozen wheel-widths from Berthelot who is still having difficulty with the pace, the Nationals are being supported by the Conservatives, the Pan-Europeans respond and Wolkenhove dribbles, charges off ball at his feet down the space to his the right, comes up against centre-back Kuhn, good ball control by Wolkenhove, a dribble leftward then a flick of the foot, the ball goes to the right of Kuhn, Wolkenhove goes round Kuhn on the left, a terrific sidestep, Wolkenhove reconnects with the ball behind the wrong-footed Kuhn but is then brought down by Tardieu, defender of the gold standard, free-kick taken by Maynes, the only currency worth having is thought, a left hook, the spectators are on their feet, Regel takes the punch, Merken follows up with an uppercut to the liver for today the gregarianisation of man nowadays must go under the name of Europe.

Regel back-pedals, keeps his guard low, rapid movements of his upper body, ducks, regains control of his legs, philosophy will never solve the crisis of Europe, the concept of crisis is consubstantial with philosophy, Regel very elegant, keeps pegging away with his left to make Merken keep his distance, Europe, said Hegel, is the absolute end of History, Merken is off-balance, Regel does not hit him very hard, he boxes the way you keep up a conversation, the crowd jeers Regel, it's women's stuff, as elegant as Al Brown, philosophy and Europe are locked in a permanent symmetry, Regel's blind spot! Merken the Boar from the Black Forest tries to get under his opponent's guard, the disarray of Europe stems from the neglect of Being, at the back of the scrum Maynes releases his three-quarters, a high kick over the curtain of the back line to chase, Kappler and Wolkenhove, a gap such as you dream about, the only proper expression is that which is concertedly European, they're in their opponents' twenty-two but Bainville relieves the pressure on his side, finds touch on the left of the field, around the halfway line, it's taken quickly, Van Ryssel catches for the Pan-Europeans, the United States of Europe, the move is closed down by the opponents of federalism, Jacques Seydoux, deputy director of the Quai d'Orsay, this Pan-European union reeks of the Hun, ball recovered by Regel who passes it to Kappler.

A superb cross pass from Kappler to Briand, the bell clangs, still twenty laps to go, a cash prize will be given by the Van Ryssel Company to the fastest time on the next lap, Merken feeds his backs, if you don't want Europe to be annihilated you will have to deploy new spiritual forces, Kappler has taken over the lead, ups the pace, a ripple runs through the stands, spectators drained by fatigue and lack of sleep roar but do not applaud, Kappler isn't French.

New counter-attack by Merken from his twenty-two, eight-hundred kilos, the combined weight of the eight forwards, a heavy pack, gives no quarter, we're on our way to Being without knowing where we're at with Beingness, a long kick into touch, it's up to our people, heart of the West, to resist the darkness that is descending on the world, on the ground the League of Nations is using a very promising tactic, WM formation, Stresemann, has the ball at his feet, attacking half-back, behind the centre circle, steadies the play, I've visited the factories of the Cash Register Co. at Dayton, the huge canteen with the firm's motto: 'The World is my Country', Stresemann dribbles, long reverse pass out to the left wing, the Europeans are going to have to unite very quickly otherwise they'll end up being nothing more than an outpost of American companies, players in WM, a football revolution, three defenders, two defensive backs and two offensive, three attackers, Europe is a threat to the universal character of the League of Nations, Briand watches Stresemann, never trusted the man, Regel providing support for his Chancellor, the ball is back in the centre circle again, the spirit of Weimar is the spirit of Kant, a terrific long one-two between Regel and Stresemann who passes down the right wing to Wolkenhove who centres, Kappler chests it down, a quick flick over the opposing back, a half deflection, a volley, the future of Europe must be guided by some ideal, fine save by the Nationals' keeper who boots the ball straight back into the centre circle.

The ball is trapped by Henderson, the League of Nations left winger who is also the British Empire's representative at the Waldhaus, he backs Europe, Henderson leaving the ball behind him makes a run down the touch line, we've just banned *Dawn*, a dangerous English film which tells the story of the alleged fate of Miss Cavell and in so doing has threatened Anglo-German relations, Henderson followed by Kuhn who is marking him very closely and falls into the trap, then realises his mistake and turns just as the number 7 passes the ball back to Henderson, Henderson also wants a European Social Charter, rise of the opponents of a Social Charter, free market! free movement! regrouping of the Nationals and supporters of laissez-faire, rejection of the Social Charter, they stay on the high shoulder of the track, the Pan-Europeans run of out steam, a tight pack of sprinters, the spectators in the velodrome sing 'Ramona', litres of alcohol to overcome the searing heat of the sausage, the amazing machine continues spinning on its wooden ring, for the young Drieu Europe is an abstract civilisation, mechanical and surrealist, given to sport and drugs, onanistic, Malthusian and mystical, not artistic, in the Quai d'Orsay some voices are demanding that Russia should not be forgotten, but first Bolshevism will need to be brought to heel, the latest form of Asiatic pride!

Frédérique tells Max that his sporting number wasn't in the best taste, he replied that it was as well it was just a number because the whole thing could end in tears.

*

The great Waldhaus Seminar ended with two motions and a summary of conclusions. In the end, Hans turned down the Presidency of the Association for the United States of Europe.

People found the way Madame Hellström had sung during her recital at the closing ceremony rather odd, fortunately Stirnweiss had also been there, her voice rather husky, but it all went off very nicely, well sung, expressive, lively.

The first of the motions put off plans for the political union of Europe until the Greek calends, the other invited the League of Nations to take responsibility for setting up a committee on European affairs.

The philosophers went their separate ways smiling. By the morning they all left, Professor Regel was fully himself again, a telegram had arrived from Berlin.

'He's turned it down, turned the job down, ah! what a man! Merken has refused the Berlin chair, he says it's mine, such generosity!'

In the vast lobby, Regel has paid a vigorous tribute to Merken, Merken said:

'I shall go back to the country, philosophy thrives under a sun which sets on slopes green with vine and forest, the soil alone can shape the true power of will, it's there that the body of the people and the body of ideas are made whole again.'

In Hans's view, Merken's refusal did him honour. Merken replied that he refused to think of himself as a democrat, there had been an unfortunate concatenation of circumstances but it was not the business of philosophy to take advantage of circumstances. Regel was very moved:

'Erna, Professor and Madame Merken have offered you an outstanding position, I shall be sorry to lose you.'

To Merken and the others, he also added:

'Unlike you, I am not a man of the soil, I take the view that it is the air of great cities which makes us free, I shall sell my estate in Pomerania, I shall move to Berlin, you know my passion for the industry of men, for their ventures, I shall buy shares to support our factories, the economy, the Stock Exchange, the market, all growing healthily, tomorrow we shall live in an age of magnificent cities!'

The previous evening, things had got somewhat out of hand, dances and chases along corridors smelling pleasantly of beeswax, night cream, larch wood, Virginia tobacco, the great perfumes, the tyranny of beautiful women, rat-a-tat-tat on a door, you either got an answer or you didn't, people went looking for each other, others were sent to look in the lounge, the library, smoking room, terrace, the paths and drives in the grounds, the billiard room, music room, eagerly they went, a man looking for a woman who was looking for a man just as in farce, then a culminating movement, the pairing-off of lovers, they make haste but proceed tastefully, in evening dress, words had been exchanged as they danced, I'd like to ask you two little questions, very little ones, ask away, feel free:

'Where and when?'

'If I gave you a quick answer you'd be the first to pull a face.'

'Me? Not at all.'

'In that case, straight away, darling, and in your room, for instance. Any objections? Somebody might come and knock on the door? Fixed something up with someone else? For later? You're surely not going to suggest we use the garage? I think you're cute but not cute enough for me to want to agree to a session of gymnastics on the bonnet of a car, oh, I'm no prude, I did it once, but never again, so, since it's chilly outside, it's your room or nothing, you can sort it out with your wife, you're best placed to know if she'll come looking for you before eight in the morning, and I shan't make a sound, I can control myself, if you hesitate for one more second it'll be because you've made another arrangement, and if you have then so have I.'

A smart alec walking along a corridor which wasn't his, a sports jacket in his hand.

'Have you seen the hotel's housekeeper? I've got a little sewing job for her.'

'If you're looking for the housekeeper, you won't find her before tomorrow morning, on the other hand I know someone else who was asking after you on the third floor, she wants to return a book of yours, no, not that way, to go back down to the third floor you have to go via the small stairs, otherwise the main staircase will take you directly to the third floor in the left wing, but the person who's looking for you is in the right wing, and when you go down the small stairs turn left.'

Lilstein is sixteen, he looks two years older, he is standing outside Lena's door, he must be mad to be doing this, if she asks you in what'll you do? Jump on her? Or will you say please I beg you? And what if she's with someone? If she's alone invite her to have a last drink downstairs, and she'll say no thanks, good night, see you in the morning, no, not downstairs, she might say come in, or slam the door in your face, you're about to ruin everything with a knock on a door, my boy, what on earth are you thinking of? You should be in bed, are you really that keen to be called 'my boy'? How beautiful she is! Be clear with yourself, is there the smallest objective reason why she should ask you in? It's not a question of objective reason, the whole time you were walking together she kept reaching for your arm, to make you walk slower, to speak to you, to point out an ibex, each time a slight pressure on your arm, calling you my boy, but it was to cover up the pressure on your arm, what is a woman who squeezes a man's arm trying to say? The real question is to find out if in her eyes you are a man, her, now or never!

She'll never forgive you for turning up at her door, Lilstein has just knocked on Lena's door, two little taps, light, casual, friendly, ah, Lena, I was beginning to think we'd never find time to spend five minutes together, that's the tack, light, friendly, chirpy, but there's no reply, Lilstein now knocks loudly enough for her to hear, and more loudly again so that she'll hear even if she's with someone, don't care if it does disturb them, no reply, she isn't in, hasn't come up to bed yet, or else she's already with somebody, he goes back down the main staircase, glances round as he reaches each floor, returns to the lounge, does not see her, I saw her just this minute someone tells him, she seemed to be heading for the garage, or out on to the terrace.

Lilstein finds no one on the terrace. He goes into the library which is lit only by a large desk lamp and the fire in the hearth. He doesn't see anyone, at last spots Madame Merken in a corner, she is looking up at the topmost shelves. Lilstein doesn't like the woman, he has no wish to be asked to reach down a book for her, he leaves, closing the door quietly behind him. Madame Merken is thinking in the library at the Waldhaus, it's the right time for it, semi-darkness. Madame Merken has a nickname, they call her the tank, there are many reasons why, a tank with big green eyes, they stare, slow and oily, thick eyebrows, she has sensed that someone had come in and then gone out again closing the door behind them, good, she prefers being alone, she has no wish to know where her husband's got to, she doesn't care what other people are doing this evening, she is meditating upon greatness, the poetry of greatness, epic deeds, the heroes of legend, the heroines of legend, the future, her thoughts are interrupted by another intruder, makes more noise, a Frenchman, it's young Moncel, all scowls, he's short, thin as a rake, flat hair, steel-rimmed glasses, always wears dark grey, voice reedy but forceful, he has come to the library to be alone, he likes thinking out loud, by himself, surrounded by all these books.

When he's alone the miracle happens, everyone starts listening to him, he becomes the epicentre of the whole Seminar, his eloquence carries all before it, it can last for a whole hour of blessed solitude, but this fat German woman is already here in the library. She doesn't like Moncel, he's silent, detestable, a megalomaniac, good evening young Moncel, not much is seen of this young French philosopher outside the philosophical sessions of the Seminar, he grunts a reply, he twangs a small elastic band, Madame Merken does not care for grunts, elastic bands or little peacocks, is this what they call French urbanity, young man? he pulls himself together, good evening Madame, it seems young Moncel doesn't like women, not very much Madame, rather convenient, Madame Merken doesn't either, especially this evening, Moncel says women are all deceivers, and moreover they're always trying to belittle us, hmph! I most certainly did not come here to listen to this weedy little Frenchman trot out a string of clichés.

'And what, young man, about Germans, do you like them? I imagine no more than you like women?'

'My uncle was killed at Verdun, Madame.'

'No doubt, like many Germans.'

'But they weren't invited, Madame.'

If we're talking invitations, what on earth does any young Frenchman hope to find in German-speaking Waltenberg? he must surely have observed that there is a great deal of talk about reconciliation, you speak excellent German and you take notes as if your life depended on it every time my husband opens his mouth, this hotel is full of Germans, and women, and yet you come and shut yourself away in here, I think that is very peculiar in someone who doesn't like us, is young Moncel that keen on suffering?

'No, I'm here to size you Teutons up, get an idea of your strength, you have surrendered nothing and once more you are attempting to do us down.'

'Do *you* down? your African soldiers litter our streets with their bastards, you proclaim your main frontier is the Rhine, and it's we who are trying to do you down?'

'And where do you suppose that frontier ought to be, Madame, if it's not the Rhine?'

La Merken has come closer, voice low, you must calm yourself, young man, here a gentleman does not shout in the presence of ladies, not even German ladies, there is now only one meaningful frontier, there, Madame Merken's large chin points to the night outside the windows, a frontier lying much further east than is visible to your myopic eye, the frontier which faces the barbarian horses of the Steppes, the vital frontier which your country's stupidity weakens with every passing day, not the Rhine, no, on the other side, in the East, other great rivers, the Vistula is a frontier, we never speak of it but it is in our thoughts, you should think of it so too, and the irony of History is that by establishing your presence on the Rhine and humiliating us with your Senegalese and Arabs, to contain us as you put it, you have opened the doors of the East to new invasions of hordes which pour into your own towns and cities by the trainful, such smells, the tribal food, the pullulation of squalid infants, got nothing to say for yourself, Moncel? Do you prefer your vermin in the style of Corneille and Goethe?

'I have never thought that.'

'Comes to the same thing, and you haven't seen the worst, when people like that, who overrun you, who live fifteen to a room, who were intended to live fifteen to a room and go round saying that other people aren't entitled to more, what could be worse than there being fifteen of them in a room, thousands of rooms occupied every day, and there they congregate in tribes and there they reproduce, and you know what is the worst thing of all, Monsieur Moncel, be honest enough to admit it!'

'The worst thing of all, Madame, is when they go out.'

'The philosopher speaks! Yes, they go out, they become dress-makers, journalists, restaurateurs, policemen, philosophers, lawyers, sometimes you don't recognise them for what they are, the worst of them become gynaecologists, they strip us of our wealth, they're in Berlin, Munich, Paris.'

'And they buy up estates as far afield as Brittany, where I was born.'

Good old Brittany, such larks, Arthur, the Round Table, the Grail, the only right to the ownership of land should be birth, now the peacock is giving me his full attention, he has stopped fiddling with his wretched elastic band, it is now dawning on him that there are such things as real ideas, and powerful, he knew it; now we, Monsieur Moncel, we say that the strong must work together if they are to resist the domination of the weak, instead of imagining that the frontier should run along the banks of the Rhine, are you making a genuine effort to understand us Germans?

'You don't make it very easy, Madame.'

Moncel will never understand the first thing about the Germans unless he can come to understand their attachment to the land, the marriage of river and crag, to emphatic deeds and gentle people, do you know *Die Walküre*, young man? 'The Ride of the Valkyrie', and the song of Brünnhilde? Moncel knows neither, at the seminary he attended opera was not allowed, one of his classmates had referred to *Carmen* one day to make the point that 'toreador' wasn't an authentic

Spanish word, he'd been sent for by the Superior, a month's penitence, no need for this woman to know that, look up there, young man, those four large volumes, the end one, pass it down to me, the ride and the lyricism, I just ask for your attention for five minutes, no more, and I shall tell my husband to give you the interview you've been hoping for ever since you got here, but first I want to make you understand my country!

Moncel has taken half a pace back. He doesn't want to? You hate us that much? You hate us more than the scum?

'I didn't say that, Madame, but I can't stand . . .'

'So you are in favour of these invasions?'

Moncel knows what he can't stand, the presence of this woman, her fat body, the smell of face-powder and sweet perfume, the underlying acid odours, those eyes, the beefy arms which could reach out and collar him in a flash, the sturdy hiking shoes, a woman a foot taller than him, this woman is in herself her own male, if she attacks him he won't be able to fight her off, she has positioned herself between him and the door, she could flatten him, crush him, I'd have to grab one of the chairs, put a chair between me and her, she has a mammoth bosom, she'll punch me and then say she was forced to defend herself, they will believe her, I shall be a laughing-stock, I should have turned tail and fled the instant I saw her here in the library, she's got fists like giant hams, hands that could wring the neck of just about anything.

She's quite capable of rushing out of the library shouting Moncel attacked me, like the maid in the presbytery at Rethel, she'd run out into the street, she'd torn the front of her blouse, screamed blue murder, and now she's bearing down on him, what is it you can't stand, Monsieur Moncel? A bare thirty centimetres now separate her from Moncel, a smell of sweetness and German sweat, Moncel is forced to raise his head to meet her eye, they say she has a foul temper, whatever you do don't provoke her, I can't stand ladders, Madame, I get giddy . . .

'What? strong lad like you! with those athlete's arms and nimble legs . . .'

La Merken has grabbed hold of one of Moncel's arms, I know it's silly, Madame, her hand has crept back up on to Moncel's shoulder, weighty, enveloping but not aggressive, a heavy smell, sweet, but not essence of cabbage, thank God! La Merken's green eyes, her bosom swells, she breathes more sterterously, you can overcome it, you've got muscles and a back as strong as a mountain climber's, Madame, I hate it, La Merken takes him by the shoulder, a mountain of flesh and a small man, a head shorter than her.

She leads him to a set of library steps, the maid from the presbytery had been dismissed, a hysteric, but the *curé* of Rethel never got a living at Rheims, her movements become more and more ponderous, she is quite capable of yelling at him, she circles his shoulders with her other arm, he feels La Merken's bosom against his shoulder, the breasts are more pliant than he would have thought, have faith, it won't come to anything, one rung at a time, just let yourself go, steady now, sometimes you have to do what you're told if you want to get on.

Too late now for putting a chair between them, there'll be no obligation on you to like us, Monsieur Moncel, but you'll have learnt to climb a ladder, and the benefit of reaching the top is well worth the effort, *citius, altius, fortius,* let me guide you, steady, if he goes up the rungs of the ladder she'll have to let go of him, he'll no longer feel the pressure of that bosom on his shoulder nor the weight of her stomach against his hip, the door opened, I'm sure the door opened and closed, anyone might come in, someone has come in, there's someone watching us, she's going to scream, she's too near, he climbs up a few rungs, she has let go of his shoulder and arm, he can breathe again, fewer smells, his hand trembles on the higher rungs, go on, young man, you see, it's a lot easier than it looks.

Moncel would have been perfectly happy staying right there, not too high up, but out of La Merken's reach, not feeling giddy either, just there at eye-level with the works of Kipling, now there's an Englishman who is not ashamed of his Empire, *Kim,* a book he's never read, he doesn't want to go any higher to get Wagner's librettos, find an excuse, there's a book here I've been trying to find for ages, I'll come down and put it to one side then I'll come back up and help out, if she's so keen on Wagner she can shin up the damn ladder herself on those great big feet of hers, she's afraid I'll see her large feet, Moncel stretches out a hand for *Kim,* he feels two hands settle firmly around his calves, strong hands, but not aggressive.

It's not very high, young man, go on, take your time, slowly now, I don't feel at all well, Madame, do you know the author of *Kim?* The one who wrote 'one day you'll be a man', I'd like to come down and put it aside, no, go on, you've done the hardest part, and the hands grow harder, keep calm, keep looking up, she releases one of his calves, gives it a tap, now now, no childishness, just a few more little rungs, there's nothing to it, come along, the hand seizes his calf again, forces his leg up on to the next rung, again, now the other leg.

This is crazy, what am I doing here? the ladder shakes, don't be afraid, look there, the ladder is secured high up by hooks, there's no need for this woman to tell me not to be afraid, it's not fear, the other leg now, breathe, she doesn't have to force me, her right hand has gone all the way up to the back of Moncel's knee, she's hampering my movements, she doesn't have to paw me, what would she say if I started pawing the back of her knee, I could assault her too, bite the back of her knee, and her breasts, keep going, one more, La Merken's voice grows softer and softer, the solution is to get this over and done with as quickly as possible, get her bloody book for her, don't look down, I'm not feeling the least giddy, it's weird, maybe it's because she's holding me.

It's the first time I've managed to get past the fifth rung of a ladder, bite her backside, that sweet smell, who does this woman think she is? In Paris, in the establishment run by Madame Blanche, there are women who look like her and are much sweeter-natured, Moncel is nearing the top, his hand is on one of the Wagner volumes, I have it, Madame, I'm coming down now, no, open it, read, read from your great height, the last scene, the legato passage, now I'm really starting to feel dizzy, she's mad, I want to come down, I can't read standing up on top of a ladder, I'm going to fall, Madame, no, I'm holding you, relax, La Merken was almost shouting, breathe, read, the last scene, the song of Brünnhilde, it's sung in a subdued voice, you're not afraid now, read *trat ich vor ihm,* read, I walked towards him, and you can come down, I don't read German very well, *trat ich vor ihm*, ladder's slipping Madame.

She put her hand under his backside, I walked towards him, you're not afraid any more, her large paw under Moncel's backside, the woman's thumb, he shudders, do what she says, quickly, La Merken is careful, mustn't hurt, but she doesn't move her hand, it's at this precise moment that it happens, before there was nothing, now it's done, La Merken has no respect for what she's holding in her hand but she's careful with it, Moncel says nothing, in Madame Blanche's establishment the woman had taken him firmly saying this way, he was excited, she had squeezed very hard, around the base, stay calm sweetie, I'm not going to short-change you, must have your money's worth, I'm an honest girl! she was hurting him, to calm him, see it's not so terrible! Read, Moncel, *Ich vernahm des Heldens*, yes I beheld the hero's sacred pain, Madame, it's moving, there's nothing to be afraid of, I've got you, Madame Merken's hand, no giddiness, the lament of the bravest of the brave has reached my ear, read, Moncel, read.

The ladder shakes, your thumb Madame, if you wouldn't mind, *furchtbares Leid*, do you understand, Moncel? Translate, the horrid suffering of the freest love, go on, I'm holding you, the ladder, your thumb, Madame, *mein Aug'*, that's it, Moncel, my eye has seen what struck my heart with a sacred jolt, do you like that? now do you understand us?

Yes, Madame, Moncel on the top of his ladder, La Merken's right hand is firm and alive, it supports Moncel, Moncel glances down, eyes wide, she cranes her head up to him, her double chin has disappeared, he doesn't think her ugly any more, someone has come into the library, La Merken has removed her hand, he doesn't know how he managed to climb back down again, La Merken was now talking to her husband's new secretary.

Lena walks through the lobby, have you seen Monsieur Kappler? She can't find him, a Scotsman sitting in an armchair with his legs crossed watches as she goes, I don't know what's the matter with people tonight, it's the altitude, the medics say that altitude multiplies the number of red blood corpuscles, this makes us more active, more resilient, sometimes it prevents us sleeping, it can also bring on migraines but tonight nobody's got a headache, a woman says to Lena:

'Monsieur Kappler? He was with young Mademoiselle de Valréas just a few minutes ago.'

That Frédérique, arrogant, a know-all, as silly as girls are at eighteen, Lena searches for Hans in the lounges, she know Frédérique isn't really silly or arrogant, she's just young, that's exactly why you don't like her, see things as they are, she's going to do what you have failed to do for the last ten years, a farandole jigs past, the dancers try to sweep Lena along with them, she shakes free of them, Lilstein is looking for her.

Max as usual has taken refuge in his role as observer, he thinks Hans is mad, he's been trying to find Lena for more than ten years, she's here, they say she's never looked more beautiful and Hans is having a pleasant chat with a brazen young hoyden who is at the same time also being kept under surveillance by Merken, the wild boar, young Frédérique is flattered, Philosophy and Fiction are looking at her, Max feels sure that she is even now saying no to Hans, and Hans will be free but in a way that Lena won't like, actually it's not at all certain the girl will say no to Hans, she gives him a playful tap, they both laugh affectionately, Hans is telling Frédérique about his walk two days ago, along a path through the forest, there were children playing, very young, two nannies to take care of them:

'I pretended to be taking a breather, among the children there was a little girl called Frédérique.'

'Loving and obedient?'

'Frédérique, I would like to have a little girl by you.'

'Hans, you know very well that motherhood interests young women not at all, or at best inadvertently.'

'I'd settle for that, I'll give anything, at once!'

'So that you can demand everything?'

'Are you going to remain single? Grow old alone?'

'I intend to wait, Hans, we're all waiting for Mr Right, like Natasha at the ball in *War and Peace*, we wait and suddenly he's coming straight towards us, the handsomest of men, the most heroic, he comes to us and he asks us to dance, then he is killed in the war and we turn into ladies of property and live on our country estates, I shan't have the patience to wait, I shall anticipate events.'

'You're going to travel?'

'No, I think travel narrows the mind, but I do want to get away from my mother, work, read, write, walk, fight, weep, make the running, apparently you always find a man in the end.'

'Who are you looking for?'

'A teddy bear, Hans, a teddy bear, like before, he has to be strong as an ox, and artistic, but intelligent with it, I've no idea what he should look like, like you? Or nobody? Or he'll just be someone I'll miss where he's not around.'

Further along, snatches of salon conversation are heard it seems that women belong to the men who love them most, true, but the man who loves a woman the most puts himself at her mercy and eventually suffers for it, there's no getting away from that.

Max has observed that Lilstein looked unhappy, he said if you want to be loved you must hold your cards closer to your chest, it only takes one look and they can tell you're a novice.

And Lilstein got systematically drunk, German-style, on French cognac, in a corner, without stirring, with reflections gyrating in the mirrors, sudden fascinations with the shape of a wineglass, a stool, words which stay inside, words which have diminishing success in getting themselves into the correct order.

Hans caught up again with Michael Lilstein at three in the morning, on the edge of coma, he took him back to his room, helped him be sick, at eleven a.m. Lilstein woke up, feeling nauseous, headache, dizziness in waves, he's wearing only his pyjama top, remembers nothing, by his bedside Hans Kappler is fast asleep in a deep armchair, he must have stayed to keep an eye on him, Lilstein doesn't dare get out of bed, he can't see any of his clothes within arm's reach.

*

The day they all left Max accompanied Hans down into the valley, as far as Klosters station. Max feared his every word. Hans said:

'You mustn't think I blame you, you're more unhappy than I am.'

Hans is referring to what happened the evening before last, but he doesn't mention Lena's name, he says again:

'Don't think I blame you.'

He adds:

'We must go on working together on our plans.'

Max didn't understand what Hans meant by plans, Hans reminded him of another conversation, the one in the Jardin du Luxembourg, the sets and props for your novel, *The Madwoman*, you know you promised I could do them, the story of the one-legged man and his wife, you didn't finish it that day in the gardens, you broke off to tell me about Ensor and some young writer, you told me the woman had been cared for, in '17 she'd protested against the war and she'd been given treatment.

'You'll like it,' said Max, 'a very interesting episode, very scientific.'

A chance to talk about something other than the night before last: with a bit of luck Max might be able to spin it out until the train pulled in without any mention of him and Lena cropping up, 1917, a very scientific episode, the wife of a hero shouting denunciations of the war, she couldn't be anything except mad, the most modern treatments were used, first the milk diet but there was a shortage of dairy products, balneotherapy, diuretics, sedatives, a lot of sedatives, then her temperature was artificially raised and she was given long, invigorating cold showers, it made her shake uncontrollably, they tied her down, she still shook, there was no improvement, so they proceeded to the final weapon, faradism, the latest thing in war psychiatry, electricity, her husband told me all about it, I never really understood if he was for or against, in any case he was invited to be present at the treatments, the purpose was to counter a neurosis of the ego, hence the resort to electric energy to free her by shocks from her negative ego, persuasive faradism.

According to the doctors, this was a way of linking modern technology to the permanent moral battle, the basic idea was the assumption that the patient maintained a degree of lucidity, a latent cooperative will which would be awakened by means of drastic therapy, they would have to eradicate her anxiety and emotional fragility, the egotistical emotivity which had taken possession of her when she had first seen her husband with one leg missing, a disorienting, self-destructive hyperactivity, Hans, what do you think of the vocabulary? It was a symptom of psychopathy but not inaccessible to aggressive treatment.

The whole of French medical opinion fought hard to force upon Hélène de Vèze the ability to turn back into the honourable wife of a soldier who had fought with valour, she had sought refuge in illness, she had to be made to reject illness, make it so horrible that she would have only one thought in her head, to escape the bright sparks on the ends of the copper wires, the sound of the discharges just before the treatments began, the humming of the coils, the thick copper and metal bracelets, the urging of the doctors, the pain.

Diseased organs are subjected to the same treatment, in cases of localised paralysis, current is applied to the hand which has stopped moving, the patient screams, proof that his hand exists, therefore that it can be made to function, he can reacquire as function what he feels as pain, and for the head, in mental cases, it's the same, she had lost the feeling of victory and honour, the fact that she was Swiss made her less tough, same treatment.

It took four strong nuns to hold her down, she had fled the war into illness, four, five brawny nuns and a medic to force her to flee from illness and back to health, the faradaic current delivered by a pencil of copper wires, it was played over skin, belly, thighs, nails of hands and feet, not town electricity, too strong, too risky, they used a Faraday machine, progressive current, but it had to be forcibly felt, it had to shock, the patient should not be allowed time to get used to it.

She was a neurotic, all neurotics dissemble, they dissemble without knowing that they're doing it, that is what their illness is, it was crucial not to allow the illness to erect defences against faradisation, hence the sizzling offensive, no warning given, as in war, surprise, shock, the woman held out for a long time, a foreigner, she was even used in demonstrations given to other patients, those awaiting the treatment, she resisted.

One of the doctors said that her resistance came from a deep-seated displacement of the maternal instinct. She had no child, she had no country, she could not have any feeling of a motherland; and at the same time she looked on her husband as her child, now the husband was a defender of the motherland, she blamed her husband for defending the wrong mother.

He was an extremely subtle doctor, the wrong mother, so they decided to apply the electric beams to areolas and nipples, not easy to take such a decision, it needed sturdy sisters who volunteered to restrain her, the question was raised whether male patients waiting their turn should be allowed to watch, in the end they were made to attend these sessions, that's right, three sessions, results were inconclusive.

At one point, the woman started muttering:

'Victory, victory.'

She stared at the Faraday machine, most impressive, the doctors realised that they had won, in the theatre everyone started mouthing victory, she was exhausted, she is always exhausted, but she has returned to her own, into the community, a fine victory, and one which paved the way for others.

Two of the patients waiting to be treated got up one morning saying that they felt better, that they wouldn't need to have the treatment, but they were given it all the same. With the woman, it had been extra difficult because she was French by adoption, she was very brave, the doctors congratulated her.

'All that will have to go in your novel, Max.'

'Putting everything in is a German speciality, Hans, in France we call it being long-winded. A novel is not an encyclopaedia.'

'You can't just ignore the knowledge of the age you live in.'

'But you don't have to import it wholesale, what you want is a quick turn over, create an impression.'

'*Nein*, that would be bluffing!'

'Whether I describe or don't describe, the main thing is that it changed our militant heroine permanently, with lifelong after-care, the *ne plus ultra*, at the army's expense.'

'And for years your Thomas de Vèze has been taking Hélène out for walks of an afternoon, whenever it's fine, a great love, is she able to speak?'

'Very slowly, all she can say are the usual hellos and thank-yous, the neighbours call her the Madwoman, especially those who had almost believed what she'd said, the ones the gendarmes questioned at the time and did not prosecute, no charges were brought, there were only statements from witnesses, it was put down to a minor outbreak of hysteria foreign in origin, they concluded that the stock was healthy, it didn't stop Hélène having a kid.'

'And will *The Madwoman* be the title of this novella?'

'Of my novel, Monsieur Kappler!'

'You're going to have to pad it out if you want to make it look like a novel, so you'll need to stir in some factual stuff.'

'You said there was a knack to writing descriptions?'

'Yes, a secret, and a secret it will stay.'

'I'll swap you, the secret for a beautiful object I've spotted here-abouts.'

'No object is worth a trade secret, Max.'

'This one is.'

'At least tell me what it's called.'

'It's a spanking chair.'

'Trust you French, such dirty minds! What's it like? Did you find it in some knocking shop? How is the victim strapped in?'

'Your trade secret first.'

'No, Max, your secret, then I promise I'll hand over mine.'

'In fact, there's nothing so special about it to qualify as secret, no mechanism to immobilise the partially unclothed victim, no hatch, it's a perfectly inoffensive chair, looks like any other carver's chair, with arm-rests, except that one of the arm-rests has been removed so that it doesn't impede the pedagogue who is free to swish whoever he has forced on to his or her knees, every school in France has one, the one I saw was actually designed for a left-handed swisher.'

*

Hans refuses to include this hogwash in the backdrop to the novel, Max tries to negotiate, it would be fun, push the reader into a spot of dirty-minded adult fantasising, when he comes round he finds there are small children within reach and it's his fault . . . As you wish . . . Over to you now: the secret of describing.

'It's not much of a secret either, Max, it's simple, for a description you need a clash, a conflict, the conflict is much more important than the details otherwise the reader gets bored, the wind and the trees, if you show the wind bending the trees, you've soon finished, but if the trees resist you have a struggle, a lull, battle rejoined, suspense, drama, a structure, La Fontaine knew all this long ago, you can also do it along lines very fashionable nowadays, abandon descriptions alto-gether, take out plot, dialogue, things, you stand the character in front of a mirror or insert him into a waking dream, he talks to himself, you fracture grammar and thought, you make things easier for yourself, with short sentences, very curt.'

'I prefer conflict,' says Max.

'In that case your sentence must brawl with itself, that is the whole point of describing, it's not to be lifelike, nowadays photos are far better at doing that, you have to describe without knowing where you're going, Max you see that light through the foliage? On the other side of the track? The flowers? I tell myself that if I succeed in getting them down interestingly on the page, not to remind the reader of what he has already seen and heard, but to make him hear what is unwonted in language, there, look, between the railway posters, the leaves and the purple dress that woman is wearing, there on the platform oppo-site, that couple, don't stare, the dark-haired woman in the purple dress, the background ochre of the poster behind the purple dress and the belladonna shade of the scarf, I don't know yet, there you have all the power of daylight, or there's nothing, but if words start brawling with one another over the poster and the face of the woman in the purple dress, then my German language will become less useful for giving orders with, you've seen that face, Max? We've been through catastrophic times, but pretty women are always with us.'

Max doesn't think there's anything particularly extraordinary about the woman, but now that Hans has stopped talking about Lena he feels disposed to admire all the women travelling on Swiss railways who come within his friend's ambit.

'A sentence brawling with itself. Today the fashion is the exact opposite, the curt sentence, Max, it's perfectly good, no affectation, it packs a punch, it has a youthful ring, but actually it's exactly like giving an order, there's nothing ambiguous about it, it leaves nothing unsaid, the curt sentence is omniscience in a dozen words, it intimidates, it connives with order, the sentence must fight against order, Max, it must stretch its limbs and fight against everything it has been made to do up to now, we must invent a longer sentence, different from what it was before we began, a sentence that is without order, chiaroskewered words, the feeling that they've missed something out, don't start a sentence if you know how to end it, because the reader will also know, and when you reread it you will rage at what you have not succeeded in doing, and if the whole thing suddenly starts to sing, even if it's only in the proper name of plants for example, in the setting sun, Nerine, Torch Lily, Chinese Lantern, some day I'd like to write a poem with Chinese Lantern.

'You've got to let it sing and when it starts to sing you must say to yourself the song is merely the conceit of what you have failed to achieve, you wanted to flay bare and you describe, you sough, you rage, and you start again, if necessary you jettison flowers, you start again with fungi, the underwoods, the colours which change, something to do with the name of fungi, Max, or the movements of a dancer or a woman singing.'

Hans has managed to say a woman singing without stumbling, he would like to embrace Max and send him away saying kiss her for me, he says nothing, looking across at the woman on the platform he resumes:

'You have to hurl words, otherwise all that remains will be curt sentences and telegramese.'

'Hans, this couple of mine, Thomas and Hélène, eventually they had a kid, I don't know what to do with kids in stories.'

Chapter 11

1969

A Funeral and an Ambush

In which a great writer is buried and no stone is left unturned to capture a spy who is present among the mourners.

In which Henri de Vèze reads aloud a passage from Le Grand Meaulnes.

In which we learn what transpired long ago at Waltenberg between a boar and a young woman.

In which Lilstein warns you against the fine sentiments which can be so prejudicial to good moles.

Grindisheim, October 1969

One day the self stops spinning its own tales.
What sort of people ever get over it?

Charles Juliet

Someone has taken Max by the elbow, Max said nothing to begin with; they walked on together for a moment without speaking, in the main body of the funeral cortege. Sometimes, at a bend, they could see shiny reflections of the brass band, the black plumes of the horses.

'You're late, young Lilstein, where were you?'

'Forty years ago your face was exactly as it is now, Max, you haven't changed a bit.'

'The face of a man who'd seen it all, young Lilstein, and you had the face of an angel, an opinionated boy and as beautiful as the angel who says no, you stand very straight, cheeks smooth, still very presentable in your fifties, and you take me by the elbow as Hans used to when we went for walks, I don't mention it to make you let go of me, today I need the familiar gesture, is the friendly arm a new custom in the GDR?'

'It's the first time I've ever done it, I saw Monsieur Kappler do it when you used to walk together.'

'He did it for my sake, to be more French than the French, I rather liked it, you still call him *Monsieur* Kappler?'

'I admired you, at Waltenberg I didn't agree with either of you but I admired you, you knew so many things, a whole culture . . .'

'. . . which had been through Hell, four years of Hell, you saw Hans again, after his final return to Rosmar in '56?'

'Two or three times.'

'That all? Doubtless what you call "negative talks"?'

'He fulminated, Max.'

'Like you when you were sixteen, young Lilstein. And eighteen months later you helped him return to the West?'

'I told whoever it might have concerned that we shouldn't try to stop him.'

'And whoever it did concern muttered into his little goatee, wiped his little glasses, and said in that famous reedy voice *so sei es*, let it be so. What sort of angel are you, young Lilstein, that whoever it concerned should, in your presence, start talking like God the Father in the land of atheists?'

'When Monsieur Kappler said he'd like to come back to us, the general secretary of the Politburo himself gave the green light, I said it was a mistake, that it wouldn't be long before he was off again, and when he did want to go . . .'

'You performed your self-criticism, comrade, as if the green light had been given by you personally.'

'Max, how well you know us.'

'It's age, young man, as you know, I've seen it all. You took the blame for the Politburo secretariat's mistake, I mean the mistake made by *whoever it might have concerned*, and then, as your reward, *whoever it did concern* allowed Hans to leave.'

'We couldn't have done otherwise.'

'And in any case *whoever it did* or his little comrades would have made you carry the can, which you would have found more painful than a session of self-criticism.'

Early that morning, at seven o'clock, in a large house in the centre of Grindisheim, the Director of the Federal Office for the Protection of the Constitution had reminded them of the orders: during the funeral itself they were only to keep the subject under surveillance, surround him, but in no circumstances approach him, it was not yet known if these would be the final instructions, that decision would be taken at the top, in Bonn, in the Chancellery, we have thirty agents on the ground, I don't want a shambles, Colonel Sebald will be coordinating all services, orders can come only from him and he will get his orders from me alone.

Around Max and Lilstein, the crowd walks slowly behind the antique hearse and the trade union brass band, banners, tubas, drums, and clarinettes. The band started with funeral marches, Chopin and Verdi, but as they proceeded the music became less gloomy, faces lifted. The procession was strung out along the tarmac road which rose in broad loops through the vine slopes of Grindisheim.

'What sort of wine do they make in these parts, Max?'
   'Don't you know? A German who doesn't recognise wine on the vine bang in the middle of the Rhineland only a few days before they start the grape harvest?'
   'If it's in a glass I can manage, but otherwise I'm a bit of a dunce.'
   'The leaves, my boy, the leaves: fleshy, ridged, veins like the veins on the back of the hand, pubescent, fruit very round, brown and russet blemishes, thick skin.'
   'Max, you learned that by heart.'
   'Just what you need! And the soil, young Lilstein, want me to recite that too?'
   Max's forefinger aimed at the sky, his eye on the head of the procession:
   'Listen to that, unusual, eh?'
   The band is playing 'Lilli Marlene', very slow tempo.

Hans had written: 'Since it is out of the question for me to make my final journey along the sea front of my native town, I wish my funeral to be held at Grindisheim, in the vineyard between the Rhine and the forest, I ask for a band, flowers, wreaths, sunshine and would like people to drink.' The council chose the route, from the town hall to the cemetery, taking a wide detour through the terraces of the vine slopes with a few deviations into the forest higher up.

'A sandy soil,' says Lilstein.

'A good point, and that gives?'

'A wine tending to the sweet, as the guidebooks say, Max.'

'Two good points. And if you give a certain clever little fungus its head?'

'I'm not illiterate either, but that said, I prefer a wine that's more sinewy.'

'In that case we'll have to go higher up. Hans would have approved of my feeding you little titbits about life and wine, like in the good old days. The ground just before you get to the forest, not so much loess and more slate, more wind, more cold, less mist, more sun, and more risk as well, but a definite flintiness in the back of the throat, just enough bitterness to make you want to drink more, you know, like life!'

Max and Lilstein are halfway up the slope, Lilstein looks down, then up towards the top: the crowd is now strung out over nearly a kilometre. The terraces are retained by walls of pink sandstone, large blocks mellowed by the late-afternoon sun. At some bends in the road there are fountains; Max has seen one date, 1853. With a gesture of his hand, he points to the cortege:

'You know the old saying, young Lilstein, "One eye to weep, the other to measure the length of the cortege"?'

'And the name of the grape, Max?'

'Noblesse, poor yield, virile on the tongue, young Lilstein, one of my great memories is of a bottle I drank in 1922 at Weimar with Rathenau; he asked me to communicate to the French that by threatening to occupy the Ruhr we were handing Germany over to the extreme right, Riesling, young Lilstein, the best! Hans would never have agreed to his coffin being paraded past second-rate vines!'

As far as the Director of the Federal Office for the Protection of the Constitution was concerned, if someone in the cortege showed hostility of any sort towards the suspect, that person would have to be discreetly neutralised:

'We must be the only ones able to create problems for the suspect.

He will doubtless exchange greetings with a number of people, do not become distracted by trying to identify them, that's the job of another team; if a well-known member of parliament shakes his hand, don't start thinking that the member of parliament in question is a traitor, our man has known many people for a very long time, and the traitor is perhaps somebody who pretends not to know him or knows that we know that they know each other and so goes out of his way to say hello to him, or even someone who knows that he is innocent and will say hello because he knows that our suspicions will fall first on those who keep their distance, and if you think we're going to have problems working all this out, then you've understood where our target's strength lies.'

In the cortege, around Max and Lilstein are many people of their age, over fifty.

There are also some who are younger, often in twos. Readers? Max draws Lilstein's attention to a woman, mourning suit, fair hair, fleshy, black toque, pearl-grey scarf, dark leather boots, she is alone and she is beautiful.

'From some points of view, Hans would have really loved this cortege, do you fancy her, young man?'

'She's probably a representative of the association of thirty-year-old women who read novels. Max, she has no husband, reading is an exclusive occupation.'

'Ah, sociology, but tell me, for you to have been allowed out of the GDR to come here, you must be a person of some standing?'

'Or of no account whatsoever, Max, I never asked them for anything, they never asked me for anything.'

'And at the frontier were the Vopos on strike?'

'I came via Vienna and Switzerland, I don't give a damn now, since he died I've been like you, sleepwalking.'

'And your eyes are red-rimmed, young Lilstein.'

'Two deaths in six months, Max, it's hard, but at least I've been able to be here for this funeral.'

'Yes, and Lena's would have cost you dearer than the price of a

509

wreath. If I've the strength I'll tell you all, and also if you tell me a couple of things in confidence.'

*

Lilstein told you:

'You know, young gentleman of France, in 1956 I'd arranged to meet Kappler, here, at Waltenberg, not in the Waldhaus, the Waldhaus was for you, the Kappler meeting was in the Konditorei, that same morning.'

You look at Lilstein, he takes his time to sit down, he casts an eye all round the large hotel lobby. Some distance away, a table is occupied by a group of about fifteen people. The men are dressed in cycling gear. They are very noisy.

'They drive up here in Mercedes,' says Lilstein, 'with their bikes on the roof. They have a good meal and then they ride sedately down again. Their wives are left with the job of driving the cars back.'

He looks suddenly serious:

'Authentic German athletes.'

He sits down, gives you an affectionate look:

'You'll see, when you're at Grindisheim, a funeral is not an easy thing, all your failures come charging back to you at the double. In '56, Kappler and I had known each other for more than a quarter of a century, since my first visit to Waltenberg in '29. He knew a great many things about life, he smiled, he treated me like an equal, I was almost sixteen, he called me young Lilstein, and every time I call you young man, or young Frenchman, I recall Kappler's voice.

'In '56, I tried to persuade him not to return to the Democratic Republic, I did not succeed, he returned, set up house at Rosmar, by the sea, he held out for a few years and then left again. He'd already tried it once late in '46, it hadn't worked. He didn't know where to settle, he went backwards and forwards between East and West.'

He breaks off, gets up to greet the hotelière who is heading for your table. You stand too. She has changed very little. She has put on weight but her face is unlined. Lilstein orders two glasses of white wine and two portions of Linzer, without even asking you. You sit down again, he resumes:

'By the way, have you noticed? In the village they've knocked down the Konditorei; Waltenberg has changed a lot. The Waldhaus seminars are expanding, they're going to set up a kind of forum for the great decision-makers of the Western world, they're looking for willing helpers. You wouldn't fancy making yourself indispensable to these people? They earn a lot of money but can't write for toffee, it would make the perfect excuse for all your comings and goings, we might even be able to drop the guff about classified ads for bibliophiles.'

*

In the cortege, Max asked Lilstein if he knew the young woman with the pearl-grey scarf, she's a few steps behind them, the face means nothing to Max but Lilstein isn't so sure, might she look a little like Hans? A niece? A daughter?

'He never had children,' says Max, 'nor any relatives of her age, he'd have told me, mistress maybe? I don't see him committing suicide when he had a royal dish like her in his bed, or perhaps she'd stopped wanting to warm it for him.'

'In that case, would she come to his funeral? Max, she really does look like him.'

'No, the face is completely different.'

'She looks at people just the way he did, as if she were constantly trying to force the world to give her a reason for living. In any case, she's been looking this way as if she knew us, maybe I'm imagining things, Max, why suicide?'

'Perhaps for the same reasons as Socrates?'

'No one sentenced him to death, Max, on the contrary, we let him go back to the West as soon as he asked to go, we said nothing, he was immensely respected, a man who encapsulated his century.'

'He wanted a lot more, young Lilstein, he wanted to see the GDR become the land he'd dreamed of, it was an awful lot to ask. He went back to you in '56 as a gesture of provocation, at a time when you were committing your biggest foul-ups, and because he realised that the CIA was using him, that famous association "for the freedom of culture", he believed in it implicitly, a genuine realignment of intellectuals to further the freedom of culture, and then he found out that the meals, plane tickets, hotel bills, everything was paid for by the CIA, that didn't bother people like Spender or Koestler, but it stuck in Hans's craw, he slammed the door, went back to Rosmar, at the worst possible time, Budapest, to provoke, and also to punish himself, and it didn't work, so he went back to the West, and when he'd got sick of you, of both you and them, he threw his death in your faces.'

'Moral rigidity, that's why he killed himself,' says Lilstein, 'because he couldn't forgive himself for dreaming his dreams.'

'Or because he'd run out of the kind of books he could read before going to sleep, or couldn't remember the name of a friend he was at school with, or because some dog kept barking all night, or because he realised that he was beginning to sound querulous, like me, all those days when you could have worked but instead you let them be filled by stupid things, you can kill yourself for that, because you've had enough of living with your own remains, or because of something entirely trivial, you're making me cross with your questions, he almost died once of a broken heart, in 1914, and he also wanted to kill himself when he left his house at Rosmar the first time, in 1934.'

'We let him have it back, fully restored.'

'Yes, but you stayed exactly the same, I mean your wonderful regime. Last year you and yours rode into Czechoslovakia to do a spot more restoration work, that also made his day.'

An argument carried on in an undertone in the nerve-centre of the Federal Office for the Protection of the Constitution: some wanted to lift the suspect immediately, in the middle of the funeral, must know how to make the most of an opportunity, the fact that it was a funeral will soon be forgotten, the fact that they got him will be all that's remembered, I tell you the target's a heavyweight, it's been going on for years and years, we hold him responsible for the denunciation and deaths of dozens of our agents in the East, no, I'm not exaggerating, and even if those deaths were indirect, he is still *objectively* complicit in a number of murders because he undermines our position. Actually, replies a voice, I think it's funny that you should use the word *objectively* the way the people on the other side do.

And the man who said *objectively* and has just attracted the remark about the people on the other side turns pale, because he is in fact from the other side.

Lilstein leans towards Max, in a quick whisper, voice cautious or broken, or ironic:

'Hans never recovered from his experience of real socialism.'

'If anyone wrote anything like that in your amazing Democratic Republic, young Lilstein, they'd shunt him off to prison, you are a stirrer, you should be someone really important over there, you know what he left on his bedside table? A quote from a poet: "Do not let me into your Paradise, there I should suffer torment more terrible than anything Hell has to offer, I choose Hell, Hell is all I want." Obviously you know the poet is the one who penned your national, democratic, people's anthem, no less?'

'And now, Max, the Germans are going to fight to find out who it really was that Monsieur Kappler did his talking to, "your Paradise", I can just imagine the next few weeks in the papers.'

'Is it true what they say? that you are now in charge of inter-German relations? that is, of selling your dissidents to the Federal Republic? Give me an interview on that subject, and I'll tell you about Lena's funeral?'

'Max! A truce, a few hours!'

The young woman with the fair hair and the pearl-grey scarf has come up to Max and Lilstein:

'Good morning, my mother isn't well, she asked me to come instead of her, she knew you'd be here, I have a photo, you're Max and you're Lilstein, my mother told me: "You'll have no trouble recognising Max Goffard, he'll be more or less the same as in the photo, the one with the big ears, the other one is the tall adolescent who's standing next to them, he must be about fifty-five now, he'll certainly be there, by Max's side." I'm Frédérique's daughter. My mother also said: "Give them my love, you must stick close to them, it'll stop them getting into arguments during the funeral." That's all.'

There are five of them in the photo, skis on feet, plus-fours, Norwegian sweaters, Max is wearing a Basque beret, Hans and Lilstein have caps, Lena a soldier's beret, Erna a woolly hat with a pompon, behind them the façade of a hotel, an immense double chalet, with flowers in the windows.

'Period kitsch,' says Max, 'it was Frédérique who took the photo outside the Waldhaus, I took one too, of Frédérique and the other four, have you got it with you?'

'I've seen it, my mother wouldn't let me have it, she admitted that you were a crazy gang, all in love with each other and none of you knowing how you stood with the others. She also said the men weren't very good at it.'

'Young Lilstein lost sleep over it.'

'Max wanted to move from Erna to Frédérique,' said Lilstein with a smile, 'and one evening there he was back in the corridor, all the doors closed, actually, not all of them: he had the luck for which Monsieur Kappler and I would have given our eye-teeth, but he didn't seem any the happier for it.'

'That's not strictly true,' said Max, 'but you can understand why we were crazy: what beautiful creatures those women are! What became of your mother, young woman? You know, to us she is immortal.'

Lilstein does not listen to the answer the young woman gives Max, he is at Waltenberg with those beautiful skiing girls, forty years ago, with one of them, the slope of a coomb, a breath-stopping diagonal, having got up at four in the morning, there were about ten of them, I'd never have missed a session of the Seminar but she wanted to trek across country on skis, she had nothing else to do, she was there for the closing recital, needed fresh air, it was the guide who'd come and roused Lilstein, a cross-country with her, a whole day, as I got up I banged my forehead, under the eaves, a room with twin beds, thick waxed beam, just above the bed.

Max is launched into a series of wild questions, did your mother ever talk about Maynes? Or Merken? Splendid fellows! And that young philosopher who looked like a Boy Scout, Hans and I used to pull his leg, a young Catholic, took Madame Merken's fancy, name of Moncel, nowadays he's a very big name in theatre.

'My mother knows less about him than I do,' the young woman said, 'I often bump into him, I'm an actress.'

She said this gravely, for Max's benefit she adds:

'I know Monsieur Kappler didn't like the theatre.'

'It wasn't quite that, young lady, he was suspicious of theatre, for instance he couldn't stand *Lorenzaccio*.'

Lilstein knocked his head, when you get out of bed in this room under the eaves you always forget to pay attention, afterwards he took more care, I got ready keeping out of that beam's way, I went out, forgot my scarf, I went back up to my room, retrieved my scarf from the bed, I took care and I still knocked the back of my neck as I stood up, my brother grunted, without waking up, departure four thirty, still dark, three-quarter moon, incipient headache, headaches always made me slow-witted, I'm going to be with her for a whole day and already I've got a headache.

Max and Hans had been to see *Lorenzaccio* in Paris in the early fifties, as they came out afterwards Hans looked unhappily at Max, he hadn't been able to stand the play.

'And it was the Théâtre National Populaire too,' resumes Max, 'Gérard Philipe, Ivernel, big production, full house, enthusiastic audience, not at all the regular Comédie Française audience, more tweedy people, often with no tie, mix of middle-class, civil servants, clerks, workmen in their Sunday best like in Russia, a lot of young people, either in couples or in groups.'

Forefinger towards the face of Frédérique's daughter:

'You know, young lady, when people talk about the theatre-goer they are mistaken, the theatre-goer is never in the singular, but almost invariably a couple, formed, or about to be formed, or to split, who knows? The basic unit is the couple and what happens within the couple who go to the theatre, you act for couples, Hans and I were an exception, a pair of old friends. I told him to watch the couples, all those attractive women, I'd have preferred seats in the balcony so I could look down their cleavages, he said I had a dirty mind. He found the play very peculiar.'

Skis and sticks over one shoulder, hat pulled down, measured pace, two by two along the road, the clunk of steel-tipped boots, some use a ski-stick like a walking-stick, after half an hour they leave the road, a path already flattened in the snow, overlaid by a few centimetres of fresh frosted powder, the bracing air in the chest, the trachea, Lena is chatting to one of the young French girls, Lilstein is just behind her with an Englishman, the hardest part for me is to stay in contact with London, the Englishman is as tall as Lilstein, thick lips, hair already receding though he's not yet forty, it's Maynes, he makes a point of seeking Lilstein out, the path winds up gently towards the first col, they are making towards Davos, the guide has a sing-song voice, 'not so fast', 'not so fast', he stops two men who have gone on ahead, 'halt!', he tells them to go to the back, puts Lena and Lilstein at the front, with himself just behind them, it's the first time Lilstein has ever wanted to kiss a mountain guide, he tells the guide our English friends are not best pleased, a woman has been put at the head of the group.

'The theatre is a tough business to be in, Monsieur Goffard,' says the young woman. 'You shouldn't speak ill of it.'

Max decides that she looks like her mother, the same modulation, low and categorical, in the young woman's voice. She adds:

'I prefer Monsieur Moncel even if he's unfair about what I act in, with his *Figaro* reviews.'

'Oh, he's turned over a new leaf,' says Max, 'you were there for *The Cherry Orchard*, last year? Or when he went to see *The Days of the Commune*? When the curtain comes down, the audience gives the Berliner Ensemble a standing ovation, La Weigel comes down off the stage, imagine, she's there in the stalls, with Aragon, Elsa, the leading communists, the left-wing intellectuals. In the centre aisle a silence settles from the back, a man walks forward slowly, on the arm of a friend, a woman, he goes up to La Wiegel, it's Moncel greeting Brecht's widow! And everyone smiles at him, that too was a great spectacle.'

The guide tells Lilstein:

'Fräulein Hotspur, excuse me, Fräulein Hellström, is very much at home in these mountains, she knows this route very well, she's already done it several times.'

'Was that a long time ago, Madame Hellström?'

'You can call me Lena, Michael, if you call me Lena and not Madame I'll teach you to put your questions more graciously, yes, I've been on a good number of these cross-country treks, here, with our guide, before the war, before '14, now don't go repeating that even though it doesn't really matter, look!'

She points to a mountain top just beginning to turn pink, the Rikshorn.

'You see those little clouds, they say the old man's smoking his pipe, fine weather, with a small risk of becoming unsettled, in the mountains a small risk can turn into something big, unleash equinoctial fury. Maybe this wasn't the right day for a jaunt.'

They come across the tracks of weasel or stoat, a bend every three hundred metres or so, what's after the col? Another col, it's a theorem of a mountain, every col is followed by another and higher col, one of the French girls shouts:

'My sunglasses! I've forgotten my sunglasses!'

The guide smiles, pulls another pair out of his anorak, holds them out to her, that's his job, to think of everything, especially think for people who forget their sunglasses, he'd lined up his charges outside the hotel, the list out loud, gloves, hat, biscuits, flask, sunglasses, he himself carries a bag which must weigh all of twenty kilos, plus two spare ski tips and a rope slung over the top; the French girl had said yes without checking if she really had her sunglasses; Lena has even thought to bring a sort of small pad which she inserts between her shoulder and the skis, the going is becoming harder now, it's not long before people aren't talking, throats burning, time to adjust, the guide repeats 'not so fast', Lilstein has a tendency to go faster, Lena puts one hand on his arm, squeezes his biceps:

'You must do what the grown-ups tell you.'

Lilstein does not care at all for the remark.

'Hans didn't like *Lorenzaccio* one bit,' says Max, 'not the play, Hans said here you find it exaggerated but for a German it'll do, he added: "What I don't understand is why it should be such a success here in the heart of Paris in front of all these people, how long is it? Hardly six, seven years since the Occupation ended, great left-wing actor, left-wing director, people's theatre, civic theatre to use your word, and what's the play about? A tyrant protected by a German garrison, have I got it wrong? The Duke has a stronger libido than Pétain but that's what it is, a tyrant who has the backing of the Church and is protected by a German garrison, and on the other side the people resisting them talk too much or behave without thinking, incompetents, think about it, Max, three hours of incompetent resistance, the stuff of cock-ups or cowardice, and it's barely half a dozen years that France has been free, and the audience cheers, power wielded by bastards, resistance mounted by morons, the only character to carry out a plan to the end is the effeminate one who's so handy with a knife, and the regime which follows is presented as being rotten to the core, as rotten as the one before, it orders students to be fired on, and everyone applauds, the right, the left, the moderates in between, the activists, the wait-and-sees, the collaborators, the resisters, everybody anxious to get their snout in the trough, Max, I don't like this method of being in agreement!" '

Lilstein has quickened his pace, deliberately, right, so she's put her hand on my arm but that's no reason for saying I have to do what the grown-ups say, she said it so she could put her hand on my arm, or else she put her hand on my arm so that she could say it, and then she smiles, it's true that it's only at me that she smiles like that. A hand once again on Lilstein's arm, just a little muttered *tsk tsk*, she's not talking about grown-ups now, she's not saying anything, so agreeable, headache's gone. She adds:

'You'll get a telling off.'

They've been going for an hour and a half already, heartbeat normal, Waltenberg looks very small down in the valley below, all that can be made out is the bulk of the Waldhaus and the annexe, a few street lights outside the hotel, a wisp of hair has escaped from under Lena's hat, flutters on the nape of her neck, I would like to be that wisp of hair.

Then the halt, a col from where at last they can see another valley, about eight in the morning, no village, they are right on top of the col, they can see both valleys, day is breaking in earnest now, it is still very cold, thermos and flacket of schnapps do the rounds.

The guide points to another col, much higher, the sealskins, everyone ski-shod, one behind the other, one of the men branches off, starts climbing splay-footed, the guide says no, you wouldn't last half an hour, he puts Lena at the head, Fräulein Hotspur, sorry, Hellström, will set the pace, Lilstein is just behind Lena, from time to time the guide says 'halt!' He moves up to the front, ropes up, gives the other end to three men, he moves across the slope stamping with his skis as he goes, once a small layer breaks away, just one, the guide doesn't even fall over, Lena gives Lilstein a running commentary and points to a number of clouds which are beginning to come together.

They are on the terrace of the Palais de Chaillot, Hans wanted to see the Eiffel Tower, the view down the Champs-de-Mars, terraces like this are good for the spirits, if it wasn't for those dreadful buildings . . .

'They're NATO's, defence of the free world, Hans, it's worth it, Hans, for a spot of architectural jumble.'

Max turns, gestures to the façade of the TNP, that's theatre for you, Sir Novelist, if you want a full house you have to have mistaken identities and suchlike, you've got to have good box-office, otherwise no theatre, no *Lorenzaccio*, the people who cheered Pétain now come and applaud this rubbish about resisters, the people who cheered de Gaulle turn out to applaud the death of the tyrant, they're often the same people, the resisters who had ideals applaud the denunciation of the new regime, the older women turn into duchesses, the girls die deliciously, everyone believes different things at the same time, that's the togetherness of theatre.

'This guide knows the region like the back of his hand,' says Lena, 'in summer it's a reserve, he's a gamekeeper, he takes care of chamois and moufflon, he knows every tree, every rock for twenty kilometres round about, he started with his father when he was six, once he brought me back down through fog.'

Around noon, they reached their destination, another col. From here, they can see the wide valley of Davos, through their binoculars they can make out black dots moving down the slopes.

And then the ski descent, after a five-hour trek, heading back towards Waltenberg, long diagonal traverses, a few breath-stopping slopes, there are two schools of thought, those who favour the Telemark turn – a full bend of the leading knee, followed by a dip of the trailing knee, the front ski starts pointing inward, engage turn, then straighten up slowly bringing skis together, not too hasty, skis exactly parallel – and those, like Lena and the guide, who take risks and execute the move called the christiania or christie stem turn, or even the classic christiania, madness, you turn by kicking one ski against the other, Lilstein tried it, he fell over.

Lena didn't laugh.

'Michael, promise me you'll stop fooling around and I'll teach you how to do christianias tomorrow.'

Now and then they pass through clumps of larch, sometimes it's level going for a kilometre or more, they push themselves along with their sticks, the silence of the forest, they come out into full sunlight, then they can ski some more, Lena teaches Lilstein the secrets of the stem turn, he is euphoric, his headache has gone, she laughs at him with unexpected sweetness, the guide restrains members of the group who feel like trying short cuts, they climb back up to a small col, no, says the guide, not the Hirschkuh, you'd need to spend the night on the mountain, Lilstein dreams of spending the night on the mountain, Misha, you will behave yourself, won't you? they are both in the Hirschkuh refuge, flames in the hearth, they are frozen, she has taken her clothes off, she has wrapped herself in several blankets, he's lying next to her, no, there are two beds, each of them sleeps in a separate bed, Lilstein is cold, Lena says I'm cold too, no, they're sitting in front of the fire, she smiles, Lilstein lays his head on Lena's lap, Lena doesn't speak, yes she does, when the guide says 'not the Hirschkuh' she halts, leans on her sticks, looks at Lilstein, and in a serious voice:

'Not a night on the mountain, no *berceuse* for you, you don't ski as well as a Swiss light infantryman.'

They resume their descent, they arrive at the Waldhaus when the sky has already turned cherry red, she turns to Lilstein:

'You don't ski that badly, actually we could have taken the detour across the Hirschkuh.'

He throws a snowball at her, she chases him, he falls, rolls over and over, he is on his back in the snow, she looks at him, standing over him, evening gathers, there's no one about. They are there, listening to themselves breathe. She says:

'Let's go in, it's going to turn cold.'

Frédérique's daughter points to the woman in the woolly hat in the middle of the photo:

'What happened to Erna? My mother lost track of her.'

'It's a long story, isn't that right Max?'

'She's director of Merken's study centre,' says Max, 'in Munich, conservative philosophy, whereas at Waltenberg she was very Red Front.'

Max looks around them:

'You know we've got watchers all around us, Lilstein? Hobnail boots. Are they here on your account?'

'There's a fair chance they won't do anything,' says Lilstein.

'What sort of chance?'

'At least one in two.'

'If they do nab you, it will present you with quite a dilemma; either they convert you and you become a CIA agent, or else you deny everything, then they'd be forced to send you back to the socialist paradise. And once there you'd be shot, young rebel, for attending a friend's funeral without authorisation, for being soft-hearted.'

'Still, a one in two chance of getting away with it, Max, maybe better, they're shooting fewer and fewer people these days.'

'Anyway, if you are suspect in the heart department, it will be a relief for the comrades in the GDR. Thriving are they? Will you tell me what you're up to at the moment? A little interview on the sale, or should we say exchange, of dissidents for non-redeemable credits. And how do you get on these days with the Ivans?'

'I'm not sure I know them any better than you do, Max.'

*

'What is interesting,' Lilstein had told you between two ritual mouthfuls of Linzer, 'is that everyone will be there, in Grindisheim, you'll bump into all kinds of acquaintances, people you met in Paris, Berne, Rome, even Singapore, not all of them, but a high proportion, from the diplomatic, journalists, intellectuals, fans of Herr Kappler, other writers, people who've come to be in the photos or because it would look peculiar if they didn't turn up, and all those who're called the Europeans, a lot of people, a whole way of life, there'll also be large numbers of policemen, information-gathering agents, counter-espionage people, the crème de la crème, it should be great fun, a mixture of the unflappable and the hysterical, it'll be like a fair or a festival, a place to do deals in, it's risky but you've got to be there.'

*

The CIA had also sent a large contingent to Grindisheim, along with one of its heads, rather young for his rank, name of Walker, pleasant and mild-mannered, in a battered tweed jacket with a rather loud handkerchief, orange and black, in the breast pocket. He never needed to repeat what he had to say. He'd confined himself to a role of observer by saying that the situation should stay under control. Concerning the suspect, there was nothing definite in any file but he wasn't in the clear either.

'That's no good to us,' the West German minister had commented.

In the view of other Bonn officials, no action should be taken, a small chance that he really was a spy, but a very good chance of provoking a diplomatic incident which they wouldn't be able to contain.

As time goes on in the large house in the centre of Grindisheim the tension mounts, they talk to each other with increasing frankness:

'You don't give a shit about creating a scandal, you want to nail him, spy or no spy that's frankly not your problem, you just want to stir things up, you're not interested in détente, you're trying to scupper the agreements favouring détente, the new policy in the East and our good relationships with our allies.'

While they waited for a decision from the Chancellery, the watchers from the Federal Office for the Protection of the Constitution keep the subject under surveillance. In the main room of the house the PA continuously relayed messages from walkie-talkies, a whole network of them in a ring around the suspect and the people he talks to. He'd been given a code name, Blanchot, this gave rise to exchanges like 'Big Loaf, Blanchot now with Granny', Granny would say 'understood, Blanchot under wraps'.

And in the cortege, men in mourning clothes or sometimes a woman, would take up positions according to instructions relayed by the command unit set up in the house.

A man has come up to Frédérique's daughter, medium build, monkey-arse beard, he kissed the young woman, she begins to introduce him to Max.

'Oh, I know Monsieur Poirgade very well,' said Max.

A nod in Lilstein's direction:

'Monsieur Lilstein, import and export. Monsieur Poirgade, specialises in strategy. So, Poirgade, still with the Foreign Office?'

'Still there, Monsieur Goffard.'

Poirgade and Frédérique's daughter have moved off.

'How amusing,' said Max, 'the Valréas baton picked up by the likes of Poirgade, when I say amusing . . .'

'Are they engaged?'

'At least that would explain why they made off like thieves. But Poirgade converted to women? Now that would be something. Still, why not? A pretty girl, and her address book full of the names of the old European aristocracy. You didn't answer my question about the Ivans, young Lilstein.'

'Look, Max!'

Lilstein's hand points to the river, the sun is raising backlit mists all over the landscape, the movement of his hand is awkward, Lilstein turns away and looks at Max:

'I don't see Soviets very often these days, we're getting old, Max, we are consulted less and less. I don't read much from you at the moment either. Started keeping your distance? Thinking of retiring?'

Max's reply is instant:

'Never! I want to kick the bucket like Albert Londres, in harness, one day, in the middle of a story, a liner, a hole in the water, that's the way a journalist should go, it would be grand!'

Max has just finished writing a long article about concentration camps, the collusion, the Nazis, and the collaborators who fled in 1945, their escape channels, the Italian monasteries, but he has problems, no one wants the piece, three chief editors already, all telling him:

'Max, it's too long, too detailed, time's not right, everybody knows about this stuff, best wait for a more favourable moment, readers don't give a damn.'

Max went back to the camps, Buchenwald, Birkenau, he also traced survivors, here and there throughout the world.

'People who knew you, Misha, they were pleasant with me, an honest conversation, I talk to them so they trust me, when they trust me then they talk, good cordial talk, and rereading my notes I see they told me only what I'd said to them.'

One woman agreed to talk, she asked Max not to add any adjectives, there are the things they did to us, Monsieur Goffard, it was monstrous, they can be talked about but don't write monstrous, just be direct, and then there are the things they made us do, for those the word is unspeakable and I'm not sure I'll be able to speak to you about them, she tried to tell Max, she still felt guilty for a crust of bread she had hidden, for not offering her shoulder to someone on a forced march, for having stayed in the infirmary, she believed she owed her life to the death of others, she found great difficulty speaking, others told Max he'd be adding grist to the mill of Bolshevik propaganda, reminding the Poles about what the Germans had done to them or what they themselves didn't want to know, a few photos, a few phrases, a row of women and kids on the left-hand page with an SS officer, and on the right a photo of the new *Bundeswehr*, the Soviets are very good at this type of montage, this isn't the moment, it's a very good piece about the Nazi camps, but later, when things have settled down, there are times, young Lilstein, when I can't come up with any subject that's suitable for the times.

'Want to give me your piece for one of our papers?' asks Lilstein.

'Never!'

'Max, why not write a biography.'

'You mean, like Ulbricht's? Got any unpublished material? On the early thirties?'

'You wouldn't fancy a few leads about Beria, would you, Max? It would go down very well, I don't know much myself but I'll give you whatever I can find, how you get to be someone like Beria, you set out in life to be an engineer and you end up being Beria, a biography, you could reconstruct a whole slice of history, and you'd tell me everything you found, you'd know the life of Beria inside out.'

They have now emerged from under the trees, the air is cooler, wind from the Rhine.

'Misha, let's save time, you tell me now what it is you want me to find on Beria. Are you planning some propaganda job?'

'No, Max, really, it's personal.'

'A woman? Misha, you're in love with Beria's wife! Does she live in Berlin? Can you arrange an interview for me?'

'Max, this is serious, it's just between the two of us, if you were working on a biography of Beria and you could let me know why and how I managed to survive, how it happened, the son of a German Bolshevik Jewess eliminated in Moscow for Trotskyism who outlives his mother. I survived Auschwitz and Stalin, didn't get a bullet in the back of the head in '46 or in '51, I wonder if the explanation isn't somewhere close to Beria, at least up until the time of his death, why did Beria let me live?'

'Maybe because you were like him? Even so, he put you behind bars in 1951, Misha, you have a selective memory.'

'Surely, but at the start it wasn't so hard, I mean compared with the Nazis, hours and days on a stool, it didn't seem like out-and-out torture, they called it the endless screw, the hardest thing to bear about the whole business is that they don't hit you, if you hurt it's because it hurts to remain sitting all that time on the edge of a stool, hurts more and more, but you can't honestly say that these men who are talking to you are hurting you on a level with beating you with a length of hose pipe, that's the clever bit, you think that if you're hurting then it's the fault of your backbone, no way can you use hatred as a way of resisting.'

'So how did you manage it?'

'I needed to hate, I kept thinking this doesn't come from Stalin, nor from Beria, it must come from someone else, that bastard Abakumov, the swine who gets his vengeance in first, Max, I'll give you a few leads on Abakumov, you must always have someone available to hate, that's how I never buckled, and because they weren't trying to destroy me, I could hear other noises in the corridor, it was horrible, but they never did anything like that to me, why?

'And with my leads, Max, you could write a fine biography of Beria, full of detailed facts, for example their favourite game, when the small inner circle got tanked up with Stalin, at least four times a week, you don't know what their favourite game was? Everyone played, except the victim, it consisted of putting a tomato on Mikoyan's chair before he sat down – sometimes they pulled the same stunt on Malenkov – he gets up to go for a leak and they stick a tomato on his chair, he might glance down at his chair just as he is about to sit down, but Stalin chooses that precise moment to shout "Anastasius, what are you plotting these days?" and Anastasius makes very sure he's looking Stalin straight in the eye.

'He forgets everything else, and *splatt*! goes the tomato, like schoolboys, but no one ever tried it on with Beria, too scared, Stalin wasn't, but Stalin was never the one who placed the tomato, Beria had too much on him that he could spill, you'd need to stress the serious side of Beria, Max, the way he managed things, you could never stress Beria's managerial skills enough, you do realise that in the United States he could have been head of IBM or United Fruit?'

'Yes, that's good, young Misha, when Stalin dies Beria seeks asylum in the United States, locked up for a few months, many debriefings with the top brass, as there'd been for some Nazis, his abilities as a manager are spotted, turn him loose, but for business purposes only, as to personal preferences he is made to conform, no more teenage girls, not so? Mistresses yes but not underage girls brought in off the street? Even your wife could confirm this? What she says is that she can't see where you could have found the time, rumours, vulgar rumours? Agreed, but we don't want any rumours either, if you feel the slightest urge ask Ted, your driver, no, that's not what I mean, Ted knows the right people, want to make love? Buy it outright. And Beria becomes vice-president of United Fruit, chief of operations, you can forget the rest, exactly the same as with Gehlen or von Braun, that's the way to do it!'

'Yes, Max, it surely is, Beria as a Yankee manager, I like it! Beria crazy about development, becomes the world number one in the banana business, and like all world number ones he hates taxes, a five per cent tax is slapped on his bananas by a Guatemalan president, so Beria dines in town, plays golf, poker, maybe with you, and the CIA sets up a military regime in Guatemala to protect his plantations of untaxed bananas, thousands dead, heavy hand of the military, dirtier and dirtier as the years roll by, but no Gulags, just safeguarding free enterprise and top-grade bananas, and Beria, a top-grade manager, keeps his hands clean.

'A biography, Max! True, false, plausible, you would tell it very well, you'd discover why he protected me, include stories about little girls if you want, help make it sell.'

'I don't want,' says Max.

At Grindisheim at around five in the evening, everyone gathered again around the grave, a thousand people in a semi-circle.

At a sign from the funeral director a man steps up to the microphones, from his pocket he takes a book, opens it, in accordance with the last wishes of our friend I shall now read, in French, a passage from the chapter headed 'The Picnic', which is chapter five of the third part of *Le Grand Meaulnes*, through the gathered crowd runs a ripple not of hostility but of sporadic surprise, merely what happens whenever certain people in a crowd recognise the person who is the object of every gaze and circulate an unexpected name, yes, you can see it's him, it really is the French Ambassador, not Monsieur Gillet, no, this one's the French Ambassador at Berne, Monsieur de Vèze, I wasn't aware they knew each other, it's odd, a Frenchman reading *Le Grand Meaulnes* in the middle of a German cemetery, with the president of the Bundestag here, and de Vèze has begun: 'Everything seemed to have come so perfectly together with a view to making us happy, and yet we have known so little happiness . . .'

Through de Vèze's slow, careful delivery is evoked a world of small meadows, grey hills, the baying of hounds and turreted castles . . . 'how beautiful the banks of the Cher looked . . .' hedges, copses, a lawn . . . 'a wide, closely cut lawn where it seemed there was room only for endless games . . .' knowing Kappler, old man, I was expecting something more acerbic than this old picture postcard stuff, he traversed the century and he got a Frenchman to read out bits of an adolescent novel, it doesn't surprise me, you know, there are at least two Kapplers, the man who wrote those virtually unreadable great works between the two wars, crisis of values, crisis of the novel, a martyr to chiaroscuro, and the bestselling author after '45, the easy turn of phrase, realist transparency, his last period, stories that everyone can read, he even wanted to launch a literature series which rewrote great books in everyday language, they would have been condensed, pruned, he even wanted to do it with *Ulysses* and *The Magic Mountain*, I think he'd even have simplified his beloved *Grand Meaulnes*, tell me, any idea what will happen to French foreign policy now de Gaulle has gone?

Then the same funeral director said:

'I now call upon Monsieur Max Goffard.'

Three days earlier, the notary had summoned Max:

'Your name is expressly mentioned in connection with one of your friend's last wishes, Herr Kappler requested that you read out a brief passage from the *Scenes from the Life of a Good-for-Nothing*, he specifies, I quote, "Once Max has stopped protesting you might add that the passage from Eichendorff is to be read in German, he'll like that very much, from the time we first met all our discussion were in French, now it'll be my turn to listen to him speaking German and have a good laugh." Herr Kappler only wants these two readings, Monsieur de Vèze and you.'

*

At the Waldhaus, Lilstein's face is calm, you have both finished your portions of tart at the same time, like an old married couple. He gives you a kindly look, then he stares out at the cable cars and the village below the hotel, those large pale eyes come back to you, he yawns, a little laugh:

'The advantage of big funerals like Herr Kappler's on Friday next is that they allow the expression of deep feelings. In our line of business, that's refreshing, I shall be burying one of my two greatest friends and I will have every right to be red-eyed, whereas in normal circumstances we must unfortunately avoid showing fine sentiments, our fondest hopes, gush can lead to disaster, I mean to the catastrophic dashing of illusions, I don't want you to end up like that, I don't like it when you're discouraged, but I surely do not want you going in for displays of fine feelings, speaking for myself I have learned to show my feelings only at funerals, you can't do our kind of work with an artichoke heart. Shall we order more wine?'

You don't really want to take up Lilstein's suggestion. White wine doesn't particularly agree with you. But you're feeling anxious. You say yes. Lilstein raises one hand, a young Waldhaus waitress arrives with the new drinks, sets them down, leaves, you want to look at her legs, Lilstein watches you, you reach out your hand to your glass to avoid catching his eye, good legs that waitress, you turn back to face Lilstein, his eye has not wavered, he smiles.

'You must be wary of the finer feelings, young man. A woman I knew before the war, Austrian, fought against Nazism, old aristocratic family, became an administrator for the Soviets, she had fine feelings, one May Day she'd paraded in Red Square, tears in her eyes, a Marxist with an artichoke heart, you'll see if I'm right, she worked for Red Army intelligence.

'One day in 1937 or '38, in Frankfurt, the leader of her network showed her a letter from Voroshilov, that's right, already the absolute head of the Red Army, a handwritten letter, this happened by a small lake, in a public park, to the casual observer a women is reading a moving letter, she reads it, reads it again, tears in her eyes, her network boss averts his gaze modestly, a fine letter, "I wanted particularly to thank you in the name of the USSR and comrade Stalin for all the sacrifices you are making, for your devotion to the cause of proletarian internationalism and the cradle of socialism", her network leader speaks to her again, must tear up the letter, small pieces, for the waters of the lake and the little ducks who at first think they are bits of bread and then swim off, dive and show their backsides.

'But the big ducks haven't moved, they can tell the difference between bread and bits of paper, Voroshilov in person, "I wanted particularly to thank you." A few years later she comes face to face with Voroshilov, tears in her eyes, she thanks him in turn, that letter meant a great deal at a very difficult time, it was nothing, comrade, nothing out of the ordinary, oh but it was, those were very difficult days, Voroshilov has no wish to be reminded of those days in detail, but she carries on regardless, that letter was worth ten times more to me than all the gold in the whole wide world, it was the beating heart of the proletariat. Voroshilov smiles at her, she senses that he hasn't understood, the penny drops, the letter was a sham, she cursed herself for being so gullible, Voroshilov turned on his heel, she can't even lay the blame on her network head, he had been shot, so let's be wary of fine feelings, even if they count for a lot, can you see yourself, in tears, on the little bridge just outside the village, holding a letter from my minister, the bastard?

'Who was the network head shot by? Guess. As to her, she stopped doing good work, and she disappeared. I don't want you to end up like that.'

*

When the funeral was over, collation in Grindisheim's main hotel, Max and Lilstein have ordered tea, they have looked round for Frédérique's daughter, haven't located her.

'Her mother was a very impressive girl,' says Lilstein, 'Hans was genuinely in love with her. She wanted to fall in love but didn't want to make it the big thing in her life. Was she really Merken's mistress?'

As far as Max was concerned, that was all tittle-tattle, people had it in for Madame de Valréas, for being so close to the Merkens, Huns, she'd entrusted Frédérique to them for a year at Heidelberg, La Valréas was official mistress to the great philosopher, people made the most of this to stoke up a scandal, Merken sleeping with the mother and the daughter, gossip.

At the time Frédérique scares the professor, but only when philosophy is involved, she can recite back to him an article of his, twenty pages, two hours after reading it, Max and Lilstein remember, superb intellectual equipment, very passionate tone of voice, very much at home in the 1929 Waldhaus Seminar, an idea a minute, she believed Merken was the greatest philosopher of his time, she held it against him for competing for a job with Regel, the Berlin chair, she would have preferred him to be above that sort of thing, at Waltenberg she spoke to him about reactions to the news from Berlin, on the whole people don't care for this sort of wrangling over a job, they don't like it to be talked about, they defend Regel who is made ill by the idea of not getting the job, they even say he's more or less gone mad, Merken says it's nothing to do with him, Frédérique knows that a majority of the professors prefer Regel, by appointing Merken the Minister would be ignoring this majority.

Merken doesn't like the idea that one of his students should be so outspoken, this fuss over the job is trumped-up, and if Regel really is in as bad a way as people say it's not because the Minister is about to do something high-handed, people like Regel have a permanent need to stand up to high-handed behaviour, it doesn't mean they're mad, they just like it, in fact Regel can't say what really happened during the professors' meeting which was held behind closed doors, that would be wrong with regard both to the institution and faculty rules, but truth still exists even if it cannot be made public, and the truth is that Regel did not come top of the list for the Berlin job, he ought by rights to have had the biggest vote but he only came second, it's nothing to do with Merken, the fact is Regel's friends were split, they wanted to use the ballot as a marker for another colleague, younger and more left-wing and very deserving.

It was very useful to have a junior colleague's name put on this prestigious shortlist, yes, the result of the vote is published, but not the minutes of the discussion, not the line of argument developed by each member of the committee, so there was a third thief, the supporters of Regel split and some voted for the third thief.

One of Regel's best friends, a political friend and holiday companion, made out a very solid case in favour of the deserving junior colleague, a member of the same union as he himself belonged to, but it was another of Regel's best friends who felt it was his duty to report all this to Regel over the phone the moment the meeting was over, no one actually wanted to elect the young colleague, it was merely to put down a marker, so it is quite true to say that the majority was favourable to Regel, Merken knew this, he merely put his name forward as a matter of principle, so that there'd be a debate about ideas under cover of the election, but Regel's friends split, the vote gave third place to the third thief, with Regel second and Merken heading the poll, although the majority were not for him.

Regel's friends were happy with this first round of voting, and in the second round, the final vote, they would all unite behind the name of Regel, and Regel would be elected.

Except that faculty rules did not allow for a second ballot, there could be a second ballot only if there were more than three candidates, a first round to test the water, a second round to select three names, but there were only three candidates, therefore the first vote was the sole and final vote, rules are rules, as everyone knew, except that Regel's friends had forgotten it in their fine haste to raise the profile of their promising young colleague, Regel was not the victim of high-handed interference by the Minister, they called the Minister on the telephone and the Minister very legally refused them permission to organise a second ballot.

It was the stupidity of Regel's friends which made Regel lose, he was the victim of the genial goodwill of his friends.

It's what is called a three-cornered election, it cannot be made public, because the deliberations take place behind closed doors, but that was the truth of it, and it was that which sent Regel off his head, caused him to dance a jig in public, the young woman told Merken that it won't stop his, Merken's, enemies laying the blame at his door, or telling him that he'd connived with the brutal way Regel was treated, no, it's just words, people who don't like Merken have had their words ready for a long time, whatever he might do, Merken and young Frédérique are on one of the terraces on the north side of the Waldhaus, the discussion is animated.

They are alone. Where is Frédérique's mother this morning? Surely not with Regel? No, but she is in a shaky state too, all through today's discussions Madame de Valréas has behaved as she used to when she suspected her daughter of stealing her bras, she has not let her out of her sight, someone must have said something to her, Merken does not like idle whispers, at the back of them there's always somebody but never anybody, a monster, with eyes proliferating cancerously by the million, millions of viper's tongues and one singular vocal cord, gossip-mongering, ah what misery!

Frédérique protests, is it enough to make her miserable?

'My dear Frédérique, it's not for philosophy to save anyone, it does not have to take over the role of Christ after retrieving it from some ancient shelf, philosophy is there to return us to nothingness, everything else, lust for life . . . will to shape the future . . . just fairy stories.'

Frédérique resists:

'That's no reason to let ourselves get discouraged.'

Eulogy of despondency by Professor Merken, it gives us the strength to throw the inkwell at our looking glass, Merken wishes to withdraw, to return to the lounge, Frédérique detains him, she hadn't wanted to make the professor angry, she can't understand all this business about despondency, Merken remains on the terrace, all thought is despondency, the moment we cease behaving like dogs we become sad.

'Did she make a scene?'

'Frédérique!'

'Did my mother make a scene?'

'That's not the point . . .'

'Why "sad"? It's insulting! Dogs? The bitch salutes you, Professor! Go sleep with the bitch!'

Frédérique leaving the terrace, departing in disarray, Merken catches up with her.

'Frédérique, the situation . . .'

'You've got nothing to lose! Everyone assumes I'm still running after you, you are sad, it's all over, let me be!'

'It's not those people who are at issue, it's deeper than that.'

'I don't like this sadness of yours, it's out to get me.'

Frédérique is mistaken if she thinks it's that easy, Frédérique will not listen to reason:

'Picture it, Sir comes back from his walk, Sir meets up with his sweet Frédérique and Sir's sad! What a shame!'

The poor man begs Frédérique not to shout, in vain.

'Sad are you? When a man is sad it's because he's found another woman, you're sad because you're forcing yourself to stay here with me, you don't like me making a noise any more, you didn't always say that!'

'Please, Gretchen, don't shout, there's no one else.'

Each of them says 'no one', Frédérique so that she can go on yelling, her anger feeding off her anger, and the poor man also says 'no one', he means his life in general, without anyone else but Frédérique.

'Don't shout, I need you.'

'He needs me and he's sad, though you're really quite attractive with those creased trousers and the feather in your hat, come here, nearer, there's nothing to be sad about, your cheeks are red, a pleasing mix of melancholy and the heat, and you're unhappy, come along now, let's have this little chagrin out in the open, let's wrap it up in ribbon for the lady, let's take a walk under the trees, the cool Alpine air blowing on your little chagrin.'

'Frédérique, we're becoming ridiculous.'

It's Merken's turn to try to walk off the terrace. Then Frédérique:

'Has the Professor really got no more bullets left to shoot?'

'Don't be crude.'

'And who started calling the other person "my little beaver"?'

She has shouted the last word.

It's at this exact moment that La Valréas came out on to the terrace, she understood.

'Frédérique, you will never convert the professor to your silly nonsense, stop pestering him with your revolution and stop shouting, young women nowadays are insufferable, they want everything, and they want it straight away, has she been annoying you?'

'Certainly not, my dear.'

'We were talking about Thought, mama, and about the sadness of the tasks it requires us to perform.'

Chapter 12

1969

Twice as Strong

In which Lilstein tries to worm out of Max secrets of his private life.

In which the net tightens around the spy who is there at the funeral.

In which the man named Walker comes up with a muscular plan to capture the spy.

In which Max pieces together the life of his friend Lena in the years between the two wars and during a short period after it.

In which Lilstein again warns you to beware of noble sentiments.

In which a clear idea emerges of Lena's talents as a singer of Lieder.

Grindisheim, October 1969

In the hotel at Grindisheim, Max and Lilstein sit in a secluded corner, next to a sideboard on which the head waiter has just carefully set down a large bilberry tart, sprinkling it with sugar from an antique-style sugar-shaker, crystal cut-glass sides and silver spout, the dark surface of the sideboard, the silver, the transparencies of the glass, the ochre rim of the tart dish, the dark red of the bilberries, the golden sheen of the shortcrust pastry. Lilstein:

'That tart might just reconcile me with this place, I loathe this new fashion for putting neon and plastic everywhere, they tear out old wood panelling to make way for it, you remember the Waldhaus, Max, the lounge-cum-library, Hans loved it, he used to arrange to meet Frédérique there, the french windows opened on to the terrace, the lake, the mountains, with the coffee and bilberry tart on low tables, they hadn't started serving Linzer at that stage, the bilberries covered with icing sugar in the corner by the glass door, wooden floor, Hungarian marquetry, the settees, the worn club chairs, instead of all this formica rubbish!'

'Misha, in those days you called it bourgeois comfort, you wanted to destroy it, you despised teak-lined walls, the engravings of William Tell, the wire-fronted bookcases full of Balzac, Goethe and Dickens.'

'And the books about botany, Max, do you remember the books about botany? And bound sets of *L'Illustration* and the *Neue Zürcher*

Zeitung? It was so restful, and how about the piano? The grand piano on the small stage? The room with the red and gold easy chairs, a dark brown piano, marquetry also, always well-tuned.'

Max has sneered at Lilstein's nostalgia for bourgeois values, the comfort of the privileged. Lilstein protested, library, piano, old armchairs, no one rates that kind of privilege any more, the privileged now have different tastes, they want loudspeakers and screens, things you have less need to learn, they finance them, they sell them to the masses and they borrow them back from the masses, it promotes the idea that privilege is no more, they no longer need long novels, engravings, teak, the piano, all that, and icing sugar on bilberry tart will become a thing of the past.

'Look, Max, here they've kept just one piece of furniture to give the impression of a library but it's pathetic, I had a look, full of drivel, large-print, conspicuous by its absence is anything literary, *Reader's Digest*, would you believe, a library that contains no literature, a brand of literature which has been stripped of literature so that a place for it will be found in libraries where there'll be no literature.'

'Misha, don't they ever censor literature where you come from?'

After a few minutes, a waiter comes round, he has nodded discreetly to Max and Lilstein, he stares at the board, the sugar which the head waiter had poured has been absorbed by the bilberries, the waiter now sprinkles the tart generously, six waiters in the room, each as scrupulous as the next and all enthusiastic sugar-sprinklers, six turns with the sugar-shaker in a few minutes, when the head waiter recommended his bilberry tart after giving it one last sprinkle Lilstein declined, the head waiter suggested the Linzer but I don't see why I should order a portion of Linzer from oiks who sabotage their bilberries.

Max and Lilstein have not spoken any more about Hans, Max was not keen, Lilstein did not push it, they changed the subject, Max hasn't asked questions about the expulsion of dissidents and the interest-free loans, no doubt because he already knew all he wanted to, really they talked only of Lena, plus a little about the death of Stalin, because of Beria, Max insisted on telling Lilstein the tale of Stalin's death and Lilstein felt like letting him talk, not because Max was about to tell him anything new but because he thought it might be interesting to see if Max believed he was telling him something he didn't know, and also because if Max was willing to hold forth best let him get on with it so that maybe later on he'd be as forthcoming about Lena.

To this extent you might think that it was Lilstein who made Max talk but Max needed no urging, he'd never said a word about her to anyone, he talked to Lilstein because first, Lilstein agreed to hear part of the death of Stalin, second because Lilstein asked him to talk about Lena and also to allow what happened a chance of surviving the all-consuming dust.

Max filled Lilstein in on what he did not know about the final evenings of the '29 Waltenberg Seminar, they completed their memories, for Lilstein also told the story of his outing on skis with Lena.

'When we got back, I threw a snowball at her, I ran off, she ran after me, I fell over.'

Max listened, they recalled Lena's tangos, the dancing parties. With such a large gathering of older people you might have expected the evening entertainment to be fairly sedate, but there were also a lot of young people, at least in the audience at discussions, La Valréas insisted on it, she wanted the best students in Europe, she paid all their expenses, including evening dress, there were also hotel guests who were there for the skiing, at least a good hundred of these, sporty types, quite a few Americans, amusing to see the evening abruptly overrun by all these people looking as if they had just stepped straight out of a cinema screen, the dresses of some of the European women suddenly became unwearable.

The American women laughed loudly, smoked, drank, skittered, kissed, skipped, bare arms, bare backs, throats, breasts, napes of necks, knees exposed to the universal gaze, beautiful faces, fresh and pink, blackheadless nostrils, and every hairstyle had its finery, its headband of cloth, velvet, satin, the fabric acting as a setting for small clusters of precious stones or gold or silver medallions, and used also to anchor a feather, they had long cigarette-holders and strings of pearls hanging down to their waists, short hair showing the back of the neck, bare shoulder-blades, straight barrel-line dresses, tubular frocks, very simple, soft material, flare-effect panels low down, the material tight across the hips but fitting more loosely thereafter to allow full play to the flare, the whole lower section of the dress whirling in the gyrations of the dance, whipping the air, rising as they whirled, allowing a glimpse of a flesh-coloured petticoat and the tops of stockings held up by flesh-coloured garters.

Dresses without gathers or pleats, green, golden-yellow or saffron, champagne, Veronese, the occasional gilt hat, no brim, darker-coloured stockings, maroon or grey, or misty blue, couples suddenly grown more serious, left arm of the man and right arm of his partner pointing horizontally towards a distant horizon on which eyes are fastened, affected stiffness, caricatured gravity displayed by some, tango for trumpets, clarinets, double-bass, drums, young women rushing on to the dance floor with a gusto which consigned to the dustbin all theories concerning neurasthenia in the modern world, in a rout of dance steps, fox-trot, charleston, scornful glances from spectators, sometimes hate, people who'd come along only to feel the desire to destroy the whole lot of them, to see they got their come-uppance some day, then they went away, leaving the others to enjoy a medley of dances, women humming, crooning 'Don't Cry Baby' or 'Mí Noche Triste' to some spring-heeled sure-footed dancer, head thrown back or a sudden look straight into the eyes of another man, drinking and laughing and glass held out on the side of the dance floor, the evening turning into folly after the twelve strokes, one single thought, dresses clinging to body, flared for the legs, garish petticoats, shoes with straps, high heels, dazzling gems, very long necklaces, coiled several times, worn round the neck, and those young women know how to shake a leg, they are as hard as champions and when they laugh they throw back their heads and show all their teeth, Aristide Briand watching, he was born during the Second Empire, makes an observation about 'breasts for lean times' but goes on watching the women with very long false eyelashes, plucked eyebrows, redrawn in pencil, bright red lipsticked lips, dark foundation, violet nails, glossy pearl-fringed cloche hat, blue-grey, eyes upturned under it, occasional outburst, out of the question that I should let him, woman butting in on the conversation of two people, I'm going to whisk him away but I shall let you have him back in just a jiffy, you won't have time to grow one minute older, imitation feather fan, orange and beige cameo, gold lamé here and there, and a boa for the women staying in the annexe, the annexe apparently less prestigious, but much more comfortable, ultramodern bathrooms, telephones less temperamental, V-shaped necklines, edged with small sparkling stones, hair flaunting a kiss-curl, fox-trot, quick tempo, steps you dance in sequence, strict tempo, steps you improvise, feet thrashing, whirling, crossing, fox-trot and its less hurried variant, the slow fox-trot, glissé, cake-walk, movements weird and bodies contorted, give a cake to the black slave who walks the most complicated dance, body extravagantly arched backwards, arms out, advance raising the knees as high as they will go, dress which shucks down on uneven tasselled fringes and which a twitch of the hips sends shooting back up again, beyond the bounds of possibility, in the carefree unconcern of the music.

'You were watching the skirts, Misha, there were two of you ogling the skirts, you and Briand, a revolutionary and a social-traitor, same struggle, on the look-out for skirt!'

Lilstein has grown misty-eyed, he has even recounted the episode of the shower cubicle in the swimming pool at the Waldhaus.

'I pushed a door, she'd forgotten to bolt it, then it was gone, Max!'

Max has realised he shouldn't have listened, Lilstein in this state had dropped his guard low enough to tell him about the business with the shower cubicle and was now on the verge of tears, Lilstein has outmanoeuvred you, you listened, he's got you now, it's a trade, you're going to have to tell him something.

There was a silence, Lilstein is never as dangerous as when the line of his mouth softens, when he looks as if he has a great deal to blame life for.

'Max, what was it like, with her?'

Max looked into Lilstein's look:

'You've been mulling over that question for forty years, young Lilstein, I won't tell you anything.'

Surely Max isn't going to chat about the only wedding night of his entire life to this blundering German, a hand placed on Max's hand, in the Waldhaus, it's getting late, all those taking part in the European Seminar have dispersed to their rooms, Hans is nowhere to be seen, there is no sign of Erna, nor of Merken, Frédérique has vanished, Stirnweiss has vanished, Lena has vanished, doors have been locked, Lilstein too has vanished, Moncel isn't around any more, Max is in the bar, doing some serious drinking, he's there with a group of young English girls, the barman has got out a map of Scotland and tulip glasses, the north coast, Speyside, the home of whisky.

Map laid out on the bar, they follow the route and stop for a dram at each distillery, turning names and tastes into song, glass after glass. The English girls are sporty, clean-scrubbed, brazen, built like boxers. They want Max to pronounce Craigellachie and Mannochmore, Inverboyndie, Ballindalloch. He makes them laugh, he tries to teach them to sing 'Amélie, cache tes genous'.

The barman has just poured the umpteenth whisky, Max grabs it, a hand is placed on his, a voice asks:

'Do you really have to?'

She's the only woman who doesn't interest Max, she's beautiful, she's the one Hans dreams of, but she is no longer just Hans's dream, though she might as well be, the wives of my friends are sexless. Forty years ago Lena pushed his glass to one side saying:

'Do you really have to?'

And she drank the whisky, straight.

'Come along, Max, I don't love you.'

Young Lilstein would very much like to know what happened forty years ago, to make love to the memory of Lena through the memories of his friend Max Goffard, if I told him he was lucky that night, the poor muddlehead would never believe me.

That night Max behaved like an idiot, he even told Lena:

'The wives of my friends are sexless.'

To which she replied:

'You have much too conventional an idea of sex.'

Lena was twice as strong as Max, let that be part of the detail which our blundering German friend certainly does not need to know, twice as strong as a Max Goffard who is no longer sure of anything, it was wonderful and at the same time I was like the goat who sees a very determined lady coming towards him, several ladies in that lady, or the same one in various guises, several rather determined ladies, and the goat wonders why they have started dancing, I'd drunk a lot of whisky that evening but I've never known what it's like to be drunk, Lena wasn't drunk, the pretty ladies dance and suddenly they toss the goat up in air, and the goat thinks this is strange, they catch him neatly and throw him up again even higher, and he doesn't know what's happening, he's falling and at the very last moment they catch him, they throw up him again, a game, no way of stopping it, he's airborne, he doesn't dislike it, down he falls, up he goes again, getting into the swing of it, he falls, they catch him with their teeth, women dancing, throwing wine in each other's faces, they toss the goat up in the air again, compare what happened with Monsieur Seguin and the wolf and it's small beer.

Women who dance, who perspire, who glow, they shout, the goat panics, doesn't know which way to turn, understands that it's also a very bad time, they're mad, they're doing themselves harm, don't even realise, a moonless carnival, the next person who talks to me about gentleness, intuition, affection, caring natures, I will knock his block off, frenzy, the goat has got it at last, one of the women has a scrap of goat flesh in her mouth, she's laughing.

She holds a torch of burning pine, shakes her hair, shakes the brand like a madwoman, when you say goat it's to get people used to the idea from the word go, but these crazy women have now begun attacking lots of other beasties, even bears, one swipe of a bear's paw can do a crazy woman serious damage but they don't care, these women didn't come here to bandage anybody's wounds, they scream, they sing, they run, stop, die, come back to life, a place where forces collide, they throw the goat up in the air once more, life at its most intense, the screams quicken the race which quickens the screams.

They do not feel the limb twist nor the claw strike, to feel that would require a bearing, they have lost their bearings, they are far away, they come back, they shake their hair, scream, throw their loins to the flames, tearing themselves open with their hands, subside, eyes wild open, splash their faces with water, vine and wine, death looms up in their midst, by way of a greeting they grab their ration of raw flesh as they pass by, wound themselves, feed themselves, plead, run away, they hurt, madness in their eyes, hands, mouth, they call, death watches them, joy of living, joy of dying, they curl up, seethe, tear themselves to pieces, fingers white from being clenched, the madness which tears itself apart, which engulfs.

They depart in a whirling cloud, roll, crash to the ground, throw down the torch, pick it up, take revenge like wounded creatures with nothing to lose, death claims his wages, the goat in a coffin of sensations, a force which persists as long as their sharp piercing cries and then tears to tatters, then it begins again, scraps of goat, a flower muscle, murmurs of chaos.

Escaped by the skin of his teeth, lucky sod.

Next morning Lena was so sweet, she sat down in front of her pierglass, slow expansive movements, she was combing her hair, she looked in the mirror, her life she says is giving recitals or appearing in opera, the day before you mustn't, on the day it makes the voice dull, the day after she doesn't feel like it, she sings often.

'Tot up what's left, Max, and to make my condition worse I forbid you to go elsewhere, I can be an utterly demonic Carmen, jealousy is physically so demanding, I don't allow anyone to walk over me, I stay ahead of the game, sometimes I get it wrong but at least no one laughs at me, I'm a very jealous person, didn't used to be, but the older I get the more jealous I become.

'Sometimes I never say anything to the man I'm with, I stay nice, and loving, and I go straight for the other woman, no altercations, I leave that to shop girls, what I do is jump in my car, then I ram her car, I yank her out by the hair, I once did that in the middle of a cross-roads, in Duluth, and I swotted her with the starting handle, you don't know Duluth, you need to if you want an idea of what sort of scandal it made, a large De Soto starting handle, a huge scandal, they didn't dare charge me, it's possible the judge had slept with the woman, she slept with everybody, he didn't dare do a thing, and my lover at the time didn't say anything either, a free action that looks free, not very subtle but effective, men are cowards.

'I could do even better than that, Max, know what a woman can do to keep her lover? To get him to marry her? You're jealous of the wife, you want marriage, you corner your lover in the kitchen, a good talk, you feel he wants to break it off, go home, you're not going to let him get away with it, it starts in the kitchen and it stays in the kitchen, the man has qualified as a pharmacist, he tries to speak calmly, he's about to set himself up, buy a dispensary, in Linz, the town's leading pharmacy, he starts building his case, a turning point in his life, he has children, twins, just starting school, they're going to need him home every evening, so you don't mess with the children's education, but you can mess with a mistress? The man is making the most tactless case imaginable.

'In any case, a man who is ending a relationship and insists on talking is always tactless, there's an explosion, one word is all it takes, he actually dared to say I don't deserve you, that's the point when you explode, a bastard, a man who wants to end an affair is essentially a bastard, the storm breaks very quickly, in a kitchen it's very bad, table suddenly cleared with a backhand swipe from the woman, tears in her voice, in her eyes, on her cheeks, the woman's hands held out in front of her, ready for battle, out of control, though not really, not really out of control those hands, one hand which opens the top of the stove, the ceramic stove, one hot plate open, the biggest.

'The crazy woman is about to do something stupid, hurt herself, put her right hand in, she's yelling, the man keeps a close eye on her right hand, the roar of the fire in the stove, how hot can it get inside a ceramic stove? the intake of air, how do you treat burns? the flames burn higher, a thousand degrees? If the wood's really dry, eight hundred, eleven hundred degrees? The fire roars, burning hotter and hotter, her hand, not the right hand, the left, she holds her left hand over the hole in the top of the stove.

'What is the man's academic and professional file doing in that left hand? The originals of the documents in his file, the woman screams, on your knees! It's an order, the kind of order that can be given by a woman in a rage who knows that without the originals of his diplomas the man might just about be able to open a grocery but not a pharmacy, especially not in Linz, and it's not only his file, there are bearer bonds, half the capital he needs is being dangled over the flames, in the hand of this mad woman, the woman is not threatening to throw his papers into a fire in a fireplace, they should have stayed in the living room, papers thrown into a fire in a fireplace can be rescued, here, the central hole of the stove, a thousand degrees, final, vocal cords ready to snap, the woman screeches, you'll swear on the heads of your children, you swear on the Bible!

'On the Bible, Max, absurd! But in the end he stays with her. He divorced. He married her. Men love being loved like this, a woman who would not hesitate to reduce you to a state of administrative non-existence in Austria fully deserves to earn her marriage, an utterly harmonious marriage, a blast of jealous rage, the originals of diplomas and bearer bonds, that's not a matter of small importance, they married.

'Later the woman divorced the man, she discovered he had a weak character. She said I'd married my bad self. I refer to dear Elisabeth, Max, sweet, fair-haired Elisabeth Stirnweiss.

'Let's stay friends, Max, with the life I lead I need to talk without what I say turning into love or loathing.'

At Grindisheim, in the hotel, people have started taking their leave of each other, they came to say goodbye to Max, still sitting with Lilstein, at one point he loses his temper:

'Look here, I'm not Kappler's widow!'

People said farewell looking somewhat abashed and he laughed. One man came up and Max stopped laughing, the man had only one arm, a German, he said to Max:

'I met Herrr Kappler not long ago, we talked about her.'

Max asked Lilstein to excuse him, he went off to one side with the man, Lilstein remained sitting at their table, after a moment Max came back, Max didn't explain but he forced Lilstein to listen to his account of Stalin's death, the Party leaders waited a very long time indeed before they called in the doctors, a big drinking session, five of them, correct me if I start talking nonsense, young Lilstein, anyway Stalin, Beria, Malenkov, Bulganin, Khrushchev, the night of the first and second of March 1953, around four or five in the morning the guests leave. Stalin goes off to bed, by noon not a peep, the domestic staff start to worry but a ban on entering the boss's room without being summoned, that evening, around eleven, someone at last goes in, no one knows exactly who, people vacillate between an old cleaning woman, Matrena Butussova, and Captain Lozgachev, his job is to bring the mail from the Kremlin, he or she discovers Stalin lying on the floor, conscious but unable to speak, that same evening Stalin got one hundred per cent of the votes cast in the eight constituencies of the local soviets where he had been a candidate, at three in the morning, 3 March, the little gang of Khrushchev, Beria, Malenkov and co. returns, they learn that Stalin has urinated in his trousers, they decide not to go in, a matter of propriety, says Khrushchev.

Max paused, looked over Lilstein's shoulder, de Vèze was coming towards them, Max got to his feet, Lilstein did the same, de Vèze said hello to Max.

'Ambassador, let me introduce you to Monsieur Lilstein, Monsieur Lilstein first met Hans forty years ago, Hans was very fond of him, he used to say Michael Lilstein would be the salt of the earth if he didn't make too many mistakes.'

'I've made lots,' says Lilstein, 'my respects, Ambassador, I am most grateful to you for not avoiding me, although many people assume I am a trafficker in living souls.'

'My dear Monsieur Lilstein, I don't give a damn, as long as it lets me get up the noses of the informers and low-life who forced de Gaulle out, and I am very, very pleased to meet you.'

De Vèze has frozen, Max has looked in the direction de Vèze is looking, he has recognised Philippe Morel, the historian, he has just been elected to the Collège de France, unusual for one so young, he's in his forties but it's still very young for the Collège, Max knows why de Vèze has frozen, Morel is coming over, he is alone, surprising that Morel should come over, or maybe he intends to cause an incident, the cuckolded husband who slaps his rival across the face at a funeral, the rival is the Ambassador, a very French scandal, this is going to look bad, de Vèze isn't the sort who'll let himself be slapped across the face without reacting, he's perfectly capable of forestalling Morel, a punch, no, he can't, he'll have to wait for the slap, so he can block it? Is Morel worth all the fuss? Max could step forward, that's it, I'm stepping forward, on with the tomfoolery, Professor! This is a surprise! you know Hans was telling me all about you just recently, no, Morel has executed a quarter turn to his left, he walks off towards the terrace, from a distance Max sees him shaking hands with Poirgade.

Among the watchers gathered around Colonel Sebald and the head of the Federal Office for the Protection of the Constitution, some had reached the end of their tether, others hadn't, no point getting all worked up, if we haven't got the green light now, we'll lift the suspect when he travels back, before he crosses the frontier, on the road, that'll make less of a splash than if we do it at the funeral, we've got thirty agents around him, the Minister only has to give us the nod and we'll be on him, I'm sure he won't try to get away, with people like that they're often relieved when it's all over, if the Minister gives the green light we'll be on him within three seconds.'

'Big Loaf calling,' said the radio, 'Blanchot stuck in a bunch, it's getting difficult, he's with the French Ambassador and an American journalist.'

It was at that moment that the cat was set among the pigeons. When it was announced that the suspect had left with the French Ambassador at Berne.

Walker blanched. Radio again:

'The French Ambassador has driven off with our client in a DS.'

It was de Vèze who suggested it. He was with Lilstein, Max and the correspondent of the *Washington News*, Linus Mosberger. Mosberger is a top-notch interviewer, he tries to get de Vèze to talk, departure of de Gaulle, Pompidou's speech in Rome, before the referendum, saying he was ready to undertake great tasks if the opportunity presented itself, that is if de Gaulle lost the elections. Getting an old Gaullist to talk, persuading him to say what he thinks of Pompidou, checking what he says, Pompidou has betrayed his own side, he is assumed to have betrayed his own side because his wife had been insulted.

'Is there any truth in what they say, Ambassador? that Pompidou dropped the Gaullists because certain Gaullists had slandered his wife?'

De Vèze reckons the American is very direct.

'I'm sure, Monsieur Mosberger, that certain services of the American government could tell you far more about it than I can.'

And suddenly de Vèze:

'Goffard, I'll give you a lift.'

Mosberger and Lilstein took their leave.

It was Max who got into the DS with de Vèze.

The CIA man, Walker, asked wasn't there anything they could do while they were on the road? He had a quiet voice:

'We could blow a tyre with a rifle with telescopic sights, I'll take the shot myself if you don't want to, or we could stage an accident along their route, they stop, get out, take a look, and we can hold Goffard as a witness.'

Everyone started coming out with theories better suited to the pages of crime thrillers, Walker is now in charge of operations, an incident on the road taken by the French Ambassador, he's returning to Berne, the best spot would be around Winzig, an hour's drive away, that would allow enough time to set it all up, they've decided to go for it, mad rush to get away before de Vèze, maybe ten vehicles, Walker in one of them, Winzig here we come!

The Ambassador's DS drove out of Grindisheim and two kilometres further on dropped de Vèze and Max at a small flying club on the banks of the Rhine, setting them down by a twin-engined aircraft, high wings, metallic grey with a red stripe along the fuselage.

'Max, if you promise not to go round telling everybody I use an air taxi instead of tooling around in a DS, I'll take you to Basle.'

De Vèze stroked the nose of the plane.

'Same model as Eisenhower had, an Aerocommander, the 680, no, I'm not in that much of a hurry, actually it's so I can fly a plane. An Ambassador isn't allowed to pilot his own plane, so I hire a taxiplane, always the same one, an Aerocommander, high wing, gives you the best view of the landscape. And now and then the pilot lets me have the double controls. But that stays between the two of us! Climb aboard, we can talk, Grindisheim–Basle, we fly over the Rhine, beauty, legends.'

In the plane, de Vèze has given Max a big surprise.

Max assumes that de Vèze would start where they'd left off in a conversation they'd both had four years earlier when, a month after that evening in Singapore, he'd visited de Vèze in the Embassy in Rangoon. They'd sat in de Vèze's office, Max had looked upon the Ambassador with an affection he couldn't explain and had started telling him about a trip through Haute-Savoie, it happened a long time ago.

A trip taken in 1929, Max on Alpine roads in the company of a lady, a very great lady, a journey that took them from Waltenberg to the French Alps, a road rimmed by precipices but negotiated without mishap, Max had come to see de Vèze's parents with this lady.

'She'd agreed to come with me, as friends, we set out from Waltenberg, I'd told her everything, she knew how your mother was. When we got to Araches she sang for your mother, *a capella*, in German and in French, your mother cried and held Lena close in her arms, you were five, Ambassador, Lena had brought you a present, a big wooden roundabout, fully working, we'd bought it from Weber's in Zurich, the Blue Dwarf there, you loved it. A two-tier Limonaire, wooden horses. In those days you had an Irish setter who was jealous of your merry-go-round and wanted to play with you, I had long talks with your father and Lena sang for your mother, later your father wrote to me saying that for years afterwards your mother went on singing what Lena had sung to her.'

De Vèze could have talked about all that with Max as a preliminary to more important business, and then tell him how sad he'd been for never having seen Lena again and for not being there when she was buried, he could also have talked about Hans, the way he'd finally met up with him in Geneva, they'd had dinner together, on a boat which sailed round the lake, de Vèze never mentioned a word of all that, in the cabin of the plane he had given Max a big surprise, came straight out with it:

'How was Arlington?'

'Terrifying, Ambassador.'

That's what Lena's funeral at Arlington was, terrifying, respond at once with something forceful, don't behave like someone who's caught off balance and hides behind anodyne comments, move smartly to a point beyond where de Vèze expects Max to be.

'Terrifying, I wept, in the middle of a military cemetery, I didn't last out, they folded the flag and they gave it to me, to me, Goffard, a foreigner. And Leone Trice sang "Voi che sapete", terrifying, much more terrifying than today's proceedings, Arlington, Americans in full dress uniform, three salvos and bagpipes, military funeral though she hadn't asked for anything.

'Two or three top officials had pulled every string in the CIA, the Pentagon, the White House, can you imagine who was there? Music lovers, spooks, generals, aesthetes, patricians, liberals, singers and blackmailers, all clustered round the coffin of Lena Hellström, star-spangled banner, it was mainly the CIA who organised the show, important for them to show that she was one of theirs, that they don't only work with schmucks and finks, everybody there was wondering how long it was since the CIA recruited her.

'No one can possibly say they'd never recruited her, she was grand-mother to the lot of them, she'd watched them cut their teeth, and before the CIA she'd been in at the birth of the outfit that came before it, the OSS, she'd started before all that, she sang, she had lots of useful contacts among the Germans, the English, they loved her in Berlin, eternal youth, Belle Époque, the great eagle above a frozen lake, she started with the war, in '14, pre-dated even the OSS, as it happened, she was living in Switzerland with Hans, he left her to go off and play heroes, or rather she walked out on him when she realised he was going to leave her, that he wouldn't desert just to please her, she felt it was like being at the opera, she left him without saying where she was going, or rather they left each other, Hans always said "over a stupid thing".

'She wasn't all that anxious to see him again but on the off-chance she decided to go to Berlin and take a few singing lessons before returning to the United States, to improve her command of music, the world goes up in flames and she decides to improve her singing.'

Max had gradually pieced together Lena's story, he felt he could tell it to de Vèze but he didn't tell all of it, he was afraid to say too much that was definitive, to be too careful about choosing a particular way of putting the events together, the sequences, afraid of suddenly finding he'd gone out on a limb because he'd said too much, he relived Lena's story as he had relived it in his seat, in the front row at Arlington, in flashes, with clear moments, brief scenes, snatches of dialogue.

He didn't tell de Vèze everything, he remained the low-voiced enunciator of Lena's past, enunciating because he had to, but keeping unvoiced the things that were important to him alone, de Vèze catching only what Max allowed to go in his direction, and being happy with that because the last thing he wanted was to have to ask Max to be more specific, letting Max bask in his low murmur, with occasional glances down at the course of the Rhine, everything on the west bank made golden in the sunshine, Lena in 1914, in Berlin, received by her father's business contacts, rich people, who know titled people who also invite her, she sings well, listens well, she is refreshing say the hostesses, she understands what's being said, her father made her sit at the dinner table as soon as she was ten, he had many Europeans come to the house.

She knows exactly what expression to put on her face when a man starts talking politics, the pupil who is bored and the pupil who listens, that's how she learned, her big eyes slow and bored or wide and alert depending on what people tell her, and the men who talk to her have only one desire which is to see her eyes change from bored to bright, they stop caring about what they say and only about the way she listens to them, she never hesitates to interrupt, switching from one subject to another, the content is of no interest to her.

It pleases the Germans to see an American woman who is not hostile, she even goes so far as to pull her hair back behind her right ear, they admire her right ear and her fine head of red hair, they don't dare admit to themselves what they would like to do to that right ear, they talk and talk just to see her smile and do that again, her hair, the lobe which reappears, can you imagine, a woman who dares touch her body in public, she doesn't care, she's American, when she gets bored with a man it's painful, you're there with your suit or your uniform, your titles, respected, and this American looks at you as though you were an old tin can.

Mademoiselle Hellström is a test, when you speak in front of other people, the other people listen to you, out of respect, she's the only one among them who focuses solely on your face and your intelligence, with all the others it's just manners, so when you're with her you talk, sometimes she smiles at you and does that thing with her hair, apparently her perfume is French, she tells everyone that her perfume comes from America but in fact it's more likely to be some bergamot-based French aphrodisiac perfume, no, I've not worn 'Jicky' since the war, seems in it there's plum-tree evernia, vetiver and a hint of leather, an American woman, in Berlin, who touches her hair and her ear in the company of men and once a week takes tea at the American Embassy.

She tells her German friends she doesn't much like going, but that she has to because of her exit-visa from the USA, as a matter of fact the Ambassador is a friend of her father and President Wilson, all three graduates of Princeton, the Ambassador finds his chats with Lena very enlightening, he sends regular cables to the White House, in time Lena found out a great many things, about the politics of the Reich, about the blockade, about forthcoming changes in the Imperial General Staff, they say Americans are slow on the uptake, maybe Lena does not fully understand everything she repeats to the Ambassador but it's pure gold, she sings in German drawing rooms for their pleasure, and one day for her pleasure, they tip her off.

She must go, without delay, leave the Reich, things are going to get worse and worse, she goes back to Switzerland in 1917 on the eve of America's entry into the war, she stays in Switzerland, she is unhappy, she continues to move in diplomatic circles, complains about the stupid war, she maintains a level of nostalgia for the Belle Époque, she rarely sees Germans these days, but lots of Swedes and a few Brazilians who do see Germans, and she also sees the United States Ambassador at Berne, she stays in Switzerland until the end of the war.

At the time of the Armistice she goes back to America, once more calls herself Hellström, she has agreeable discussions with presidential advisers, begins to appreciate exactly what she's doing, and she does it better and better, she also sings better and better, throaty voice, strange, her drawing-room conversation is more or less unremarkable, large mouth, large eyes, but when she sings it is as though that voice has been touched by the sorrows of the whole wide world, in Washington another of her father's friends asks her if she wouldn't like to return to Europe, go back to France, Paris, Versailles.

She sets sail, she is invited into the salons of French ladies, the ladies who love to play ducks and drakes with politics through their ministerial lovers, she also runs across German friends who tell her things in confidence, a group of young Englishmen around an economist, an eccentric, name of Maynes, he disapproves of the fact that the French and the English insist on making Germany pay exorbitant war reparations, he's brilliant, it's so pleasant to go out with you, dear Lena, you attract them, he's homosexual, she's very fond of him.

In the end she gets to know all about the in-fighting within each delegation, French, English, German, she passes it all on to Wilson, when he comes to France they think he's very naïve but he knows everything, you're doing a terrific job, dear Lena, I'd like you to do me a favour, it's not Lena who is asking for something in return for all she does for the United States, but her President who is asking her for a favour, let me come to one or two of your rehearsals, that's Lena's reward, in Paris: a President who sits in a corner and makes himself very small while she works on her singing, that's all.

Max doling out a part of all this to de Vèze, voice low, lingering occasionally upon a desire, he would like to write a piece on that celebrated Congress of Versailles, Lena in implausible hats, her expertise in any discussion about frontiers, the rights of people and the payment of war debts.

In the twenties it seems she put a temporary stop to these little parallel activities, she doesn't like the Republicans, Coolidge, Harding, Hoover, she comes from a Democrat background, the new Europe scares her a little, she re-immerses herself in things American, concentrates on her singing, she was present at the great Waltenberg Seminar of 1929, but only in her capacity as a singer.

Max says to de Vèze:

'One of these days you must ask our good friend Lilstein to tell you about Lena, Hans was her lover for a year, Lilstein never was, neither of them ever got over it.'

'What about you, Max?'

De Vèze could not contain himself, he has made the mistake of interrupting Max, he regrets it immediately.

'If you had a half-decent intelligence service, Ambassador, you'd know, it's as if I were to ask you whether Madame Morel said yes in the end, what would you reply?'

De Vèze got off lightly, a crude mention of Muriel, he does not take offence, the main thing is that Max should go on with his tale, de Vèze takes particular care not to make Max take up where he left off, he concentrates on flying the plane, then hands the controls back to the pilot but doesn't dare turn round to look at Max, who gazes down at the landscape lost in his thoughts and slowly resumes because he'd feel bad now if he failed to make the most of the opportunity to relive those years, no doubt it was Roosevelt who asked Lena to go back to Europe, in 1933, to Germany primarily, the moment Hitler took over, she is very much in favour at court, as they say, not the innermost circle maybe, not always, but she works prodigiously hard.

In Berlin a radio operator has been placed at her disposal, an Australian, that's right, an Aussie who works for the Intelligence Service, it was the English who supplied the radio operator, because Roosevelt did not trust his own services, people reluctant to intercept German or Japanese communications, a gentleman simply doesn't do that, it was the English who taught them to be gentlemen but they at least have no qualms about spying, Lena regularly contacts her radio man, nothing ever written down, she gives him a few sentences, off he goes, encodes, transmits.

It is thought she even ran across Lilstein in about 1937, nothing definite, spring of '37, could be coincidence, Berlin, music shop, a man she can't quite place at first, except the voice, and also his large build, the light-coloured eyes, close-cropped hair, small moustache, a good-looking young man of about twenty-five, a splendid advert for Aryan propaganda, instinctively both behaved as if they did not know each other, the man came up to her talking about the recital she'd given the previous evening, Beethoven, arias from *Fidelio*, she autographed a score for him, a fan encountered by chance.

Obviously an army officer in civvies, the mark left on the back of his neck by an officer's cap, tall, hair short, arrogant manner, pure chance, although meeting a fan in a shop which sold romantic sheet music wasn't really that much of a coincidence, he told her he played the piano, she answered I hope you always keep a fire burning at home because it's going to get very cold soon, and that's not very good for pianos.

She held out her hand to him, great lady, aloof, I was happy to sign a score for you, exchange a few words, now that's an end to it, a smile like a Greek statue, the smile of the omniscient blind seer, she knew many things, maybe a dignitary in the Gestapo had just asked her to postpone a private recital, maybe on the same day another dignitary had just had her informed that he couldn't make it this week, perhaps a sign, or even other indications no one will ever know about, something big was brewing, the tall man left.

Two cops had walked into the shop behind Lena, with faces blank and big feet, one of them was about to follow the tall man, she thrust her parcels into his hands, since you've now taken to following me into shops, you can take these and put them in my car, the men probably hadn't dared report the incident, though it was interesting, the lady had spoken to a man she didn't seem to know, in a specialist music shop, they exchanged a few words about falling temperatures and then she'd said goodbye, the men with blank faces and big feet couldn't have filed a report, didn't want to explain why they hadn't followed the man with the slow movements, arrogant manner and light-coloured eyes.

If this is true, it gave the big man a breathing space, and if the man really is Lilstein the Gestapo won't pick him up until the end of 1937.

Two weeks after the business in the music shop, Lena spoke to Goebbels, an excellent evening, he had just listened to her singing, they were in a window recess, covert looks directed at them, respectful of their privacy, they spoke about Goethe, Goebbels was paying attention, he was just realising that she knew Goethe better than he did, yes, I also acted in Schiller, *The Brigands*, while I was still at school, Minister, and in German, I learned German when I was very young, it's very easy for us northern peoples, Lena was almost one metre eighty tall, just by standing next to him she was saying to him I at least am a true Aryan, he asked if she would come on a visit to a new motor-car factory.

He was then in the process of organising a grand occasion, present would be the Prince of Wales, Herr Neuville, Herr Lindberg, the aristocratic old guard, capitalist success, airborne audacity, the German people, its leaders, a vehicle for the people, the participation of Fraülein Hellström would impress on the day the seal of art, surely you're not short of fine singers in the Reich, Minister, women whom I think of as examples, in the end she accepted, they'd started discussing what she'd sing, something by Wolf, a setting to a poem by Goethe, and something by Wagner, she was very keen to do the song of Mignon, as to the Wagner, she left the Minister free to choose, she hummed a few arias, Goebbels in seventh heaven.

In the middle of an aria she broke off, which would you rather, Minister, a friend of Germany whom one does not have followed by morons, or a singer who returns suddenly to New York saying Berlin is becoming intolerable? I can also have the question put to the Führer by one of my friends, or ask him myself next week.

Goebbels knew full well why she wanted to be rid of her guardian angels, mature woman, the bourgeois women of the Third Reich do not like her, imagine, she has lovers but no husband.

The greedy forties, the age for large-scale consumption of airmen, classically handsome lieutenants not eager to continue consorting with a woman watched by the Gestapo, nor attracted by the idea of having one fine morning to write a report which would include everything they'd done with the lady.

Also hint of a smoke-screen. You know how diplomats hate this kind of complication, de Vèze. Well, to relieve the pressure, she resumed her routine activities, boldness, cool head, professionalism, Washington recognises that she is doing great work and she makes the most of the situation to idolise aviators, a passion for airborne encounters, the new production models, sometimes she disappears for two days with an airman, in the country, once I was in Berlin, she'd just returned from one such fling, I said to her these are the days of your youth, she understood and said I had a mind like a sewer, we laughed a lot.

Until one night when it all goes very wrong, she's at the wheel of her big Mercedes, road between Stuttgart and Tübingen, late '37, on the back seat a man, asleep, smelling of whisky, actually it wasn't a Mercedes, those big Mercedes had Nazi written all over them, she had a more unusual car, more aristocratic, superb wire wheels, the man on the back seat is wearing a dinner jacket, but next to him is the cap and tunic of a *Luftwaffe* officer, Lena is driving fast, too fast, her passion, night-driving, headlights of approaching vehicles visible from afar, sporty driving style, double-declutch, avoid braking, she can throw a twelve-cylinder beast into a bend, a controlled skid.

Star-filled night, she hums a tune and has to stop at a large security road-block, not road police but a mixture of gendarmes and SS, papers please, American passport, the voices of the men as metallic as ever but less brutal, they're not going to bother her, smell of whisky, torch shining on the back seat, the sleeper is in an ethylic stupor, silence all round, the soldiers tense up, an NCO has gone to get an officer, who sends for another officer, Lena caught something like *Oberst* or *Oberstleutnant*, she never understood about ranks, must be a commanding officer.

When he comes the soldiers stand to attention, he walks with a limp, more torch waving, the tunic on the back seat, commanding officer's voice, a soft fashionable drawl, may I ask the identity of your passenger, Madame? she gets out of the car, opens the back door, pushing a soldier out of her way: his name's Ulrich, he's my lover.

She lights a cigarette to calm her rising fury, throws it down after the second drag on it, my lover is drunk as a skunk, a session with his colleagues, he's not in the mood for love, I can't stand it, I leave him to you, write a report and take him back to his field-marshal, he should have been back on duty by this time, let this be a lesson to him.

Around her half a dozen SS have suddenly replaced the gendarmes, one of the SS men is holding a lantern, the commanding officer has burn scars over all his face, he has recognised Lena, he is sinister, he too peers into the back of the car, the triage at the gates of hell, deliberate movements, the deliberation of the sadist, eyes boring into Lena's eyes, anything but a fool, a man in this state at your side Madame is, to say the least, surprising, at this hour, on this road? Will you allow me another question? another glance inside the car, at the cap and the tunic, you said Ulrich, is that *Flugleutnant* Ulrich? And the conclusion comes: by your side, in this state, is he not sufficiently punished? He is a warrior, flying is an extremely dangerous occupation, he is already sufficiently punished, you may go, Madame, solid drinking with comrades is a tradition of the German people and her warriors, sometimes we have to drink to forget and to be the better man the next day, a man is a man, forgive him on this occasion, in this state, by your side, sufficiently punished, dangerous occupation.

The commanding officer gives a sign to an SS man who steps forward, chalks a mark on the inside of the windscreen, my regards, Madame, and my unalloyed admiration, he clicks his heels, points to the chalk mark, that will ensure you won't be bothered again, he then limps back towards the next vehicle, Lena sets off again.

Two days later Ulrich is sent for by Goering, three generals are there, Goering curtly: Lieutenant Ulrich, when an officer of my *Luftwaffe* has his eye on one of the most alluring weapons in the enemy's arsenal what should he do? Ulrich standing to attention, voice metallic, impeccable: fire all guns, quick bursts, direct hits, Marshal – laughs all round which bounce back off the marble walls of the huge office, quick bursts!

Goering laughs until the tears come, he resumes, slow and serious voice, the killer, in future if ever your inveterate drinking prevents you from carrying out the mission of an officer of the Reich you will get six months' latrine fatigues and be banned from flying, dismiss, and get yourself married fast to some good young German girl, we need children. Ulrich does not understand everything Goering tells him but he does not try to defend himself, he does drink a lot, he is let off lightly, usually an order to appear before the fat man turns out rather more painfully, he reckons he's been fortunate, he'll follow the Marshal's recommendation, get married.

That is how Lena succeeded in ferrying her radio operator as far as the Swiss frontier, with whisky sprinkled over a *Flugleutnant*'s uniform, a seamstress at the opera house in Stuttgart had brought her a shawl one evening where there was no performance, to her hotel, for you, tonight also it's going to turn very cold, very quickly.

Instead of keeping out of sight, Lena makes a few arrangements and speeds off in her car to pick up her radio operator before he can set foot in the street where they're waiting for him, she was lucky, a good tip about the cold, and for a while in London an Australian transmissions instructor repeated to students training to be spies, this is a very interesting business to be in, take me for example, it gave me an opportunity to be the lover of a great singer, for one night only, in a car, somewhere in Europe, a very fine motor, a Maybach Zeppelin.

Lena had given herself a real fright, anyone else would have fled Germany after pulling a stunt like that, would have taken a harmless little trip for example to Lucerne, in fact she did go to Lucerne, a visit to a very old girlfriend, but she went back to Germany immediately afterwards, not the sort who gave up easily, and whatever she might say she loved the atmosphere, the uniforms against which her dress could positively shine, she loved the parties, the last time I met her in Berlin was at the Opera, a gala for the *Wehrmacht*, in 1938, at the time of the Munich talks.

She was radiant surrounded by all those uniforms, I pointed this out to her, she got angry, she said, 'Goffard, you're just a footling Frenchman', she bawled me out in front of everyone, said I was small-minded, I thought she was going to slap my face, I beat a retreat, I felt quite ill for the rest of the evening, I was aware that she had just shattered our friendship, it was my fault, I watched out for an opportunity to have another word with her, she saw me coming, she withered me with a look, the people around us, Nazi dignitaries and generals in full dress uniform, the swine were waiting for her to slap my face, she spat a few words in my direction, she spoke through gritted teeth, white-hot fury, I hardly heard what she said, I walked out of the Opera, got into my car, left Berlin, I was weeping, I took the Munich road, Lena had just said to me 'Max, you see the company I keep these days, go back to your poker-playing friends, tell them not to sign, they are to be told not to sign, you see the company I keep?'

I ran the errand, told the English and the French, but in Munich sign they did, they weren't interested in knowing what German generals were telling them not to do.

In the cockpit of the plane, Max's voice has grown louder, more articulate, anxious to hide nothing from de Vèze:

'I spent nearly twenty years, de Vèze, twenty years adding it all up, sifting through it, then it all became perfectly clear one evening in Paris in the early fifties, in the Officers' Club, the room for Senior Men and special guests, a dinner for Allied Generals, with Marlene Dietrich and other luminaries, press barons who were being honoured for their efforts on behalf of the cause of freedom, when Lena came in there was a ripple of interest which took in Marlene too, they'd both sung that afternoon in support of the charitable work of the Allied armies, Lena was magnificent, very handsome at fifty, figure like a model but with talents and ideas, the most important man there that evening was Gruenther, the NATO boss, he was first to get to his feet, he went over to her.

'He gave a military salute, saluted a woman, a civilian, the farm-boy from Nebraska, a yokel, instead of bringing his heels together smartly and lowering his head to kiss her hand he gave a soldier's salute, very snappy, parade-ground stuff, the other men all stood up, she was their guest, clicking of heels, bows, hand-kissing, only Gruenther blundered, he saluted military fashion, everyone thought it was a bloomer, and then he compounded his mistake, proud to be standing next to her, not the way a man is when he has swept a beautiful woman off her feet, proud as if he'd been standing next to Patton.

'At that moment I more or less got it, in London I'd seen French officers salute sober family men in grey suits who wore a small ribbon in their buttonhole, a shot-silk ribbon, green, black edging, you know, the sort of men who derail trains using only a mackintosh, she wasn't wearing a ribbon, the other officers did not salute, she responded by offering Gruenther her hand, smiled like a lady of fashion, it was perfect.

'Other things came back to me, in the end I knew all of it, just had to get the right angle, in 1947 she sang with Stirnweiss, Elisabeth Stirnweiss, no one protested, picture it, Madame Stirnweiss, once a card-carrying member of the Nazi Party, not one of the top names, nothing terrible against her, Austrian, with a big heart, but even so, she'd sung for the Führer, she'd dined with him, Stirnweiss wasn't a Nazi but she had an NSDAP card, during the post-war years it was enough to limit her to giving private lessons to middle-class Viennese citizens for ten years, long enough for her to lose her voice.

'And dear scatterbrained Lena agrees to sing with her, yes, in '47 the request came directly from Stirnweiss, or indirectly, and Lena did not respond indirectly, she came to Stirnweiss, tears in Stirnweiss's eyes, their paths had crossed in Berlin and Vienna, in the thirties, two friends, Stirnweiss had given her an entrée to the best salons, the best society, and Lena loved that, once she'd turned up with Lindbergh, she saw the Prince of Wales and Mrs Simpson, but Lena never went as far as those people, she loved a party but she got angry every time the Nazis tried to exploit her presence, and the Nazis back-pedalled because she knew a few personal telephone numbers and because she wasn't afraid to give people a roasting.

'So in '47 she reopened doors closed to Stirnweiss, from friendship, with no second thoughts, out of artistic preference, but there was also something else, she must have discussed it with Washington before leaving, people from the East should not be allowed to deliver Persil-white certificates of cleanliness to wayward talents, with or without NSDAP cards, like Furtwängler or Stirnweiss, or Karajan, people like that should not be allowed to scoot off to Dresden or East Berlin, the

Soviets had just reopened the Staatsoper, with *Orpheus, Eugene Onegin, Rigoletto*, to which add a magnificent Arts Centre on *Unter den Linden*, the cold war was just beginning, shifting alliances, one side salvaged von Braun, the other von Whoever, Lena whisked Stirnweiss off to Salzburg, for the festival, and no one turned a hair.

'My old friend Linus Mosberger told me that a newspaper columnist in New York had decided to get the knives out for Lena and her taste for ex-Nazis, he was called in, he shut up, she was very protected, she handled the whole Stirnweiss business with panache.

'No one knows why but there was not one West German who could say no to Lena, no one ever said anything, but the great and the good were at each other's throats to get her round their dinner tables or into their drawing rooms, to hear her talking about Toscanini or the Waltenberg Seminar or the Congress of Versailles from which so much evil had flowed, they trusted her implicitly, told her everything, and as the evening drew to a close people would start saying how they'd secretly opposed Hitler, Lena would listen, one day she'd remarked "many Germans opposed Hitler, such a shame they never got together".

'She always had a slightly mad streak, in 1956 I was in West Berlin, everywhere things were getting tense, the Poles, the Hungarians especially, summer of '56. One of Berlin's main shopping streets, I bump into a man, he drops his parcels, I apologise, I give him a hand, he raises his hat, old-style polite gesture, I respond in kind, we spend as long as is required by Berlin courtesy, we go our separate ways, I never saw him again, I'd just had time to hear a few words "she's in Budapest, hasn't got a diplomatic passport, it's going to turn extremely cold".

'I got on a train, I ran the errand for Lena, she wouldn't listen, she stayed in Budapest, she had a lot of guts, she was giving a master-class for singers, and between lessons she busied herself with various small matters concerning well-meaning people, to move things on, she loves that city, the weather was fine.

'She took me and three Hungarian friends to a spot a few kilometres out of the city, on the banks of the Danube, a boat house, they took a boat which could carry several people, not a rowing-skiff, one of those very narrow jobs they use for racing, for coxed fours, the three Hungarians row well, I try not to make a fool of myself, she's cox, she pretends to be our trainer, giving us the tempo as if she were conducting an orchestra, we laughed liked kids, we turned when we reached the Parliament building, it was great, the return was slower, rowing to our starting point but this time against the current, couldn't sit down for a week.

'Another evening we went in a gang down to the water's edge, she laughed a lot, a riverside eating place, she swallowed a bellyful of fried gudgeon, she ate them as they were, bones and all, she dipped the gudgeon in the mayonnaise then gulp, and a swig of red to help them down, afterwards she asked the accordionist to play a tango, she danced, at her age, no one said anything, magnificent legs, she was very much admired, also had a big following, marked out, the people she mixed with were being watched by the Hungarian security services, and those people didn't go in for half-measures, a hundred kilos of explosives, but she was long gone. A great lady, de Vèze, a great lady. At Arlington I cried my heart out, and I wasn't the only one.'

In the large house in the middle of Grindisheim, after it was all over, the head of the Federal Office for the Protection of the Constitution did an operation assessment of sorts, as a consolation for the men who were about to disperse:

'It's as well that Monsieur Goffard left with his Ambassador, he was already dining with Prime Ministers before you people were born, he'd finish the evening with them, played poker, and he's still at it, you never know what he'll say next, he's opened too many cupboards, I'd bet that before the week's out he'll be invited to dine with the Chancellor. Why? To understand that you need long memories, in 1945 the Americans had a plan for us, Germany would become one big farm, the Morgenthau Plan, you'd all have grown up in the shadow of cows' backsides, and de Gaulle wanted to be given the right bank of the Rhine, the very same as where we're speaking at this moment,

Goffard wrote two long articles saying that the mistakes made in 1918 should not repeated, in his view Morgenthau was making the same stupid blunders as Poincaré.'

On the side of the Americans and Walker, things didn't go as well. When he was told that Max and de Vèze had taken a touring plane he blanched, he ordered cars heading for Winzig to stop, lovely late afternoon on a road over the tops, looking down on the Rhine, he cursed, traitors the lot of them, he even kicked a tyre, he demanded an immediate line to the Schiltighaus airbase, to speak into the microphone he recovered his clear, soft voice, it's only an air-taxi, no diplomatic status, got to show them what happens when you try to make monkeys out of people, no, not fighter planes.

'I want three attack helicopters, Cobras, his Aero is a slowpoke, and I want live ammo, yes, I'm fully authorised, and this French Ambassador isn't clean, warning salvo with live rounds, I want pilots who'll go the whole nine yards, we're going to make him so scared he'll land on the first piece of level ground he comes to! Hear this, he must land on the German side! And I want live ammunition!'

*

In the lounge at the Waldhaus, Lilstein continues to abuse your patience, he talks as though he were confiding in you, as if you were his last hope, he asks if you know what it was that had been scaring him most these last few weeks, prior to setting off for Waltenberg.

'It was in one of those very attractive French magazines of yours, a story about your *force de frappe*, the pilots of planes that carry atomic bombs, no, they didn't look very threatening, clean-cut boys, soldiers from the abyss with short back and sides, very wholesome manner, but two of them are ready to scramble, ready to jump into their Mirages, in the photo they're all reading issues of the same magazine, you can make out the title, I asked my research department to find out about the magazine your pilots read, I was told that *Planète* is a para-psychology magazine, UFOs, Inca bas-reliefs showing a figure holding his erect penis in his hands, fertility gods, the sort of thing you get everywhere the moment men started making images, but for *Planète* they are real, authentic extraterrestrial pilots clutching broom handles, *Gott verdamnt*, young gentleman of France, those boys fly around with hell between their knees and they read magazines written by morons who confuse a large *Pimmel* with the handle of an extra-terrestrial's broom, what scared the living daylights out of me was the fact that it's the same on the Russian side.

'An evening with the Russians in Berlin, a dinner, all went smoothly until midnight, and then they started telling stories about fortune-telling, magic, Martians, they all were members of the Party, the KGB, and the Red Army, two generals, a half-century of Marxism and that's all these morons can think of to talk about after midnight, stories about extraterrestrials, clairvoyance, thought transmission, at the time it made me laugh, to myself.

'But when I saw that your pilots were reading the same sort of rubbish, I started to feel scared, you've already seen photos of Americans, each of the men whose job is to fire the rockets has a military policeman standing behind him holding a gun to the back of his head, just in case he goes mad, we've got the same thing, it's reassuring, but what happens if the general who gives the orders to all these men, or his Soviet opposite number, or the Frenchman in his Mirage hears an extraterrestrial telling him go ahead, lad, do it? Our work as cultivated, serious people is to prevent that kind of accident, to pass round rational information, we regulate the tension, that's what we are, regulators!

'It's not even in your interest to remain an orthodox Marxist, I mean deep down, if you cling to all your ideals and all your thoughts life will become impossible, there'll be no one left you can talk to frankly, except me, and I'm becoming more and more sceptical as I grow older.'

*

Seen from the plane, the Rhine is beautiful, altitude three hundred metres, vineyards, woods, bends in the river, villages, the great flood-gates, the slanting sun lights up the river bank on their left.

'Look, Max,' says de Vèze, 'to the west, where the Moselle joins, makes you think of some pretty little valley, it was the great highway for invasions, massacres, we'll soon be passing Bacharach.'

A dreamy look in de Vèze's eye:

'Don't speak, Ambassador, concentrate on flying the plane, if you tell me about the Lorelei and her lilac-coloured comb, I'll denounce you.'

De Vèze smiles, allows Max a lot of latitude.

'I don't give a damn for legends, Max, nor for the wild beauties of the river.'

He points to one of the engines through the plane's window:

'Intake stroke, compression, combustion, outlet stroke, thousands of times every minute, long live technology, Max! There's a thousand times more crazy beauty in the pistons of that rig there than in the entire history of the Rhine.'

He leans on the joystick, the Rhine comes nearer.

De Vèze turns to Max. He knows Max won't tell him any more about Lena.

'Your friend Linus Mosberger, when we were all together earlier, he took the opportunity to ask me for an interview. He'd like to hear about Pompidou. Was it you who put him up to it? Is your chum Linus to be trusted? Known him long?'

Linus Mosberger, an old story about a contract, which still does the rounds of editorial offices, writes extremely well, drips experience, de Vèze can trust him, Max is very fond of him, Max and Linus got to know each other properly in Prague in 1938. In those days Mosberger was freelance, an independent reporter, but he'd just signed a contract with the *Chicago Guardian*, becomes their European correspondent, fifty dollars a week, eighty if war breaks out and for three extra weeks after the armistice which would end the war. For those days it's pretty good pay but the paper thinks it's got a bargain, that the war won't last long.

When Max meets Linus in Prague, in May 1938, he gets a fright. Linus is just back from Vienna. He is ashen-faced, attack of the shivers, covered with spots, one giant itch, he tries to write two or three pages, a scoop, he could do without this, what he has is more like an anxiety attack.

Three days earlier, in Vienna, a very thin man shut a door on Linus, turned the bolt, eleven at night, Linus is alone, locked in for the night, he wanders among the tables, Linus has an article to write about what he is about to discover, he wants to begin the article with that, the man shutting the door on him and turning the key, it's dark, Linus has only a torch for light, he feels as if he's going to be sick.

'I didn't want to be sick when I was in that room in Vienna, Max, it's now that it's come on me, now that I've nothing to fear any more, now that I'm here, in Prague, sitting at my Underwood.'

The man pushed the bolt home, it's dark, Linus wanders among the tables, on a large desk there are ledgers, Max, I can't even write that properly, ledgers, the very thin man, with his black cap and oniony breath left me alone in this room, at that point I was terrified, Max, but not anguished, I was in Vienna, in a large room, I was taking action, didn't have spots all over my body, not like now, terror in action.

Linus reads what has been entered with a dip pen in the ledgers, he deciphers what is written, his torch dims, in the ledgers are names and dates, he moves among the tables, then returns to the ledgers, six names of people who have committed suicide.

'Max, I'm never going to be able to write the story, my hands are shaking all over the keyboard, whisky doesn't help, I went back to the tables with those names in my head.'

Back to the tables, bodies laid out on the tables, with labels, Linus locates the names of the suicides.

'One of them committed suicide by beating himself over the head, Max, so hard his eyes were expelled from their sockets, another had this serene expression on his face, I lift the sheet, bruises everywhere, only suicides, I wanted to describe what I'd seen but I dropped everything, the medic in Prague told me what was wrong with me, he advised me to go to Carlsbad, I'm about to leave, fields of wheat, hops, rape, the Jewish section, I'd paid the man to shut me up for a night in the Jewish section of the Vienna morgue, only bodies of suicides and urns.'

Linus had given three dollars baksheesh to an Austrian functionary to let him spend one night in the Vienna morgue, the functionary returned at dawn.

'I asked him about the urns, he said "no family has ever turned up to claim any of them", according to the functionary all members of all the families were already dead, Max, I'm going away now to see those hop fields, no, there's no point even in trying to see for yourself, I've no idea where they put them nowadays, there are more and more, I'll try later, ever since the Nazis came the American Embassy in Vienna has been issuing twenty visas a week to refugees, and it's practically the only one doing so, today the morgue symbolises the whole of History, Max, and I'm going to Carlsbad.'

Max has fallen silent, de Vèze has concentrated on flying the plane, at one moment he said, without looking at Max:

'What was it like when she sang, Max?'

*

As he left the Waldhaus, Lilstein said this to you:

'The greatest danger in our profession comes from noble sentiments and ideals, young gentleman of France, look at what happened to Tellheim, one of the great men of the East-West balancing act, he was part of the team that made the Hiroshima bomb, it's partly down to him that there wasn't an atomic war, he gave us the information we needed, Soviet laboratories made up for lost time, he kept them informed for eight years, they only started to have suspicions from 1949 onward, when an H-bomb was exploded in Kazakhstan, the Americans and the British thought that the USSR was still ten years away from doing that, Beria was in charge of the nuclear programme.

'By '49 Tellheim has already been gone from the United States for some time, he was at Harwell, he sensed that the Intelligence Service had identified him but he didn't try to save himself, you grasp the situation, everyone suspects him, in his lab at Harwell no one speaks to him any more, he moves forward in a vacuum, the British question him, let him go, question him again two weeks later, he feels relieved, he dreams of giving it all up, of returning to the GDR, his father is there, now retired, a Protestant, member of the consistory for the town where he lives.

'Instead of slipping quietly away, Tellheim turns up for questioning, and he admits everything, even owns up to things they do not ask him about – well, almost everything, let's be honest, he kept two or three small items to himself – he threw his hand in, like a man who believes too much in what he was doing and drops everything all at once, the fox snared, but he didn't get away by biting his leg or tail off, he gave himself up, according to my Russian colleagues it was because he was ideologically under-nourished, he jettisoned the part of himself he could no longer feed.

'In the end, the antifascist man of science packed the game in and made way for the angler fishing for his debts, a gloomy fox, he lived among the English, in a world whose ideas he had to pretend to share, he had two systems of thought, the one he despised and the one he kept hidden, the kind of thinking he despised loomed increasingly large, while the other continued to be valid. The strain was too much for him, he talked to the English who actually would have preferred him not to say as much.

'Today he is a sad man, he lives in the GDR, he's still a useful physicist for his age, but he doesn't do much thinking now, in the thirties and forties he was really one of the three or four top men in world physics, he's gone into a decline, he believed in too many things at the same time, Marxism-Leninism and democracy, science, free debate, he celebrated the benefits of the group but he was one of the strangest individuals of his generation, tremendous pride, he wanted to do everything.

'For our work as regulators, it's vital from the very start that we shouldn't believe too ardently in what we do, when I was a young man, too many people advised me to read Lenin, you're better off reading Shakespeare and *Faust* instead.'

*

When she sang? In the small plane Max does not answer de Vèze's question immediately, he doesn't look at him, he looks at the Rhine, the landscape.

Lena's singing, now if he could say what it was like, he'd have written it down long ago, once I tried to get it down on paper but I never succeeded, I lack the flair for it, Malraux was right, not bold enough, I'm just not capable of expressing it, all that happens is a tightening of the pharynx when I think about it, I could say a few words but not to de Vèze, too complicated, he likes planes, women, adventure stories, motor cars, novels for men, Max can't imagine saying to de Vèze very simple harmony, start of the last *Lied*, Schumann, D minor, first note, fourth, dominant, tonic, the voice initially on a single note, the D, simple chords, then the diminished sevenths, she stood before us, she had arranged her red hair in thick twists coiled in spirals at each side, neckline low, marvellous shoulders, no jewellery, the great lounge of the Waldhaus, just one Schumann, the penultimate evening of the 1929 Seminar, the recital, Stirnweiss cannot continue, Madame de Valréas has said we're not slave drivers, Stirnweiss sang first, Mozart, then a few *Lieder* from *Woman's Love and Life*, the altitude caused her throat to go dry, she ignored it, Stirnweiss sang very well, surprise, joy, love, fragile voice, Max listened to La Stirnweiss, pure sung delight, everyone reconciled with everyone else.

Then there'd been a halt in the proceedings, Madame de Valréas had looked daggers at a few smokers and then introduced an American artiste idolised throughout Europe, Lena and her nerve, sheer nerve to start with the last *Lied* of the cycle Stirnweiss had just been singing, Stirnweiss had said with a smile I'll leave the last one for you, Lena had accepted, like a shot, actually not a very nice thing to do when you think about it, off she started, *Nun hast du mir den ersten Schmerz getan . . .* you were the cause of my first pain.

Not much in the bass for the left hand for the first few bars, beginning of a recitative not in strict time, without the bass notes differences in tempo are less noticeable, the first beat is a rest, and on the third beat the piano attacks with its major chord of D, ditto at the start of the second line, a rising scale of sleep and death, her man is dead, Max did you practise your scales? How old was I? Ten, twelve? I was already on the living-room carpet eating bread and butter and caster sugar, I loved sight-reading on the piano but scales less, for the following lines, from *Es blicket*, harmonies held longer and the negative of the sorrowing recitative, the diminished sevenths, the high point on *leer*, in the *Lied*'s high compass, another day Lena lying on the floor, on her back, Maxie, be a sweetie, pass me that big book next to the croissants, quarto, glossy paper, at least two kilos, she rests it on her abdomen, breathes in, holds her breath, breathes out slowly, the book sinks back down, what are you doing Lena? Singing exercises, Max, diaphragm and muscles low down, very low down, says Max, if I may say so it's not very far from a certain spot, are you sure pubic muscles are used in singing? Absolutely Max, that's where it all starts, if you want to put feeling into a high note you start from there; does a few minutes' exercise, gets up, stands back to the wall, heels, buttocks, back, head all pressed against the wall, legs apart, hands against her ribs, her red hair thick and untamed, she breathes out, that, says Max, is more decent, still working on those high notes? Maxie, if you knew what I'm doing, I can see, you're stretching your back straight, you're controlling the expansion of your rib-cage, that I can understand, she laughs, you don't know everything, well never mind.

Then she sang.

To start with that last *Lied*, the sad one, the one her friend had been unable to sing, the one she had left to her, the moment of death, like the one which had to be sung with even more expression than the previous ones, which had conveyed surprise, pleasure or joy, the last one, death, the one which called for a strength of feeling even greater and more intense than the six others, gentle Elisabeth had left it for her friend as a homage, so that she might go one better than her, there was that hiatus in the lounge of the Waldhaus, while Madame de Valréas had withered a few smokers with her glance, then the resumption, she did it cold in a sense, the second part of the recital beginning with Schumann's last *Lied*, the most dramatic, the audience waited with a certain impatience to hear what an American could do with this masterpiece of European romantic sensibility, there was silence.

She sang, and people in the audience knew what was coming, that was why, from the start, for singing like this, it was crucial to be possessed of an unsuspected power of feeling, the declaration, with the very first notes, of the very heart of the piece, the death of the beloved, all the women in the audience are ready to live, relive, anticipate, imagine, transpose, imitate the death of the beloved in music, the pain she makes them feel, not one of them who has not at some point imagined the death of her beloved to see what it feels like, and all the men are ready to listen to the pain a woman feels when death deprives her of the companion life has given her, not one of them who has not already imagined himself dead so that he can see an inner picture of the pain of a woman he loves when she is confronted by the spectacle of his death.

And all of them, men and women, know how great the need for a delicate quality of voice, the dying fall of one accent into the next, seesawing syncopated notes running trippingly in pursuit of each other, full of pain, they wander, lacerated by pleas, as if the soul were suddenly discovering what it carries within it and to which it cannot deny expression, moans, distress, desires, memories and nameless terrors, syncopated rhythms harassed by quavers, while the spurts of fear take shape, gather into a melody, and the moment ends with a surge in which they become a song of entreaty which calms the milling agitation of the pain, then the initial theme returns, the subsiding of one tone into another, violent agitation of accents laden with savage resolve, all of which makes everyone at the same moment wonder: what is happening?

Everyone expectant of that succession of tonal adventures sustained by the deep-eyed, lost expression on a beautiful American face, red hair gleaming in swaying coils at her temples, hands clasped so tight they are snow white, a rising chromatic scale full of wild nostalgia, stippled with sudden pianissimi, convulsions of a pain it's no longer possible to contain.

And the initial theme returns yet again, trembling, lyrical, exulting, sobbing, advancing in triumph, clad in all the growling splendour of the left hand, a melody almost perverse in the avidity with which it is savoured and exploited, until at last, slowed by lassitude, a long, languid, minor arpeggio wells up, rises a tone, resolves into the major and fades to silence with melancholy diffidence.

Then she sang, *Nun hast du mir . . .* you were the cause of my first pain, suddenly everyone in the lounge of the Waldhaus is drawn as one towards this voice.

But it was not that at all.

It wasn't a song, strictly speaking, it was close to recitative, the words resist, refuse to be caught up and swept away, the diction remains in advance of the melodic line, the voice virtually hangs on one note, the D, at the beginning, a repeated note, and the piano accompaniment tracks it, sustained chords, as if to suspend the time, diminished sevenths, few openings here for pathos, very simple harmonies, D minor, first note, fourth, dominant.

In the lounge the audience is wrong-footed, music without wings, with nothing in which to trust, with nothing to which one's soul might be entrusted, you must keep it with you, weighed down by the world, the tonal system reduced to its most simple form, utter simplicity in the sequence of chords, very little in the bass for the left hand, a recitative not in strict tempo, then the harmonies become more tense but not lyrical, drift up the scale, Lena's magnificent top notes, she used to say high notes aren't on the top of a ladder, not in Schumann, the voice must be like a wave which breaks on to the high note, makes off with it, *leer*, the world is empty, the culmination, a D flat, a far cry from the basic key of D minor.

Not far away in terms of intervals, but far in terms of tonal systems; so to have a D flat in the signature there must be at least four flats, in the key of D minor there's only one flat, here B flat minor, ears disoriented, embryonic cadence on the fifth, and this D flat is resolved only in the C which follows, for the voice this resolution is achieved after the piano, the cadence will not end, I'm lost, Lena, I want you to tell me what you were doing standing pressed against the wall that day, they are in a car driving up to a village in Haute-Savoie, I was loosening up the small of my back, Max, by straightening my spine I was loosening the small of my back, it's crucial if you want ringing, free-flowing high notes, to express unhappiness, the lounge in the Waldhaus.

Previously, the other songs, Stirnweiss, altogether more lively, the ring, the wedding, the child, and the last *Lied* for Lena, my first pain, a break with the whole cycle.

Then she sang, another tempo begins, in the cycle and for the public, something is happening, she had begun at the limits of recitative, neither tune nor melody, diction foregrounded, in advance of the melodic line, then the D flat, *leer*, and for the voice the resolution comes after the piano, a tension, friction of a half-tone, delay in the resolution of the note, for the voice the descent from D flat to C occurs only on the second quaver of the fourth beat, whereas on the piano it occurs on the third, a very powerful dissonance, and that's what music is.

She sang, leaving her soul where she stood, with the dross of the world, none of the emotions they had been prepared to feel, it was cold, not cold exactly, the song brought you face to face with death, said plainly I'm not here to spoon-feed you emotion, to hold your emotion by the hand, they had simply been confronted by a song of death, all the work was left for them to do.

The purpose of music is not to redeem the life you live so badly.

Max hasn't answered de Vèze, and de Vèze has respected his silence, then he pointed out divers landscapes for Max to admire. In the distance, in the gathering autumnal gloom, they made out Strasbourg cathedral. They flew on, following the course of the river. At one point, de Vèze got excited:

'Look, magnificent!'

He gestured to the right bank of the Rhine.

'Not allowed to go anywhere near.'

Max couldn't see anything.

'Look, on the bank of the canal, that big construction site, soon two revolutionary hyperboles, two pure forms reaching heavenward, exuding water vapour. Matter in the service of two revolutionary hyperboles, coming soon. Two towers, each almost a hundred metres tall. Not allowed to go anywhere near them. They'll emit billions of droplets and people have the gall to say that they'll be a blot on the landscape, I wouldn't exchange them for all the cathedrals built during their wars of religion!'

'Is that Fessenheim?'

'Yes, they've begun work on the site, designed to produce nine hundred megawatts.'

'Then I fear I must disappoint you, Ambassador, there won't be any cooling towers, the Rhine will do the cooling, old *Vater Rhein*. River-cooled nuclear, no hyperboles there!'

De Vèze has sulked for a few minutes, Max asks him to tell him about his meeting with Hans in Geneva.

'You knew?'

'I always do.'

'Kappler was on top form. We went out on the lake in a boat.'

'Did he give you the Winterthur turbine routine?'

Hans had shown de Vèze the boat's splendid mechanism; they'd also managed to see Coppet, the tall willows, Hans had perked up, he'd talked about the tomb of Madame de Staël and especially about the pages in which Chateaubriand evokes the soul of his dead fellow toiler.

'Oh yes, Max, Hans greatly admired those pages, the thought of Chateaubriand, devout Catholic, showing the soul of Madame de Staël the way to Paradise via Byron, Voltaire and Rousseau! Sound values, but enough to ensure she was refused admittance for all eternity!'

'Kappler was very fond of the grotesque side of the *Mémoires*.'

'I think, my dear Ambassador, that he thought of Chateaubriand as essentially a sylph, anyone who could write a book like that while dreaming of a creature of cloud reassured him, justified the unproductive hours.'

Walker failed to get authorisation to force de Vèze's plane to land.

Next day, in the CIA Boeing which was flying him back to Washington, he cursed Europe one or twice then reviewed the situation with Garrick, his deputy:

'We're not even sure Goffard's the goddam French mole or even the guy who acts as decoy.'

Garrick asked him if Lena Hellström had come up with anything at the beginning of the year and Walker answered quietly:

'She died before she could find out anything at all, it's an irreparable loss.'

Chapter 13

1991

Is Reason Historical?

In which Lilstein finds himself once more in a trap and we discover the identity of the mole.

In which a young bookseller's assistant keeps an eye on her customers while attempting to answer a philosophical question.

In which Lilstein realises that The Adventures of Gédéon *is a most instructive book.*

In which we also learn how the story of the bear ends.

Paris, Passage Marceau, September 1991

If reason ruled the world, nothing would ever happen.
Bernard de Fontenelle

It's very quiet, the untroubled quiet of bookshops, there is a young woman at the cash desk, dark auburn hair, square face, dark eyes, slightly turned-up nose, she has glanced up at Lilstein then looked back down at her notes.

Lilstein's Paris friend is already there, beige overcoat, he nods a greeting but does not come over to him, never act as if you didn't know each other, when people know each other it's always obvious, it's barely noticeable but no one is ever taken in, we'll behave as if we already knew each other vaguely, young gentleman of France, a nod of the head, a gesture of the hand, whichever, we know each other but each refrains from bothering the other, it gives an opportunity to scout out the terrain, assess the atmosphere.

Lilstein is perusing a large illustrated volume, my young friend assured me there was no risk, but I'm not too keen, a passageway debouching into the Grands Boulevards, block up both ends and you've got a trap, they locate me in the bookshop and they pick me up at one of the exits from the passage, a car waiting at each end, an effective trap, it's what I'd have done myself, I'm making too much of this, everything's quiet enough, that beige coat is new, he didn't have it last year, makes him look younger, these illustrated books are rather entertaining, a collection of drawings, rabbits, three rabbits and a duck, the edge of a wood, Sunnyside Woods, the duck has one thought and one thought only: 'to protect the weak against the strong, no more and no less'.

Lilstein turns the pages of the book, lingers over the drawings, a story about a duck and some rabbits, I too was a duck, the strong, the weak, a decent enough aim. Escorted by the rabbits the duck does the rounds of the animals in the woods, 'I will take you to a place of delights, the best paradise of all', that yellow is just right for the duck, not yellow, ochre, light ochre, I like ochre, the colour of completed things, when the redundant shine has been rubbed off them, someone said that to me one day, the village has tiled roofs, a sort of rusty red, and the grass in full sunlight, the dream of people from northern climes, the duck looks out of the side of his eyes the way sweet-talkers do, 'you will be rid of your most implacable enemies', the animals listen to him.

When I was a boy I really liked drawing animals, a town kid who dreamed of forests, the ochre, the rejection of unnecessary ostentation, it was Lena who talked to me about ochre, she loved it, to describe alto voices people usually talk about grey voices, she tried to put ochre tints in hers, she used to say it takes hours to get a good ochre tone into the voice, this bookshop isn't making my head spin, what I like about bookshops in the West is that they make your head spin, you go in, you don't know what to look at first, but here there's no chance of being disoriented, lots of pictures, not much printed text, children's books.

My young friend is watching me, it's clumsy, not as young as he was, it's true, despite his beige coat, he's still my young Frenchman, known each other for thirty-five years, he looks as if he's absorbed in the book he's reading but he's watching me as if he's up to some tomfool nonsense, personally I'd never have arranged to meet him in an alley, too many risks, no, there's no risk with him, no trap, he said there's something I need to buy, come with me, at your age it's time you got into what we call the comic book.

Rather droll these rabbits, they're watching the duck, they're sitting on their back legs, one front paw against their cheek wondering, they prattle, they listen to the duck's promises, 'a good life of peace and calm will take the place of terror and dread', I don't like alleyways.

The young woman at the cash desk saw the two men come in, the beige coat and the grey mackintosh, the older man, the one who's parked himself in the corner with the *Gédéons* and the *Babars*, he's the same build as Gilles, Gilles isn't so tall, he's the older of the two but he stands up straighter, he looks nice, shy and nice, afraid he's going to bump into things, of upsetting things, but he holds himself straight, it must be the first time in his life he's been in a place like this, they must have known each other for yonks, they don't need to be forever talking to each other and smiling as they talk, it's their fault I've lost the thread of my plan, just three days before the essays are due in and I still don't have a plan, a simple question, why are they asking it? because there's a chance that reason isn't historical, that there's no reason in History, because it eludes History, which means that what goes on in History isn't rational, careful, don't change the question, it's not 'Is History rational?' it's 'Is reason Historical', that said, it's linked, one of the two men looks as if he knows about books, the one with the beard and the beige overcoat, what sort of Reason would not be historical? if Reason looms over History, I don't even know where I'm heading, three days before it has to be in, the one with the beard must have been insufferable when as a young man, like Gilles, no, I'm being too hard on Gilles, I'm going to need at least twelve pages, last time the prof said you're not developing your thought enough, I'm too concise, Mum is always saying it takes forty years to make a man, I've been living with Gilles now for over a year.

The duck is talking to the fox, the snail, and with Ursula Owl, Salsifis the badger, Lilstein smiles, Ursula is also ochre, the rabbits are either grey or ochre, a quite solid grey which lightens into blue-grey for the walls of the houses, the sky, the church steeple, a play of graded shades, there's also a deer, just like in the poem by Johannes Becher, Becher didn't merely write the words for the GDR national anthem, 'Risen from the Ruins', he also wrote about nature, he included a deer in one of his poems, 'in your goodness, as you pass through the Black Forest you will permit the approach of a wary deer', that was in 1953, the death of Stalin, the goodness is Stalin's, now Gédéon the duck is trying to convince Martin, the big bear, 'you'll be able to laze in the grass in the meadows all the livelong day'.

Exactly the sort of thing to promise comrade Big Bear, Lilstein knows a bear who not that long ago would have landed Gédéon a hefty wallop with his paw, not for lazing around but for encouraging others to, it was possible not to work, though without overdoing it of course, taking it easy, provided you gave the impression of working very hard indeed, though not so much giving the impression since no one believed you, but behaving as if you really were, and if everyone can manage the 'as if' part then you really are in the land of workers and there is no such thing as laziness.

It wasn't laziness, people over-exerted themselves with being lazy but it wasn't laziness, they pretended to be working because other people pretended to pay them, or else the opposite, during the war it must have been different, but I never fought in the real war, not in the classic sense, in the camps we went even more slowly, except when a guard came along, and besides war doesn't last for ever, it wasn't the same for actors, they went at a proper pace, got properly paid too, the Berliner Ensemble four days before a dress rehearsal was a virtual cyclotron, the actors worked really well, and fast, and they weren't the only ones who didn't pretend.

Gédéon is holding a meeting at Burntwood crossroads, a tall copse, the trunks of trees with holes big enough for a boar to hide in, there are two deer in the listening crowd.

In Becher's poem, the '53 poem, there was only one deer, it had just sat down on a bench, by the bust of Stalin, Lilstein suddenly remembers 'you will stand tall there, Stalin, and in your goodness you will permit the approach of a wary deer; with Lenin, at eventide, it will settle on a bench, and Ernst Thälmann will come and join them there', in the background the rabbits watch, they look as if they're having a good time.

For a rabbit to have a good time, all you need do is give him a mouth shaped like a V, all the animals are there, their eyes have the pupils in the corners, that leaves a lot of the whites of the eyes showing in the drawing, makes them look attentive, drawing is a very suitable activity for a man's retirement, I'll go back to it, an activity that doesn't cost much, table, chair, paper, pencil, four walls around you, it all depends on what kind of space they enclose, nine square metres, that's a prison, actually you can live in nine square metres in a town, but if you don't have enough money to go out much it's like a prison, fortunately there are supermarkets, and an electric hot plate to cook on, my room is ten square metres at most, that's what's left when I subtract the floor-space of the lavatory and shower, a maid's room, apparently I was extremely lucky to have found one on the Boulevard de Port-Royal, especially with lavatory and shower.

Every evening around ten the woman next door plays the accordion, I'll have to revise my budget, the cost of living is very high here, food, I was good at drawing, until fifteen, sixteen, especially objects, turn-of-the-century telephones I could do very well, and cars, I even did some watercolours, but I wasn't as good at bodies, I never knew how, my cousin Agatha was the one who was really good at bodies.

Terrific nudes, genuine art studies, during the slump she used to sell them to lads from the *lycée* so she could buy food and clothes, one day a boy showed me a drawing of a woman with her legs wrapped round a man's waist, head back, unsigned, Agatha's style, twenty times more expensive, I thought she can't be short of anything, she went to America, found work as a draughtsman.

Another glance in Lilstein's direction from the girl at the counter, the older man, the one ensconced in the corner with the *Gédéons* and *Babars*, he's not the shop-lifting sort, the man who owns the shop told me you must never go by appearances, I'm too hard on Gilles, he's not that awful, the only thing that grates is the bin-bag, last night he got home at eleven, he saw the bin-bag in the middle of the hallway, he said it smells, I was in bed, the only chore down to him is to take out the bin-bag now and then, that's a journalist for you.

When I said that he didn't like it one bit, he said that if philosophers started seriously bothering with bin-bags no one would believe them any more, that's got nothing to do with it, and philosophers don't ask to be believed, they try to be rational, does Reason have a date of birth? That's not the problem, the question of the historicity of Reason isn't about the date of its birth, or death, you see the trap, the ready-made answer, Reason died at Auschwitz, the sort of remark that leaves the exercise of Reason to the brutes, the dominants, be careful with 'dominants', the prof doesn't like Bourdieu, I was in bed, Gilles went down to the yard with the bin-bag, when he came back up he rang the bell so I'd have to get out of bed, I didn't, the neighbour banged on the wall, I went and opened the door, I turned my back to him and returned to the bedroom, and he had his keys all the time, he said no I left them here.

Don't forget Fontenelle, 'If reason ruled the world, nothing would ever happen', sounds OK, yes, but it's not enough, that said it's the first arm of the pincer, if Reason dominates History there are no more events, no, that's not my pincer, first hypothesis, if reason isn't historical then History cannot be rational, but second hypothesis, second arm of my pincer, if reason is historical there can be no absolute of Reason, that's where you stick Fontenelle in, Gilles made a lot of noise in the living room, it lasted half an hour, finally he came to bed, with the newspaper, it's amazing how much noise a newspaper makes, Gilles sighs, seen my keys? that really made me see red, but he put on his helpless voice, like he does when I've got to help him do his accounts, he said I'm sodding fed up, can't find them anywhere.

Lilstein turns the pages, the wolf looks a nasty piece of work, maybe it's just because he's showing his teeth, a lot of the white of his eyes showing too, it's like in the cinema, eyes very wide open, black and white comedies, Cary Grant shows a lot of the white of his eyes, I'll have to buy another video of *Philadelphia Story*, in Berlin it must have been Honecker who forgot to return the one I had, it's a damned peculiar life where you lend the leader of your democratic republic an American video, he could end your career by raising one finger, everyone watched everyone else, end the career of the first person who made a mistake, but watching a film with Cary Grant and James Stewart was no longer thought of as an error though there was a time when you could have paid a heavy price for doing so, I'm exaggerating, no one ever paid a heavy price, that being said, you lend a video to the leader of your democratic republic, you can hardly ask him for it back, you realise things are changing the day he says Misha I must give you that video back.

Where videos were concerned, Honecker wasn't the worst offender, he'd return them, he would even lend some of his without making a big fuss about it.

He was easy to deal with compared to Mathias, the former trade union owner, then retired, Mathias had a superb collection of videos, recordings that had come from the West, he had *Angel* with Marlene Dietrich, he loaned out his videos, he would offer to lend, he'd stand by his shelves, raise one finger and say:

'From each according to his needs . . .'

Gives me a tape:

'. . . to each according to his abilities, culture must circulate.'

I always returned his videos, but over time he began saying I'd lost some, he ticked me off for not going to see him, when I did go he was delighted, and within five minutes he'd throw the business of the non-returned videos in my face, his wife used to give him funny looks, they probably talked about it all the time, I'd arrived after leaving the office, about nine one evening, they gave me a warm welcome, I carefully avoiding talking about films, we were snug and warm, I was pleased to see them, but Mathias never lasted out for more than five minutes, he always found a way of bringing up the videos I was supposed to have lost, it wasn't true, and he knew it would make me want to leave earlier than planned, if he hadn't I'd have been glad to drink a tisane and a small plum brandy, but I'd go away without having anything, he wife would say 'So soon?' it wasn't quite a question, it sounded like a question but the sort of question to which you know the answer, as though it confirmed something she'd said before I got there, something like:

'You'll see, he'll hardly have his foot through the door before he'll be off again.'

People like Mathias criticise you for not going to see them, so you go, they criticise you over the business of the videos, you decide to leave, they criticise you for going, Mathias would nod in my direction and say to his wife 'this is his idea of a visit to old friends', we'd be chatting in the hallway, the conversation might very well revert to being pleasant, I might almost have drunk that tisane, with a plum brandy, but Mathias would always get round to saying:

'Go, don't strain yourself.'

I always fell into the trap, I was really rather fond of them both, 'using his persuasive eloquence Gédéon convinced his assembled listeners, he made them understand that there were better things to do in life than going round gobbling each other up', that's well said, do they have video recorders in the prisons of the reunified Germany? I'll have to ask Honecker's lawyer, when are they going to cart me off to jail? as I'm leaving this kiddies' shop? No, prison is official, with these people there'll be an interrogation first, out in the sticks, with a medic to keep an eye on my blood pressure.

About the keys, I said to Gilles we'll see tomorrow, but I got up, I didn't say he was becoming impossible, he had them when he came home from work, they weren't lost, we'd agreed we would always leave them in the plate on top of the central heating, where mine are, you see, we were both starting to feel cold, both of us in just T-shirts, while we were hunting for the keys, I found Dilthey, I must use Dilthey, *A Critique of Historical Reason*, also find a place for that quote from *Faust*, 'In the beginning was the deed' and don't fall into the trap, there's also Ortega y Gasset, got to see clearly that historical reason, the affirmation that reason is historical, is for Ortega the means of putting an end to pure reason, the Enlightenment and the Revolution, mustn't mix up the first 'reason', extra-historical, which can or may seem to be realised in History, with the second, the historical reason which literally refers back to what has befallen man, so use Ortega as a way of shifting towards Heidegger, even if I'm not all that keen, about the keys, search instituted high and low, hallway, living room, kitchen, I was sleepy, Gilles waited for the moment when I was about to get angry so that he could criticise me for being angry, I said to him:

'A metallic sound.'

'What metallic sound?'

'Like the noise keys make when they fall.'

'Keys falling?'

'Are you positive you didn't hear the tinkle of keys falling in a dustbin?'

The deer, the partridges, the tawny owl, the young wild boar, the heron, the pheasant, the rabbits, the dogs march past beneath Lilstein's fingers, see how the duck leads them all to an old abandoned farm, they are going to build the house of peace.

When things were going well in the country which Lilstein calls home, they called it the house of peace and socialism, the duck and his friends haven't got to the socialism bit yet, good for them, just plain peace, not a bad start though, peace, the end of savagery, in the poem by Becher, the one with the bust of Stalin and the deer on the park bench with Lenin and Thälmann, there was also an accordion, 'an accordion will play to say thank you to them and they, grateful and modest, will smile', here there's no accordion, no bust, but there's food, Gédéon arranges for them to be fed.

'Grub and lots of it', actually it's practically the route to socialism, we'd almost succeeded on the grub front, not like the Russians or Poles, our cars were pathetic but the grub wasn't that bad, 'made with all the kitchen left-overs garnered throughout the land'.

Now that's not socialism, that's sabotage, or shall we say a malfunction of the bodies responsible for forward planning, 'left-overs' indeed!

This will be corrected for the next mobilisation campaign, we'll rectify, add a few abstract words.

The alleyway outside is too quiet, my young French friend hasn't a clue about organising a meeting, the bookshop's too quiet, it's like the block of flats in Moscow in 1945, some evenings everything would seem normal except there were no kids making a racket, no slanging matches between neighbours, too quiet, somewhere up on one of those floors everyone knew there was a flat that was going to be raided, during the night or around dawn, no one had said anything but everyone knew, does the girl at the counter, with her turned-up nose, know anything?

And here come the real enemy, the hunters, feathers in their hats, leather breeches, genuine Bavarians, the swine, a slaughter in the farm of peace, when no one's expecting it, they rush in altogether and start shooting, that being said, animals who live in the forest can't afford to forget about hunters, just because you say you've moved into the farm of peace doesn't mean you're safe from attack, from an Operation Barbarossa, buckshot, that's for the head and belly of deer and partridge, though in the drawing there aren't any deer or partridge.

But there were, in the house of peace, only a little while ago, but there are none now in the slaughter, there's no blood either, just green, ochre and pale blue, a boar lying on the ground, a stag, a bear, a big one, they're not bleeding, they've crumpled, exactly right for tough-looking victims, no kids on the ground, no women, just the death of the big males, that's all, no sign of blood anywhere, an expertly executed massacre.

Hunting, first light, my first time, trudging, the hinterland around Rosmar, the dog, a wire-haired dachshund, the friends, the field of carrots, schnapps, the dachshund disappearing among the carrot leaves, when he stops to point, all you saw was the end of his tail wagging vertically above the greenery, I shot my first hare, bravo Misha, my comrades congratulated me, I put my hare in the back pocket of my jerkin, I went on, lovely country, the plain, a light headwind over the ploughed fields, the occasional knoll, a spinney against the sky, and the hare started moving against my back, very disconcerting.

I must tell my young French friend, he's always talking about skeletons in cupboards, it sounds sinister but at least inside a cupboard a skeleton doesn't move, whereas a rabbit that starts kicking you in the spine when you thought it was good and dead is quite something, not to mention that you have to get him out so you can break his neck.

'No, not with a stone, you must learn to do it cleanly, a chop with the side of the hand!'

The sole effect of comrade Gédéon's militant naivety has been to provide an easy target for the class enemies of the workers of the forest, a fine old slaughter, that's what you get when you build the house of peace before wiping out the class enemy, in our case we wiped out the class enemy, when I say we I include everything that's happened since '17, and then we went on wiping out so that we wouldn't be wiped out ourselves, that's what we used to say when we felt the need to talk about it.

In this unhappy hour, the denizens of the forest have one last piece of good fortune, which is that it's the enemy who is killing them, not their friends who have turned into public prosecutors, these Gédéon books are so sweet, very educational. I don't like being here, it's a rat-trap.

Gilles didn't like my idea about the keys falling into the dustbin, in the middle of the night, two overcoats over our T-shirts, shoes but no socks, the outhouse where the dustbins are kept at the far end of the courtyard, I hate all this nonsense with keys, no light in the outhouse, the bin's full, did you bring the torch? He dared asked me that, and it's a month since he was supposed to buy a battery.

We pulled the dustbin out into the yard, under the timed light, we heard a window go up, whoever opened it didn't put the light on, Gilles said in quite a loud voice:

'I bet he's going to phone the Gestapo.'

We didn't hear another peep, we took the bags out, they smelled.

On the right in the hallway, Gilles had left his keys on a bookshelf, on the right as you go in, I found them there when we went back up, lying on the cut edge of *The Critique of Dialectical Reason*, there's nothing worse than bookshelves for swallowing things, even books, day before yesterday I lost my Kojève again, I need it for my essay, historical reason can be the opposite of pure reason, of the faculty for generating principles, you see what's at issue here, the link between pure reason and Revolution, do away with pure reason in order to do away with the idea of Revolution itself, Ortega y Gasset-style historical reason, it's the end of reason-in-History, is historical reason still reason? How am I going to pull all this together? Go back to the two notions, reason and History, and examples, got to have examples, references, reason of State for instance, and against that the reason that gave the Rights of Man, State reason as a negative example against the requirements of law, yes, but can there be human rights where there is no State? State against instinct, man as a reasonable animal, reasonable or rational? going to have to dig deeper.

Poor Gédéon, 'he who was so happy to see the rabbits dance the fox-trot to the sound of a harmonica, he whose soul had thrilled with delight to see the chicks disporting themselves on the sweet grass of the meadow', very flowery turn of phrase Gédéon old man, but you must learn to grow up, to stare disaster in the face, the disaster that comes after the fox-trot.

We used to dance the fox-trot at the Waldhaus, Lena danced the fox-trot, Kappler would say, go ahead, young Lilstein, I'm too old for that sort of thing, but he wasn't really that old at the time, *Fox-trot in Waltenberg*, could be the title of a sophisticated novel, late twenties, Lena also danced the tango, she held me very close to her, she lifted her thigh against my hip, she was American so people waited to see her do the fox-trot and she would deliberately kick off with tangos, Gédéon wanted a ballroom, and he got a disaster, it took me a long time to grow up, when you looked at Lena's fox-trot, it was as good as her tango, of disasters I've seen a few, starting in the thirties.

The worst is when the spring uncoils, when it was you who screwed up because you didn't see it coming, no, that's too easy, too many people about nowadays who say I never saw it coming, I was still a child, the age of illusions, I had too much to do with the enemy, I went on believing too long, no, the illusions were inertia, I've never had illusions.

An amusing half-page, rabbits dancing in a circle around the head of a dead bear.

Very representative, the bears, in the Gulag a poet, a Bukharinian, jailed for Bukharinian deviation even though he never had the first clue about what Bukharinism was, this poet had told a bear story, he'd got it from a German, a Silesian joke, we were talking one evening to take our minds off how hungry we were, the Bukharinian poet decided he would tell the story of the rabbit and the fox in *Alexander Nevsky*, we all jumped down his throat, then he said:

'I know what the moral of my life-story is, I thought I wanted to be part of the Revolution, my story is also yours.'

We let him speak, trying to stop someone speaking is only funny if you know that you will actually be able to stop him, we knew that he didn't have that much time left, he was too thin, he talked like an actor at his farewell appearance, he retreated a few steps, put a broom on his shoulder, walked back towards us sticking his chest out, a hunter in the middle of the forest, a very jaunty step, suddenly he's facing this huge bear, on its hind legs, more than two metres tall, the dream of every self-respecting hunter, takes aim with his broom, the bristles against his shoulder, bang! the bear goes down, the hunter goes up to it, take care, gives it a kick, no reaction, places his foot on the bear.

The Bukharinian poet was in the middle of the cell, we'd formed a circle, he'd put his foot on a stool, he was holding his broom vertical, the bear doesn't move, the hunter stays there for a moment with his bear, walks round it, struts his hour all by himself, decides to go and fetch the villagers, returns singing, the old man heads back towards the cell-door, he's making for the village, faint coils of wood smoke, the houses nice and warm, as he walks there comes a tap on the hunter's shoulder, from behind, it's the bear, on two legs, fifty centimetres away, the bear gives him a great big smile, very friendly, you can see his teeth, he raises his right paw, palm as big as a hunter's head, splendid claws, with traces of blood on them, the bear slowly lowers its left paw, shows what he has between his legs, he smiles, says to the hunter:

'Jollywobbles please, or I'll eat you up!'

The hunter does what he's told, the bear lets him go, the hunter goes back to the village puking every hundred metres, locks himself in his house, washes his mouth out, reloads his gun, leaves his house, plunges into the forest, determined step, looks for the bear, finds the bear.

For the dissertation I've got to have at least two examples from the history of science, reason that's patently historical is the kind whose history can be constructed, the history of a scientific concept, which one? Canguilhem? the reflex concept, the history of a series of theories, but there's the other sort of reason, that of the reasonable man, who gives up killing, everything in reason that relates to the reasonable rather than to the rational, I'm going to get this wrong, it's always the same, I manage to cope with the first two parts, describing, trawling through the works, but the minute I have to start thinking for myself I get lost or I knock it all over and can't put it back together again, I do terrible essays. Old people don't break the spines of books when they open them, no need for me to worry there, they know the value of things, and when they pinch stuff it's always specifically targeted, I'm sure it was some old guy who stole that special edition of *Tintin in America* two months back, the one priced seven thousand francs, fortunately it was an afternoon when I wasn't here, it was an old guy did that because the owner keeps a close eye on the young ones, dead twitchy straight away, he'll go and tidy the shelves just near where they are, he stands quite close to them, doesn't let them alone for one second:

'May I help you? Something you want to ask, perhaps?'

The owner's 'perhaps' is a masterpiece, unlikely that even the cops have got a 'perhaps' as good as that.

Actually that story about the bear, I've let the poet tell it, but I recognised it, I'd known it from way back, Müller had told me it, Müller loved that story, claimed to have got it from Kappler, one day he told me he intended to use it for one of his plays but he never did, here it's a children's book, the big bear is dead and the rabbits are dancing round his head, a huge head, larger than life, on the ground, might easily be Stalin's head when people started dancing round it.

When Becher stood up in front the Central Committee and recited his poem about the bust of Stalin, the deer and the accordion, people wept, it was at the time of Stalin's death, I personally never had any occasion to shed a tear, I was still at Magadan, not the worst in the Gulag, but it was already very cold, I saw grown men weep at Magadan when the news of Stalin's death was announced, and not just among the ones who were guarding us, I saw Stalin's bust lying on the ground later, in 1956, lying between two tram rails, Budapest, trust the Hungarians!

My young friend has spoken just once to the girl behind the counter, they don't know each other, or maybe he's already been here before to buy something, still it seems odd, a man as serious, as important, in a shop like this, he looks very elegant in that beige coat, this place a really good find for a meeting, too good, I'm spending my time wondering about this shop and I'm forgetting to be careful, I honestly couldn't say whom I've seen walking past the shop window in the last ten minutes.

Those Hungarians danced a merry jig in '56, the first bust of Stalin to get knocked off its pedestal, no the first was earlier, in '53, lying in a gutter, that's when I became aware of the disaster, hardly out of Magadan I get to Berlin and I'm treated to the spectacle of the German proletariat knocking over statues of the great leader, I got the picture, I'd understood before, before the war, I got the picture very early on, I didn't dare speak the word aloud, but I knew very early on what Stalinism was.

I've always known, by day I was active and at night I thought, I knew, there was someone who knew and someone who acted, two someones who went under the same name, Lilstein, the Lilstein who knew took care not to get in the way of the Lilstein who acted, and the Lilstein who acted tried not to cramp the style of the Lilstein who knew, and there was never a right time to clarify things, confronting us was the counter-revolutionary threat, the fascist threat, the Nazi threat, the imperialist threat, the hawks of Washington, today there are clever people who tell us you could have seen what you were doing and who you were doing it with, I did see, but confronting me were people who wanted to send me up a chimney as smoke or melt me down with the H-bomb, I always preferred keeping my sights on the people facing me.

Rewind the spring, I knew but I said nothing, I acted, even in Magadan I never said anything, in the end I was convinced I was going to die in that bloody Gulag, and I never said a word, wasn't fear, wasn't to save the essential thing, even in the camp I never said anything because the Lilstein who knew had no wish to break with the Lilstein who had acted, two Lilsteins, every evening there's one of them who says to the other cosy up to the butcher but change the world, and the other one laughs.

Siamese twins, they can't bear to be together, and they know that to be separated would mean that one would die, no one knows which, both would have died, maybe I might permit myself to know because I used to be pro-active, perhaps I did certain things because I could still tell myself that they were foul things, at the end of a working day you ring for a secretary, you hold out a folder containing a single sheet of paper, you could hold out just the sheet of paper, three names are on it, but in a folder it becomes a file, even if the men haven't done much, and all you have to do is say:

'Close the file.'

With all the closing of files we did we eventually built a wall and when we started shooting the people who wanted to climb over the wall as if they were rabbits Lilstein said to Lilstein quick let's do something which will enable us to dispense with the wall, let's be better spies, let's be better plotters, let's work smarter, it'll be better, come off it, I knew, I acted, I never said anything, first prize for silence, in Moscow one day Markov said to me:

'Mustn't drink too much.'

He already had a diseased liver, he told me people die because they chatter like magpies, a few glasses of vodka and they feel the need to express themselves, in them there is nothing but silence and sobriety, usually they keep quiet, they vote for the most nonsensical proposals in silence, and the same evening in front of thirty people, at the tenth glass, they shout today we did something really bloody stupid, they want to save their souls, bear witness at the tops of their voices, with the courage of vodka, they know that a team will come looking for them at five in the morning and will ask them to be more specific about the witness they'd borne, sober this time, a lot less amusing, when I say sober I mean them, because the men asking the questions can go on drinking, I personally never tried to bear witness, because I don't drink.

He was all right, Markov, he looked after me, I looked after my young French friend, that's what History is.

With Hegel and his flame, and the bear.

In historical reason, the idea of reason modifies the idea of History and vice versa, Ortega y Gasset is logical, he simultaneously demolishes a concept of reason, a concept of History and a policy, his own policy is how to keep the masses quiet, how to connect with the political, some statements which are designed to disqualify the real, so as to leave place only for market forces, go back to Marx, even if he's no longer fashionable, the link with exploitation, apparently exploitation has disappeared, take someone like me who is paid for half-time in a bookshop but actually works two-thirds of a week, could you say this was exploitation? You're getting off the point, irrelevant, an honest conscience which leads you off the point, the owner is always telling me that he wants me to share the results, that means he wants me to work for a commission, he knows I'm not keen, what he wants is for me to work as if I was on a commission but for a fixed wage, I'm going to have to keep an eye on those two old guys, a reasonable animal or a rational animal, I'd also like to work in the idea that man is an animal who cooks, I'm sure Kant stole stuff from Samuel Johnson.

My Bukharinian poet and his bear, he told it well, the hunter washing his mouth out, going back into the forest, in a furious rage, finds the bear, bang! bear on the ground, kick in the ribs, bear doesn't move, the hunter stays with his victim, second lap of honour around the bear, hunter decides to go back and get the villagers, goes home singing, on the way a tap on the shoulder from behind, it's the bear, on its hind legs, fifty centimetres, broad grin, the teeth, the right paw, palm as big as a hunter's head, great big claws, the bear slowly lowers its left paw, shows what he's got between his legs, smiles, says to the hunter:

'Jollywobbles please, or I'll eat you up!'

The hunter does what he's told, the bear lets him go, the hunter goes back to the village puking every hundred metres, house, reloads his gun, comes back out again, returns at a run, bang! bear falls down, kick in the ribs, bear doesn't move, glorious forest, third lap of honour.

'Cut it short! Bloody poet!'

In the hut some of the men were starting to get restless, but they let the poet carry on, he was really very thin, fairly tall, beard, all you could make out were his green eyes and his teeth, very odd, he still had all his teeth and they were white, again he talked of claws, of traces of blood on the claws, the bear slowly lowers its left paw, points to what it has between its legs, jollywobbles please or I'll eat you up, the hunter who goes home, throws up every hundred metres, locks himself up in his house, goes out again, charges back.

He finds the bear, fourth shot, kick, fourth lap of honour, all alone again, decides to go get people from village, tap on shoulder, the bear, big smile, paw rising, the claws, the blood, the bear crosses his arms and asks the hunter:

'Is killing bears the real reason why you come into the forest?'

The bear and the flame, to have loved the flame so intensely that we ourselves become what feeds it, it was a French poet who said that, a great poet, you have a small chance of surviving it if you don't drink, if you don't play around with words, if you don't try to bear witness to save your soul.

In Magadan I saw men die yelling at the tops of their voices to save the flame, shouting 'long live Stalin!' and 'long live the Party!' a volley of rifle fire and down they went like rags.

Not forgetting the one who made everybody laugh, back to the wall, facing the firing squad, he yelled 'long live the Tsar!' crazy laughter, we close our eyes, clamp eyeballs, lips, jaws, we titter, we're spotted, we're in prison clothes, an officer shouts at us:

'Think that's funny, do we, my little woodchips?'

Comic or tragic we couldn't say, some of the others were crying, the officer said:

'You're right to think that's funny, my little woodchips, or maybe it's the *tchaïfir* that's making you laugh?'

You sensed he wasn't going to punish us, he smiled, he called us his little woodchips, Stalin's woodchips, because when you chop wood you always leave woodchips, he added:

'Humour is no way out.'

Apart from us no one has come into this shop, where's that young woman got to? She's disappeared, now there's only my young Parisian friend and me here, a traitor and me, this is it, they're going to get me, for the third time in my life they're going to get me, instead of admiring his beige coat you should have made a run for it the moment you saw him so firmly settled in this awful bookshop, they'll get you for the third time and there won't be a fourth, too old, it's like when you say I'll never have time to reread the whole of Goethe, never have time to live another kind of life, no one has come into the shop, the girl has vanished, this has got to stop, at least I can make up my mind to put an end to this ridiculous farce.

No, she's there.

Where did she go? Where can a shop assistant be when you can't see her? there she is, by the till, she must have bent down, nothing out of the usual.

The officer barked:

'Fire!'

File on the Trotskyite-tsarist closed, the man was right to yell 'long live the Tsar!', they couldn't take his death away from him, everybody remembered it, some men sentenced to death never said anything, sometimes they had faces like children who couldn't cry, I didn't say anything at Magadan either, for a while I still felt protected, and I never understood that things were going pear-shaped until another prisoner, a big-time gangster, gave me an order:

'Scratch my feet!'

Among the young crowd, it's only with Gilles that the owner is at all pleasant, that's because Gilles writes for the papers, usually the owner is never pleasant with young persons, he says they never buy anything, I correct him, they are tomorrow's customers, when they'll have money, he replies by the time they've got money I'll be six feet under, for the essay the main thing is to get as fast as I can to the problem part, though actually it's a double problem, if reason is historical, it's to the detriment of pure reason, but when reason is pure it's got nothing whatsoever to do with History, if I dramatise this paradox, I'll have part one, and into the second I'll stick Hegel and the ruse of reason, find reason in History all the same, thanks to the ruse of reason, using what as examples?

That's how it goes, the gangster saying scratch my feet, a sign, you thought up until then that you were going to get away with it and suddenly you have to start thinking it's all over, it's the opposite in this bookshop, I know this is the end but I don't see a sign, an alleyway which is a trap, all it takes is a car at each end, you imagine that a friend can never betray you, but though I keep looking I can't see anything, scratch my feet.

   Until then no thug had ever dared say anything like that to me, they probably knew that I'd made men like them toe the line at Buchenwald, but that day, when their chief said, here, you, politician man, scratch my feet, I knew I no longer had any choice, he must have learned something, he knew more than I did, he looked at me as if I was already dead:

   'Scratch my feet for me!'

   The other thugs were watching me, and then he said:

   'No, not now.'

   I never had to scratch his feet for him, I could invent and say that at that moment I looked him squarely in the eye, the guy had almost no nose left, his skin was very swarthy, very pitted, the middle of his face an agglomeration of rolls of fat, a sort of hole for a nose, and between the rolls of fat two light-coloured eyes, maybe he backed down because he was scared by the strength he could sense in me, a whole life of Bolshevik strength, a prisoner at Magadan and the experience of Buchenwald and Birkenau, but no, he probably just wanted to check his facts one last time, it was a bet, if you lost the bet your losses would be too high, his feet were unspeakably disgusting.

He had almost no nose left, you could smell the stench of him at ten paces and he was meticulously cutting his nails as he said scratch my feet, I never had to scratch them for him but I knew that death was creeping up on me, it had just set off on my trail, it was merely hesitating about the speed it would travel at, it was a signal, a thug told you scratch my feet and you knew that the guards had given the go-ahead, that the commandant had spoken to the guards, that the regional rep had spoken to the commandant, that in Moscow some-one had taken a decision, not even a decision, decisions require a report-card, a signature or a stamp, no need for all that, someone must have just said:

'Him? Surely he's not still there?'

And a subordinate gets the message at once.

I was put in a group which went out cutting wood in temperatures of minus twenty, very heavy work, especially when you were with youngsters, those youngsters in the Gulag went at it like mad things, they wanted to prove that an injustice had been done when they'd been found guilty, I was with a man who taught natural science, about my age, he nodded to the trees:

'See, the trees have faith, they've seen the axes but they have faith, they're not afraid, and do you know why the trees have faith although they've seen the axes? Because the handles are made of wood too, you know what you can do with faith, comrade.'

I let the teacher of natural science ramble on, he was not a Trotskyite nor right-wing nor a Stalinist, he just liked natural science.

I started sleeping like a hare, with my eyes open. When I realised that I was on the point of dying I knew what I'd yell at them:

'Long live Gogol!'

Up to that point I had said nothing, it would be:

'Long live Gogol!'

To the guards, the gangster, the men in Moscow and Berlin, it wouldn't have seemed very political but it was all I had, I could have said bunch of traitors, or up with the Revolution, not yours, but long live socialism anyway, 'long live Gogol!' was much wider, less political but much wider, my hatred suggested something else, 'bunch of bastards' but that was too predictable, I'd drink *tchaïfir*, I'd continue keeping a tight rein on my hatred and I'd shout 'long live Gogol!' yes, *tchaïfir*, four hundred grams of tea in a quarter of a litre of water, the tannin acts exactly like opium.

It was at that point that I was freed, the death of Iosif Vissarionovich, I am alive because a gang of yes-men took a long time to go into the bedroom of the man with the moustache to give first aid, dead drunk he was, we had *tchaïfir*, but the man with the moustache had real vodka, he took three days to die, looking furious.

About that copy of *Tintin in America*, the one that was stolen, the owner told me he was a prize idiot, that he couldn't see straight any more, that he was gaga, I don't like it when the owner has a go at himself, because immediately afterwards he has a go at me, he says I'll get a job at Gibert's, Gibert's second-hand department, books by the kilo, he gives himself a right roasting and then it's my turn, he blames me, you being bloody part-time, if there were two of us here full-time nothing would get nicked, what good will having a philosophy degree do you? Qualify you to sort peaches? He's pleased with his little joke, the ruse of reason, the passion which acts in its stead, reason which takes the form of a flame, that supposes an overly optimistic vision, go back to the origins, *ratio*, it's both the power of knowledge and the content of knowledge, there's also the rationality of ends and means and the beige coat that's heading this way.

The head of the bear on the ground, it wrings the heart of comrade Gédéon, ah! next chapter, Gédéon gives alley cats the milk intended for pet moggies, I don't see the connection, a sequence in which you get told about a massacre and on the next page milk gets given to alley cats, no transition, no link, after all maybe there never is, there are also rabbits tied up in a sack, how can they be freed? first a sequence showing a massacre in a forest, Gédéon has disappeared, then with no transition we're confronted with the rabbits tied up in a sack.

And they're going to get me too, it's in the bag, all tied up, my friend has sold me down the river to the CIA, no way out, for years I told him I want you to be inventive, I want you to tell me things I don't know, I'll try to be inventive, out loud, here and now, we shall invent two roles, young gentleman of France, just the two of us and nobody else, when we're together nobody will be able to make a move against us because we shall invent, you will see me inventing and you will invent in turn, and today he's being inventive by arranging for me to be stuffed in a sack, for thirty-five years I've kept him safe from every threat and now he ties me up in a sack, but it's all over for him, lackey of the Americans, from the outside it looks like he's in clover, in reality he's turning into a slave, in his shoes I'd rather be dead, when it was just us two we were in charge.

I'm going to die.

The hunters have gone, the job of freeing the rabbits is taken on by the mole, a very mole-ish idea, dig a tunnel under the sack, why do it the easy way, instead of just opening the sack the mole lets off a huge banger underneath it, curtains for the rabbit comrades, bang! 'gone away, destination unknown'.

Fine ring to those words, in Berlin we used to say 'unknown in Records' or 'not known at this address', I've known smarter moles, a mole was never meant to work with explosives.

The two youths who've just come in, long hair, yobs, like the ones we have back home, trainers, jeans, bomber-jacket, one of them is carrying a Coca-Cola bag, I know why, the bag is because you can't get a walkie-talkie in a bomber-jacket.

The other one has a slightly longer jacket, that's for when you carry your revolver behind your back, a holster on your belt at the back American-style, now he's in the back of the shop, the other one has stayed to the right of the door, normally they'd send in a couple, the woman looks at me, stares at me and while she does I stop looking at the man in the back of the shop and I wonder why arms grab me from behind, a bear-hug, my young friend smiles, I'm not even trembling, I'm driven out into the country, to a forest, there you can make a noise, and this time there's no one telling me it's going to get very cold.

Now Gédéon is attacking the wolf, attacking the wolf is always the right thing to do, especially when you're powerless against the hunters, the French wolf is called Ysengrin, terror of the farmyard, 'Gédéon and his friend Briffault the dog saw Ysengrin hiding in a barrel where he could keep watch through the bung-hole for the flock of harmless sheep who passed by', I never liked sheep, someone always eats them in the end.

The wolf is hiding in the barrel, his tail is sticking out through the bung-hole, Briffault sinks his teeth into the part of the tail that's sticking out, won't let go, caudal appendage, in children's books, a tail is called a caudal appendage, French kiddies don't know how lucky they are, the wolf can't get out, he values his tail too much, and the farmer's wife fills the barrel with milk, terrible mess, in the background there's a very nice half-timbered building, the outline is clearly recognisable.

The beige overcoat has stopped by the Flash Gordons, the grey raincoat hasn't moved, the two youths in trainers have walked out, we don't do underground stuff, the owner doesn't like it, pity, I sent them round to the Thé Troc, the bookseller there is a friend of Crumb and Shelton, they'll find what they're looking for. And four customers to keep an eye on was hard, the nub of the question is whether reason is autonomous with regard to every other principle liable to deny or transcend it, that's Hegel, everything which is rational is real, everything that is real is rational, except that reason can only be a product of the interaction of men with the world, that interaction being set in time, in other words in History, I'm sure the owner prefers it when I'm the one who gets conned, I hate all this watching, he says theft is death to us.

The wolf starts struggling about all by himself in the barrel, he keeps trying to get out but the dog Briffault has sunk his fangs into the part of his caudal appendage which sticks out of the bung-hole, he won't let go 'his legs thrashed for so long and with such vigour that the creamy drink turned to butter, and in the end the wolf was so worn out that he was forced to stop', good children, mark and learn, it is quite all right to be cruel if you're being cruel to wolves, and only wolves, the hard part comes when you've learned to be cruel and you can't break the habit, especially if people don't call it cruelty, the sort of cruelty where you don't see any blood, the butter must be revolting, a slab of at least forty kilos, they've removed it from the barrel.

An enormous pat of well-churned butter with a wolf inside it, they're going to kill the wolf, no, they leave the butter in the farmyard, they go off elsewhere to celebrate, and the wolf is able to escape because the butter softens overnight, a grave oversight.

Dangerous chap, oversight, on our side we too were capable of cruelty towards the careless, all you had to do was come up with solid evidence and if the evidence wasn't solid enough then there was the evidence of the question, the revealing question, an effective by-product of prosecution dialectic:

'We do not yet know, ex-comrade, if you have been guilty merely of an oversight or if you are deliberately engaged in sabotaging the tasks entrusted to you by the people of our Democratic Republic, but the very fact that we have been led to ask ourselves the question and specifically with you in mind . . .'

Crucial that word 'specifically', meaningless in the context, but effectiveness guaranteed.

'. . . this simple question which we've been led to ask about you is revealing in itself of the threat which you may well represent.'

Clever, that 'which you may well', poor sod's as good as in jail already, there is nothing more he can do, but he is still allowed a 'may', they used it on me, this revealing question, on my stool, with jabs to my liver and kidneys, the wolf managed to get away, and now we see the farmers selling the wolf butter, eight francs a kilo, nauseating, I must ask my young friend how much eight francs was worth at the time the book was written, he's bound to know, bloody kulaks, always

the same, selling butter that smells of wolf for eight francs a kilo, and
they'll find buyers, when you've got butter to sell, you can always find
buyers.

Also I mustn't look as if I've got my eye on these two older men all the
time, shop window's really filthy, I'll have to clean it, that being said
it doesn't get as dirty here as on the Boulevard, the woman from
Unilivres was telling me that if she didn't keep the dust down every
couple of days the books would get a sort of greasy film on them which
spoilt everything, she said imagine our lungs, I didn't fancy imagining
her lungs because on top of everything else she smokes like a chimney,
I said to her:

'You should try to give up smoking.'

'I'm fifty-three years old and I'm not afraid of dying, what I'm
afraid of is getting the sack.'

Last year they sacked her most experienced assistant, she was too
expensive, the girl in question went home, to Orange, it wouldn't be
as hard there for her in the provinces, also she had her parents living
close by.

Outside the window of the bookshop, in the middle of the alleyway,
a man has stopped, oddly dressed, a workman straight off the job or a
house painter or a window-cleaner, in a vest, but all he's carrying is a
large plastic bag with 'Tati' written on it, the girl at the till is also
looking at him, the man has a mop of blond hair, very pale eyes, he's
not looking at the bookshop nor the shop opposite which sells African
artefacts, he's standing motionless in the middle of the alleyway, he's
looking intently towards the end which opens on to the Boulevard,
he's strongly built, muscles like a boxer, you can hear him shout:

'You bloody wogs can keep your traps shut!'

I knew it, it's starting.

'This is France!

It was too quiet.

Lilstein has stopped moving. This is it, it's now, an agitator, an
incident, the police, they're going to pick me up, classic trap, this is

what they've cooked up, a man starts shouting, he comes into the shop, he starts on me, the police, everyone is nicked, the man is tough, a voice that carries, a passer-by just centimetres from him, and it's as if the man didn't see him, the passer-by is there in support, this is it, another passer-by, and they say nothing, and if I'd had an escort . . .

'Foreigners, shut your mouths, in France, declaration, rights of man, article one . . .'

The two passers-by would be used to block my escort, if I had one.

'. . . a foreigner should keep his trap shut!'

The man has stopped shouting, he looks at me, a trap, that's it, I've had enough.

Lilstein moves three paces towards his friend in the beige overcoat, he shouts:

'That's enough!'

I've been protecting him for thirty-five years, a bastard, beige is a bastard's colour.

'D'you hear, Morel? tell them to end this charade, it's over! Are you happy now? Tell them to stop! Make them shut that lout up, him and his insults, there's no point, I've had enough! Let them come and take me away!'

Lilstein has grasped Philippe Morel by the arm, the beige coat is very soft, cashmere, Lilstein speaks savagely but in an undertone, in the alleyway the man in the vest with the plastic bag with 'Tati' on it continues shouting, the two passers-by stare at him, nobody else.

'Constitution, article two, shut your traps, especially political asylum seekers!'

The girl sacked by Unilivres went a year and a half without finding a job, and the day she found something she grabbed it, taking the money in a motorway tollbooth, in the provinces, works nights, a hundred and fifty francs a month more, some nights she notches up almost two thousand vehicles, drivers telling her she's a waste of space if she can't tell them if it's raining in Paris, she's lucky because she works in a toll area where gendarmes are stationed, the rest of it, drivers who snarl obscenities then zoom off, she's got used to, and there are two meanings of 'History', first a means of knowing which is used for matters for which there can be no rational, theoretical explanation, this sort of history is when theory does not suffice as a means of explaining, and the other meaning is the one which refers to the way societies change over time, that crazy loon with the 'Tati' bag is putting the wind up everybody. The man in the grey raincoat looks worried. He's looking every which way. They're going to leave without buying anything.

Philippe Morel smiles at his friend Lilstein, he pays no attention to his savagery:

'Nothing to worry about, the man's going it a bit strong, but our universal declaration isn't quite like that yet.'

'Wogs should keep their traps shut, especially the political refugees.'

'Stop worrying, Misha,' says Philippe Morel, 'he's just some crackpot.'

It's the first time Morel has ever called him Misha, what gives him the right? Hans used to call him Misha, Max was allowed to call him Misha, what right does Morel have to call him that? No right at all, rather the superiority of the one who betrays, I'm finished, he calls me Misha for short, that's how the bastard's mind works.

'Misha, calm down, that man's no threat, he'll be off soon, I know, you remember there was a time when five men in grey raincoats would have arrested him, and you with him, today he can shout his head off in public without getting into trouble because we don't have enough trained men in grey raincoats, it's progress, you don't agree? He'll move on, Misha, and besides there are foreigners and foreigners, you aren't one of the kind he doesn't like.'

The man raises a fist, punches the air, cracked voice of one who sleeps rough:

'And why? I'll tell you! Why are there all these political refugees in France who're gonna have to keep their traps shut, eh? Why don't they bugger off back where they came from and keep their traps shut there?'

'Don't be scared, Misha, he's just another crackpot, you're in France, the police aren't looking for you, why are you getting so worked up?'
  'Morel, tell me what I'm doing here! It's a trap!'

I've protected Morel for thirty-five years and now he betrays me, he works for the CIA, he arranges a meet in a trap, been in the business more than fifty years and I end up sitting in a trap, Morel says there's a book he has to buy and we meet up in this alleyway to which there are two exits, they're waiting for me, an ambulance, Morel has sold me out, he behaves with all the casualness of people who've got themselves a cushy number, a lackey of the CIA.
  'I've spent my life protecting you, Morel, I never had you down as linked to the CIA, you really that fond of Coca-Cola? Let's go, let's finish this, an ambulance? or a van? I can't stay in this place any longer, all these reactionary books, your squalid little manoeuvres, hand me over and let's have done with it.'
  I'm shaking, I never shook in my life, nowhere, I'm shaking like Regel, that day he threw a fit, he just crumpled in the middle of the lounge of the Waldhaus, that's exactly how I must look, let's get it over and done with.

Morel needed a few moments to calm Lilstein down, nothing was wrong. In the alleyway the madman with the vest and the 'Tati' bag had finally moved on. Morel reasoned with Lilstein, no one was out to get him, everything was fine.

The girl at the till hasn't even moved a finger, she's used to seeing the madman pass by, here the owner pays me for working part-time, that's half the minimum wage, not a penny more, whereas I actually do twenty-five hours, he says he's teaching me the business, that I've got time to go to the university, that if I was working in a half-decent hotel with a restaurant for the same pay I'd be doing ten hours a day, and working late every night, so either reason encompasses History, it has the power to dominate History because it is a permanent entity which resists the temporal flow, or else there is a historicity of reason because thought does not recognise the same possibilities in the ages of Plato, Hegel or Heidegger, but that's still rationalising History, you could also say that what happens is subject to contingency, I'm getting lost now, in the hotel trade the more tired you are the less you smile, the less you smile the fewer the tips you get says the owner, and the sack the first time you ask for a rise, a reference that guarantees you'll never get another job, written by an ecological hotelier who grows his own rosemary, gives interviews to the *Nouvel Obs* and collects money for the rights of man, at least here, in the bookshop, you can complain, but I can't afford to pay you more, and you can read your philosophy books, you can leave whenever you want, I'll find someone else soon enough, some young girl, who actually likes being young,

Morel did not even take umbrage at having been suspected by Lilstein of betraying him:

'Par for the course, Misha, you're so jittery.'

Lilstein calmed down, he felt cross with himself for panicking, it was on account of this place, an alleyway, an enclosed place in an alleyway, I like bookshops to open straight into the street and I can't stand these reactionary books.

'"Regressive", my dear Misha, "regressive" is the word, "reactionary" is incorrect, besides there's no such thing any more, there aren't any reactionaries around now, that was in the days when you had thousands of people working for you, "regressive" is the word you want, but, look at this, yes, this is the book I came to buy, a monument to Yankee ideology, as you say, Misha, I want to show you just how far "reactionary" books can go.

'Look, *Flash Gordon*, amusing enough, no? Aircraft carriers, aeroplanes, a surprise attack on the United States, by aircraft carrier, planes which sink the American fleet at anchor, yes, you're right, not original, a carbon-copy of Pearl Harbor, a well-known story, but look here, this page, at the bottom, the date, yes, the date of publication, October 1941, got it? That's two months before the real Pearl Harbor, two months before!

'Now isn't that amusing? The Americans are attacked by an enemy fleet, and they counter-attack, it's still October 1941, can you guess what they counter-attack with? Look at this, that's right, with atomic explosives, a great story, two months before Pearl Harbor!

'Did Roosevelt and his admirals read comic books? Yes, because comic strips were published every day in a great many newspapers, this particular one appeared on 11 October 1941 syndicated in at least a hundred and fifty newspapers, Roosevelt and his admirals must all have read it in one or other of the papers, over breakfast, two months before the Japanese attack, a stab in the back, all because they didn't pay enough attention to cartoon strips!'

Lilstein has calmed down, he turns the pages of *Flash Gordon*, he smiles, he feels better, Morel has not betrayed him, Morel is a historian, a great historian, Roosevelt and the Japanese dagger between the shoulder-blades.

At last Morel and Lilstein have left the bookshop, they have made for the southern exit of the Passage Marceau, the girl watches them leave, she is alone again, she has decided to ring Gilles, they'll meet up at the Turk's, then they'll come back to the bookshop for a coffee, I'm not fair on Gilles, I love his skin, best if Gilles comes here at lunchtime, we'll eat in the back of the shop, I'll pop out and buy a few things, mayo salad, two small quiches, half-bottle of wine, apple tart, I'll behave as if we had all the time in the world, we behave as if we didn't know, without rushing, and when I'm on the table, I can stroke Gilles's ears with my feet.

Lilstein has begun to feel a lot better. Just before they reached the exit from the alleyway, an object turning in a shop window caught his attention, a rotating disc about fifty centimetres in diameter, on it a representation of the Knights of the Round Table, Lilstein cheers up, eleven miniature knights standing by their chairs, around the Table, and King Arthur in front of his throne, tin figures, less than ten centimetres tall, their right arms extended horizontally, pointing with their swords to the middle of the table, and on their left arms each holds a large helmet with a more or less fabulous creature on it, wolf, dragon, boar or hippocampus. Lilstein looks at the price-tag, six hundred francs for each Knight, nine hundred for the King, five hundred per chair, the Table is priced at one thousand three hundred francs and Lilstein bursts out laughing:

'See that? Electric motor for turning the disc one thousand francs!'

They have emerged on to the Boulevard des Italiens, Lilstein repeated 'a thousand francs for legend-turning, a thousand francs', Morel is happy to see him so relaxed. Lilstein had gone through a brief persecution crisis, he had doubted his friend, had come close to breaking off almost half a century of friendship, he blames himself, he feels he can trust him again, they have walked up the Boulevard des Italiens towards the Opera, grey sky, with blue breaks in it and a few drops of non-threatening rain.

'Could we take a leisurely stroll down the avenue de l'Opéra?' asked Lilstein, 'I'd like to stay with you.'

'Misha, sure it won't tire you?'

Lilstein said it was probably the last chance of a walk he'd have, the people in Bonn, oh yes, I know, these days we have to say the people in Berlin, but I haven't got used to it yet, strolling, it won't be long before the people in Bonn won't be letting me do much strolling.

They started making their way down the avenue de l'Opéra, after they'd gone a couple of dozen metres Morel stopped. He asked Lilstein:

'Are you really sure you want to go all the way to the end? No cinemas, no restaurants, just the one bookshop, stocks books for tourists, there are just banks, bureaux de change and travel agents.'

Morel's hand pointing to the signs around them:

'Voyages Melia, Thomas Cook, Tourscope, Czech Airlines! All that's left of this row of shop are businesses which enable you to get the hell out of here. Come on!'

Morel took Lilstein's arm, Lilstein put up no resistance, they went along the rue Daunou, emerged on to the Boulevard des Capucines, then on to the Madeleine.

Lilstein's mood was gloomy:

'Gorbachev, *perestroika*, *glasnost*, truth, socialism with a human face, we almost won, a whole life vindicated, Morel, I'm going to turn myself in to the people in Bonn, I won't say anything about us, I'm embarrassed that I suspected you of betraying me, please forgive me, very sincerely, if they interrogate me about you I'll say I came to see you because you are a historian, I'll make them believe I told you things for a big article you're writing about the Cold War, that will give you something to exert pressure with, do you remember, my first words at Waltenberg, "You won't be caught because there'll be nothing to get caught for", Morel, you have nothing to fear.'

They went as far as the Madeleine, which Lilstein thought very ugly. Morel pointed out to his friend the old shop front of Berck's, the stamp-dealer's, and the mustard maker's emporium just next to it. In the distance, to the north, they could make out the church of Saint-Augustin, Morel talked about a small square next to the church, he'd grazed his knees there and pushed toy cars around it over a period of years, he added:

'There's also the Army Club, you can't see it from here, it's on the left, just before you get to Saint-Augustin, you've never been there? not even by proxy?'

In the end they walked along the rue Royale, towards the Place de la Concorde. Morel was moved. At last Lilstein found a note of gentleness in Morel's voice. When they reached the rue Saint-Honoré, Morel stopped, he looked at the Obélisque, he asked:

'Misha, do you know why I betrayed you?'

Chapter 14

1991

We Never Suspected You for One Moment!

In which we learn the reasons that motivated the mole after the fall of the Berlin Wall.

In which we hear final revelations concerning the life of Lena and the death of Hans.

In which the question arises of who should serve the tea in the White House.

In which young people have a great time without giving a second thought to what old persons think.

Paris, the *quais* of the Seine, September 1991

What's the good of a vacuum cleaner if the power's cut off?
Graham Greene, *Our Man in Havana*

Lilstein did not react to Morel's question.

Morel continued:

'Do you know why I went over to the CIA, Misha? Because I'm a better Marxist than you.

'I betrayed you because I realised it was all over. You remember advising me to have two souls? I went over to the Americans when I realised your precious socialism was fucked, that Gorbachev wouldn't last long, that my idealistic soul would never float back down to earth, Gorby is currently making a hash of it, and is taking the old dream down with him.

'I had a head start on you, for a long time I'd been seeing it clearly, output potential, production outcomes, fifteen million Germans available and all that could be manufactured was plastic motor cars, I ask you!

'The Trabant on the motorway, next to the Audis, the Mercedes, and the official slogan, "Overtaking – our way", I had a start on you because I'm more materialistic than you are, Misha, you'd placed all your hopes in Gorbachev but without having an "objective reason" for doing so, you had too much faith in the spirits you'd been summoning to the rescue since you were a teenager, whereas I knew that Gorbachev couldn't rely on those "real social forces" as they used to be called once, *perestroika, glasnost*, hot air. The future isn't something to put on a pedestal.

'I'm a historian, a historian has a feel for these things, the role of material conditions, and that held even truer for Honecker, you remember Honecker with his panama hat and big round glasses, saluting youth march-pasts by waving a small yellow and red teddy bear? That's all there ever was, march-pasts, and a regime which was only right twice a day, like a stopped watch, and to get a lawn-mower you had to recycle an electric drill and to make an electric drill you had to recycle a hair-drier, and you fingered dissidents in order to hide what you were really up to, those were the material conditions, the housewife saying to her hubby "go to town and even if you can't find anything bring me back something!"

'Hardly surprising you needed a wall to protect all that! And the USSR, even more grotesque! Those two souls, Misha! One dreamy, the other cynical, no, you're wrong, it wasn't the cynical soul that came off best, it was the idealistic soul which stuck its heels in, the one you'd offered the leading role. I intend to go on being part of the game.

'I went to the CIA because I'm a better Marxist than you, I told them everything about the past, I had several interviews, handsome office, windows, lost in a corner of a vast room full of computers, just like the offices of a large newspaper; when the people I talked to wanted privacy they lowered the blinds, they didn't do it often, there were half-a-dozen of them, six civil servants and a tape-recorder, lists of questions, and no one departed from his script, to begin with I found this dangerous, a bogus kind of professionalism, I thought I'd made a stupid mistake in coming to them, I'd thought I'd walk into the realms of alternative truths and I had come to earth among yahoos clutching questionnaires and pencils for ticking boxes with, I was very scared, I almost warned you, told you to vanish.'

Lilstein says nothing. Nothing more to say. He looks at the Obélisque on the Place de la Concorde, a couple of hundred metres away. Talking won't help. He's not surprised. He'd been expecting betrayal. Now it's Morel's turn to do the talking. It's his day. In one single moment their friendship has ended, gone without anger. The anger had been earlier, in the bookshop, with the first suspicion. And now that Lilstein would be needing it, there is no anger. Lilstein listens, he tries to get the hang of some of what Morel is telling him, he tries to get a grip, he has always succeeded in getting a grip, but that was because other people didn't know him very well. Morel is different, Lilstein always told Morel everything, transparency, it was transparency which had kept them together all this time, Morel knows that Lilstein now wants to take back the initiative, so no point in trying to react, Morel will have anticipated this.

Lilstein listens while the man he trained tells him how he betrayed him, because Morel didn't just defect, he could have gone over to the CIA and covered his old friend, giving his name but remaining selective, giving Lilstein space and time. But he did none of that. Where will the threat come from now? Another car? Lilstein steps back from the kerb.

Morel takes a step forward:

'Come on, Misha, I'll show you, Place de la Concorde, the Obélisque, the Hôtel Crillon, the American Embassy.'

At these last words, Lilstein tensed up. He had no wish to go to the Place de la Concorde. Morel agreed to turn left, along the rue Saint-Honoré, towards the Palais-Royal. Lilstein let him talk, all the while steering clear of the kerb.

'One morning a woman invited me to lunch, Misha, in Washington, I'd seen her around a couple of times, she'd come into the room where I was being interrogated, some of the men would stand, she was black, African-American as they say nowadays.

'She'd cast an eye over some papers, exchange a few words, look at me without saying a word, then leave, very beautiful, dazzling smile, firm calves, tall, but not too tall, middling height, the invitation was to a French restaurant, yes, she insisted on paying, a restaurant with photos of Toulouse on the walls and rugby pennants, black and white, the proprietor of the restaurant came by, kissed her on both cheeks saying "Bonjour, Maisie", corner-table, and three men came and sat at another table, between us and the rest of the room, Maisie chose for us, cassoulet, an authentic Toulouse cassoulet, made the previous day, lamb, *confit de canard*, not forgetting the bacon rind and pork hock, a spiral of Toulouse sausage, covering of breadcrumbs, for the gratin and browning, spoon in it sticking straight up, when the *patron* asked what wine she said, in accentless French "no fucking contest a Madiran!" The *patron* laughed, his Madiran is dark cherry, with hints of strawberry and blackcurrant, but it's an assertive wine, it's not there to accompany anything, it shouts out for attention with every mouthful.

'A very hearty lunch, yet Maisie is slim, "I eat whatever I want, this evening the gym, need the energy", I insisted on serving her, I dropped a bean in her Madiran, I also spilled sauce on the tablecloth, clumsy Frenchman stuff, they love it.'

Lilstein and Morel are now on the corner of the rue Richepance, outside the windows of the Blue Dwarf, in one there's a display of electronic games, in the other a collection of dolls from around the world. Morel goes on:

'Maisie's skin is light, black but light, just as I'm thinking about this she said "some not very great white chief must have raped one of my ancestors", she started by chewing on a bean, a solitary bean, she smiled at the *patron*, she loves Europe, two years in Toulouse and one in Berlin, political science at Toulouse and musicology in Berlin, great big eyes, teeth to smile with, emphasises her cheekbones, she added "we've decided to cooperate with you, we never suspected you for one moment, that's why we're going to cooperate with you".

'I was very proud when I heard Maisie say "cooperate", it meant I wouldn't get a penny, but at the same time it was high praise, "we saw you come and go several times, but we never suspected you, our big blunder."

'Americans are like that, Misha, they conform to type, they make a mistake, its creates a problem, so solve the problem, a beautiful woman, just into her forties, face to go with it, no stretching of the skin, fine lines denoting intelligence, clear eyes, curly hair, she has relaxed, she just loved the South of France, walking through the South of France with friends, got as far as the Gers, "we walked through farmyards and had such fun telling the fowl they used for *foie gras* apart from the fowl they used for *confit*", they did bed and breakfast, for breakfast their hosts served them *foie gras* and pork scratchings, "I can still hear the voice of the guy who said eat up, it won't do you any harm, there's no butter just goose-fat."

'Maisie even wanted to settle down in one of those out-of-the-way places, one morning a van stopped, a pick-up, the driver had come to have breakfast with them, on the pick-up were hives, he'd come a long way, he was moving them to the lavender, he talked to her about beekeeping, she'd spent a quarter of an hour working out whether she could give up everything and become an itinerant apiarist moving between fir and lavender.

'At one point she signalled to one of the men who were watching us in this Washington restaurant, I was surprised because the man shook his head, the signal she gave looked like an order, it wasn't a question like when you open your eyes wide as you look at someone, it was a frown, brows down, and the man said no with a great deal of authority, I couldn't make it out, they wouldn't have fooled you, I had misled myself, she wasn't as high-grade as I'd thought, the top man was sitting at the other table, and he'd sent my African-American on her way, elbows on table, hand under his chin, he'd said no with his head.

'I'd taken him for a bodyguard, and he had the power! Maisie had cleared the ground, now we were going to get to the serious stuff, with the real top man, I'd never seen him before, I'd made a mistake, I'd opened up to a subordinate, good cop and now I'd located the bad cop, too late, the guy who'll say "my assistant here somewhat overstepped the mark, you're here simply to do what you're told, cooperation is out of the question", but the man wasn't ready to get out of his chair, he sent his Afro-American assistant on her way, she had style, she smiled, she tried to save face, she closed her eyes. Then the man got up, very athletic type, he came over to us, not the cooperating kind.

It's at this point that Lilstein began to relax. He's happy about what happened to Morel in that American restaurant, caught in the act of over-reaching himself, through excessive self-confidence, Morel is still an amateur, he still lets himself be guided by his reactions, especially with women. Lilstein has long believed Morel to be invulnerable because he no longer had a wife, no more Marguerite, but all the Americans had to do was dangle a women with a modicum of allure in front of Morel for him to stop thinking straight, Lilstein would never have made the same mistake, he would have spotted the second team, he reminds Morel of this as they stand looking at the dolls in the window of the Blue Dwarf, he reminds him of basic principles, he regains the initiative in a few slow sentences, just like in the good old days: the professional first puts up a curtain, my young French friend, he watches everything that passes in front of the curtain, and if all is well only then does he move on to the stage himself. Morel had walked into a trap, such a comfort. Lilstein does not say this last thought aloud, he looks around him, he's not going to let himself be lifted.

Morel heard Lilstein out, thanked him, then went on with a kind of amused affection in his voice:

'The sporty type took out a packet of cigarettes, he offered one to Maisie, lit it, went back to his table. He was only a bodyguard, Misha, just a bodyguard, a gun-carrier and cigarette-dispenser, for a lady who wanted to cut down on her smoking. I'd given myself a scare. Maisie inhaled deeply, she glanced at her cigarette and said "I'm trying to give up too, you managed it twenty years ago, that right? after a six-month stint with Gallia, the day they elected you to the Collège de France? smoke bother you? we're going to cooperate seriously."

'For all these years they hadn't managed to pin me down, Misha, and yet they knew all about Gallia, you really protected me well. You shouldn't have bet your shirt on Gorbachev. The CIA hadn't managed to get to me. I told them all about the past, but that wouldn't have been enough to make me interesting, they need a project, they have a thing about projects, programmes.

624

'If they were talking about cooperation it meant that I had a future I could sell them. I told them Gorbachev is going to fail. At the time, they really liked my analysis of Gorbachev's future.

'Maisie invited me to dinner a second time insisting "it's still on me", same Toulouse restaurant, same cigarette-carrying bodyguards, same cassoulet.

'But sitting at our table was another man, well-dressed, relaxed, tweed jacket, handkerchief in his breast pocket, corduroy trousers, Maisie's real boss this time, you're going to meet him very soon now, you're going to have fascinating conversations at the highest level, the man's name is Walker, they refer to him as Richard F. T. Walker, the American mania for initials, F. T. is for flame-thrower, Richard Flame-Thrower Walker, I don't know why, but it says what it means, with you he's promised not to go any further than the lie-detector, he'll keep his word, after all you're going to be one of his colleagues, he gets on very well with Maisie, he's deputy-director of the CIA, he's Maisie's boss, but it's more complicated than that, sometimes he talks to her as if she's a subordinate, at others as if he's talking to someone who could one day be giving him orders, their relationship is very ambiguous.

'I explained my assessments of Gorbachev for Maisie and Walker, the imminent failure of *perestroika*, the absence of genuine material conditions, they said "you're talking Marx but that's our kind of Marxism".

'It's given them an edge, over the State Department and even the British, thanks to me, for once, the CIA got it right before everyone else did, they got it right for their president when Thatcher was giving him a hard time over her beloved Gorby, a desperate survivor hanging on to power, he misses his footing and to save himself reaches out and grabs a nest of vipers.

'Maisie and Walker are both very pleased with me, Thatcher said "we must make cash payments to Gorby, we mustn't let the West Germans absorb the GDR, we didn't win the war for nothing", she went off and told Gorbachev "don't let go of the GDR", the French also had the wind up them, no one wanted a greater Germany, not straight away, not for fifteen, twenty years.

'I told the Americans Gorbachev is just a doctor who makes dying last longer, I also told them that German reunification was a done thing, it was unfortunate, but it was all settled, I sold them a slice of the future, think of what comes next, strengthen the ties with Poland, the Czechs, the Hungarians, in the old days they called them reverse alliances, I told them that my assessments came in part from you, don't look like that, Misha, I really needed to embed you in the business, you'll see why soon, I also said about you "there's a man you could rescue".'

By now Lilstein and Morel are no longer in the rue Saint-Honoré, they have walked under the colonnades of the Louvre, they emerge into the Place du Carrousel. Lilstein is happy to have put some distance between himself and the road and the cars which brush past pedestrians, he heads off to the Pei pyramid. Morel trails meekly behind him, takes up his thread:

'The Americans found our friendship very touching, they want it to continue, with them as a third party, and I need your help to go on with my work, you may perhaps have wronged some innocent people, my dear scapegoat, but don't give way to romantic impulse and turn yourself in to restore the order that's been upset, though we must go on believing in order . . .

'I know, Misha, you'd like the German police to arrest you, your new compatriots, they can only do that for your pre-war activities against Hitler, and you want to force them to do it, it would be droll, a great moral victory, but then what? A short spell in jail, slopping out in your cell, officially there's no blood on your hands, officially, they'd be forced to release you fairly quickly, you'd be just a guilty man with no ideals left, a senile Cassandra, paid less and less handsomely by newspapers that become more and more vulgar.

'Misha, I don't want to see you eating up your days in melancholy, I'm offering you a hand in the big game until the end, a chance to go out in style, you're holding a file out to a secretary and at that very moment, curtains, your arm drops, heart attack halfway through a file, better, ruptured aneurysm, a death like de Gaulle's but when you're still working, truly a gift, that's what I'm offering you, you were born to die in harness, tempting, no? Yes, you're right, I'm reversing the roles, today the tempter, the Devil, is me, the world turned inside out? The reverse of Goethe's world? No, the world isn't Goethean, we don't need to turn it inside out, you're wrong, I'm going to let you in on a secret, there's no need to turn the world inside out.

'The world never has had a right side except in the eyes of those who are paid to make us believe that it has, a world without God or the Devil, temptation rushing round and round in a whirlwind, and that's it, you just never had the bottle to be honest with yourself.

'The Americans, at least the ones I know, my new friends, believe in their God, they grapple with the Devil, and keep their end up by resorting to a theory of the necessary lie, since they believe truth has no opposite they are forced to lie, they sit in the Devil's seat, they're convinced they can get up off it whenever they like, with a prayer.

'They haven't even asked me to align myself with their point of view, they've got enough ostensible allies, I'm going to write an article about the war in Iraq, about the bombing of the motorway just outside Kuwait City, all the cars incinerated by United States Airforce napalm, though the victims were civilians. They're perfectly willing for me to express my reservations, the role of the man who asks himself questions, just a ploy to suit the people who will want to answer my questions.

'It's what they call luring the wolf out of the forest, the idea is to go on getting myself invited to places where it's important, then tell them what goes on there, my little entrées into grand houses, I've got the taste for it.

'Are you coming, Misha? Penny for your thoughts? Looking at the water? Remember, you can't swim twice in the same river.'

They are now on the Quai du Louvre, at the entrance to the Pont du Carrousel. How stupid, being afraid this was going to be a lift, Lilstein stares down at the Seine. He has allowed a small gap to open up between him and Morel. The same river! Morel turns, comes back towards him, tells him to stop watching the water flow by, it numbs the brain, never twice in the same river, Morel is mocking him, Morel is invulnerable, because he no longer has a Marguerite, his own wife dumped him though she was no Marguerite, Morel is alone, that's his strength, this man has never felt the cold, he'd lost hope momentarily in '56, he'd almost become a penny-plain bourgeois, and it was Lilstein who offered him meaning, and when that meaning had unravelled Lilstein offered him a game. Today, Morel mocks both the game and the meaning, he shoves Lilstein's head under the water and laughs, saying 'never twice in the same river'.

'Come out of the river, Misha, Gorby has dumped you, if it's any consolation he won't last much longer, this you already know but you've got out of the habit of believing anything that might do you some good.

'There isn't even a river any more. Let's get to the point, why we're both here, why you won't go to Berlin but to Washington: my new friends don't know the right way to make a Linzer, they'd like to try but they'll never acquire the knack, all they're asking from you is a few files, not many names, no one's going to ask you to foul your own nest, not important, all in the past, you can even keep the agents you've been running and arrange a meet with them now and then over a couple of drinks, to sing the "Chant des marais" and such like.

'What my new friends need is whatever you've got on your opponents: the Christian-democrats, the socio-democrats, the pluto-democrats, the eco-democrats, the liberal-democrats, any and all the groups that have claimed the moral high ground and would like to see you in jail, we want to know exactly what the new Germany is planning to do in Europe, in Poland, Austria, Hungary, Bohemia, Mittel-Europa, all that stuff.

'When Herr Kohl says "in this country of ours", we watch his hand, the one that sweeps up the space in front of him, we want to know how far it intends to reach, you can help us, when the old Warsaw Pact countries gain entry to Europe, the Germans will have the right to buy all the land they want, in Poland, Bohemia, Danzig, the Sudetenland, it will cost them much less than a world war, we'll need to keep an eye on that, and moreover you know the Russians pretty well, the Evil Empire is dead but Russia is still an empire.

'That's what they'll want of you. Say yes, there's no point any more in always saying no. I know, it's not a very attractive prospect, lackeys of the CIA, if that was all I'd be embarrassed suggesting it to you, Misha.'

They are now at the middle of the Pont du Carrousel, leaning on the parapet. Lilstein can't stop looking eastwards. The air is cool. The city is beautiful in the breeze. Lilstein has deliberately not responded to Morel's last remark, he allows him to continue.

'I'd blush. You suspect there's more to it than that, crumbs of information for the CIA, everything you taught me to despise, which has its importance, on a daily basis, we'll do our duty, but we must have a good time, Misha, my new friends have given me to understand that we'll have the wherewithal to have us a whale of a time, they didn't agree to that willingly, it wasn't cynicism, they are cynics but it was when they were being most frank with me that they taught me things, had they but known it.

'Walker, for example, one day he mentioned the name of Lena Hellström, Walker had tears in his eyes, he said she was his god-mother, that she'd cuddled him when he was a babe in arms, Maisie laughed saying, "FT, if you're going to go all dewy-eyed on us we'll bounce you out of your job as director of operations." Ever since that day, Walker has not said another word about Lena Hellström. You like it when I talk about Lena, Misha?

'It was Maisie who brought her name up again, in the restaurant, Maisie gave the impression she'd fallen in love with Lena, I had a lot of discussions with her, we talked about heavy stuff, and in the end, to unwind, she'd ask me to tell her about Lena. And to make me talk she'd talk about herself, and she let her own friends talk about her, Maisie said I can skate on ice too, and ski, and play Beethoven. It's true, Maisie doesn't sing but she can play piano sonatas, high standard, top amateur level, and chamber music too, plays with colleagues, they call themselves the "National Security Chamber Orchestra", they give concerts two or three times a year, Maisie is a great lady.

'In the good years, when you could still say that civil rights were something which communists demanded, an eminent professor declared in a seminar that the white race was gifted with superior abilities, Maisie was there, she let him have it, deathly silence, important seminar, forty or so students, and colleagues of the professor, assistants, the kind of place where you find a lot of future leaders, clear careful minds, the prof is a little out of touch in his philosophical views but he's the top man for international law, you let him say his piece even if you don't agree with him, Maisie didn't stand up, sat right there in her seat to speak, very calm, seminar voice, she looked at her pen all the time, they looked her, she said "you study philosophy and you don't read German, I do, you study international law and you don't know Russian, I can speak it, I can read it and I can write it, along with German, French and Spanish, these are things any human being can learn, you like to think you're a man of culture, but I'm the one who plays Beethoven sonatas".

'Up to this point, you could say that Maisie's comments were brave, fine role for a woman, she bore witness, birth of a new muse of civil rights, I am the exception but I refuse to prove your rule, it's just a question of being out of sync, just a question of catching up, she was right, you can guess the rest, and the big finish on "I have a dream", she had a fine job ready and waiting for her in the farce that is politics, queen of civil rights, positive discrimination, etc. But there was something else.

'And the people around her felt that Maisie had taken her first step along a very long road, that she wouldn't just be playing the role of representative of the Blacks.

'To be sure she said "I'm the only black person here", it was enough to get her looked at with a mix of sympathy, a trace of shame and a guilty conscience prepared to do whatever it took to atone, they were going to make it easier for her, recognise all the talents she'd talked about, defend her against the professor if they had to.

'Looking up and including the other students present she added "you use the fact that Blacks have a way to go as a lesson to white students that all they have to do is be white, your ideas encourage laziness; but Blacks have got the message, only real work should count, this country doesn't need easygoing ways, ten years from now being an easygoing White won't be enough".

'She also spoke about the strength of the individual, about personal will and the help of God which is offered to all, they didn't clap, not with the professor sitting there, but you could hear "yeah" and "hear hear" like in the House of Commons, all very discreet, it made its impression on people's minds and the professor didn't like it one little bit.

'At the end of the year, for her oral exam, the Dean of the Faculty and a couple other members of the Board sat in the public seats, she performed brilliantly, passed with the highest honours, *summa cum laude.*'

They crossed the Seine, and bore left along the Quai towards Notre-Dame. Lilstein tries to think while listening to Morel. If the people in Berlin have put out a warrant for him, he's going to need the Americans to get out of Europe. Who would make the best jailers? Morel says he needs Lilstein, but if that's not true he'll drop Lilstein like a hot potato the moment he confirms his statements to the Americans. And then the Americans will drop Lilstein. They'll send him back to Berlin. Lilstein will have allowed himself to be caught in a trap consisting of a story about an American woman and some cassoulet, Morel has turned out to be an excellent pupil.

'That said, Misha, Maisie may very well be a woman, but she has a man's weakness, she works for the CIA but she wants better than that, she wants to be a politician, today she listens but some day she'll only want to hear what she chooses to hear, she'll insist on it, she'll be our friend, first she'll try to catch us out, we'll look as if we're in the wrong, so inferior to her! We'll give her what she wants, Misha, she has a little weakness: masculine ambition.

'She defended the United States to my face, she doesn't like my scepticism, it's the land of "just do it", when she was young her father told her over and over "this is the country where they can refuse to let you into a diner but you can also get to be President of the whole country".

'Only once did she ever remind me of that to my face, the presidency, "just do it", that's why she's settled into the role of unlikeliest republican, with a faultless European culture, consistent stance, rights of the individual, "I'd rather be ignored than helped", Lena fascinates her, she wonders if she lived alone, did she have a man in her life? Did she like women? American questions, Misha you must have lots to tell her on that subject.

'Maisie ate her profiteroles and went right on drinking the Madiran, putting off the moment when she'd ask her bodyguard for a cigarette, amazing woman, not at all the type of African-American you get in magazines, more the feminist who specialises in the folk-tales of Zimbabwe, her thing is the history of the USSR, the Komintern, and Europe, from Talleyrand to Bismarck, and Schubert, yes, "like Madame Hellström, but I can't play Schubert's sonatas, just the accompaniment to some of the *Lieder*".

'She's a Presbyterian, so was Lena, in the Toulouse restaurant in Washington she ate her profiteroles with a mixture of hunger and gluttony, you should have seen her, especially after the hole she'd made in the cheese board, never mind, forget the gym we'll go and listen to her play the piano.

'Her father thought, if you're black you got to be twice as good, the same thing old man Hellström must have said to his daughter, he was white, from the South, a Presbyterian democrat from the South, "when you've got a name like Hellström you've got to be twice as good", and those good little girls with ribbons in their hair, one Black and one White, start doing their very best, piano, singing, giving twice their best, sixty years apart, and with big, big differences, in the sixties Maisie was still a nigger, in a school for niggers.

'Nigger part of town, with buses for niggers, restrooms ditto, that said there are niggers and niggers, the father for example was a teacher and a Presbyterian minister, there were also Baptists, one day in the Baptist church an explosion, four little girls died, KKK, never did find out who did it, one of the girls was Maisie's best friend at school.'

Morel has stopped. He has grabbed Lilstein's arm. He looks him in the eye, tells him there'll be no trap, that there'll be no car to lift him, Lilstein must trust him because it's the only way out for both of them, because the solution is called Maisie, whether Lilstein likes it or not.

'Maisie's father isn't a democrat, Misha, he's a republican, a black man registered as a republican voter in the deep south of the United States, because the first time he tried to get his name on the electoral roll he came across a good southern-thinking democrat who made him sit an aptitude test for Blacks, a great big salad bowl full of dry beans, to get your name on to the electoral roll they had to guess how many beans there were in that bowl.

'The father walked out, went back another day and came across a republican who said he'd register him but only if he could register him as a republican voter, one long childhood, for a little African-American girl, of being told "you can get to be President", Maisie told me she'd like to have met Lena, that she was fascinated, an American fascinated by Europe now that's fascinating, "Europe" Maisie would say, "interests me, but it doesn't fascinate me", Maisie with this very methodical approach to the profiteroles, didn't pour all the hot chocolate sauce at once, poured it on the first one to begin with, sheeny black topping, Maisie brings her nose down real close so she won't miss any of the chocolate aromas, she laughs, starts telling a story, "in Toulouse there was this other pâtisserie, it was called 'Au Bon Nègre', I used to make a point of going there."

'Misha, she's every bit as greedy as you are, wouldn't I just love to see all three of us in a Washington *salon de thé*. The *patron* had brought the hot chocolate sauce in a small silver dish, it had the logo of the General Transatlantic Company on it, Maisie serves herself very methodical spoonfuls.

'Each time a little chou pastry, a little ice-cream, a little chocolate sauce, "you want a taste? No? Chocolate gives you a headache? Me too, but if I'm good and careful I manage to avoid it, what you mustn't do is mix alcohol, chocolate and lack of sleep, when I've managed to get a good night's sleep I know I can eat a good dinner, with wine and chocolate, provided I can work it off afterwards at the gym, I studied the decline of European diplomacy in the twentieth century, I was taught by a great Austrian professor, Madame Hellström interests me a lot, she really seems to have known everybody, I would have spent hours listening to her, we'd have gotten ensconced at Demel's, in Vienna, over a Linzer."

'Maisie seemed to say Linzer in all innocence but I suspect she knows a great deal, Misha, she talked about Lena and Linzer, lost the urge to interrupt me? Feel like you want to run away? I find your silence disloyal. Is it because we're talking about Lena?

'Maisie asked if I knew that Lena had been buried at Arlington, I said yes, there'd been a piece in *Newsweek*, I haven't told her yet that your friend Max gave me the whole story, the low hill, Arlington, bagpipes, dress uniforms, shiny medals on a cushion, triple salvo, all the razzmatazz, no they didn't do the body-on-the-gun-carriage routine, but it seems people got pretty emotional, top brass and ordinary citizens, music-lovers, women in veils, students, they all admired her, Madame Hellström was a big draw, the occasion even had a humorous side.

'Who was to be given the flag draped over the coffin? No family members present, she had cousins, second-cousins, but if you're Southern Presbyterians of any standing you don't want to draw attention to yourself by being seen by the coffin of a woman who never wanted a husband, it was to Max that the honour went, Lena had organised the whole thing.

'The guard of honour presented the flag to your friend Max, who'd stopped believing in anything a long time ago, and especially in the American flag, he'd lost his faith the day he'd lost his boater, at the start of the century, he held up firm when they put the flag in his hands, dry-eyed, like everyone there, Lena didn't have a sentimental bone in her body, Max saying as he got to the cemetery, "I have a feeling that there's something intelligent inside me that stops me crying", and Max found himself shedding tears when Leone Trice started to sing, everyone had been ready for Schumann, something robust, or even a Schubert melody, they'd been expecting the tears to well up but to be able to hold them back, a moment without ostentation, an ochre-coloured moment, the sort she liked.

'And then Leone Trice started singing "Voi che sapete", people were seated, and the aria, instead of rising through the air, spoke directly to them, "you who know", Max in tears, half a century crowding back on him with those tears, and he stroked the flag on his knees, Arlington was because of what Lena had done during both wars, a military cemetery, didn't Max tell you the full story? So what did you two talk about? On a cushion there were medals, Max said to me in his inimitable way "a few bloody medals, they'd make any story-book hero turn pale at the sight".

'Maisie wants to know everything about how to make Linzer, we shall do what she says, Misha, she's one of Walker's deputies, the CIA big man, a decorated veteran of the Korean War and the Cold War, he wants to be appointed an adviser to the White House, Maisie does whatever Walker advises her to do, she follows his lead, a good little black Republican girl, she's the one we'll have to deal with, she wants to know all there is to know about Lena, Lena who held Walker in her arms when he was a baby.

'Maisie ate her profiteroles after finishing the cassoulet, she would have liked Lena to tell her what happened during the war, not just the Arlington connection, Maisie is curious, she wants to get her hands on the real file.

'The one that doesn't yet exist, Lena in 1943, the strained relations with her controllers, the trips to Spain or Portugal, neutral countries, Lena must have met a whole gang of people there, old contacts, she returned to Washington, set off again for Lisbon by way of Ireland, she was one of the few civilians entitled to travel by air, PanAm's great transatlantic seaplanes, the same ones that she'd travelled in before the war, luxury birds converted for carrying generals and ministers, anyway, tense relations with her controllers, Lisbon, really means nothing to you? Not got a record of anything to do with it? We can picture the scene, dinner in a restaurant for lovers overlooking the port, "dear Lena, I'm so happy to have found you again, it's hell and yet here you are", the half-lit restaurant, with Portuguese watchers sitting just a few tables away.

'The man strokes her leg, she kisses his ear, an old friend, he pets her leg under the tablecloth with his right hand, the left he'd lost along with the rest of his arm, was it at Stalingrad? Is he a soldier? Or an intelligence agent? What the hell is he doing there? Lena cuts his meat for him, she laughs, she makes him laugh, she holds out a forkful to him and laughs, the man's right hand can stay under the table, Lena doesn't try to stop him, two Lenas, one, high-end, eats, holds out a fork, prattles, the other, low rent, lets a man stroke her leg, is the man a hero of the *Wehrmacht*? Or a civilian? An aristocrat sickened by the regime? A huge problem, she has the beginnings of an explanation, no doubt when that hand finds its way into her knickers, not too much, I mean don't let out too much of a sigh, just enough to show the man that she feels something.

'In any case, the watchers have already taken note, you never saw a record of any of this, Misha? You are listening, aren't you? I think you're paying more attention now, the lady allowed the man named Berg to stroke her leg in the most outrageous way, she smiled, placed her lips on the man's ear, at one point he said to her you aren't just beautiful, you're worse, the man's hand sometimes moved out on to the table again, the lady kissed his hand, the hand went down again, the lady became hysterical, she laughed as she stroked the cheeks of the man named Berg, lots of detail of that kind in the watchers' notes, a crippled German who was now out of control, a hysterical singer, it's pretty clear to the watchers that this pair wouldn't take much longer now, the restaurant is dark, many foreign lovers, but that's no reason, the details are obscene, the watchers are careful about what they say in their report.

'The man named Berg was recalled, never seen again, yes he was, once, remember? As to the hysterical American woman who was sleeping with a German in the middle of a war, she didn't stay long in Lisbon, in America they must have reopened her file.

'Always the same story, she'd been friendly with the Krauts since 1915, no one ever clarified exactly what role she'd played after 1933, maybe she was just a hysterical case, the people employed by the Portuguese secret police to spy on her submitted their report, and their superiors cheerfully circulated it widely via every one of their administrative channels, and lurking somewhere in those channels there was someone to pass the report on to the German Embassy, and someone else to do likewise for the Americans, a high price to pay for an evening of short-lived excitement, Lena was supposed to be gathering information about the state of mind of the German army, and Berg had presumably been given the job of sounding out this American woman about the possibility of an armistice, you can imagine that dear Lena would have given the Germans information about the state of mind of Roosevelt and his advisers, we had to walk on eggshells, because she was closely linked to the older Kennedy, the Germanophile.

'Mustn't get uptight, Misha, I'm not trying to make out that your Lena was a Nazi, that's not what the file's about, that's all hearsay, but if I know all about it it's because like you I know the rest, which Maisie would love to know, because she gets some very feminine intuitions, does our Maisie.

'And also because she's a musician capable of taking an interest in something that nobody spotted at the time of the funeral at Arlington, a sharp eye, on the list of all the wreaths was one which had been sent on behalf of "the Friends of the *Winter Journey*", she's certain you have things to tell her about that, she also found a note from your colleagues in Bonn, the ones who'd like to see you behind bars, there's an issue concerning a former civil servant in your Ministry, I mean the real Ministry, a woman, an ex-civil servant in your *Aufklärung* who allegedly talked to them, story is they gave her a mission in 1956, no big deal, escort a woman on a trip by car from Budapest to the

Austrian frontier, a strong-arm expulsion, end of August '56, no need to get uptight, Misha.

'I realise everyone knows the story, it's been told often enough, but there's one small para, "I was instructed to tell the American woman 'it's going to turn very cold', just those six words", that's what interests Maisie, what your ex-civil servant said, just those few words, "it's going to turn very cold", apparently Lena never said anything about that, she told her debriefing in '56 that she was one hundred per cent sure that the Soviets were about to attack, she told about how she'd been lifted, a very precise operation, but she never quoted those six little words "it's going to turn very cold" nor said what they might have meant to her.

'Maisie thinks Lena should have denounced you in 1956, Misha, she wants to know why it never happened; after all, you'd had her expelled from Hungary in '56 and saved her life, she should have been in the building in Budapest which the secret services of the Warsaw Pact countries blew up the night before the Russian tanks returned, Lena was in touch with the resisters, sorry, the plotters, but you know that we say resisters nowadays, people in the best parts of town, enlightened communists, cosmopolitans, friends of Imre Nagy, bang! a present from Markov, thirty enlightened communist lackeys of imperialism fewer, but not Lena, gone off in a car just before, not willingly, it saved her life.

'Maisie would like to fill a few of the little gaps in the file, she'll interrogate you about that, and also about the year 1943 and the aftermath, you weren't there in '43 but apparently you know.

'After her hysterical hand-in-the-knickers session with the one-armed man, Berg, colonel or civilian? Was he really at Hans Kappler's funeral? Or did I dream it? Anyway, Lena had got back from Lisbon, took the first plane, in the watchers' notes the most interesting bit was missing: the envelope, neatly slipped into Lena's knickers.

'The envelope was very small, microfilm of a report, on a stage in the middle of the room a fado singer almost drowns the conversation, one hand under the table, the hysterical lady returned to the United States in her splendid seaplane, with information about what was going on in Poland, a report comes from various sources, rail tracks all arriving bang in the middle of camp huts, chimney stacks, women, kids, Jews.'

Lilstein and Morel stopped when they were level with the Pont des Arts. They stare at the building of the Institut. Morel gestures to the left wing of the pile:

'That's where the Tour de Nesle used to be, a period which people imagine was full of tragic love affairs. For more cheerful kinds of chivalry we have another symbol, look yonder, way along there, the equestrian statue, King Henri IV. In those days . . . Am I boring you with my talk of kings? You're surely not thinking of jumping into a taxi? Back from Portugal, with her microfilm, no one was prepared to believe her, apparently she got desperate, she went back in the finest plane in existence, she watched the wing through the window, a marvel of technology, they told her it's the same wing that's used for the big bombers that are sent over Germany, she could see herself making her report, Berg's words, the microfilm. And now they were sending planes to bomb railway tracks in Portugal. And in Washington they just say thank you and do nothing. Don't they believe her?

'No, they believe her but give the issue a low priority, Lena desperate, nothing's being done! The question is whether she kept her desperation to herself or whether she did something which was beyond her remit, do I know too much, Misha? How did I manage that? If I told you that in the end I spoke to de Vèze, would that make you happy? Can you see me having drinkies with the man who ran off with my wife? Or was it more simple, that Maisie shared her hypotheses with me? But I prefer talking about Lena, about the way she felt, about what she told her friend Max, who also talked to de Vèze from time to time, lives might have been saved thanks to her and nothing was done, maybe she had a breakdown, the future which turns into an empty-handed ghost.

'Maisie asked what it was with Lena, so categorical in her choices, "you know, Philippe", that's right, Maisie calls me Philippe, occasionally "my dear Mr Morel", but most often it's Philippe, "you know, Philippe, I don't trust these categorical characters, agents lose heart if they see their controllers are dragging their feet with their file and invalidating the information they supply, in which case they hand over all they know to people who are more active".

'To Uncle Joe, for example, Lena and Uncle Joe, that's what Maisie suspects, at least Uncle Joe ensures the rule of order and purity, and he's on the march, give Uncle Joe the means of getting to Poland sooner, Stalin's no tyrant, the whole of the American press have stopped saying he's a tyrant and are calling him Uncle Joe, because the Americans are refusing to bomb those installations, I'll hand all I know over to Uncle Joe, everything that's being said in Roosevelt's entourage.

'And so, Misha, at a given moment for one reason or another, on account of some tale about railway lines that are allowed to reach certain camps or because of some civil servant asleep on the job, your precious Lena loses confidence, runs out of respect for her colleagues, for her superiors, she didn't betray anybody, she just started speaking more freely with a different set of people, people whom she quite liked but whose ideas she'd disliked from the very beginning, certain of your sympathisers in the United States, scientists, intellectuals.

'She knew Roosevelt's entourage pretty well, and she also had equally close links with all the people who might be in contact with Moscow, Maisie thinks that it was while the war was going on that certain items of intelligence material were passed to the Russians using Lena as go-between, leaks of a diplomatic nature before the Conference at Yalta for example, or even before the Tehran Conference, leaks which allowed Stalin to know just how angry he could allow himself to get, and what quantities of equipment they were prepared to let him have, or basic verbal suggestions, all this started long before you were freed, as early as 1943.

'And in '45 it was maybe that which saved your life. Your pre-war relationship with Lena, at the Liberation you don't rate the attentions of Stalin's sorters, you rush off to Asia to rebuild your strength, a few

months, then back you go to Rosmar, you still have the profile of the
sort of man they continue to eradicate in large numbers, a thirties communist, you keep a dangerous photo in your head, comrade Lilstein,
I'm sure you were there in 1932 when Ulbricht and Goebbels staged
their joint meeting in Berlin, the great hall of the *Friedrichshain*, it went
very badly, general brawl instead of a confrontation of two anti-
bourgeois points of view, but you're one of the witnesses, Ulbricht and
Goebbels on the same platform, in the same photo that you keep in
your head, not the sort of thing you can boast about.

'And then you resisted, were part of the home-grown resistance,
prisoner of the Nazis, cosmopolitan profile, they could fix you up with
a file as a cosmopolitan collaborating with the English or even the
Nazis, they don't do it, in 1945 they hesitate, in '46 they spare you,
Misha, they give you responsibilities, so there are more important
things in life than hunting down trotsko-cosmopolitans, normally
you'd be a candidate for a bullet in a corridor and then somebody talks
about a woman and says maybe Lilstein could restore her confidence
and keep her on board, that's it, someone in Beria's entourage says
that you could resume contact and restore the confidence of a friendly
American woman who is beginning to have doubts about the virtues
of Uncle Joe, from 1946 onwards, Madame Hellström must be asking
a whole heap of questions.

'The Iron Curtain, the tensions, Poland, Czechoslovakia, that
woman is worth far more than her weight in gold, but for some time
she hasn't passed anything to Uncle Joe, she's lost confidence in him.
And she's due to sing in Berlin, lovely surprise, for whom?

'You went to hear her, "Misha I'm so pleased!" she trusts you, she
realises that Uncle Joe is turning out badly, but if you're there all is not
lost, problem is Uncle Joe's entourage, one part of his entourage, his
negative face, so you resurface, such an old friend, the positive face of
Uncle Joe, you natter away with Lena, everyone's there, the Russians,
the Americans, the English, the Germans, the French, they stare at
you, and between the blah-blahing and Lena's wide eyes, those large
deep-blue eyes, you are there, it's not all over yet, the cause of peace is

not dead, in Berlin in '37 Lena saved you, and you saved her six months later.

'So she quickly makes up her mind, everybody starts feeling scared that there's going to be another world war, got to redress the balance in favour of peace, discovering an old friend is like discovering yourself, she strokes your cheek, she checks that you are still as young as ever, she weeps genuine tears, "Misha, you haven't changed one bit, how do you do it? You use a cream?" she laughs, "I'm sure you use a night cream, like women do", then she reels off a list of creams and laughs at you saying "personally I just use water, it has to disperse, especially crows' feet, water straight out of the tap, my beautician can't get over it, plain water, there's nothing better, in the end my beautician had to agree", she strokes your cheek some more, top of the cheekbone, she says "hydration, can't beat it, my beautician uses a similar word but I couldn't tell you what it is, never mind, and she's even given up using a pencil on my eyes, pencil's bad, doesn't stop you having to use a good cream, but mustn't overdo it", that's all.

'And so on and so forth, Misha, love and kisses, she might well have said something to you along those lines, that and nothing else.

'"It has to disperse, tap water, crows' feet, and no pencil", it sounds silly, but when you know that these words come from atomic physicists as gifted as Tellheim or Mzilar, by a direct route from American and British labs, the whole thing acquires a certain charm, at the time Beria must have loved it.

'Means nothing to you, Misha? Tired? How about a drink, a café, sit outside? Don't want to? You do? Look, across the street, a few tables outside that bistro, it's called The Lock Gate, come on, a sentimental journey for me, I'll explain, a couple of good beers, it'll do us good. So Beria must have loved this stuff about make-up. You're not interrupting me but it really doesn't mean anything to you? Fact is though that Maisie has found a summary of that meeting in Vienna in Lena's file, there were watchers making notes there too, just notes, woman's talk about make-up, no one wanted to translate, and almost nothing is said about you, get it? they didn't identify you! You don't want to tell me anything? You'd rather I embroidered? that I send you back to Rosmar the day after this meeting? You leave Vienna for Rosmar, not your office but the airbase at Rosmar and on to Moscow by a direct flight specially laid on for comrade Lilstein, Moscow, Markov, he writes down what Lilstein dictates, sitting beside Markov is another man, according to Max it seems his name was Kolymaguine.

'This Kolymaguine has written down only a few words when suddenly he says to Markov "we must report directly to the comrade Commissar", to Lilstein he says "you're coming with us also", and the top-ranking Commissar sees all three immediately, it's Kolymaguine who does the talking, right?

'Extraction by dispersal, water channel, Misha, when Maisie talks about it she gets furious, she's certain Lena even said "a good, heavy water", the watchers didn't pick up on it, idiots, Maisie asked me if I knew many women who give out their beauty secrets in public, Kolymaguine went on, the comrade Commissar listening, "dispersal, heavy water, this cross-checks with the two other sources, the woman spoke of hydration but said it wasn't the right word, the only word which sounds like it in the area which interests us is hydride, she doesn't want to say the exact word because it's too specific, uranium hydride, so extraction by dispersal, heavy water channel, uranium 235, and no pencil, that is no graphite, it all checks, comrade Commissar."

'And Beria places his left forefinger in front of his lips as he stares at the sheet containing Markov's notes, there are two other sheets of paper on the desk, he compares them, elbow on the desktop, the forefinger moves to his cheekbone, "your opinion, comrades?"

'Kolymaguine says "it's a pure lead, comrade Commissar", Beria turns to Markov, "can you guarantee the source?" Markov says simply "yes, comrade Commissar", Beria to Lilstein, same question, and you say "yes, comrade Commissar".

'Beria is happy, "if this works out all three of you will be on list A", did that make you feel good, Misha?

'Later Markov must surely have said something along these lines to you "there are two lists, the first, if things work out right, is the list of heroes of the Soviet Union, the second is the list of the Order of Lenin, and if things don't work out, those on the first list are lined up and shot, those on the second are sent to the Gulag, we must be proud that we are on the first list".

'Beria really has good grounds for being pleased, he is director of espionage, counter-espionage, the police and atomic research, does it all concurrently, first-rate manager, he's pleased with you and Markov, a good team, under the direction of a good manager, that's more than a year gained.

'Maisie reckons Lena must have passed you this information about the bomb, Misha, at least part of it, a very interesting operation.

'An operation centring on a nucleus, a nucleus of scientists who had the first ideas, who went to Roosevelt and told him it was time to move to the practical phase, the bomb, at the outset it was scientists who convinced the politicians and the military, and the same scientists decided among themselves to share the secret with their Soviet ally, that they wouldn't give it exclusively to the American military, such a thing was too dangerous in just one pair of hands, so Beria didn't go looking for the scientists, a few scientists just decided from the very beginning to scale down their own knowledge, they had a world vision, no one camp shall hold a decisive advantage, they sent out information through a variety of channels.

'For Maisie, in this whole atomic business, your friend Lena was one of the major go-betweens, because she didn't like Truman and because she liked you a lot.

'Maisie's got it wrong, hasn't she? Lena wasn't just an intermediary between Moscow and the core of scientists, she was part of the core, an old friend of Tellheim, the period when this small circle debated very freely just before they were shut away in their atomic laboratories in the desert, the period when they discussed, agreed, set it all to music.

'Lena loved setting things to music, that was her main reason, setting things to music, her contempt for Truman was secondary, and she liked Eisenhower, it has to be said that he kept her out of McCarthy's way, he sent Walker to take care of McCarthy, it's funny: with all his faults, McCarthy had understood exactly what was going on, and it was Walker who told Eisenhower that he had to get Lena out of McCarthy's clutches.

'A riddle, dear Misha: who was it slipped a few items of information to McCarthy in 1954 to put him on Lena's track? And arrange for her to be defended by Eisenhower in person? It was risky but she was becoming terminally untouchable, a brilliant move, do you accept belated compliments? But it didn't work, because it rebounded against you, the McCarthy business turned her into a close friend of Eisenhower.

'And Lena has principles, you never betray a friend, so nothing more comes your way, she stops singing, and later she adored Kennedy, she campaigned for Kennedy, she was a member of the clan, I'm sure she only worked for them, she must have put you out to pasture the moment Eisenhower defended her, same thing in Kennedy's day too, or maybe you understood that there were things you couldn't ask her any more, though in fact did you ever ask her anything? I think she always gave you what she wanted to give you, that's all.

'And one day she just stopped, you didn't say anything, there was even better than that, as with me, roles reversed, right? I'm very fond of this little bistro, let's say I'm very fond of what it used to be, it's changed a great deal since the days when I used to come here, end of the fifties early sixties, it was already called The Lock Gate, hardly seats for fifty customers inside, I saw the best female singers of the time pass through here, Barbara, Anne Sylvestre, Cora Vaucaire, I used to come with my wife. That's all gone now, it's expensive, but I still come from time to time and stay for half an hour, just long enough to read a newspaper.

'It was you who passed information to Lena, in 1961, Cuba, the missile crisis, you cozened me into telling my pet minister "got to stay firm, the Russians will back off", that was designed to land Mister K in a fix, when did your friend Markov become a member of the Politburo?

'And when Mister K runs the risk of getting himself booted out by the warmongers, he gets support, a brief message is passed to the

Americans, "you don't invade Cuba and we'll withdraw the missiles", I know, in Washington, it was Linus Mosberger, an old pal of Max, who was used to pass the message directly to Kennedy, but I'm sure the same message reached the White House by way of a certain great lady of the world of opera, you always need confirmation.

'Markov landed Khrushchev in a fix, then he helped him get out of it, and finally he had him removed, did Lena actually make a lightning Vienna–Washington trip at that time? To make music? For her, the best outcome was Kennedy emerging as winner and for you it was Markov coming out on top.

'That said, if all this pother in the forties about uranium and heavy water was all finally to come out into the open the Americans would be capable of digging up Arlington Lena and dumping her on some municipal rubbish tip, but Maisie won't do that, Lena won't be touched, she's more or less committed to that, she'll tell you she's committed to it, she told me "I've got a heart, you can tell by the way I cover it with my hand every time I hear the last post or the national anthem, especially when it happens at Arlington".

'It's something I have in common with Maisie, Misha, those cemetery emotions, Arlington, the star-spangled banner draped over the coffin, the band, the impeccable folding of said banner, eleven movements, I counted, very fine the way they do it, I think it's so impressive that I decided to go and see it done properly, at Colleville-sur-mer, the lowering of the colours at Colleville-sur-mer, beautiful site, ten thousand American solders buried there, overlooking the sea, the colours are lowered at about a quarter to six, no bagpipes, a pre-recorded last post, ten thousand graves, I was half-expecting gleaming white caps, the guard of honour, there was none of that, no doubt problems of cost, the flag was brought and folded by civilians, pants with pockets at the knees, just guys who looked after the site, they fold it along the creases, still they must have been shown how to do it, but without the threat of ten days in the calaboose if they screw up on the job, it lacks class, if I want to see the flag folded properly I have to go to the cinema, funeral of the hero, sometimes it happens right at the start of the film, it tends to spoil what comes after.

'Misha, have you seen through our new American lady friend's little game? You've got to wise up! Why does the lovely Maisie want to know all there is to know about Lena? So she can write a report? So she can look good by uncovering yet another mole story? So she can trample all over us?

'Or rather is it because Walker protected Lena? Because he snatched her from the clutches of McCarthy and because in 1954 he wasn't seeing straight? Because she was his godmother, as he is fond of pointing out? Would Maisie take action to protect Walker? Now that would be swell. As swell as if we were acting simply to protect Lena's memory.

'It seems Walker best likes working when he's got protection, in Korea he was a flame-thrower, came under the wing of Garrick who was a marksman, he went on working with Garrick but Garrick gets sick. Maybe Maisie replaced Garrick, a beautiful friendship between Maisie and Walker, you believe in friendship? I'd like to see all this more clearly, Misha, let's imagine that one day Walker said something gross.

'Something like "I'll never let Maisie set foot inside the White House, not even to pour the coffee, not even with a big white bow in her hair", Walker is a careful man, it looked as if he were merely casting doubt on Maisie's abilities, he wasn't a racist, he chose to say something that he didn't think, the better to control, but words like that turned the clock back a few years, the remark about the coffee and the white bow was made in the presence of two leaders of the Republican Party, the old style of boss man, very reactionary, Walker is a liberal, a liberal republican, he doesn't believe a word of what he said to those guys, but said it all the same, to make them laugh, to get them eating out of his hand.

'Walker wants to be a White House adviser, he can't afford to look like a liberal, unfortunately that's his reputation, although he took part in the Phœnix programme in Vietnam, the eradication of tens of thousands of civilians by the CIA, but he still has a name for being liberal, with his pipe, tweed jackets and his Princeton degree.

'And he can't very well go round shouting from the rooftops "I too have had civilians killed" just to defend himself against being thought a wicked liberal. Then he made that crack about waitresses, pouring the coffee, with a bow in their hair, that should do it, they laughed all right, and so Walker gets the discreet support of the Republican right for the price of a crack.

'One day Maisie smiled at Walker, an even broader smile than usual, cheekbones, teeth, even more dazzling, large eyes sparkling, she held out a cup of coffee to him with a smile, and he knew she'd heard about the crack.

'And also with that big smile that she was offering to make peace, Walker realised he should have killed her and not made cracks about who serves the coffee at the White House, not even in front of two Republican chiefs, one of the two chiefs must have made progress, or the wife of one of them, or an aide, doesn't matter which, it was too late, Maisie didn't get angry, it meant that she had him where she wanted him, no need for getting angry, one of the two chiefs would be prepared to testify, and the other one would corroborate.

'She talked to Walker with increasing regularity, about this and that, she'd smile "FT it's so good having you for a boss and as a friend, nothing can wreck our friendship", and Walker can only agree with her or kill her, too late to kill her now, they are allies, Maisie will help Walker get to the White House and Walker will help her in turn to join him there. That's the new deal.

'They talk, Walker likes educating Maisie, passing on the history and tradition of the company, they go together to the coffee-machine.

'Walker is anxious, he's a liberal, it's the old CIA from the Cold War days, when it was in bed with the non-communist left, or the ex-communist left, which was responsible for the downfall of McCarthy.

'The new chiefs of the White House don't care for tweed jackets and liberals, of course Walker has taken down communists, Viets, civilians, Phœnix and guys with red gloves, but he overdid it, liberals are like that, when they roll their sleeves up they always go too far, Walker really needs Maisie's support, he talks to her a lot, confides in her so that she confides in him, he knows she has free access to the

President's family, the crack about coffee was the big mistake of his life, to try and make people forget it he confides in her more and more, he lays out his whole life for Maisie, anyone who listens to him the way she does must be on his side, and in the long run Maisie pieces together the coincidences in what Walker tells her.

'Some coincidences! She became his ally, she listened to him, she understood him, she took as an ally a man who wouldn't have let her pour the coffee in the White House, "a country where they can refuse to let you into a diner but you can also get to be President of the whole country", she'll never get to pour the coffee, they use army orderlies to do that, guys a metre eighty tall, who like Maisie a lot because she pays attention to them, Walker and Maisie talked about the history of Europe, Maisie's special area, the Cold War, and the story of Lena is a superb illustration of those years.

'Walker hadn't spotted the coincidences, sometimes Maisie would lay out what she could see for him, that is everything that happened between 1943 and let's say the election of Eisenhower as President, when Walker defended Lena against McCarthy, Maisie only showed Walker coincidences in a half-light, no one sees much and it's better that way.

'Walker became Maisie's sponsor, he'd made fun of her, she had picked up on the coincidences, Walker caught on, until then he had noticed nothing, but Maisie had noticed, she knows everything Walker didn't know, in the end she said "FT, I'm convinced that woman knew how to move faster than her shadow".

'Maisie can speak or shut up, at last Walker gets the message: he's been left for dead.

'And when they ask Walker for his opinion with respect to the job in the White House so that he'll talk about himself he'll say that Maisie's the one to cross the river, to become an adviser in the Oval Office.

'He's too old, Maisie will be able to come up with the new scenarios needed to take us into the twenty-first century, you get the picture, Walker makes a good case, "Maisie's the one you want, she weighs as much as millions of votes", and it works, people are actually relieved to see him backing Maisie, Maisie becomes a White House adviser and sometimes she it is who invites Walker, who has stayed with the CIA, to meetings in the holy of holies, imagine the holy of holies, Misha, you never made it inside, imagine it!

'So one day it will dawn on Walker that he's not going to go any higher, he's indebted to this woman who knows the full story of Lena, he'll watch Maisie operate, he's already the originator of an expression which is bandied about a great deal between Langley and Washington, "the lower slopes are littered with guys who were wrong about Maisie."

'And the sooner our little princess learns things about Walker's mistakes and the truth about Lena, the better she'll feel, I've no idea how high she'll go, but Walker's not going anywhere, Deputy Director of Operations, and Maisie is going to love us for this, thanks to us she's going to discover the full richness of Lena's character, all the coincidences, great singer and great teacher, great lover of men, a great American lady, she was that and much more and Maisie will be very pleased when she finds out.

'No, I don't think they'll be digging up Lena at Arlington, we won't allow it, you're going to help me and together we'll keep her in their hearts, it'll emerge that the hand she played was at times a little personal but all things considered she always played on the side of freedom, it's what they want to believe, because Maisie doesn't want to kill Walker.

'Walker will become her main backer, he'll get her into the White House, into the job he should have got himself, Maisie's security adviser, and Lena's memory will be piously guarded, splendid way to bear witness, Maisie won't kill FT, I'm beginning to know her, she'll protect him, they'll work together, he never understood women, not Lena not Maisie, Maisie gets into the White House and now and then arranges for him to be invited, he'll reach retirement age, he won't like the idea and Maisie will help him, she'll work it so he gets an exceptional extension of three years, "Richard, I'm so sorry, it was the best I could do."

'And Richard will thank her, a decent stay of execution, three years of doing work he loves, a dish of gladness served up by his loyal friend, Maisie is his best investment, he'd made a mistake, he'd put it right, the dividends are now flowing his way, a Walker thirsting to be in the know, he's not old, he signs up for his three-year extension with the CIA, reads the clauses, a kind of cut-price stint, he takes it back to Maisie, she is scandalised by the way her friend FT is being treated, she'll speak to the director of the CIA, two months later the director in person tells Walker in Maisie's presence that there's no way of fixing things differently, and only the first six months are guaranteed, queer street, Walker ages badly in a matter of weeks, pays a high price for his dish of gladness, no more permanent pass, has to be renewed every month, and the fear that the sojourn on queer street might be extended.

'It won't be extended, in the fifth month the orderly on duty in the parking lot informs him his pass is no longer valid, this won't prevent Maisie having Walker come in now and again, for a chat, "FT, you all right?" Walker answers yes, he looks well, face getting increasingly crumpled but there's a spring in his step, Maisie is glad to see that Walker has kept the spring in his step despite what's been happening to him, a sign of pain vanquished, the pain of a man who won't give up.

'Maisie just wants the truth about Lena, all facets, Misha, you're going to tell her, from the beginning, everything Hans told you, everything Max knew from Hans and from his own experience, all you yourself know, we'll offer Maisie a secret which opens many doors, she'll love that, she'll keep it to herself, everyone will come out of it smelling of roses, and we'll go back to Waltenberg.'

Lilstein turns white, in a hiss:

'Never, Morel! Waltenberg? Never again!'

Lilstein on his feet, he walks away from the *terrasse* of The Lock Gate, Morel hurries to pay, Lilstein has crossed over, has set off along the river bank towards the Pont Neuf, Lilstein has got to calm down, but Lilstein's voice rises, shrill:

'Their Forum, pointless claptrap! Never! People droning on and on, peddling meaningless drivel, they've even got the conductor of a Boston orchestra to give pre-concert talks to the wives of industrialists, cocktail parties for parvenus, everyone stands all the time, all you needed in '29 was ideas and you could just walk into any group, nowadays even Neuville seems to me to have his good points, I even thought Merken was magnificent, when he spoke there was the same silence as Lena got when she sang, half the audience was thinking "what a bastard" and at the same time they admired him, Merken poeticised philosophy, a perverse undertaking, but it was truly something to behold, and then the evening concert, today conductors don't conduct orchestras any more, they give pre-concert talks to silly, fat old women!'

'Calm down, Misha.'

'Merchants selling garbage! And the philosophers they invite: self-publicists who lick the boots of the garbage-merchants!'

'Misha, I never said a thing, look, the equestrian statue of Henri IV, halfway across the bridge, I'm now going to cheer you up, it dates from the Restoration, calm down, it was Louis XVIII who ordered it, the sculptor was an ex-Bonapartist, equestrian statue of Good King Henri. Know what the sculptor does? When no one's looking he stuffs the horse's belly full of Napoleonic proclamations, bulletins from Napoleon's Grande Armée, Ulm, Austerlitz, Iéna, he must have been weeping with laughter.

'Imagine it, Misha, the unveiling, the voices of all those ministers, and hidden deep in the horse's belly the voice of Napoleon: "they'll say, what a splendid fellow . . . I saved the Revolution which was dying . . .", the voice of the Emperor, in the horse's belly, "you are shit in a silk stocking", the sculptor torn between hate and delight, I love that story with its multiple voices, a legacy left for future generations, you see, Misha? it's calmed you down, I promise you, no more Waltenberg, let's walk on, Misha, no car, no one's going to be lifted, we'll pick up the game where we left off.

'And for the time being the most urgent business is Germany which isn't an ashen-faced mother any more nor a winter's tale, it's still the German question, has been for centuries.

'My friends in America didn't like the way the new Germany refused to help them when they went to take a look-see in Iraq, Misha, no one's asking you to switch direction, you can keep the same targets, you can keep your old moles and you'll be one of us, don't look like that, don't tell me your faith isn't strong enough, you can stay in the Devil's kitchen, we'll go on doing the cooking, it'll be our pleasure, with new technologies, these new technologies are fascinating, I must show you my model train layout.

'I've upgraded it all, electronic controls, we're going to have some splendid afternoons, we're not even obliged to tell them everything, no one can get to you, Misha, it may all be creaking like an imminent shipwreck but that's no reason for losing heart.

'And we'll talk about the main issue, Misha, I have a fine scheme in mind, youth, think of the girl we saw in the bookshop earlier, must start again from square one, on the invisible front, with young people, ten or so, I know a nice bunch of students, they have dinner once a week in a restaurant I go to, been observing them for almost a year, we'll go have dinner one Friday, their day, my usual table is on the mezzanine, against the balustrade, good seats to watch from.

'Those young people are amazing, a journalist just out of journalism school, a medical student who'll be a great, no, not a surgeon, in Paris we've got this definition, a surgeon has to have the strength of an ox and a brain to match, this boy already wants to specialise in what we call in-house medicine, the cases no one else can diagnose, he'll try, he'll study the symptoms no one understands and now and then he'll understand them, there's also a girl with a turned-up nose, very good at philosophy, that's right, you've got it, it's the girl from the bookshop, but she didn't want to get locked into speculation, which is just words, so she's also studying political science, I'll try and fix it so that she's diverted into my seminar, reliable as a clock, some day she'll be a government minister or the general editor of France's leading newspaper.

'To these we can add a young Japanese, a physicist, he's working on plasmas, he's currently based in the university which turns out our infrequent Nobel Prize winners, in France he learned how to laugh, there's a German, a Franco-German, an IT hotshot, already has a contract with IBM's centre for computation, and there are two sisters, one's doing law and the other one doesn't know yet what she'll do, she's the cleverer of the two, around them there are five or six others, these young people are bursting with energy, they have dinner, they go out places, they have fun, they work, they go swimming, they dream, they kick tin cans in the street when they find them, the girls protest, try to make the boys a little more couth, I've watched them all, it's a Vietnamese restaurant just by the Collège de France, spicy sauce and large fans in the ceiling, not at all expensive, there are about ten of them, all young, they comment on everything, they are intolerant, demanding, the other evening they put everyone and everything through the mincer, Cabinet ministers, the husband of the Prime Minister, Madame Cresson, he claimed he taught his wife Mozart and elegance, they left no stone unturned.

'They mock our cinema stars, journalists, money, self-importance, everything, they imitate our singers, have you heard of Johnny Halliday? You don't surprise me, his name's everywhere. Last week the young Japanese quoted the singer as saying "I realised that changing your body comes about through changing your mind-set", one of the boys stood up and starting pumping iron and looking Neanderthal, another straddled his chair and raced around the table going "vroum-vroum", Misha, they were doing what I never dared all my life, they were behaving badly.

'They chased each other round the table laughing uproariously, they started singing Johnny's greatest hits, they shouted at each other, they hugged, ordered bowls of rice, poured the spicy sauce while they laughed some more, swapped plates, drank toasts to Chinese beer, imitated their teachers, said where they could go.

'The journalist did an impression of his editor-in-chief who wants to get rid of hot type and bring in computers for everything, the budding doctor gave the journalist a helping hand, he arched his back and the journalist played on it like a computer keyboard, the editor tries to write his editorial and the machine won't let him, there's a computer program in the hardware which blocks long sentences, long words, unusual words, repeated words, the editor gets angry, the angrier he gets the more often the machine goes "beep-beep" instead of validating his sentences, it refuses to write "politics", "responsible", "unacceptable", "constitution", "institutions" and even "republic", too long, it also rejects "brazen", not sufficiently current, and refuses to write proper names when linked with the word "fraud", a very funny number, Misha, they strung it out for a full five minutes, a very political editorial, very succinct, which ends up "one cannot, in the face of public opinion, do such things", of which only "one", "opinion" and "things" remained, the editor-in-chief Coqueret, he's quite famous, also has his own TV show.

'After the sketch the hurly-burly started up again, they interrupted each other, stopped interrupting each other, sang a mix of current hits and 'O sole mio' and 'Marinella', took each other by the shoulders, made a tremendous racket, told each other the plots of films, of books, about the struggle between Yeltsin and Gorbachev, and a cat-fight between top models, you know how . . . you know our ways, I've forgotten the names of the models, all I recall are three numbers, 88, 61, 92, it's not at all the same with your girl-swimmers, they talked very fast, about the way African hair-styles are designed, the new fashion, very expensive, I know now that it can cost five thousand francs, with gold-thread in the braiding, one boy's hand glided over the table, through the bottles, he was imitating the overturning of a statue.

'The statue of your Dzerzhinsky, a giant crane in the Moscow night and the archangel of the Cheka rises into the heavens, they laughed, one of the girls turned to the young IT whiz-kid you must be a prodigy, he replied there's no such thing, there are no precocious children, only the spawn of fuckwits, a good crowd, if one started getting uppity the rest would merrily saw through the branch he was sitting on, and then they were off again, on the next table to mine a man had a few words with the proprietor who answered "that's life, sir, the future, I weep tears for Saigon and they put the world to rights", the man said "some world that'll be", the proprietor laughed, he added "in any case we won't be there to see it".

'I like this notion of putting the world to rights, Misha, the temperature in the restaurant started rising, people thought these young people were loud, vulgar, too much alcohol, at this point the journalist stood up, good-looking boy, tall, dark, hair cut very short, dressed in denim dungarees, he tapped his glass with a knife, another lapse of taste, and he started reciting a poem, "La Chanson du mal-aimé", of course, you know it, it's more than thirty years since you told me you knew kilometres of poems by heart, you see, on he goes, in the restaurant something happened, people stopped eating, the boy didn't leave out the Zaporogues, he recited the whole thing, slowly, the half-mist, the waves of brick, the scar, the people who sell their shadows, the graceful ship, the burning beehives, the derrière of a Damascene damsel, the demons of chance, the backwards descent, the cafés swollen with smoke and the white bodies of women in love, a long poem, he had the knack, Misha, the secret is not to speed up.

'Mustn't hurry the words, on the contrary, let them hang, make the audience wait for the rhymes, the words, the rhythms, if you go too fast people start waiting for you to get to the end, they stop listening, but if you let the words hang they wait for every little occurrence, does what I'm saying ring any bells with you? Slow down, keep 'em waiting, interpretation as a form of suspense, that's right, it's Kappler's last lecture, at Freiburg, three weeks before he died, he spoke about Goethe and the work of the actor in *Faust*.

'When he got to the end of "La Chanson du mal-aimé" the whole room applauded, the *patron* came bearing a large Norwegian omelette, shouts, sparklers, the little group sang "Happy Birthday" to one of the girls, the presents came out, the girl shrieked with delight, yes, Misha, it was the one who was at the till, earlier, she nearly recognised me, she took the hand of the boy in the dungarees and never let it go. A girl's face, Misha, when she senses she's holding the man of her life!

'She was holding him by his right hand, eating with her left hand, that's the advantage of Asian restaurants and Norwegian omelettes, you can eat without ever letting go of the hand of the person you're with, the *patron* said champagne on the house, the other tables grew more animated, everyone clinked glasses, heads spun, they drank head-spinningly like in the old days, when there was a wedding, then the young people left, through the window I watched them go for a moment, they were heading for the Seine playing leap-frog, it was eleven o'clock, they hadn't used up a tenth of their energy yet.

'It won't be any ordinary recruitment exercise. Recruiting them on whose behalf? I'll tell them the story of the *Histoire des Treize*, and no one will ever again be able to make them believe that they are here to serve a sentence.

'They'll go off to the United States, Yale, Columbia, the whole nine yards, they'll make new friends, they'll come back, they'll circulate, some might run a think tank, people are obsessed with working in small groups behind the scenes, the Bilderberg Group, the Institut Montaigne, the Boston Thinking Group, the Fondation Jean-Jaurès, the Schiller Gesellschaft, even the Russians are at it, the Stolypine Society, people who tell each other everything, you've got to know how to glean, these young people will be a quick study, they'll meet up on the ski slopes or in Martinique, Brussels, San Francisco, they'll go round and round the world whereas we used to spend just a few hours in a train.

'It's getting late, Misha, let's try to be something once again, let's introduce these young people to the recipe for a good Linzer, those young people are seeking, they want to know, they want to reshape the world, they want to be empowered, and let's not forget the most important thing of all, the thing that for so long enabled us to get up in the morning because it dispersed the melancholy which makes you look at things as they are, let's not forget the risk, Misha, you know they don't look as if they would but sometimes these youngsters do get depressed, they believe that there are no forbidden pleasures, we'll show them that there is at least one, that it comes with a risk every morning.

'Your friend Kappler was like you, but he didn't play, he was a puritan, and that's why he spent all his life shuttling to and fro between two worlds and why he killed himself, he neither got to the forbidden fruit nor what you called the third shore.

'We'll invite some of these young people to step right into the wizards' lair, in Washington, I'm sure the girl who studies political science will appeal to Maisie, then we'll send one or two to earnest old Walker to give him something to do in his retirement, the bitterness, the coarseness, the disagreements, he'll get them hooked, he'll tell them about Lena, that's right, Misha, I've also met Walker in private, Walker's last visit to the old lady, a chalet by a lake in Vermont, she feels weary, she's shrinking more and more into herself, "FT, I'm so glad to see you, it's so sweet", the stroll along the lake shore, Misha, Lena walking slowly on the arm of a man she knew first as a baby, Lena's great big eyes looking into Walker's, "FT, why did you come?" – "Lena, we've got a problem".

'Will you help me to envisage the scene, Misha? March 1969, Lena has heart problems, Walker has come to suggest ways she can get a whiff of springtime in her nostrils again, a trip with him, it's vital we give a voice to what happened that day, Misha, it cannot be allowed to die, Walker came to ask Lena something, the lakeside is so beautiful, they walk slowly, when he told me about it Walker was sitting in his kitchen, he spoke slowly, he tried to describe the shore of the lake, he tried not to omit any of the words she had spoken, slowly he repeated the suggestion he'd made to her, on 12 March 1969, "Lena there's someone in Paris someone who does for the Russians what you've been doing for us for fifty years, you're the only one who can pick up on this, we're chasing a tone, Lena, scattered notes, maybe you can find the key, and the signature for the key", that's what Walker said, Misha, this is happening in the time of Nixon and Brezhnev, you once called them mangy sheepdogs, Lena Hellström was set on the trail of the mole, seven hours in a plane, she has heart trouble, happy as Larry, she looks out the window, the ocean, the clouds, cathedrals of clouds under the wings of the Boeing.

'She watches out for Europe, to Walker she says in confidence "I'm going to make the most of this, I'm going to meet up with a man I should never have stopped loving, I should have married him before the war, the First War, an argument, he wanted to go and play soldiers, we could have stayed in Switzerland, a life without troubles, I tried to persuade him, he left".

'Misha, Walker told me that this story mustn't be allowed to turn to dust, Lena had met up again with Hans Kappler between the wars, at a time when they might have picked up the pieces, 1929, the Waltenberg Seminar, remember? How you used to bend my ear about that damned Seminar! In '29 Kappler told Lena that he'd gone off to fight in that abomination that was the First World War because she'd slapped his face, it was the most painful of his memories, but Lena didn't remember any of that, no doubt Kappler was making up painful memories to justify walking out on her at the time, "FT, I never slapped him, he swore I did, apparently that day he tried to kiss me but I wanted an argument, he said he'd told me he hadn't come to argue, I know him, he would never have said anything as vulgar, according to him that was when I slapped him, I stayed very cool, I slapped him and off he went to the war, it's all so long ago, FT, I can't remember anything, maybe the slap was intended to gain time."
'Walker related all that as though he was the one who'd been slapped, Misha, his chin was resting in the palm of his right hand, he was talking about two lovers who meet up again fifteen years later at the Waldhaus, I told him you were there too, Lena thought that Kappler had made up the slap to justify himself, because in 1929 he was in love again, not with Lena but with a much younger girl, all he was really interested in was the girl whereas Lena wanted to live with him again, "I skied, I sang, I was beautiful, FT, my best years, he didn't want to, I don't think the girl wanted to either, it was too late", in the plane from Paris Lena was happy, she said "We had plenty of time to calm down, I'll help you, FT, and then I'm going to join him in Geneva, I've written to him".

'Max blamed Walker, he said the trip killed Lena, her last mission. In Paris they'd had to open the files for her so she could see the extent of the damage done by the mole, she knew a lot of things and she died in that city, without seeing Kappler again, Kappler died six months later.

'In Paris she didn't come up with anything on the mole, or if she did she didn't say, Misha. At the time you didn't warn me, never even put me on my guard, why? Was there really no danger? Would she find nothing? Did she die in Paris without unmasking anyone? With a smile on her face?

'Heart failure, Misha, she didn't like Nixon any more than you liked Brezhnev. Did you manage some *readjustment* with her? Will you tell me about it? Arlington, that wreath from the 'Friends of the *Winter Journey*', who sent it? Was it Max? What happened to Max? You don't know? Disappeared? De Vèze told me that the last time he saw Max was in a garden, a cat jumped into Max's arms and Max said "Orpheus, the time's come!" He vanished along with the cat, no one ever saw him again.

'We'll listen to what Walker tells the youngsters we send him, and you can tell Walker all about Waltenberg, we need him, he's not a happy man, we must also find a few sound brains in Russia, Spain, a likely bunch of young friends, and a girl who's studying singing, I absolutely insist we have a girl who's studying singing.

'We're going to disappear, Misha, nowadays our eyes water more when we wake up of a morning, no, I'm not mad, let's not be late, the big game, the third shore!

'And even if I was mad, let's not forget the most urgent task, saving your skin, today Kohl's star is highest in the firmament, an enlarged Germany in the centre of Europe, with lots of money to buy territory with, Maisie doesn't like it at all, you wouldn't have something on Herr Kohl, would you?'